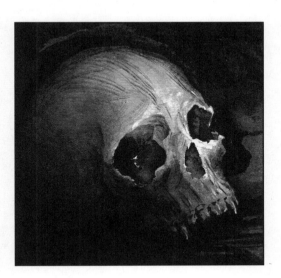

IN THE SHADOW OF DRACULA

IN THE SHADOW OF DRACULA

CLASSIC VAMPIRE FICTION 1816–1914

Edited with Introductions and Notes by

LESLIE S. KLINGER

& JEFF CONNER

ILLUSTRATED BY

MICHAEL MANOMIVIBUL

IDW®

SAN DIEGO

2011

Book Design by Jeff Conner • Assistant Design by Robbie Robbins

Family of the Vourdalak, translation used by permission of Christopher Frayling.

ISBN: 978-1-60010-957-7

14 13 12 11   1 2 3 4

IDW®

Ted Adams, CEO & Publisher
Greg Goldstein, Chief Operating Officer
Robbie Robbins, EVP/Sr. Graphic Artist
Chris Ryall, Chief Creative Officer/Editor-in-Chief
Matthew Ruzicka, CPA, Chief Financial Officer
Alan Payne, VP of Sales

Become our fan on Facebook **facebook.com/idwpublishing**
Follow us on Twitter **@idwpublishing**
Check us out on YouTube **youtube.com/idwpublishing**
www.IDWPUBLISHING.com

"…I live in your warm life,
and you shall die—die, sweetly die—into mine."

— J. SHERIDAN LE FANU,
Carmilla

CONTENTS

CONTENTS

ILLUSTRATIONS

INTRODUCTION

Leslie S. Klinger

"…he is known everywhere that men have been."
—*Professor Abraham Van Helsing*

Throughout the whole vast shadowy world of ghosts and demons," writes Montague Summers, "there is no figure so terrible, no figure so dreaded and abhorred, yet dight with such fearful fascination, as the vampire, who is himself neither ghost nor demon, but yet who partakes the dark natures and possesses the mysterious and terrible qualities of both." What is a vampire? For purposes of this collection, the simplest definition may be applied: a formerly dead person returned to life, the "undead." Here the vampire is distinguished from the zombie, an animated corpse with no intelligence. According to the 1888 *Encyclopædia Britannica*, the vampire was supposed to be the soul of a decedent that had quit the buried body by night to suck the blood of living persons.

> Hence, when the vampire's grave is opened, his corpse is found to be fresh and rosy from the blood which he has thus absorbed. To put a stop to his ravages, a stake is driven

through the corpse, or the head cut off, or the heart torn out
and the body burned, or boiling water and vinegar are poured
on the grave. . . . The belief in vampires chiefly prevails in
Slavonic lands, as in Russia (especially White Russia and the
Ukraine), Poland and Servia and among the Czechs of Bohemia and the other Slavonic races of Austria. It became especially prevalent in Hungary between the years 1730 and
1735, whence all Europe was filled with reports of the ex-
ploits of vampires. Several treatises were written on the subject, among which may be mentioned Ranft's *De masticatione
mortuorum in tumulis* [1734] and [Dom Augustine] Calmet's
Dissertation on the Vampires of Hungary [1751]...

Although vampires had been in the public eye for hundreds
of years, it was *Dracula* (1897), written by Abraham "Bram" Stoker,
an Irishman best known in his day as the confidante of the great
actor Sir Henry Irving, that caught the imagination of the world
and led "the triumphal march of the un-dead Transylvanian vampire," in the words of one critic, "through the newspapers, books,
cinema screens and stages of the Anglo-Saxon world." For most,
the shadow of the monumental novel has obliterated recognition
of other vampires in legend and literature, just as the 1931 film of
Dracula with Bela Lugosi became the standard by which all further
film portrayals of vampires are measured.

As will be seen in this volume, the undead appeared in English
fiction as early as the second decade of the nineteenth century. In
addition, many fine vampire stories appeared before and after *Dracula* and deserve to be more familiar to modern readers. The vampire, the revenant (as it was termed by Calmet), the undead, is
reportedly of ancient origins, with myths and legends traced back
to Egyptian, Chinese, Greek, Babylonian, Assyrian, and other Eastern cultures of antiquity. Not all associate the undead with blood
and blood-sucking, and some tales report the vampire as having
the ability to change shape or to pass through the earth or a coffin
or tomb. There is little resemblance among these early accounts,

and only after 1670 did a pattern of observations of vampires begin to emerge—labeled by some as "epidemics" of vampirism.

The first widely published report (1672) related to Istria, in modern Croatia, on the Adriatic. Subsequently widespread incidents were recorded in East Prussia (1710 and 1721), Hungary (1725-30), Austrian Serbia (1725-32), East Prussia (1750), Silesia (1755), Wallachia (1756), and Russia (1772). Some of these early cases related to named individuals—Giure Grando (Istria), Peter Plogojowitz (Serbia), Arnold Paole (Medvegia, near Belgrade), and several villagers from Olmutz, Austria—and government reports record in detail the testimony of reputable churchmen, scientists, and military personnel who examined the bodies of the alleged vampires. The signs of vampirism were unmistakable to these witnesses: corpses bloated with blood, often with luxuriant hair and nails, evidence of movement of the corpses, and sounds of protest emitted when the corpses were impaled or punctured with wooden or iron stakes. Of course, later generations dismissed these as simple examples of normal human decomposition (see, for example, the splendid *Vampire Forensics* by Mark Collins Jenkins published in 2010), but the stories continued to echo.

One of the most persistent legends is that of the Countess Elizabeth Bathory. Bathory was a Magyar who, in the late sixteenth and early seventeenth century, murdered young woman to bathe in their blood and so, she believed, preserve her beauty and youth. While she was not, strictly speaking, a vampire, she has become closely associated with the undead and, in some fictionalized accounts, made into a classical vampire. Similarly, the Wallachian prince Vlad Draculya, also known as Vlad Tepeş, has repeatedly been identified as the "model" for Stoker's Dracula (this is patently untrue, as is explored in detail in this editor's *New Annotated Dracula* [2008]), and has been twisted into a vampire in many novels and films.

What caused the appearance of these vampires? That is, what made some corpses into vampires, while others rested in peace? Dozens of cultures have traditions of vampires and vampire-like beings, and perhaps not surprisingly, there are almost as many ascriptions of causes as there are such cultures. For example, the *nachtzehrer* of Bavaria is the end result of being born with a second skin or caul; the *pijavica* of Croatia is cursed by reason of incestuous relations with the mother; the *kuzlak* of Dalmatia has been weaned too early; the *upir* of Poland are born with teeth; the *myertovets*, *vurdalak*, and *upirzhy* of Russia are the offspring of a witch or werewolf, while the *strigoil* and *muronul* of Roumania were born out of wedlock to parents also born out of wedlock; and the *bruxsa* of Portugal are the product of witchcraft.

And how may the vampire be destroyed? Again, remedies are contradictory and various, although many involve decapitation, staking (with wood or iron), burning, and other means of assuring that the corpse will not be in a physical condition to be mobile. Some of the more unusual prophylactics are burial of the corpse at a crossroads (Bohemia), chaining the corpse to the grave with wild roses (Bulgaria), piling stones on the grave (Ireland), burial face downward, which presumably confuses the revenant so that he or she cannot escape *upward* (Poland), placing a lemon in the corpse's mouth (Saxony), and burying poppy seeds in the grave—this for the curious reason that the undead cannot resist obsessively counting the seeds to the point of ignoring everything else and therefore will not bother the family (Prussia).

One of the more pleasant remedies is that prescribed in the village of Căzăneşti, in Roumania: In order to be rid of a *strigoi* generated by a cat or a dog walking over or under an unburied body, bury a bottle of wine near the person's grave, wait six weeks, dig up the bottle, and share it with those whom you wish to protect.

Of course, not all corpses become vampires, and tests have

been devised to determine the true vampire from the merely bloated corpse. Folklorist Agnes Murgoçi, writing in 1927 about Roumanian traditions, explains the local tests:

1. The vampire's household, his family, and his livestock, and possibly even the livestock of the whole village, die off rapidly.

2. The vampire comes back in the night and speaks with the family. This intercourse may be disruptive or helpful; for example, some vampires have helped with the housework and cut wood. Female vampires are reported to return to their children.

3. If the local priest reads a service at the grave and the evil that is occurring does not cease, the occupant of the grave must be a vampire.

4. A hole about the size of a serpent may be found near the tombstone of the dead man. This is the exit of the vampire from the grave.

5. Neither a white horse nor a gander will walk over the grave of a vampire.

6. On exhuming the corpse, if it is a vampire it will be found to be:
   (a) red in the face, even for months and years after burial,
   (b) with the face turned downward,
   (c) with a foot retracted and forced into a corner of the grave or coffin.

7. If relations have died, the mouth will be red with blood. If the vampire has ruined things at home, the mouth will be covered with maize meal.

Murgoçi warns that if the vampire is not destroyed, it will pursue its evil ways for seven years, preying on its family, its village, its country, and eventually travelling to another country, where it may become a man again.

Many artistic records of vampires appear in the literature of Europe after the seventeenth century epidemics ran their courses and before *Dracula*. The earliest long account is found in Johann Ludwig Tieck's "Wake Not the Dead" (included in this volume), which tells of Brunhilda, a Burgundian noble who preyed mainly on children The first account published in English is John Polidori's "The Vampyre" (1819), a very popular and significant tale that spawned several stage plays of equal popularity. Just as notable is "Varney the Vampire", an immensely successful "penny dreadful," first published serially between 1845 and 1847, which also enjoyed several stage versions. "Carmilla," written by Joseph Sheridan Le Fanu in 1871, was also highly influential, both then and now.

Sir Christopher Frayling divides these records into four categories: the folkloric vampire, the female vampire, the aristocratic vampire, and the "unseen force." While there is wild disparity among the records, the consensus regarding the characteristics of the vampire seems to be that (a) the vampire drinks blood, usually that of a carefully selected victim, (b) the drinking of blood not only sustains the vampire but produces a youthful appearance or "rejuvenates" the creature, and (c) the vampire is affected by holy artifacts and can be destroyed by decapitation, burning, or a wooden or iron stake. Of course, the vampires recorded in *Dracula* exhibit further characteristics not necessarily in evidence in these earlier accounts: the lack of a shadow, unphotographability, supernatural strength, shape-shifting abilities, telepathic command, and the need to sleep in a coffin or box filled with earth. Dracula himself, contrary to his image in films, is described as a tall, thin, old man with a long white moustache, hair growing on the palms of his hands, a thick pair of eyebrows meeting in the middle, and bad breath (the smell of the grave). Only shape-shifting is part of the folkloric record. In some cultures, the werewolf (or other were-beast) and vampire are linked by the common shape-shifting trait.

The literature of the nineteenth century failed to provide a coherent description of the origin of the vampire, and in the following pages, a variety of vampiric types will be seen. Some do not appear to drink blood; rather, they "suck" energy or life-force from their victims. Some live in society and pursue romantic relationships with their victims; others abide in grave sites or ruins, treating humans as mere prey. Some are men, many are women; some are quite young in appearance, others old and apparently decrepit. As will be seen in these tales, however, all fascinate us. Vampires embody the ideas that life does not end in the grave, that death need not conquer, and that if we are willing to pay the price, immortality is at hand. For those reasons, we continue to be thrilled, terrorized, and taught by their stories.

IN THE
SHADOW OF
DRACULA

John Polidori

"THE VAMPYRE" was the first truly popular piece of vampire fiction published in England (*New Monthly Magazine*, April 1819). Written by Dr. John William Polidori (1795-1821), the story is important not just for its primacy but also for its originality, creating the mold for the pedigree of Count Dracula and many other high-born creatures of the night. Prior to this, vampires were derived directly from folklore and were little more than the risen dead, walking corpses without personality or style.

Polidori's inspiration was the scandalous and world-renowned Lord George Gordon Byron, who is still one of the most famous poets in the English language. In 1816, young Polidori, who harbored literary aspirations of his own, was commissioned by Byron's publisher to accompany the great poet, already well traveled, on a trip to Italy and Switzerland.[1] It was common, if not prudent, to have a private physician along on such excursions, but the doctor's main duty was to record Byron's conversations for posterity.

That summer the Byron entourage encamped at the Villa Diodati near Lake Geneva. There they were visited by the leading Romantic poet of the day, Percy Bysshe Shelley, along with his young lover Mary Wollstonecraft Godwin (Shelley was married to another at the time) and his sister. Due to massive volcanic eruptions in 1815 (the largest ever recorded) in Indonesia, 1816 became

---

[1] The trip was a self-exile from England in order to escape financial and romantic entanglements; unfortunately it would be a permanent vacation for Byron.

known as "the year without summer," with near-constant bad
weather and major food shortages throughout the Northern Hemi-
sphere. When incessant rain kept Byron and company trapped
indoors, the party turned to reading aloud from a three-volume
French edition of supernatural stories which had recently been
translated from German (*Fantasmagoriana: Tales of the Dead*).

With science and "rationalism" impacting modern society, a
cultural counter-reaction also developed. The Romantic movement
in literature (which Byron rejected, though many mistakenly regard
him as an adherent) was but one response, and an interest in folktales and legends was another (a trend that originated in Germany).

As later recounted by Mary Shelley,[2] Byron suggested that
they each compose a story to rival those in *Fantasmagoriana*. This
parlor game (really an informal contest between the two poets)
would in fact produce two genre-defining works of fiction—neither
from Lord Byron or Percy Shelley.

Byron started on a story but soon abandoned it,[3] while Percy
Shelley found the challenge too emotionally draining and couldn't
write at all. Mary Shelley's effort would eventually become the
novel *Frankenstein*, published two years later (after heavy editing
by Percy). Polidori's inital story was also stillborn, and shortly thereafter Byron discharged him and he returned to England.

Polidori's relationship with Byron was complicated, alternating between hero worship and intense jealousy, so it was perhaps
inevitable that he would use Byron's "Fragment," and indeed the
poet himself, as inspiration for his belated entry in the ghost story
challenge. The result would establish a new literary genre.

"The Vampyre" was originally heralded as a new work by
Byron,[4] who often cast versions of himself in his long narrative
poems (thus adding to his celebrity).[5] But soon the story was rec-

---

[2] She married Percy Shelley following his sickly wife's death.
[3] It is usually reprinted as "Fragment of a Novel" or "Augustus Darvell."

ognized as a dark satire of Byron's controversial public persona,[6] recasting the notorious lord as a new kind of predator.

"The Vampyre" blends the famed poet's scandalous reputation with the then-exotic folktales of undead blood-drinkers from Eastern Europe, recasting these monstrous denizens of dark haunted forests and ruined country churches as sophisticated nobility, seeking out prey from within the most fashionable social circles. The result was an immediate sensation, and it was soon adapted into several stage plays (often unauthorized), which ran for years, spreading the story's fame and influence even further.

Whether carefully crafted or not, some eighty years later this one compelling tale from John Polidori would establish the foundation for Bram Stoker's *Dracula*, and thus establish most of the core elements found in modern vampire fiction. (As a former theatre critic, and then a stage manager for twenty-seven years, it is more than likely that Stoker saw "The Vampyre" performed.)

Lord Byron's poetry remains popular (his "She Walks in Beauty" is considered a classic), and the term "Byronic hero"—an idealized but flawed character—is coined in his honor.

Aside from an essay on the evils of classism, Polidori wrote but one other work of note, the novel *Ernestus Brechtold*, but neither it nor his medical practice was very successful. Plagued by gambling debts he died at the age of twenty-seven, an apparent suicide.

---

[4] The story was apparently issued without Polidori's knowledge, and there is some mystery as to how the publisher actually acquired it in the first place.

[5] Byron skillfully used the emerging mass media (i.e., print journalism) to create an image of himself for popular consumption (which he later came to regret). Because of this Byron is considered the first modern "rock star."

[6] The story's "Lord Ruthven" character intentionally echoes the "Lord Ruthven" featured in *Glenarvon*, a scandalous, thinly disguised novel by Lady Caroline Lamb, one of Lord Byron's more vengeful ex-lovers; thus the public already equated Lord Ruthven with Byron. It appears that when Polidori discovered his manuscript had been published under Byron's name, he attempted to "reclaim" ownership by amending "Ruthven" to "Strongmore," which appears in the fifth book edition, the first one edited by Polidori.

THE VAMPYRE

JOHN POLIDORI

It happened that in the midst of the dissipations attendant upon a London winter, there appeared at the various parties of the leaders of the *ton,*[1] a nobleman more remarkable for his singularities than his rank. He gazed upon the mirth around him, as if he could not participate therein. Apparently the light laughter of the fair only attracted his attention, that he might by a look quell it, and throw fear into those breasts where thoughtlessness reigned.

Those who felt this sensation of awe could not explain whence it arose. Some attributed it to the dead grey eyes which, while fixing upon the object's face did not seem to penetrate, falling upon the cheek with a leaden ray that weighed upon the skin it could not pass—yet at one glance did pierce through to the inward workings of the heart.

His peculiarities caused him to be invited to every house; all wished to see him, and those who had been accustomed to violent excitement, and now felt the weight of *ennui,*[2] were pleased at having something in their presence capable of engaging their attention.

In spite of the deadly hue of his face—which never gained a warmer tint, either from the blush of modesty or the strong emotion of passion, though its form and outline were beautiful—many of the female hunters of notoriety attempted to win his attentions, and gain, at least, some marks of what they might term affection. Lady Mercer, who had been the mockery of every monster shown in drawing-rooms[3] since her marriage, threw herself in his way. She did all but put on the dress of a mountebank[4] to attract his notice, in vain.

When she stood before him, though his eyes were apparently fixed upon hers, still it seemed as if they were unperceiving. Even her

[1] French; meaning high fashion; stylishness; used here to denote the current crop of fashionistas.

[2] Boredom (*French*).

[3] In Britain, a formal private dance party or reception, usually where young ladies are introduced to "society"; similar to a debutante ball in America.

[4] Here meaning a juggler or street entertainer who dressed distinctively and was paid by the crowd.

unappalled impudence was baffled, and she left the field.

But though the common adulteress could not influence even the guidance of his eyes, it was not that the female sex was indifferent to him. Yet such was the apparent caution with which he spoke to the virtuous wife and innocent daughter that few knew he ever addressed himself to females. He had, however, the reputation of a winning tongue, and whether it was that it even overcame the dread of his singular character, or that they were moved by his apparent hatred of vice. He was as often among those females who form the boast of their sex from their domestic virtues, as among those who sully it by their vices.

About the same time, there came to London a young gentleman of the name of Aubrey. He was an orphan left with an only sister in the possession of great wealth by parents who died while he was yet in childhood. Left also to himself by guardians, who thought it their duty merely to take care of his fortune while they relinquished the more important charge of his mind to the care of mercenary subalterns,[5] he cultivated more his imagination than his judgment.

He had, hence, that high romantic feeling of honor and candor, which daily ruins so many milliners' apprentices.[6] He believed all to sympathize with virtue, and thought that vice was thrown in by Providence merely for the picturesque effect of the scene, as we see in romances. He thought that the misery of a cottage merely consisted in the vesting of clothes, which were as warm, but which were better adapted to the painter's eye by their irregular folds and various colored patches. He thought, in fine, that the dreams of poets were the realities of life. He was handsome, frank, and rich; for these reasons, upon his entering into society's circles, many mothers surrounded him, striving which should describe with least truth their languishing or romping favorites. Their daughters at the same time, by their brightening countenances when he approached and by their sparkling eyes, when he opened his lips soon led him into false notions of his talents and his merit.

Attached as he was to the romance of his solitary hours, he was startled at finding that, except in the tallow and wax candles that flickered, not from the presence of a ghost but from want of snuffing, there was no foundation in real life for any of that congeries[7] of pleasing pictures and descriptions contained in those volumes from which he had formed his study. Finding, however, some compensation in his gratified vanity, he was about to relinquish his dreams, when the extraordinary being we have above described crossed him in his career.

Aubrey watched him; and the very impossibility of forming an idea of the character of a man entirely absorbed in himself, who gave few other signs of his observation of external objects, than the tacit assent to their existence, implied by the avoidance of their contact. Allowing his imagination to picture every thing that flattered its propensity to extravagant ideas, he soon formed this object into the hero of a romance, and determined to observe the offspring of his fancy, rather than the person before him.

Aubrey became acquainted with him,

---

[5] That is, the guardians turned over his education to paid tutors rather than do it themselves.

[6] "Milliner's apprentices" refers to shop girls, that is, naïve youths (as in "just off the farm").

[7] A collection of items or parts in one mass; an assemblage.

paid him attentions, and, so far advanced upon his notice, that his presence was always recognized. He gradually learnt that Lord Ruthven's affairs were embarrassed and soon found, from the notes of preparation in —— Street, that he was about to travel.[8]

Desirous of gaining some information respecting this singular character, who till now had only whetted his curiosity, he hinted to his guardians that it was time for him to perform the tour,[9] which for many generations has been thought necessary to enable the young to take some rapid steps in the career of vice towards putting themselves upon an equality with the aged, and not allowing them to appear as if fallen from the skies whenever scandalous intrigues are mentioned as the subjects of pleasantry or of praise, according to the degree of skill shown in carrying them on.

They consented, and Aubrey, immediately mentioning his intentions to Lord Ruthven, was surprised to receive from him a proposal to join him. Flattered by such a mark of esteem from him, who apparently had nothing in common with other men, he gladly accepted it, and in a few days they had passed the circling waters.[10]

Hitherto, Aubrey had had no opportunity of studying Lord Ruthven's character, and now he found that, though many more of his actions were exposed to his view, the results offered different conclusions from the apparent motives to his conduct. His companion was profuse in his liberality—the idle, the vagabond, and the beggar received from his hand more than enough to relieve their immediate wants. But Aubrey could not avoid remarking, that it was not upon the virtuous, reduced to indigence by the misfortunes attendant even upon virtue, that he bestowed his alms—these were sent from the door with hardly suppressed sneers.

Yet when the profligate came to ask something, not to relieve his wants but to allow him to wallow in his lust or to sink him still deeper in his iniquity, he was sent away with rich charity. This was, however, attributed by him to the greater importunity of the vicious, which generally prevails over the retiring bashfulness of the virtuous indigent.

There was one circumstance about the charity of his Lordship which was still more impressed upon his mind: all those upon whom it was bestowed inevitably found that there was a curse upon it, for they were all either led to the scaffold, or sunk to the lowest and the most abject misery.

At Brussels and other towns through which they passed, Aubrey was surprised at the apparent eagerness with which his companion sought for the centers of all fashionable vice. There he entered into all the spirit of the faro table.[11] He betted, and always gambled with success, except where the known sharper was his antagonist, and then

---

8 That is, Ruthven was broke; to avoid creditors and debtors' prison, he was going abroad (as did Byron).

9 Refers to "the Grand Tour" in which British aristocracy traveled to Europe to improve their minds and perhaps gain experience in other areas as well ("what happens in Paris, stays in Paris").

10 The waters around England.

11 Faro: a popular fast-moving card game of French origin. (The name derives from the "Pharaoh"; depicted on the original French decks.) Players wager with a house banker, matching dealt cards with ones already exposed. When done fairly, faro offers players better odds than similar games of chance, but widespread cheating by professional players ("sharpers") and gaming parlors led to its being banned in many countries.

he lost even more than he gained. But it was always with the same unchanging face, with which he generally watched the society around. It was not, however, so when he encountered the rash youthful novice, or the luckless father of a numerous family; then his very wish seemed fortune's law—this apparent abstractedness of mind was laid aside, and his eyes sparkled with more fire than that of the cat whilst dallying with the half-dead mouse.

In every town, he left the formerly affluent youth torn from the circle he adorned—cursing, in the solitude of a dungeon, the fate that had drawn him within the reach of this fiend; whilst many a father sat frantic, amidst the speaking looks of mute hungry children, without a single farthing of his late immense wealth wherewith to buy even sufficient to satisfy their present craving.

Yet he took no money from the gambling table, but immediately lost, to the ruiner of many, the last gilder he had just snatched from the convulsive grasp of the innocent. This might but be the result of a certain degree of knowledge, which was not, however, capable of combating the cunning of the more experienced.

Aubrey often wished to represent this to his friend[12] and beg him to resign that charity and pleasure which proved the ruin of all, and did not tend to his own profit. But he delayed it—for each day he hoped his friend would give him some opportunity of speaking frankly and openly to him. However, this never occurred.

Lord Ruthven, in his carriage and amidst the various wild and rich scenes of nature, was always the same: his eye spoke less than his lip. And though Aubrey was near the object of his curiosity, he obtained no greater grati-

fication from it than the constant excitement of vainly wishing to break that mystery, which to his exalted imagination began to assume the appearance of something supernatural.

They soon arrived at Rome, and Aubrey for a time lost sight of his companion; Lord Ruthven left him in daily attendance upon the morning circle of an Italian countess, whilst he went in search of the memorials of another almost deserted city. Whilst he was thus engaged, letters arrived from England, which he opened with eager impatience.

The first was from his sister, breathing nothing but affection. The others were from his guardians, the latter astonished him. If it had before entered into his imagination that there was an evil power resident in Lord Ruthven, these seemed to give him almost sufficient reason for the belief. His guardians insisted upon his immediately leaving his friend, and urged that his character was dreadfully vicious, for that the possession of irresistible powers of seduction rendered his licentious habits more dangerous to society.

It had been discovered that Lord Ruthven's contempt for the adulteress had not originated in hatred of her character, but that he had required, to enhance his gratification, that his victim, the partner of his guilt, should be hurled from the pinnacle of unsullied virtue down to the lowest abyss of infamy and degradation. In fine, that all those females whom he had sought, apparently on account of their virtue, had since his departure thrown even the mask aside and had not scrupled[13] to expose the whole deformity of their vices to the public gaze.

Aubrey determined upon leaving one

---

[12] That is, point this out to Ruthven.

[13] Hesitated due to conscience.

whose character had not yet shown a single bright point on which to rest the eye. He resolved to invent some plausible pretext for abandoning him altogether, purposing, in the meanwhile, to watch him more closely and to let no slight circumstances pass by unnoticed.

He entered into the same circle and soon perceived that his Lordship was endeavoring to work upon the inexperience of the daughter of the lady whose house he chiefly frequented. In Italy, it is seldom that an unmarried female is met with in society; he was therefore obliged to carry on his plans in secret. But Aubrey's eye followed him in all his windings and soon discovered that an assignation had been appointed, which would most likely end in the ruin of an innocent though thoughtless girl.

Losing no time, Aubrey entered the apartment of Lord Ruthven and abruptly asked him his intentions with respect to the lady, informing him at the same time that he was aware of his being about to meet her that very night. Lord Ruthven answered that his intentions were such as he supposed all would have upon such an occasion and, upon being pressed whether he intended to marry her, merely laughed.

Aubrey left and, immediately writing a note to say that from that moment he must decline accompanying his Lordship in the remainder of their proposed tour, he ordered his servant to seek other apartments. Calling upon the mother of the lady, he informed her of all he knew, not only with regard to her daughter, but also concerning the character of his Lordship. The assignation was prevented. Lord Ruthven next day merely sent his servant to notify his complete assent to a separation, but did not reveal any suspicion of his plans having been foiled by Aubrey's interposition.

Having left Rome, Aubrey directed his steps towards Greece and, crossing the Peninsula, soon found himself at Athens. He then fixed his residence in the house of a Greek and soon occupied himself in tracing the faded records of ancient glory upon monuments that apparently, ashamed of chronicling the deeds of freemen only before slaves,[14] had hidden themselves beneath the sheltering soil or many colored lichen.

Under the same roof as Aubrey existed a girl named Ianthe; a being so beautiful and delicate that she might have formed the model for a painter wishing to portray on canvas the promised hope of the faithful in Mahomet's[15] paradise, save that her eyes spoke too much mind for anyone to think she could belong to those who had no souls.

As she danced upon the plain, or tripped along the mountain's side, one would have thought the gazelle a poor type of her beauties; for who would have exchanged her eye, apparently the eye of animated nature, for that sleepy luxurious look of the animal suited but to the taste of an epicure. The light step of Ianthe often accompanied Aubrey in his search after antiquities. Often would the unconscious girl, engaged in the pursuit of a Kashmere butterfly, show the whole beauty of her form, floating as it were upon the wind, to Aubrey's eager gaze. In the contemplation of her sylph-like figure he would forget the letters he had just deciphered upon an almost effaced tablet.

[14] This was a popular sentiment of the day—that modern Greece was a degraded country when compared to its ancient glory.

[15] Mohammed. (The author's prejudiced view of Islam was common at the time.)

Often would her tresses falling, as she flitted around, exhibit in the sun's ray such delicately brilliant and swiftly fading hues, as might well excuse the forgetfulness of the antiquary, who would let escape from his mind the very object he had before thought of vital importance to the proper interpretation of a passage in Pausanias.[16]

But why attempt to describe charms which all feel, but none can appreciate? It was innocence, youth, and beauty, unaffected by crowded drawing-rooms and stifling balls. Whilst Aubrey drew those remains of which he wished to preserve a memorial for his future hours, Ianthe would stand by and watch the magic effects of his pencil tracing the scenes of her native place. She would then describe to him the circling dance upon the open plain, would paint to him in all the glowing colors of youthful memory, the marriage pomp she remembered viewing in her infancy; and then, turning to subjects that had evidently made a greater impression upon her mind, would tell him all the supernatural tales of her nurse.

Her earnestness and apparent belief of what she narrated excited Aubrey's interest. And often, as she told him the tale of the living Vampyre—who had passed years amidst his friends and dearest ties, forced every year to feed upon the life of a lovely female to prolong his existence for the ensuing months—Aubrey's blood would run cold, whilst he attempted to laugh her out of such idle and horrible fantasies.

But Ianthe cited to him the names of old men who had at last detected one living among themselves, after several of their near relatives and children had been found marked with the stamp of the fiend's appetite. When she found him so incredulous she begged of him to believe her, for it had been remarked that those who had dared to question their existence always had some proof given, which obliged them, with grief and heartbreaking, to confess it was true.

Ianthe detailed to Aubrey the traditional appearance of these monsters, and his horror was increased by hearing such an accurate description of Lord Ruthven. He, however, still persisted in persuading her that there could be no truth in her fears, though at the same time he wondered at the many coincidences, which had all tended to excite a belief in the supernatural power of Lord Ruthven.[17]

Aubrey began to attach himself more and more to Ianthe; her innocence, so contrasted with all the affected virtues of the women among whom he had sought for his vision of romance, won his heart. And while he ridiculed the idea of a young man of English habits marrying an uneducated Greek girl, still he found himself more and more enchanted by the almost fairy form before him.

At times he would tear himself from her and, forming a plan for some antiquarian research, he would depart, determined not to return until his object was attained. But he always found it impossible to fix his attention upon the ruins around him, whilst in his mind he retained an image that alone

---

[16] A Greek traveler and geographer of the second century AD; famous for *Description of Greece*, which recounts ancient Greece from first-hand observations, thus making it a crucial link between classical literature and modern archaeology. The book was popular as a guide to Greek ruins.

[17] Note that Aubrey has to go to Eastern Europe to hear about vampires; there were few legends of them in England. Greece is near the Carpathian Mountains, where Dracula had his castle.

seemed the rightful possessor of his thoughts.

Ianthe was unconscious of his love, and was ever the same frank infantile being Aubrey had first known. She always seemed to part from him with reluctance, but it was because she had no longer anyone with whom she could visit her favorite haunts whilst her guardian was occupied in sketching or un-covering some fragment which had yet escaped the destructive hand of time. She had appealed to her parents on the subject of Vampyres, and they both, with several present, affirmed their existence, pale with horror at the very name.

Soon after, Aubrey determined to pro-ceed upon one of his excursions, which was to detain him for a few hours. When they heard the name of the place, they all at once begged of him not to return at night, as he must nec-essarily pass through a wood where no Greek would ever remain after the day had closed, upon any consideration.

They described it as the haunt of the Vampyres in their nocturnal orgies, and deno-unced the most heavy evils as impending upon him who dared to cross their path. Aubrey made light of their representations and tried to laugh them out of the idea, but when he saw them shudder at his daring thus to mock a superior, infernal power—he very name of which apparently made their blood freeze—he was silent.

Next morning Aubrey set off upon his excursion unattended. He was surprised to observe the melancholy face of his host, and was concerned to find that his words mocking the belief of those horrible fiends had inspired them with such terror.

When he was about to depart, Ianthe came to the side of his horse and earnestly begged of him to return before night allowed the power of these beings to be put in action; he promised. But later he was so occupied in his research that he did not perceive that day-light would soon end, and that in the horizon there was one of those specks which, in the warmer climates, so rapidly gather into a tre-mendous mass and pour all their rage upon the devoted country.

Aubrey at last mounted his horse, deter-mined to make up by speed for his delay, but it was too late. Twilight, in these southern climates, is almost unknown; immediately the sun sets, night begins. And ere he had ad-vanced far, the power of the storm was above. Its echoing thunders had scarcely an interval of rest before its thick heavy rain forced its way through the canopying foliage, whilst the blue forked lightning seemed to fall and radi-ate at his very feet.

Suddenly his horse took fright, and he was carried with dreadful rapidity through the entangled forest. The animal at last, through fatigue, stopped, and he found, by the glare of lightning, that he was in the neighborhood of a hovel that hardly lifted itself up from the masses of dead leaves and brushwood which surrounded it. Dismounting, he approached, hoping to find someone to guide him to the town or to at least obtain shelter from the pelting of the storm.

As he approached, the thunders, for a moment silent, allowed him to hear the dreadful shrieks of a woman, mingling with the stifled, exultant mockery of a laugh, which continued in one almost unbroken sound. Startled, but roused by the thunder which again rolled over his head, with a sudden effort Aubrey forced open the door of the hut. He found himself in utter darkness; the sound, however, guided him. He was appar-ently unperceived, for though he called out, still the eerie sounds continued and no notice was taken of him.

He found himself in contact with someone, whom he immediately seized. A voice cried out, "Again baffled!"[18]—to which a loud laugh answered, and he felt himself grappled by one whose strength seemed superhuman. Aubrey struggled, determined to sell his life as dearly as he could. But it was in vain; he was lifted from his feet and hurled with enormous force against the ground. The enemy threw himself upon him and, kneeling upon his breast, had placed his hands upon his throat—when the glare of many torches penetrating through the hole that gave light in the day, disturbed him. He instantly rose and, leaving his prey, rushed through the door. In a moment, the crashing of the branches as he broke through the wood was no longer heard.

The storm was now still, and Aubrey, incapable of moving, was soon heard by those without. They entered, the light of their torches falling upon the mud walls and the thatch, loaded on every individual straw with heavy flakes of soot. Upon his pleas, they searched for the one who had attracted him by her cries; he was again left in darkness. But what was his horror when the light of the torches once more burst upon him, to perceive the airy form of Ianthe—now a lifeless corpse.

Aubrey shut his eyes, hoping that it was but a vision arising from his disturbed imagination; but when he unclosed them he again saw the same form, stretched by his side. There was no color upon her cheek, not even upon her lip; yet there was a stillness about her face that seemed almost as if life dwelt there still. Upon her neck and breast was blood, and upon her throat were the marks of teeth having opened the vein—to this the men pointed, crying, simultaneously struck with horror, "A Vampyre! A Vampyre!"

A litter was quickly made, and Aubrey was laid by the side of her who had lately been to him the object of so many bright and fairy visions, now fallen with the flower of life that had died within her. He knew not what his thoughts were—his mind was benumbed and seemed to shun reflection, and take refuge in vacancy. Almost unconsciously he held in his hand a naked dagger of a particular construction, which had been found in the hut.

They were soon met by different parties who had been engaged in the search of her whom a mother had missed. Their lamentable cries, as they approached the city, forewarned the parents of some dreadful catastrophe. To describe their grief would be impossible, but when they ascertained the cause of their child's death, they looked at Aubrey and pointed to Ianthe's corpse. They were inconsolable; both died brokenhearted.

Being put to bed, Aubrey was seized with a most violent fever and was often delirious; in these intervals he would call upon Lord Ruthven and upon Ianthe—by some unaccountable combination he seemed to beg of his former companion to spare the being he loved. At other times he would imprecate maledictions[19] upon his head and curse him as her destroyer. Lord Ruthven chanced at this time to arrive at Athens and, from whatever motive, upon hearing of the state of Aubrey, immediately placed himself in the same house and became his constant attendant.

When Aubrey recovered from his delir-

[18] This usage: to frustrate or obstruct.
[19] That is, he would wish him ill.

ium, he was horrified and startled at the sight of the one whose image he had now combined with that of a Vampyre. But Lord Ruthven, by his kind words implying almost repentance for the fault that had caused their separation, and still more by the attention, anxiety, and care which he showed, soon reconciled him to his presence.

His Lordship seemed quite changed; he no longer appeared that apathetic being who had so astonished Aubrey. But as soon as his convalescence began to be rapid, Ruthven again gradually retired into the same state of mind, and Aubrey perceived no difference from the former man, except that at times he was surprised to meet his gaze fixed intently upon him, with its smile of malicious exultation playing upon his lips.

He knew not why, but this smile haunted him. During the last stage of the invalid's recovery, Lord Ruthven was apparently engaged in watching the tideless waves raised by the cooling breeze or in marking the progress of those orbs, circling, like our world, the moveless sun—indeed, he appeared to wish to avoid the eyes of all.

Aubrey's mind, by the shock and horror of his love object's death, was much weakened. That elasticity of spirit which had once so distinguished him now seemed to have fled forever; he was now as much a lover of solitude and silence as Lord Ruthven. But much as he wished for solitude, his mind could not find it in the neighborhood of Athens.

If he sought it amidst the ruins he had formerly frequented, Ianthe's form stood by his side. If he sought it in the woods, her light step would appear wandering amidst the underwood, in quest of the modest violet, then suddenly turning round, she would show to his wild imagination her pale face and wounded throat, with a meek smile upon her lips.

He determined to flee from Athens, every feature of which created such bitter associations in his mind. He proposed to Lord Ruthven, to whom he held himself bound by the tender care he had taken of him during his illness, that they should visit those parts of Greece neither had yet seen. They traveled in every direction and sought out every spot to which a new experience could be attached; but though they thus hastened from place to place, yet they seemed not to heed what they gazed upon. They heard much of robbers, but gradually began to slight these reports, which they imagined were only the invention of individuals whose interest it was to excite the generosity of those whom they defended from pretended dangers.

In consequence of thus neglecting the advice of the inhabitants, on one occasion they traveled with only a few guards, more to serve as guides than as a defense. However, upon entering a narrow defile[20]—at the bottom of which was the bed of a torrent, with large masses of rock brought down from the neighboring precipices—they had reason to repent their negligence. Scarcely had the whole of the party entered into the narrow pass, when they were startled by the whistling of bullets close to their heads and by the echoed reports of several guns.

In an instant their guards left them, finding refuge behind rocks, and had begun to fire in the direction of the gunfire. Lord Ruthven and Aubrey, imitating this example, retired for a moment behind the sheltering turn of the defile. But ashamed of being thus detained by a foe, who with insulting shouts bade them

[20] A ravine.

advance, and being exposed to unresisting slaughter should any of the robbers climb above and take them in the rear, they determined at once to rush forward in search of the enemy.

Hardly had they lost the shelter of the rocks, when Lord Ruthven received a shot in the shoulder, which brought him to the ground. Aubrey hastened to his assistance and, no longer heeding the contest or his own peril, was soon surprised by seeing the robbers' faces around him—his guards having, upon Lord Ruthven's being wounded, immediately thrown down their arms and surrendered.

By promises of great reward, Aubrey soon induced the attackers to convey his wounded friend to a neighboring cabin. Having agreed upon a ransom, he was no more disturbed by their presence—they being content merely to guard the entrance till their comrade should return with the promised sum, for which he had an order.

Lord Ruthven's strength rapidly decreased; in two days mortification ensued, and death seemed advancing with hasty steps. His conduct and appearance had not changed; he seemed as unconscious of pain as he had been of the objects about him. But towards the close of the last evening, his mind became apparently uneasy, and his eye often fixed upon Aubrey, who was induced to offer his assistance with more than usual earnestness.

"Assist me?" uttered Ruthven. "You may save me—you may do more than that—I mean not my life, I heed the death of my existence as little as that of the passing day; but you may save my honor, your friend's honor."

"How? Tell me how—I would do anything," replied Aubrey.

"I need but little—my life ebbs apace— I cannot explain the whole—but if you would conceal all you know of me, my honor were free from stain in the world's mouth—and if my death were unknown for some time in England—I—I—but life…"

"It shall not be known," assured Aubrey.

"Swear!" cried the dying man, raising himself with exultant violence. "Swear by all your soul reveres, by all your nature fears, swear that for a year and a day you will not impart your knowledge of my crimes or death to any living being in any way, whatever may happen—or whatever you may see." His eyes seemed bursting from their sockets.

"I swear!" said Aubrey.

Lord Ruthven sunk, laughing, upon his pillow, and breathed no more.

Aubrey retired to rest, but did not sleep. The many circumstances attending his acquaintance with this man rose upon his mind, and he knew not why. When he remembered his oath a cold shivering came over him, as if from the presentiment of something horrible awaiting him.

Rising early in the morning, he was about to enter the hovel in which he had left the corpse, when a robber met him and informed him that the body was no longer there, having been conveyed by himself and comrades, upon Aubrey's retiring, to the pinnacle of a neighboring mount. According to a promise they had given his Lordship that it should be exposed to the first cold ray of the moon that rose after his death.

Astonished, Aubrey determined on taking several of the men and to go and bury the corpse upon the spot where it lay. But when he had mounted to the summit, he found no trace of either the corpse or the clothes, though the robbers swore they pointed out the identical rock on which they had laid the body. For a time his mind was bewildered in conjectures, but he at last returned, convinced that the bandits had buried the corpse for the sake of the clothes.

Weary of a country in which he had met with such terrible misfortunes, and in which all apparently conspired to heighten that superstitious melancholy that had seized upon his mind, Aubrey resolved to leave it, and soon arrived in Turkey, at Smyrna.

While waiting for a vessel to convey him to Otranto or to Naples, he occupied himself in arranging those effects he had with him belonging to Lord Ruthven. Amongst other things, there was a case containing several weapons, each more or less adapted to ensure the death of the victim. There were several daggers and *ataghans*, Turkish knives with curved blades, as like a scimitar.[21]

Whilst turning them over and examining their curious forms, to Audrey's surprise he found a sheath apparently ornamented in the same style as the dagger he discovered in the fatal hut. He shuddered, and hastening to gain further proof, then found the weapon itself. His horror may be imagined when he discovered that the blade, though peculiarly shaped, fitted perfectly the sheath he held in his hand.

His eyes seemed to need no further certainty as they gazed as if bound to the dagger, yet still he wished to disbelieve. But the weapon's particular form, the same varying tints upon the haft and sheath were alike in splendor on both, and to leave no room for doubt: there were also drops of blood on each.

He left Smyrna, and on his way home, at Rome, his first inquiries were concerning the lady he had attempted to snatch from Lord Ruthven's seductive arts. Her parents were in distress, their fortune ruined, and she had not been heard of since the departure of his lordship. Aubrey's mind became almost broken under so many repeated horrors; he was afraid that this lady had fallen a victim to the destroyer of Ianthe. He became morose and silent; his only occupation consisted in urging the speed of the postilions,[22] as if he were going to save the life of someone he held dear.

He arrived at Calais. A breeze which seemed obedient to his will soon wafted him to the English shores. Aubrey hastened to the mansion of his fathers, and there, for a moment, he appeared to lose in the embraces and caresses of his sister, all memory of the past. If she before, by her youthful caresses, had gained his affection, now that the woman began to appear, she was still more engaging as a companion.

Miss Aubrey had not that winning grace which gains the gaze and applause of the drawing-room assemblies. There was none of that light brilliancy which only exists in the heated atmosphere of a crowded apartment. Her blue eyes were never lit up by the levity of the mind beneath. There was a melancholy charm about them which did not seem to arise from misfortune, but from some feeling within that appeared to indicate a soul conscious of a brighter realm.

Her step was not that light footing which strays wherever a butterfly or a color may

---

[21] The *ataghan* was worn on the belt in a gold or silver scabbard.

[22] Type of coachman who rides the lead horse rather than guiding the team from the carriage itself.

attract—it was sedate and pensive. When alone, her face was never brightened by the smile of joy; but when her brother breathed to her his affection, and would in her presence forget those griefs she knew destroyed his rest, who would have exchanged her smile for that of the voluptuary?[23] It seemed as if those eyes, that face, were then playing in the light of their own native sphere. She was yet only eighteen and had not been presented to the world,[24] it having been thought by her guardians more fit that her presentation should be delayed until her brother's return from the continent, when he might be her protector.

It was now, therefore, resolved that the next drawing-room, which was fast approaching, should mark her entry into the "busy scene." Aubrey would rather have remained in the mansion of his fathers, and fed upon the melancholy which overpowered him.

He could not feel interest about the frivolities of fashionable strangers, when his mind had been so torn by the events he had witnessed, but he determined to sacrifice his own comfort to the protection of his sister. They soon arrived in town and prepared for the next day, which had been announced as a drawing-room.

The crowd was excessive—a drawing-room had not been held for a long time, and all who were anxious to bask in the smile of royalty hastened thither. Aubrey was there with his sister. While he was standing in a corner by himself, heedless of all around him, engaged in the remembrance that the first time he had seen Lord Ruthven was in that very place—he felt himself suddenly seized by the arm, and a voice he recognized too well sounded in his ear:—

"Remember your oath."

He had hardly courage to turn, fearful of seeing a specter that would blast him, when he perceived at a little distance, the same figure which had attracted his notice on this spot upon his first entry into society. He gazed till his limbs almost refused to bear their weight and he was obliged to take the arm of a friend. Forcing a passage through the crowd, he threw himself into his carriage and was driven home. He paced the room with hurried steps and fixed his hands upon his head, as if he were afraid his thoughts were bursting from his brain.

Lord Ruthven again before him—circumstances started up in dreadful array—the dagger—his oath. He roused himself; he could not believe it possible—the dead rise again! He thought his imagination had conjured up the image his mind was resting upon. It was impossible that it could be real. He determined, therefore, to go again into society; for though he attempted to ask concerning Lord Ruthven, the name hung upon his lips, and he could not succeed in gaining information.

Aubrey went a few nights after with his sister to the assembly of a near relation. Leaving her under the protection of a matron, he retired into an alcove and there gave himself up to his own devouring thoughts. Perceiving, at last, that many were leaving, he roused himself and, entering another room, found his sister surrounded by several, apparently in earnest conversation.

He attempted to pass and get near her

---

[23] A person whose life is devoted to the pursuit and enjoyment of luxury and sensual pleasure.

[24] She had not yet made her "debut in society" via a drawing-room reception.

when one, whom he requested to move, turned round and revealed to him those features he most abhorred. He sprang forward, seized his sister's arm and with hurried step forced her towards the street. At the door he found himself impeded by the crowd of servants who were waiting for their lords, and while he was engaged in passing them, he again heard that voice whisper close to him:

"Remember your oath!"

He did not dare to turn but, hurrying his sister, soon reached home.

Aubrey became almost distracted. If before, his mind had been absorbed by one subject, how much more completely was it engrossed now that the certainty of the monster's living again pressed upon his thoughts. His sister's attentions were now unheeded, and it was in vain that she entreated him to explain to her what had caused his abrupt conduct. He only uttered a few words, and those terrified her.

The more he thought, the more he was bewildered. His oath startled him—was he then to allow this monster to roam, bearing ruin upon his breath amidst all he held dear, and not avert its progress? His very sister might have been touched by him. But even if he were to break his oath and disclose his suspicions, who would believe him? He thought of employing his own hand to free the world from such a wretch, but death, he remembered, had been already mocked.

For days he remained in this state. Shut up in his room, he saw no one and ate only when his sister came. Her eyes streaming with tears, she besought him, for her sake, to support nature. At last, no longer capable of bearing stillness and solitude, he left his house, roamed from street to street, anxious to flee that image which haunted him. His dress became neglected, and he wandered, as often exposed to the noon-day sun as to the mid-night damps. He was no longer to be recognized; at first he returned with the evening to the house, but at last he laid himself down to rest wherever fatigue overtook him.

His sister, anxious for his safety, employed people to follow him, but they were soon outdistanced by him who fled from a pursuer swifter than any—from thought. His conduct, however, suddenly changed. Struck with the idea that he left by his absence the whole of his friends with a fiend amongst them, of whose presence they were unconscious, he determined to enter again into society and watch this menace closely, anxious to forewarn, in spite of his oath, all whom Lord Ruthven approached with intimacy.

But when he entered into a room, his haggard and suspicious looks were so striking, his inward shudderings so visible, that his sister was at last obliged to beg of him to abstain from seeking, for her sake, a society which affected him so strongly. When, however, remonstrance proved unavailing, the guardians thought proper to interpose, and fearing that his mind was becoming alienated,[25] they thought it high time to resume again that trust which had been before imposed upon them by Aubrey's parents.

Desirous of saving him from the injuries and sufferings he had daily encountered in his wanderings, and of preventing him from exposing to the general eye those marks of what they considered folly, they engaged a physician to reside in the house and take constant care of him. He hardly appeared to

---

[25] Term for insanity; psychiatrists at this time were referred to as "alienists."

notice it, so completely was his mind absorbed by one terrible subject. His incoherence became at last so great that he was confined to his chamber. There he would often lie for days, incapable of being roused.

He had become emaciated; his eyes had attained a glassy luster. The only sign of affection and recollection remaining displayed itself upon the entry of his sister. Then he would sometimes start, and seizing her hands, with looks that severely afflicted her, he would entreat her:—

"Oh, do not touch him! If your love for me is aught, do not go near him!"

When, however, she inquired to whom he referred, his only answer was, "True! True!" and again he sank into a state whence not even she could rouse him. This lasted many months; gradually, however, as the year was passing, his incoherencies became less frequent, and his mind threw off a portion of its gloom, whilst his guardians observed, that several times in the day he would count upon his fingers a definite number, and then smile.

The time had nearly elapsed, when, upon the last day of the year, one of his guardians entering his room, began to converse with his physician upon the melancholy circumstance of Aubrey's being in so awful a situation, when his sister was going next day to be married. Instantly Aubrey's attention was attracted; he asked anxiously to whom. Glad of this mark of returning intellect, of which they feared he had been deprived, they mentioned the name of the Earl of Marsden.

Thinking this was a young Earl whom he had met with in society, Aubrey seemed pleased, and astonished them still more by his expressing his intention to be present at the nuptials and desiring to see his sister. They answered not, but in a few minutes his sister was with him. He was apparently again capable of being affected by the influence of her lovely smile; for he pressed her to his breast and kissed her cheek, wet with tears flowing at the thought of her brother's being once more alive to the feelings of affection.

He began to speak with all his wonted warmth, and to congratulate her upon her marriage with a person so distinguished for rank and every accomplishment, when he suddenly perceived a locket upon her breast. Opening it, what was his surprise at beholding the features of the monster who had so long influenced his life!

He seized the portrait in a paroxysm of rage and trampled it under foot. Upon her asking him why he thus destroyed the image of her future husband, he looked as if he did not understand her. Then seizing her hands, and gazing on her with a frantic expression of countenance, he bade her swear that she would never wed this monster, for he— But he could not continue—it seemed as if that voice again bade him remember his oath. He turned suddenly round, thinking Lord Ruthven was near him, but saw no one.

In the meantime the guardians and physician, who had heard the whole and thought this was but a return of his disorder, entered and forced him from Miss Aubrey, telling her to leave. He fell upon his knees to them, he implored, he begged them to delay but for one day. They, attributing this to the insanity they imagined had taken possession of his mind, endeavored to pacify him and retired.

Lord Ruthven had called the morning after the drawing-room and had been refused with everyone else. When he heard of Aubrey's ill health, he readily understood himself to be the cause of it, but when he learned that Aubrey was deemed insane, his exultation and pleasure could hardly be concealed from those among whom he had gained this information. He hastened to the house of his former companion, and by constant attendance and the pretense of great affection for the brother and interest in his fate, he gradually won the ear of Miss Aubrey.

Who could resist his power? His tongue had dangers and toils to recount.[26] He could speak of himself as of an individual having no sympathy with any being on the crowded earth, save with her to whom he addressed himself. He could tell how, since he knew her, his existence had begun to seem worthy of preservation, if it were merely that he might listen to her soothing accents.

In fine, he knew so well how to use the serpent's art,[27] or such was the will of fate, that he gained her affections. The title of the elder branch falling at length to him, he obtained an important embassy,[28] which served as an excuse for hastening the marriage (in spite of her brother's deranged state), which was to take place the very day before his departure for the continent.

Aubrey, when he was left by the physician and his guardians, attempted to bribe the servants, but in vain. He asked for pen and paper. It was given him, and he wrote a letter to his sister, conjuring her,[29] as she valued her own happiness, her own honor, and the honor of those now in the grave, who once held her in their arms as their hope and the hope of their house, to delay but for a few hours that

marriage, on which he denounced the most heavy curses. The servants promised they would deliver it, but gave it to the physician. He thought it better not to harass any more the mind of Miss Aubrey by, what he considered, the ravings of a maniac.

Night passed on without rest for the busy inmates of the house, and Aubrey heard, with a horror that may more easily be conceived than described, the notes of busy preparation. Morning came, and the sound of carriages broke upon his ear.

Aubrey grew almost frantic. The curiosity of the servants at last overcame their vigilance; they gradually stole away, leaving him in the custody of a helpless old woman. He seized the opportunity, and with one bound was out of the room; in a moment finding himself in the apartment where all were nearly assembled. Lord Ruthven was the first to perceive him. He immediately approached and, taking Aubrey's arm by force, hurried him from the room, speechless with rage.

When on the staircase, Lord Ruthven whispered in his ear—"Remember your oath, and know, if not my bride today, your sister is dishonored. Women are frail!" So saying, he pushed him towards his attendants, who, roused by the old woman, had come in search of him.

He could no longer support himself; his rage not finding vent, had broken a bloodvessel, and he was conveyed to bed. This was not mentioned to his sister, who was not present when he entered, as the physician was

---

[26] That is, he could describe his adventures.

[27] Serpent's art: lying seductively.

[28] A relative of Ruthven's died, leaving him the title of Earl of Marsden, which he used to get appointed as a foreign ambassador. Lord Byron unexpectedly inherited his title in a similar manner.

[29] This usage, to appeal to solemnly or in earnest.

afraid of agitating her. The marriage was solemnized, and the bride and bridegroom left London.

Aubrey's weakness increased; the effusion of blood produced symptoms of the near approach of death. He desired his sister's guardians might be called, and when the midnight hour had struck, he related composedly what the reader has just perused. He died immediately after.

The guardians hastened to protect Miss Aubrey; but when they arrived, it was too late. Lord Ruthven had disappeared, and Aubrey's sister had glutted the thirst of a VAMPYRE!

Johann Ludwig Tieck

Johann Ludwig Tieck (1773-1853) was a leading German Romantic poet and novelist; he was also director of the Dresden Theatre from 1819 to 1840, before he moved to Berlin at the invitation of the emperor. Some of his *Tales* were translated by Carlyle; in turn, Tieck's German translations of *Don Quixote* (1799-1802) and Shakespeare (1825) were highly regarded. The following story has long been attributed to Tieck, but it appeared anonymously in a three-volume anthology of translations published in London under the title *Popular Tales and Romances of the Northern Nations*. The saga of Brunhilda bears a marked resemblance to the legends of Countess Elizabeth Bathory, about whom the first written accounts appeared in 1729.

WAKE NOT THE DEAD

JOHANN LUDWIG TIECK

Wilt thou forever sleep? Wilt thou never more awake, my beloved, but henceforth repose forever from thy short pilgrimage on earth? O yet once again return! And bring back with thee the vivifying dawn of hope to one whose existence hath, since thy departure, been obscured by the dunnest[1] shades. What! Dumb? Forever dumb? Thy friend lamenteth, and thou heedest him not?

He sheds bitter, scalding tears, and thou reposest unregarding his affliction? He is in despair, and thou no longer openest thy arms to him as an asylum from his grief? Say then, doth the paly[2] shroud become thee better than the bridal veil? Is the chamber of the grave a warmer bed than the couch of love? Is the spectre death more welcome to thy arms than thy enamored consort? Oh! Return, my beloved, return once again to this anxious disconsolate bosom."

Such were the lamentations which Walter poured forth for his Brunhilda, the partner of his youthful passionate love. Thus did he bewail over her grave at the midnight hour, what time the spirit that presides in the troublous atmosphere, sends his legions of monsters through mid-air; so that their shadows, as they flit beneath the moon and across the earth, dart as wild, agitating thoughts that chase each other o'er the sinner's bosom. Thus did he lament under the tall linden trees by her grave, while his head reclined on the cold stone.

Walter was a powerful lord in Burgundy, who, in his earliest youth, had been smitten with the charms of the fair Brunhilda, a beauty far surpassing in loveliness all her rivals. Her tresses, dark as the raven face of night, streaming over her shoulders, set off to the utmost advantage the beaming lustre of her slender form, and the rich dye of a cheek whose tint was deep and brilliant as that of the western heaven. Her eyes did not resemble those burning orbs whose pale glow gems the vault of night, and whose immeasurable distance fills the soul with deep thoughts of eternity, but rather as the sober beams which cheer this nether world, and

---

[1] Dun is dark brown-grey.
[2] *Archaic*: Somewhat pale; pallid.

which, while they enlighten, kindle the sons of earth to joy and love.

Brunhilda became the wife of Walter, and both being equally enamored and devoted, they abandoned themselves to the enjoyment of a passion that rendered them reckless of aught besides, while it lulled them in a fascinating dream. Their sole apprehension was lest aught should awaken them from a delirium which they prayed might continue forever. Yet how vain is the wish that would arrest the decrees of destiny! As well might it seek to divert the circling planets from their eternal course. Short was the duration of this frenzied passion; not that it gradually decayed and subsided into apathy, but death snatched away his blooming victim, and left Walter to a widowed couch. Impetuous, however, as was his first burst of grief, he was not inconsolable, and before long another bride became the partner of the youthful nobleman.

Swanhilda also was beautiful; although nature had formed her charms on a very different model from those of Brunhilda. Her golden locks waved bright as the beams of morn: only when excited by some emotion of her soul did a rosy hue tinge the lily paleness of her cheek: her limbs were proportioned in the nicest symmetry, yet did they not possess that luxuriant fullness of animal life: her eye beamed eloquently, but it was with the milder radiance of a star, tranquillizing to tenderness rather than exciting to warmth. Thus formed, it was not possible that she should steep him in his former delirium, although she rendered happy his waking hours—tranquil and serious, yet cheerful, studying in all things her husband's pleasure, she restored order and comfort in his family, where her presence shed a general influence all around. Her mild benevolence tended to restrain the fiery, impetuous disposition of

Walter; while at the same time her prudence recalled him in some degree from his vain, turbulent wishes, and his aspirings after unattainable enjoyments, to the duties and pleasures of actual life.

Swanhilda bore her husband two children, a son and a daughter; the latter was mild and patient as her mother, well contented with her solitary sports, and even in these recreations displayed the serious turn of her character. The boy possessed his father's fiery, restless disposition, tempered, however, with the solidity of his mother. Attached by his off-spring more tenderly towards their mother, Walter now lived for several years very happily; his thoughts would frequently, indeed, recur to Brunhilda, but without their former violence, merely as we dwell upon the memory of a friend of our earlier days, borne from us on the rapid current of time to a region where we know that he is happy.

But clouds dissolve into air, flowers fade, the sands of the hourglass run imperceptibly away, and even so, do human feelings dissolve, fade, and pass away, and with them too, human happiness. Walter's inconstant breast again sighed for the ecstatic dreams of those days which he had spent with his equally romantic, enamored Brunhilda—again did she present herself to his ardent fancy in all the glow of her bridal charms, and he began to draw a parallel between the past and the present. Nor did imagination, as it is wont, fail to array the former in her brightest hues, while it proportionably obscured the latter; so that he pictured to himself, the one much more rich in enjoyments, and the other, much less so than they really were.

This change in her husband did not escape Swanhilda; whereupon, redoubling her attentions towards him, and her cares towards their children, she expected, by this means, to re-unite the knot that was slackened. Yet the more she endeavored to regain his affections, the colder did he grow—the more intolerable did her caresses seem, and the more continually did the image of Brunhilda haunt his thoughts. The children, whose endearments were now become indispensable to him, alone stood between the parents as genii eager to affect a reconciliation; and, beloved by them both, formed a uniting link between them. Yet, as evil can be plucked from the heart of man, only ere its root has yet struck deep, its fangs being afterwards too firm to be eradicated; so was Walter's diseased fancy too far affected to have its disorder stopped, for, in a short time, it completely tyrannized over him. Frequently of a night, instead of retiring to his consort's chamber, he repaired to Brun-hilda's grave, where he murmured forth his dis-content, saying: "Wilt thou sleep forever?"

One night as he was reclining on the turf, indulging in his wonted sorrow, a sorcerer from the neighboring mountains entered into this field of death for the purpose of gathering, for his mystic spells, such herbs as grow only from the earth wherein the dead repose, and which, as if the last production of mortality, are gifted with a powerful and supernatural influence. The sorcerer perceived the mourner, and ap-proached the spot where he was lying.

"Wherefore, fond wretch, dost thou grieve thus, for what is now a hideous mass of mortal-ity—mere bones, and nerves, and veins? Na-tions have fallen unlamented; even worlds themselves, long ere this globe of ours was cre-ated, have mouldered into nothing; nor hath anyone wept over them; why then should'st thou indulge this vain affliction for a child of the dust—a being as frail as thyself, and like thee the creature but of a moment?"

Walter raised himself up:—"Let yon

worlds that shine in the firmament," replied he, "lament for each other as they perish. It is true, that I who am myself clay, lament for my fel-low-clay: yet is this clay impregnated with a fire—with an essence, that none of the elements of creation possess—with love: and this divine passion, I felt for her who now sleepeth beneath this sod."

"Will thy complaints awaken her: or could they do so, would she not soon upbraid thee for having disturbed that repose in which she is now hushed?"

"Avaunt,[3] cold-hearted being: thou know-est not what is love. Oh! That my tears could wash away the earthy covering that conceals her from these eyes; that my groan of anguish could rouse her from her slumber of death! No, she would not again seek her earthy couch."

"Insensate that thou art, and couldst thou endure to gaze without shuddering on one dis-gorged from the jaws of the grave? Art thou too thyself the same from whom she parted; or hath time passed o'er thy brow and left no traces there? Would not thy love rather be converted into hate and disgust?"

"Say rather that the stars would leave yon firmament, that the sun will henceforth refuse to shed his beams through the heavens. Oh! That she stood once more before me; that once again she reposed on this bosom!—how quickly should we then forget that death or time had ever stepped between us."

"Delusion! Mere delusion of the brain, from heated blood, like to that which arises from the fumes of wine. It is not my wish to tempt thee; to restore to thee thy dead; else wouldst thou soon feel that I have spoken truth."

"How! Restore her to me," exclaimed Walter

[3] *Middle English*: Forward; hence, away.

casting himself at the sorcerer's feet. "Oh! If thou art indeed able to effect that, grant it to my earnest supplication; if one throb of human feeling vibrates in thy bosom, let my tears prevail with thee: restore to me my beloved; so shalt thou hereafter bless the deed, and see that it was a good work."

"A good work! A blessed deed!"—returned the sorcerer with a smile of scorn; "for me there exists nor good nor evil; since my will is always the same. Ye alone know evil, who will that which ye would not. It is indeed in my power to restore her to thee: yet, bethink thee well, whether it will prove thy weal.[4] Consider too, how deep the abyss between life and death; across this, my power can build a bridge, but it can never fill up the frightful chasm."

Walter would have spoken, and have sought to prevail on this powerful being by fresh entreaties, but the latter prevented him, saying: "Peace! Bethink thee well! And return hither to me tomorrow at midnight. Yet once more do I warn thee, 'Wake not the dead.' "

Having uttered these words, the mysterious being disappeared. Intoxicated with fresh hope, Walter found no sleep on his couch; for fancy, prodigal of her richest stores, expanded before him the glittering web of futurity; and his eye, moistened with the dew of rapture, glanced from one vision of happiness to another.

During the next day he wandered through the woods, lest wonted objects by recalling the memory of later and less happier times, might disturb the blissful idea, that he should again behold her—again fold her in his arms, gaze on her beaming brow by day, repose on her bosom at night: and, as this sole idea filled his imagination, how was it possible that the least doubt should arise: or that the warning of the myste-

rious old man should recur to his thoughts.

No sooner did the midnight hour approach, than he hastened before the grave-field where the sorcerer was already standing by that of Brunhilda. "Hast thou maturely considered!" inquired he.

"Oh! Restore to me the object of my ardent passion," exclaimed Walter with impetuous eagerness. "Delay not thy generous action, lest I die even this night, consumed with disappointed desire; and behold her face no more."

"Well then," answered the old man, "return hither again tomorrow at the same hour. But once more do I give thee this friendly warning, 'Wake not the dead'."

All in the despair of impatience, Walter would have prostrated himself at his feet, and supplicated him to fulfill at once a desire now increased to agony; but the sorcerer had already disappeared. Pouring forth his lamentations more wildly and impetuously than ever, he lay upon the grave of his adored one, until the grey dawn streaked the east. During the day, which seemed to him longer than any he had ever experienced, he wandered to and fro, restless and impatient, seemingly without any object, and deeply buried in his own reflections, unquiet as the murderer who meditates his first deed of blood.

The stars of evening found him once more at the appointed spot. At midnight the sorcerer was there also. "Hast thou yet maturely deliberated?" inquired he, as on the preceding night.

"Oh what should I deliberate?" returned Walter impatiently. "I need not to deliberate: what I demand of thee, is that which thou hast promised me—that which will prove my bliss. Or dost thou but mock me? If so, hence from

---

[4] A prosperous state. The sorcerer is urging Walter not to act in haste.

my sight, lest I be tempted to lay my hands on thee."

"Once more do I warn thee," answered the old man with undisturbed composure. "'Wake not the dead'—let her rest."

"Aye, but not in the cold grave: she shall rather rest on this bosom which burns with eagerness to clasp her."

"Reflect, thou mayst not quit her until death, even though aversion and horror should seize thy heart. There would then remain only one horrible means."

"Dotard!"[5] cried Walter, interrupting him. "How may I hate that which I love with such intensity of passion? How should I abhor that for which my every drop of blood is boiling?"

"Then be it even as thou wishest," answered the sorcerer. "Step back."

The old man now drew a circle round the grave, all the while muttering words of enchantment. Immediately the storm began to bowl among the tops of the trees; owls flapped their wings, and uttered their low voice of omen; the stars hid their mild, beaming aspect, that they might not behold so unholy and impious a spectacle; the stone then rolled from the grave with a hollow sound, leaving a free passage for the inhabitant of that dreadful tenement. The sorcerer scattered into the yawning earth, roots and herbs of most magic power, and of most penetrating odor, so that the worms crawling forth from the earth congregated together, and raised themselves in a fiery column over the grave: while rushing wind burst from the earth, scattering the mould[6] before it, until at length the coffin lay uncovered.

The moonbeams fell on it, and the lid burst open with a tremendous sound. Upon this the sorcerer poured upon it some blood from out of a human skull, exclaiming at the same time: "Drink, sleeper, of this warm stream, that thy heart may again beat within thy bosom." And, after a short pause, shedding on her some other mystic liquid, he cried aloud with the voice of one inspired: "Yes, thy heart beats once more with the flood of life: thine eye is again opened to sight. Arise, therefore, from the tomb."

As an island suddenly springs forth from the dark waves of the ocean, raised upwards from the deep by the force of subterraneous fires, so did Brunhilda start from her earthy couch, borne forward by some invisible power. Taking her by the hand, the sorcerer led her towards Walter, who stood at some little distance, rooted to the ground with amazement.

"Receive again," said he, "the object of thy passionate sighs: mayest thou never more require my aid; should that, however, happen, so wilt thou find me, during the full of the moon, upon the mountains in that spot and where the three roads meet."

Instantly did Walter recognize in the form that stood before him, her whom he so ardently loved; and a sudden glow shot through his frame at finding her thus restored to him: yet the night-frost had chilled his limbs and palsied his tongue. For a while he gazed upon her without either motion or speech, and during his pause, all was again become hushed and serene; and the stars shone brightly in the clear heavens.

"Walter!" exclaimed the figure; and at once the well-known sound, thrilling to his heart, broke the spell by which he was bound.

"Is it reality? Is it truth?" cried he, "or a cheating delusion?"

---

[5] An old person, especially one who has become weak or senile.

[6] Dirt.

"No, it is no imposture: I am really living—conduct me quickly to thy castle in the mountains."

Walter looked around: the old man had disappeared, but he perceived close by his side, a coal-black steed of fiery eye, ready equipped to conduct him thence; and on his back laid all proper attire for Brunhilda, who lost no time in arraying herself. This being done, she cried, "Haste, let us away ere the dawn breaks, for my eye is yet too weak to endure the light of day." Fully recovered from his stupor, Walter leaped into his saddle, and catching up, with a mingled feeling of delight and awe, the beloved being thus mysteriously restored from the power of the grave, he spurred on across the wild, towards the mountains, as furiously as if pursued by the shadows of the dead, hastening to recover from him their sister.

The castle to which Walter conducted his Brunhilda was situated on a rock between other rocks rising up above it. Here they arrived, unseen by any save one aged domestic, on whom Walter imposed secrecy by the severest threats.

"Here will we tarry," said Brunhilda, "until I can endure the light, and until thou canst look upon me without trembling: as if struck with a cold chill." They accordingly continued to make that place their abode: yet no one knew that Brunhilda existed, save only that aged attendant, who provided their meals. During seven entire days they had no light except that of tapers;[7] during the next seven, the light was admitted through the lofty casements only while the rising or setting-sun faintly illumined the mountaintops, the valley being still enveloped in shade.

Seldom did Walter quit Brunhilda's side: a nameless spell seemed to attach him to her;

even the shudder which he felt in her presence, and which would not permit him to touch her, was not unmixed with pleasure, like that thrilling awful emotion felt when strains of sacred music float under the vault of some temple; he rather sought, therefore, than avoided this feeling. Often too as he had indulged in calling to mind the beauties of Brunhilda, she had never appeared so fair, so fascinating, so admirable when depicted by his imagination, as when now beheld in reality. Never till now had her voice sounded with such tones of sweetness; never before did her language possess such eloquence as it now did, when she conversed with him on the subject of the past. And this was the magic fairy-land towards which her words constantly conducted him. Ever did she dwell upon the days of their first love, those hours of delight which they had participated together when the one derived all enjoyment from the other: and so rapturous, so enchanting, so full of life did she recall to his imagination that blissful season, that he even doubted whether he had ever experienced with her so much felicity, or had been so truly happy.

And, while she thus vividly portrayed their hours of past delight, she delineated in still more glowing, more enchanting colors, those hours of approaching bliss which now awaited them, richer in enjoyment than any preceding ones. In this manner did she charm her attentive auditor with enrapturing hopes for the future, and lull him into dreams of more than mortal ecstasy; so that while he listened to her siren strain, he entirely forgot how little blissful was the latter period of their union, when he had often sighed at her imperiousness, and at her harshness both to himself and all his household. Yet even had he recalled this to mind would it have disturbed him in his present delirious trance? Had she not now left behind

---

[7] Candles.

in the grave all the frailty of mortality? Was not her whole being refined and purified by that long sleep in which neither passion nor sin had approached her even in dreams? How different now was the subject of her discourse! Only when speaking of her affection for him, did she betray anything of earthly feeling: at other times, she uniformly dwelt upon themes relating to the invisible and future world; when in descanting[8] and declaring the mysteries of eternity, a stream of prophetic eloquence would burst from her lips.

In this manner had twice seven days elapsed, and, for the first time, Walter beheld the being now dearer to him than ever, in the full light of day. Every trace of the grave had disappeared from her countenance; a roseate tinge like the ruddy streaks of dawn again beamed on her pallid cheek. The faint, mouldering taint of the grave was changed into a delightful violet scent; the only sign of earth that never disappeared. He no longer felt either apprehension or awe as he gazed upon her in the sunny light of day. It is not until now that he seemed to have recovered her completely; and, glowing with all his former passion towards her, he would have pressed her to his bosom, but she gently repulsed him, saying:—"Not yet—spare your caresses until the moon has again filled her horn."

Spite of his impatience, Walter was obliged to await the lapse of another period of seven days: but, on the night when the moon was arrived at the full, he hastened to Brunhilda, whom he found more lovely than she had ever appeared before. Fearing no obstacles to his transports, he embraced her with all the fervor of a deeply enamored and successful lover. Brunhilda, however, still refused to yield to his passion.

"What!" exclaimed she. "Is it fitting that I who have been purified by death from the frailty of mortality, should become thy concubine, while a mere daughter of the earth bears the tide of thy wife? Never shall it be. No, it must be within the walls of thy palace, within that chamber where I once reigned as queen, that thou obtainest the end of thy wishes—and of mine also," added she, imprinting a glowing kiss on the lips, and immediately disappeared.

Heated with passion, and determined to sacrifice everything to the accomplishment of his desires, Walter hastily quitted the apartment, and shortly after the castle itself. He traveled over mountain and across heath, with the rapidity of a storm, so that the turf was flung up by his horse's hooves; nor once stopped until he arrived home.

Here, however, neither the affectionate caresses of Swanhilda, or those of his children could touch his heart, or induce him to restrain his furious desires. Alas! Is the impetuous torrent to be checked in its devastating course by the beauteous flowers over which it rushes, when they exclaim:—"Destroyer, commiserate our helpless innocence and beauty, nor lay us waste"?—the stream sweeps over them unregarding, and a single moment annihilates the pride of a whole summer.

Shortly afterwards, did Walter begin to hint to Swanhilda, that they were ill-suited to each other; that he was anxious to taste that wild, tumultuous life, so well according with the spirit of his sex, while she, on the contrary, was satisfied with the monotonous circle of household enjoyments:—that he was eager for whatever promised novelty, while she felt most attached to what was familiarized to her by habit: and lastly, that her cold disposition, bordering upon indifference, but ill assorted with his ardent temperament: it was therefore more

[8] Discussing earnestly.

prudent that they should seek apart from each other, that happiness which they could not find together.

A sigh, and a brief acquiescence in his wishes was all the reply that Swanhilda made: and, on the following morning, upon his presenting her with a paper of separation, informing her that she was at liberty to return home to her father, she received it most submissively: yet, ere she departed, she gave him the following warning:—

"Too well do I conjecture to whom I am indebted for this our separation. Often have I seen thee at Brunhilda's grave, and beheld thee there even on that night when the face of the heavens was suddenly enveloped in a veil of clouds. Hast thou rashly dared to tear aside the awful veil that separates the mortality that dreams, from that which dreameth not? Oh! Then woe to thee, thou wretched man, for thou has attached to thyself that which will prove thy destruction." She ceased, nor did Walter attempt any reply, for the similar admonition uttered by the sorcerer flashed upon his mind, all obscured as it was by passion, just as the lightning glares momentarily through the gloom of night without dispersing the obscurity.

Swanhilda then departed, in order to pronounce to her children, a bitter farewell, for they, according to national custom, belonged to the father; and, having bathed them in her tears, and consecrated them with the holy water of maternal love, she quitted her husband's residence, and departed to the home of her father's.

Thus was the kind and benevolent Swanhilda, driven an exile from those halls, where she had presided with such graces—from halls which were newly decorated to receive another mistress. The day at length arrived, on which Walter, for the second time, conducted Brunhilda home, as a newly-made bride. And he caused it to be reported amongst his domestics, that his new consort had gained his affections by her extraordinary likeness to Brunhilda, their former mistress. How ineffably happy did he deem himself, as he conducted his beloved once more into the chamber which had often witnessed their former joys, and which was now newly gilded and adorned in a most costly style: among the other decorations were figures of angels scattering roses, which served to support the purple draperies, whose ample folds o'ershadowed the nuptial couch.

With what impatience did he await the hour that was to put him in possession of those beauties, for which he had already paid so high a price, but, whose enjoyment was to cost him most dearly yet! Unfortunate Walter! Reveling in bliss, thou beholdest not the abyss that yawns beneath thy feet, intoxicated with the luscious perfume of the flower thou hast plucked, thou little deemest how deadly is the venom with which it is fraught, although, for a short season, its potent fragrance bestows new energy on all thy feelings.

Happy, however, as Walter now was, his household were far from being equally so. The strange resemblance between their new lady and the deceased Brunhilda, filled them with a secret dismay—an undefinable horror; for there was not a single difference of feature, of tone of voice, or of gesture. To add too to these mysterious circumstances, her female attendants discovered a particular mark on her back, exactly like one which Brunhilda had.

A report was now soon circulated, that their lady was no other than Brunhilda herself, who had been recalled to life by the power of necromancy. How truly horrible was the idea of living under the same roof with one who had been an inhabitant of the tomb, and of being obliged to attend upon her, and acknowledge her as mistress! There was also in Brunhilda, much to increase this aversion, and favor their superstition: no ornaments of gold ever decked her person; all that others were wont to wear of this metal, she had formed of silver: no richly colored and sparkling jewels glittered upon her; pearls alone, lent their pale luster to adorn her bosom. Most carefully did she always avoid the cheerful light of the sun, and was wont to spend the brightest days in the most retired and gloomy apartments: only during the twilight of the commencing, or declining day did she ever walk abroad, but her favorite hour was, when the phantom light of the moon bestowed on all objects a shadowy appearance, and a somber hue; always too at the crowing of the cock, an involuntary shudder was observed to seize her limbs.

Imperious as before her death, she quickly imposed her iron yoke on every one around her, while she seemed even far more terrible than ever, since a dread of some supernatural power attached to her, and appalled all who approached her. A malignant withering glance seemed to shoot from her eye on the unhappy object of her wrath, as if it would annihilate its victim. In short, those halls which, in the time of Swanhilda were the residence of cheerfulness and mirth, now resembled an extensive desert tomb. With fear imprinted on their pale countenances, the domestics glided through the apartments of the castle; and, in this abode of terror, the crowing of the cock caused the living to tremble, as if they were the spirits of the departed; for the sound always reminded them of their mysterious mistress. There was no one but who shuddered at meeting her in a lonely place, in the dusk of evening, or by the light of the moon, a circumstance that was deemed to be ominous of some evil: so great was the appre-

hension of her female attendants, they pined in continual disquietude, and, by degrees, all quitted her. In the course of time even others of the domestics fled, for an insupportable horror had seized them.

The art of the sorcerer had indeed bestowed upon Brunhilda an artificial life, and due nourishment had continued to support the restored body; yet, this body was not able of itself to keep up the genial glow of vitality, and to nourish the flame whence springs all the affections and passions, whether of love or hate; for death had forever destroyed and withered it: all that Brunhilda now possessed was a chilled existence, colder than that of the snake. It was nevertheless necessary that she should love, and return with equal ardour the warm caresses of her spell-enthralled husband, to whose passion alone she was indebted for her renewed existence. It was necessary that a magic draught should animate the dull current in her veins, and awaken her to the glow of life and the flame of love—a potion of abomination—one not even to be named without a curse—human blood, imbibed whilst yet warm, from the veins of youth.

This was the hellish drink for which she thirsted: possessing no sympathy with the purer feelings of humanity; deriving no enjoyment from aught that interests in life, and occupies its varied hours; her existence was a mere blank, unless when in the arms of her paramour husband, and therefore was it that she craved incessantly after the horrible draught. It was even with the utmost effort that she could forbear sucking even the blood of Walter himself, as he reclined beside her.

Whenever she beheld some innocent child, whose lovely face denoted the exuberance of infantine health and vigor, she would entice it by soothing words and fond caresses into her most secret apartment, where, lulling it to sleep in her arms, she would suck from its bosom the warm, purple tide of life. Nor were youths of either sex safe from her horrid attack: having first breathed upon her unhappy victim, who never failed immediately to sink into a lengthened sleep, she would then in a similar manner drain his veins of the vital juice.

Thus children, youths, and maidens quickly faded away, as flowers gnawn by the cankering worm: the fullness of their limbs disappeared; a sallow line succeeded to the rosy freshness of their cheeks, the liquid luster of the eye was deadened, even as the sparkling stream when arrested by the touch of frost; and their locks became thin and grey, as if already ravaged by the storm of life. Parents beheld with horror this desolating pestilence, devouring their offspring; nor could simple charm, potion, or amulet avail aught against it.

The grave swallowed up one after the other; or did the miserable victim survive, he became cadaverous and wrinkled even in the very morn of existence. Parents observed with horror, this devastating pestilence snatch away their off-spring—a pestilence which, nor herb however potent, nor charm, nor holy taper, nor exorcism could avert. They either beheld their children sink one after the other into the grave, or their youthful forms, withered by the unholy, vampire embrace of Brunhilda, assume the decrepitude of sudden age.

At length strange surmises and reports began to prevail. It was whispered that Brunhilda herself was the cause of all these horrors; although no one could pretend to tell in what manner she destroyed her victims, since no marks of violence were discernible. Yet when young children confessed that she had fre-

quently lulled them asleep in her arms, and elder ones said that a sudden slumber had come upon them whenever she began to converse with them, suspicion became converted into certainty, and those whose off-spring had hitherto escaped unharmed, quitted their hearths and home—all their little possessions—the dwellings of their fathers and the inheritance of their children, in order to rescue from so horrible a fate those who were dearer to their simple affections than aught else the world could give.

Thus daily did the castle assume a more desolate appearance; daily did its environs become more deserted; none but a few aged decrepit old women and grey-headed menials were to be seen remaining of the once numerous retinue. Such will in the latter days of the earth, be the last generation of mortals, when child-bearing shall have ceased, when youth shall no more be seen, nor any arise to replace those who shall await their fate in silence.

Walter alone noticed not, or heeded not, the desolation around him; he apprehended not death, lapped as he was in a glowing Elysium[9] of love. Far more happy than formerly did he now seem in the possession of Brunhilda. All those caprices and frowns which had been wont to overcloud their former union had now entirely disappeared. She even seemed to dote on him with a warmth of passion that she had never exhibited even during the happy season of bridal love; for the flame of that youthful blood, of which she drained the veins of others, rioted in her own. At night, as soon as he closed his eyes, she would breathe on him till he sank into delicious dreams, from which he awoke only to experience more rapturous enjoyments. By day she would continually discourse with him on the bliss experienced by happy spirits

9 In Greek mythology Elysium is a section of the Underworld reserved for heroic and virtuous souls.

beyond the grave, assuring him that, as his af-fection had recalled her from the tomb, they were now irrevocably united. Thus fascinated by a continual spell, it was not possible that he should perceive what was taking place around him. Brunhilda, however, foresaw with savage grief that the source of her youthful ardor was daily decreasing, for, in a short time, there re-mained nothing gifted with youth, save Walter and his children, and these latter she resolved should be her next victims.

On her first return to the castle, she had felt an aversion towards the off-spring of an-other, and therefore abandoned them entirely to the attendants appointed by Swanhilda. Now, however, she began to pay considerable attention to them, and caused them to be fre-quently admitted into her presence. The aged nurses were filled with dread at perceiving these marks of regard from her towards their young charges, yet dared they not to oppose the will of their terrible and imperious mistress. Soon did Brunhilda gain the affection of the children, who were too unsuspecting of guile to appre-hend any danger from her; on the contrary, her caresses won them completely to her.

Instead of ever checking their mirthful gambols, she would rather instruct them in new sports; often too did she recite to them tales of such strange and wild interests as to exceed all the stories of their nurses. Were they wearied either with play or with listening to her narra-tives, she would take them on her knees and lull them to slumber. Then did visions of the most surpassing magnificence attend their dreams: they would fancy themselves in some garden where flowers of every hue rose in rows one above the other, from the humble violet to the tall sun-flower, forming a party-colored broi-dery of every hue, sloping upwards towards the golden clouds, where little angels, whose wings sparkled with azure and gold, descended to bring them delicious foods, or splendid jewels; or sung to them soothing melodious hymns.

So delightful did these dreams in short time become to the children, that they longed for nothing so eagerly as to slumber on Brun-hilda's lap, for never did they else enjoy such visions of heavenly forms. Thus were they most anxious for that which was to prove their destruction:—yet do we not all aspire after that which conducts us to the grave—after the enjoy-ment of life? These innocents stretched out their arms to approaching death, because it assumed the mask of pleasure; for, while they were lapped in these ecstatic slumbers, Brun-hilda sucked the life-stream from their bosoms.

On waking, indeed, they felt themselves faint and exhausted, yet did no pain, nor any mark betray the cause. Shortly, however, did their strength entirely fail, even as the summer brook is gradually dried up; their sports became less and less noisy; their loud, frolicsome laugh-ter was converted into a faint smile; the full tones of their voices died away into a mere whisper. Their attendants were filled with hor-ror and despair, too well did they conjecture the horrible truth, yet dared not to impart their sus-picions to Walter, who was so devotedly at-tached to his horrible partner. Death had already smote his prey: the children were but the mere shadows of their former selves, and even this shadow quickly disappeared.

The anguished father deeply bemoaned their loss, for, notwithstanding his apparent neglect, he was strongly attached to them, nor until he had experienced their loss was he aware that his love was so great. His affliction could not fail to excite the displeasure of Brunhilda.

"Why dost thou lament so fondly," said she, "for these little ones? What satisfaction could such unformed beings yield to thee, unless thou wert still attached to their mother? Thy heart then is still hers? Or dost thou now regret her and them, because thou art satiated with my fondness, and weary of my endearments? Had these young ones grown up, would they not have attached thee, thy spirit and thy affections more closely to this earth of clay—to this dust, and have alienated thee from that sphere to which I, who have already passed the grave, endeavor to raise thee? Say is thy spirit so heavy, or thy love so weak, or thy faith so hollow, that the hope of being mine forever is unable to touch thee?"

Thus did Brunhilda express her indignation at her consort's grief, and forbade him her presence. The fear of offending her beyond forgiveness, and his anxiety to appease her soon dried up his tears; and he again abandoned himself to his fatal passion, until approaching destruction at length awakened him from his delusion.

Neither maiden, nor youth, was any longer to be seen, either within the dreary walls of the castle, or the adjoining territory—all had disappeared; for those whom the grave had not swallowed up, had fled from the region of death. Who, therefore, now remained to quench the horrible thirst of the female vampire, save Walter himself? And his death she dared to contemplate unmoved; for that divine sentiment that unites two beings in one joy and one sorrow was unknown to her bosom. Was he in his tomb, so was she free to search out other victims, and glut herself with destruction, until she herself should, at the last day, be consumed with the earth itself. Such is the fatal law, to which the dead are subject, when awoke by the arts of necromancy from the sleep of the grave.

She now began to fix her blood-thirsty lips on Walter's breast, when cast into a profound sleep by the odor of her violet breath. He reclined beside her quite unconscious of his impending fate: yet soon did his vital powers begin to decay; and many a grey hair peeped through his raven locks. With his strength, his passion also declined; and he now frequently left her in order to pass the whole day in the sports of the chase, hoping thereby, to regain his wonted vigor.

As he was reposing one day in a wood beneath the shade of an oak, he perceived, on the summit of a tree, a bird of strange appearance, and quite unknown to him; but, before he could take aim at it with his bow, it flew away into the clouds; at the same time, letting fall a rose-colored root which dropped at Walter's feet. He immediately took it up, and, although he was well acquainted with almost every plant, he could not remember to have seen any at all resembling this. Its delightfully odoriferous scent induced him to try its flavor, but ten times more bitter than wormwood,[10] it was even as gall[11] in his mouth; upon which, impatient of the disappointment, he flung it away with violence. Had he, however, been aware of its miraculous quality, and that it acted as a counter charm against the opiate perfume of Brunhilda's breath, he would have blessed it in spite of its bitterness: thus do mortals often blindly cast away in displeasure the unsavory remedy that would otherwise work their weal.

When Walter returned home in the evening and laid him down to repose as usual by Brunhilda's side, the magic power of her breath produced no effect upon him; and for the first

---

[10] Known for its bitter taste, wormword was used in folk medicine to counteract poison; a variety is used in the preparation of absinthe.

[11] Bile; used in medicine, also very bitter.

time during many months did he close his eyes in a natural slumber. Yet hardly had he fallen asleep, ere a pungent smarting pain disturbed him from his dreams; and, opening his eyes, he discerned, by the gloomy rays of a lamp, that glimmered in the apartment, what for some moments transfixed him quite aghast, for it was Brunhilda, drawing with her lips, the warm blood from his bosom. The wild cry of horror which at length escaped him, terrified Brunhilda, whose mouth was besmeared with the warm blood.

"Monster!" exclaimed he, springing from the couch, "is it thus that you love me?"

"Aye, even as the dead love," replied she, with a malignant coldness.

"Creature of blood!" continued Walter. "The delusion which has so long blinded me is at an end! Thou art the fiend who hast destroyed my children—who hast murdered the off-spring of my vassals."

Raising herself upwards and, at the same time, casting on him a glance that froze him to the spot with dread, she replied, "It is not I who have murdered them:—I was obliged to pamper myself with warm youthful blood, in order that I might satisfy thy furious desires—thou art the murderer!"

These dreadful words summoned, before Walter's terrified conscience, the threatening shades[12] of all those who had thus perished; while despair choked his voice. "Why," continued she, in a tone that increased his horror, "why dost thou make mouths at me like a puppet? Thou who hadst the courage to love the dead—to take into thy bed one who had been sleeping in the grave, the bed-fellow of the worm—who hast clasped in thy lustful arms,

the corruption of the tomb—dost thou, unhallowed as thou art, now raise this hideous cry for the sacrifice of a few lives? They are but leaves swept from their branches by a storm. Come, chase these idiot fancies and taste the bliss thou hast so dearly purchased."

So saying, she extended her arms towards him. But this motion served only to increase his terror, and exclaiming: "Accursed Being,"—he rushed out of the apartment.

All the horrors of a guilty, upbraiding conscience became his companions, now that he was awakened from the delirium of his unholy pleasures. Frequently did he curse his own obstinate blindness, for having given no heed to the hints and admonitions of his children's nurses, but treating them as vile calumnies.[13] But his sorrow was now too late, for, although repentance may gain pardon for the sinner, it cannot alter the immutable decrees of fate—it cannot recall the murdered from the tomb.

No sooner did the first break of dawn appear, than he set out for his lonely castle in the mountains, determined no longer to abide under the same roof with so terrific a being; yet vain was his flight, for, on waking the following morning, he perceived himself in Brunhilda's arms, and quite entangled in her long raven tresses, which seemed to involve him and bind him in the fetters of his fate. The powerful fascination of her breath held him still more captivated, so that, forgetting all that had passed, he returned her caresses, until awakening as if from a dream he recoiled in unmixed horror from her embrace.

During the day he wandered through the solitary wilds of the mountains, as a culprit seeking an asylum from his pursuers; and, at night, retired to the shelter of a cave; fearing less to couch himself within such a dreary place, than to expose himself to the horror of

---

[12] Ghosts.

[13] Lies intended to harm another's reputation.

again meeting Brunhilda. But alas! It was in vain that he endeavored to flee her. Again, when he awoke, he found her the partner of his miserable bed. Nay, had he sought the centre of the earth as his hiding place; had he even imbedded himself beneath rocks, or formed his chamber in the recesses of the ocean, still had he found her his constant companion; for, by calling her again into existence, he had rendered himself inseparably hers; so fatal were the links that united them.

Struggling with the madness that was beginning to seize him, and brooding incessantly on the ghastly visions that presented themselves to his horror-stricken mind, he lay motionless in the gloomiest recesses of the woods, even from the rise of sun till the shades of eve. But, no sooner was the light of day extinguished in the west, and the woods buried in impenetrable darkness, than the apprehension of resigning himself to sleep drove him forth among the mountains.

The storm played wildly with the fantastic clouds, and with the rattling leaves, as they were caught up into the air, as if some dread spirit was sporting with these images of transitoriness and decay: it roared among the summits of the oaks as if uttering a voice of fury, while its hollow sound rebounding among the distant hills, seemed as the moans of a departing sinner, or as the faint cry of some wretch expiring under the murderer's hand: the owl too, uttered its ghastly cry as if foreboding the wreck of nature.

Walter's hair flew disorderly in the wind, like black snakes wreathing around his temples and shoulders; while each sense was awake to catch fresh horror. In the clouds he seemed to behold the form of the murdered; in the howling wind to hear their laments and groans; in the chilling blast itself he felt the dire kiss of Brunhilda; in the cry of the screeching bird he heard her voice; in the mouldering leaves he scented the charnel-bed out of which he had awakened her.

"Murder of thy own off-spring," exclaimed he in a voice making night and the conflict of the elements still more hideous. "Paramour of a blood-thirsty vampire, reveler with the corruption of the tomb!"

In his despair he rent the wild locks from his head, as just then the full moon darted from beneath the bursting clouds. The sight recalled to his remembrance the advice of the sorcerer, when he trembled at the first apparition of Brunhilda rising from her sleep of death—namely, to seek him, at the season of the full moon, in the mountains, where three roads met. Scarcely had this gleam of hope broke in on his bewildered mind, than he flew to the appointed spot.

On his arrival, Walter found the old man seated there upon a stone, as calmly as though it had been a bright sunny day, and completely regardless of the uproar around. "Art thou come then?" exclaimed he to the breathless wretch, who, flinging himself at his feet, cried in a tone of anguish:—"Oh save me—succor me—rescue me from the monster that scattereth death and desolation around her."

"And wherefore a mysterious warning? Why didst thou not perceive how wholesome was the advice:—'Wake not the dead'?"

"And wherefore a mysterious warning? Why didst thou not rather disclose to me, at once, all the horrors that awaited my sacrilegious profanation of the grave?"

"Wert[13] thou able to listen to any other voice than that of thy impetuous passions? Did not thy eager impatience shut my mouth at the

[13] *Archaic*: "were."

very moment I would have cautioned thee?"

"True, true:—thy reproof is just. But what does it avail now?—I need the promptest aid."

"Well," replied the old man, "there remains even yet a means of rescuing thyself, but it is fraught with horror, and demands all thy resolution."

"Utter it then, utter it; for what can be more appalling, more hideous than the misery I now endure?"

"Know then," continued the sorcerer, "that only on the night of the new moon, does she sleep the sleep of mortals; and then all the supernatural power which she inherits from the grave totally fails her. 'Tis then that thou must murder her."

"How! Murder her!" echoed Walter.

"Aye," returned the old man calmly, "pierce her bosom with a sharpened dagger, which I will furnish thee with; at the same time renounce her memory forever, swearing never to think of her intentionally, and that, if thou dost involuntarily, thou wilt repeat the curse."

"Most horrible! Yet what can be more horrible than she herself is?—I'll do it."

"Keep then this resolution until the next new moon."

"What, must I wait until then?" cried Walter. "Alas ere then, either her savage thirst for blood will have forced me into the night of the tomb, or horror will have driven me into the night of madness."

"Nay," replied the sorcerer, "that I can prevent," and, so saying he conducted him to a cavern further among the mountains. "Abide here twice seven days," said he; "so long can I protect thee against her deadly caresses. Here wilt thou find all due provision for thy wants; but take heed that nothing tempt thee to quit this place. Farewell, when the moon renews itself, then do I repair hither again." So saying, the sorcerer drew a magic circle around the cave, and then immediately disappeared.

Twice seven days did Walter continue in this solitude, where his companions were his own terrifying thoughts, and his bitter repentance. The present was all desolation and dread; the future presented the image of a horrible deed, which he must perforce commit; while the past was empoisoned by the memory of his guilt. Did he think on his former happy union with Brunhilda, her horrible image presented itself to his imagination with her lips defiled with dripping blood: or, did he call to mind the peaceful days he had passed with Swanhilda, he beheld her sorrowful spirit, with the shadows of her murdered children. Such were the horrors that attended him by day: those of night were still more dreadful, for then he beheld Brunhilda herself, who, wandering round the magic circle which she could not pass, called upon his name, till the cavern re-echoed the horrible sound. "Walter, my beloved," cried she, "wherefore dost thou avoid me? Art thou not mine? Forever mine—mine here, and mine hereafter? And dost thou seek to murder me?—Ah! Commit not a deed which hurls us both to perdition—thyself as well as me." In this manner did the horrible visitant torment him each night, and, even when she departed, robbed him of all repose.

The night of the new moon at length arrived, dark as the deed it was doomed to bring forth. The sorcerer entered the cavern; "Come," said he to Walter, "let us depart hence, the hour is now arrived"; and he forthwith conducted him in silence from the cave to a coal-black steed, the sight of which recalled to Walter's remembrance the fatal night. He then related to the old man Brunhilda's nocturnal visits, and anxiously inquired whether her apprehensions of eternal perdition would be fulfilled or not.

"Mortal eye," exclaimed the sorcerer, "may

not pierce the dark secrets of another world, or penetrate the deep abyss that separates earth from heaven." Walter hesitated to mount the steed. "Be resolute," exclaimed his companion, "but this once is it granted to thee to make the trial, and, should thou fail now, naught can rescue thee from her power."

"What can be more horrible than she herself?—I am determined"; and he leaped on the horse, the sorcerer mounting also behind him.

Carried with a rapidity equal to that of the storm that sweeps across the plain, they in brief space arrived at Walter's castle. All the doors flew open at the bidding of his companion, and they speedily reached Brunhilda's chamber, and stood beside her couch. Reclining in a tranquil slumber; she reposed in all her native loveliness, every trace of horror had disappeared from her countenance; she looked so pure, meek, and innocent that all the sweet hours of their endearments rushed to Walter's memory, like interceding angels pleading in her behalf. His unnerved hand could not take the dagger which the sorcerer presented to him. "The blow must be struck even now"; said the latter, "shouldst thou delay but an hour, she will lie at daybreak on thy bosom, sucking the warm life drops from thy heart."

"Horrible! Most horrible!" faltered the trembling Walter, and turning away his face, he thrust the dagger into her bosom, exclaiming— "I curse thee forever!"—and the cold blood gushed upon his hand. Opening her eyes once more, she cast a look of ghastly horror on her husband, and, in a hollow dying accent said:—

"Thou too art doomed to perdition."

"Lay now thy hand upon her corse,"[15] said the sorcerer, "and swear the oath."

15 *Archaic*: corpse.

Walter did as commanded, saying:—

"Never will I think of her with love, never recall her to mind intentionally, and, should her image recur to my mind involuntarily, so will I exclaim to it: be thou accursed."

"Thou has now done everything," returned the sorcerer; "restore her therefore to the earth, from which thou didst so foolishly recall her; and be sure to recollect thy oath: for, shouldst thou forget it but once, she would return, and thou wouldst be inevitably lost. Adieu—we see each other no more." Having uttered these words he quitted the apartment, and Walter also fled from this abode of horror, having first given direction that the corse should be speedily interred.

Again did the terrific Brunhilda repose within her grave; but her image continually haunted Walter's imagination, so that his existence was one continued martyrdom, in which he continually struggled, to dismiss from his recollection the hideous phantoms of the past; yet, the stronger his effort to banish them, so much the more frequently and the more vividly did they return; as the night-wanderer, who is enticed by a fire-wisp into quagmire or bog, sinks the deeper into his damp grave the more he struggles to escape. His imagination seemed incapable of admitting any other image than that of Brunhilda: now he fancied he beheld her expiring, the blood streaming from her beautiful bosom: at others he saw the lovely bride of his youth, who reproached him with having disturbed the slumbers of the tomb: and to both he was compelled to utter the dreadful words, "I curse thee forever."

The terrible imprecation was constantly passing his lips; yet was he in incessant terror lest he should forget it, or dream of her without being able to repeat it, and then, on awakening, find himself in her arms. Else would he recall her expiring words, and, appalled at their terrific import, imagine that the doom of his perdition was irrecoverably passed. Whence should he fly from himself? Or how erase from his brain these images and forms of horror? In the din of combat, in the tumult of war and its incessant pour of victory to defeat; from the cry of anguish to the exultation of victory—in these he hoped to find at least relief of distraction: but here too he was disappointed. The giant fang of apprehension now seized him who had never before known fear; each drop of blood that sprayed upon him seemed the cold blood that had gushed from Brunhilda's wound; each dying wretch that fell beside him looked like her, when expiring, she exclaimed:—"Thou too art doomed to perdition"; so that the aspect of death seemed more full of dread to him than aught beside, and this unconquerable terror compelled him to abandon the battlefield.

At length, after many a weary and fruitless wandering, he returned to his castle. Here all was deserted and silent, as if the sword, or a still more deadly pestilence had laid everything waste: for the few inhabitants that still remained, and even those servants who had once shewn themselves the most attached, now fled from him, as though he had been branded with the mark of Cain. With horror he perceived that, by uniting himself as he had done with the dead, he had cut himself off from the living, who refused to hold any association with him. Often, when he stood on the battlements of his castle, and looked down upon desolate fields, he compared their present solitude with the lively activity they were wont to exhibit, under the strict but benevolent discipline of Swanhilda. He now felt that she alone could reconcile him to life, but durst he hope that one, whom he so deeply aggrieved, could pardon him, and receive him again?

Impatience at length got the better of fear; he sought Swanhilda, and, with the deepest contrition, acknowledged his complicated guilt; embracing her knees he beseeched her to pardon him, and to return to his desolate castle, in order that it might again become the abode of contentment and peace. The pale form which she beheld at her feet, the shadow of the lately blooming youth, touched Swanhilda.

"The folly," said she gently, "though it has caused me much sorrow, has never excited my resentment or my anger. But say, where are my children?"

To this dreadful interrogation the agonized father could for a while frame no reply: at length he was obliged to confess the dreadful truth. "Then we are sundered forever," returned Swanhilda; nor could all his tears or supplications prevail upon her to revoke the sentence she had given.

Stripped of his last earthly hope, bereft of his last consolation, and thereby rendered as poor as mortal can possibly be on this side of the grave, Walter returned homewards. When, as he was riding through the forest in the neighborhood of his castle, absorbed in his gloomy meditations, the sudden sound of a horn roused him from his reverie. Shortly after he saw appear a female figure clad in black, and mounted on a steed of the same color: her attire was like that of a huntress, but, instead of a falcon, she bore a raven in her hand; and she was attended by a cheerful troop of cavaliers and dames.

The first salutations being passed, he found that she was proceeding the same road as himself; and, when she found that Walter's castle was close at hand, she requested that he would lodge her for that night, the evening being far advanced. Most willingly did he comply with this request, since the appearance of the beautiful stranger had struck him greatly;

so wonderfully did she resemble Swanhilda, except that her locks were brown, and her eye dark and full of fire. With a sumptuous banquet did he entertain his guests, whose mirth and songs enlivened the lately silent halls. Three days did this revelry continue, and so exhilarating did it prove to Walter, that he seemed to have forgotten his sorrows and his fears; nor could he prevail upon himself to dismiss his visitors, dreading lest, on their departure, the castle would seem a hundred times more desolate than before, and his grief be proportionately increased. At his earnest request, the stranger consented to stay seven days, and again another seven days.

Without being requested, she took upon herself the superintendence of the household, which she regulated as discreetly and cheerfully as Swanhilda had been wont to do, so that the castle, which had so lately been the abode of melancholy and horror, became the residence of pleasure and festivity, and Walter's grief disappeared altogether in the midst of so much gaiety. Daily did his attachment to the fair unknown increase; he even made her his confidant; and, one evening as they were walking together apart from any of her train, he related to her his melancholy and frightful history.

"My dear friend," returned she, as soon as he had finished his tale, "it ill beseems a man of thy discretion to afflict thyself, on account of all this. Thou hast awakened the dead from the sleep of the grave, and afterwards found—what might have been anticipated, that the dead possess no sympathy with life. What then? Thou wilt not commit this error a second time. Thou hast however murdered the being whom thou hadst

thus recalled again to existence—but it was only in appearance, for thou couldst not deprive that of life, which properly had none. Thou hast, too, lost a wife and two children: but, at thy years, such a loss is most easily repaired. There are beauties who will gladly share thy couch, and make thee again a father. But thou dreadst the reckoning of hereafter:—go, open the graves and ask the sleepers there whether that hereafter disturbs them."

In such manner would she frequently exhort and cheer him, so that, in a short time, his melancholy entirely disappeared. He now ventured to declare to the unknown the passion with which she had inspired him, nor did she refuse him her hand. Within seven days afterwards the nuptials were celebrated, and the very foundations of the castle seemed to rock from the wild tumultuous uproar of unrestrained riot. The wine streamed in abundance; the goblets circled incessantly: intemperance reached its utmost bounds, while shouts of laughter, almost resembling madness, burst from the numerous train belonging to the unknown. At length Walter, heated with wine and love, conducted his bride into the nuptial chamber: but, oh horror! Scarcely had he clasped her in his arms, ere she transformed herself into a monstrous serpent, which entwining him in its horrid folds, crushed him to death.

Flames crackled on every side of the apartment; in a few minutes after, the whole castle was enveloped in a blaze that consumed it entirely: while, as the walls fell in with a tremendous crash, a voice exclaimed aloud:—

"Wake not the dead!"

Aleksei Tolstoy

ALEKSEI TOLSTOY (1810-1875) was a Russian Count who served in the Crimean War and wrote numerous dramas, poems, and novels, including his notable play *Death of Ivan the Terrible* (1864). A distant cousin of Leo Tolstoy, Aleksei wrote a series of ghost stories, including the following. Written in French, it was first published in 1843 (under a pseudonym); it wasn't issued in Russia until 1884. Its folklore seems to be lifted straight out of the accounts of Dom Augustine Calmet (1672-1757), whose *Dissertations sur les apparitions des anges, des démons et des espirits. Et sur les revanans et vampires de Hongrie, de Boheme, de Maravie et de Silésie* was first published in Paris in 1746.

In this tale, a sophisticated nobleman finds himself in the middle of a pack of rural vampires. This translation is by Sir Christopher Frayling and is used here with his kind permission.

THE FAMILY OF THE VOURDALAK

ALEKSEI TOLSTOY

Vienna. 1815. While the Congress had been in session, the city had attracted all the most distinguished European intellectuals, the fashion leaders of the day, and, of course, members of the highest diplomatic elite.[1] But the Congress of Vienna was no longer in session.

Royalist émigrés were preparing to return to their country chateaux (hoping to stay there this time); Russian soldiers were anxiously awaiting the time when they could return to their abandoned homes; and discontented Poles—still dreaming of liberty—were wondering whether their dreams would come true, back in Cracow, under the protection of the precarious "independence" that had been arranged for them by the trio of Prince Metternich, Prince Hardenberg, and Count Nesselrode.

It was as if a masked ball were coming to an end. Of the assembled "guests," only a select few had stayed behind and delayed packing their bags in the hope of still finding some amusement, preferably in the company of the charming and glamorous Austrian ladies.

This delightful group of people (of which I was a member) met twice a week in a chateau belonging to Madame the dowager Princess of Schwarzenberg.[2] It was a few miles from the city center, just beyond a little hamlet called Hitzing. The splendid hospitality of our hostess, as well as her amiability and intellectual brilliance, made any stay at her chateau extremely agreeable.

Our mornings were spent *á la promenade;*[3] we lunched all together either at the chateau or somewhere in the grounds; and in the evenings, seated around a welcoming fire-

---

[1] With the defeat of Napoleonic France, all of the European powers gathered in Vienna to carve up Europe and establish new national boundaries. The principal leaders were Prince Metternich of Austria, Count Nesselrode of Russia, and Prince Hardenberg of Prussia.

[2] A fictitious princess (although her ancestor, Eleonore von Schwarzenberg, 1682-1741, was rumored to be a vampire).

[3] That is, out riding through the parks in their carriages.

side, we amused ourselves by gossiping and telling each other stories. A rule of the house was that we should not talk about anything to do with politics. Everyone had had enough of *that* subject. So our tales were based either on legends from our own countries or else on our own experiences.

One evening, when each of us had told a tale and when our spirits were in that tense state which darkness and silence usually create, the Marquis d'Urfé, an elderly émigré[4] we all loved dearly for his childish gaiety and for the piquant way in which he reminisced about his past life and good fortunes, broke the ominous silence by saying, "Your stories, gentlemen, are all out of the ordinary, of course, but it seems to me that each one lacks an essential ingredient—I mean *authenticity;* for I am pretty sure that none of you has seen with his own eyes the fantastic incidents that he has just narrated, nor can he vouch for the truth of his story on his word of honor as a gentleman."

We all had to agree with this, so the elderly gentleman continued, after smoothing down his jabot: "As for me, gentlemen, I know only one story of this kind, but it is at once so strange, so horrible, and so *authentic* that it will suffice to strike even the most jaded of imaginations with terror. Having unhappily been both a witness to these strange events and a participant in them, I do not, as a rule, like to remind myself of them—but just this once I will tell the tale, provided, of course, the ladies present will permit me."

Everyone agreed instantly. I must admit that a few of us glanced furtively at the long shadows which the moonlight was beginning to sketch out on the parquet floor. But soon our little circle huddled closer together and each of us kept silent to hear the Marquis's story. M. d'Urfé took a pinch of snuff, slowly inhaled it, and began as follows:

Before I start, mesdames (said d'Urfé), I ask you to forgive me if, in the course of my story, I should find occasion to talk of my *affaires de coeur* more often than might be deemed appropriate for a man of my advanced years. But I assure that they must be mentioned if you are to make full sense of my story. In any case, one can forgive an elderly man for certain lapses of this kind—surrounded as I am by such attractive young ladies, it is no fault of mine that I am tempted to imagine myself a young man again. So, without further apology, I will commence by telling you that in the year 1759 I was madly in love with the beautiful Duchesse de Gramont.

This passion, which I then believed was deep and lasting, gave me no respite either by day or by night, and the Duchesse, as young girls often do, enjoyed adding to my torment by her *coquetterie.*[5] So much so that in a moment of spite I determined to solicit and be granted a diplomatic mission to the hospodar[6] of Moldavia, who was then involved in negotiations with Versailles over matters that it would be as tedious as it would be pointless to tell you about.

The day before my departure I called in on the Duchesse. She received me with less mockery than usual and could not hide her emotions as she said, "D'Urfé, you are behaving like a madman, but I know you well enough

---

[4] One who fled France during the Revolution.
[5] Literally "vanity," but here the Marquis means flirtatiousness.
[6] The ruler.

to be sure that you will never go back on a decision once taken. So I will only ask one thing of you. Accept this little cross as a token of my affection and wear it until you return. It is a family relic which we treasure a great deal."

With *galanterie* that was perhaps misplaced at such a moment I kissed not the relic but the delightful hand which proffered it to me, and I fastened the cross around my neck—you can see it now. Since then, I have never been parted from it.

I will not bore you, mesdames, with the details of my journey nor with the observations that I made on the Hungarians and the Serbians, those poor and ignorant people who, enslaved as they were by the Turks, were brave and honest enough not to have forgotten either their dignity or their time-honored independence. It's enough for me to tell you that having learned to speak a little Polish during my stay in Warsaw, I soon had a working knowledge of Serbian as well—for these two languages, like Russian and Bohemian, are, as you no doubt know very well, only branches of one and the same root, which is known as Slavonian.

Anyway, I knew enough to make myself understood. One day I arrived in a small village. The name would not interest you very much. I found those who lived in the house where I intended to stay in a state of confusion, which seemed to me all the more strange because it was a Sunday, a day when the Serbian people customarily devote themselves to different pleasures, such as dancing, arquebus[7] shooting, wrestling and so on. I attributed the confusion of my hosts to some very recent misfortune and was about to withdraw when

a man of about thirty, tall and impressive to look at, came up to me and shook me by the hand.

"Come in, come in, stranger," he said. "Don't let yourself be put off by our sadness; you will understand it well enough when you know the cause."

He then told me about how his old father (whose name was Gorcha), a man of wild and unmanageable temperament, had got up one morning and had taken down his long Turkish arquebus from a rack on a wall.

"My children," he had said to his two sons, Georges and Pierre, "I am going to the mountains to join a band of brave fellows who are hunting that dog Ali Bek." (That was the name of a Turkish brigand who had been ravaging the countryside for some time.)

"Wait for me patiently for ten days and if I do not return on the tenth, arrange for a funeral mass to be said—for by then I will have been killed. But," old Gorcha had added, looking very serious indeed, "if, may God protect you, I should return after the ten days have passed, do not under any circumstances let me come in. I command you, if this should happen, to forget that I was once your father and to pierce me through the heart with an aspen stake, whatever I might say or do, for then I would no longer be human. I would be a cursed *vourdalak*, come to suck your blood."

It is important at this stage to tell you, mesdames, that the *vourdalaks* (the name given to vampires by Slavic peoples) are, according to local folklore, dead bodies who rise from their graves to suck the blood of the living. In this respect they behave like all types of vampire, but they have one other characteristic which makes them even more terrifying. The *vourdalaks*, mesdames, prefer to suck the blood of their closest relatives and their

---

[7] A muzzle-loaded gun.

most intimate friends; once dead, the victims become vampires themselves. People have claimed that entire villages in Bosnia and Hungary have been transformed into *vourdalaks* in this way. The Abbe Augustin Calmet in his strange book on apparitions cites many horrible examples.[8]

Apparently, commissions have been appointed many times by German emperors to study alleged epidemics of vampirism. These commissions collected many eyewitness accounts. They exhumed bodies, which they found to be sated with blood, and ordered them to be burned in the public square after staking them through the heart. Magistrates who witnessed these executions have stated on oath that they heard blood-curdling shrieks coming from these corpses at the moment the executioner hammered his sharpened stake into their hearts. They have formal depositions to this effect and have corroborated them with signatures and with oaths on the Holy Book.

With this information as background, it should be easier for you to understand, mesdames, the effect that old Gorcha's words had on his sons. Both of them went down on their bended knees and begged him to let them go in his place. But instead of replying, he had turned his back on them and had set out for the mountains, singing the refrain of an old ballad. The day I arrived in the village was the very day that Gorcha had fixed for his return, so I had no difficulty understanding why his children were so anxious.

This was a good and honest family. Georges, the older of the two sons, was rug-ged and weather-beaten. He seemed to me a serious and decisive man. He was married with two children. His brother Pierre, a handsome youth of about eighteen, looked rather less tough and appeared to be the favorite of a younger sister called Sdenka, who was a genuine Slavic beauty. In addition to the striking beauty of her features, a distant resemblance to the Duchesse de Gramont struck me especially. She had a distinctive line on her forehead which in all my experience I have found only on these two people. This line did not seem particularly attractive at first glance, but became irresistible when you had seen it a few times.

Perhaps I was still very naïve. Perhaps this resemblance, combined with a lively and charmingly simple disposition, was really irresistible. I do not know. But I had not been talking with Sdenka for more than two minutes when I already felt for her an affection so tender that it threatened to become something deeper still if I stayed in the village much longer.

We were all sitting together in front of the house, around a table laden with cheeses and dishes of milk. Sdenka was sewing; her sister-in-law was preparing supper for her children, who were playing in the sand; Pierre, who was doing his best to appear at ease, was whistling as he cleaned a yataghan, or long Turkish knife.

Georges was leaning on the table with his head in his hands and looking for signs of movement on the great highway. He was silent.

For my part, I was profoundly affected

---

[8] The monumental book of Calmet (1672-1757), entitled *Dissertations sur les apparitions des anges, des démons et sur les espirits. Et sur les revanans et vampires de Hongrie, de Boheme, de Maravie et de Silésie,* was first published in Paris in 1746. It was translated into English in 1850 as *The Phantom World: The Philosophy of Spirits, Apparitions, & c.* Calmet's work was a response to the plague of vampirism sweeping Europe in the early 1700s,

by the general atmosphere of sadness and, in a fit of melancholy, looked up at the evening clouds which shrouded the dying sun and at the silhouette of a monastery, which was half hidden from my view by a black pine forest.

This monastery, as I subsequently discovered, had been very famous in former times on account of a miraculous icon of the Virgin Mary which, according to legend, had been carried away by the angels and set down on an old oak tree. But at the beginning of the previous century the Turks had invaded this part of the country; they had butchered the monks and pillaged the monastery. Only the walls and a small chapel had survived; an old hermit continued to say Mass there. This hermit showed travellers around the ruins and gave hospitality to pilgrims who, as they walked from one place of devotion to another, liked to rest a while at the Monastery of Our Lady of the Oak.

As I have said, I didn't learn all this until much later, for on this particular evening my thoughts were very far from the archaeology of Serbia. As often happens when one allows one's imagination free rein, I was musing on past times—on the good old days of my childhood; on the beauties of France that I had left for a wild and faraway country. I was thinking about the Duchesse de Gramont and—why not admit it?—I was also thinking about several other ladies who lived at the same time as your grandmothers, the memory of whose beauty had quietly entered my thoughts in the train of the beautiful Duchesse. I had soon forgotten all about my hosts and their terrible anxiety.

Suddenly Georges broke the silence. "Wife," he said, "at exactly what time did the old man set out?"

"At eight o'clock. I can clearly remember hearing the monastery bell."

"Well, that's all right then," said Georges. "It cannot be more than half past seven." And he again looked for signs of movement on the great highway which led to the dark forest.

I have forgotten to tell you, mesdames, that when the Serbians suspect that someone has become a vampire, they avoid mentioning him by name or speaking of him directly, for they think that this would be an invitation for him to leave his tomb. So Georges, when he spoke of his father, now referred to him simply as "the old man."

There was a brief silence. Suddenly one of the children started tugging at Sdenka's apron and crying, "Auntie, when will grandpapa be coming back?"

The only reply he got to this untimely question was a hard slap from Georges. The child began to cry, but his little brother, who by now was surprised and frightened, wanted to know more. "Father, why are we not allowed to talk about grandpapa?"

Another slap shut him up firmly. Both children now began to howl and the whole family made a sign of the cross. Just at that moment, I heard the sound of the monastery bell. As the first chime of eight was ringing in our ears, we saw a human figure coming out of the darkness of the forest and approaching us.

"It is he, God be praised," cried Sdenka, her sister-in-law, and Pierre all at once. "May

and approached the subject from a religious perspective. He sought to distinguish the folklore tales of vampirism from the Catholic doctrine of miracles and to expose blasphemous doctrines and ignorance. Although later scholars (such as Voltaire) accused Calmet of being credulous and uncritical, his analysis represents a serious consideration of the problem of extensive reports of vampiric incidents.

the good God protect us," said Georges solemnly. "How are we to know if the ten days have passed or not?"

Everyone looked at him, terror-struck. But the human form came closer and closer. It was a tall old man with a silver moustache and a pale, stern face; he was dragging himself along with the aid of a stick. The closer he got, the more shocked Georges looked. When the new arrival was a short distance from us, he stopped and stared at his family with eyes that seemed not to see—they were dull, glazed, deep sunk in their sockets.

"Well, well," he said in a dead voice, "will no one get up to welcome me? What is the meaning of this silence, can't you see I am wounded?"

I saw that the old man's left side was dripping with blood.

"Go and help your father," I said to Georges. "And you, Sdenka, offer him some refreshment. Look at him—he is almost collapsing from exhaustion!"

"Father," said Georges, going up to Gorcha, "show me your wound. I know all about such things and I can take care of it…"

He was just about to take off the old man's coat when Gorcha pushed his son aside roughly and clutched at his body with both hands. "You are too clumsy," he said, "leave me alone … Now you have hurt me."

"You must be wounded in the heart," cried Georges, turning pale. "Take off your coat, take it off. You must, I insist."

The old man pulled himself up to his full height. "Take care," he said in a sepulchral voice. "If you so much as touch me, I shall curse you."

Pierre rushed between Georges and his father. "Leave him alone," he said. "Can't you see that he's suffering?"

"Do not cross him," Georges's wife added. "You know he has never tolerated that."

At that precise moment we saw a flock of sheep returning from pasture raising a cloud of dust as it made its way towards the house. Whether the dog which was escorting the flock did not recognize its own master, or whether it had some other reason for acting as it did, as soon as it caught sight of Gorcha it stopped dead, hackles raised, and began to howl as if it had seen a ghost.

"What is wrong with that dog?" said the old man, looking more and more furious. "What is going on here? Have I become a stranger in my own house? Have ten days spent in the mountains changed me so much that even my own dogs do not recognize me?"

"Did you hear that?" said Georges to his wife.

"What of it?"

"He admits that the ten days *have been spent.*"

"Surely not, for he has come back to us within the appointed time."

"I know what has to be done."

The dog continued to howl. "I want that dog destroyed!" cried Gorcha. "Well, did you hear me?"

Georges made no move, but Pierre got up with tears in his eyes, and grabbed his father's arquebus; he aimed at the dog, fired, and the creature rolled over in the dust.

"That was my favorite dog," he said sulkily. "I don't know why father wanted it to be destroyed."

"Because it deserved to be," bellowed Gorcha. "Come on now, it's cold and I want to go inside."

While all this was going on outside, Sdenka had been preparing a cordial for the old man consisting of pears, honey, and raisins, laced with eau-de-vie,[9] but her father pushed it aside with disgust. He seemed equally disgusted by the plate of mutton with rice that Georges offered him. Gorcha shuffled over to the fireplace, muttering gibberish from behind clenched teeth.

A pine-log fire crackled in the grate and its flickering light seemed to give life to the pale, emaciated features of the old man. Without the fire's glow, his features could have been taken for those of a corpse.

Sdenka sat down beside him. "Father," she said, "you do not wish to eat anything, you do not wish to rest; perhaps you feel up to telling us about your adventures in the mountains."

By suggesting that, the young girl knew that she was touching her father's most sensitive spot, for the old man loved to talk of wars and adventures. The trace of a smile creased his colorless lips, although his eyes showed no animation, and as he began to stroke his daughter's beautiful blonde hair, he said: "Yes, my daughter, yes, Sdenka, I would like to tell you all about my adventures in the mountains—but that must wait for another time, for I am too tired today. I can tell you, though, that Ali Bek is dead and that he perished by my hand. If anyone doubts my word," continued the old man, looking hard at his two sons, "here is the proof."

He undid a kind of sack which was slung behind his back, and pulled out a foul, bloody head which looked about as pale as his own! We all recoiled in horror, but Gorcha gave it to Pierre.

"Take it," he said, "and nail it above the door, to show all who pass by that Ali Bek is dead and that the roads are free of brigands—except, of course, for the Sultan's janissaries!"[10]

Pierre was disgusted. But he obeyed. "Now I understand why that poor dog was howling," he said. "He could smell dead flesh!"

"Yes, he could smell dead flesh," murmured Georges; he had gone out of the room without anyone noticing him and had returned at that moment with something in his hand which he placed carefully against a wall. It looked to me like a sharpened stake.

"Georges," said his wife, almost in a whisper, "I hope you do not intend to..."

"My brother," Sdenka added anxiously, "what do you mean to do? No, no—surely you're not going to..."

"Leave me alone," replied Georges, "I know what I have to do and I will only do what is absolutely necessary."

While all this had been going on, night had fallen, and the family went to bed in a part of the house which was separated from my room only by a narrow partition. I must admit that what I had seen that evening had made an impression on my imagination. My candle was out; the moonlight shone through a little window near my bed and cast blurred shadows on the floor and walls, rather like those we see now, mesdames, in this room.

I wanted to go to sleep but I could not. I thought this was because the moonlight was so clear; but when I looked for something to curtain the window, I could find nothing suitable. Then I overheard confused voices from the other side of the partition. I tried to make out what was being said.

"Go to sleep, wife," said Georges. "And you, Pierre, and you, Sdenka. Do not worry, I will watch over you."

---

[9] A cognac or brandy-like liqueur.

[10] The Sultan's household troops.

"But, Georges," replied his wife, "it is I who should keep watch over you—you worked all last night and you must be tired. In any case, I ought to be staying awake to watch over our eldest boy. You know he has not been well since yesterday!"

"Be quiet and go to sleep," said Georges. "I will keep watch for both of us."

"Brother," put in Sdenka in her sweetest voice, "there is no need to keep watch at all. Father is already asleep—he seems calm and peaceful enough."

"Neither of you understands what is going on," said Georges in a voice which allowed for no argument. "Go to sleep, I tell you, and let me keep watch."

There followed a long silence. Soon my eyelids grew heavy and sleep began to take possession of my senses.

I THOUGHT I SAW the door of my room opening slowly, and old Gorcha standing in the doorway. Actually, I did not so much see as *feel* his presence, as there was only darkness behind him. I felt his dead eyes trying to penetrate my deepest thoughts as they watched the movement of my breathing. One step forward, then another. Then, with extreme care, he began to walk towards me, with a wolf-like motion. Finally he leapt forward. Now he was right beside my bed. I was absolutely terrified, but somehow managed not to move. The old man leaned over me and his waxen face was so close to mine that I could feel his corpse-like breath. Then, with a superhuman effort, I managed to wake up, soaked in perspiration.

There was nobody in my room, but as I looked towards the window I could distinctly see old Gorcha's face pressed against the glass from outside, staring at me with his sunken eyes. By sheer willpower I stopped myself from crying out and I had the presence of mind to stay lying down, just as if I had seen nothing out of the ordinary. Luckily, the old man was only making sure that I was asleep, for he made no attempt to come in, and after staring at me long enough to satisfy himself, he moved away from the window and I could hear his footsteps in the neighboring room. Georges was sound asleep and snoring loudly enough to wake the dead.

At that moment the child coughed, and I could make out Gorcha's voice. "You are not asleep little one?"

"No, grandpapa," replied the child, "and I would so like to talk with you."

"So, you would like to talk with me, would you? And what would we talk about?"

"We would talk about how you fought the Turks. I would love to fight the Turks!"

"I thought you might, child, and I brought back a little yataghan for you. I'll give it to you tomorrow."

"Grandpapa, grandpapa, give it to me now."

"But, little one, why didn't you talk to me about this when it was daytime?"

"Because papa would not let me."

"He is careful, your papa… So you really would like to have your little yataghan?"

"Oh yes, I would love that, but not here, for papa might wake up."

"Where then?"

"If we go outside, I promise to be good and not to make any noise at all."

I thought I could hear Gorcha chuckle as the child got out of bed. I didn't believe in vampires, but the nightmare had preyed on my nerves, and just in case I should have to reproach myself in the morning I got up and banged my fist against the partition. It was enough to wake up the "seven sleepers," but there was no sign of life from the family. I threw myself against the door, determined to save the child—but it was locked from the outside and I couldn't shift the bolts. While I was trying to force it open, I saw the old man pass by my window with the little child in his arms.

"Wake up! Wake up!" I cried at the top of my voice, as I shook the partition. Even then only Georges showed any sign of movement.

"Where is the old man?" he murmured blearily.

"Quick," I yelled, "he's just taken away your child."

With one kick, Georges broke down the door of his room—which like mine had been locked from the outside—and he sprinted in the direction of the dark forest. At last I succeeded in waking Pierre, his sister-in-law, and Sdenka. We all assembled in front of the house and after a few minutes of anxious waiting we saw Georges return from the dark forest with his son. The child had apparently passed out on the highway, but he was soon revived and didn't seem to be any more ill than before. After questioning him we discovered that his grandpapa had not, in fact, done him any harm; they had apparently gone out together to talk undisturbed, but once outside the child had lost consciousness without remembering why. Gorcha himself had disappeared.

As you can imagine, no one could sleep for the rest of that night. The next day, I learned that the river Danube, which cut across the highway about a quarter of a league from the village, had begun to freeze over; drift ice now blocked my route. This often happens in these parts some time between the end of autumn and the beginning of spring. Since the highway was expected to be blocked for some days, I could not think of leaving. In any case, even if I could have left, curiosity—as well as a more powerful emotion—would have held me back. The more I saw Sdenka, the more I felt I was falling in love with her.

I am not among those, mesdames, who believe in love at first sight of the kind which novelists so often write about; but I do believe that there are occasions when love develops more quickly than is usual. Sdenka's strange beauty, her singular resemblance to the Duchesse de Gramont—the lady from whom I had fled in Paris, and who I saw again in this remote setting, dressed in a rustic costume and speaking in a musical foreign tongue—the fascinating line on her forehead, like that for which I had been prepared to kill myself at least twenty times in France: all this, combined with the incredible, mysterious situation in which I found myself… everything helped to nurture in me a passion which, in other circumstances, would perhaps have proved itself to be more vague and passing.

During the course of the day I overheard Sdenka talking to her younger brother. "What do you think of all this?" she asked. "Do you also suspect our father?"

"I dare not suspect him," replied Pierre, "especially since the child insists that he came to no harm. And as for father's disappearance, you know that he never used to explain his comings and goings."

"I know," said Sdenka. "All the more reason why we must think about saving him, for you know that Georges…"

"Yes, yes, I know. It would be useless to talk him out of it. We can at least hide the stake. He certainly won't go out looking for another one, since there is not a single aspen tree this side of the mountains."

"Yes, let's hide the stake—but don't mention it to the children, for they might chatter about it with Georges listening."

"We must take care not to let that happen," said Pierre. And they went their separate ways.

At nightfall we had still discovered nothing about old Gorcha. As on the previous night I was lying on my bed, and the moonlight again stopped me from going to sleep. When at last sleep began to confuse my thoughts, I again felt, as if by instinct, that the old man was coming towards me. I opened my eyes and saw his waxen face pressed against my window.

This time I wanted to get up but could not. All my limbs seemed to be paralysed. After taking a good long look at me, the old man disappeared. I heard him wandering around the house and tapping gently on the window of Georges's room. The child turned over on his bed and moaned as he dreamed. After several minutes' silence the tapping on the window resumed. Then the child groaned once again and woke up. "Is that you, grandpapa?" he asked.

"It is me," replied a dead voice, "and I have brought you your little yataghan."

"But I dare not go outside. Papa has forbidden it."

"There is no need to go outside; just open the window and embrace me!"

The child got up and I could hear him opening the window. Then somehow finding the strength, I leaped to the foot of my bed and ran over to the partition. I struck it hard with my fist. In a few seconds Georges was on his feet. I heard him mutter an oath. His wife screamed. In no time at all the whole household had gathered around the lifeless child. Just as on the previous occasion, there was no sign of Gorcha.

We tried carefully to revive the child, but he was very weak and breathed with difficulty. The poor little chap had no idea why he had passed out. His mother and Sdenka thought it was because of the shock of being caught talking with his grandpapa. I said nothing. However, by now the child seemed to be more calm and everybody except Georges went back to bed.

At daybreak, I overheard Georges waking his wife and whispering with her. Sdenka joined them and I could hear both the women sobbing. The child was dead.

Of the family's despair, the less said the better. Strangely enough no one blamed the child's death on old Gorcha—at least, not openly. Georges sat in silence, but his expression, always gloomy, now became terrible to behold. Two days passed and there was still no sign of the old man. On the night of the third day (the day of the child's burial) I thought I heard footsteps all around the house and an old man's voice which called out the name of the dead child's brother.

For a split second I also thought I saw Gorcha's face pressed against my window, but I couldn't be sure if I was imagining it or not, for the moon was veiled by cloud that night. Nevertheless I considered it my duty to mention this apparition to Georges. He questioned the child, who replied that he *had* in fact heard grandpapa calling and had also seen him looking in through the window. Georges strictly charged his son to wake him up if the old man should appear again.

All these happenings did not prevent my passion for Sdenka from developing more and more each day. In the daytime, I couldn't talk to her alone. At night, the mere thought that I would shortly have to leave broke my heart. Sdenka's room was separated from mine only by a kind of corridor which led to the road on one side and a courtyard on the other. When the whole family had gone to bed, I decided to go for a short walk in the fields to ease my mind.

As I walked along the corridor I saw that Sdenka's door was slightly open. Instinctively, I stopped and listened. The rustling of her dress, a sound I knew well, made my heart pound against my chest. Then I heard her singing softly. She was singing about a Serbian king who was saying farewell to his lady before going to war.

"Oh my young Poplar," said the old king, "I am going to the war and you will forget me.

"The trees which grow beneath the mountain are slender and pliant, but they are nothing beside your young body!

"The berries of the rowan tree which sway in the wind are red, but your lips are more red than the berries of the rowan tree!

"And I am like an old oak stripped of leaves, and my beard is whiter than the foam of the Danube!

"And you will forget me, oh my soul, and I will die of grief, for the enemy will not dare to kill the old King!"

The beautiful lady replied: "I swear to be faithful to you and never to forget you. If I should break my oath, come to me after your death and drink all my heart's blood!"

And the old king said: "So be it!" And he set off for the war. Soon the beautiful lady forgot him...!

At this point Sdenka paused, as if she was frightened to finish the ballad. I could restrain myself no longer. That voice—so sweet, so expressive—was the voice of the Duchesse de Gramont... Without pausing to think, I pushed open the door and went in. Sdenka had just taken off her knitted jacket

(of a kind often worn by women in those regions). All she was wearing was a nightgown of red silk, embroidered with gold, held tight against her body by a simple, brightly colored belt. Her fine blonde hair hung loose over her shoulders. She looked more beautiful than ever. She did not seem upset by my sudden entry, but she was confused and blushed slightly.

"Oh," she said, "why have you come? What will the family think of me if we are discovered?"

"Sdenka, my soul, do not be frightened! Everyone is asleep. Only the cricket in the grass and the mayfly in the air can hear what I have to say to you."

"Oh, my friend, leave me, leave me! If my brother should discover us I am lost!"

"Sdenka, I will not leave you until you have promised to love me forever, as the beautiful lady promised the king in your ballad. Soon I will have to leave... Who knows when we will see each other again? Sdenka, I love you more than my soul, more than my salvation...my life's blood is yours...may I not be granted one hour with you in return?"

"Many things can happen in an hour," said Sdenka calmly. But she did let her hand slip into mine. "You do not know my brother," she continued, beginning to tremble. "I fear he will discover us."

"Calm yourself, my darling Sdenka. Your brother is exhausted from watching late into the night; he has been lulled to sleep by the wind rustling in the trees; heavy is his sleep, long is the night, and I only ask to be granted one hour—then, farewell, perhaps forever!"

"Oh no, no, not forever!" cried Sdenka; then she recoiled, as if frightened by the sound of her own voice.

"Oh, Sdenka, I see only you, I hear only

you; I am no longer master of my own destiny; a superior strength commands my obedience. Forgive me, Sdenka!" Like a madman I clutched her to my heart.

"You are no friend to me," she cried, tearing herself from my embrace and rushing to another part of the room. I do not know what I said to her then, for I was as alarmed as she was by my own forwardness, not because such boldness had failed me in the past—far from it—but because in spite of my passion, I could not help having a sincere respect for Sdenka's innocence. It is true that I had used the language of *galanterie* with this girl at first (a language which did not seem to displease the society ladies of the time), but I was now ashamed of these empty phrases and renounced them when I saw that the young girl was too naïve to comprehend fully what I meant by them—what you, mesdames, to judge by your suggestive smiles, have understood immediately. I stood before her, at a loss as to what to say, when suddenly she began to tremble and look towards the window, terror-struck. I followed her gaze and clearly saw the corpse-like face of Gorcha, staring at us from outside.

At precisely that moment, I felt a heavy hand on my shoulder.

I froze. It was Georges. "What are you doing here!" he snapped.

Embarrassed by his tone of voice, I simply pointed towards his father, who was still staring at us through the window—but he disappeared the moment Georges turned to look at him. "I heard the old man and came to warn your sister," I stammered.

Georges looked me straight in the eye, as if trying to read my innermost thoughts. Then he took me by the arm, led me to my room, and left, without a single word.

THE NEXT DAY the family had gathered in front of the house, around a table laden with jugs of milk and cakes.

"Where is the child?" said Georges.

"In the courtyard," replied his wife. "He is playing his favourite game, imagining that he is fighting the Turks single-handed."

No sooner had she said these words, than to our amazement we saw the tall figure of Gorcha walking slowly towards us from out of the dark forest. He sat at the table just as he had done the day I arrived.

"Father, we welcome you," murmured Georges's wife in a hoarse voice. "We welcome you, father," whispered Sdenka and Pierre in unison. "My father," said Georges firmly, turning pale, "we are waiting for you to say Grace!"

The old man glared at him and turned away.

"Yes... Grace—say it now!" repeated Georges, crossing himself. "Say it this instant, or by St. George..."

Sdenka and her sister-in-law threw themselves at the old man's feet and begged him to say Grace.

"No, no, no," said the old man. "He has no right to speak to me in that way, and if he continues, I will curse him!"

Georges got up and rushed into the house. He returned almost immediately, looking furious. "Where is that stake?" he yelled. "Where have you hidden it?"

Sdenka and Pierre looked at each other.

"Corpse!" Georges shouted at the old man. "What have you done with my elder boy? Why have you killed my little child? Give me back my son, you creature of the grave!"

As he said this, he became more and more pale and his eyes began to burn with fury. The old man simply glared at him.

"The stake, the stake," yelled Georges. "Whoever has hidden it must answer for all the evils which will befall us!"

At this moment we heard the excited laughter of the younger child. We saw him galloping towards us on a wooden horse, or rather on a long aspen stake, shrieking the Serbian battle cry at the top of his voice. Georges's eyes lit up as he realized what was happening. He grabbed the stake from the child and threw himself at his father. The old man let out a fearful groan and began to sprint towards the dark forest as if possessed by demons. Georges raced after him across the fields, and soon they were both out of sight.

It was after sunset when Georges returned to the house. He was as pale as death; his hair stood on end. He sat down by the fireside, and I could hear his teeth chattering. No one could pluck up the courage to question him. By about the time the family normally went to bed he seemed to be more his usual self and, taking me to one side, said to me quite calmly:—

"My dear guest, I have been to the river. The ice has gone, the road is clear—nothing now prevents you from leaving. There is no need," he added, glancing at Sdenka, "to take your leave of my family. Through me, the family wishes you all the happiness you could desire and I hope that you will have some happy memories of the time you have spent with us. Tomorrow at daybreak, you will find your horse saddled and your guide ready to escort you. Farewell. Think about your host from time to time, and forgive him if your stay here has not been as carefree as he would have liked."

As he said this, even Georges's rough features looked almost friendly. He led me to my room and shook my hand for one last time. Then he began to tremble and his teeth chattered as if he were suffering from the cold.

Now I was alone, I had no thoughts of going to sleep—as you can imagine. Other things were on my mind. I had loved many times in my life, and had experienced the whole range of passions—tenderness, jealousy, fury—but never, not even when I left the Duchesse de Gramont, had I felt anything like the sadness that I felt in my heart at that moment. Before sunrise, I changed into my travelling clothes, hoping to have a few words with Sdenka before I departed. But Georges was waiting for me in the hall. There was no chance of my seeing her again.

I leaped into the saddle and spurred on my horse. I made a resolution to return from Jassy via this village, and although that might be some time hence, the thought made me feel easier in my mind. It was some consolation for me to imagine in advance all the details of my return. But this pleasant reverie was soon shattered. My horse shied away from something and nearly had me out of the saddle. The animal stopped dead, dug in its forelegs and began to snort wildly, as if some danger was nearby.

I looked around anxiously and saw something moving about a hundred paces away. It was a wolf digging in the ground. Sensing my presence, the wolf ran away; digging my spurs into the horse's flanks, I managed with difficulty to get him to move forward. It was then that I realized that on the spot where the wolf had been standing, there was a freshly dug grave. I seem to remember also that the end of a stake protruded a few inches out of the ground where the wolf had been digging. However, I do not swear to this, for I rode away from that place as fast as I could.

AT THIS POINT the Marquis paused and took a pinch of snuff.

"Is that the end of the story?" the ladies asked.

"I'm afraid not," replied M. d'Urfé. "What remains to be told is a very unhappy memory for me, and I would give much to cast it from my mind."

MY REASONS FOR going to Jassy (he continued) kept me there for much longer than I had expected—well over six months, in fact. What can I say to justify my conduct during that time? It is a sad fact, but a fact nonetheless, that there are very few emotions in this life which can stand the test of time. The success of my negotiations, which were very well received in Versailles—politics, in a word, vile politics, a subject which has become so boring to us in recent times—preoccupied my thoughts and dimmed the memory of Sdenka.

In addition, from the moment I arrived, the wife of the hospodar, a very beautiful lady who spoke fluent French, did me the honor of receiving my attentions, singling me out from among all the other young foreigners who were staying in Jassy. Like me, she had been brought up to believe in the principles of French *galanterie;* the mere thought that I should rebuff the advances of such a beautiful lady stirred up my Gallic blood. So I received her advances with courtesy, and since I was there to represent the interests and rights of France, I made a start by representing those of her husband the hospodar as well.

When I was recalled home, I left by the same road I had ridden to Jassy. I no longer even thought about Sdenka or her family, but

one evening when I was riding in the countryside, I heard a bell ringing the eight o'clock chime. I seemed to recognize that sound and my guide told me that it came from a nearby monastery.

I asked him the name: it was the monastery of Our Lady of the Oak. I galloped ahead and in no time at all we had reached the monastery gate. The old hermit welcomed us and led us to his hostel.

The number of pilgrims staying there put me off the idea of spending the night at the hostel, and I asked if there was any accommodation available in the village.

"You can stay where you like in the village," replied the old hermit with a gloomy sigh. "Thanks to that devil Gorcha, there are plenty of empty houses!"

"What on earth do you mean?" I asked. "Is old Gorcha still alive?"

"Oh no, he's well and truly buried with a stake through his heart! But he rose from the grave to suck the blood of Georges's little son. The child returned one night and knocked on the door, crying that he was cold and wanted to come home. His foolish mother, although she herself had been present at his burial, did not have the strength of mind to send him back to the cemetery, so she opened the door. He threw himself at her throat and sucked away her life's blood. After she had been buried, she in turn rose from the grave to suck the blood of her second son, then the blood of her husband, then the blood of her brother-in-law. They all went the same way."

"And Sdenka?"

"Oh, she went mad with grief; poor, poor child, do not speak to me of her!"

The old hermit had not really answered my question, but I did not have the heart to repeat it. He crossed himself. "Vampirism is contagious," he said after a pause. "Many families in the village have been afflicted by it, many families have been completely destroyed, and if you take my advice you will stay in my hostel tonight; for even if the *vourdalaks* of the village do not attack you, they will terrify you so much that your hair will have turned white before I ring the bells for morning mass.

"I am only a poor and simple monk," he continued, "but the generosity of passing travellers gives me enough to provide for their needs. I can offer you fresh country cheese and sweet plums which will make your mouth water; I also have some flagons of Tokay wine which are every bit as good as those which grace the cellars of His Holiness the Patriarch!"

The old hermit seemed to be behaving more like an inn-keeper than a poor and simple monk. I reckoned he had told me some old wives' tales about the village in order to make me feel grateful enough for his hospitality to show my appreciation in the usual way, by giving the holy man enough to provide for the needs of passing travellers. In any case, the word *terror* has always had the effect on me that a battle cry has on a war horse. I would have been thoroughly ashamed of myself if I had not set out immediately to see for myself. But my guide, who was less enthusiastic about the idea, asked my permission to stay in the hostel. This I willingly granted.

It took me about half an hour to reach the village. Deserted. No lights shone through the windows, no songs were being sung. I rode past many houses that I knew, all as silent as the grave. Finally I reached Georges's. Whether I was being sentimental or just rash, I don't know, but it was there I decided to spend the night. I got off my horse, and banged on the gate. Still no sign of life. I pushed the gate and the hinges creaked eerily as it slowly opened.

Then I crept into the courtyard. In one of the outerhouses I found enough oats to last the night, so I left my horse tethered there, still saddled, and strode towards the main house. Although all the rooms were deserted, no doors were locked. Sdenka's room had been occupied only a few hours before. Some of her clothes were draped carelessly over the bed. A few pieces of jewelry that I had given her, including a small enamel cross from Budapest, lay on her table sparkling in the moonlight. Even though my love for her was a thing of the past, I must admit that my heart was heavy. Nevertheless, I wrapped myself up in my cloak and stretched out on her bed. Soon I was asleep. I cannot recall everything, but I do remember that I dreamed of Sdenka, as beautiful, as simple, and as loving as she had been when first I met her.

I remember also feeling ashamed of my selfishness and my inconstancy. How could I have abandoned that poor child who loved me; how could I have forgotten her? Then her image became confused with that of the Duchesse de Gramont and I saw only one person. I threw myself at Sdenka's feet and begged her forgiveness. From the depths of my being, from the depths of my soul came an indescribable feeling of melancholy and of joy.

I lay there dreaming, until I was almost awakened by a gentle musical sound, like the rustling of a cornfield in a light breeze. I heard the sweet rustling of the corn and the music of singing birds, the rushing of a waterfall and the whispering of trees. Then I realized that all these sounds were merely the swishing of a woman's dress and I opened my eyes. There was Sdenka standing beside my bed. The moon was shining so brightly that I could distinguish every single feature which had been so dear to me and which my dream made me love again as if for the first time. Sdenka seemed more beautiful, and somehow more mature. She was dressed as she had been when last I saw her alone: a simple nightgown of red silk, gold embroidered, and a colored belt, clinging tightly above her hips.

"Sdenka!" I cried, sitting up. "Is it really you, Sdenka?"

"Yes, it is me," she replied in a sweet, sad voice. "It is that same Sdenka you have forgotten. Why did you not return sooner? Everything is finished now; you must leave; a moment longer and you are lost! Farewell my friend, farewell forever!"

"Sdenka, you have seen so much unhappiness they say! Come, let us talk, let us ease your pain!"

"Oh, my friend, you must not believe everything they say about us; but leave me, leave me now, for if you stay a moment longer you are doomed."

"Sdenka, what are you afraid of? Can you not grant me an hour, just one hour to talk with you?"

Sdenka began to tremble and her whole being seemed to undergo a strange transformation. "Yes," she said, "one hour, just one hour, the same hour you begged of me when you came into this room and heard me singing the ballad of the old king. Is that what you mean? So be it, I will grant you one hour! But no, no!" she cried, as if fighting her inclinations. "Leave me, go away!—leave now, I tell you, fly! Fly, while you still have the chance!"

Her features were possessed with a savage strength. I could not understand why she should be saying these things, but she was so beautiful that I determined to stay, whatever she said. At last she surrendered, sat down beside me, and spoke to me of the past; she blushed as she admitted that she had fallen in love with me the moment she set eyes on me. But little by little I began to notice that Sdenka was not as I had remembered her. Her former timidity had given way to a strange wantonness of manner. She seemed more forward, more knowing. It dawned on me that her behavior was no longer that of the naïve young girl I recalled in my dream. Is it possible, I mused, that Sdenka was never the pure and innocent maiden that I imagined her to be? Did she simply put on an act to please her brother? Was I gulled by an affected virtue? If so, why insist that I leave? Was this perhaps a refinement of *coquetterie*? And I thought I knew her! What did it matter? If Sdenka was not a Diana, as I thought, she began to resemble another goddess at least as attractive— perhaps more so. By God! I preferred the role of Adonis to that of Actaeon.[11]

If this classical style that I adopted seems a little out of place, mesdames, remember that I have the honor to be telling you of incidents which occurred in the year of grace 1759. At that time mythology was *very* fashionable, and I am trying to keep my story in period. Things have changed a lot since then, and it was not so long ago that the Revolution, having overthrown both the traces of paganism and the Christian religion, erected the goddess Reason in their place. This goddess, mesdames, has never been my patron saint, least

---

[11] Greek legend told that Actaeon saw the goddess Diana while she was bathing; she then changed him into a stag and he was chased and slain by his own hunting dogs.

of all when I am in the presence of other god-
desses, and, at the time I am referring to, I was
less disposed than ever to worship at her
shrine.

I abandoned myself passionately to Sdenka,
and willingly outdid even her in the provoca-
tive game she was playing. Some time passed
in sweet intimacy, until, as Sdenka was amusing me by trying on various pieces of jewelry;
I thought it would be a good idea to place the
little enamel cross around her neck. But as I
tried to do this, Sdenka recoiled sharply.

"Enough of these childish games, my
dearest," she said. "Let us talk about you and
what is on your mind!"

This sudden change in Sdenka's behavior made me pause a moment and think.
Looking at her more closely I noticed that she
no longer wore around her neck the cluster of
tiny icons, holy relics, and charms filled with
incense which Serbians are usually given as
children, to wear for the rest of their lives.

"Sdenka," I asked, "where are those
things you used to wear around your neck?"

"I have lost them," she replied impatiently, and hastily changed the subject.

I do not know exactly why, but at that
moment I began to feel a strong sense of foreboding. I wanted to leave, but Sdenka held me
back. "What is this?" she said. "You asked to
be granted an hour, and here you are trying to
leave after only a few minutes!"

"Sdenka, you were right when you tried
to persuade me to leave; I think I hear a noise
and I fear we will be discovered!"

"Calm yourself, my love, everyone is
asleep; only the cricket in the grass and the
mayfly in the air can hear what I have to say!"

"No, no, Sdenka, I must leave now...!"

"Stay, stay," she implored, "I love you
more than my soul, more than my salvation.

You once told me that your life's blood belonged to me...!"

"But your brother—your brother, Sdenka—
I have a feeling he will discover us!"

"Calm yourself, my soul; my brother has
been lulled to sleep by the wind rustling in the
trees; heavy is his sleep, long is the night, and
I ask only to be granted one hour!"

As she said this, Sdenka looked so
ravishing that my vague sense of foreboding
turned into a strong desire to remain near her.
A strange, almost sensual feeling, part fear,
part excitement, filled my whole being. As I
began to weaken, Sdenka became more tender, and I resolved to surrender, hoping to
keep up my guard. However, as I told you at
the beginning, I have always overestimated
my own strength of mind, and when Sdenka,
who had noticed that I was holding back, suggested that we chase away the chill of the
night by drinking a few glasses of the good
hermit's full-blooded wine, I agreed with a
readiness which made her smile. The wine
had its desired effect. By the second glass, I
had forgotten all about the incident of the cross
and the holy relics; Sdenka, with her beautiful
blonde hair falling loose over her shoulders,
with her jewels sparkling in the moonlight,
was quite irresistible. Abandoning all restraint,
I held her tight in my arms.

Then, mesdames, a strange thing happened. One of those mysterious revelations
that I can never hope to explain. If you had
asked me then, I would have denied such
things could happen, but now I know better.
As I held Sdenka tightly against my body, one
of the points of the cross which the Duchesse
de Gramont gave me before I left stuck
sharply into my chest. The stab of pain that I
felt affected me like a ray of light passing right
through my body.

Looking up at Sdenka I saw for the first time that her features, though still beautiful, were those of a corpse; that her eyes did not see; and that her smile was the distorted grimace of a decaying skull. At the same time, I sensed in that room the putrid smell of the charnel-house. The fearful truth was revealed to me in all its ugliness, and I remembered too late what the old hermit had said to me. I realized what a fearsome predicament I was in. Everything depended on my courage and my self-control.

I turned away from Sdenka to hide the horror which was written on my face. It is then that I looked out of the window and saw the satanic figure of Gorcha, leaning on a bloody stake and staring at me with the eyes of a hyena. Pressed against the other window were the waxen features of Georges, who at that moment looked as terrifying as his father. Both were watching my every movement, and I knew that they would pounce on me the moment I tried to escape. So I pretended not to know they were there, and, with incredible self-control, continued—yes, mesdames, I actually continued—passionately to embrace Sdenka, just as I had done before my horrifying discovery.

Meanwhile, I desperately racked my brains for some means of escape. I noticed that Gorcha and Georges were exchanging knowing glances with Sdenka and that they were showing signs of losing patience. Then, from somewhere outside, I heard a woman's shriek and the sound of children crying, like the howling of wild cats; these noises set my nerves on edge.

Time to make for home, I said to myself, *and the sooner the better!*

Turning to Sdenka, I raised my voice so that her hideous family would be sure to hear me: "I am tired, my dear child; I must go to bed and sleep for a few hours. But first I must go and see whether my horse needs feeding. I beg you to stay where you are and to wait for me to come back." I then pressed my mouth against her cold, dead lips and left the room.

I found my horse in a panic, covered with lather and crashing his hooves against the outhouse wall. He had not touched the oats, and the fearful noise he made when he saw me coming gave me gooseflesh, for I feared he would give the game away.

But the vampires, who had almost certainly overheard my conversation with Sdenka, did not appear to think that anything suspicious was happening. After making sure that the main gate was open, I vaulted into the saddle and dug my spurs into the horse's flanks.

As I rode out of the gates I just had time to glimpse a whole crowd gathered around the house, many of them with their faces pressed against the windows. I think it was my sudden departure which first confused them, but I cannot be sure: the only sound I could hear at that moment was the regular beat of my horse's hooves which echoed in the night.

I was just about to congratulate myself on my cunning, when all of a sudden I heard a fearful noise behind me, like the sound of a hurricane roaring through the mountains. A thousand discordant voices shrieked, moaned, and contended with one another. Then complete silence, as if by common assent. And I heard a rhythmic stamping, like a troop of foot soldiers advancing in double-quick time.

I spurred on my horse until I tore into his flanks. A burning fever coursed through my veins. I was making one last effort to preserve my sanity, when I heard a voice behind me which cried out: "Stop, don't leave me, my dearest! I love you more than my soul, I love you more than my salvation! Turn back, turn back, your life's blood is mine!"

A cold breath brushed my ear and I sensed that Sdenka had leaped on to my horse from behind. "My heart, my soul!" she cried. "I see only you, hear only you! I am not mistress of my own destiny—a superior force commands my obedience. Forgive me, my dearest, forgive me!"

Twisting her arms around me she tried to sink her teeth into my neck and to wrench me from my horse. There was a terrible struggle. For some time I had difficulty even defending myself, but eventually I managed to grab hold of Sdenka by curling one arm around her waist and knotting the other hand in her hair. Standing bolt upright in my stirrups, I threw her to the ground!

Then my strength gave out completely and I became delirious. Frenzied shapes pursued me—mad, grimacing faces. Georges and his brother, Pierre, ran beside the road and tried to block my way. They did not succeed, but just as I was about to give thanks, I looked over my shoulder and caught sight of old Gorcha, who was using his stake to propel himself forward as the Tyrolean mountain men do when they leap over Alpine chasms.

But Gorcha did not manage to catch up with me. Then his daughter-in-law, dragging her children behind her, threw one of them to him; he caught the child on the sharpened point of his stake.

Using the stake as a catapult, he slung the creature towards me with all his might. I fended off the blow, but with the true terrier instinct the little brat sunk his teeth into my horse's neck, and I had some difficulty tearing him away. The other child was propelled towards me in the same way, but he landed beyond the horse and was crushed to pulp. I do not know what happened after that, but when I regained consciousness it was daylight, and I found myself lying near the road next to my dying horse.

So ended, mesdames, a love affair which should perhaps have cured me forever of the desire to become involved in any others. Some contemporaries of your grandmothers could tell you whether I had learned my lesson or not. But, joking aside, I still shudder at the thought that if I had given in to my enemies, I would myself have become a vampire.

As it was, Heaven did not allow things to come to that, and so far from wishing to suck your blood, mesdames, I only ask—old as I am—to be granted the privilege of shedding my own blood in your service!

Théophile Gautier

PIERRE JULES THÉOPHILE GAUTIER (1811-1872) was a French poet and romance writer and a leader of the romantic school. He wrote travel books, novels, and plays and was recognized as an officer of the Legion of Honor. He frequently wrote criticism of art, literature, and drama, including major works on his friends Balzac and Baudelaire. His writing was greatly esteemed by Marcel Proust and Oscar Wilde. This story—Gautier's only notable short work—is more about faith and renunciation than vampirism, and the vampire is a pitiable, romantic creature.

THE DEATHLY LOVER

THÉOPHILE GAUTIER

You ask me, brother, if I have ever loved. I have. It is a strange story, and though I am sixty, I scarce venture to stir the ashes of that remembrance. I mean to refuse you nothing, but to no soul less tried than yours would I tell the story.

The events are so strange that I can hardly believe they did happen. I was for more than three years the plaything of a singular and diabolical illusion. I, a poor priest, I led in my dreams every night—God grant they were dreams only!—the life of the damned, the life of the worldly, the life of Sardana-palus.[1] A single glance, too full of approval, cast upon a woman, nearly cost me the loss of my soul. But at last, by the help of God and of my holy patron, I was able to drive away the evil spirit which had possessed me. My life was complicated by an entirely different nocturnal life.

During the day I was a priest of God, chaste, busied with prayers and holy things; at night, as soon as I had closed my eyes, I became a young nobleman, a connoisseur of women, of horses and dogs, gambling, drinking, and cursing, and when at dawn I awoke, it seemed to me rather that I was going to sleep and dreaming of being a priest.

Of that somnambulistic life there have remained in my remembrance things and words I cannot put away, and although I have never left the walls of my presbytery, you will be apt to think, on hearing me, that I am a man who, having worn out everything and having given up the world and entered religion, means to end in the bosom of God days too greatly agitated, rather than a humble student in a seminary, who has grown old in a forgotten parish in the depths of a forest, and who has never had anything to do with the things of the day.

Yes, I have loved, as no one on earth ever loved, with an insensate and furious love, so violent that I wonder it did not break my

[1] According to Greek historians, the last king of Assyria (7th Century B.C.E.), legendary for his decadence, who died in an orgy of self-destruction.

heart. Ah! What nights, what nights I have had! From my youngest childhood I felt the vocation to the priesthood and all my studies were therefore bent in that direction. My life until the age of twenty-four was nothing but one long novitiate. Having finished my theological studies, I passed successfully through the minor orders, and my superiors considered me worthy, in spite of my youth, of crossing the last dread limit. The day of my ordination was fixed for Easter week. I had never gone into the world. The world, to me, lay within the walls of the college and of the seminary.

I knew vaguely that there was something called a woman, but my thoughts never dwelt upon it; I was utterly innocent. I saw my old, infirm mother but twice a year; she was the only connection I had with the outer world. I regretted nothing; I felt not the least hesitation in the presence of the irrevocable engagement I was about to enter into; nay, I was joyous and full of impatience. Never did a young bridegroom count the hours with more feverish ardor. I could not sleep; I dreamed that I was saying Mass; I saw nothing more glorious in the world than to be a priest. I would have refused, had I been offered a kingdom, to be a king or a poet instead, for my ambition conceived nothing finer.

What I am telling you is to show you that what happened to me ought not to have happened, and that I was the victim of the most inexplicable fascination.

The great day having come, I walked to the church with so light a step that it seemed to me that I was borne in the air, or that I had wings on my shoulders; I thought myself an angel, and I was amazed at the somber and preoccupied expression of my companions—for there were several of us. I had spent the night in prayer, and was in a state bordering on ecstasy. The bishop, a venerable old man, seemed to me like God the Father bending from eternity, and I beheld the heavens through the vault of the dome.

You are acquainted with the details of the ceremony: the benediction, the Communion in both kinds, the anointing of the palms of the hands with the oil of the catechumens,[2] and finally the sacred sacrifice offered in conjunction with the bishop. I will not dwell on these things. Oh! How right was Job, "Imprudent is he who has not made a covenant with his eyes"! I happened to raise my head, which until then I had kept bent down, and I saw before me, so close that I might have touched her, although in reality she was a long way off, on the other side of the railing, a young woman of wondrous beauty dressed with regal magnificence.

It was as though scales had fallen from my eyes. I felt like a blind man suddenly recovering his sight. The bishop, so radiant but now, was suddenly dimmed, the flame of the tapers on their golden candlesticks turned pale like stars in the morning light, and the whole church was shrouded in deep obscurity. The lovely creature stood out against this shadow like an angelic revelation. She seemed illumined from within, and to give forth light rather than to receive it.

I cast down my eyes, determined not to look up again, so as to avoid the influence of external objects, for I was becoming more and more inattentive and I scarcely knew what I was about. Yet a moment later I opened my eyes again, for through my eyelids I saw her dazzling with the prismatic colors in a radiant

---

[2] Disciples studying for baptism.

penumbra, just as when one has gazed upon the sun.

Oh, how beautiful she was! The greatest painters had never approached this fabulous reality, even when, pursuing ideal beauty in the heavens, they brought back to earth the divine portrait of the Madonna. Neither the verse of the poet nor the palette of the painter can give you an idea of her. She was rather tall, with the figure and the port of a goddess. Her hair, of a pale gold, was parted on her brow and flowed down her temples like two golden streams; she looked like a crowned queen. Her forehead, of a bluish whiteness, spread out broad and serene over the almost brown eyebrows, a singularity which added to the effect of the sea-green eyes, the brilliancy and fire of which were unbearable. Oh, what eyes! With one flash they settled a man's fate. They were filled with a life, a limpidity, an ardor, a moist glow, which I have never seen in any other human eyes. From them flashed glances like arrows, which I distinctly saw striking my heart. I know not whether the flame that illumined them came from heaven or hell, but undoubtedly it came from one or the other place.

That woman was an angel or a demon, perhaps both. She certainly did not come from the womb of Eve, our common mother. Teeth of the loveliest pearl sparkled through her rosy smile, and little dimples marked each inflection of her mouth in the rosy satin of her adorable cheeks. As to her nose, it was of regal delicacy and pride, and betrayed the noblest origin. An agate polish played upon the smooth, lustrous skin of her half-uncovered shoulders, and strings of great fair pearls, almost similar in tone to her neck, fell upon her bosom. From time to time she drew up her head with the undulating movement of an adder or of a peacock, and made the tall embroidered ruff that surrounded her like a silver trellis tremble slightly. She wore a dress of orange-red velvet, and out of the broad, ermine-lined sleeves issued wondrously delicate patrician hands, with long, plump fingers, so ideally transparent that the light passed through them as through the fingers of Dawn.

All these details are still as vivid to me as if I had seen her but yesterday, and although I was a prey to the greatest agitation, nothing escaped me; the faintest tint, the smallest dark spot on the corner of the chin, the scarcely perceptible down at the corners of the lips, the velvety brow, the trembling shadow of the eyelashes on her cheeks—I noted all with astonishing lucidity.

As I gazed at her, I felt open within me doors hitherto fast-closed; passages obstructed until now were cleared away in every direction and revealed unsuspected prospects; life appeared in a new guise; I had just been born into a new order of ideas. Frightful anguish clutched my heart, and every minute that passed seemed to me a second and an age. Yet the ceremony was proceeding, and I was being carried farther from the world, the entrance to which was fiercely besieged by my nascent desires. I said "yes," however, when I meant to say "no," when everything in me was revolting and protesting against the violence my vow was doing to my will. An occult force dragged the words from my mouth in spite of myself.

It is perhaps just what so many young girls do when they go to the altar with a firm resolve to boldly refuse the husband forced upon them. Not one carries out her intention. It is no doubt the same thing which makes so many poor novices take the veil, although they are quite determined to tear it to pieces at the moment of speaking their vows. No one dares to cause such a scandal before everybody, nor to deceive the expectations of so many present. The numerous wills, the numerous glances, seem to weigh down on one like a leaden cloak. And then, every precaution is so carefully taken, everything is so well settled beforehand in a fashion so evidently irrevocable that thought yields to the weight of fact and completely gives way.

The expression of the fair unknown changed as the ceremony progressed. Her glance, tender and caressing at first, became disdainful and dissatisfied as if to reproach me with dullness of perception. I made an effort, mighty enough to have overthrown a mountain, to cry out that I would not be a priest, but I could not manage it; my tongue clove to the roof of my mouth and it was impossible for me to express my will by the smallest negative sign. I was, although wide-awake, in a state similar to that of nightmare, when one seeks to call out a word on which one's life depends, and yet is unable to do so.

She seemed to understand the martyrdom I was suffering, and as if to encourage me, she cast upon me a look full of divine promise. Her eyes were a poem, her every glance was a canto; she was saying to me, "If you will come with me, I will make you more happy than God Himself in Paradise. The angels will be jealous of you. Tear away the funeral shroud in which you are about to wrap yourself. I am beauty and youth and love; come to me, and together we shall be Love.

"What can Jehovah offer you in compensation? Our life shall pass like a dream, and will be but one eternal kiss. Pour out the wine in that cup and you are free. We will go away to unknown isles and you shall sleep on my bosom on a bed of massive gold under a pavilion of silver. For I love you and mean to take you from your God, before whom so many youthful hearts pour out floods of love that never reach Him."

It seemed to me that I heard these words on a rhythm of infinite sweetness, for her glance was almost sonorous, and the phrases her eyes sent me sounded within my heart as if invisible lips had breathed them. I felt myself ready to renounce God, but my hand was mechanically accomplishing the formalities of the ceremony. The beauty cast upon me a second glance so beseeching, so despairing that sharp blades pierced my heart, and I felt more swords enter my breast than did the Mother of Sorrows.

Never did any human face exhibit more poignant anguish. The maiden who sees her betrothed fall suddenly dead by her side, the mother by the empty cradle of her child, Eve seated on the threshold of the gate of Paradise, the miser who finds a stone in place of his treasure, the poet who has accidentally dropped into the fire the only manuscript of his favorite work—not one of them could look more inconsolable, more stricken to the heart. The blood left her lovely face and she turned pale as marble.

Her beautiful arms hung limp by her body as if the muscles had been unknotted, and she leaned against a pillar, for her limbs were giving way under her. As for me, livid, my brow covered with a sweat more bloody than that of Calvary, I staggered towards the church door. I was stifling; the vaulting seemed to press down on me and my hand to upbear alone the weight of the cupola.

As I was about to cross the threshold, a woman's hand suddenly touched mine. I had never touched one before. It was cold like the skin of a serpent, yet it burned me like the print of a red-hot iron. It was she. "Oh, unfortunate man! Unfortunate man! What have you done?" she whispered; then disappeared in the crowd.

The old bishop passed by. He looked severely at me. My appearance was startlingly strange. I turned pale, blushed red, and flames passed before my eyes. One of my comrades took pity on me and led me away; I was incapable of finding alone the road to the seminary. At the corner of a street, while the young priest happened to look in another direction, a quaintly dressed negro page approached me and without staying his steps handed me a small pocket-book with chased gold corners, signing to me to conceal it. I slipped it into my sleeve and kept it there until I was alone in my cell. I opened it.

It contained but two leaves with these words: "Clarimonda, at the Palazzo Concini." I was then so ignorant of life that I did not know of Clarimonda, in spite of her fame, and I was absolutely ignorant where the Palazzo Concini was situated. I made innumerable conjectures of the most extravagant kind, but the truth is that, provided I could see her again, I cared little what she might be, whether a great lady or a courtesan.

This new-born love of mine was hopelessly rooted within me. I did not even attempt to expel it from my heart, for I felt that that was an impossibility. The woman had wholly seized upon me; a single glance of hers had been sufficient to change me; she had breathed her soul into me, and I no longer lived but in her and through her.

I indulged in countless extravagant fancies; I kissed on my hand the spot she had touched, and I repeated her name for hours at a time. All I needed to do to see her as plainly as if she had been actually present was to close my eyes; I repeated the words which she had spoken to me, "Unfortunate man! Unfortunate man! What have you done?"

I grasped the full horror of my situation, and the dread, somber aspects of the state which I had embraced were plainly revealed to me. To be a priest; that is, to remain chaste, never to love, never to notice sex or age; to turn aside from beauty, to voluntarily blind myself, to crawl in the icy shadows of a cloister or a church, to see none but the dying, to watch by strangers' beds, to wear mourning for myself in the form of the black cassock, a robe that may readily be used to line your coffin.

Meanwhile I felt life rising within me like an internal lake, swelling and overflowing; my blood surged in my veins; my youth, so long suppressed, burst out suddenly like the aloe that blooms but once in a hundred years, and then like a thunder-clap. How could I manage to see Clarimonda again? I could find no pretext to leave the seminary, for I knew no one in town. Indeed, my stay in it was to be very short, for I was merely waiting to be appointed to a parish.

I tried to loosen the bars of the window, but it was at a terrific height from the ground, and having no ladder, I had to give up that plan. Besides, I could go out at night only, and how should I ever find my way through the labyrinth of streets? All these difficulties, which would have been slight to other men, were tremendous for me, a poor seminarist, in love since yesterday, without experience, without money, and without clothes.

"Ah, if only I had not been a priest, I might have seen her every day; I might have been her lover, her husband," I said to myself in my blindness. Instead of being wrapped in my gloomy shroud, I should have worn silk and velvet, chains of gold, a sword and a plume, like handsome young cavaliers. My hair, instead of being dishonored by a broad tonsure,[3] would have fallen in ringlets around my neck; I should have worn a handsome waxed moustache; I should have been a valiant man. A single hour spent before an altar, a few words scarcely breathed, had cut me off forever from the living; I had myself sealed the stone of my tomb; I had pushed with my own hand the bolts of my prison door.

I looked out of the window. The heavens were wondrously blue, the trees had assumed their springtime livery, nature exhibited ironical joy. The square was full of people coming and going. Young dandies and young beauties in couples were going towards the gardens and the arbors; workmen passed by, singing drinking songs. There was an animation, a life, a rush, a gaiety, which contrasted all the more painfully with my mourning and my solitude. A young mother was playing with her child on the threshold of a door. She kissed its little rosy lips still pearly with drops of milk, and indulged, as she teased it, in those many divine puerilities which mothers alone can invent. The father, who stood a little way off, was smiling gently at the charming group, and his crossed arms pressed his joy to his heart. I could not bear the sight. I closed the window and threw myself on my bed, my heart filled with frightful hatred and jealousy, and I bit my fingers and my coverlet as if I had been a tiger starving for three days.

I know not how long I remained in this condition, but in turning over in a furious spasm, I perceived Father Serapion standing in the middle of the room gazing attentively at me. I was ashamed of myself, and letting fall my head upon my breast, I covered my face with my hands.

"Romualdo, my friend, something extraordinary is taking place in you," said Serapion after a few moments' silence. "Your conduct is absolutely inexplicable. You, so pious, so calm, and so gentle, you have been raging in your cell like a wild beast. Beware, my brother, and do not listen to the suggestions of the devil. The evil spirit, angered at your having devoted yourself to the Lord, prowls around you like a ravening wolf, and is making a last effort to draw you to himself.

"Instead of allowing yourself to be cast down, dear Romualdo, put on the breastplate of prayer, take up the shield of mortification, and valiantly fight the enemy. You will overcome him. Trial is indispensable to virtue, and gold emerges finer from the crucible. Be not dismayed nor discouraged; the best guarded and the strongest souls have passed through just such moments. Pray, fast, meditate, and the evil one will flee from you."

The father's discourse brought me back to myself, and I became somewhat calmer. "I was coming," he said, "to inform you that you are appointed to the parish of C—. The priest who occupied it has just died, and his lordship the Bishop has charged me to install you there. Be ready tomorrow."

I signed that I would be ready, and the father withdrew.

I opened my breviary[4] and began to read

---

[3] The part of a cleric's head, usually the crown, left bare by shaving the scalp.

[4] A book of daily prayers and readings.

my prayers, but the lines soon became confused; I lost the thread of my thoughts, and the book slipped from my hands without my noticing it.

To leave tomorrow without having seen her again.

To add one more impossibility to all those that already existed between us! To lose forever the hope of meeting her unless a miracle occurred! Even if I were to write to her, how could I send my letter? Considering the sacred functions which I had assumed, to whom could I confide, in whom could I trust? I felt terrible anxiety.

Then what Father Serapion had just said to me of the wiles of the devil recurred to my memory. The strangeness of the adventure, the supernatural beauty of Clarimonda, the phosphorescent gleam of her glance, the burning touch of her hand, the trouble into which she had thrown me, the sudden change which had occurred in me, my piety vanished in an instant—everything went to prove plainly the presence of the devil, and that satin-like hand could only be the glove that covered his claws. These thoughts caused me much terror. I picked up the breviary that had fallen to the ground from my knees, and I again began to pray.

THE NEXT DAY Serapion came for me. Two mules were waiting for us at the door, carrying our small valises. He got on one and I on the other as well as I could. While traversing the streets of the town, I looked at every window and every balcony in the hope of seeing Clarimonda, but it was too early; and the town was not yet awake. My glance tried to pierce through the blinds and curtains of all the palaces in front of which we were passing. No doubt Serapion thought my curiosity was due to the admiration caused in me by the beauty of the architecture, for he slackened his mule's speed to give me time to look.

Finally we reached the city gate and began to ascend the hill. When we reached the top, I turned around once again to gaze at the spot where lived Clarimonda. The shadow of a cloud covered the whole town; the blue and red roofs were harmonized in one uniform half-tint, over which showed, like flecks of foam, the morning smoke. By a singular optical effect there stood out bright under a single beam of light a building that rose far above the neighboring houses, wholly lost in the mist. Although it was certainly three miles away, it seemed quite close; the smallest detail could be made out—the turrets, the platforms, the windows, even the swallow-tailed vanes.

"What is that palace yonder lighted by a sunbeam?" I asked Serapion.

He shaded his eyes with his hand, and after having looked, answered: "That is the old palazzo which Prince Concini gave to Clarimonda the courtesan. Fearful things take place there."

At that moment—I have never known whether it was a reality or an illusion—I thought I saw on the terrace a slender white form that gleamed for a second and vanished. It was Clarimonda. Oh! Did she know that at that very moment, from the top of the rough road which was taking me away from her, ardent and restless, I was watching the palace she dwelt in, and which a derisive effect of light seemed to draw near to me as if to invite me to enter it as its master? No doubt she knew it, for her soul was too much in sympathy with mine not to have felt its every emotion, and it was that feeling which had urged her, still wearing her night-dress, to ascend to the terrace in the icy-cold dew of morning.

The shadow reached the palace, and all turned into a motionless ocean of roofs and attics in which nothing was to be distinguished save swelling undulations. Serapion urged on his mule; mine immediately started too, and a turn in the road concealed forever from me the town of S—, for I was never to return there. After three days' travelling through a monotonous country, we saw rising above the trees the weathercock of the steeple of the church to which I had been appointed; and after having traversed some tortuous streets bordered by huts and small gardens, we arrived before the façade, which was not very magnificent. A porch adorned with a few moldings and two or three sandstone pillars roughly cut, a tiled roof, and buttresses of the same sandstone as the pillars—that was all. On the left, the cemetery overgrown with grass, with a tall iron cross in the centers to the right, in the shadow of the church, the presbytery,[5] a very plain, poor, but clean house.

We entered. A few hens were picking up scattered grain. Accustomed, apparently, to the black dress of ecclesiastics, they were not frightened by our presence, and scarcely moved out of the way. A hoarse bark was heard, and an old dog ran up to us; it was my predecessor's dog. Its eye was dim, its coat was gray, and it exhibited every symptom of the greatest age a dog can reach. I patted it gently with my hand, and it immediately walked beside me with an air of inexpressible satisfaction.

An old woman, who had been house-keeper to the former priest, also came to meet us, and after having shown us, into the lower room, asked me if I intended to keep her. I told her that I should do so, and the dog and the hens also, and whatever furniture her master had left her at his death, which caused her a transport of joy, Father Serapion having at once paid her the price she had set upon it.

Having thus installed me, Father Serapion returned to the seminary. I therefore remained alone and without any other help than my own. The thought of Clarimonda again began to haunt me, and in spite of the efforts I made to drive it away, I was not always successful. One evening as I was walking through the box-edged paths of my little garden, I thought I saw through the shrubbery a female form watching my movements, and two sea-green eyes flashing amid the foliage, but it was merely an illusion. Having passed on the other side of the walk, I found only the imprint of a foot on the sand, so small that it looked like a child's foot. The garden was shut in by very high walls. I visited every nook and corner of it, but found no one. I have never been able to explain the fact, which, for the matter of that, was nothing by comparison with the strange things that were to happen to me.

I had been living in this way for a year, carefully fulfilling all the duties of my profession: praying, fasting, exhorting, and succoring the sick, giving alms even to the extent of depriving myself of the most indispensable necessaries; but I felt within me extreme aridity, and the sources of grace were closed to me. I did not enjoy the happiness which comes of fulfilling a holy mission; my thoughts were elsewhere, and Clarimonda's words often recurred to me. O my brother, ponder this care-

[5] The clergy's home.

fully. Because I had a single time looked at a woman, because I had committed a fault apparently so slight, I suffered for several years the most dreadful agitation and my life was troubled forever.

I shall not dwell longer upon these inward defeats and victories which were always followed by greater falls, but I shall pass at once to a decisive circumstance. One night there was a violent ringing at my door. The housekeeper went to open it, and a dark complexioned man, richly dressed in a foreign fashion, wearing a long dagger, showed under the rays of Barbara's lantern. Her first movement was one of terror, but the man reassured her, and told her that he must see me at once on a matter concerning my ministry. Barbara brought him upstairs. I was just about to go to bed. The man told me that his mistress, a very great lady, was dying and asking for a priest. I replied that I was ready to follow him, took what was needed for extreme unction, and descended quickly.

At the door were impatiently pawing and stamping two horses black as night, breathing out long jets of smoke. The man held the stirrup for me and helped me to mount one, then sprang on the other, merely resting his hand upon the pommel of the saddle. He pressed in his knees and gave his horse its head, when it went off like an arrow. My own, of which he held the bridle, also started at a gallop and kept up easily with the other. We rushed over the ground, which flashed by us gray and streaked, and the black silhouettes of the trees fled like the rout of an army. We traversed a forest, the darkness of which was so dense and icy that I felt a shudder of superstitious terror.

The sparks which our horses' hoofs struck from the stones formed a trail of fire,

and if anyone had seen us at that time of night, he would have taken us for two spectres bestriding nightmares. From time to time will-o'-the-wisps flashed across the road, and the jackdaws croaked sadly in the thickness of the wood, in which shone here and there the phosphorescent eyes of wildcats. Our horses' manes streamed out wildly, sweat poured down their sides, and their breath came short and quick through their nostrils; but when the equerry[6] saw them slackening speed, he excited them by a guttural cry which had nothing of human in it, and the race began again madder than ever.

At last our whirlwind stopped. A black mass dotted with brilliant points suddenly rose before us. The steps of our steeds sounded louder upon the ironbound flooring, and we entered under an archway the somber mouth of which yawned between two huge towers. Great excitement reigned in the chateau. Servants with torches in their hands were traversing the courts in every direction, and lights were ascending and descending from story to story. I caught a confused glimpse of vast architecture—columns, arcades, steps, stairs, a perfectly regal and fairy-like splendor of construction.

A negro page, the same who had handed me Clarimonda's tablets, and whom I at once recognized, helped me to descend, and a majordomo, dressed in black velvet, with a gold chain around his neck and an ivory cane, advanced towards me. Great tears fell from his eyes and flowed down his cheeks upon his white beard.

"Too late," he said, shaking his head. "Too late, my lord priest. But if you have not been able to save the soul, come and pray for

---

[6] An officer charged with the care of the horses.

the poor body." He took me by the arm and led me to the room of death. I wept as bitterly as he did, for I had understood that the dead woman was none else than Clarimonda, whom I had loved so deeply and madly.

A *prie-dieu*[7] was placed by the bedside; a bluish flame rising from a bronze cup cast through the room a faint, vague light, and here and there brought out of the shadow the corner of a piece of furniture or of a cornice. On a table, in a chased urn, was a faded white rose, the petals of which, with a single exception, had all fallen at the foot of the vase like perfumed tears. A broken black mask, a fan, and disguises of all kinds lay about on the armchairs, showing that death had entered this sumptuous dwelling unexpectedly and without warning.

I knelt, not daring to cast my eyes on the bed, and began to recite the psalms with great fervor, thanking God for having put the tomb between the thought of that woman and myself, so that I might add to my prayers her name, henceforth sanctified.

Little by little, however, my fervor diminished, and I fell into a reverie. The room had in no wise the aspect of a chamber of death. Instead of the fetid and cadaverous air which I was accustomed to breathe during my funeral watches, a languorous vapor of Oriental incense, a strange, amorous odor of woman, floated softly in the warm air. The pale light resembled less the yellow flame of the night-light that flickers by the side of the dead than the soft illumination of voluptuousness. I thought of the strange chance which made me meet Clarimonda at the very moment when I had lost her forever, and a sigh of regret escaped from my breast.

7 A small kneeling bench.

I thought I heard someone sigh behind me, and I turned involuntarily. It was the echo. As I turned, my eyes fell upon the state-bed which until then I had avoided looking at. The red damask curtains with great flowered pattern, held back by golden cords, allowed the dead woman to be seen, lying full length, her hands crossed on her breast.

She was covered with a linen veil of dazzling whiteness, made still more brilliant by the dark purple of the hangings; it was so tenuous that it concealed nothing of the charming form of her body, and allowed me to note the lovely lines, undulating like the neck of a swan, which even death itself had been unable to stiffen. She looked like an alabaster statue, the work of some clever sculptor, intended to be placed on a queen's tomb, or a young sleeping girl on whom snow had fallen.

I was losing my self-mastery. The sensuous air intoxicated me, the feverish scent of the half-faded rose went to my brain, and I strode up and down the room, stopping every time before the dais to gaze at the lovely dead woman through her transparent shroud. Strange thoughts came into my mind; I imagined that she was not really dead, that this was but a feint she had employed to draw me to her château and to tell me of her love. Once indeed I thought I saw her foot move under the white veil, disarranging the straight folds of the shroud.

Then I said to myself, "But is it Clarimonda? How do I know? The black page may have passed into some other woman's service. I am mad to grieve and worry as I am doing." But my heart replied, as it beat loud, "It is she—it is none but she."

I drew nearer the bed and gazed with increased attention at the object of my uncertainty. Shall I confess it? The perfection of her form, though refined and sanctified by the shadow of death, troubled me more voluptuously than was right, and her repose was so like sleep that anyone might have been deceived by it. I forgot that I had come there to perform the funeral offices, and I imagined that I was a young husband entering the room of his bride who hides her face through modesty and will not allow herself to be seen.

Sunk in grief, mad with joy, shivering with fear and pleasure, I bent towards her and took up the corner of the shroud; I raised it slowly, holding in my breath for fear of waking her. My arteries palpitated with such force that I felt the blood surging in my temples and my brow was covered with sweat as if I had been lifting a marble slab. It was indeed Clarimonda, such as I had seen her in the church on the day of my ordination. She was as lovely as then, and death seemed to be but a new coquetry of hers.

The pallor of her cheeks, the paler rose of her lips, the long-closed eyelashes showing their brown fringes against the whiteness, gave her an inexpressibly seductive expression of melancholy chastity and of pensive suffering. Her long hair, undone, in which were still a few little blue flowers, formed a pillow for her head and protected with its curls the nudity of her shoulders. Her lovely hands, purer and more diaphanous than the Host, were crossed in an attitude of pious repose and of silent prayer that softened the too great seduction, even in death, of the exquisite roundness and the ivory polish of her bare arms from which the pearl bracelets had not been removed.

I remained long absorbed in mute contemplation. The longer I looked at her, the less I could believe that life had forever forsaken that lovely frame. I know not whether it was an illusion or a reflection of the lamp, but it seemed to me that the blood was beginning to course again under the mat pallor; yet she still remained perfectly motionless.

I gently touched her arm; it was cold, yet no colder than her hand on the day it touched me under the porch of the church. I resumed my position, bending my face over hers, and let fall upon her cheeks the warm dew of my tears. Oh, what a bitter despair and powerlessness I felt! Oh, what agony I underwent during that watch! I wished I could take my whole life in order to give it to her, and breathe upon her icy remains the flame that devoured me.

Night was passing, and feeling the moment of eternal separation approaching, I was unable to refuse myself the sad and supreme sweetness of putting one kiss upon the dead lips of her who had had all my love. But, oh, wonder! A faint breath mingled with mine, and Clarimonda's lips answered to the pressure of mine. Her eyes opened, became somewhat brighter, she sighed, and moving her arms, placed them around my neck with an air of ineffable delight.

"Oh, it is you, Romualdo!" she said in a voice as languishing and soft as the last faint vibrations of a harp. "I waited for you so long that I am dead. But now we are betrothed; I shall be able to see you and to come to you. Farewell, Romualdo, farewell! I love you; that is all I wish to say to you, and I give you back the life which you have recalled to me for one moment with your kiss. Good-bye, but not for long."

Her head fell back, but her arms were still around me as if to hold me. A wild gust of wind burst in the window and rushed into the room; the last leaf of the white rose fluttered for a moment like a wing at the top of the stem, then broke away and flew out of the casement, bearing Clarimonda's soul. The lamp went out and I swooned away on the bosom of the lovely dead.

When I recovered my senses, I was lying on my bed in my little room in my house, and the old dog of the former priest was licking my hand that was hanging out from under the blanket. Barbara, shaky with old age, was busy opening and closing drawers and mixing powders in glasses. On seeing me open my eyes, the old woman uttered a cry of joy, while the dog yelped and wagged his tail; but I was so weak that I could neither move nor speak.

I learned later that I had remained for three days in that condition, giving no other sign of life than faint breathing. These three days are cut out of my life. I do not know where my mind was during that time, having absolutely no remembrance of it. Barbara told me that the same copper-complexioned man who had come to fetch me during the night, had brought me back the next morning in a closed litter and had immediately departed.

As soon as I could collect my thoughts, I went over in my own mind all the circumstances of that fatal night. At first I thought I had been the dupe of some magical illusion, but real and palpable circumstances soon shattered that supposition. I could not believe I had been dreaming, since Barbara had seen, just as I had, the man with two black horses, and described his dress and appearance accurately. Yet no one knew of any chateau in the neighborhood answering to the description of that in which I had again met Clarimonda.

One morning I saw Father Serapion enter. Barbara had sent him word that I was ill, and he had hastened to come to me. Although this eagerness proved affection for and interest in me, his visit did not give me the pleasure I should have felt. The penetration and the inquisitiveness of his glance troubled me; I felt embarrassed and guilty in his presence. He had been the first to notice my inward trouble, and I was annoyed by his clear-sightedness. While asking news of my health in a hypocritically honeyed tone he fixed upon me his two yellow, lion-like eyes, and plunged his glance into my soul like a sounding-rod.

Then he asked me a few questions as to the way in which I was working my parish, if I enjoyed my position, how I spent the time which my duties left me, if I had made any acquaintances among the inhabitants of the place, what was my favorite reading, and many other details of the same kind. I answered as briefly as possible, and he himself, without waiting for me to finish, passed on to something else. The conversation evidently had nothing to do with what he meant to say to me. Then, without any preparation, as if it were a piece of news which he had just recollected and which he was afraid to again forget, he said, in a clear, vibrant voice that sounded in my ear like the trump of the Last Judgment:—

"The great courtesan Clarimonda died recently, after an orgy that lasted eight days and nights. It was infernally splendid. They renewed the abominations of the feasts of Belshazzar and Cleopatra. What an age we are living in! The guests were served by dark slaves speaking an unknown language, who, I think, must have been fiends; the livery of the meanest of them might have served for the gala dress of an emperor. There have always been very strange stories about this Clarimonda; all her lovers have died a wretched and violent death. It is said that she was a ghoul, a female vampire, but I am of opinion that she was Beelzebub in person."

He was silent and watched me more attentively than ever to see the effect his words produced upon me. I had been unable to repress a start on hearing the name of Clarimonda, and the news of her death, besides the grief it caused me, through the strange coincidence with the nocturnal scene of which I had been a witness, filled me with a trouble and terror that showed in my face in spite of the efforts I made to master myself. Serapion looked at me anxiously and severely; then he said, "My son, I am bound to warn you that you have one foot over the abyss. Beware lest you fall in. Satan has a long arm, and tombs are not always faithful. The stone over Clarimonda should be sealed with a triple seal, for it is not, I am told, the first time that she has died. May God watch over you, Romualdo!"

With these words he walked slowly towards the door, and I did not see him again, for he left for S— almost immediately.

I HAD AT LAST entirely recovered, and had resumed my usual duties. The remembrance of Clarimonda and the words of the old priest were ever present to my mind; yet no extraordinary event had confirmed Serapion's gloomy predictions. I therefore began to believe that his fears and my terrors were exaggerated; but one night I dreamed a dream. I had scarcely fallen asleep when I heard the curtains of my bed open and the rings sliding over the bars with a rattling sound. I sat up abruptly, leaning on my elbow, and saw the shadow of a woman standing before me.

I at once recognized Clarimonda. In her hand she bore a small lamp, of the shape of those put into tombs, the light of which gave to her slender fingers a rosy transparency that melted by insensible gradations into the opaque milky whiteness of her bare arm. Her sole vestment was the linen shroud that had covered her upon her state bed, and the folds of which she drew over her bosom as if she were ashamed of being so little clothed, but her small hand could not manage it. It was so white that the color of the drapery was confounded with that of the flesh under the pale light of the lamp.

Enveloped in the delicate tissue which revealed all the contours of her body, she resembled an antique marble statue of a bather rather than a woman filled with life. Dead or living, statue or woman, shadow or body, her beauty was still the same; only the green gleam of her eyes was somewhat dulled, and her mouth, so purple of yore, had now only a pale, tender rose-tint almost like that of her cheeks. The little blue flowers which I had noticed in her hair were dried up and had lost most of their leaves. And yet she was charming, so charming that in spite of the strangeness of the adventure and the inexplicable manner in which she had entered the room, I did not experience a single thrill of terror.

She placed the lamp on the table and sat down on the foot of my bed. Then bending towards me, she said in the silvery, velvety voice which I had heard from no one but her:—

"I have made you wait a long time, dear Romualdo, and you must have thought I had forgotten you. But I have come from a very long distance, from a bourne[8] whence no traveler has yet returned. There is neither moon nor sun in the country whence I have come;

---

[8] Destination.

neither road nor path; naught but space and shadow; no ground for the foot, no air for the wing; and yet I am here, for love is stronger than death and overcomes it.

Ah, what worn faces, what terrible things I have seen on my way! What difficulty my soul, which returned to this world by the power of will, experienced before it could find its own body and re-enter it! What efforts I had to make before I could push up the tombstone with which they had covered me! See! The palms of my poor hands are all bruised. Kiss them and cure them, my dear love." And one after the other, she put the cold palms of her hands upon my lips. I did kiss them many a time, and she watched me with a smile of ineffable satisfaction.

I confess it to my shame—I had wholly forgotten the counsels of Father Serapion and my own profession; I had fallen without resisting and at the first blow; I had not even endeavored to drive away the tempter. The freshness of Clarimonda's skin penetrated mine, and I felt voluptuous thrills running through my body. Poor child! In spite of all that I have seen of her, I find it difficult to believe that she was a demon; she certainly did not look like one, and never did Satan better conceal his claws and horns. She had pulled her feet up under her, and was curled up on the edge of my bed in an attitude full of nonchalant coquetry.

From time to time she passed her little hand through my hair and rolled it into ringlets as if to try how different ways of dressing it would suit my face. I allowed her to go on with the most guilty complaisance, and while she toyed with me she chatted brightly. The remarkable thing is that I experienced no astonishment at so extraordinary an adventure, and with the facility we enjoy in dreams of admitting as quite simple the most amazing events, it seemed to me that everything that was happening was quite natural.

"I loved you long before I had seen you, dear Romualdo, and I had looked for you everywhere. You were my dream, and when I saw you in church at that fatal moment, I at once said, 'It is he!' I cast on you a glance in which I put all the love which I had had, which I had, and which I was to have for you; a glance that would have damned a cardinal and made a king kneel before my feet in the presence of his whole court. But you remained impassible; you preferred your God to me. Oh, I am jealous of God, whom you loved, and whom you still love more than me! Unfortunate that I am—oh, most unfortunate! Your heart will never be wholly mine, though you brought me back to life with a kiss, though I am Clarimonda, who was dead and who for your sake burst the cerements of the tomb, and has come to devote to you a life which she has resumed only to make you happy!"

With these words she mingled intoxicating caresses which penetrated my senses and my reason to such a degree that I did not hesitate, in order to console her, to utter frightful blasphemies and to tell her that I loved her as much as I did God.

Her eyes brightened and shone like chrysoprase.[9] "True? Quite true? As much as God?" she said, clasping me in her lovely arms. "Since that is so, you will go with me, you will follow me where I will. You shall cast off your ugly black clothes, you shall be the proudest and most envied of men, you shall be my lover. Oh, the lovely, happy life we shall lead! When shall we start?"

[9] An apple-green translucent mineral.

"Tomorrow! Tomorrow!" I cried in my delirium.

"Tomorrow be it," she replied. "I shall have time to change my dress, for this one is rather scanty and not of much use for travelling. Then I must also warn my people, who think me really dead, and who are mourning as hard as they can. Money, clothes, and carriage—everything shall be ready, and I shall call for you at this same hour. Good-bye, dear heart," and she touched my brow with her lips.

The lamp went out, the windows were closed, and I saw no more. A leaden, dreamless sleep overcame me and held me fast until the next morning. I awoke later than usual, and the remembrance of the strange vision agitated me the livelong day. At last I managed to persuade myself that it was a mere fever of my heated brain. Yet the sensation had been so intense that it was difficult to believe it was not real, and it was not without some apprehension of what might happen that I went to bed, after having prayed God to drive away from me evil thoughts and to protect the chastity of my sleep.

I soon fell fast asleep and my dream continued. The curtains were opened, and I saw Clarimonda, not as the first time, wan in her pale shroud, and the violets of death upon her cheeks, but gay, bright, and dainty, in a splendid travelling-dress of green velvet with gold braid, caught up on the side and showing a satin under-skirt. Her fair hair escaped in great curls from below her broad black felt hat with capriciously twisted white feathers. She held in her hand a small riding-whip ending in a golden whistle. She touched me lightly with it and said: "Well, handsome sleeper, is that the way you get ready? I expected to find you up. Rise quickly, we have no time to lose."

I sprang from my bed.

"Come, put on your clothes and let us go," she said, pointing to a small parcel which she had brought. "The horses are impatiently champing their bits at the door. We ought to be thirty miles away by now."

I dressed hastily, and she herself passed me the clothes, laughing at my awkwardness and telling me what they were when I made a mistake. She arranged my hair for me, and when it was done, she held out a small pocket-mirror of Venice crystal framed with silver filigree and said to me, "What do you think of yourself? Will you take me as your valet?"

I was no longer the same man and did not recognize myself. I was no more like myself than a finished statue is like a block of stone. My former face seemed to me but a coarse sketch of the one reflected in the mirror. I was handsome, and my vanity was sensibly tickled by the metamorphosis. The elegant clothes, the rich embroidered jacket, made me quite a different person, and I admired the power of transformation possessed by a few yards of stuff cut in a certain way. The spirit of my costume entered into me, and in ten minutes I was passably conceited. I walked up and down the room a few times to feel more at my ease in my new garments. Clarimonda looked at me with an air of maternal complaisance and appeared well satisfied with her work.

"Now, that is childishness enough. Let us be off, dear Romualdo; we are going a long way and we shall never get there." As she touched the doors they opened, and we passed by the dog without waking it.

At the door we found Margheritone, the equerry who had already conducted me. He held three horses, black like the first, one for me, one for himself, and one for Clarimonda. The horses must have been Spanish jennets,[10] sired by the gale, for they went as fast as the wind, and the moon, which had risen to light us at our departure, rolled in the heavens like a wheel detached from its car. We saw it on our right spring from tree to tree, breathlessly trying to keep up with us.

We soon reached a plain where by a clump of trees waited a carriage drawn by four horses. We got into it and the horses started off at a mad gallop. I had one arm around Clarimonda's waist and one of her hands in mine; she leaned her head on my shoulder, and I felt her half-bare bosom against my arm. I had never enjoyed such lively happiness. I forgot everything at that moment. I no more remembered having been a priest, so great was the fascination which the evil spirit exercised over me.

From that night my nature became in some sort double. There were in me two men unknown to each other. Sometimes I fancied myself a priest who dreamed every night he was a nobleman; sometimes I fancied I was a nobleman who dreamed he was a priest. I was unable to distinguish between the vision and the waking, and I knew not where reality began and illusion ended. The conceited libertine rallied the priest; the priest hated the excesses of the young nobleman. Two spirals, twisted one within the other and confounded without ever touching, very aptly represent this bicephalous[11] life of mine.

Yet, in spite of the strangeness of this position, I do not think that for one instant I was mad. I always preserved very clearly the perception of my double life. Only there was an absurd fact which I could not explain: it was that the feeling of the same self should exist in two men so utterly different. That was an anomaly which I did not understand, whether I believed myself to be the parish priest of the little village of —— or il Signor Romualdo, the declared lover of Clarimonda.

What is certain is that I was, or at least believed that I was, in Venice. I have never yet been able to make out what was true and what was imaginary in that strange adventure. We dwelt in a great marble palace on the Canaleio, full of frescoes and statues, with two paintings in Titian's best manner in Clarimonda's bedroom. It was a palace worthy of a king. Each of us had his own gondola and gondoliers, his own livery, music-room, and poet. Clarimonda liked to live in great style, and she had something of Cleopatra in her nature.

As for me, I lived like a prince's son, and acted as if I belonged to the family of the twelve Apostles or the four Evangelists of the Most Serene Republic; I would not have got out of my way to let the Doge pass, and I do not think that since Satan fell from heaven there was anyone so proud and so insolent as I. I used to go to the Ridotto[12] and gamble fearfully. I met the best society in the world, ruined eldest sons, swindlers, parasites, and swashbucklers, yet in spite of this dissipated life, I remained faithful to Clarimonda. I loved her madly. She would have awakened satiety itself and fixed inconstancy.

I should have been perfectly happy but for the accursed nightmare which returned every night, and in which I thought myself a parish priest living an ascetic life and doing penance for his excesses of the daytime. Reassured by the habit of being: with her, I

[10] A breed of small Spanish horses.

[11] Having two heads.

[12] A famous government-owned casino in Venice.

scarcely ever thought of the strange manner in which I had made her acquaintance. However, what Father Serapion had told me about her occasionally occurred to my mind and caused me some uneasiness.

For some time past Clarimonda's health had been failing. Her complexion was becoming paler and paler every day. The doctors, when called in, failed to understand her disease and knew not how to treat it. They prescribed insignificant remedies, and did not return. Meanwhile she became plainly paler, and colder and colder. She was almost as white and as dead as on that famous night in the unknown chateau. I was bitterly grieved to see her thus slowly pining away. She, touched by my sorrow, smiled gently and sadly at me with the smile of one who knows she is dying.

One morning I was seated by her bed breakfasting at a small table, in order not to leave her a minute. As I pared a fruit I happened to cut my finger rather deeply. The blood immediately flowed in a purple stream, and a few drops fell upon Clarimonda. Her eyes lighted up, her face assumed an expression of fierce and savage joy which I had never before beheld. She sprang from her bed with the agility of an animal, of a monkey or of a cat, and sprang at my wound, which she began to suck with an air of inexpressible delight.

She sipped the blood slowly and carefully like a gourmand who enjoys a glass of sherry or Syracuse wine; she winked her eyes, the green pupils of which had become oblong instead of round. From time to time she broke off to kiss my hand, then she again pressed the wound with her lips so as to draw out a few more red drops. When she saw that the blood had ceased to flow, she rose up, rosier than a

May morn, her face full, her eyes moist and shining, her hand soft and warm; in a word, more beautiful than ever and in a perfect state of health.

"I shall not die! I shall not die!" she said, half mad with joy, as she hung around my neck. "I shall be able to love you a long time yet. My life is in yours, and all that I am comes from you. A few drops of your rich, noble blood, more precious and more efficacious than all the elixirs in the world, have restored my life."

The scene preoccupied me a long time and filled me with strange doubts concerning Clarimonda. That very evening, when sleep took me back to the presbytery, I saw Father Serapion, graver and more care-worn than ever. He looked at me attentively, and said to me: "Not satisfied with losing your soul, you want to lose your body also. Unfortunate youth, what a trap you have fallen into!" The tone in which he said these few words struck me greatly, but in spite of its vivacity, the impression was soon dispelled and numerous other thoughts effaced it from my mind.

However, one evening I saw in my mirror, the perfidious position of which she had not taken into account, Clarimonda pouring a powder into the cup of spiced wine she was accustomed to prepare for me after the meal. I took the cup, feigned to carry it to my lips, and put it away as if to finish it later at leisure, but I profited by a moment when my beauty had turned her back, to throw the contents under the table, after which I withdrew to my room and went to bed, thoroughly determined not to sleep, and to see what she would do.

I had not long to wait. Clarimonda entered in her night-dress, and having thrown it off, stretched herself in the bed by me. When she was quite certain that I was asleep, she bared my arm, drew a golden pin from her hair, and whispered, "One drop, nothing but a little red drop, a ruby at the end of my needle! Since you still love me, I must not die. Oh, my dear love! I shall drink your beautiful, brilliant, purple blood.

"Sleep, my sole treasure, my god and my child. I shall not hurt you, I shall only take as much of your life as I need not to lose my own. If I did not love you so much, I might make up my mind to have other lovers whose veins I would drain; but since I have known you, I have a horror of everyone else. Oh, what a lovely arm, how round and white it is! I shall never dare to prick that pretty blue vein."

And as she spoke, she wept, and I felt her tears upon my arm which she held in her hands. At last she made up her mind, pricked me with the needle, and began to suck the blood that flowed. Though she had scarcely imbibed a few drops, she feared to exhaust me. She tied my arm with a narrow band, after having rubbed my wound with an unguent which healed it immediately.

I could no longer doubt; Father Serapion was right. However, in spite of the certainty, I could not help loving Clarimonda, and I would willingly have given her all the blood she needed in order to support her factitious existence. Besides, I was not much afraid, for the woman guarded me against the vampire; what I had heard and seen completely reassured me. At that time I had full-blooded veins which would not be very speedily exhausted, and I did not care whether my life went drop by drop. I would have opened my arm myself and said to her, "Drink, and let my life enter your body with my blood." I avoided alluding in the least to the narcotic which she had poured out for me and the scene of the pin—and we lived in the most perfect harmony.

Yet my priestly scruples tormented me more than ever, and I knew not what new penance to invent to tame and mortify my flesh. Although all these visions were involuntary and I in no wise took part in them, I dared not touch the crucifix with hands so impure and a mind so soiled by such debauch, whether real or imaginary. After falling into these fatiguing hallucinations, I tried to keep from sleeping. I kept my eyes open with my fingers, and remained standing by the wall struggling against slumber with all my strength; but soon it would force itself into my eyes, and seeing that the struggle was useless, I let fall my arms with discouragement and weariness, while the current carried me again to the perfidious shores. Father Serapion exhorted me most vehemently, and harshly reproached me with weakness and lack of fervor. One day, when he had been more agitated than usual, he said to me:—

"There is but one way of ridding you of this obsession, and although it is extreme, we must make use of it. Great evils require great remedies. I know where Clarimonda is buried. We must dig her up, and you shall see in what a pitiful condition is the object of your love. You will no longer be tempted to lose your soul for a loathsome body devoured by worms and about to fall into dust. It will assuredly bring you back to your senses."

For myself, I was so wearied of my double life that I accepted, wishing to know once for all whether it was the priest or the nobleman who was the dupe of an illusion. I was determined to kill, for the benefit of the one or the other, one of the two men who were in me, or to kill them both, for such a life as I had been leading was unendurable.

Father Serapion provided a pick, a crowbar, and a lantern, and at midnight we repaired to the cemetery of the place of which he knew accurately, as well as the disposition of the graves. Having cast the light of our lantern upon the inscriptions on several tombs, we at last reached a stone half hidden by tall grass and covered with moss and parasitical plants, on which we made out this partial inscription: "Here lies Clarimonda, who in her lifetime was the most beautiful woman in the world..."

"This is the spot," said Serapion, and putting down the lantern, he introduced the crowbar in the joints of the stone and began to raise it. The stone yielded, and he set to work with the pick. I watched him, darker and more silent than the night itself. As for him, bending over this funereal work, he perspired heavily and his quick breath sounded like the rattle in a dying man's throat. It was a strange spectacle, and anyone who might have seen us would have taken us rather for men profaning the tomb and robbing the shrouds than for priests of God.

Serapion's zeal had something harsh and savage which made him resemble a demon rather than an apostle or an angel, and his face, with its austere features sharply brought out by the light of the lantern, was in no wise reassuring. I felt an icy sweat break out on my limbs, my hair rose upon my head. Within myself I considered the action of the severe Serapion an abominable sacrilege, and I wished that from the somber clouds that passed heavily over our heads might flash a bolt that would reduce him to powder. The owls, perched on the cypresses, troubled by the light of the lantern, struck the glass with their dusty wings and uttered plaintive cries. The foxes yelped in the distance, and innumerable sinister noises rose in the silence.

At last Serapion's pick struck the coffin, which gave out the dull, sonorous sound which nothingness gives out when it is touched. He pulled off the cover, and I saw Clarimonda, pale as marble, her hands clasped, her white shroud forming but one line from her head to her feet. A little red drop shone like a rose at the corner of her discolored lips. Serapion at the sight of it became furious.

"Ah! There you are, you demon, you shameless courtesan! You who drink blood and gold!" and he cast on the body and the coffin quantities of holy water, tracing with the sprinkler a cross upon the coffin.

The holy dew no sooner touched poor Clarimonda than her lovely body fell into dust and became only a hideous mass of ashes and half-calcined bones.

"There is your mistress, my lord Romualdo," said the inexorable priest, as he pointed to the remains. "Are you now still tempted to go to the Lido and Fusino with your beauty?"

I bowed my head. Something had been shattered within me. I returned to my presbytery, and lord Romualdo, the lover of Clarimonda, left the poor priest with whom he had so long kept such strange company. Only the next night I saw Clarimonda. She said to me, as the first time under the porch of the church, "Unfortunate man! Unfortunate man! What have you done? Why did you listen to that foolish priest? Were you not happy? What have I done to you, that you should go and violate my poor tomb and lay bare the wretchedness of my nothingness? All communion between our souls and bodies is henceforth broken. Farewell; you will regret me."

She vanished in air like a vapor, and I never saw her again. Alas! She spoke the truth. I have regretted her more than once, and I still regret her. I purchased the peace of my soul very dearly. The love of God was not too much to replace her love.

Such, brother, is the story of my youth. Never look upon a woman, and walk always with your eyes cast on the ground, for chaste and calm though you may be, a single minute may make you lose eternity.

James Malcolm Rymer

VARNEY THE VAMPIRE; or the Feast of Blood first appeared in 1845 as a series of inexpensive pamphlets, the so-called "penny dreadfuls." There were 109 weekly installments before the lurid, sprawling narrative finally concluded; then was collected and issued in book form in 1847 (a strategy that comic book publishers still use today).

There remains some controversy over whether the 667,000-word vampire epic was written by James Malcolm Rymer. Virtually nothing is known about Rymer (1814-1881), except that he was probably a civil engineer and wrote dozens of thrillers in the 1830s to 1850s, in his own name, under the pseudonyms Malcolm J. Merry, Malcolm J. Errym, and probably using other names in American publications. Some have claimed that *Varney* was the product of Thomas Pecket Prest (1810-1859), a prolific penny dreadful scribe and creator of the demon barber Sweeney Todd. The editor-scholar E. F. Bleiler concluded that *Varney* was "almost certainly" that of Rymer. Whatever the case, Varney's bloody adventures held the general public enthralled and were hugely influencial, popularizing many elements associated with modern vampire fiction, such as nubile female victims menaced by an aristocratic vampire with sharp fangs, superhuman strength, and hypnotic powers. (It should also be noted that Varney's vampirism was portrayed as a kind of malady, manifesting itself only when he needed to feed; he was human otherwise.)

VARNEY THE VAMPYRE
or *The Feast of Blood*

JAMES MALCOLM RYMER

CHAPTER I

*"How graves give up their dead,
And how the night air hideous grows
With shrieks!"*

MIDNIGHT.—THE HAIL-STORM.—
THE DREADFUL VISITOR.—
THE VAMPYRE.

The solemn tones of an old cathedral dock have announced midnight—the air is thick and heavy—a strange, death-like stillness pervades all nature. Like the ominous calm which precedes some more than usually terrific outbreak of the elements, they seem to have paused even in their ordinary fluctuations, to gather a terrific strength for the great effort.

A faint peal of thunder now comes from far off. Like a signal gun for the battle of the winds to begin, it appeared to awaken them from their lethargy, and one awful, warring hurricane swept over a whole city, producing more devastation in the four or five minutes it lasted, than would a half century of ordinary phenomena. It was as if some giant had blown upon some toy town, and scattered many of the buildings before the hot blast of his terrific breath; for as suddenly as that blast of wind had come did it cease, and all was as still and calm as before.

Sleepers awakened, and thought that what they had heard must be the confused chimera[1] of a dream. They trembled and turned to sleep again.

All is still—still as the very grave. Not a sound breaks the magic of repose. What is that—a strange pattering noise, as of a million fairy feet? It is hail—yes, a hailstorm has burst over the city. Leaves are dashed from the trees, mingled with small boughs; windows that lie most opposed to the direct fury of the pelting particles of ice are broken, and the rapt repose that before was so remarkable in its intensity, is exchanged for a noise which, in its accumu-

---

[1] A mythological fire-breathing creature, part lioness, part snake, part goat; here, metaphorically, a creature of fantasy.

lation, drowns every cry of surprise or consternation which here and there arose from persons who found their houses invaded by the storm.

Now and then, too, there would come a sudden gust of wind that in its strength, as it blew laterally, would, for a moment, hold millions of the hailstones suspended in mid air, but it was only to dash them with redoubled force in some new direction, where more mischief was to be done.

Oh, how the storm raged! Hail—rain—wind. It was, in very truth, an awful night.

There was an antique chamber in an ancient house. Curious and quaint carvings adorn the walls, and the large chimneypiece is a curiosity of itself. The ceiling is low, and a large bay window, from roof to floor, looks to the west. The window is latticed and filled with curiously painted glass and rich stained pieces, which send in a strange, yet beautiful light, when sun or moon shines into the apartment. There is but one portrait in that room, although the walls seem paneled for the express purpose of containing a series of pictures. That portrait is of a young man, with a pale face, a stately brow, and a strange expression about the eyes, which no one cared to look on twice.

There is a stately bed in that chamber, of carved walnut-wood is it made, rich in design and elaborate in execution; one of those works which owe their existence to the Elizabethan era. It is hung with heavy silken and damask furnishing; nodding feathers are at its corners—covered with dust are they, and they lend a funereal aspect to the room.[2] The floor is of polished oak.

God! How the hail dashes on the old bay window! Like an occasional discharge of mimic musketry, it comes clashing, beating, and cracking upon the small panes; but they resist it—their small size saves them; the wind, the hail, the rain, expend their fury in vain.

The bed in that old chamber is occupied. A creature formed in all fashions of loveliness lies in a half sleep upon that ancient couch—a girl young and beautiful as a spring morning. Her long hair has escaped from its confinement and streams over the blackened coverings of the bedstead; she has been restless in her sleep, for the clothing of the bed is in much confusion.

One arm is over her head, the other hangs nearly off the side of the bed near to which she lies. A neck and bosom that would have formed a study for the rarest sculptor that ever Providence gave genius to, were half disclosed. She moaned slightly in her sleep, and once or twice the lips moved as if in prayer—at least one might judge so, for the name of Him who suffered for all came once faintly from them.

She had endured much fatigue, and the storm does not awaken her; but it can disturb the slumbers it does not possess the power to destroy entirely. The turmoil of the elements wakes the senses, although it cannot entirely break the repose they have lapsed into.

Oh, what a world of witchery was in that mouth, slightly parted, and exhibiting within the pearly teeth that glistened even in the faint light that came from that bay window. How sweetly the long silken eyelashes lay upon the cheek. Now she moves, and one shoulder is entirely visible—whiter, fairer than

---

[2] Black ostrich feathers, in the form of plumes on hats and horses, as well as decorations, were featured at upscale Victorian funerals.

the spotless clothing of the bed on which she lies, is the smooth skin of that fair creature, just budding into womanhood, and in that transition state which presents to us all the charms of the girl—almost of the child, with the more matured beauty and gentleness of advancing years.

Was that lightning? Yes—an awful, vivid, terrifying flash—then a roaring peal of thunder, as if a thousand mountains were rolling one over the other in the blue vault of Heaven! Who sleeps now in that ancient city? Not one living soul. The dread trumpet of eternity could not more effectually have awakened anyone.

The hail continues. The wind continues. The uproar of the elements seems at its height. Now she awakens—that beautiful girl on the antique bed; she opens those eyes of celestial blue, and a faint cry of alarm bursts from her lips. At least it is a cry which, amid the noise and turmoil without, sounds but faint and weak. She sits upon the bed and presses her hands upon her eyes. Heavens! What a wild torrent of wind, and rain, and hail! The thunder likewise seems intent upon awakening sufficient echoes to last until the next flash of forked lightning should again produce the wild concussion of the air.

She murmurs a prayer—a prayer for those she loves best; the names of those dear to her gentle heart come from her lips; she weeps and prays; she thinks then of what devastation the storm must surely produce, and to the great God of Heaven she prays for all living things.

Another flash—a wild, blue, bewildering flash of lightning streams across that bay window, for an instant bringing out every color in it with terrible distinctness. A shriek bursts from the lips of the young girl, and then, with eyes fixed upon that window, which, in another moment, is all darkness, and with such an expression of terror upon her face as it had never before known, she trembled, and the perspiration of intense fear stood upon her brow.

"What—what was it?" she gasped, "real or delusion? Oh, God, what was it? A figure tall and gaunt, endeavoring from the outside to unclasp the window. I saw it. That flash of lightning revealed it to me. It stood the whole length of the window."

There was a lull of the wind. The hail was not falling so thickly—moreover, it now fell, what there was of it, straight, and yet a strange clattering sound came upon the glass of that long window. It could not be a delusion—she is awake, and she hears it. What can produce it? Another flash of lightning—another shriek—there could be now no delusion.

A tall figure is standing on the ledge immediately outside the long window. It is its fingernails upon the glass that produces the sound so like the hail, now that the hail has ceased. Intense fear paralyzed the limbs of the beautiful girl. That one shriek is all she can utter—with hand clasped, a face of marble, a heart beating so wildly in her bosom, that each moment it seems as if it would break its confines, eyes distended and fixed upon the window, she waits, froze with horror.

The pattering and clattering of the nails continue. No word is spoken, and now she fancies she can trace the darker form of that figure against the window, and she can see the long arms moving to and fro, feeling for some mode of entrance. What strange light is that which now gradually creeps up into the air? Red and terrible—brighter and brighter it grows. The lightning has set fire to a mill, and the reflection of the rapidly consuming building falls upon that long window.

There can be no mistake. The figure is there, still feeling for an entrance, and clattering against the glass with its long nails, that appear as if the growth of many years had been untouched. She tries to scream again but a choking sensation comes over her, and she cannot. It is too dreadful—she tries to move—each limb seems weighted down by tons of lead—she can but in a hoarse faint whisper cry:—

"Help—help—help—help!"

And that one word she repeats like a person in a dream. The red glare of the fire continues. It throws up the tall gaunt figure in hideous relief against the long window. It shows, too, upon the one portrait that is in the chamber, and the portrait appears to fix its eyes upon the attempting intruder, while the flickering light from the fire makes it look fearfully lifelike. A small pane of glass is broken, and the form from without introduces a long gaunt hand, which seems utterly destitute of flesh. The fastening is removed, and one-half of the window, which opens like folding doors, is swung wide open upon its hinges.

And yet now she could not scream—she could not move. "Help!—help!—help!" was all she could say. But, oh, that look of terror that sat upon her face, it was dreadful—a look to haunt the memory for a lifetime—a look to obtrude itself upon the happiest moments, and turn them to bitterness.

The figure turns half round, and the light falls upon its face. It is perfectly white—perfectly bloodless. The eyes look like polished tin; the lips are drawn back, and the principal feature next to those dreadful eyes is the teeth—the fearful-looking teeth—projecting like those of some wild animal, hideously, glaringly white, and fang-like.

It approaches the bed with a strange, gliding movement. It clashes together the long nails that literally appear to hang from the finger ends. No sound comes from its lips. Is she going mad—that young and beautiful girl exposed to so much terror? She has drawn up all her limbs; she cannot even now say help. The power of articulation is gone, but the power of movement has returned to her; she can draw herself slowly along to the other side of the bed from that towards which the hideous appearance is coming.

But her eyes are fascinated. The glance of a serpent could not have produced a greater effect upon her than did the fixed gaze of those awful, metallic-looking eyes that were bent down on her face. Crouching down so that the gigantic height was lost, and the horrible, protruding white face was the most prominent object, came on the figure. What was it?—what did it want there?—what made it look so hideous—so unlike an inhabitant of the earth, and yet be on it?

Now she has got to the verge of the bed, and the figure pauses. It seemed as if when it paused she lost the power to proceed. The clothing of the bed was now clutched in her hands with unconscious power. She drew her breath short and thick. Her bosom heaves, and her limbs tremble, yet she cannot withdraw her eyes from that marble-looking face. He holds her with his glittering eye.

The storm has ceased—all is still. The winds are hushed; the church clock proclaims the hour of one: a hissing sound comes from the throat of the hideous being, and he raises his long, gaunt arms—the lips move. He advances. The girl places one small foot on to the floor. She is unconsciously dragging the clothing with her.

The door of the room is in that direction—can she reach it? Has she power to walk?—can she withdraw her eyes from the face of the intruder, and so break the hideous charm? God of Heaven! Is it real, or some dream so like reality as to nearly overturn judgment forever?

The figure has paused again, and half on the bed and half out of it that young girl lies trembling. Her long hair streams across the entire width of the bed. As she has slowly moved along she has left it streaming across the pillows. The pause lasted about a minute—oh, what an age of agony. That minute was, indeed, enough for madness to do its full work in.

With a sudden rush that could not be foreseen—with a strange howling cry that was enough to awaken terror in every breast, the figure seized the long tresses of her hair, and twining them round his bony hands he held her to the bed.

Then she screamed—Heaven granted her then power to scream. Shriek followed shriek in rapid succession. The bed-clothes fell in a heap by the side of the bed—she was dragged by her long silken hair completely on to it again. Her beautifully rounded limbs quivered with the agony of her soul. The glassy, horrible eyes of the figure ran over that angelic form with a hideous satisfaction—horrible profanation.

He drags her head to the bed's edge. He forces it back by the long hair still entwined in his grasp. With a plunge he seizes her neck in his fang-like teeth—a gush of blood, and a hideous sucking noise follows. *The girl has swooned, and the vampyre is at his hideous repast!*

THE VAMPYRE'S STORY *

In the reign of the First Charles,[3] I resided in a narrow street, in the immediate neighborhood of Whitehall. It was a straggling, tortuous thoroughfare, going down to the Thames; it matters little what were my means of livelihood, but I have no hesitation in saying that I was a well-paid agent in some of the political movements which graced and disgraced that period.

London was then a mass of mean-looking houses, with here and there one that looked like a palace, compared with its humbler neighbors. Almost every street appeared to be under the protection of some great house situated somewhere in its extent, but such of those houses as have survived the wreck of time rank now with their neighbors, and are so strangely altered, that I, who knew many of them well, could now scarcely point to the place where they used to stand.

I took no prominent part in the commotions of that period, but I saw the head of a king held up in its gore at Whitehall as a spectacle for the multitude.

There were thousands of persons in England who had aided to bring about that result, but who were the first to fall under the ban of the gigantic power they had themselves raised.

Among these were many of my employers; men, who had been quite willing to shake the stability of a throne so far as the individual occupying it was concerned; but who certainly never contemplated the destruction of monar-

---

* NOTE: This chapter is told in the first person by Varney himself, a narrative device never before applied to a vampire tale. This perspective on vampiric existence remained a unique entry in the canon for decades.

[3] That is, Charles I of England (1600-1649), who struggled with Parliament for control of the country and was succeeded by the Cromwellian "Commonwealth of England" until the restoration of Charles II in 1660.

chy; so the death of the First Charles, and the dictatorship of Cromwell, made royalists in abundance.

They had raised a spirit they could not quell again, and this was a fact which the stern, harsh man, Cromwell, with whom I had many interviews, was aware of.

My house was admirably adapted for the purposes of secrecy and seclusion, and I became a thriving man from the large sums I received for aiding the escape of distinguished loyalists, some of whom lay for a considerable time *perdu*[4] at my house, before an eligible opportunity arrived of dropping down the river quietly to some vessel which would take them to Holland.

It was to offer me so much per head for these royalists that Cromwell sent for me, and there was one in particular who had been private secretary to the Duke of Cleveland, a young man merely, of neither family nor rank, but of great ability, whom Cromwell was exceedingly anxious to capture.

I think there likewise must have been some private reasons which induced the dictator of the Commonwealth to be so anxious concerning this Master Francis Latham, which was the name of the person alluded to.

It was late one evening when a stranger came to my house, and having desired to see me, was shown into a private apartment, when I immediately waited upon him.

"I am aware," he said, "that you have been confidentially employed by the Duke of Cleveland, and I am aware that you have been very useful to distressed loyalists, but in aiding Master Francis Latham, the duke's secretary,

you will be permitted almost to name your own terms."

I named a hundred pounds, which at that time was a much larger sum than now, taking into consideration the relative value. One half of it was paid to me at once, and the other promised within four-and-twenty hours after Latham had effected his escape.

I was told that at half past twelve o'clock that night, a man dressed in common working apparel, and with a broom over his shoulder would knock at my door and ask if he could be recommended to a lodging, and that by those tokens I should know him to be Francis Latham. A Dutch lugger,[5] I was further told, was lying near Gravesend, on board of which, to earn my money, I was expected to place the fugitive.

All this was duly agreed upon; I had a boat in readiness, with a couple of watermen upon whom I could depend, and I was far from anticipating any extraordinary difficulties in carrying out the enterprise.

I had a son about twelve years of age, who being a sharp acute lad, I found very useful upon several occasions, and I never scrupled to make him acquainted with any such affair as this that I am recounting. Half past twelve o'clock came, and in a very few minutes after that period of time there came a knock at my door, which my son answered, and according to arrangement, there was the person with a broom, who asked to be recommended to a lodging, and who was immediately requested to walk in.

He seemed rather nervous, and asked me if I thought there was much risk.

"No," said I, "no more than ordinary risk in all these cases, but we must wait half an hour 'till the tide turns. For just now to struggle against it down the river would really be nothing else but courting observation."

---

[4] Hidden or concealed.

[5] A short-masted vessel, often used for fishing.

To this he perfectly agreed, and sat down by my fireside.

I was as anxious as he to get the affair over, for it was a ticklish job, and Oliver Cromwell, if he had brought anything of the kind exactly home to me, would as lief[6] order me to be shot as he would have taken his luncheon in the name of the Lord.

I accordingly went down to the water-side to speak to the men who were lying there with the boat, and had ascertained from them that in about twenty minutes the tide would begin to ebb in the center of the stream, when two men confronted me.

Practiced as I was in the habits and appearances of the times, I guessed at once who they were. In fact, a couple of Oliver Cromwell's dismounted dragoons[7] were always well known.

"You are wanted," said one of them to me.

"Yes, you are particularly wanted," said the other.

"But, gentlemen, I am rather busy," said I. "In an hour's time I will do myself the pleasure, if you please, of waiting upon you anywhere you wish to name."

The only reply they made to this was the practical one, of getting on each side of me, and then hurrying me on, past my own door.

I was taken right away to St. James's at a rapid pace, being hurried through one of the court yards; we paused at a small door, at which was a sentinel.

My two guides communicated something to him, and he allowed us to pass. There was a narrow passage without any light, and through another door, at which was likewise a sentinel, who turned the glare of a lantern upon me and my conductors. Some short explanation was given to him likewise during which I heard the words His Highness,[8] which was the title which Cromwell had lately assumed.

They pushed me through this doorway, closed it behind me, and left me inside in the dark.

BEING PERFECTLY IGNORANT of where I was, I thought the most prudent plan was to stand stock still, for if I advanced it might be into danger, and my retreat was evidently cut off.

Moreover, those who brought me there must have some sort of intention, and it was better for me to leave them to develop it than to take any steps myself, which might be of a very hazardous nature.

That I was adopting the best policy I was soon convinced, for a flash of light suddenly came upon me, and I heard a gruff voice, say:—

"Who goes there? Come this way."

I walked on, and passed through an open door way into a small apartment, in the center of which, standing by a common deal table on which his clenched hand was resting, I found Oliver Cromwell himself.

"So, sirrah," he said, "royalists and pestilent characters are to ravage the land, are they so? Answer me."

"I have no answer to make, your highness," said I.

"God's mercy, no answer, when in your own house the Duke of Cleveland's proscribed secretary lies concealed."

---

6 Gladly, willingly.

7 The dragoons were the mounted infantry or light cavalry.

8 In 1653, Oliver Cromwell was officially appointed "Lord Protector" and had taken to signing his name in the regal style of "Oliver P."

I felt rather staggered, but was certain I had been betrayed by some one, and Cromwell continued rapidly, without giving me time to speak.

"The Lord is merciful, and so are we, but the malignant must be taken by the beloved soldiers of the Commonwealth, and the gospel God-fearing men, who always turn to the Lord, with short carbines, will accompany you. The malignant shall be taken from your house, by you, and the true God-fearing dragoons shall linger in the shade behind. You will take him to the river side, where the Lord willing, there will be a boat with a small blue ensign, on board of which you will place him, wishing him good speed."

He paused, and looked fixedly upon me by the aid of the miserable light that was in the apartment.

"What then, your highness?" I said.

"Then you will probably call upon us to-morrow for a considerable sum, which will be due to you for this good service to the Commonwealth; yea, it shall be profitable to fight the battles of the Lord."

I must confess, I had expected a very different result from the interview, which I had been greatly in fear would have resulted, in greatly endangering my liberty. Cromwell was a man not to be tampered with; I knew my danger, and was not disposed to sacrifice myself for Master Latham.

"Your highness shall be obeyed," I said.

"Ay, verily," he replied, "and if we be not obeyed, we must make ourselves felt with a strong arm of flesh. What ho! God-fearing Simpkins, art thou there?"

"Yes, the Lord willing," said a dragoon, making his appearance at the door.

Cromwell merely made him a sign with his hand, and he laid hold of the upper part of my arm, as though it had been in a vise, and led me out into the passage again where the sentinels were posted.

In the course of a few moments, I was duly in custody of my two guards again, and we were proceeding at a very rapid pace towards my residence.

It was not a very agreeable affair, view it in whatever light I might; but as regarded Cromwell, I knew my jeopardy, and it would be perceived that I had not hesitated a moment in obeying him. Moreover, I considered, for I knew he was generous, I should have a good round sum by the transaction, which added to the fifty pounds I had received from the royalists, made the affair appear to me in a pleasant enough light. Indeed, I was revolving in my mind as I went along, whether it would not be worth while, almost entirely to attach myself to the protector.

"If," I reasoned with myself, "I should do that, and still preserve myself a character with the royalists, I should thrive."

But it will be seen that an adverse circumstance put an end to all those dreams.

When we reached the door of my house, the first thing I saw was my son wiping his brow, as if he had undergone some fatigue; he ran up to me, and catching me by the arm, whispered to me.

I was so angered at the moment, that heedless of what I did, and passion getting the mastery over me, I with my clenched fist struck him to the earth. His head fell upon one of the hard round stones with which the street was paved, and he never spoke again. I had murdered him.

I DON'T KNOW what happened immediately subsequent to this fearful deed; all I can recollect is, that there was a great confusion and a flashing of lights, and it appeared to me as if something had suddenly struck me down to the earth with great force.

When I did thoroughly awaken, I found myself lying upon a small couch, but in a very large apartment dimly lighted, and where, there were many such couches ranged against the walls. A miserable light just enabled me to see about me a little, and some dim dusky-looking figures were creeping about the place.

It was a hospital that the protector had lately instituted in the Strand.

I tried to speak, but could not; my tongue seemed glued to my mouth, and I could not, and then a change came upon my sense of sight, and I could scarcely see at all the dim dusky-looking figures about me.

Some one took hold of me by the wrist, and I heard one say, quite distinctly:—

"He's entirely going, now."

Suddenly it seemed as if something had fallen with a crushing influence upon my chest, and then a consciousness that I was gasping for breath, and then I thought I was at the bottom of the sea. There was a moment, only a moment, of frightful agony, and then came a singing sound, like the rush of waters, after which, I distinctly felt some one raising me in their arms. I was dropped again, my limbs felt numbed and chill, a universal spasm shot through my whole system, I opened my eyes, and found myself lying in the open air, by a newly opened grave.

A full moon was sailing through the sky and the cold beams were upon my face; a voice sounded in my ears, a deep and solemn voice—and painfully distinct was every word it uttered.

"Mortimer," it said, for that was my name, "Mortimer, in life you did one deed which at once cast you out from all hope that anything in that life would be remembered in the world to come to your advantage. You poisoned the pure font of mercy, and not upon such as you can the downy freshness of Heaven's bounty fall. Murderer, murderer of that being sacredly presented to your care by the great Creator of all things, live henceforth a being accused. Be to yourself a desolation and a blight, shunned by all that is good and virtuous, armed against all men, and all men armed against thee, Varney the Vampyre."

I STAGGERED TO my feet, the scene around me was a churchyard, I was gaunt and thin, my clothes hung about me in tattered remnants. The damp smell of the grave hung about them, I met an aged man, and asked him where I was. He looked at me with a shudder, as though I had escaped from some charnel house.

"Why, this is Isledon," said he.

A peal of bells came merrily upon the night air.

"What means that?" said I.

"Why this is the anniversary of the Restoration."

"The Restoration! What Restoration?"

"Why of the royal family to the throne, to be sure, returned this day last year. Have you been asleep so long that you don't know that?"

I shuddered and walked on, determined to make further inquiries, and to make them with so much caution, that the real extent of my ignorance should scarce be surmised, and the result was to me of the most astonishing character.

I found that I had been in the trance of death for nearly two years, and that during that period, great political changes had taken place. The exiled royal family had been restored to the throne, and the most remarkable revulsion of feeling that had ever taken place in a nation had taken place in England.

But personally I had not yet fully awakened to all the horror of what I was. I had heard the words addressed to me, but I had attached no very definite meaning to them.

I HAVE ALREADY said that I was not yet fully alive to the horror of what I was, but I soon found what the words which had been spoken to me by the mysterious being who had exhumed me meant; I was a thing accursed, a something to be shunned by all men, a horror, a blight, and a desolation.

I felt myself growing sick and weak, as I traversed the streets of the city, and yet I loathed the sight of food, whenever I saw it.

I reached my own house, and saw that it had been burned down; there lay nothing but a heap of charred ruins where it once stood.

But I had an interest in those ruins, for from time to time I had buried considerable sums of money beneath the flooring of the lowest apartments, and I had every reason to believe, as such a secret treasure was only known to myself, that it remained untouched.

I waited until the moon became obscured by some passing clouds, and then having a most intimate knowledge of the locality, I commenced groping about the ruins, and removing a portion of them, until I made my way to the spot where my money was hidden.

The morning came, however, and surprised me at my occupation; so I hid myself among the ruins of what had once been my home for a whole day, and never once stirred from my concealment.

Oh, it was a long and weary day. I could hear the prattle of children at play, an inn or change-house was near at hand, and I could hear noisy drinkers bawling forth songs that had been proscribed in the Commonwealth.

I saw a poor wretch hunted nearly to death, close to where I lay concealed, because from the fashion of his garments, and the cut of his hair, he was supposed to belong to the deposed party.

But the long expected night came at last. It was a dark one, too, so that it answered my purpose well.

I had found an old rusty knife among the ruins, and with that I set to work to dig up my hidden treasure; I was successful, and found it all. Not a guinea had been removed, although in the immediate neighborhood, there were those who would have sacrificed a human life for any piece of gold that I had hoarded.

I made no enquiries about anyone that had belonged to me, I dreaded to receive some horrible and circumstantial answer, but I did get a slight piece of news, as I left the ruins, although I asked not for it.

"There's a poor devil," said one; "did you ever see such a wretch in all your life?"

"Why, yes," said another, "he's enough to turn one's canary[9] sour, he seems to have come up from the ruins of Mortimer's house. By-the-by did you ever hear what became of him?"

"Yes, to be sure, he was shot by two of Cromwell's dragoons in some fracas or another."

"Ah, I recollect now, I heard as much. He murdered his son, didn't he?"

I passed on. Those words seemed to send a bolt of fire through the brain, and I dreaded that the speaker might expatiate upon them. A slow misty rain was falling, which caused

---

[9] Canary sack, a potent fortified wine imported from the Canary Islands.

the streets to be very much deserted, but being extremely well acquainted with the city, I passed on till I came to that quarter which was principally inhabited by money-lenders who I knew would take my money without any troublesome questions being asked me, and also I could procure every accommodation required; and they did so, for before another hour had passed over my head, I emerged richly habited as a chevalier of the period, having really not paid to the conscientious man much more than four times the price of the clothing I walked away with.

And thus I was in the middle of London, with some hundreds of pounds in my pocket, and a horrible uncertainty as to what I was.

I was growing fainter and fainter still, and I feared that unless I succeeded in housing myself shortly, I should become a prey to someone who, seeing my exhausted condition, would, notwithstanding I had a formidable rapier by my side, rob me of all I possessed.

My career has been much too long and too checkered a one even to give the briefest sketch of. All I purpose here to relate is how I became convinced I was a vampyre, and that blood was my congenial nourishment and the only element of my new existence.

I passed on until I came to a street where I knew the houses were large but unfashionable, and that they were principally occupied by persons who made a trade by letting out apartments, and there I thought I might locate myself in safety.

As I made no difficulty about terms, there was no difficulty at all of any sort, and I found myself conducted into a tolerably handsome suite of rooms in the house of a decent-looking widow woman, who had two daughters, young and blooming girls, both of whom regarded me as the new lodger, with looks of anything but favor, considering my awful and cadaverous appearance most probably as promising nothing at all in the shape of pleasant companionship.

This I was quite prepared for—I had seen myself in a mirror—that was enough; and I could honestly have averred that a more ghastly and horrible looking skeleton, attired in silks and broad-cloth, never yet walked the streets of the city.

When I retired to my chamber, I was so faint and ill, that I could scarcely drag one foot after the other; and was ruminating what I should do, until a strange feeling crept over me that I should like—what? Blood!—raw blood, reeking and hot, bubbling and juicy, from the veins of some gasping victim.

A clock upon the stairs struck one. I arose and listened attentively; all was still in the house—still as the very grave.

It was a large old rambling building, and had belonged at one time, no doubt, to a man of some mark and likelihood in the world. My chamber was one of six that opened from a corridor of a considerable length, and which traversed the whole length of the house.

I crept out into this corridor, and listened again for full ten minutes, but not the slightest sound, save my own faint breathing, disturbed the stillness of the house; and that emboldened me so that, with my appetite for blood growing each moment stronger, I began to ask myself from whose veins I could seek strength and nourishment.

But how was I to proceed? How was I to know in that large house which of the sleepers I could attack with safety, for it had now come to that, that I was to attack somebody. I stood like an evil spirit, pondering over the best means of securing a victim.

And there came over me the horrible

faintness again, that faintness which each moment grew worse, and which threatened completely to engulf me. I feared that some flush of it would overtake me, and then I should fall to rise no more; and strange as it may appear, I felt a disposition to cling to the new life that had been given to me. I seemed to be acquainted already with all its horrors, but not all its joys.

Suddenly the darkness of the corridor was cleared away, and soft and mellow light crept into it, and I said to myself:—

"The moon has risen."

Yes, the bright and beautiful moon, which I had felt the soft influence of when I lay among the graves, had emerged from the bank of clouds along the eastern sky, its beams descending through a little window. They streamed right through the corridor, faintly but effectually illuminating it, and letting me see clearly all the different doors leading to the different chambers.

And thus it was that I had light for anything I wished to do, but not information.

The moonbeams playing upon my face seemed to give me a spurious sort of strength. I did not know until after experience what a marked and sensible effect they would always have upon me, but I felt it even then, although I did not attribute it wholly to the influence of the queenly planet.

I walked on through the corridor, and some sudden influence seemed to guide me to a particular door. I know not how it was, but I laid my hand upon the lock, and said to myself:—

"I shall find my victim here."

I PAUSED YET a moment, for there came across me even then, after I had gone so far, a horrible dread of what I was about to do, and a feeling that there might be consequences arising from it that would jeopardize me greatly. Perhaps even then if a great accession of strength had come to my aid—mere bodily aid I mean—I should have hesitated and the victim would have escaped; but, as if to mock me, there came that frightful feeling of exhaustion which felt so like the prelude to another death.

I no longer hesitated; I turned the lock of the door, and I thought that I must be discovered. I left it open about an inch, and then flew back to my own chamber.

I listened attentively; there was no alarm, no movement in any of the rooms—the same death-like stillness pervaded the house, and I felt that I was still safe.

A soft gleam of yellow looking light had come through the crevice of the door when I had opened it. It mingled strangely with the moonlight, and I concluded correctly enough, as I found afterwards, that a light was burning in the chamber.

It was at least another ten minutes before I could sufficiently reassure myself to glide from my own room and approach that of the fated sleeper; but at length I told myself that I might safely do so, and the night was waning fast, and if anything was to be accomplished it must be done at once, before the first beams of early dawn should chase away the spirits of the night, and perhaps should leave me no power to act.

"What shall I be," I asked myself; "after another four-and-twenty hours of exhaustion? Shall I have power then to make the election of what I will do or what I will not? No, I may suffer the pangs of death again, and the scarcely less pangs of another revival."

This reasoning—if it may be called reasoning—decided me; and with cautious and cat-like footsteps, I again approached the bedroom door which I had opened.

I no longer hesitated, but at once crossed the threshold, and looked around me. It was the chamber of the youngest of my landlady's daughters, who, as far as I could judge, seemed to be about sixteen years of age; but they had evidently been so struck with my horrible appearance, that they had placed themselves as little as possible in my way, so that I could not be said to be a very good judge of their ages or of their looks.

I only knew she was the youngest, because she wore her hair long, and wore it in ringlets, which were loose and streaming over the pillow on which she slept, while her sister, I remarked, wore her hair plaited up, and completely off her neck and shoulders.

I stood by the bedside, and looked upon this beautiful girl in all the pride of her young beauty, so gently and quietly slumbering. Her lips were parted, as though some pleasant images were passing in her mind, and induced a slight smile even in her sleep. She murmured twice, too, a word, which I thought was the name of some one—perchance the idol of her young heart—but it was too indistinct for me to catch it, nor did I care to hear; that which was perhaps a very cherished secret, indeed, mattered not to me. I made no pretensions to her affections, however strongly in a short time I might stand in her abhorrence.

One of her arms, which was exquisitely rounded, lay upon the coverlet; a neck, too, as white as alabaster, was partially exposed to my gaze, but I had no passions—it was food I wanted.

I sprung upon her. There was a shriek, but not before I had secured a draught of life blood from her neck. It was enough. I felt it dart through my veins like fire, and I was restored. From that moment I found out what was to be my sustenance; it was blood—the blood of the young and the beautiful.

The house was thoroughly alarmed, but not before I had retired to my own chamber. I was but partially dressed, and those few clothes I threw off me, and getting into my bed, I feigned to be asleep; so that when a gentleman who slept likewise in the house, but of whose presence I knew nothing, knocked hardly at my door, I affected to awaken in a fright, and called out:—

"What is it? What is it?—for God's sake tell me if it is a fire."

"No, no—but get up, sir, get up. There's some one in the place. An attempt at murder, I think, sir."

I arose and opened the door; so by the light he carried he saw that I had to dress myself—he was but half attired himself, and he carried his sword beneath his arm.

"It is a strange thing," he said; "but I have heard a shriek of alarm."

"And I likewise," said I; "but I thought it was a dream."

"Help! help! help!" cried the widow, who had risen, but stood upon the threshold of her own chamber. "Thieves! Thieves!" By this time I had got on sufficient of my apparel that I could make an appearance, and, likewise with my sword in my hand, I sallied out into the corridor.

"Oh, gentlemen—gentlemen," cried the landlady, "did you hear anything?"

"A shriek, madam," said my fellow-lodger; "have you looked into your daughters' chambers?"

The room of the youngest daughter was the nearest, and into that she went at once. In another moment she appeared on the threshold again with a face as white as a sheet, then she wrung her hands, and said:—

"Murder! Murder!—my child is murdered—my child is murdered, Master Harding,"—which I found was the name of my fellow-lodger. "Fling open one of the windows, and call for the watch," said he to me, "and I will search the room, and woe be to anyone that I may find within its walls unauthorized."

I did as he desired, and called the watch, but the watch came not, and then, upon a second visit to her daughter, the landlady found she had only fainted, and that she had been deceived in thinking she was murdered by the sudden sight of the blood upon her neck, so the house was restored to something like quiet again, and the morning being now near at hand, Mr. Harding retired to his chamber, and I to mine, leaving the landlady and her eldest daughter assiduous in their attentions to the younger.

How wonderfully revived I felt—I was quite a new creature when the sunlight came dancing into my apartment. I dressed and was about to leave the house, when Mr. Harding came out of one of the lowest rooms, and intercepted me.

"Sir," he said, "I have not the pleasure of knowing you, but I have no doubt that an ordinary feeling of chivalry will prompt you to do all in your power to obviate the dread of such another night as the past."

"Dread, sir," said I, "the dread of what?"

"A very proper question," he said, "but one I can hardly answer; the girl states, she was awakened by someone biting her neck, and in proof of the story she actually exhibits the marks of teeth, and so terrified is she, that she declared that she shall never be able to sleep again."

"You astonish me."

"No doubt—it is sufficiently astonishing to excuse even doubts; but if you and I, who are both inmates of the house, were to keep watch to-night in the corridor, it might have the effect of completely quieting the imagination of the young girl, and perhaps result in the discovery of this nocturnal disturber of the peace."

"Certainly," said I, "command me in any way, I shall have great pleasure."

"Shall it be understood, then, that we meet at eleven in your apartment or in mine."

"Whichever you may please to consider the most convenient, sir."

"I mention my own then, which is the furthest door in the corridor, and where I shall be happy to see you at eleven o'clock."

There was a something about this young man's manner which I did not altogether like, and yet I could not come to any positive conclusion as to whether he suspected me, and therefore I thought it would be premature to fly, when perhaps there would be really no occasion for doing so; on the contrary, I made up my mind to wait the result of the evening, which might or might not be disastrous to me. At all events, I considered that I was fully equal to taking my own part, and if by the decrees of destiny I was really to be, as it were, repudiated from society, and made to endure a new, strange, and horrible existence, I did not see that I was called upon to be particular how I rescued myself from difficulties that might arise.

Relying, then, upon my own strength, and my own unscrupulous use of it, I awaited with tolerable composure the coming of night.

During the day I amused myself by walking about, and noting the remarkable changes which so short a period as two years had made in London. But these happened to be two years most abundantly prolific in change. The feelings and habits of people seemed to have undergone a thorough revolution, which I was the more surprised at when I learned by what thorough treachery the restoration of the exiled family was effected.

The day wore on; I felt no need of refreshment, and I began to feel my own proper position, and to feel that occasionally a draught of delicious life-blood, such as I had quaffed the night before was fresh marrow to my bones.

I could see, when I entered the house where I had made my temporary home, that notwithstanding that I considered my appearance wonderfully improved, that feeling was not shared in by others, for the whole family shrunk from me as though there had been a most frightful contamination in my touch, and as though the very air I had breathed was hateful and deleterious. I felt convinced that there had been some conversation concerning me, and that I was rather more than suspected. I certainly could then have left the place easily and quietly, but I had a feeling of defiance, which did not enable me to do so.

I felt as if I were an injured being, and ought to resist a something that looked like oppression.

"Why," I said to myself, "have I been rescued from the tomb to be made the sport of a malignant destiny? My crime was a great one, but surely I suffered enough, when I suffered death as an expiation of it, and I might have been left to repose in the grave."

The feelings that have since come over me held no place in my imagination, but with a kind of defiant desperation I felt as if I should like to defeat the plan by which I was attempted to be punished, and even in the face of Providence itself, to show that it was a failure entailing far worse consequences upon others than upon me.

This was my impression, so I would not play the coward, and flee upon the first flash of danger.

I sat in my own room until the hour came for my appointment with Mr. Harding, and then I walked along the corridor with a confident step, and let the hilt end of my scabbard clank along the floor. I knocked boldly at the door, and I thought there was a little hesitation in his voice as he bade me walk in, but this might have been only my imagination.

He was seated at a table, fully dressed, and in addition to his sword, there was lying upon the table before him a large holster pistol, nearly half the size of a carbine.

"You are well prepared," said I, as I pointed to it.

"Yes," he said, "and I mean to use it."

"What do they want now?" I said.

"What do who want?"

"I don't know," I said, "but I thought I heard some one call you by name from below."

"Indeed, excuse me a moment, perhaps they have made some discovery. "

There was wine upon the table, and while he was gone, I poured a glass of good Rhenish down the barrel of the pistol. I wiped it carefully with the cuff of my coat, so there was no appearance upon the barrel of anything of the sort, and when he came back, he looked at me very suspiciously, as he said:—

"Nobody called me, how could you say I was called."

"Because I thought I heard you called; I

suppose it is allowable for human nature to be fallible now and then."

"Yes, but then I am so surprised how you could make such a mistake."

"So am I."

It was rather a difficult thing to answer this, and looking at me very steadily, he took up the pistol and examined the priming. Of course, that was all right, and he appeared to be perfectly satisfied.

"There will be two chairs and a table," he said, "placed in the corridor, so that we can sit in perfect ease. I will not anticipate that anything will happen, but if it should, I can only say that I will not be backward in the use of my weapons."

"I don't doubt it," said I, "and commend you accordingly. That pistol must be a most formidable weapon. Does it ever misfire?"

"Not that I know of," he said, "I have loaded it with such extraordinary care that it amounts to almost an impossibility that it should. Will you take some wine?"

At this moment there came a loud knocking at the door of the house. I saw an expression of satisfaction come over his face, and he sprung to his feet, holding the pistol in his grasp.

"Do you know the meaning of that knocking," said I, "at such an hour?" and at the same time with a sweep of my arm I threw his sword off the table and beyond his reach.

"Yes," he said, rather excitedly. "You are my prisoner; it was you who caused the mischief and confusion last night. The girl is ready to swear to you, and if you attempt to escape, I'll blow your brains out."

"Fire at me," said I, "and take the consequences—but the threat is sufficient, and you shall die for your temerity."

I drew my sword, and he evidently thought his danger imminent, for he at once snapped the pistol in my face. Of course it only flashed in the pan, but in one moment my sword went through him like a flash of light. It was a good blade the money-lender had sold me—the hilt struck against his breast bone, and he shrieked.

Bang! bang! bang! came again at the outer door of the house. I withdrew the reeking blade, dashed it into the scabbard just in time to prevent my landlady from opening the door, which she was almost in the act of doing. I seized her by the back of the neck, and hurled her to a considerable distance, and then opening the door myself, I stood behind it, and let three men rush into the house. After which I quietly left it, and was free to continue my existence as—*VARNEY, THE VAMPYRE!*

⚜

Anonymous

NUMEROUS EFFORTS to discover the author of this tale have failed. Translated from German, its first English appearance was in *Odds and Ends* magazine (1860). The story may well have been known to Bram Stoker, for *Dracula* shares a number of elements: The vampire lives in the ruins of a castle; he sleeps in a coffin; he does not eat or drink; he must be invited into the victim's home; and he must be killed in his coffin. The author introduces the notion that only the victim has power over the creature, however, and the nailing shut of the coffin is a unique element, resembling the wooden or iron stake of legend while evoking the common fear of "premature burial" as well.

THE MYSTERIOUS STRANGER

ANONYMOUS

"To die, to sleep,
To sleep, perchance to dream, ay, there's the rub."
Hamlet

Boreas, that fearful northwest wind, which in the spring and autumn stirs up the lowest depths of the wild Adriatic, and is then so dangerous to vessels, was howling through the woods, and tossing the branches of the old knotty oaks in the Carpathian Mountains[1], when a party of five riders, who surrounded a litter drawn by a pair of mules, turned into a forest path, which offered some protection from the April weather, and allowed the travelers in some degree to recover their breath.

It was already evening, and bitterly cold; the snow fell every now and then in large flakes. A tall old gentleman, of aristocratic appearance, rode at the head of the troop. This was the Knight of Fahnenberg, in Austria. He had inherited from a childless brother a con-

siderable property, situated in the Carpathian Mountains; and he had set out to take possession of it, accompanied by his daughter Franziska, and a niece about twenty years of age, who had been brought up with her.

Next to the knight rode a fine young man of some twenty and odd years—the Baron Franz von Kronstein. He wore, like the former, the broad-brimmed hat with hanging feathers, the leather collar, the wide riding-boots—in short, the traveling-dress which was in fashion at the commencement of the seventeenth century.

The features of the young man had much about them that was open and friendly, as well as some mind; but the expression was more that of dreamy and sensitive softness than of youthful daring, although no one could deny that he possessed much of youthful beauty. As the cavalcade turned into the oak wood the young man rode up to the litter, and chatted with the ladies who were seated therein. One of these—and to her his conversation was principally addressed—was of dazzling beauty.

[1] Home of Castle Dracula.

Her hair flowed in natural curls round the fine oval of her face, out of which beamed a pair of star-like eyes, full of genius, lively fancy, and a certain degree of archness.

Franziska von Fahnenberg seemed to attend but carelessly to the speeches of her admirer, who made many kind inquiries as to how she felt herself during the journey, which had been attended with many difficulties: she always answered him very shortly, almost contemptuously; and at length remarked, that if it had not been for her father's objections, she would long ago have requested the baron to take her place in their horrid cage of a litter, for, to judge by his remarks, he seemed incommoded by the weather; and she would so much rather be mounted on the spirited horse, and face wind and storm, than be mewed up[2] there, dragged up the hills by those long-eared animals, and mope herself to death with *ennui*.

The young lady's words, and, still more, the half-contemptuous tone in which they were uttered, appeared to make the most painful impression on the young man: he made her no reply at the moment, but the absent air with which he attended to the kindly-intended remarks of the other young lady, showed how much he was disconcerted.

"It appears, dear Franziska," said he at length in a kindly tone, "that the hardships of the road have affected you more than you will acknowledge. Generally so kind to others, you have been very often out of humor during the journey, and particularly with regard to your humble servant and cousin, who would gladly bear a double or triple share of the discomforts, if he could thereby save you from the smallest of them."

[2] Confined.

Franziska showed by her look that she was about to reply with some bitter jibe, when the voice of the knight was heard calling for his nephew, who galloped off at the sound.

"I should like to scold you well, Franziska," said her companion somewhat sharply, "for always plaguing your poor Cousin Franz in this shameful way; he who loves you so truly, and who, whatever you may say, will one day be your husband."

"My husband!" replied the other angrily. "I must either completely alter my ideas, or he his whole self, before that takes place. No, Bertha! I know that this is my father's darling wish, and I do not deny the good qualities Cousin Franz may have, or really has, since I see you are making a face; but to marry an effeminate man—never!"

"Effeminate! You do him great injustice," replied her friend quickly. "Just because instead of going off to the Turkish war, where little honor was to be gained, he attended to your father's advice, and stayed at home, to bring his neglected estate into order, which he accomplished with care and prudence; and because he does not represent this howling wind as a mild zephyr—for reasons such as these you are pleased to call him effeminate."

"Say what you will, it is so," cried Franziska obstinately. "Bold, aspiring, even despotic, must be the man who is to gain my heart; these soft, patient, and thoughtful natures are utterly distasteful to me. Is Franz capable of deep sympathy, either in joy or sorrow? He is always the same—always quiet, soft and tiresome."

"He has a warm heart, and is not without genius," said Bertha.

"A warm heart! That may be," replied the other; "but I would rather be tyrannized over, and kept under a little by my future husband, than be loved in such a wearisome manner. You say he has genius, too. I will not exactly contradict you, since that would be impolite, but it is not easily discovered. But even allowing you are right in both statements, still the man who does not bring these qualities into action is a despicable creature.

"A man may do many foolish things, he may even be a little wicked now and then, provided it is in nothing dishonorable; and one can forgive him, if he is only acting on some fixed theory for some special object. There is, for instance, your own faithful admirer the Castellan of Glogau, Knight of Woislaw; he loves you most truly, and is now quite in a position to enable you to marry comfortably.

"The brave man has lost his right hand—reason enough for remaining seated behind the stove, or near the spinning-wheel of his Bertha; but what does he do?—He goes off to the war in Turkey; he fights for a noble thought—"

"And runs the chance of getting his other hand chopped off, and another great scar across his face," put in her friend.

"Leaves his lady-love to weep and pine a little," pursued Franziska, "but returns with fame, marries, and is all the more honored and admired! This is done by a man of forty, a rough warrior, not bred at court, a soldier who has nothing but his cloak and sword. And Franz—rich, noble—but I will not go on. Not a word more on this detested point, if you love me, Bertha."

Franziska leaned back in the corner of the litter with a dissatisfied air, and shut her eyes as though, overcome by fatigue, she wished to sleep.

"This awful wind is so powerful, you say, that we must make a detour to avoid its full force," said the knight to an old man, dressed in a fur-cap and a cloak of rough skin, who seemed to be the guide of the party.

"Those who have never personally felt the Boreas storming over the country between Sessano and Trieste, can have no conception of the reality," replied the other. "As soon as it commences, the snow is blown in thick long columns along the ground. That is nothing to what follows. These columns become higher and higher, as the wind rises, and continue to do so until you see nothing but snow above, below, and on every side—unless, indeed, sometimes, when sand and gravel are mixed with the snow, and at length it is impossible to open your eyes at all. Your only plan for safety is to wrap your cloak around you, and lie down flat on the ground. If your home were but a few hundred yards off, you might lose your life in the attempt to reach it."

"Well, then, we owe you thanks, old Kumpan," said the knight, though it was with difficulty he made his words heard above the roaring of the storm; "we owe you thanks for taking us this round as we shall thus be enabled to reach our destination without danger."

"You may feel sure of that, noble sir," said the old man. "By midnight we shall have arrived, and that without any danger by the way, if—" Suddenly the old man stopped. He drew his horse sharply up, and remained in an attitude of attentive listening.

"It appears to me we must be in the neighborhood of some village," said Franz von Kronstein; "for between the gusts of the storm I hear a dog howling."

"It is no dog, it is no dog!" said the old man uneasily, and urged his horse to a rapid pace. "For miles around there is no human dwelling; and except in the castle of Klatka, which indeed lies in the neighborhood, but has been deserted for more than a century, probably no one has lived here since the creation. But there again," he continued; "well, if I wasn't sure of it from the first."

"That howling seems to bother you, old Kumpan," said the knight, listening to a long-drawn fierce sound, which appeared nearer than before, and seemed to be answered from a distance.

"That howling comes from no dogs," replied the old guide uneasily. "Those are reed-wolves. They may be on our track; and it would be as well if the gentlemen looked to their firearms."

"Reed-wolves? What do you mean?" inquired Franz in surprise.

"At the edge of this wood," said Kumpan, "there lies a lake about a mile long, whose banks are covered with reeds. In these a number of wolves have taken up their quarters, and feed on wild birds, fish and such like. They are shy in the summer-time, and a boy of twelve might scare them; but when the birds migrate, and the fish are frozen up, they prowl about at night, and then they are dangerous.

"They are worst, however, when the Boreas rages, for then it is just as if the fiend himself possessed them: they are so mad and fierce that man and beast become alike their victims; and a party of them have been known even to attack the ferocious bears of these mountains, and, what is more, to come off victorious."

The howl was now again repeated more distinctly, and from two opposite directions. The riders in alarm felt for their pistols and the old man grasped the spear which hung at his saddle.

"We must keep close to the litter; the wolves are very near us," whispered the guide.

The riders turned their horses, surrounded the litter, and the knight informed the ladies, in a few quieting words, of the cause of this movement.

"Then we *shall* have an adventure—some little variety!" cried Franziska with sparkling eyes.

"How can you talk so foolishly?" said Bertha in alarm.

"Are we not under manly protection? Is not Cousin Franz on our side?" said the other mockingly.

"See, there is a light gleaming among the twigs; and there is another," cried Bertha. "There must be people close to us."

"No, no," cried the guide quickly. "Shut up the door, ladies. Keep close together, gentlemen. It is the eyes of wolves you see sparkling there."

The gentlemen looked towards the thick underwood, in which every now and then little bright spots appeared, such as in summer would have been taken for glowworms; it was just the same greenish-yellow light, but less unsteady, and there were always two flames together. The horses began to be restive, they kicked and dragged at the rein; but the mules behaved tolerably well.

"I will fire on the beasts, and teach them to keep their distance," said Franz, pointing to the spot where the lights were thickest.

"Hold, hold, Sir Baron!" cried Kumpan quickly, and seized the young man's arm. "You would bring such a host together by the report, that, encouraged by numbers, they would be sure to make the first assault. However, keep your arms in readiness, and if an old she-wolf springs out—for these always lead the attack—take good aim and kill her, for then there must be no further hesitation."

By this time the horses were almost unmanageable, and terror had also infected the mules. Just as Franz was turning towards the litter to say a word to his cousin, an animal, about the size of a large hound, sprang from the thicket and seized the foremost mule.

"Fire, Baron! A wolf!" shouted the guide. The young man fired, and the wolf fell to the ground. A fearful howl rang through the wood.

"Now, forward! Forward without a moment's delay!" cried Kumpan. "We have not above five minutes' time. The beasts will tear their wounded comrade to pieces, and, if they are very hungry, partially devour her.

"We shall, in the meantime, gain a little start, and it is not more than an hour's ride to the end of the forest. There—do you see—there are the towers of Klatka between the trees—out there where the moon is rising, and from that point the wood becomes less dense."

The travelers endeavored to increase their pace to the utmost, but the litter slowed their progress. Bertha was weeping with fear, and even Franziska's courage had diminished, for she sat very still. Franz endeavored to reassure them. They had not proceeded many moments when the howling recommenced, and approached nearer and nearer.

"There they are again and fiercer and more numerous than before," cried the guide in alarm.

The lights were soon visible again, and certainly in greater numbers. The wood had already become less thick, and the snowstorm having ceased, the moonbeams discovered many a dusky form amongst the trees, keeping together like a pack of hounds and advancing nearer and nearer till they were within twenty paces, and on the very path of the travelers.

From time to time a fierce howl arose from their centre which was answered by the whole pack, and was at length taken up by single voices in the distance.

The party now found themselves some few hundred yards from the ruined castle of which Kumpan had spoken. It was, or seemed by moonlight to be, of some magnitude. Near the tolerably preserved principal building lay the ruins of a church which must have once been beautiful, placed on a little hillock dotted with single oak trees and bramble-bushes. Both castle and church were still partially roofed in, and a path led from the castle gate to an old oak tree, where it joined at right angles the one along which the travelers were advancing.

The old guide seemed in much perplexity. "We are in great danger, noble sir," said he. "The wolves will very soon make a general attack. There will then be only one way of escape: leaving the mules to their fate, and taking the young ladies on your horses."

"That would be all very well, if I had not thought of a better plan," replied the knight. "Here is the ruined castle; we can surely reach that, and then, blocking up the gates, we must just await the morning."

"Here? In the ruins of Klatka?—Not for all the wolves in the world!" cried the old man. "Even by daylight no one likes to approach the place, and, now, by night!—The castle, Sir Knight, has a bad name."

"On account of robbers?" asked Franz.

"No; it is haunted," replied the other.

"Stuff and nonsense!" said the baron. "Forward to the ruins; there is not a moment to be lost."

And this was indeed the case. The ferocious beasts were but a few steps behind the travelers. Every now and then they retired, and set up a ferocious howl. The party had just arrived at the old oak before mentioned and were about to turn into the path to the ruins, when the animals, as though perceiving the risk they ran of losing their prey, came so near that a lance could easily have struck them.

The knight and Franz faced sharply about, spurring their horses amidst the advancing crowds, when suddenly, from the shadow of the oak stepped forth a man who in a few strides placed himself between the travelers and their pursuers.

As far as one could see in the dusky light the stranger was a man of a tall and well-built frame; he wore a sword by his side and a broad-brimmed hat was on his head. If the party were astonished at his sudden appearance, they were still more so at what followed. As soon as the stranger appeared the wolves gave over their pursuit, tumbled over each other, and set up a fearful howl. The stranger now raised his hand, appeared to wave it, and the wild animals crawled back into the thickets like a pack of beaten hounds.

Without casting a glance at the travelers, who were too much overcome by astonishment to speak, the stranger went up the path which led to the castle and soon disappeared beneath the gateway.

"Heaven have mercy on us!" murmured old Kumpan in his beard, as he made the sign of the cross.

"Who was that strange man?" asked the knight with surprise, when he had watched the stranger as long as he was visible, and the party had resumed their way.

The old guide pretended not to understand, and riding up to the mules, busied himself with arranging the harness, which had become disordered in their haste: more than

a quarter of an hour elapsed before he rejoined them.

"Did you know the man who met us near the ruins and who freed us from our four-footed pursuers in such a miraculous way?" asked Franz of the guide.

"Do I know him? No, noble sir; I never saw him before," replied the guide hesitatingly.

"He looked like a soldier, and was armed," said the baron. "Is the castle, then, inhabited?"

"Not for the last hundred years," replied the other. "It was dismantled because the possessor in those days had iniquitous dealings with some Turkish-Sclavonian hordes, who had advanced as far as this; or rather"—he corrected himself hastily—"he is *said* to have had such, for he might have been as upright and good a man as ever ate cheese fried in butter."

"And who is now the possessor of the ruins and of these woods?" inquired the knight.

"Who but yourself, noble sir?" replied Kumpan. "For more than two hours we have been on your estate, and we shall soon reach the end of the wood."

"We hear and see nothing more of the wolves," said the baron after a pause. "Even their howling has ceased. The adventure with the stranger still remains to me inexplicable, even if one were to suppose him a huntsman—"

"Yes, yes; that is most likely what he is," interrupted the guide hastily, whilst he looked uneasily round him. "The brave good man, who came so opportunely to our assistance, must have been a huntsman. Oh, there are many powerful woodsmen in this neighborhood! Heaven be praised!" he continued, taking a deep breath, "there is the end of the wood, and in a short hour we shall be safely housed."

And so it happened. Before an hour had elapsed the party passed through a well-built village, the principal spot on the estate, towards the venerable castle, the windows of which were brightly illuminated, and at the door stood the steward and other dependents, who, having received their new lord with every expression of respect, conducted the party to the splendidly furnished apartments.

NEARLY FOUR WEEKS passed before the traveling adventures again came on the *tapis*.[3] The knight and Franz found such constant employment in looking over all the particulars of the large estate, and endeavouring to introduce various German improvements, that they were very little at home.

At first Franziska was charmed with everything in a neighborhood so entirely new and unknown. It appeared to her so romantic, so very different from her German Fatherland, that she took the greatest interest in everything, and often drew comparisons between the countries, which generally ended unfavorably for Germany.

Bertha was of exactly the contrary opinion: she laughed at her cousin, and said that her liking for novelty and strange sights must indeed have come to a pass when she preferred hovels in which the smoke went out of the doors and windows instead of the chimney, walls covered with soot, and inhabitants not much cleaner, and of unmannerly habits, to the comfortable dwellings and polite people of Germany.

However, Franziska persisted in her notions, and replied that everything in Austria was flat, *ennuyant*,[4] and common; and that a wild peasant here, with his rough coat of skin, had ten times more interest for her than a quiet Austrian in his holiday suit, the mere sight of whom was enough to make one yawn.

As soon as the knight had gotten the first arrangements into some degree of order the party found themselves more together again. Franz continued to show great attention to his cousin, which, however, she received with little gratitude, for she made him the butt of all her fanciful humors, which soon returned when after a longer sojourn she had become more accustomed to her new life. Many excursions into the neighborhood were undertaken but there was little variety in the scenery, and these soon ceased to amuse.

The party was one day assembled in the old-fashioned hall, dinner had just been removed, and they were arranging in which direction they should ride. "I have it," cried Franziska suddenly, "I wonder we never thought before of going to view by day the spot where we fell in with our night-adventure with wolves and the Mysterious Stranger."

"You mean a visit to the ruins—what were they called?" said the knight.

"Castle Klatka," cried Franziska gaily. "Oh, we really must ride there! It will be so charming to go over again by daylight, and in safety, the ground where we had such a dreadful fright."

"Bring round the horses," said the knight to a servant; "and tell the steward to come to

---

[3] "On the *tapis*" means "on the table"—that is, came to pass.
[4] Tiresome, tedious.

me immediately." The latter, an old man, soon after entered the room.

"We intend taking a ride to Klatka," said the knight; "we had an adventure there on our road—"

"So old Kumpan told me," interrupted the steward.

"And what do you say about it?" asked the knight.

"I really don't know what to say," replied the old man, shaking his head. "I was a youth of twenty when I first came to this castle, and now my hair is grey; half a century has elapsed during that time. Hundreds of times my duty has called me into the neighborhood of those ruins, but never have I seen the Fiend of Klatka."

"What do you say? Whom do you call by that name?" inquired Franziska, whose love of adventure and romance was strongly awakened.

"Why, people call by that name the ghost or spirit who is supposed to haunt the ruins," replied the steward. "They say he only shows himself on moonlight nights—"

"That is quite natural," interrupted Franz smiling. "Ghosts can never bear the light of day; and if the moon did not shine, how could the ghost be seen, for it is not supposed that anyone for a mere freak would visit the ruins by torch light."

"There are some credulous people who pretend to have seen this ghost," continued the steward. "Huntsmen and woodcutters say they have met him by the large oak on the cross-path. That, noble sir, is supposed to be the spot he inclines most to haunt, for the tree was planted in remembrance of the man who fell there."

"And who was he?" asked Franziska with increasing curiosity.

"The last owner of the castle, which at that time was a sort of robbers' den, and the headquarters of all depredators in the neighborhood," answered the old man. "They say this man was of superhuman strength, and was feared not only on account of his passionate temper, but of his treaties with the Turkish hordes. Any young woman, too, in the neighborhood to whom he took a fancy, was carried off to his tower and never heard of more. When the measure of his iniquity was full, the whole neighborhood rose in a mass, besieged his stronghold, and at length he was slain on the spot where the huge oak tree now stands."

"I wonder they did not burn the whole castle, so as to erase the very memory of it," said the knight.

"It was a dependency of the church, and that saved it," replied the other. "Your great-grandfather afterwards took possession of it, for it had fine lands attached. As the Knight of Klatka was of good family, a monument was erected to him in the church, which now lies as much in ruin as the castle itself."

"Oh, let us set off at once! Nothing shall prevent my visiting so interesting a spot," said Franziska eagerly. "The imprisoned damsels who never reappeared, the storming of the tower, the death of the knight, the nightly wanderings of his spirit round the old oak, and lastly, our own adventure, all draw me thither with an indescribable curiosity."

When a servant announced that the horses were at the door, the young girls tripped laughingly down the steps which led to the coach-yard. Franz, the knight, and a servant well acquainted with the country followed; and in a few minutes the party was on the road to the forest.

The sun was still high in the heavens when they saw the towers of Klatka rising above the trees. Everything in the wood was still except the cheerful twitterings of the birds as they hopped about amongst the bursting buds and leaves and announced that spring had arrived.

The party soon found themselves near the old oak at the bottom of the hill on which stood the towers, still imposing in their ruin. Ivy and bramble bushes had wound themselves over the walls, and forced their deep roots so firmly between the stones that they in a great measure held these together. On the top of the highest spot a small bush in its young fresh verdure swayed lightly in the breeze.

The gentlemen assisted their companions to alight, and leaving the horses to the care of the servant, ascended the hill to the castle. After having explored this in every nook and cranny, and spent much time in a vain search for some trace of the extraordinary stranger whom Franziska declared she was determined to discover, they proceeded to an inspection of the adjoining church.

This they found to have better withstood the ravages of time and weather; the nave, indeed, was in complete dilapidation, but the chancel and altar were still under roof, as well as a sort of chapel which appeared to have been a place of honor for the families of the old knights of the castle. Few traces remained, however, of the magnificent painted glass which must once have adorned the windows, and the wind entered at pleasure through the open spaces.

The party was occupied for some time in deciphering the inscriptions on a number of tombstones, and on the walls, principally within the chancel. They were generally memorials of the ancient lords, with figures of men in armor, and women and children of all ages. A flying raven and various other devices were placed at the corners.

One gravestone, which stood close to the entrance of the chancel, differed widely from the others: there was no figure sculptured on it, and the inscription, which on all besides was a mere mass of flattering eulogies, was here simple and unadorned; it contained only these words: "Ezzelin von Klatka fell like a knight at the storming of the castle"—on such a day and year.

"That must be the monument of the knight whose ghost is said to haunt these ruins," cried Franziska eagerly. "What a pity he is not represented in the same way as the others—I should so like to have known what he was like!"

"Oh, there is the family vault, with steps leading down to it, and the sun is lighting it up through a crevice," said Franz, stepping from the adjoining vestry.

The whole party followed him down the eight or nine steps which led to a tolerably airy chamber, where were placed a number of coffins of all sizes, some of them crumbling into dust. Here, again, one close to the door was distinguished from the others by the simplicity of its design, the freshness of its appearance, and the brief inscription: "Ezzelinus de Klatka, Eques."

As not the slightest effluvium was perceptible, they lingered some time in the vault; and when they reascended to the church, they had a long talk over the old possessors, of whom the knight now remembered he had heard his parents speak. The sun had disappeared, and the moon was just rising as the explorers turned to leave the ruins. Bertha had made a step into the nave, when she uttered a slight exclamation of fear and surprise.

Her eyes fell on a man who wore a hat

with drooping feathers, a sword at his side, and a short cloak of somewhat old-fashioned cut over his shoulders. The stranger leaned carelessly on a broken column at the entrance; he did not appear to take any notice of the party; and the moon shone full on his pale face.

The party advanced towards the stranger.

"If I am not mistaken," commenced the knight; "we have met before."

Not a word from the unknown.

"You released us in an almost miraculous manner," said Franziska, "from the power of those dreadful wolves. Am I wrong in supposing it is to you we are indebted for that great service?"

"The beasts are afraid of me," replied the stranger in a deep fierce tone, while he fastened his sunken eyes on the girl, without taking any notice of the others.

"Then you are probably a huntsman," said Franz, "and wage war against the fierce brutes."

"Who is not either the pursuer or the pursued? All persecute or are persecuted, and Fate persecutes all," replied the stranger without looking at him.

"Do you live in these ruins?" asked the knight hesitatingly.

"Yes; but not to the destruction of your game, as you may fear, Knight of Fahnenberg," said the unknown contemptuously. "Be quite assured of this; your property shall remain untouched—"

"Oh! My father did not mean that," interrupted Franziska, who appeared to take the liveliest interest in the stranger. "Unfortunate events and sad experiences have, no doubt, induced you to take up your abode in these ruins, of which my father would by no means dispossess you."

"Your father is very good, if that is what he meant," said the stranger in his former tone; and it seemed as though his dark features were drawn into a slight smile; "but people of my sort are rather difficult to turn out."

"You must live very uncomfortably here," said Franziska, half vexed, for she thought her polite speech had deserved a better reply.

"My dwelling is not exactly uncomfortable, only somewhat small—still quite suitable for quiet people," said the unknown with a kind of sneer. "I am not, however, always quiet; I sometimes pine to quit the narrow space, and then I dash away through forest and field, over hill and dale; and the time when I must return to my little dwelling always comes too soon for me."

"As you now and then leave your dwelling," said the knight, "I would invite you to visit us, if I knew—"

"That I was in a station to admit of your doing so," interrupted the other; and the knight started slightly, for the stranger had exactly expressed the half-formed thought. "I lament," he continued coldly, "that I am not able to give you particulars on this point—some difficulties stand in the way: be assured, however, that I am a knight, and of at least as ancient a family as yourself."

"Then you must not refuse our request," cried Franziska, highly interested in the strange manners of the unknown. "You must come and visit us."

"I am no boon-companion,[5] and on that account few have invited me of late," replied the other with his peculiar smile. "Besides, I generally remain at home during the day; that is my time for rest. I belong, you must know, to that class of persons who turn day into

[5] A good or convivial friend.

night, and night into day, and who love everything uncommon and peculiar."

"Really? So do I! And for that reason, you must visit us," cried Franziska. "Now," she continued smiling, "I suppose you have just risen, and you are taking your morning airing. Well, since the moon is your sun, pray pay a frequent visit to our castle by the light of its rays. I think we shall agree very well, and that it will be very nice for us to be acquainted. "

"You wish it?—You press the invitation?" asked the stranger earnestly and decidedly.

"To be sure, for otherwise you will not come," replied the young lady shortly.

"Well, then, come I will!" said the other, again fixing his gaze on her. "If my company does not please you at any time, you will have yourself to blame for an acquaintance with one who seldom forces himself, but is difficult to shake off."

When the unknown had concluded these words he made a slight motion with his hand, as though to take leave of them, and passing under the doorway, disappeared among the ruins. The party soon after mounted their horses and took the road home.

IT WAS EVENING of the following day, and all were again seated in the hall of the castle. Bertha had that day received good news. The knight Woislaw had written from Hungary that the war with the Turks would soon be brought to a conclusion during the year, and that although he had intended returning to Silesia, hearing of the Knight of Fahnenberg having gone to take possession of his new estates, he should follow the family there, not doubting that Bertha had accompanied her friend.

He hinted that he stood so high in the opinion of his duke on account of his valuable services, that in future his duties would be even more important and extensive; but before settling down to them, he should come and claim Bertha's promise to become his wife. He had been much enriched by his master, as well as by booty taken from the Turks.

Having formerly lost his right hand in the duke's service, he had essayed to fight with his left; but this did not succeed very admirably, and so he had an iron one made by a very clever artist. This hand performed many of the functions of a natural one, but there had been still much wanting; now, however, his master had presented him with one of gold, an extraordinary work of art, produced by a celebrated Italian mechanic. The knight described it as something marvelous, especially as to the superhuman strength with which it enabled him to use the sword and lance.

Franziska naturally rejoiced in the happiness of her friend, who had had no news of her betrothed for a long time before. She launched out every now and then, partly to plague Franz, and partly to express her own feelings, in the highest praise and admiration of the bravery and enterprise of the knight, whose adventurous qualities she lauded to the skies. Even the scar on his face and his want of a right hand were reckoned as virtues; and Franziska at last saucily declared that a rather ugly man was infinitely more attractive to her than a handsome one, for as a general rule handsome men were conceited and effeminate. Thus, she added, no one could term their acquaintance of the night before handsome, but attractive and interesting he certainly was.

Franz and Bertha simultaneously denied this. The stranger's gloomy appearance, the deadly hue of his complexion, the tone of his voice, were each in turn depreciated by Bertha, while Franz found fault with the contempt and arrogance obvious in his speech. The knight stood between the two parties.

He thought there was something in his bearing that spoke of good family, though much could not be said for his politeness; however, the man might have had trials enough in his life to make him misanthropical. Whilst they were conversing in this way, the door suddenly opened and the subject of their remarks himself walked in.

"Pardon me, Sir Knight," he said coldly, "that I come, if not uninvited, at least unannounced; there was no one in the ante-chamber to do me that service."

The brilliantly lighted chamber gave a full view of the stranger. He was a man of about forty, tall, and extremely thin. His features could not be termed uninteresting—there lay in them something bold and daring—but the expression was on the whole anything but benevolent. There were contempt and sarcasm in the cold grey eyes, whose glance, however, was at times so piercing that no one could endure it long.

His complexion was even more peculiar than the features: it could neither be called pale nor yellow; it was a sort of grey, or, so to speak, dirty white, like that of an Indian who has been suffering long from fever; and was rendered still more remarkable by the intense blackness of his beard and short cropped hair. The dress of the unknown was knightly, but old-fashioned and neglected; there were great spots of rust on the collar and breastplate of his armor; and his dagger and the hilt of his finely worked sword were marked in some places with mildew.

As the party was just going to supper, it was only natural to invite the stranger to partake of it; he complied, however, only in so far that he seated himself at the table, for he ate no morsel. The knight, with some surprise, inquired the reason.

"For a long time past I have accustomed myself never to eat at night," he replied with a strange smile. "My digestion is quite unused to solids, and indeed would scarcely confront them. I live entirely on liquids."

"Oh, then we can empty a bumper of Rhine-wine together," cried the host.

"Thanks; but I neither drink wine nor any cold beverage," replied the other; and his tone was full of mockery.[6] It appeared as if there was some amusing association connected with the idea.

"Then I will order you a cup of hippocras"—a warm drink composed of herbs—"it shall be ready immediately," said Franziska.

"Many thanks, fair lady; not at present," replied the other. "But if I refuse the beverage you offer me now, you may be assured that as soon as I require it—perhaps very soon—I will request that, or some other of you."

Bertha and Franz thought the man had something inexpressibly repulsive in his whole manner, and they had no inclination to engage him in conversation; but the baron, thinking that perhaps politeness required him to say something, turned towards the guest, and commenced in a friendly tone: "It is now many weeks since we first became acquainted with you; we then had to thank you for a singular service—"

"And I have not yet told you my name, although you would gladly know it," interrupted the other dryly. "I am called Azzo; and as"—this he said again with his ironical smile—"with the permission of the Knight of

---

[6] Compare Dracula's statement in Tod Browning's film of *Dracula* (1931): "I don't drink—wine."

Fahnenberg, I live at the castle of Klatka, you can in future call me Azzo von Klatka."

"I only wonder you do not feel lonely and uncomfortable amongst those old walls," began Bertha. "I cannot understand—"

"Why my business is there? Oh, about that I will willingly give you some information, since you and the young gentleman there take such a kindly interest in my person," replied the unknown in his tone of sarcasm.

Franz and Bertha both started, for he had revealed their thoughts as though he could read their souls. "You see, my lady," he continued, "there are a variety of strange whims in the world. As I have already said, I love what is peculiar and uncommon, at least what would appear so to you. It is wrong in the main to be astonished at anything, for, viewed in one light, all things are alike; even life and death, this side of the grave and the other, have more resemblance than you would imagine.

"You perhaps consider me rather touched a little in my mind, for taking up my abode with the bat and the owl; but if so, why not consider every hermit and recluse insane? You will tell me that those are holy men. I certainly have no pretension that way; but as they find pleasure in praying and singing psalms, so I amuse myself with hunting. Oh, away in the pale moonlight, on a horse that never tires, over hill and dale, through forest and woodland! I rush among the wolves, which fly at my approach, as you yourself perceived, as though they were puppies fearful of the lash."

"But still it must be lonely, very lonely for you," remarked Bertha.

"So it would by day; but I am then asleep," replied the stranger dryly; "at night I am merry enough."

"You hunt in an extraordinary way," remarked Franz hesitatingly.

"Yes; but, nevertheless, I have no communication with robbers, as you seem to imagine," replied Azzo coldly.

Franz again started—that very thought had just crossed his mind. "Oh, I beg your pardon; I do not know—" he stammered.

"What to make of me," interrupted the other. "You would therefore do well to believe just what I tell you, or at least to avoid making conjectures of your own, which will lead to nothing."

"I understand you: I know how to value your ideas, if no one else does," cried Franziska eagerly. "The humdrum, everyday life of the generality of men is repulsive to you; you have tasted the joys and pleasures of life, at least what are so called, and you have found them tame and hollow. How soon one tires of the things one sees all around!

"Life consists in change. Only in what is new, uncommon, and peculiar, do the flowers of the spirit bloom and give forth scent. Even pain may become a pleasure if it saves one from the shallow monotony of everyday life— a thing I shall hate till the hour of my death."

"Right, fair lady—quite right! Remain in this mind: this was always my opinion, and the one from which I have derived the highest reward," cried Azzo; and his fierce eyes sparkled more intensely than ever. "I am doubly pleased to have found in you a person who shares my ideas. Oh, if you were a man, you would make me a splendid companion; but even a woman may have fine experiences when once these opinions take root in her, and bring forth action!"

As Azzo spoke these words in a cold tone of politeness, he turned from the subject, and for the rest of his visit only gave the knight monosyllabic replies to his inquiries, taking leave before the table was cleared. To an invitation from the knight, backed by a still more pressing one from Franziska to repeat his visit, he replied that he would take advantage of their kindness, and come sometimes.

When the stranger had departed, many were the remarks made on his appearance and general deportment. Franz declared his most decided dislike of him. Whether it was as usual to vex her cousin, or whether Azzo had really made an impression on her, Franziska took his part vehemently. As Franz contradicted her more eagerly than usual, the young lady launched out into still stronger expressions; and there is no knowing what hard words her cousin might have received had not a servant entered the room.

The following morning Franziska lay longer than usual in bed. When her friend went to her room, fearful lest she should be ill, she found her pale and exhausted. Franziska complained she had passed a very bad night; she thought the dispute with Franz about the stranger must have excited her greatly, for she felt quite feverish and exhausted, and a strange dream, too, had worried her, which was evidently a consequence of the evening's conversation.

Bertha, as usual, took the young man's part, and added that a common dispute about a man whom no one knew, and about whom anyone might form his own opinion, could not possibly have thrown her into her present state. "At least," she continued, "you can let me hear this wonderful dream."

To her surprise, Franziska for a length of time refused to do so.

"Come, tell me," inquired Bertha, "what can possibly prevent you from relating a dream—a mere dream? I might almost think it credible, if the idea were not too horrid, that poor Franz is not very far wrong when he says

that the thin, corpse-like, dried-up, old-fashioned stranger has made a greater impression on you than you will allow."

"Did Franz say so?" asked Franziska. "Then you can tell him he is not mistaken. Yes, the thin, corpse-like, dried-up, whimsical stranger is far more interesting to me than the rosy-cheeked, well-dressed, polite, and prosy cousin."

"Strange," cried Bertha. "I cannot at all comprehend the almost magic influence which this man, so repulsive, exercises over you."

"Perhaps the very reason I take his part, may be that you are all so prejudiced against him," remarked Franziska pettishly. "Yes, it must be so; for that his appearance should please my eyes is what no one in his senses could imagine. But," she continued, smiling and holding out her hand to Bertha, "is it not laughable that I should get out of temper even with you about this stranger?—I can more easily understand it with Franz—and that this unknown should spoil my morning, as he has already spoiled my evening and my night's rest?"

"By that dream, you mean?" said Bertha, easily appeased, as she put her arm round her cousin's neck and kissed her. "Now, do tell it to me. You know how I delight in hearing anything of the kind."

"Well, I will, as a sort of compensation for my peevishness towards you," said the other, clasping her friend's hands. "Now, listen! I had walked up and down my room for a long time; I was excited—out of spirits—I do not know exactly what. It was almost midnight ere I lay down, but I could not sleep. I tossed about, and at length it was only from sheer exhaustion that I dropped off.

"But what a sleep it was! An inward fear

ran through me perpetually. I saw a number of pictures before me, as I used to do in childish sicknesses. I do not know whether I was asleep or half awake. Then I dreamed, but as clearly as if I had been wide awake, that a sort of mist filled the room, and out of it stepped the knight Azzo.

"He gazed at me for a time, and then letting himself slowly down on one knee, imprinted a kiss on my throat. Long did his lips rest there; and I felt a slight pain, which always increased, until I could bear it no more. With all my strength I tried to force the vision from me, but succeeded only after a long struggle. No doubt I uttered a scream, for that awoke me from my trance. When I came a little to my senses I felt a sort of superstitious fear creeping over me, how great you may imagine when I tell you that, with my eyes open and awake, it appeared to me as if Azzo's figure were still by my bed, and then disappearing gradually into the mist, vanished at the door!"[7]

"You must have dreamed very heavily, my poor friend," began Bertha, but suddenly paused. She gazed with surprise at Franziska's throat. "Why, what is that?" she cried. "Just look: how extraordinary—a red streak on your throat!"

Franziska raised herself, and went to a little glass that stood in the window. She really saw a small red line about an inch long on her neck, which began to smart when she touched it with her finger.

"I must have hurt myself by some means in my sleep," she said after a pause; "and that in some measure will account for my dream."

The friends continued chatting for some time about this singular coincidence—the dream and the stranger; and at length it was all turned into a joke by Bertha.

SEVERAL WEEKS passed. The knight had found the estate and affairs in greater disorder than he at first imagined; and instead of remaining three or four weeks, as was originally intended, their departure was deferred to an indefinite period. This postponement was likewise in some measure occasioned by Franziska's continued indisposition. She who had formerly bloomed like a rose in its young fresh beauty was becoming daily thinner, more sickly and exhausted, and at the same time so pale, that in the space of a month not a tinge of red was perceptible on the once glowing cheek.

The knight's anxiety about her was extreme, and the best advice was procured which the age and country afforded; but all to no purpose. Franziska complained from time to time that the horrible dream with which her illness commenced was repeated, and that always on the day following she felt an increased and indescribable weakness. Bertha naturally set this down to the effects of fever, but the ravages of that fever on the usually clear reason of her friend filled her with alarm.

The knight Azzo repeated his visits every now and then. He always came in the evening, and when the moon shone brightly. His manner was always the same. He spoke in monosyllables, and was coldly polite to the knight; to Franz and Bertha, particularly to

---

[7] The entire scene—the vampire taking the form of a mist, coalescing into a solid figure, drinking from the neck of his half-sleeping victim, and then disappearing into a mist—appears in *Dracula* (1897), in the climactic bedroom confrontation between Dracula, Mina Harker, Jonathan Harker, Dr. Seward, and Dr. Van Helsing (see Chapter 21).

the former, contemptuous and haughty; but to Franziska, friendliness itself. Often when, after a short visit, he again left the house, his peculiarities became the subject of conversation. Besides his odd way of speaking, in which Bertha said there lay a deep hatred, a cold detestation of all mankind with the exception of Franziska, two other singularities were observable. During none of his visits, which often took place at supper-time, had he been prevailed upon to eat or drink anything, and that without giving any good reason for his abstinence.

A remarkable alteration, too, had taken place in his appearance: he seemed an entirely different creature. The skin, before so shriveled and stretched, seemed smooth and soft, while a slight tinge of red appeared in his cheeks, which began to look round and plump. Bertha, who could not at all conceal her ill-will towards him, said often, that much as she hated his face before, when it was more like a death's-head than a human being's, it was now more than ever repulsive; she always felt a shudder run through her veins whenever his sharp piercing eyes rested on her.

Perhaps it was owing to Franziska's partiality, or to the knight Azzo's own contemptuous way of replying to Franz, or to his haughty way of treating him in general, that made the young man dislike him more and more. It was quite observable that whenever Franz made a remark to his cousin in the presence of Azzo, the latter would immediately throw some ill-natured light on it or distort it to a totally different meaning. This increased from day to day, and at last Franz declared to Bertha that he would stand such conduct no longer, and that it was only out of consideration for Franziska that he had not already called him to account.

At this time the party at the castle was increased by the arrival of Bertha's long-expected guest. He came just as they were sitting down to supper one evening, and all jumped up to greet their old friend. The knight Woislaw was a true model of the soldier, hardened and strengthened by war with men and elements. His face would not have been termed ugly, if a Turkish sabre had not left a mark running from the right eye to the left cheek, and standing out bright red from the sunburned skin.

The frame of the Castellan of Glogau might almost be termed colossal. Few would have been able to carry his armor, and still fewer move with his lightness and ease under its weight. He did not think little of this same armor, for it had been a present from the palatine[8] of Hungary on his leaving the camp. The blue wrought-steel was ornamented all over with patterns in gold; and he had put it on to do honor to his bride-elect, together with the wonderful gold hand, the gift of the duke.

Woislaw was questioned by the knight and Franz on all the concerns of the campaign; and he entered into the most minute particulars relating to the battles, which, with regard to plunder, had been more successful than ever. He spoke much of the strength of the Turks in a hand-to-hand fight, and remarked that he owed the duke many thanks for his splendid gift, for in consequence of its strength many of the enemy regarded him as something superhuman.

The sickliness and deathlike paleness of Franziska was too perceptible not to be immediately noticed by Woislaw; accustomed to see her so fresh and cheerful, he hastened to inquire into the cause of the change. Bertha

---

[8] This meaning, a powerful feudal lord.

related all that had happened, and Woislaw listened with the greatest interest. This increased to the utmost at the account of the often-repeated dream, and Franziska had to give him the most minute particulars of it; it appeared as though he had met with a similar case before, or at least had heard of one.

When the young lady added that it was very remarkable that the wound on her throat which she had at first felt had never healed, and still pained her, the knight Woislaw looked at Bertha as much as to say that this last fact had greatly strengthened his idea as to the cause of Franziska's illness.

It was only natural that the discourse should next turn to the knight Azzo, about whom everyone began to talk eagerly. Woislaw inquired as minutely as he had done with regard to Franziska's illness about what concerned this stranger, from the first evening of their acquaintance down to his last visit, without, however, giving any opinion on the subject.

The party were still in earnest conversation, when the door opened, and Azzo entered. Woislaw's eyes remained fixed on him, as he, without taking any particular notice of the new arrival, walked up to the table, and seating himself, directed most of the conversation to Franziska and her father, and now and then made some sarcastic remark when Franz began to speak.

The Turkish war again came on the *tapis*, and though Azzo only put in an occasional remark, Woislaw had much to say on the subject. Thus they had advanced late into the night, and Franz said smiling to Woislaw: "I should not wonder if day had surprised us, whilst listening to your entertaining adventures."

"I admire the young gentleman's taste," said Azzo, with an ironical curl of the lip. "Stories of storm and shipwreck are, indeed, best heard on *terra firma*, and those of battle and death at a hospitable table or in the chimney-corner. One has then the comfortable feeling of keeping a whole skin, and being in no danger, not even of taking cold."

With the last words, he gave a hoarse laugh, and turning his back on Franz, rose, bowed to the rest of the company, and left the room. The knight, who always accompanied Azzo to the door, now expressed himself fatigued, and bade his friends good night.

"That Azzo's impertinence is unbearable," cried Bertha when he was gone. "He becomes daily more rough, unpolite, and presuming. If only on account of Franziska's dream, though of course he cannot help that, I detest him. Now, tonight, not one civil word has he spoken to anyone but Franziska, except, perhaps, some casual remark to my uncle."

"I cannot deny that you are right, Bertha," said her cousin. "One may forgive much to a man whom fate had probably made somewhat misanthropical; but he should not overstep the bounds of common politeness. But where on earth is Franz?" added Franziska, as she looked uneasily round. The young man had quietly left the room whilst Bertha was speaking.

"He cannot have followed the knight Azzo to challenge him?" cried Bertha in alarm.

"It were better he entered a lion's den to pull his mane!" said Woislaw vehemently. "I must follow him instantly," he added, as he rushed from the room.

He hastened over the threshold, out of the castle, and through the court before he came up to them. Here a narrow bridge with a slight balustrade passed over the moat by which the castle was surrounded. It appeared that Franz had only just addressed Azzo in a few hot words, for as Woislaw, unperceived by either, advanced under the shadow of the wall, Azzo said gloomily: "Leave me, foolish boy—leave me; for by that sun"—and he pointed to the full moon above them—"you will see those rays no more if you linger another moment on my path."

"And I tell you, wretch, that you either give me satisfaction for your repeated insolence, or you die," cried Franz, drawing his sword.

Azzo stretched forth his hand, and grasping the sword in the middle, it snapped like a broken reed. "I warn you for the last time," he said in a voice of thunder as he threw the pieces into the moat. "Now, away—away, boy, from my path, or, by those below us, you are lost!"

"You or I! You or I!" cried Franz madly as he made a rush at the sword of his antagonist and strove to draw it from his side. Azzo replied not; only a bitter laugh half escaped from his lips; then seizing Franz by the chest, he lifted him up like an infant, and was in the act of throwing him over the bridge when Woislaw stepped to his side.

With a grasp of his wonderful hand, into the springs of which he threw all his strength, he seized Azzo's arm, pulled it down, and obliged him to drop his victim. Azzo seemed in the highest degree astonished. Without concerning himself further about Franz, he gazed in amazement on Woislaw.

"Who art thou who darest to rob me of my prey?" he asked hesitatingly. "Is it possible? Can you be—"

"Ask not, thou bloody one! Go, seek thy nourishment! Soon comes thy hour!" replied Woislaw in a calm but firm tone.

"Ha, now I know!" cried Azzo eagerly. "Welcome, blood-brother! I give up to you this worm, and for your sake will not crush him. Farewell; our paths will soon meet again."

"Soon, very soon; farewell!" cried Woislaw, drawing Franz towards him. Azzo rushed away and disappeared.

Franz had remained for some moments in a state of stupefaction, but suddenly started as from a dream. "I am dishonored, dishonored forever!" he cried, as he pressed his clenched hands to his forehead.

"Calm yourself; you could not have conquered," said Woislaw.

"But I will conquer, or perish!" cried Franz incensed. "I will seek this adventurer in his den, and he or I must fall."

"You could not hurt him," said Woislaw. "You would infallibly be the victim."

"Then show me a way to bring the wretch to judgment," cried Franz, seizing Woislaw's hands, while tears of anger sprang to his eyes. "Disgraced as I am, I cannot live."

"You shall be revenged, and that within twenty-four hours, I hope; but only on two conditions—"

"I agree to them! I will do anything—" began the young man eagerly.

"The first is, that you do nothing, but leave everything in my hands," interrupted Woislaw. "The second, that you will assist me in persuading Franziska to do what I shall represent to her as absolutely necessary. That young lady's life is in more danger from Azzo than your own."

"How? What?" cried Franz fiercely. "Franziska's life in danger! And from that man? Tell me, Woislaw, who is this fiend?"

"Not a word will I tell either the young

lady or you, until the danger is passed," said Woislaw firmly. "The smallest indiscretion would ruin everything. No one can act here but Franziska herself, and if she refuses to do so she is irretrievably lost."

"Speak, and I will help you. I will do all you wish, but I must know——"

"Nothing, absolutely nothing," replied Woislaw. "I must have both you and Franziska yield to me unconditionally. Come now, come to her. You are to be mute on what has passed, and use every effort to induce her to accede to my proposal."

Woislaw spoke firmly, and it was impossible for Franz to make any further objection; in a few moments they both entered the hall, where they found the young girls still anxiously awaiting them.

"Oh, I have been so frightened," said Franziska, even paler than usual, as she held out her hand to Franz. "I trust all has ended peaceably."

"Everything is arranged; a couple of words were sufficient to settle the whole affair," said Woislaw cheerfully. "But Master Franz was less concerned in it than yourself, fair lady."

"I! How do you mean?" said Franziska in surprise.

"I allude to your illness," replied the other.

"And you spoke of that to Azzo? Does he, then, know a remedy which he could not tell me himself?" she inquired, smiling painfully.

"The knight Azzo must take part in your cure; but speak to you about it he cannot, unless the remedy is to lose all its efficacy," replied Woislaw quietly.

"So it is some secret elixir, as the learned doctors who have so long attended me say, and through whose means I only grow worse," said Franziska mournfully.

"It is certainly a secret, but is as certainly a cure," replied Woislaw.

"So said all, but none has succeeded," said the young lady peevishly.

"You might at least try it," began Bertha.

"Because your friend proposes it," said the other smiling. "I have no doubt that you, with nothing ailing you, would take all manner of drugs to please your knight; but with me the inducement is wanting, and therefore also the faith."

"I did not speak of any medicine," said Woislaw.

"Oh! A magical remedy! I am to be cured—what was it the quack who was here the other day called it?—'by sympathy.' Yes, that was it."

"I do not object to your calling it so, if you like," said Woislaw smiling; "but you must know, dear lady, that the measures I shall propose must be attended to literally, and according to the strictest directions."

"And you trust this to me?" asked Franziska.

"Certainly," said Woislaw hesitating; "but—"

"Well, why do you not proceed? Can you think that I shall fail in courage?" she asked.

"Courage is certainly necessary for the success of my plan," said Woislaw gravely; "and it is because I give you credit for a large share of that virtue, I venture to propose it at all, although for the real harmlessness of the remedy I will answer with my life, provided you follow my directions exactly."

"Well, tell me the plan, and then I can decide," said the young lady.

"I can only tell you that when we commence our operations," replied Woislaw.

"Do you think I am a child to be sent here, there, and everywhere, without a reason?" asked Franziska, with something of her old pettishness.

"You did me great injustice, dear lady, if you thought for a moment I would propose anything disagreeable to you, unless demanded by the sternest necessity," said Woislaw; "and yet I can only repeat my former words."

"Then I will not do it," cried Franziska. "I have already tried so much—and all ineffectually."

"I give you my honor as a knight, that your cure is certain, but you must pledge yourself solemnly and unconditionally to do implicitly what I shall direct," said Woislaw earnestly.

"Oh, I implore you to consent, Franziska. Our friend would not propose anything unnecessary," said Bertha, taking both her cousin's hands.

"And let me join my entreaties to Bertha's," said Franz.

"How strange you all are!" exclaimed Franziska, shaking her head; "You make such a secret of that which I must know if I am to accomplish it, and then you declare so positively that I shall recover, when my own feelings tell me it is quite hopeless."

"I repeat, that I will answer for the result," said Woislaw, "on the condition I mentioned before, and that you have courage to carry out what you commence."

"Ha! Now I understand; this, after all, is the only thing which appears doubtful to you," cried Franziska. "Well, to show you that our sex are neither wanting in the will nor in the power to accomplish deeds of daring, I give my consent."

With the last words, she offered Wois-law her hand. "Our compact is thus sealed," she pursued smiling. "Now say, Sir Knight, how am I to commence this mysterious cure?"

"It commenced when you gave your consent," said Woislaw gravely. "Now, I have only to request that you will ask no more questions, but hold yourself in readiness to take a ride with me tomorrow an hour before sunset. I also request that you will not mention to your father a word of what has passed."

"Strange!" said Franziska.

"You have made the compact; you are not wanting in resolution; and I will answer for everything else," said Woislaw encouragingly.

"Well, so let it be. I will follow your directions," said the lady, although she still looked incredulous.

"On our return you shall know everything; before that, it is quite impossible," said Woislaw in conclusion. "Now go, dear lady, and take some rest; you will need strength for tomorrow."

IT WAS ON the morning of the following day; the sun had not risen above an hour, and the dew still lay like a veil of pearls on the grass or dripped from the petals of the flowers swaying in the early breeze, when the knight Woislaw hastened over the fields towards the forest, and turned into a gloomy path, which by the direction one could perceive led towards the towers of Klatka.

When he arrived at the old oak tree we have before had occasion to mention, he sought carefully along the road for traces of human footsteps, but only a deer had passed that way. Seemingly satisfied with his search, he proceeded on his way, though not before he had half drawn his dagger from its sheath, as though to assure himself that it was ready for service in time of need.

Slowly he ascended the path; it was evident he carried something beneath his cloak. Arrived in the court, he left the ruins of the castle to the left, and entered the old chapel. In the chancel he looked eagerly and earnestly around. A deathlike stillness reigned in the deserted sanctuary, only broken by the whispering of the wind in an old thorn-tree which grew outside. Woislaw had looked round him ere he perceived the door leading down to the vault; he hurried towards it and descended. The sun's position enabled its rays to penetrate the crevices, and made the subterranean chamber so light that one could read easily the inscriptions at the head and feet of the coffins.

The knight first laid on the ground the packet he had hitherto carried under his cloak, and then going from coffin to coffin, at last remained stationary before the oldest of them. He read the inscription carefully, drew his dagger thoughtfully from its case, and endeavored to raise the lid with its point. This was no difficult matter, for the rusty iron nails kept but a slight hold of the rotten wood. On looking in, only a heap of ashes, some remnants of dress, and a skull were the contents.

He quickly closed it again, and went on to the next, passing over those of a woman and two children. Here things had much the same appearance, except that the corpse held together till the lid was raised, and then fell into dust, a few linen rags and bones being alone perceptible. In the third, fourth, and nearly the next half-dozen, the bodies were in better preservation: in some, they looked a sort of yellow-brown mummy; whilst in others a skinless skull covered with hair grinned from the coverings of velvet, silk, or mildewed

embroideries; all, however, were touched with the loathsome marks of decay.

Only one more coffin now remained to be inspected; Woislaw approached it, and read the inscription. It was the same that had before attracted the Knight of Fahnenberg: Ezzelin von Klatka, the last possessor of the tower, was described as lying therein. Woislaw found it more difficult to raise the lid here; and it was only by the exertion of much strength that he at length succeeded in extracting the nails. He did all, however, as quietly as if afraid of rousing some sleeper within; he then raised the cover, and cast a glance on the corpse. An involuntary "Ha!" burst from his lips as he stepped back a pace. If he had less expected the sight that met his eyes, he would have been far more overcome.

In the coffin lay Azzo as he lived and breathed, and as Woislaw had seen him at the supper-table only the evening before. His appearance, dress, and all were the same; besides, he had more the semblance of sleep than of death—no trace of decay was visible—there was even a rosy tint on his cheeks. Only the circumstance that the breast did not heave distinguished him from one who slept. For a few moments Woislaw did not move; he could only stare into the coffin. With a hastiness in his movements not usual with him, he suddenly seized the lid, which had fallen from his hands, and laying it on the coffin, knocked the nails into their places. As soon as he had completed this work, he fetched the packet he had left at the entrance, and laying it on the top of the coffin, hastily ascended the steps, and quitted the church and the ruins.

The day passed. Before evening, Franziska requested her father to allow her to take a ride with Woislaw, under pretense of showing him the country. He, only too happy to think this a sign of amendment in his daughter, readily gave his consent; so followed by a single servant, they mounted and left the castle. Woislaw was unusually silent and serious. When Franziska began to rally him about his gravity and the approaching sympathetic cure, he replied that what was before her was no laughing matter; and that although the result would be certainly a cure, still it would leave an impression on her whole future life.

In such discourse they reached the wood, and at length the oak, where they left their horses. Woislaw gave Franziska his arm, and they ascended the hill slowly and silently. They had just reached one of the half-dilapidated outworks where they could catch a glimpse of the open country, when Woislaw, speaking more to himself than to his companion, said: "In a quarter of an hour, the sun will set, and in another hour the moon will have risen; then all must be accomplished. It will soon be time to commence the work."

"Then, I should think it was time to entrust me with some idea of what it is," said Franziska, looking at him.

"Well, my lady," he replied, turning towards her, and his voice was very solemn, "I entreat you, Franziska von Fahnenberg, for your own good, and as you love the father who clings to you with his whole soul, that you will weigh well my words, and that you will not interrupt me with questions which I cannot answer until the work is completed. Your life is in the greatest danger from the illness under which you are laboring; indeed, you are irrecoverably lost if you do not fully carry out what I shall now impart to you.

"Now, promise me to do implicitly as I shall tell you; I pledge you my knightly word it is nothing against Heaven, or the honor of your house; and, besides, it is the sole means for saving you." With these words he held out his right hand to his companion, while he raised the other to heaven in confirmation of his oath.

"I promise you," said Franziska, visibly moved by Woislaw's solemn tone, as she laid her little white and wasted hand in his.

"Then, come; it is time," was his reply, as he led her towards the church. The last rays of the sun were just pouring through the broken windows. They entered the chancel, the best preserved part of the whole building; here there were still some old kneeling-stools, placed before the high altar, although nothing remained of that but the stonework and a few steps; the pictures and decorations had all vanished.

"Say an *Ave*,[9] you will have need of it," said Woislaw, as he himself fell on his knees. Franziska knelt beside him, and repeated a short prayer. After a few moments, both rose. "The moment has arrived! The sun sinks, and before the moon rises, all must be over," said Woislaw quickly.

"What am I to do?" asked Franziska cheerfully.

"You see there that open vault!" replied the knight Woislaw, pointing to the door and flight of steps. "You must descend. You must go alone; I may not accompany you. When you have reached the vault you will find, close to the entrance, a coffin, on which is placed a small packet. Open this packet, and you will find three long iron nails and a hammer. Then pause for a moment; but when I begin to re-

---

[9] Here meaning "Ave Maria" (Latin); a traditional Catholic prayer asking for the intercession of the Virgin Mary, the mother of Jesus.

peat the *Credo*[10] in a loud voice, knock with all your might, first one nail, then a second, and then a third, into the lid of the coffin, right up to their heads."

Franziska stood thunderstruck; her whole body trembled, and she could not utter a word. Woislaw perceived it.

"Take courage, dear lady!" said he. "Think that you are in the hands of Heaven, and that, without the will of your Creator, not a hair can fall from your head. Besides, I repeat, there is no danger."

"Well, then, I will do it," cried Franziska, in some measure regaining courage.

"Whatever you may hear, whatever takes place inside the coffin," continued Woislaw, "must have no effect upon you. Drive the nails well in, without flinching: your work must be finished before my prayer comes to an end."

Franziska shuddered, but again recovered herself. "I will do it; Heaven will send me strength," she murmured softly.

"There is one thing more," said Woislaw hesitatingly; "perhaps it is the hardest of all I have proposed, but without it your cure will not be complete. When you have done as I have told you, a sort of"—he hesitated—"a sort of liquid will flow from the coffin; in this dip your finger, and besmear the scratch on your throat."

"Horrible!" cried Franziska. "This liquid is blood. A human being lies in the coffin."

"An *unearthly one* lies therein! That blood is your own, but it flows in other veins," said Woislaw gloomily. "Ask no more; the sand is running out."

Franziska summoned up all her powers of mind and body, went towards the steps which led to the vault, and Woislaw sank on his knees before the altar in quiet prayer. When the lady had descended, she found herself before the coffin on which lay the packet before mentioned. A sort of twilight reigned in the vault, and everything around was so still and peaceful, that she felt more calm, and going up to the coffin, opened the packet. She had hardly seen that a hammer and three long nails were its contents when suddenly Woislaw's voice rang through the church, and broke the stillness of the aisles.

Franziska started, but recognized the appointed prayer. She seized one of the nails, and with one stroke of the hammer drove it at least an inch into the cover. All was still; nothing was heard but the echo of the stroke. Taking heart, the maiden grasped the hammer with both hands, and struck the nail twice with all her might, right up to the head into the wood.

At this moment commenced a rustling noise; it seemed as though something in the interior began to move and to struggle. Franziska drew back in alarm. She was already on the point of throwing away the hammer and flying up the steps, when Woislaw raised his voice so powerfully, and so entreatingly, that in a sort of excitement, such as would induce one to rush into a lion's den, she returned to the coffin, determined to bring things to a conclusion. Hardly knowing what she did, she placed a second nail in the centre of the lid, and after some strokes this was likewise buried to its head.

The struggle now increased fearfully, as if some living creature were striving to burst the coffin. This was so shaken by it that it cracked and split on all sides. Half distracted, Franziska seized the third nail; she thought

[10] Latin for "I Believe"; as used here, the Nicene-Constantinopolitan Creed (the Apostles' Creed) in the Mass.

no more of her ailments, she only knew herself to be in terrible danger, of what kind she could not guess: in an agony that threatened to rob her of her senses and in the midst of the turning and cracking of the coffin, in which low groans were now heard, she struck the third nail in equally tight. At this moment, she began to lose consciousness. She wished to hasten away, but staggered; and mechanically grasping at something to save herself by, seized the corner of the coffin, and sank fainting beside it on the ground.

A quarter of an hour might have elapsed when she again opened her eyes. She looked around her. Above was the starry sky, and the moon, which shed her cold light on the ruins and on the tops of the old oak trees. Franziska was lying outside the church walls, Woislaw on his knees beside her, holding her hand in his.

"Heaven be praised that you live!" he cried, with a sigh of relief. "I was beginning to doubt whether the remedy had not been too severe, and yet it was the only thing to save you."

Franziska recovered her full consciousness very gradually. The past seemed to her like a dreadful dream. Only a few moments before, that fearful scene; and now this quiet all around her. She hardly dared at first to raise her eyes, and shuddered when she found herself only a few paces removed from the spot where she had undergone such terrible agony. She listened half unconsciously, now to the pacifying words Woislaw addressed to her, now to the whistling of the servant, who stood by the horses, and who, to while away his time, was imitating the evening-song of a belated cowherd.

"Let us go," whispered Franziska, as she strove to raise herself. "But what is this? My shoulder is wet, my throat, my hand—"

"It is probably the evening dew on the grass," said Woislaw gently.

"No; it is blood!" she cried, springing up with horror in her tone. "See, my hand is full of blood!"

"Oh, you are mistaken—surely mistaken," said Woislaw, stammering. "Or perhaps the wound on your neck may have opened! Pray, feel whether this is the case." He seized her hand and directed it to the spot.

"I do not perceive anything; I feel no pain," she said at length, somewhat angrily.

"Then, perhaps, when you fainted you may have struck a corner of the coffin, or have torn yourself with the point of one of the nails," suggested Woislaw.

"Oh, of what do you remind me!" cried Franziska shuddering. "Let us away—away! I entreat you, come! I will not remain a moment longer near this dreadful, dreadful place."

They descended the path much quicker than they came. Woislaw placed his companion on her horse, and they were soon on their way home.

When they approached the castle, Franziska began to inundate her protector with questions about the preceding adventure; but he declared that her present state of excitement must make him defer all explanations till the morning, when her curiosity should be satisfied. On their arrival, he conducted her at once to her room, and told the knight his daughter was too much fatigued with her ride to appear at the supper-table.

ON THE FOLLOWING morning, Franziska rose earlier than she had done for a long time. She assured her friend it was the first time since her illness commenced that she had been really refreshed by her sleep, and, what was still more remarkable, she had not been troubled by her old terrible dream. Her improved looks were not only remarked by Bertha, but by Franz and the knight; and with Woislaw's permission, she related the adventures of the previous evening. No sooner had she concluded, than Woislaw was completely stormed with questions about such a strange occurrence.

"Have you," said the latter, turning towards his host, "ever heard of Vampires?"

"Often," replied he; "but I have never believed in them."

"Nor did I," said Woislaw; "but I have been assured of their existence by experience."

"Oh, tell us what occurred," cried Bertha eagerly, as a light seemed to dawn on her.

"It was during my first campaign in Hungary," began Woislaw, "when I was rendered helpless for some time by this sword-cut of a janissary across my face, and another on my shoulder. I had been taken into the house of a respectable family in a small town. It consisted of the father and mother, and a daughter about twenty years of age. They obtained their living by selling the very good wine of the country, and the taproom was always full of visitors.

"Although the family was well-to-do in the world, there seemed to brood over them a continual melancholy, caused by the constant illness of the only daughter, a very pretty and excellent girl. She had always bloomed like a rose, but for some months she had been getting so thin and wasted, and that without any satisfactory reason: they tried every means to restore her, but in vain.

"As the army had encamped quite in the neighborhood, of course a number of people of all countries assembled in the tavern. Amongst these there was one man who came every evening, when the moon shone, who struck everybody by the peculiarity of his manners and appearance; he looked dried up and deathlike, and hardly spoke at all; but what he did say was bitter and sarcastic. Most attention was excited towards him by the circumstance, that although he always ordered a cup of the best wine, and now and then raised it to his lips, the cup was always as full after his departure as at first."

"This all agrees wonderfully with the appearance of Azzo," said Bertha, deeply interested.

"The daughter of the house," continued Woislaw, "became daily worse, despite the aid not only of Christian doctors, but of many amongst the heathen prisoners, who were consulted in the hope that they might have some magical remedy to propose. It was singular that the girl always complained of a dream, in which the unknown guest worried and plagued her."

"Just the same as your dream, Franziska," cried Bertha.

"One evening," resumed Woislaw, "an old Sclavonian—who had made many voyages to Turkey and Greece, and had even seen the New World—and I were sitting over our wine, when the stranger entered, and sat down at the table. The bottle passed quickly between my friend and me, whilst we talked of all manner of things, of our adventures, and of passages in our lives, both horrible and amusing. We went on chatting thus for about an hour, and drank a tolerable quantity of wine.

"The unknown had remained perfectly silent the whole time, only smiling contemptuously every now and then. He now paid his money, and was going away. All this had quietly worried me—perhaps the wine had gotten a little into my head—so I said to the stranger: 'Hold, you stony stranger; you have hitherto done nothing but listen, and have not even emptied your cup. Now you shall take your turn in telling us something amusing, and if you do not drink up your wine, it shall produce a quarrel between us.'

" 'Yes,' said the Sclavonian, 'you must remain; you shall chat and drink, too'; and he grasped—for although no longer young, he was big and very strong—the stranger by the shoulder, to pull him down to his seat again: the latter, however, although as thin as a skeleton, with one movement of his hand flung the Sclavonian to the middle of the room, and half stunned him for a moment.

"I now approached to hold the stranger back. I caught him by the arm; and although the springs of my iron hand were less powerful than those I have at present, I must have gripped him rather hard in my anger, for after looking grimly at me for a moment, he bent towards me and whispered in my ear: 'Let me go: from the grip of your fist, I see you are my brother, therefore do not hinder me from seeking my bloody nourishment. I am hungry!'

"Surprised by such words, I let him loose, and almost before I was aware of it, he had left the room. As soon as I had in some degree recovered from my astonishment, I told the Sclavonian what I had heard. He started, evidently alarmed. I asked him to tell me the cause of his fears, and pressed him for an explanation of those extraordinary words. On our way to his lodging, he complied with my request. 'The stranger,' said he, 'is a Vampire!'"

"How?" cried the knight, Franziska, and Bertha simultaneously, in a voice of horror. "So this Azzo was—"

"Nothing less. He also was a Vampire!" replied Woislaw. "But at all events *his* hellish thirst is quenched forever; he will never return. But I have not finished. As in my country Vampires had never been heard of, I questioned the Sclavonian minutely. He said that in Hungary, Croatia, Dalmatia, and Bosnia, these hellish guests were not uncommon. They were deceased persons, who had either once served as nourishment to Vampires, or who had died in deadly sin, or under excommunication; and that whenever the moon shone, they rose from their graves, and sucked the blood of the living."

"Horrible!" cried Franziska. "If you had told me all this beforehand, I should never have accomplished the work."

"So I thought; and yet it must be executed by the sufferers themselves, while someone else performs the devotions," replied Woislaw. "The Sclavonian," he continued after a short pause, "added many other facts with regard to these unearthly visitants. He said that whilst their victim wasted, they themselves improved in appearance, and that a Vampire possessed enormous strength—"

"Now I can understand the change your false hand produced on Azzo," interrupted Franz.

"Yes, that was it," replied Woislaw. "Azzo, as well as the other Vampire, mistook its great power for that of a natural one, and concluded I was one of his own species. You may now imagine, dear lady," he continued, turning to Franziska, "how alarmed I was at your appearance when I arrived: all you and Bertha told me increased my anxiety; and when I saw Azzo, I could doubt no longer that he was a Vampire.

"As I learned from your account that a grave with the name Ezzelin von Klatka lay in the neighborhood, I had no doubt that you might be saved if I could only induce you to assist me. It did not appear to me advisable to impart the whole facts of the case, for your bodily powers were so impaired, that an idea of the horrors before you might have quite unfitted you for the exertion; for this reason, I arranged everything in the manner in which it has taken place."

"You did wisely," replied Franziska shuddering. "I can never be grateful enough to you. Had I known what was required of me, I never could have undertaken the deed."

"That was what I feared," said Woislaw; "but fortune has favored us all through."

"And what became of the unfortunate girl in Hungary?" inquired Bertha.

"I know not," replied Woislaw. "That very evening there was an alarm of Turks, and we were ordered off. I never heard anything more of her."

The conversation upon these strange occurrences continued for some time longer. The knight determined to have the vault at Klatka walled up for ever. This took place on the following day; the knight alleging as a reason that he did not wish the dead to be disturbed by irreverent hands.

Franziska recovered gradually. Her health had been so severely shaken, that it was long ere her strength was so much restored as to allow of her being considered out of danger. The young lady's character underwent a great change in the interval. Its former strength was, perhaps, in some degree diminished, but in place of that, she had acquired a benevolent softness, which brought out all her best qualities.

Franz continued his attentions to his cousin; but, perhaps owing to a hint from Bertha, he was less assiduous in his exhibition of them. His inclinations did not lead him to the battle, the camp, or the attainment of honors; his great aim was to increase the good condition and happiness of his tenants; and to this he contributed the whole energy of his mind.

Franziska could not withstand the unobtrusive signs of the young man's continued attachment; and it was not long ere the credit she was obliged to yield to his noble efforts for the welfare of his fellow-creatures, changed into a liking, which went on increasing, until at length it assumed the character of love.

As Woislaw insisted on making Bertha his wife before he returned to Silesia, it was arranged that the marriage should take place at their present abode. How joyful was the surprise of the Knight of Fahnenberg, when his daughter and Franz likewise entreated his blessing, and expressed their desire of being united on the same day! That day soon came round, and it saw the bright looks of two happy couples.

❧❧❧

J. Sheridan Le Fanu

JOSEPH SHERIDAN LE FANU (1814-1873) began his career as a staff writer for the *Dublin University Magazine*; later he became editor and proprietor. Trained as a lawyer, he preferred journalism. He wrote several popular Irish novels, including *Uncle Silas* (1864) and *Guy Deverell* (1865), but is best remembered for his ghost stories. "Carmilla" was first published in the magazine *The Dark Blue* in the December 1871 and January-March 1872 issues, and appeared in revised form in the collection entitled *In a Glass Darkly*, published in 1872.

It is certain that Le Fanu crossed paths with Bram Stoker when Stoker worked as a theater critic at the magazine, and Stoker acknowledged reading "Carmilla," but there is no evidence that Le Fanu and Stoker ever compared notes about vampires. Note that "Carmilla" is set in Styria. In Stoker's notes for *Dracula*, examined in detail in this editor's *New Annotated Dracula*, it is clear that Stoker originally planned to place the events of his narrative there, only later changing the locale to Transylvania.

"Carmilla" is a highly important story, not least for its popularity: Its heavily charged sexual elements set the tone for the erotic undercurrents of *Dracula* and sparked countless imitations in the twentieth century.

CARMILLA

J. SHERIDAN LE FANU

PROLOGUE

UPON A PAPER attached to the Narrative which follows, Doctor Hesselius[1] has written a rather elaborate note, which he accompanies with a reference to his Essay on the strange subject which the MS. illuminates. This mysterious subject he treats, in that Essay, with his usual learning and acumen, and with remarkable directness and condensation. It will form but one volume of the series of that extra-ordinary man's collected papers.

As I publish the case, in this volume, simply to interest the "laity," I shall forestall the intelligent lady, who relates it, in nothing; and after due consideration, I have deter-mined, therefore, to abstain from presenting any *précis* of the learned Doctor's reasoning, or extract from his statement on a subject which he describes as "involving, not improb-ably, some of the profoundest arcana of our dual existence, and its intermediates."

I was anxious on discovering this paper, to reopen the correspondence commenced by Doctor Hesselius, so many years before, with a person so clever and careful as his informant seems to have been. Much to my regret, how-ever, I found that she had died in the interval.

She, probably, could have added little to the Narrative which she communicates in the following pages, with, so far as I can pro-nounce, such a conscientious particularity.

CHAPTER I
An Early Fright

In Styria,[2] we, though by no means magnifi-cent people, inhabit a castle, or schloss. A

---

[1] Hesselius is the psychic-physician who is the narrator of the tales in *In a Glass Darkly*, the collection in which "Carmilla" appeared. He is in some ways the progenitor of Dr. Abraham Van Helsing, the vampire-hunter of Bram Stoker's *Dracula*.

[2] A province of Austria. Stoker originally planned to set *Dracula* there as well; however, he shifted the story to Transylvania. Stoker undoubtedly had read "Carmilla," although there is no evidence that he ever discussed vampires with Le Fanu.

small income, in that part of the world, goes a great way. Eight or nine hundred a year does wonders. Scantily enough ours would have answered among wealthy people at home. My father is English, and I bear an English name, although I never saw England. But here, in this lonely and primitive place, where everything is so marvelously cheap, I really don't see however so much more money would at all materially add to our comforts, or even luxuries.

My father was in the Austrian service, and retired upon a pension and his patrimony, and purchased this feudal residence, and the small estate on which it stands, a bargain.

Nothing can be more picturesque or solitary. It stands on a slight eminence in a forest. The road, very old and narrow, passes in front of its drawbridge, never raised in my time, and its moat, stocked with perch, and sailed over by many swans, and floating on its surface white fleets of water-lilies.

Over all this the schloss shows its many-windowed front, its towers, and its Gothic chapel.

The forest opens in an irregular and very picturesque glade before its gate, and at the right a steep Gothic bridge carries the road over a stream that winds in deep shadow through the wood.

I have said that this is a very lonely place. Judge whether I say truth. Looking from the hall door towards the road, the forest in which our castle stands extends fifteen miles to the right, and twelve to the left. The nearest inhabited village is about seven of your English miles to the left. The nearest inhabited schloss of any historic associations, is that of old General Spielsdorf, nearly twenty miles away to the right.

I have said "the nearest *inhabited* village," because there is, only three miles westward, that is to say in the direction of General Spielsdorf's schloss, a ruined village, with its quaint little church, now roofless, in the aisle of which are the mouldering tombs of the proud family of Karnstein, now extinct, who once owned the equally-desolate chateau which, in the thick of the forest, overlooks the silent ruins of the town.

Respecting the cause of the desertion of this striking and melancholy spot, there is a legend which I shall relate to you another time.

I must tell you now, how very small is the party who constitute the inhabitants of our castle. I don't include servants, or those dependents who occupy rooms in the buildings attached to the schloss. Listen, and wonder! My father, who is the kindest man on earth, but growing old; and I, at the date of my story, only nineteen. Eight years have passed since then. I and my father constituted the family at the schloss. My mother, a Styrian lady, died in my infancy, but I had a good-natured governess, who had been with me from, I might almost say, my infancy. I could not remember the time when her fat, benignant face was not a familiar picture in my memory. This was Madame Perrodon, a native of Berne, whose care and good nature in part supplied to me the loss of my mother, whom I do not even remember, so early I lost her. She made a third at our little dinner party. There was a fourth, Mademoiselle De Lafontaine, a lady such as you term, I believe, a "finishing governess." She spoke French and German, Madame Perrodon French and broken English, to which my father and I added English, which, partly to prevent its becoming a lost language among us, and partly from patriotic motives, we spoke every day. The consequence was a

Babel, at which strangers used to laugh, and which I shall make no attempt to reproduce in this narrative. And there were two or three young lady friends besides, pretty nearly of my own age, who were occasional visitors, for longer or shorter terms; and these visits I sometimes returned.

These were our regular social resources; but of course there were chance visits from "neighbors" of only five or six leagues' distance. My life was, notwithstanding, rather a solitary one, I can assure you.

My governantes had just so much control over me as you might conjecture such sage persons would have in this case of a rather spoiled girl, whose only parent allowed her pretty nearly her own way in everything.

The first occurrence in my existence, which produced a terrible impression upon my mind, which, in fact, never has been effaced, was one of the very earliest incidents of my life which I can recollect. Some people will think it so trifling that it should not be recorded here. You will see, however, by-and-by, why I mention it. The nursery, as it was called, though I had it all to myself, was a large room in the upper story of the castle, with a steep oak roof. I can't have been more than six years old, when one night I awoke, and looking round the room from my bed, failed to see the nursery-maid. Neither was my nurse there; and I thought myself alone. I was not frightened, for I was one of those happy children who are studiously kept in ignorance of ghost stories, of fairy tales, and of all such lore as makes us cover up our heads when the door creaks suddenly, or the flicker of an expiring candle makes the shadow of a bed-post dance upon the wall, nearer to our faces. I was vexed and insulted at finding myself, as I conceived, neglected,

and I began to whimper, preparatory to a hearty bout of roaring; when to my surprise, I saw a solemn, but very pretty face looking at me from the side of the bed. It was that of a young lady who was kneeling, with her hands under the coverlet. I looked at her with a kind of pleased wonder, and ceased whimpering. She caressed me with her hands, and lay down beside me on the bed, and drew me towards her, smiling; I felt immediately delightfully soothed, and fell asleep again. I was wakened by a sensation as if two needles ran into my breast very deep at the same moment, and I cried loudly. The lady started back, with her eyes fixed on me, and then slipped down upon the floor, and, as I thought, hid herself under the bed.

I was now for the first time frightened, and I yelled with all my might and main. Nurse, nursery-maid, housekeeper, all came running in, and hearing my story, they made light of it, soothing me all they could meanwhile. But, child as I was, I could perceive that their faces were pale with an unwonted look of anxiety, and I saw them look under the bed, and about the room, and peep under tables and pluck open cupboards; and the housekeeper whispered to the nurse; "Lay your hand along that hollow in the bed; some one *did* lie there, so sure as you did not; the place is still warm."

I remember the nursery-maid petting me, and all three examining my chest, where I told them I felt the puncture, and pronouncing that there was no sign visible that any such thing had happened to me.

The housekeeper and the two other servants who were in charge of the nursery, remained sitting up all night; and from that time a servant always sat up in the nursery until I was about fourteen.

I was very nervous for a long time after this. A doctor was called in, he was pallid and elderly. How well I remember his long saturnine face, pitted with small-pox, and his chestnut wig. For a good while, every second day, he came and gave me medicine, which of course I hated.

The morning after I saw this apparition I was in a state of terror, and could not bear to be left alone, daylight though it was, for a moment.

I remember my father coming up and standing at the bedside, and talking cheerfully, and asking the nurse a number of questions, and laughing very heartily at one of the answers; and patting me on the shoulder, and kissing me, and telling me not to be frightened, that it was nothing but a dream and could not hurt me.

But I was not comforted, for I knew the visit of the strange woman was *not* a dream; and I was *awfully* frightened.

I was a little consoled by the nursery-maid's assuring me that it was she who had come and looked at me, and lain down beside me in the bed, and that I must have been half-dreaming not to have known her face. But this, though supported by the nurse, did not quite satisfy me.

I remember, in the course of that day, a venerable old man, in a black cassock, coming into the room with the nurse and house-keeper, and talking a little to them, and very kindly to me; his face was very sweet and gentle, and he told me they were going to pray, and joined my hands together, and desired me to say, softly, while they were praying, "Lord, hear all good prayers for us, for Jesus' sake." I think these were the very words, for I often repeated them to myself, and my nurse used for years to make me say them in my prayers.

I remember so well the thoughtful sweet face of that white-haired old man, in his black cassock, as he stood in that rude, lofty, brown room, with the clumsy furniture of a fashion three hundred years old, about him, and the scanty light entering its shadowy atmosphere through the small lattice. He kneeled, and the three women with him, and he prayed aloud with an earnest quavering voice for, what appeared to me, a long time. I forget all my life preceding that event, and for some time after it is all obscure also; but the scenes I have just described stand out vivid as the isolated pictures of the phantasmagoria surrounded by darkness.

CHAPTER II
A Guest

I AM NOW going to tell you something so strange that it will require all your faith in my veracity to believe my story. It is not only true, nevertheless, but truth of which I have been an eyewitness.

It was a sweet summer evening, and my father asked me, as he sometimes did, to take a little ramble with him along that beautiful forest vista which I have mentioned as lying in front of the schloss.

"General Spielsdorf cannot come to us so soon as I had hoped," said my father, as we pursued our walk.

He was to have paid us a visit of some weeks, and we had expected his arrival next day. He was to have brought with him a young lady, his niece and ward, Mademoiselle Rheinfeldt, whom I had never seen, but whom I had heard described as a very charming girl, and in whose society I had promised myself many happy days. I was more disappointed than a young lady living in a town, or a bustling neighborhood can possibly imagine. This visit, and the new acquaintance it promised, had furnished my day dream for many weeks.

"And how soon does he come?" I asked.

"Not till autumn. Not for two months, I dare say," he answered. "And I am very glad now, dear, that you never knew Mademoiselle Rheinfeldt."

"And why?" I asked, both mortified and curious.

"Because the poor young lady is dead," he replied. "I quite forgot I had not told you, but you were not in the room when I received the General's letter this evening."

I was very much shocked. General Spielsdorf had mentioned in his first letter, six or seven weeks before, that she was not so well as he would wish her, but there was nothing to suggest the remotest suspicion of danger.

"Here is the General's letter," he said, handing it to me. "I am afraid he is in great affliction; the letter appears to me to have been written very nearly in distraction."

We sat down on a rude bench, under a group of magnificent lime trees. The sun was setting with all its melancholy splendor behind the sylvan horizon, and the stream that flows beside our home, and passes under the steep old bridge I have mentioned, wound through many a group of noble trees, almost at our feet, reflecting in its current the fading crimson of the sky. General Spielsdorf's letter was extraordinary, so vehement, and in some places so self-contradictory, that I read it twice over—the second time aloud to my father—and was still unable to account for it, except by supposing that grief had unsettled his mind.

It said, "I have lost my darling daughter, for as such I loved her. During the last days of dear Bertha's illness I was not able to write to you. Before then I had no idea of her danger. I have lost her, and now learn *all*, too late. She died in the peace of innocence and in the glorious hope of a blessed futurity. The fiend who betrayed our infatuated hospitality has done it all. I thought I was receiving into my house innocence, gaiety, a charming companion for my lost Bertha. Heavens! What a fool I have been! I thank God my child died without a suspicion of the cause of her sufferings. She is gone without so much as conjecturing the nature of her illness, and the accursed passion of the agent of all this misery. I devote my remaining days to tracking and extinguishing a monster. I am told I may hope to accomplish my righteous and merciful purpose. At present there is scarcely a gleam of light to guide me. I curse my conceited incredulity, my despicable affectation of superiority, my blindness, my obstinacy—all—too late. I cannot write or talk collectedly now. I am distracted. So soon as I shall have a little recovered, I mean to devote myself for a time to inquiry, which may possibly lead me as far as Vienna. Some time in the autumn, two months hence, or earlier if I live, I will see you—that is, if you permit me; I will then tell you all that I scarce dare put upon paper now. Farewell. Pray for me, dear friend."

In these terms ended this strange letter. Though I had never seen Bertha Rheinfeldt, my eyes filled with tears at the sudden intelligence; I was startled, as well as profoundly disappointed.

The sun had now set, and it was twilight by the time I had returned the General's letter to my father.

It was a soft clear evening, and we loitered, speculating upon the possible meanings of the violent and incoherent sentences which

I had just been reading. We had nearly a mile to walk before reaching the road that passes the schloss in front, and by that time the moon was shining brilliantly. At the drawbridge we met Madame Perrodon and Mademoiselle De Lafontaine, who had come out, without their bonnets, to enjoy the exquisite moonlight.

We heard their voices gabbling in animated dialogue as we approached. We joined them at the drawbridge, and turned about to admire with them the beautiful scene.

The glade through which we had just walked lay before us. At our left the narrow road wound away under clumps of lordly trees, and was lost to sight amid the thickening forest. At the right the same road crosses the steep and picturesque bridge, near which stands a ruined tower, which once guarded that pass; and beyond the bridge an abrupt eminence rises, covered with trees, and showing in the shadow some grey ivy-clustered rocks.

Over the sward and low grounds, a thin film of mist was stealing, like smoke, marking the distances with a transparent veil; and here and there we could see the river faintly flashing in the moonlight.

No softer, sweeter scene could be imagined. The news I had just heard made it melancholy; but nothing could disturb its character of profound serenity, and the enchanted glory and vagueness of the prospect.

My father, who enjoyed the picturesque, and I, stood looking in silence over the expanse beneath us. The two good governesses, standing a little way behind us, discoursed upon the scene, and were eloquent upon the moon.

Madame Perrodon was fat, middle-aged, and romantic, and talked and sighed poetically. Mademoiselle De Lafontaine—in right of[3] her father, who was a German, assumed to be psychological, metaphysical, and something of a mystic—now declared that when the moon shone with a light so intense it was well known that it indicated a special spiritual activity. The effect of the full moon in such a state of brilliancy was manifold. It acted on dreams, it acted on lunacy, it acted on nervous people; it had marvelous physical influences connected with life. Mademoiselle related that her cousin, who was mate of a merchant ship, having taken a nap on deck on such a night, lying on his back, with his face full in the light of the moon, had wakened, after a dream of an old woman clawing him by the cheek, with his features horribly drawn to one side; and his countenance had never quite recovered its equilibrium.

"The moon, this night," she said, "is full of odylic[4] and magnetic influence—and see, when you look behind you at the front of the schloss, how all its windows flash and twinkle with that silvery splendor, as if unseen hands had lighted up the rooms to receive fairy guests."

There are indolent states of the spirits in which, indisposed to talk ourselves, the talk of others is pleasant to our listless ears; and I gazed on, pleased with the tinkle of the ladies' conversation.

"I have got into one of my moping moods tonight," said my father, after a silence, and quoting Shakespeare, whom, by way of keeping up our English, he used to read aloud, he said:—

---

[3] Meaning "derived from."

[4] The supposed "life force"; the name is derived from the Norse god Odin.

" 'In truth I know not why I am so sad:
    It wearies me; you say it wearies you;
    But how I got it—came by it.'

"I forget the rest. But I feel as if some great misfortune were hanging over us. I suppose the poor general's afflicted letter has had something to do with it."

At this moment the unwonted sound of carriage wheels and many hoofs upon the road, arrested our attention.

They seemed to be approaching from the high ground overlooking the bridge, and very soon the equipage emerged from that point. Two horsemen first crossed the bridge, then came a carriage drawn by four horses, and two men rode behind.

It seemed to be the travelling carriage of a person of rank; and we were all immediately absorbed in watching that very unusual spectacle. It became, in a few moments, greatly more interesting, for just as the carriage had passed the summit of the steep bridge, one of the leaders, taking fright, communicated his panic to the rest, and, after a plunge or two, the whole team broke into a wild gallop together, and dashing between the horsemen who rode in front, came thundering along the road towards us with the speed of a hurricane.

The excitement of the scene was made more painful by the clear, long-drawn screams of a female voice from the carriage window. We all advanced in curiosity and horror; my father in silence, the rest with various ejaculations of terror. Our suspense did not last long. Just before you reach the castle drawbridge, on the route they were coming, there stands by the roadside a magnificent lime tree, on the other side stands an ancient stone cross, at sight of which the horses, now going at a pace that was perfectly frightful, swerved so as to bring the wheel over the projecting roots of the tree.

I knew what was coming. I covered my eyes, unable to see it out, and turned my head away; at the same moment I heard a cry from my lady-friends, who had gone on a little.

Curiosity opened my eyes, and I saw a scene of utter confusion. Two of the horses were on the ground, the carriage lay upon its side, with two wheels in the air; the men were busy removing the traces, and a lady, with a commanding air and figure had got out, and stood with clasped hands, raising the handkerchief that was in them every now and then to her eyes. Through the carriage door was now lifted a young lady, who appeared to be lifeless. My dear old father was already beside the elder lady, with his hat in his hand, evidently tendering his aid and the resources of his schloss. The lady did not appear to hear him, or to have eyes for anything but the slender girl who was being placed against the slope of the bank.

I approached; the young lady was apparently stunned, but she was certainly not dead. My father, who piqued himself on being something of a physician, had just had his fingers to her wrist and assured the lady, who declared herself her mother, that her pulse, though faint and irregular, was undoubtedly still distinguishable. The lady clasped her hands and looked upward, as if in a momentary transport of gratitude; but immediately she broke out again in that theatrical way which is, I believe, natural to some people.

She was what is called a fine-looking woman for her time of life, and must have been handsome; she was tall, but not thin, and dressed in black velvet, and looked rather pale, but with a proud and commanding countenance, though now agitated strangely.

"Was ever being so born to calamity?" I heard her say, with clasped hands, as I came up. "Here am I, on a journey of life and death, in prosecuting which to lose an hour is possibly to lose all. My child will not have recovered sufficiently to resume her route for who can say how long. I must leave her; I cannot, dare not, delay. How far on, sir, can you tell, is the nearest village? I must leave her there; and shall not see my darling, or even hear of her till my return, three months hence."

I plucked my father by the coat, and whispered earnestly in his ear, "Oh! Papa, pray ask her to let her stay with us—it would be so delightful. Do, pray."

"If Madame will entrust her child to the care of my daughter, and of her good governante, Madame Perrodon, and permit her to remain as our guest, under my charge, until her return, it will confer a distinction and an obligation upon us, and we shall treat her with all the care and devotion which so sacred a trust deserves."

"I cannot do that, sir, it would be to task your kindness and chivalry too cruelly," said the lady, distractedly.

"It would, on the contrary, be to confer on us a very great kindness at the moment when we most need it. My daughter has just been disappointed by a cruel misfortune, in a visit from which she had long anticipated a great deal of happiness. If you confide this young lady to our care it will be her best consolation. The nearest village on your route is distant, and affords no such inn as you could think of placing your daughter at; you cannot allow her to continue her journey for any considerable distance without danger. If, as you say, you cannot suspend your journey, you must part with her tonight, and nowhere could you do so with more honest assurances of care and tenderness than here."

There was something in this lady's air and appearance so distinguished, and even imposing, and in her manner so engaging, as to impress one, quite apart from the dignity of her equipage, with a conviction that she was a person of consequence.

By this time the carriage was replaced in its upright position, and the horses, quite tractable, in the traces again.

The lady threw on her daughter a glance which I fancied was not quite so affectionate as one might have anticipated from the beginning of the scene; then she beckoned slightly to my father, and withdrew two or three steps with him out of hearing; and talked to him with a fixed and stern countenance, not at all like that with which she had hitherto spoken.

I was filled with wonder that my father did not seem to perceive the change, and also unspeakably curious to learn what it could be that she was speaking, almost in his ear, with so much earnestness and rapidity.

Two or three minutes at most, I think, she remained thus employed, then she turned, and a few steps brought her to where her daughter lay, supported by Madame Perrodon. She kneeled beside her for a moment and whispered, as Madame supposed, a little benediction in her ear; then hastily kissing her, she stepped into her carriage, the door was closed, the footmen in stately liveries jumped up behind, the outriders spurred on, the postilions cracked their whips, the horses plunged and broke suddenly into a furious canter that threatened soon again to become a gallop, and the carriage whirled away, followed at the same rapid pace by the two horsemen in the rear.

CHAPTER III
We Compare Notes

WE FOLLOWED the *cortège*[5] with our eyes until it was swiftly lost to sight in the misty wood; and the very sound of the hoofs and wheels died away in the silent night air.

Nothing remained to assure us that the adventure had not been an illusion of a moment but the young lady, who just at that moment opened her eyes. I could not see, for her face was turned from me, but she raised her head, evidently looking about her, and I heard a very sweet voice ask complainingly, "Where is Mamma?"

Our good Madame Perrodon answered tenderly, and added some comfortable assurances.

I then heard her ask:—

"Where am I? What is this place?" and after that she said, "I don't see the carriage; and Matska, where is she?"

Madame answered all her questions in so far as she understood them; and gradually the young lady remembered how the misadventure came about, and was glad to hear that no one in, or in attendance on, the carriage was hurt; and on learning that her mamma had left her here, till her return in about three months, she wept.

I was going to add my consolations to those of Madame Perrodon when Mademoiselle De Lafontaine placed her hand upon my arm, saying:

"Don't approach, one at a time is as much as she can at present converse with; a very little excitement would possibly overpower her now."

As soon as she is comfortably in bed, I thought, I will run up to her room and see her. My father in the meantime had sent a servant on horseback for the physician, who lived about two leagues away; and a bedroom was being prepared for the young lady's reception.

The stranger now rose, and leaning on Madame's arm, walked slowly over the drawbridge and into the castle gate.

In the hall, servants waited to receive her, and she was conducted forthwith to her room.

The room we usually sat in as our drawing-room is long, having four windows, that looked over the moat and drawbridge, upon the forest scene I have just described.

It is furnished in old carved oak, with large carved cabinets, and the chairs are cushioned with crimson Utrecht velvet. The walls are covered with tapestry, and surrounded with great gold frames, the figures being as large as life, in ancient and very curious costume, and the subjects represented are hunting, hawking, and generally festive. It is not too stately to be extremely comfortable; and here we had our tea, for with his usual patriotic leanings he insisted that the national beverage should make its appearance regularly with our coffee and chocolate.

We sat here this night, and with candles lighted, were talking over the adventure of the evening.

Madame Perrodon and Mademoiselle De Lafontaine were both of our party. The young stranger had hardly lain down in her bed when she sank into a deep sleep; and those ladies had left her in the care of a servant.

"How do you like our guest?" I asked, as soon as Madame entered. "Tell me all about her?"

"I like her extremely," answered Ma-

---

[5] The servants and carriage; the *entourage*.

dame, "she is, I almost think, the prettiest creature I ever saw; about your age, and so gentle and nice."

"She is absolutely beautiful," threw in Mademoiselle, who had peeped for a moment into the stranger's room.

"And such a sweet voice!" added Madame Perrodon.

"Did you remark a woman in the carriage, after it was set up again, who did not get out," inquired Mademoiselle, "but only looked from the window?"

No, we had not seen her.

Then she described a hideous black woman, with a sort of colored turban on her head, who was gazing all the time from the carriage window, nodding and grinning derisively towards the ladies, with gleaming eyes and large white eye-balls, and her teeth set as if in fury.

"Did you remark what an ill-looking pack of men the servants were?" asked Madame.

"Yes," said my father, who had just come in, "ugly, hang-dog looking fellows, as ever I beheld in my life. I hope they mayn't rob the poor lady in the forest. They are clever rogues, however; they got everything to rights in a minute."

"I dare say they are worn out with too long travelling," said Madame. "Besides looking wicked, their faces were so strangely lean, and dark, and sullen. I am very curious, I own; but I dare say the young lady will tell us all about it tomorrow, if she is sufficiently recovered."

"I don't think she will," said my father, with a mysterious smile, and a little nod of his head, as if he knew more about it than he cared to tell us.

This made me all the more inquisitive as to what had passed between him and the lady in the black velvet, in the brief but earnest interview that had immediately preceded her departure.

We were scarcely alone, when I entreated him to tell me. He did not need much pressing.

"There is no particular reason why I should not tell you. She expressed a reluctance to trouble us with the care of her daughter, saying she was in delicate health, and nervous, but not subject to any kind of seizure—she volunteered that—nor to any illusion; being, in fact, perfectly sane."

"How very odd to say all that!" I interpolated. "It was so unnecessary."

"At all events it *was* said," he laughed, "and as you wish to know all that passed, which was indeed very little, I tell you. She then said, 'I am making a long journey of *vital* importance'—she emphasized the word—'rapid and secret; I shall return for my child in three months; in the meantime, she will be silent as to who we are, whence we come, and whither we are travelling.' That is all she said. She spoke very pure French. When she said the word 'secret,' she paused for a few seconds, looking sternly, her eyes fixed on mine. I fancy she makes a great point of that. You saw how quickly she was gone. I hope I have not done a very foolish thing, in taking charge of the young lady."

For my part, I was delighted. I was longing to see and talk to her; and only waiting till the doctor should give me leave. You, who live in towns, can have no idea how great an event the introduction of a new friend is, in such a solitude as surrounded us.

The doctor did not arrive till nearly one o'clock; but I could no more have gone to my bed and slept, than I could have overtaken, on foot, the carriage in which the princess in black velvet had driven away.

When the physician came down to the drawing-room, it was to report very favorably upon his patient. She was now sitting up, her pulse quite regular, apparently perfectly well. She had sustained no injury, and the little shock to her nerves had passed away quite harmlessly. There could be no harm certainly in my seeing her, if we both wished it; and with this permission, I sent, forthwith, to know whether she would allow me to visit her for a few minutes in her room.

The servant returned immediately to say that she desired nothing more.

You may be sure I was not long in availing myself of this permission.

Our visitor lay in one of the handsomest rooms in the schloss. It was, perhaps, a little stately. There was a somber piece of tapestry opposite the foot of the bed, representing Cleopatra with the asps to her bosom; and other solemn classic scenes were displayed, a little faded, upon the other walls. But there was gold carving, and rich and varied color enough in the other decorations of the room, to more than redeem the gloom of the old tapestry.

There were candles at the bed side. She was sitting up; her slender pretty figure enveloped in the soft silk dressing-gown, embroidered with flowers, and lined with thick quilted silk, which her mother had thrown over her feet as she lay upon the ground.

What was it that, as I reached the bed side and had just begun my little greeting, struck me dumb in a moment, and made me recoil a step or two from before her? I will tell you.

I saw the very face which had visited me in my childhood at night, which remained so fixed in my memory, and on which I had for so many years so often ruminated with horror, when no one suspected of what I was thinking.

It was pretty, even beautiful; and when I first beheld it, wore the same melancholy expression. But this almost instantly lighted into a strange fixed smile of recognition.

There was a silence of fully a minute, and then at length *she* spoke; *I* could not.

"How wonderful!" she exclaimed. "Twelve years ago, I saw your face in a dream, and it has haunted me ever since."

"Wonderful indeed!" I repeated, overcoming with an effort the horror that had for a time suspended my utterances. "Twelve years ago, in vision or reality, *I* certainly saw you. I could not forget your face. It has remained before my eyes ever since."

Her smile had softened. Whatever I had fancied strange in it, was gone, and it and her dimpling cheeks were now delightfully pretty and intelligent.

I felt reassured, and continued more in the vein which hospitality indicated, to bid her welcome, and to tell her how much pleasure her accidental arrival had given us all, and especially what a happiness it was to me.

I took her hand as I spoke. I was a little shy, as lonely people are, but the situation made me eloquent, and even bold. She pressed my hand, she laid hers upon it, and her eyes glowed, as, looking hastily into mine, she smiled again, and blushed.

She answered my welcome very prettily. I sat down beside her, still wondering; and she said:

"I must tell you my vision about you; it is so very strange that you and I should have had, each of the other, so vivid a dream, that each should have seen, I you and you me, looking as we do now, when of course we both were mere children. I was a child, about six years old, and I awoke from a confused and troubled dream, and found myself in a room, unlike my nursery, wainscoted clumsily in some dark wood, and with cupboards and bedsteads, and chairs and benches placed about it. The beds were, I thought, all empty, and the room itself without anyone but myself in it; and I, after looking about me for some time, and admiring especially an iron candlestick, with two branches, which I should certainly know again, crept under one of the beds to reach the window; but as I got from under the bed, I heard some one crying; and looking up, while I was still upon my knees, I saw *you*—most assuredly you—as I see you now; a beautiful young lady, with golden hair and large blue eyes, and lips—your lips—you, as you are here. Your looks won me; I climbed on the bed and put my arms about you, and I think we both fell asleep. I was aroused by a scream; you were sitting up screaming. I was frightened, and slipped down upon the ground, and, it seemed to me, lost consciousness for a moment; and when I came to myself, I was again in my nursery at home. Your face I have never forgotten since. I could not be misled by mere resemblance. You *are* the lady whom I then saw."

It was now my turn to relate my corresponding vision, which I did, to the undisguised wonder of my new acquaintance.

"I don't know which should be most afraid of the other," she said, again smiling. "If you were less pretty I think I should be very much afraid of you, but being as you are, and you and I both so young, I feel only that I have made your acquaintance twelve years ago, and have already a right to your intimacy; at all events, it does seem as if we were destined, from our earliest childhood, to be friends. I wonder whether you feel as strangely drawn towards me as I do to you; I have never had a friend—shall I find one now?" She sighed, and her fine dark eyes gazed passionately on me.

Now the truth is, I felt rather unaccountably towards the beautiful stranger. I did feel, as she said, "drawn towards her," but there was also something of repulsion. In this ambiguous feeling, however, the sense of attraction immensely prevailed. She interested and won me; she was so beautiful and so indescribably engaging.

I perceived now something of languor and exhaustion stealing over her, and hastened to bid her good night.

"The doctor thinks," I added, "that you ought to have a maid to sit up with you tonight; one of ours is waiting, and you will find her a very useful and quiet creature."

"How kind of you, but I could not sleep, I never could with an attendant in the room. I shan't require any assistance—and, shall I confess my weakness, I am haunted with a terror of robbers. Our house was robbed once, and two servants murdered, so I always lock my door. It has become a habit—and you look so kind I know you will forgive me. I see there is a key in the lock."

She held me close in her pretty arms for a moment and whispered in my ear, "Good-night, darling, it is very hard to part with you, but good-night; tomorrow, but not early, I shall see you again."

She sank back on the pillow with a sigh, and her fine eyes followed me with a fond and melancholy gaze, and she murmured again, "Good-night, dear friend."

Young people like, and even love, on impulse. I was flattered by the evident, though as yet undeserved, fondness she showed me. I liked the confidence with which she at once received me. She was determined that we should be very dear friends.

Next day came and we met again. I was delighted with my companion; that is to say, in many respects.

Her looks lost nothing in daylight—she was certainly the most beautiful creature I had ever seen, and the unpleasant remembrance of the face presented in my early dream, had lost the effect of the first unexpected recognition.

She confessed that she had experienced a similar shock on seeing me, and precisely the same faint antipathy that had mingled with my admiration of her. We now laughed together over our momentary horrors.

CHAPTER IV
Her Habits—A Saunter

I TOLD YOU that I was charmed with her in most particulars.

There were some that did not please me so well.

She was above the middle height of women. I shall begin by describing her. She was slender, and wonderfully graceful. Except that her movements were languid—*very* languid—indeed, there was nothing in her appearance to indicate an invalid. Her complexion was rich and brilliant; her features were small and beautifully formed; her eyes large, dark, and lustrous; her hair was quite wonderful, I never saw hair so magnificently thick and long when it was down about her shoulders; I have often placed my hands under it, and laughed with wonder at its weight. It was exquisitely fine and soft, and

in color a rich very dark brown, with something of gold. I loved to let it down, tumbling with its own weight, as, in her room, she lay back in her chair talking in her sweet low voice, I used to fold and braid it, and spread it out and play with it. Heavens! If I had but known all!

I said there were particulars which did not please me. I have told you that her confidence won me the first night I saw her; but I found that she exercised with respect to herself, her mother, her history, everything in fact connected with her life, plans, and people, an ever-wakeful reserve. I dare say I was unreasonable, perhaps I was wrong; I dare say I ought to have respected the solemn injunction laid upon my father by the stately lady in black velvet. But curiosity is a restless and unscrupulous passion, and no one girl can endure, with patience, that hers should be baffled by another. What harm could it do anyone to tell me what I so ardently desired to know? Had she no trust in my good sense or honor? Why would she not believe me when I assured her, so solemnly, that I would not divulge one syllable of what she told me to any mortal breathing?

There was a coldness, it seemed to me, beyond her years, in her smiling melancholy persistent refusal to afford me the least ray of light.

I cannot say we quarreled upon this point, for she would not quarrel upon any. It was, of course, very unfair of me to press her, very ill-bred, but I really could not help it; and I might just as well have let it alone.

What she did tell me amounted, in my unconscionable estimation—to nothing.

It was all summed up in three very vague disclosures:

First.—Her name was Carmilla.

Second.—Her family was very ancient and noble.

Third.—Her home lay in the direction of the west.

She would not tell me the name of her family, nor their armorial bearings, nor the name of their estate, nor even that of the country they lived in.

You are not to suppose that I worried her incessantly on these subjects. I watched opportunity, and rather insinuated than urged my inquiries. Once or twice, indeed, I did attack her more directly. But no matter what my tactics, utter failure was invariably the result. Reproaches and caresses were all lost upon her. But I must add this, that her evasion was conducted with so pretty a melancholy and deprecation, with so many, and even passionate declarations of her liking for me, and trust in my honor, and with so many promises that I should at last know all, that I could not find it in my heart long to be offended with her.

She used to place her pretty arms about my neck, draw me to her, and laying her cheek to mine, murmur with her lips near my ear, "Dearest, your little heart is wounded; think me not cruel because I obey the irresistible law of my strength and weakness; if your dear heart is wounded, my wild heart bleeds with yours. In the rapture of my enormous humiliation I live in your warm life, and you shall die—die, sweetly die—into mine. I cannot help it; as I draw near to you, you, in your turn, will draw near to others, and learn the rapture of that cruelty, which yet is love; so, for a while, seek to know no more of me and mine, but trust me with all your loving spirit."

And when she had spoken such a rhapsody, she would press me more closely in her trembling embrace, and her lips in soft kisses gently glow upon my cheek.

Her agitations and her language were unintelligible to me.

From these foolish embraces, which were not of very frequent occurrence, I must allow, I used to wish to extricate myself; but my energies seemed to fail me. Her murmured words sounded like a lullaby in my ear, and soothed my resistance into a trance, from which I only seemed to recover myself when she withdrew her arms.

In these mysterious moods I did not like her. I experienced a strange tumultuous excitement that was pleasurable, ever and anon, mingled with a vague sense of fear and disgust. I had no distinct thoughts about her while such scenes lasted, but I was conscious of a love growing into adoration, and also of abhorrence. This I know is paradox, but I can make no other attempt to explain the feeling.

I now write, after an interval of more than ten years, with a trembling hand, with a confused and horrible recollection of certain occurrences and situations, in the ordeal through which I was unconsciously passing; though with a vivid and very sharp remembrance of the main current of my story. But, I suspect, in all lives there are certain emotional scenes, those in which our passions have been most wildly and terribly roused, that are of all others the most vaguely and dimly remembered.

Sometimes after an hour of apathy, my strange and beautiful companion would take my hand and hold it with a fond pressure, renewed again and again; blushing softly, gazing in my face with languid and burning eyes, and breathing so fast that her dress rose and fell with the tumultuous respiration. It was like the ardour of a lover; it embarrassed me; it was hateful and yet overpowering; and with gloating eyes she drew me to her, and her hot lips travelled along my cheek in kisses; and she would whisper, almost in sobs, "You are mine, you *shall* be mine, and you and I are one for ever." Then she had thrown herself back in her chair, with her small hands over her eyes, leaving me trembling.

"Are we related," I used to ask; "what can you mean by all this? I remind you perhaps of some one whom you love; but you must not, I hate it; I don't know you—I don't know myself when you look so and talk so."

She used to sigh at my vehemence, then turn away and drop my hand.

Respecting these very extraordinary manifestations I strove in vain to form any satisfactory theory—I could not refer them to affectation or trick. It was unmistakably the momentary breaking out of suppressed instinct and emotion. Was she, notwithstanding her mother's volunteered denial, subject to brief visitations of insanity; or was there here a disguise and a romance? I had read in old story books of such things.

What if a boyish lover had found his way into the house, and sought to prosecute his suit in masquerade, with the assistance of a clever old adventuress? But there were many things against this hypothesis, highly interesting as it was to my vanity.

I could boast of no little attentions such as masculine gallantry delights to offer. Between these passionate moments there were long intervals of common-place, of gaiety, of brooding melancholy, during which, except that I detected her eyes so full of melancholy fire, following me, at times I might have been as nothing to her. Except in these brief periods of mysterious excitement her ways were girlish; and there was always a languor about her, quite incompatible with a masculine system in a state of health.

In some respects her habits were odd. Perhaps not so singular in the opinion of a town lady like you, as they appeared to us rustic people. She used to come down very late, generally not till one o'clock, she would then take a cup of chocolate, but eat nothing; we then went out for a walk, which was a mere saunter, and she seemed, almost immediately, exhausted, and either returned to the schloss or sat on one of the benches that were placed, here and there, among the trees. This was a bodily languor in which her mind did not sympathize. She was always an animated talker, and very intelligent.

She sometimes alluded for a moment to her own home, or mentioned an adventure or situation, or an early recollection, which indicated a people of strange manners, and described customs of which we knew nothing. I gathered from these chance hints that her native country was much more remote than I had at first fancied.

As we sat thus one afternoon under the trees a funeral passed us by. It was that of a pretty young girl, whom I had often seen, the daughter of one of the rangers of the forest. The poor man was walking behind the coffin of his darling; she was his only child, and he looked quite heartbroken. Peasants walking two-and-two came behind, they were singing a funeral hymn.

I rose to mark my respect as they passed, and joined in the hymn they were very sweetly singing.

My companion shook me a little roughly, and I turned surprised.

She said brusquely, "Don't you perceive how discordant that is?"

"I think it very sweet, on the contrary," I answered, vexed at the interruption, and very uncomfortable, lest the people who composed the little procession should observe and resent what was passing. I resumed, therefore, instantly, and was again interrupted. "You pierce my ears," said Carmilla, almost angrily, and stopping her ears with her tiny fingers. "Besides, how can you tell that your religion and mine are the same; your forms wound me, and I hate funerals. What a fuss! Why, *you* must *die—everyone* must die; and all are happier when they do. Come home."

"My father has gone on with the clergyman to the churchyard. I thought you knew she was to be buried today."

"*She?* I don't trouble my head about peasants. I don't know who she is," answered Carmilla, with a flash from her fine eyes.

"She is the poor girl who fancied she saw a ghost a fortnight ago, and has been dying ever since, till yesterday, when she expired."

"Tell me nothing about ghosts. I shan't sleep tonight if you do."

"I hope there is no plague or fever coming; all this looks very like it," I continued. "The swineherd's young wife died only a week ago, and she thought something seized her by the throat as she lay in her bed, and nearly strangled her. Papa says such horrible fancies do accompany some forms of fever. She was quite well the day before. She sank afterwards, and died before a week."

"Well, *her* funeral is over, I hope, and *her* hymn sung; and our ears shan't be tortured with that discord and jargon. It has made me nervous. Sit down here, beside me; sit close; hold my hand; press it hard—hard—harder."

We had moved a little back, and had come to another seat.

She sat down. Her face underwent a change that alarmed and even terrified me for a moment. It darkened, and became horribly livid; her teeth and hands were clenched, and she frowned and compressed her lips, while she stared down upon the ground at her feet, and trembled allover with a continued shudder as irrepressible as ague. All her energies seemed strained to suppress a fit, with which she was then breathlessly tugging; and at length a low convulsive cry of suffering broke from her, and gradually the hysteria subsided. "There! That comes of strangling people with hymns!" she said at last. "Hold me, hold me still. It is passing away."

And so gradually it did; and perhaps to dissipate the somber impression which the spectacle had left upon me, she became unusually animated and chatty; and so we got home.

This was the first time I had seen her exhibit any definable symptoms of that delicacy of health which her mother had spoken of. It was the first time, also, I had seen her exhibit anything like temper.

Both passed away like a summer cloud; and never but once afterwards did I witness on her part a momentary sign of anger. I will tell you how it happened.

She and I were looking out of one of the long drawing-room windows, when there entered the courtyard, over the drawbridge, a figure of a wanderer whom I knew very well. He used to visit the schloss generally twice a year.

It was the figure of a hunchback, with the sharp lean features that generally accompany deformity. He wore a pointed black beard, and he was smiling from ear to ear, showing his white fangs. He was dressed in buff, black, and scarlet, and crossed with more straps and belts than I could count, from which hung all manner of things. Behind, he carried a magic-lantern,[6] and two boxes, which I well knew, in one of which was a salamander, and in the other a mandrake.[7] These monsters used to make my father laugh. They were compounded of parts of monkeys, parrots, squirrels, fish, and hedgehogs, dried and stitched together with great neatness and startling effect. He had a fiddle, a box of conjuring apparatus, a pair of foils and masks attached to his belt, several other mysterious cases dangling about him, and a black staff with copper ferrules in his hand. His companion was a rough spare dog, that followed at his heels, but stopped short, suspiciously at the drawbridge, and in a little while began to howl dismally.

In the meantime, the mountebank, standing in the midst of the courtyard, raised his grotesque hat, and made us a very ceremonious bow, paying his compliments very volubly in execrable French, and German not much better. Then, disengaging his fiddle, he began to scrape a lively air, to which he sang with a merry discord, dancing with ludicrous airs and activity, that made me laugh, in spite of the dog's howling.

Then he advanced to the window with many smiles and salutations, and his hat in his left hand, his fiddle under his arm, and with a fluency that never took breath, he gabbled a long advertisement of all his accomplishments, and the resources of the various arts which he placed at our service, and the cu-riosities and entertainments which it was in his power, at our bidding to display.

"Will your ladyships be pleased to buy an amulet against the oupire,[8] which is going like the wolf, I hear, through these woods," he said, dropping his hat on the pavement. "They are dying of it right and left, and here is a charm that never fails; only pinned to the pillow, and you may laugh in his face."

These charms consisted of oblong slips of vellum, with cabalistic ciphers and diagrams upon them.

Carmilla instantly purchased one, and so did I.

He was looking up, and we were smiling down upon him, amused; at least, I could answer for myself. His piercing black eye, as he looked up in our faces, seemed to detect something that fixed for a moment his curiosity.

In an instant he unrolled a leather case, full of all manner of odd little steel instruments.

"See here, my lady," he said, displaying it, and addressing me, "I profess, among other things less useful, the art of dentistry. Plague take the dog!" he interpolated. "Silence, beast! He howls so that your ladyships can scarcely hear a word. Your noble friend, the young lady at your right, has the sharpest tooth—long, thin, pointed, like an awl, like a needle; ha, ha![9] With my sharp and long sight, as I look up, I have seen it distinctly; now if it happens to hurt the young lady, and I think it must, here am I, here are

---

[6] A lighted device for entertainments; an early form of projector for pictures.

[7] Both legendary creatures, the salamander was supposed to be a fire elemental, the mandrake a homunculus or miniature figure.

[8] A vampire. This is the Russian form of the word (usually spelled *upir*).

[9] The hunchback observes, as the narrator does not, that Carmilla has fang-like teeth (or at least one such tooth).

my file, my punch, my nippers; I will make it round and blunt, if her ladyship pleases; no longer the tooth of a fish, but of a beautiful young lady as she is. Hey? Is the young lady displeased? Have I been too bold? Have I offended her?"

The young lady, indeed, looked very angry as she drew back from the window.

"How dares that mountebank insult us so? Where is your father? I shall demand redress from him. My father would have had the wretch tied up to the pump, and flogged with a cart-whip, and burnt to the bones with the castle brand!"

She retired from the window a step or two, and sat down, and had hardly lost sight of the offender, when her wrath subsided as suddenly as it had risen, and she gradually recovered her usual tone, and seemed to forget the little hunchback and his follies.

My father was out of spirits that evening. On coming in he told us that there had been another case very similar to the two fatal ones which had lately occurred. The sister of a young peasant on his estate, only a mile away, was very ill, had been, as she described it, attacked very nearly in the same way, and was now slowly but steadily sinking.

"All this," said my father, "is strictly referable to natural causes. These poor people infect one another with their superstitions, and so repeat in imagination the images of terror that have infested their neighbors."

"But that very circumstance frightens one horribly," said Carmilla.

"How so?" inquired my father.

"I am so afraid of fancying I see such things; I think it would be as bad as reality."

"We are in God's hands; nothing can happen without His permission, and all will end well for those who love Him. He is

our faithful creator; He has made us all, and will take care of us."

"Creator! *Nature!*" said the young lady in answer to my gentle father. "And this disease that invades the country is natural. Nature. All things proceed from Nature—don't they? All things in the heaven, in the earth, and under the earth, act and live as Nature ordains? I think so."

"The doctor said he would come here today," said my father, after a silence. "I want to know what he thinks about it, and what he thinks we had better do."

"Doctors never did me any good," said Carmilla.

"Then you have been ill?" I asked.

"More ill than ever you were," she answered.

"Long ago?"

"Yes, a long time. I suffered from this very illness; but I forget all but my pain and weakness, and they were not so bad as are suffered in other diseases."

"You were very young then?"

"I dare say; let us talk no more of it. You would not wound a friend?" She looked languidly in my eyes, and passed her arm round my waist lovingly, and led me out of the room. My father was busy over some papers near the window.

"Why does your papa like to frighten us?" said the pretty girl, with a sigh and a little shudder.

"He doesn't, dear Carmilla, it is the very furthest thing from his mind."

"Are you afraid, dearest?"

"I should be very much if I fancied there was any real danger of my being attacked as those poor people were."

"You are afraid to die?"

"Yes, everyone is."

"But to die as lovers may—to die together, so that they may live together. Girls are caterpillars while they live in the world, to be finally butterflies when the summer comes; but in the meantime there are grubs and larvae, don't you see—each with their peculiar propensities, necessities and structure. So says Monsieur Buffon, in his big book, in the next room."[10]

Later in the day the doctor came, and was closeted with Papa for some time. He was a skillful man, of sixty and upwards, he wore powder, and shaved his pale face smooth as a pumpkin. He and Papa emerged from the room together, and I heard Papa laugh, and say as they came out:—

"Well, I do wonder at a wise man like you. What do you say to hippogriffs and dragons?"

The doctor was smiling, and made answer, shaking his head:—

"Nevertheless, life and death are mysterious states, and we know little of the resources of either." And so they walked on, and I heard no more. I did not then know what the doctor had been broaching, but I think I guess it now.

CHAPTER V
A Wonderful Likeness

THIS EVENING there arrived from Gratz[11] the grave, dark-faced son of the picture-cleaner, with a horse and cart laden with two large packing-cases, having many pictures in each. It was a journey of ten leagues, and whenever a messenger arrived at the schloss from our little capital of Gratz, we used to crowd about him in the hall, to hear the news.

This arrival created in our secluded quarters quite a sensation. The cases remained in the hall, and the messenger was taken charge of by the servants till he had eaten his supper. Then with assistants, and armed with hammer, ripping chisel, and turnscrew, he met us in the hall, where we had assembled to witness the unpacking of the cases.

Carmilla sat looking listlessly on, while one after the other the old pictures, nearly all portraits, which had undergone the process of renovation, were brought to light. My mother was of an old Hungarian family, and most of these pictures, which were about to be restored to their places, had come to us through her.

My father had a list in his hand, from which he read, as the artist rummaged out the corresponding numbers. I don't know that the pictures were very good, but they were, undoubtedly, very old, and some of them very curious also. They had, for the most part, the merit of being now seen by me, I may say, for the first time; for the smoke and dust of time had all but obliterated them.

"There is a picture that I have not seen yet," said my father. "In one corner, at the top of it, is the name, as well as I could read, 'Marcia Karnstein,' and the date '1698'; and I am curious to see how it has turned out."

I remembered it; it was a small picture, about a foot and a half high, and nearly square, without a frame; but it was so blackened by age that I could not make it out.

The artist now produced it, with evident

---

[10] Georges-Louis LeClerc, Comte de Buffon (1707-1788), was the greatest naturalist of his time.

[11] Gratz, the capital of Styria, is also the place in which the Countess von Dollingen, another vampire, died (see Stoker's tale "Dracula's Guest," pp. 379, below).

pride. It was quite beautiful; it was startling; it seemed to live. It was the effigy of Carmilla!

"Carmilla, dear, here is an absolute miracle. Here you are, living, smiling, ready to speak, in this picture. Isn't it beautiful, Papa? And see, even the mole on her throat."

My father laughed, and said, "Certainly it is a wonderful likeness," but he looked away, and to my surprise seemed but little struck by it, and went on talking to the picture-cleaner, who was also something of an artist, and discoursed with intelligence about the portraits or other works, which his art had just brought into light and color, while *I* was more and more lost in wonder the more I looked at the picture.

"Will you let me hang this picture in my room, Papa?" I asked. "Certainly, dear," said he, smiling, "I'm very glad you think it so like. It must be prettier even than I thought it, if it is."

The young lady did not acknowledge this pretty speech, did not seem to hear it. She was leaning back in her seat, her fine eyes under their long lashes gazing on me in contemplation, and she smiled in a kind of rapture.

"And now you can read quite plainly the name that is written in the corner. It is not Marcia; it looks as if it was done in gold. The name is Mircalla, Countess Karnstein, and this is a little coronet over it, and underneath A.D. 1698. I am descended from the Karnsteins; that is, mamma was."

"Ah!" said the lady, languidly, "so am I, I think, a very long descent, very ancient. Are there any Karnsteins living now?"

"None who bear the name, I believe. The family was ruined, I believe, in some civil wars, long ago but the ruins of the castle are only about three miles away."

"How interesting!" she said, languidly. "But see what beautiful moonlight!" She glanced through the hall door, which stood a little open. "Suppose you take a little ramble round the court, and look down at the road and river."

"It is so like the night you came to us," I said.

She sighed, smiling.

She rose, and each with her arm about the other's waist, we walked out upon the pavement.

In silence, slowly we walked down to the drawbridge, where the beautiful landscape opened before us.

"And so you were thinking of the night I came here?" she almost whispered. "Are you glad I came?"

"Delighted, dear Carmilla," I answered.

"And you ask for a picture you think like me, to hang in your room," she murmured with a sigh, as she drew her arm closer about my waist, and let her pretty head sink upon my shoulder.

"How romantic you are, Carmilla," I said. "Whenever you tell me your story, it will be made up chiefly of some one great romance."

She kissed me silently.

"I am sure, Carmilla, you have been in love; that there is, at this moment, an affair of the heart going on."

"I have been in love with no one, and never shall," she whispered, "unless it should be you."

How beautiful she looked in the moonlight!

Shy and strange was the look with which she quickly hid her face in my neck and hair, with tumultuous sighs, that seemed almost to sob, and pressed in mine a hand that trembled.

Her soft cheek was glowing against mine. "Darling, darling," she murmured, "I live in you; and you would die for me, I love you so."

I started from her.

She was gazing on me with eyes from which all fire, all meaning had flown, and a face colorless and apathetic.

"Is there a chill in the air, dear?" she said drowsily. "I almost shiver; have I been dreaming? Let us come in. Come, come; come in."

"You look ill, Carmilla; a little faint. You certainly must take some wine," I said.

"Yes, I will. I'm better now. I shall be quite well in a few minutes. Yes, do give me a little wine," answered Carmilla, as we approached the door. "Let us look again for a moment; it is the last time, perhaps, I shall see the moonlight with you."

"How do you feel now, dear Carmilla? Are you really better?" I asked.

I was beginning to take alarm, lest she should have been stricken with the strange epidemic that they said had invaded the country about us.

"Papa would be grieved beyond measure," I added, "if he thought you were ever so little ill, without immediately letting us know. We have a very skillful doctor near this, the physician who was with Papa today."

"I'm sure he is. I know how kind you all are: but, dear child, I am quite well again. There is nothing ever wrong with me, but a little weakness. People say I am languid; I am incapable of exertion; I can scarcely walk as far as a child of three years old; and every now and then the little strength I have falters, and I become as you have just seen me. But after all I am very easily set up again; in a moment I am perfectly myself. See how I have recovered."

So, indeed, she had; and she and I talked a great deal, and very animated she was; and the remainder of that evening passed without any recurrence of what I called her infatuations. I mean her crazy talk and looks, which embarrassed, and even frightened me.

But there occurred that night an event which gave my thoughts quite a new turn, and seemed to startle even Carmilla's languid nature into momentary energy.

CHAPTER VI
A Very Strange Agony

WHEN WE GOT into the drawing-room, and had sat down to our coffee and chocolate, although Carmilla did not take any, she seemed quite herself again, and Madame, and Mademoiselle De Lafontaine, joined us, and made a little card party, in the course of which Papa came in for what he called his "dish of tea."

When the game was over he sat down beside Carmilla on the sofa, and asked her, a little anxiously, whether she had heard from her mother since her arrival.

She answered "No."

He then asked her whether she knew where a letter would reach her at present.

"I cannot tell," she answered, ambiguously, "but I have been thinking of leaving you; you have been already too hospitable and too kind to me. I have given you an infinity of trouble, and I should wish to take a carriage tomorrow, and post in pursuit of her; I know where I shall ultimately find her, although I dare not yet tell you."

"But you must not dream of such a thing," exclaimed my father, to my great relief. "We can't afford to lose you so, and I won't consent to your leaving us, except under the care of your mother, who was so good as to consent to your remaining with us till she should herself return. I should be quite happy if I knew that you heard from her; but this evening the accounts of the progress of the mysterious disease that has invaded our neighborhood, grow even more alarming; and my beautiful guest, I do feel the responsibility, unaided by advice from your mother, very much. But I shall do my best; and one thing is certain, that you must not think of leaving us without her distinct direction to that effect. We should suffer too much in parting from you to consent to it easily."

"Thank you, sir, a thousand times for your hospitality," she answered, smiling bashfully. "You have all been too kind to me; I have seldom been so happy in all my life before, as in your beautiful château, under your care, and in the society of your dear daughter."

So he gallantly, in his old-fashioned way, kissed her hand, smiling, and pleased at her little speech.

I accompanied Carmilla as usual to her room, and sat and chatted with her while she was preparing for bed.

"Do you think," I said, at length, "that you will ever confide fully in me?"

She turned around smiling, but made no answer, only continued to smile on me.

"You won't answer that?" I said. "You can't answer pleasantly; I ought not to have asked you."

"You were quite right to ask me that, or anything. You do not know how dear you are to me, or you could not think any confidence too great to look for. But I am under vows, no nun half so awfully, and I dare not tell my story yet, even to you. The time is very near when you shall know everything. You will think me cruel, very selfish, but love is always selfish; the more ardent the more selfish.

How jealous I am you cannot know. You must come with me, loving me, to death; or else hate me, and still come with me, and *hating* me through death and after. There is no such word as indifference in my apathetic nature."

"Now, Carmilla, you are going to talk your wild nonsense again," I said hastily.

"Not I, silly little fool as I am, and full of whims and fancies; for your sake I'll talk like a sage. Were you ever at a ball?"

"No; how you do run on. What is it like? How charming it must be."

"I almost forget, it is years ago."

I laughed.

"You are not so old. Your first ball can hardly be forgotten yet."

"I remember everything about it—with an effort. I see it all, as divers see what is going on above them, through a medium, dense, rippling, but transparent. There occurred that night what has confused the picture, and made its colors faint. I was all but assassinated in my bed, wounded *here*," she touched her breast, "and never was the same since."

"Were you near dying?"

"Yes, a very—cruel love—strange love, that would have taken my life. Love will have its sacrifices. No sacrifice without blood. Let us go to sleep now; I feel lazy. How can I get up just now and lock my door?"

She was lying with her tiny hands buried in her rich wavy hair, under her cheek, her little head upon the pillow, and her glittering eyes followed me wherever I moved, with a kind of shy smile that I could not decipher.

I bid her good-night, and crept from the room with an uncomfortable sensation.

I often wondered whether our pretty guest ever said her prayers. *I* certainly had never seen her upon her knees. In the morning she never came down until long after our family prayers were over, and at night she never left the drawing room to attend our brief evening prayers in the hall.

If it had not been that it had casually come out in one of our careless talks that she had been baptised, I should have doubted her being a Christian. Religion was a subject on which I had never heard her speak a word. If I had known of the world better, this particular neglect or antipathy would not have so much surprised me.

The precautions of nervous people are infectious, and persons of a like temperament are pretty sure, after a time, to imitate them. I had adopted Carmilla's habit of locking her bedroom door, having taken into my head all her whimsical alarms about midnight invaders, and prowling assassins. I had also adopted her precaution of making a brief search through her room, to satisfy herself that no lurking assassin or robber was "ensconced."

These wise measures taken, I got into my bed and fell asleep. A light was burning in my room. This was an old habit, of very early date, and which nothing could have tempted me to dispense with.

Thus fortified I might take my rest in peace. But dreams come through stone walls, light up dark rooms, or darken light ones, and their persons make their exits and their entrances as they please, and laugh at locksmiths.

I had a dream that night that was the beginning of a very strange agony.

I cannot call it a nightmare, for I was quite conscious of being asleep. But I was equally conscious of being in my room, and lying in bed, precisely as I actually was. I saw, or fancied I saw, the room and its furniture just as I had seen it last, except that it was very dark, and I saw something moving round the foot of the bed, which at first I could not accurately distinguish. But I soon saw that it was a sooty-black animal that resembled a monstrous cat.[12] It appeared to me about four or five feet long, for it measured fully the length of the hearth-rug as it passed over it; and it continued to-ing and fro-ing with the lithe sinister restlessness of a beast in a cage. I could not cry out, although as you may suppose, I was terrified. Its pace was growing faster, and the room rapidly darker and darker, and at length so dark that I could no longer see anything of it but its eyes. I felt it spring lightly on the bed. The two broad eyes approached my face, and suddenly I felt a stinging pain as if two large needles darted, an inch or two apart, deep into my breast. I waked with a scream. The room was lighted by the candle that burnt there all through the night, and I saw a female figure standing at the foot of the bed, a little at the right side. It was in a dark loose dress, and its hair was down and covered its shoulders. A block of stone could not have been more still. There was not the slightest stir of respiration. As I stared at it, the figure appeared to have changed its place, and was now nearer the door; then, close to it, the door opened, and it passed out.

I was now relieved, and able to breathe

---

[12] We will understand later that this is the vampire Carmilla in shape-shifted form. Dracula, it will be recalled, had the power to transform himself into the shape of a wolf or bat. The long connection between shape-shifters—were-bears, were-wolves, and other were-animals—and vampires is too convoluted to explore, but there is a great deal of overlapping mythology, and the dentition of vampires (including Carmilla) is markedly similar to that of werewolves.

and move. My first thought was that Carmilla had been playing me a trick, and that I had forgotten to secure my door. I hastened to it, and found it locked as usual on the inside. I was afraid to open it—I was horrified. I sprang into my bed and covered my head up in the bedclothes, and lay there more dead than alive till morning.

CHAPTER VII
Descending

IT WOULD BE vain my attempting to tell you the horror with which, even now, I recall the occurrence of that night. It was no such transitory terror as a dream leaves behind it. It seemed to deepen by time, and communicated itself to the room and the very furniture that had encompassed the apparition.

I could not bear the next day to be alone for a moment. I should have told Papa, but for two opposite reasons. At one time I thought he would laugh at my story, and I could not bear its being treated as a jest; and at another, I thought he might fancy that I had been attacked by the mysterious complaint which had invaded our neighborhood. I had myself no misgivings of the kind, and as he had been rather an invalid for some time, I was afraid of alarming him.

I was comfortable enough with my good-natured companions, Madame Perrodon, and the vivacious Mademoiselle Lafontaine. They both perceived that I was out of spirits and nervous, and at length I told them what lay so heavy at my heart.

Mademoiselle laughed, but I fancied that Madame Perrodon looked anxious. "By-the-by," said Mademoiselle, laughing, "the long lime tree walk, behind Carmilla's bedroom window, is haunted!"

"Nonsense!" exclaimed Madame, who probably thought the theme rather inopportune, "and who tells that story, my dear?"

"Martin says that he came up twice, when the old yard-gate was being repaired before sunrise, and twice saw the same female figure walking down the lime tree avenue."

"So he well might, as long as they have cows to milk in the river fields," said Madame.

"I daresay; but Martin chooses to be frightened, and never did I see fool *more* frightened."

"You must not say a word about it to Carmilla, because she can see down that walk from her room window," I interposed, "and she is, if possible, a greater coward than I."

Carmilla came down rather later than usual that day.

"I was so frightened last night," she said, as soon as we were together, "and I am sure I should have seen something dreadful if it had not been for that charm I bought from the poor little hunchback whom I called such hard names. I had a dream of something black coming round my bed, and I awoke in a perfect horror, and I really thought, for some seconds, I saw a dark figure near the chimney piece, but I felt under my pillow for my charm, and the moment my fingers touched it, the figure disappeared, and I felt quite certain, only that I had it by me, that something frightful would have made its appearance, and, perhaps, throttled me, as it did those poor people we heard of."

"Well, listen to me," I began, and recounted my adventure, at the recital of which she appeared horrified.

"And had you the charm near you?" she asked, earnestly.

"No, I had dropped it into a china vase in the drawing-room, but I shall certainly take it with me tonight, as you have so much faith in it."

At this distance of time I cannot tell you, or even understand, how I overcame my horror so effectually as to lie alone in my room that night. I remember distinctly that I pinned the charm to my pillow. I fell asleep almost immediately, and slept even more soundly than usual all night.

Next night I passed as well. My sleep was delightfully deep and dreamless. But I wakened with a sense of lassitude and melancholy, which, however, did not exceed a degree that was almost luxurious.

"Well, I told you so," said Carmilla, when I described my quiet sleep, "I had such delightful sleep myself last night; I pinned the charm to the breast of my nightdress. It was too far away the night before. I am quite sure it was all fancy, except the dreams. I used to think that evil spirits made dreams, but our doctor told me it is no such thing. Only a fever passing by, or some other malady, as they often do, he said, knocks at the door, and not being able to get in, passes on, with that alarm."

"And what do you think the charm is?" said I.

"It has been fumigated or immersed in some drug, and is an antidote against the malaria," she answered.

"Then it acts only on the body?"

"Certainly; you don't suppose that evil spirits are frightened by bits of ribbon, or the perfumes of a druggist's shop? No, these complaints, wandering in the air, begin by trying the nerves, and so infect the brain; but before they can seize upon you, the antidote repels them. That I am sure is what the charm has

done for us. It is nothing magical, it is simply natural."

I should have been happier if I could quite have agreed with Carmilla, but I did my best, and the impression was a little losing its force.

For some nights I slept profoundly; but still every morning I felt the same lassitude, and a languor weighed upon me all day. I felt myself a changed girl. A strange melancholy was stealing over me, a melancholy that I would not have interrupted. Dim thoughts of death began to open, and an idea that I was slowly sinking took gentle, and, somehow, not unwelcome possession of me. If it was sad, the tone of mind which this induced was also sweet. Whatever it might be, my soul acquiesced in it.

I would not admit that I was ill; I would not consent to tell my papa, or to have the doctor sent for.

Carmilla became more devoted to me than ever, and her strange paroxysms of languid adoration more frequent. She used to gloat on me with increasing ardor the more my strength and spirits waned. This always shocked me like a momentary glare of insanity.

Without knowing it, I was now in a pretty advanced stage of the strangest illness under which mortal ever suffered. There was an unaccountable fascination in its earlier symptoms that more than reconciled me to the incapacitating effect of that stage of the malady. This fascination increased for a time, until it reached a certain point, when gradually a sense of the horrible mingled itself with it, deepening, as you shall hear, until it discolored and perverted the whole state of my life.

The first change I experienced was

rather agreeable. It was very near the turning point from which began the descent of Avernus.[13]

Certain vague and strange sensations visited me in my sleep. The prevailing one was of that pleasant, peculiar cold thrill which we feel in bathing, when we move against the current of a river. This was soon accompanied by dreams that seemed interminable, and were so vague that I could never recollect their scenery and persons, or anyone connected portion of their action. But they left an awful impression, and a sense of exhaustion, as if I had passed through a long period of great mental exertion and danger. After all these dreams there remained on waking a remembrance of having been in a place very nearly dark, and of having spoken to people whom I could not see; and especially of one clear voice, of a female's, very deep, that spoke as if at a distance, slowly, and producing always the same sensation of indescribable solemnity and fear. Sometimes there came a sensation as if a hand was drawn softly along my cheek and neck. Sometimes it was as if warm lips kissed me, and longer and more lovingly as they reached my throat, but there the caress fixed itself. My heart beat faster, my breathing rose and fell rapidly and full drawn; a sobbing, that rose into a sense of strangulation, supervened, and turned into a dreadful convulsion, in which my senses left me, and I became unconscious.

It was now three weeks since the commencement of this unaccountable state. My sufferings had, during the last week, told upon my appearance. I had grown pale, my eyes were dilated and darkened underneath, and the languor which I had long felt began to display itself in my countenance.

My father asked me often whether I was ill; but, with an obstinacy which now seems to me unaccountable, I persisted in assuring him that I was quite well.

In a sense this was true. I had no pain, I could complain of no bodily derangement. My complaint seemed to be one of the imagination, or the nerves, and, horrible as my sufferings were, I kept them, with a morbid reserve, very nearly to myself.

It could not be that terrible complaint which the peasants call the oupire, for I had now been suffering for three weeks, and they were seldom ill for much more than three days, when death put an end to their miseries.

Carmilla complained of dreams and feverish sensations, but by no means of so alarming a kind as mine. I say that mine were extremely alarming. Had I been capable of comprehending my condition, I would have invoked aid and advice on my knees. The narcotic of an unsuspected influence was acting upon me, and my perceptions were benumbed.

I am going to tell you now of a dream that led immediately to an odd discovery.

One night, instead of the voice I was accustomed to hear in the dark, I heard one, sweet and tender, and at the same time terrible, which said, "Your mother warns you to beware of the assassin." At the same time a light unexpectedly sprang up, and I saw Carmilla, standing, near the foot of my bed, in her white nightdress, bathed, from her chin to her feet, in one great stain of blood.

I wakened with a shriek, possessed with

---

[13] A crater that, according to legend, leads to the underworld, as recounted by Virgil in *The Æneid*.

the one idea that Carmilla was being murdered. I remember springing from my bed, and my next recollection is that of standing on the lobby, crying for help.

Madame and Mademoiselle came scurrying out of their rooms in alarm; a lamp burned always on the lobby, and seeing me, they soon learned the cause of my terror.

I insisted on our knocking at Carmilla's door. Our knocking was unanswered. It soon became a pounding and an uproar. We shrieked her name, but all was vain.

We all grew frightened, for the door was locked. We hurried back, in panic, to my room. There we rang the bell long and furiously. If my father's room had been at that side of the house, we would have called him up at once to our aid. But, alas! He was quite out of hearing, and to reach him involved an excursion for which we none of us had courage.

Servants, however, soon came running up the stairs; I had got on my dressing-gown and slippers meanwhile, and my companions were already similarly furnished. Recognizing the voices of the servants on the lobby, we sallied out together; and having renewed, as fruitlessly, our summons at Carmilla's door, I ordered the men to force the lock. They did so, and we stood, holding our lights aloft, in the doorway, and so stared into the room.

We called her by name; but there was still no reply. We looked round the room. Everything was undisturbed. It was exactly in the state in which I left it on bidding her good night. But Carmilla was gone.

CHAPTER VIII
Search

AT SIGHT OF the room, perfectly undisturbed

except for our violent entrance, we began to cool a little, and soon recovered our senses sufficiently to dismiss the men. It had struck Mademoiselle that possibly Carmilla had been wakened by the uproar at her door, and in her first panic had jumped from her bed, and hid herself in a press, or behind a curtain, from which she could not, of course, emerge until the majordomo and his myrmidons[14] had withdrawn. We now recommenced our search, and began to call her by name again.

It was all to no purpose. Our perplexity and agitation increased. We examined the windows, but they were secured. I implored of Carmilla, if she had concealed herself, to play this cruel trick no longer—to come out, and to end our anxieties. It was all useless. I was by this time convinced that she was not in the room, nor in the dressing-room, the door of which was still locked on this side. She could not have passed it. I was utterly puzzled. Had Carmilla discovered one of those secret passages which the old housekeeper said were known to exist in the schloss, although the tradition of their exact situation had been lost? A little time would, no doubt, explain all—utterly perplexed as, for the present, we were.

It was past four o'clock, and I preferred passing the remaining hours of darkness in Madame's room. Daylight brought no solution of the difficulty.

The whole household, with my father at its head, was in a state of agitation next morning. Every part of the chateau was searched. The grounds were explored. Not a trace of the missing lady could be discovered. The stream was about to be dragged; my father was in distraction; what a tale to have to tell the poor

---

[14] That is, the chief steward and his male assistants.

girl's mother on her return. I, too, was almost beside myself, though my grief was quite of a different kind.

The morning was passed in alarm and excitement. It was now one o'clock, and still no tidings. I ran up to Carmilla's room, and found her standing at her dressing-table. I was astounded. I could not believe my eyes. She beckoned me to her with her pretty finger, in silence. Her face expressed extreme fear.

I ran to her in an ecstasy of joy; I kissed and embraced her again and again. I ran to the bell and rang it vehemently, to bring others to the spot, who might at once relieve my father's anxiety.

"Dear Carmilla, what has become of you all this time? We have been in agonies of anxiety about you," I exclaimed. "Where have you been? How did you come back?"

"Last night has been a night of wonders," she said.

"For mercy's sake, explain all you can."

"It was past two last night," she said, "when I went to sleep as usual in my bed, with my doors locked, that of the dressing-room, and that opening upon the gallery. My sleep was uninterrupted, and, so far as I know, dreamless; but I awoke just now on the sofa in the dressing-room there, and I found the door between the rooms open, and the other door forced. How could all this have happened without my being wakened? It must have been accompanied with a great deal of noise, and I am particularly easily wakened; and how could I have been carried out of my bed without my sleep having been interrupted, I whom the slightest stir startles?"

By this time, Madame, Mademoiselle, my father, and a number of the servants were in the room. Carmilla, was, of course, overwhelmed with inquiries, congratulations, and welcomes. She had but one story to tell, and seemed the least able of all the party to suggest any way of accounting for what had happened. My father took a turn up and down the room, thinking. I saw Carmilla's eye follow him for a moment with a sly, dark glance.

When my father had sent the servants away, Mademoiselle having gone in search of a little bottle of valerian and sal-volatile,[15] and there being no one in the room with Carmilla except my father, Madame, and myself, he came to her thoughtfully, took her hand very kindly, led her to the sofa, and sat down beside her.

"Will you forgive me, my dear, if I risk a conjecture, and ask a question?"

"Who can have a better right?" she said. "Ask what you please, and I will tell you everything. But my story is simply one of bewilderment and darkness. I know absolutely nothing. Put any question you please. But you know, of course, the limitations Mamma has placed me under."

"Perfectly, my dear child. I need not approach the topics on which she desires our silence. Now, the marvel of last night consists in your having been removed from your bed and your room without being wakened, and this removal having occurred apparently while the windows were still secured, and the two doors locked upon the inside. I will tell you my theory, and first ask you a question."

Carmilla was leaning on her hand dejectedly; Madame and I were listening. breathlessly.

"Now, my question is this. Have you ever

---

[15] A homemade remedy, part sedative, part tonic.

been suspected of walking in your sleep?"[16]

"Never since I was very young indeed."

"But you did walk in your sleep when you were very young?"

"Yes; I know I did. I have been told so often by my old nurse."

My father smiled and nodded.

"Well, what has happened is this. You got up in your sleep, unlocked the door, not leaving the key, as usual, in the lock, but taking it out and locking it on the outside; you again took the key out, and carried it away with you to some one of the five-and-twenty rooms on this floor, or perhaps upstairs or downstairs. There are so many rooms and closets, so much heavy furniture, and such accumulations of lumber, that it would require a week to search this old house thoroughly. Do you see, now, what I mean?"

"I do, but not all," she answered.

"And how, Papa, do you account for her finding herself on the sofa in the dressing-room, which we had searched so carefully?"

"She came there after you had searched it, still in her sleep, and at last awoke spontaneously, and was as much surprised to find herself where she was as anyone else. I wish all mysteries were as easily and innocently explained as yours, Carmilla," he said, laughing. "And so we may congratulate ourselves on the certainty that the most natural explanation of the occurrence is one that involves no drugging, no tampering with locks, no burglars, or poisoners, or witches—nothing that need alarm Carmilla, or anyone else, for our safety."

Carmilla was looking charmingly. Nothing could be more beautiful than her tints.

Her beauty was, I think, enhanced by that graceful languor that was peculiar to her. I think my father was silently contrasting her looks with mine, for he said:—

"I wish my poor Laura was looking more like herself"; and he sighed.

So our alarms were happily ended, and Carmilla restored to her friends.

CHAPTER IX
The Doctor

AS CARMILLA would not hear of an attendant sleeping in her room, my father arranged that a servant should sleep outside her door, so that she could not attempt to make another such excursion without being arrested at her own door.

That night passed quickly; and next morning early, the doctor, whom my father had sent for without telling me a word about it, arrived to see me.

Madame accompanied me to the library; and there the grave little doctor, with white hair and spectacles, whom I mentioned before, was waiting to receive me.

I told him my story, and as I proceeded he grew graver and graver.

We were standing, he and I, in the recess of one of the windows, facing one another. When my statement was over, he leaned with his shoulders against the wall, and with his eyes fixed on me earnestly, with an interest in which was a dash of horror.

After a minute's reflection, he asked Madame if he could see my father.

He was sent for accordingly, and as he entered, smiling, he said:—

---

[16] Sleep-walking or somnambulism features prominently in *Dracula* as well; Lucy Westenra and her father both suffered from it. Romantic writers saw the sleepwalker as caught between heaven and earth, suspended between dreams and reality, similar to the perceived effects of mesmeric attraction and animal magnetism.

"I dare say, doctor, you are going to tell me that I am an old fool for having brought you here; I hope I am."

But his smile faded into shadow as the doctor, with a very grave face, beckoned him to him.

He and the doctor talked for some time in the same recess where I had just conferred with the physician. It seemed an earnest and argumentative conversation. The room is very large, and I and Madame stood together, burning with curiosity, at the further end. Not a word could we hear, however, for they spoke in a very low tone, and the deep recess of the window quite concealed the doctor from view, and very nearly my father, whose foot, arm, and shoulder only could we see: and the voices were, I suppose, all the less audible for the sort of closet which the thick wall and window formed.

After a time my father's face looked into the room; it was pale, thoughtful, and, I fancied, agitated.

"Laura, dear, come here for a moment. Madame, we shan't trouble you, the doctor says, at present."

Accordingly I approached, for the first time a little alarmed; for, although I felt very weak, I did not feel ill; and strength, one always fancies, is a thing that may be picked up when we please.

My father held out his hand to me as I drew near, but he was looking at the doctor, and he said:

"It certainly *is* very odd; I don't understand it quite. Laura, come here, dear; now attend to Doctor Spielsberg, and recollect yourself."

"You mentioned a sensation like that of two needles piercing the skin; somewhere about your neck, on the night when you ex-perienced your first horrible dream. Is there still any soreness?"

"None at all," I answered.

"Can you indicate with your finger about the point at which you think this occurred?"

"Very little below my throat—*here*," I answered.

I wore a morning dress, which covered the place I pointed to.

"Now you can satisfy yourself," said the doctor. "You won't mind your papa's lowering your dress a very little. It is necessary, to detect a symptom of the complaint under which you have been suffering."

I acquiesced. It was only an inch or two below the edge of my collar.

"God bless me!—so it is," exclaimed my father, growing pale.

"You see it now with your own eyes," said the doctor, with a gloomy triumph.

"What is it?" I exclaimed, beginning to be frightened.

"Nothing, my dear young lady, but a small blue spot, about the size of the tip of your little finger; and now," he continued, turning to Papa, "the question is what is the best to be done?"

"Is there any danger?" I urged, in great trepidation.

"I trust not, my dear," answered the doctor. "I don't see why you should not recover. I don't see why you should not begin *immediately* to get better. That is the point at which the sense of strangulation begins?"

"Yes," I answered.

"And—recollect as well as you can—the same point was a kind of centre of that thrill which you described just now like the current of a cold stream running against you?"

"It may have been; I think it was."

"Ay, you see?" he added, turning to

my father. "Shall I say a word to Madame?"

"Certainly," said my father.

He called Madame to him, and said:

"I find my young friend here far from well. It won't be of any great consequence, I hope; but it will be necessary that some steps be taken, which I will explain by-and-by; but in the meantime, Madame, you will be so good as not to let Miss Laura be alone for one moment. That is the only direction I need give for the present. It is indispensable."

"We may rely upon your kindness, Madame, I know," added my father.

Madame satisfied him eagerly.

"And you, dear Laura, I know you will observe the doctor's direction."

"I shall have to ask your opinion upon another patient, whose symptoms slightly resemble those of my daughter, that have just been detailed to you—very much milder in degree, but I believe quite of the same sort. She is a young lady—our guest; but as you say you will be passing this way again this evening, you can't do better than take your supper here, and you can then see her. She does not come down till the afternoon."

"I thank you," said the doctor. "I shall be with you, then, at about seven this evening."

And then they repeated their directions to me and to Madame, and with this parting charge my father left us, and walked out with the doctor; and I saw them pacing together up and down between the road and the moat, on the grassy platform in front of the castle, evidently absorbed in earnest conversation.

The doctor did not return. I saw him mount his horse there, take his leave, and ride away eastward through the forest. Nearly at the same time I saw the man arrive from Dranfeld[17] with the letters, and dismount and hand the bag to my father.

In the meantime, Madame and I were both busy, lost in conjecture as to the reasons of the singular and earnest direction which the doctor and my father had concurred in imposing. Madame, as she afterwards told me, was afraid the doctor apprehended a sudden seizure, and that, without prompt assistance, I might either lose my life in a fit, or at least be seriously hurt.

This interpretation did not strike me; and I fancied, perhaps luckily for my nerves, that the arrangement was prescribed simply to secure a companion, who would prevent my taking too much exercise, or eating unripe fruit, or doing any of the fifty foolish things to which young people are supposed to be prone.

About half-an-hour after my father came in—he had a letter in his hand—and said:—

"This letter has been delayed; it is from General Spielsdorf. He might have been here yesterday, he may not come till tomorrow, or he may be here today."

He put the open letter into my hand; but he did not look pleased, as he used to when a guest, especially one so much loved as the General, was coming. On the contrary, he looked as if he wished him at the bottom of the Red Sea. There was plainly something on his mind which he did not choose to divulge.

"Papa, darling, will you tell me this?" said I, suddenly laying my hand on his arm, and looking, I am sure, imploringly in his face.

"Perhaps," he answered, smoothing my hair caressingly over my eyes.

[17] A fictitious location. There is a Dransfeld, in Germany, about 500 miles distant.

"Does the doctor think me very ill?"

"No, dear; he thinks, if right steps are taken, you will be quite well again, at least on the high road to a complete recovery, in a day or two," he answered, a little drily. "I wish our good friend, the General, had chosen any other time; that is, I wish you had been perfectly well to receive him."

"But do tell me, Papa," I insisted, "*what* does he think is the matter with me?"

"Nothing; you must not plague me with questions," he answered, with more irritation than I ever remember him to have displayed before; and seeing that I looked wounded, I suppose, he kissed me, and added, "You shall know all about it in a day or two; that is, all that *I* know. In the meantime, you are not to trouble your head about it."

He turned and left the room, but came back before I had done wondering and puzzling over the oddity of all this; it was merely to say that he was going to Karnstein, and had ordered the carriage to be ready at twelve, and that I and Madame should accompany him; he was going to see the priest who lived near those picturesque grounds, upon business, and as Carmilla had never seen them, she could follow, when she came down, with Mademoiselle, who would bring materials for what you call a picnic, which might be laid for us in the ruined castle.

At twelve o'clock, accordingly, I was ready, and not long after, my father, Madame and I set out upon our projected drive. Passing the drawbridge we turn to the right, and follow the road over the steep Gothic bridge, westward, to reach the deserted village and ruined castle of Karnstein.

No sylvan drive can be fancied prettier.

The ground breaks into gentle hills and hollows, all clothed with beautiful wood, totally destitute of the comparative formality which artificial planting and early culture and pruning impart.

The irregularities of the ground often lead the road out of its course, and cause it to wind beautifully round the sides of broken hollows and the steeper sides of the hills, among varieties of ground almost inexhaustible.

Turning one of these points, we suddenly encountered our old friend, the General, riding towards us, attended by a mounted servant. His portmanteaus[18] were following in a hired *waggon*, such as we term a cart.

The General dismounted as we pulled up, and, after the usual greetings, was easily persuaded to accept the vacant seat in the carriage, and send his horse on with his servant to the schloss.

CHAPTER X
Bereaved

IT WAS ABOUT ten months since we had last seen him; but that time had sufficed to make an alteration of years in his appearance. He had grown thinner; something of gloom and anxiety had taken the place of that cordial serenity which used to characterize his features. His dark blue eyes, always penetrating, now gleamed with a sterner light from under his shaggy grey eyebrows. It was not such a change as grief alone usually induces, and angrier passions seemed to have had their share in bringing it about.

We had not long resumed our drive, when the General began to talk, with his

---

[18] A traveling bag or case, especially a leather trunk or suitcase that opens into two halves.

usual soldierly directness, of the bereavement, as he termed it, which he had sustained in the death of his beloved niece and ward; and he then broke out in a tone of intense bitterness and fury, inveighing against the "hellish arts" to which she had fallen a victim, and expressing with more exasperation than piety, his wonder that Heaven should tolerate so monstrous an indulgence of the lusts and malignity of hell.

My father, who saw at once that something very extraordinary had befallen, asked him, if not too painful to him, to detail the circumstances which he thought justified the strong terms in which he expressed himself.

"I should tell you all with pleasure," said the General, "but you would not believe me."

"Why should I not?" he asked.

"Because," he answered testily, "you believe in nothing but what consists with your own prejudices and illusions. I remember when I was like you, but I have learned better."

"Try me," said my father; "I am not such a dogmatist as you suppose. Besides which, I very well know that you generally require proof for what you believe and am, therefore, very strongly predisposed to respect your conclusions."

"You are right in supposing that I have not been led lightly into a belief in the marvelous—for what I have experienced *is* marvelous—and I have been forced by extraordinary evidence to credit that which ran counter, diametrically, to all my theories. I have been made the dupe of a preternatural conspiracy."

Notwithstanding his profession of confidence in the General's penetration, I saw my father, at this point, glance at the General, with, as I thought, a marked suspicion of his sanity.

The General did not see it, luckily. He was looking gloomily and curiously into the glades and vistas of the woods that were opening before us.

"You are going to the Ruins of Karnstein?" he said. "Yes, it is a lucky coincidence; do you know I was going to ask you to bring me there to inspect them. I have a special object in exploring. There is a ruined chapel, ain't there, with a great many tombs of that extinct family?"

"So there are—highly interesting," said my father, "I hope you are thinking of claiming the title and estates?"

My father said this gaily, but the General did not recollect the laugh, or even smile, which courtesy exacts for a friend's joke; on the contrary, he looked grave and even fierce, ruminating on a matter that stirred his anger and horror.

"Something very different," he said, gruffly. "I mean to unearth some of those fine people. I hope by God's blessing, to accomplish a pious sacrilege here, which will relieve our earth of certain monsters, and enable honest people to sleep in their beds without being assailed by murderers. I have strange things to tell you, my dear friend, such as I myself would have scouted[19] as incredible a few months since."

My father looked at him again, but this time not with a glance of suspicion—with an eye, rather, of keen intelligence and alarm.

"The house of Karnstein," he said, "has been long extinct: a hundred years at least. My dear wife was maternally descended from the Karnsteins. But the name and title have long

[19] Mocked.

ceased to exist. The castle is a ruin; the very village is deserted; it is fifty years since the smoke of a chimney was seen there; not a roof left."

"Quite true. I have heard a great deal about that since I last saw you; a great deal that will astonish you. But I had better relate everything in the order in which it occurred," said the General. "You saw my dear ward—my child, I may call her. No creature could have been more beautiful, and only three months ago none more blooming."

"Yes, poor thing! When I saw her last she certainly was quite lovely," said my father. "I was grieved and shocked more than I can tell you, my dear friend; I knew what a blow it was to you."

He took the General's hand, and they exchanged a kind pressure. Tears gathered in the old soldier's eyes. He did not seek to conceal them. He said:

"We have been very old friends; I knew you would feel for me, childless as I am. She had become an object of very dear interest to me, and repaid my care by an affection that cheered my home and made my life happy. That is all gone. The years that remain to me on earth may not be very long; but by God's mercy I hope to accomplish a service to mankind before I die, and to subserve[20] the vengeance of Heaven upon the fiends who have murdered my poor child in the spring of her hopes and beauty!"

"You said, just now, that you intended relating everything as it occurred," said my father. "Pray do; I assure you that it is not mere curiosity that prompts me."

By this time we had reached the point at

which the Drunstall road, by which the General had come, diverges from the road which we were travelling to Karnstein.

"How far is it to the ruins?" inquired the General, looking anxiously forward. "About half a league," answered my father. "Pray let us hear the story you were so good as to promise."

CHAPTER XI
The Story

"WITH ALL MY heart," said the General, with an effort; and after a pause in which to arrange his subject, he commenced one of the strangest narratives I ever heard.

"My dear child was looking forward with great pleasure to the visit you had been so good as to arrange for her to your charming daughter." Here he made me a gallant but melancholy bow. "In the meantime we had an invitation to my old friend the Count Carlsfeld, whose schloss is about six leagues to the other side of Karnstein. It was to attend the series of fêtes which, you remember, were given by him in honor of his illustrious visitor, the Grand Duke Charles."

"Yes; and very splendid, I believe they were," said my father.

"Princely! But then his hospitalities are quite regal. He has Aladdin's lamp.[21] The night from which my sorrow dates was devoted to a magnificent masquerade. The grounds were thrown open, the trees hung with colored lamps. There was such a display of fireworks as Paris itself had never witnessed. And such music—music, you know, is my weakness—such ravishing music! The finest instrumental band, perhaps, in the world, and the finest singers who could be collected from all the great operas in Europe. As you

---

[20] Promote, further.
[21] Proverbially, the source of good fortune.

wandered through those fantastically illuminated grounds, the moon-lighted chateau throwing a rosy light from its long rows of windows, you would suddenly hear these ravishing voices stealing from the silence of some grove, or rising from boats upon the lake. I felt myself, as I looked and listened, carried back into the romance and poetry of my early youth.

"When the fireworks were ended, and the ball beginning, we returned to the noble suite of rooms that were thrown open to the dancers. A masked ball, you know, is a beautiful sight; but so brilliant a spectacle of the kind I never saw before.

"It was a very aristocratic assembly. I saw myself almost the only 'nobody' present.

"My dear child was looking quite beautiful. She wore no mask. Her excitement and delight added an unspeakable charm to her features, always lovely. I remarked a young lady, dressed magnificently, but wearing a mask, who appeared to me to be observing my ward with extraordinary interest. I had seen her, earlier in the evening, in the great hall, and again, for a few minutes, walking near us, on the terrace under the castle windows, similarly employed. A lady, also masked, richly and gravely dressed, and with stately air, like a person of rank, accompanied her as a chaperon. Had the young lady not worn a mask, I could of course, have been much more certain upon the question whether she was really watching my poor darling. I am now well assured that she was.

"We were in one of the *salons*. My poor dear child had been dancing, and was resting a little in one of the chairs near the door; I was standing near. The two ladies I have mentioned had approached, and the younger took the chair next my ward; while her companion stood beside me, and for a little time addressed herself, in a low tone, to her charge.

"Availing herself of the privilege of her mask, she turned to me, and in the tone of an old friend, and calling me by my name, opened a conversation with me, which piqued my curiosity a good deal. She referred to many scenes where she had met me—at Court, and at distinguished houses. She alluded to little incidents which I had long ceased to think of, but which, I found, had only lain in abeyance in my memory, for they instantly started into life at her touch.

"I became more and more curious to ascertain who she was, every moment. She parried my attempts to discover very adroitly and pleasantly. The knowledge she showed of many passages in my life seemed to me all but unaccountable; and she appeared to take a not unnatural pleasure in foiling my curiosity, and in seeing me flounder, in my eager perplexity, from one conjecture to another.

"In the meantime the young lady, whom her mother called by the odd name of Millarca, when she once or twice addressed her, had, with the same ease and grace, got into conversation with my ward.

"She introduced herself by saying that her mother was a very old acquaintance of mine. She spoke of the agreeable audacity which a mask rendered practicable; she talked like a friend; she admired her dress, and insinuated very prettily her admiration of her beauty. She amused her with laughing criticisms upon the people who crowded the ballroom, and laughed at my poor child's fun. She was very witty and lively when she pleased, and after a time they had grown very good friends, and the young stranger lowered her mask, displaying a remarkably beautiful face. I had never seen it before, neither had my dear child. But though it was new to us, the features were so engaging, as well as lovely, that it was impossible not to feel the attraction powerfully. My poor girl did so. I never saw anyone more taken with another at first sight, unless, indeed, it was the stranger herself, who seemed quite to have lost her heart to her.

"In the meantime, availing myself of the license of a masquerade, I put not a few questions to the elder lady.

" 'You have puzzled me utterly,' I said, laughing. 'Is that not enough? Won't you, now, consent to stand on equal terms, and do me the kindness to remove your mask?'

" 'Can any request be more unreasonable?' she replied. 'Ask a lady to yield an advantage! Beside, how do you know you should recognize me? Years make changes.'

" 'As you see,' I said, with a bow, and, I suppose, a rather melancholy little laugh.

" 'As philosophers tell us,' she said; 'and how do you know that a sight of my face would help you?'

" 'I should take chance for that,' I answered. 'It is vain trying to make yourself out an old woman; your figure betrays you.'

" 'Years, nevertheless, have passed since I saw you, rather since you saw me, for that is what I am considering. Millarca, there, is my daughter; I cannot then be young, even in the opinion of people whom time has taught to be indulgent, and I may not like to be compared with what you remember me. You have no mask to remove. You can offer me nothing in exchange.'

" 'My petition is to your pity, to remove it.'

" 'And mine to yours, to let it stay where it is,' she replied.

" 'Well, then, at least you will tell me whether you are French or German; you speak both languages so perfectly.' "

" 'I don't think I shall tell you that, General; you intend a surprise, and are meditating the particular point of attack.'

" 'At all events, you won't deny this,' I said, 'that being honored by your permission to converse, I ought to know how to address you. Shall I say Madame la Comtesse?'

"She laughed, and she would, no doubt, have met me with another evasion—if, indeed, I can treat any occurrence in an interview every circumstance of which was pre-arranged, as I now believe, with the profoundest cunning, as liable to be modified by accident.

" 'As to that,' she began; but she was interrupted, almost as she opened her lips, by a gentleman, dressed in black, who looked particularly elegant and distinguished, with this drawback, that his face was the most deadly pale I ever saw, except in death. He was in no masquerade—in the plain evening dress of a gentleman; and he said, without a smile, but with a courtly and unusually low bow:—

" 'Will Madame la Comtesse permit me to say a very few words which may interest her?'

"The lady turned quickly to him, and touched her lip in token of silence; she then said to me, 'Keep my place for me, General; I shall return when I have said a few words.'

"And with this injunction, playfully given, she walked a little aside with the gentleman in black, and talked for some minutes, apparently very earnestly. They then walked away slowly together in the crowd, and I lost them for some minutes.

"I spent the interval in cudgeling my brains for conjecture as to the identity of the lady who seemed to remember me so kindly, and I was thinking of turning about and joining in the conversation between my pretty ward and the Countess's daughter, and trying whether, by the time she returned, I might not have a surprise in store for her, by having her name, title, chateau, and estates at my fingers' ends. But at this moment she returned, accompanied by the pale man in black, who said:—

" 'I shall return and inform Madame la Comtesse when her carriage is at the door.'

"He withdrew with a bow."

CHAPTER XII
A Petition

" 'THEN WE ARE to lose Madame la Comtesse, but I hope only for a few hours,' I said, with a low bow.

" 'It may be that only, or it may be a few weeks. It was very unlucky his speaking to me just now as he did. Do you now know me?'

"I assured her I did not.

" 'You shall know me,' she said, 'but not at present. We are older and better friends than, perhaps, you suspect. I cannot yet declare myself. I shall in three weeks pass your beautiful schloss about which I have been making enquiries. I shall then look in upon you for an hour or two, and renew a friendship which I never think of without a thousand pleasant recollections. This moment a piece of news has reached me like a thunderbolt. I must set out now, and travel by a devious route, nearly a hundred miles, with all the dispatch I can possibly make. My perplexities multiply. I am only deterred by the compulsory reserve I practice as to my name from making a very singular request of you. My poor child has not quite recovered her

strength. Her horse fell with her, at a hunt which she had ridden out to witness, her nerves have not yet recovered the shock, and our physician says that she must on no account exert herself for some time to come. We came here, in consequence, by very easy stages—hardly six leagues a day. I must now travel day and night, on a mission of life and death—a mission the critical and momentous nature of which I shall be able to explain to you when we meet, as I hope we shall, in a few weeks, without the necessity of any concealment.'

"She went on to make her petition, and it was in the tone of a person from whom such a request amounted to conferring, rather than seeking a favor. This was only in manner, and, as it seemed, quite unconsciously. Then the terms in which it was expressed, nothing could be more deprecatory. It was simply that I would consent to take charge of her daughter during her absence.

"This was, all things considered, a strange, not to say, an audacious request. She in some sort disarmed me, by stating and admitting everything that could be urged against it, and throwing herself entirely upon my chivalry. At the same moment, by a fatality that seems to have predetermined all that happened, my poor child came to my side, and, in an undertone, besought me to invite her new friend, Millarca, to pay us a visit. She had just been sounding her, and thought, if her mamma would allow her, she would like it extremely.

"At another time I should have told her to wait a little, until, at least, we knew who they were. But I had not a moment to think in. The two ladies assailed me together; and I must confess the refined and beautiful face of the young lady, about which there was something extremely engaging, as well as the elegance and fire of high birth, determined me; and quite overpowered, I submitted, and undertook, too easily, the care of the young lady, whom her mother called Millarca.

"The Countess beckoned to her daughter, who listened with grave attention while she told her, in general terms, how suddenly and peremptorily she had been summoned, and also of the arrangement she had made for her under my care, adding that I was one of her earliest and most valued friends.

"I made, of course, such speeches as the case seemed to call for, and found myself, on reflection, in a position which I did not half like.

"The gentleman in black returned, and very ceremoniously conducted the lady from the room.

"The demeanor of this gentleman was such as to impress me with the conviction that the Countess was a lady of very much more importance than her modest title alone might have led me to assume.

"Her last charge to me was that no attempt was to be made to learn more about her than I might have already guessed, until her return. Our distinguished host, whose guest she was, knew her reasons.

" 'But here,' she said, 'neither I nor my daughter could safely remain more than a day. I removed my mask imprudently for a moment, about an hour ago, and, too late, I fancied you saw me. So I have resolved to seek an opportunity of talking a little to you. Had I found that you *had* seen me, I should have thrown myself on your high sense of honor to keep my secret for some weeks. As it is, I am satisfied that you did not see me; but if you now *suspect,* or, on reflection, *should* suspect, who I am, I commit myself, in like manner,

entirely to your honor. My daughter will observe the same secrecy, and I well know that you will, from time to time, remind her, lest she should thoughtlessly disclose it.'

"She whispered a few words to her daughter, kissed her hurriedly twice, and went away, accompanied by the pale gentleman in black, and disappeared in the crowd.

" 'In the next room,' said Millarca, 'there is a window that looks upon the hall door. I should like to see the last of mamma, and to kiss my hand to her.'

"We assented, of course, and accompanied her to the window. We looked out, and saw a handsome old-fashioned carriage, with a troop of couriers and footmen. We saw the slim figure of the pale gentleman in black, as he held a thick velvet cloak, and placed it about her shoulders and threw the hood over her head. She nodded to him, and just touched his hand with hers. He bowed low repeatedly as the door closed, and the carriage began to move.

" 'She is gone,' said Millarca with a sigh.

" 'She is gone,' I repeated to myself, for the first time—in the hurried moments that had elapsed since my consent—reflecting upon the folly of my act.

" 'She did not look up,' said the young lady, plaintively.

" 'The Countess had taken off her mask, perhaps, and did not care to show her face,' I said; 'and she could not know that you were in the window.'

"She sighed and looked in my face. She was so beautiful that I relented. I was sorry I had for a moment repented of my hospitality, and I determined to make her amends for the unavowed churlishness of my reception.

"The young lady, replacing her mask, joined my ward in persuading me to return to the grounds, where the concert was soon to be renewed. We did so, and walked up and down the terrace that lies under the castle windows. Millarca became very intimate with us, and amused us with lively descriptions and stories of most of the great people whom we saw upon the terrace. I liked her more and more every minute. Her gossip, without being ill-natured, was extremely diverting to me, who had been so long out of the great world. I thought what life she would give to our sometimes lonely evenings at home.

"This ball was not over until the morning sun had almost reached the horizon. It pleased the Grand Duke to dance till then, so loyal people could not go away, or think of bed.

"We had just got through a crowded salon, when my ward asked me what had become of Millarca. I thought she had been by her side, and she fancied she was by mine. The fact was, we had lost her.

"All my efforts to find her were in vain. I feared that she had mistaken, in the confusion of the momentary separation from us, other people for her new friends, and had, possibly, pursued and lost them in the extensive grounds which were thrown open to us.

"Now, in its full force, I recognized a new folly in my having undertaken the charge of a young lady without so much as knowing her name; and fettered as I was by promises, of the reasons for imposing which I knew nothing, I could not even point my inquiries by saying that the missing young lady was the daughter of the Countess who had taken her departure a few hours before.

"Morning broke. It was clear daylight before I gave up my search. It was not till near two o'clock next day that we heard anything of my missing charge.

"At about that time a servant knocked at my niece's door, to say that he had been earnestly requested by a young lady, who appeared to be in great distress, to make out where she could find the General Baron Spielsdorf and the young lady, his daughter, in whose charge she had been left by her mother.

"There could be no doubt, notwithstanding the slight inaccuracy, that our young friend had turned up; and so she had. Would to Heaven we had lost her!

"She told my poor child a story to account for her having failed to recover us for so long. Very late, she said, she had got into the housekeeper's bedroom in despair of finding us, and had then fallen into a deep sleep which, long as it was, had hardly sufficed to recruit her strength after the fatigues of the ball.

"That day Millarca came home with us. I was only too happy, after all, to have secured so charming a companion for my dear girl.

CHAPTER XIII
The Wood-Man

"THERE SOON, however, appeared some drawbacks. In the first place, Millarca complained of extreme languor—the weakness that remained after her late illness—and she never emerged from her room till the afternoon was pretty far advanced. In the next place, it was accidentally discovered, although she always locked her door on the inside, and never disturbed the key from its place, till she admitted the maid to assist at her toilet, that she was undoubtedly sometimes absent from her room in the very early morning, and at various times later in the day, before she wished it to be understood that she was stirring. She was repeatedly seen from the windows of the schloss, in the first faint grey of the morning, walking through the trees, in an easterly direction, and looking like a person in a trance. This convinced me that she walked in her sleep. But this hypothesis did not solve the puzzle. How did she pass out from her room, leaving the door locked on the inside. How did she escape from the house without unbarring door or window?

"In the midst of my perplexities, an anxiety of far more urgent kind presented itself.

"My dear child began to lose her looks and health, and that in a manner so mysterious, and even horrible, that I became thoroughly frightened.

"She was at first visited by appalling dreams; then, as she fancied, by a spectre, sometimes resembling Millarca, sometimes in the shape of a beast, indistinctly seen, walking round the foot of her bed, from side to side. Lastly came sensations. One, not unpleasant, but very peculiar, she said, resembled the flow of an icy stream against her breast. At a later time, she felt something like a pair of large needles pierce her, a little below the throat, with a very sharp pain. A few nights after, followed a gradual and convulsive sense of strangulation; then came unconsciousness."

I could hear distinctly every word the kind old General was saying, because by this time we were driving upon the short grass that spreads on either side of the road as you approach the roofless village which had not shown the smoke of a chimney for more than half a century.

You may guess how strangely I felt as I heard my own symptoms so exactly described

in those which had been experienced by the poor girl who, but for the catastrophe which followed, would have been at that moment a visitor at my father's chateau. You may suppose, also, how I felt as I heard him detail habits and mysterious peculiarities which were, in fact, those of our beautiful guest, Carmilla!

A vista opened in the forest; we were on a sudden under the chimneys and gables of the ruined village, and the towers and battlements of the dismantled castle, round which gigantic trees are grouped, overhung us from a slight eminence.

In a frightened dream I got down from the carriage, and in silence, for we had each abundant matter for thinking; we soon mounted the ascent, and were among the spacious chambers, winding stairs, and dark corridors of the castle.

"And this was once the palatial residence of the Karnsteins!" said the old General at length, as from a great window he looked out across the village, and saw the wide, undulating expanse of forest. "It was a bad family, and here its blood-stained annals were written," he continued. "It is hard that they should, after death, continue to plague the human race with their atrocious lusts. That is the chapel of the Karnsteins, down there."

He pointed down to the grey walls of the Gothic building, partly visible through the foliage, a little way down the steep. "And I hear the axe of a wood-man," he added, "busy among the trees that surround it; he possibly may give us the information of which I am in search, and point out the grave of Mircalla, Countess of Karnstein. These rustics preserve the local traditions of great families, whose stories die out among the rich and titled so soon as the families themselves become extinct."

"We have a portrait, at home, of Mircalla, the Countess Karnstein; should you like to see it?" asked my father.

"Time enough," dear friend, replied the General. "I believe that I have seen the original; and one motive which has led me to you earlier than I at first intended, was to explore the chapel which we are now approaching."

"What! See the Countess Mircalla," exclaimed my father; "why, she has been dead more than a century!"

"Not so dead as you fancy, I am told," answered the General.

"I confess, General, you puzzle me utterly," replied my father, looking at him, I fancied, for a moment with a return of the suspicion I detected before. But although there was anger and detestation, at times, in the old General's manner, there was nothing flighty.

"There remains to me," he said, as we passed under the heavy arch of the Gothic church—for its dimensions would have justified its being so styled—"but one object which can interest me during the few years that remain to me on earth, and that is to wreak on her the vengeance which, I thank God, may still be accomplished by a mortal arm."

"What vengeance can you mean?" asked my father, in increasing amazement.

"I mean, to decapitate the monster," he answered, with a fierce flush, and a stamp that echoed mournfully through the hollow ruin, and his clenched hand was at the same moment raised, as if it grasped the handle of an axe, while he shook it ferociously in the air.

"What!" exclaimed my father, more than ever bewildered.

"To strike her head off."

"Cut her head off!"

"Aye, with a hatchet, with a spade, or with anything that can cleave through her murderous throat. You shall hear," he answered, trembling with rage. And hurrying forward he said:

"That beam will answer for a seat; your dear child is fatigued; let her be seated, and I will, in a few sentences, close my dreadful story."

The squared block of wood, which lay on the grass-grown pavement of the chapel, formed a bench on which I was very glad to seat myself, and in the meantime the General called to the wood-man, who had been removing some boughs which leaned upon the old walls; and, axe in hand, the hardy old fellow stood before us.

He could not tell us anything of these monuments; but there was an old man, he said, a ranger of this forest, at present sojourning in the house of the priest, about two miles away, who could point out every monument of the old Karnstein family; and, for a trifle, he undertook to bring back with him, if we would lend him one of our horses, in little more than half-an-hour.

"Have you been long employed about this forest?" asked my father of the old man.

"I have been a wood-man here," he answered in his *patois*,[22] "under the forester, all my days; so has my father before me, and so on, as many generations as I can count up. I could show you the very house in the village here, in which my ancestors lived."

"How came the village to be deserted?" asked the General.

[22] His country dialect—that is, the wood-man spoke like a "hick."

"It was troubled by *revenants*,[23] sir; several were tracked to their graves, there detected by the usual tests, and extinguished in the usual way, by decapitation, by the stake, and by burning; but not until many of the villagers were killed.

"But after all these proceedings according to law," he continued—"so many graves opened, and so many vampires deprived of their horrible animation—the village was not relieved. But a Moravian nobleman,[24] who happened to be travelling this way, heard how matters were, and being skilled—as many people are in his country—in such affairs, he offered to deliver the village from its tormentor. He did so thus: There being a bright moon that night, he ascended, shortly after sunset, the tower of the chapel here, from whence he could distinctly see the churchyard beneath him; you can see it from that window. From this point he watched until he saw the vampire come out of his grave, and place near it the linen clothes in which he had been folded, and glide away towards the village to plague its inhabitants.

"The stranger, having seen all this, came down from the steeple, took the linen wrappings of the vampire, and carried them up to the top of the tower, which he again mounted. When the vampire returned from his prowlings and missed his clothes, he cried furiously to the Moravian, whom he saw at the summit of the tower, and who, in reply, beckoned him to ascend and take them.[25] Whereupon the vampire, accepting his invitation, began to climb the steeple, and so soon as he had reached the battlements, the Moravian, with a stroke of his sword, clove his skull in twain, hurling him down to the churchyard, whither, descending by the winding stairs, the stranger followed and cut his head off, and next day delivered it and the body to the villagers, who duly impaled and burnt them.

"This Moravian nobleman had the authority from the then head of the family to remove the tomb of Mircalla, Countess Karnstein, which he did effectually, so that in a little while its site was quite forgotten."

"Can you point out where it stood?" asked the General, eagerly.

The forester shook his head and smiled.

"Not a living soul could tell you that now," he said; "besides, they say her body was removed; but no one is sure of that either." Having thus spoken, as time pressed, he dropped his axe and departed, leaving us to hear the remainder of the General's strange story.

CHAPTER XIV
The Meeting

"MY BELOVED child," he resumed, "was now growing rapidly worse. The physician who at-

---

[23] The walking dead—the undead, the classic vampire of folklore, escaped from their graves. Dom Augustine Calmet's *The Phantom World* (1746) is filled with accounts of revenants, whom he described as those who "have been dead a considerable time, sometimes more, sometimes less; who leave their tombs, and come and disturb the living, sucking their blood, appearing to them, making a noise at their doors and in their houses, and lastly, often causing their death."

[24] Moravia, now part of the Czech Republic, is bounded in part by the Carpathian mountains—prime vampire country, according to superstition (and *Dracula*).

[25] In folkloric tradition vampires are often described as childish; for example, it was thought that if a vampire's grave was strewn with beans, the creature would busy itself counting the beans and not pursue the living.

tended her had failed to produce the slightest impression upon her disease, for such I then supposed it to be. He saw my alarm, and suggested a consultation. I called in an abler physician, from Gratz. Several days elapsed before he arrived. He was a good and pious, as well as a learned man. Having seen my poor ward together, they withdrew to my library to confer and discuss. I, from the adjoining room, where I awaited their summons, heard these two gentlemen's voices raised in something sharper than a strictly philosophical discussion. I knocked at the door and entered. I found the old physician from Gratz maintaining his theory. His rival was combating it with undisguised ridicule, accompanied with bursts of laughter. This unseemly manifestation subsided and the altercation ended on my entrance.

" 'Sir,' said my first physician, 'my learned brother seems to think that you want a conjuror, and not a doctor.'

" 'Pardon me,' said the old physician from Gratz, looking displeased, 'I shall state my own view of the case in my own way another time. I grieve, Monsieur le Général, that by my skill and science I can be of no use. Before I go I shall do myself the honor to suggest something to you.'

"He seemed thoughtful, and sat down at a table, and began to write. Profoundly disappointed, I made my bow, and as I turned to go, the other doctor pointed over his shoulder to his companion who was writing, and then, with a shrug, significantly touched his forehead.

"This consultation, then, left me precisely where I was. I walked out into the grounds, all but distracted. The doctor from Gratz, in ten or fifteen minutes, overtook me. He apologized for having followed me, but said that he could not conscientiously take his leave without a few words more. He told me that he could not be mistaken; no natural disease exhibited the same symptoms; and that death was already very near. There remained, however, a day, or possibly two, of life. If the fatal seizure were at once arrested, with great care and skill her strength might possibly return. But all hung now upon the confines of the irrevocable. One more assault might extinguish the last spark of vitality which is, every moment, ready to die.

" 'And what is the nature of the seizure you speak of?' I entreated.

" 'I have stated all fully in this note, which I place in your hands, upon the distinct condition that you send for the nearest clergyman, and open my letter in his presence, and on no account read it till he is with you; you would despise it else, and it is a matter of life and death. Should the priest fail you, then, indeed, you may read it.'

"He asked me, before taking his leave finally, whether I would wish to see a man curiously learned upon the very subject, which, after I had read his letter, would probably interest me above all others, and he urged me earnestly to invite him to visit him there; and so took his leave.

"The ecclesiastic was absent, and I read the letter by myself. At another time, or in another case, it might have excited my ridicule. But into what quackeries will not people rush for a last chance, where all accustomed means have failed, and the life of a beloved object is at stake?

"Nothing, you will say, could be more absurd than the learned man's letter. It was monstrous enough to have consigned him to a madhouse. He said that the patient was suffering from the visits of a vampire! The punctures which she described as having occurred near the throat, were, he insisted, the insertion of those two long, thin, and sharp teeth which, it is well known, are peculiar to vampires; and there could be no doubt, he added, as to the well defined presence of the small livid mark which all concurred in describing as that induced by the demon's lips, and every symptom described by the sufferer was in exact conformity with those recorded in every case of a similar visitation.

"Being myself wholly skeptical as to the existence of any such portent as the vampire, the supernatural theory of the good doctor furnished, in my opinion, but another instance of learning and intelligence oddly associated with some one hallucination. I was so miserable, however, that, rather than try nothing, I acted upon the instructions of the letter.

"I concealed myself in the dark dressing-room, that opened upon the poor patient's room, in which a candle was burning, and watched there until she was fast asleep. I stood at the door, peeping through the small crevice, my sword laid on the table beside me, as my directions prescribed, until, a little after one, I saw a large black object, very ill-defined, crawl, as it seemed to me, over the foot of the bed, and swiftly spread itself up to the poor girl's throat, where it swelled, in a moment, into a great, palpitating mass.

"For a few moments I had stood petrified. I now sprang forward, with my sword in my hand. The black creature suddenly contracted toward the foot of the bed, glided over it, and, standing on the floor about a yard below the foot of the bed, with a glare of skulking ferocity and horror fixed on me, I saw Millarca. Speculating I know not what,

I struck at her instantly with my sword; but I saw her standing near the door, unscathed. Horrified, I pursued, and struck again. She was gone!—and my sword flew to shivers against the door.

"I can't describe to you all that passed on that horrible night. The whole house was up and stirring. The spectre Millarca was gone. But her victim was sinking fast, and before the morning dawned, she died."

The old General was agitated. We did not speak to him. My father walked to some little distance, and began reading the inscriptions on the tombstones; and thus occupied, he strolled into the door of a side chapel to prosecute his researches. The General leaned against the wall, dried his eyes, and sighed heavily. I was relieved on hearing the voices of Carmilla and Madame, who were at that moment approaching. The voices died away.

In this solitude, having just listened to so strange a story, connected, as it was, with the great and titled dead, whose monuments were moulding among the dust and ivy round us, and every incident of which bore so awfully upon my own mysterious case—in this haunted spot, darkened by the towering foliage that rose on every side, dense and high above its noiseless walls—a horror began to steal over me, and my heart sank as I thought that my friends were, after all, now about to enter and disturb this triste[26] and ominous scene.

The old General's eyes were fixed on the ground, as he leaned with his hand upon the basement of a shattered monument.

Under a narrow, arched doorway, surmounted by one of those demoniacal gro-

[26] Dismal, depressing.

tesques in which the cynical and ghastly fancy of old Gothic carving delights, I saw very gladly the beautiful face and figure of Carmilla enter the shadowy chapel.

I was just about to rise and speak, and nodded smiling, in answer to her peculiarly engaging smile; when with a cry, the old man by my side caught up the wood-man's hatchet, and started forward. On seeing him a brutalized change came over her features. It was an instantaneous and horrible transformation, as she made a crouching step backwards. Before I could utter a scream, he struck at her with all his force, but she dived under his blow, and unscathed, caught him in her tiny grasp by the wrist. He struggled for a moment to release his arm, but his hand opened, the axe fell to the ground, and the girl was gone.

He staggered against the wall. His grey hair stood upon his head, and a moisture shone over his face, as if he were at the point of death.

The frightful scene had passed in a moment. The first thing I recollect after, is Madame standing before me, and impatiently repeating again and again, the question, "Where is Mademoiselle Carmilla?"

I answered at length, "I don't know—I can't tell—she went there," and I pointed to the door through which Madame had just entered; "only a minute or two since."

"But I have been standing there, in the passage, ever since Mademoiselle Carmilla entered; and she did not return."

She then began to call "Carmilla" through every door and passage and from the windows, but no answer came.

"She called herself Carmilla?" asked the General, still agitated.

"Carmilla, yes," I answered.

"Aye," he said, "that is Millarca. That is the same person who long ago was called Mircalla, Countess Karnstein. Depart from this accursed ground, my poor child, as quickly as you can. Drive to the clergyman's house, and stay there till we come. Begone! May you never behold Carmilla more; you will not find her here."

CHAPTER XV
Ordeal and Execution

AS HE SPOKE one of the strangest-looking men I ever beheld, entered the chapel at the door through which Carmilla had made her entrance and her exit. He was tall, narrow-chested, stooping, with high shoulders, and dressed in black. His face was brown and dried in with deep furrows; he wore an oddly-shaped hat with a broad leaf. His hair, long and grizzled, hung on his shoulders. He wore a pair of gold spectacles, and walked slowly, with an odd shambling gait, with his face sometimes turned up to the sky, and sometimes bowed down toward the ground, seemed to wear a perpetual smile; his long thin arms were swinging, and his lank hands, in old black gloves ever so much too wide for them, waving and gesticulating in utter abstraction.

"The very man!" exclaimed the General, advancing with manifest delight. "My dear Baron, how happy I am to see you, I had no hope of meeting you so soon." He signed to my father, who had by this time returned, and leading the fantastic old gentleman, whom he called the Baron, to meet him. He introduced him formally, and they at once entered into earnest conversation. The stranger took a roll of paper from his pocket, and spread it on the worn surface of a tomb that stood by. He had a pencil case in his fingers, with which he traced imaginary lines from point to point on the paper, which from their often glancing from it, together, at certain points of the building, I concluded to be a plan of the chapel. He accompanied, what I may term his lecture, with occasional readings from a dirty little book, whose yellow leaves were closely written over.

They sauntered together down the side aisle, opposite to the spot where I was standing, conversing as they went; then they begun measuring distances by paces, and finally they all stood together, facing a piece of the side wall, which they began to examine with great minuteness; pulling off the ivy that clung over it, and rapping the plaster with the ends of their sticks, scraping here, and knocking there. At length they ascertained the existence of a broad marble tablet, with letters carved in relief upon it.

With the assistance of the wood-man, who soon returned, a monumental inscription, and carved escutcheon, were disclosed. They proved to be of those of the long lost monument of Mircalla, Countess Karnstein.

The old General, though not I fear given to the praying mood, raised his hands and eyes to heaven, in mute thanksgiving for some moments.

"Tomorrow," I heard him say; "the commissioner will be here, and the Inquisition will be held according to law." Then turning to the old man with the gold spectacles, whom I have described, he shook him warmly by both hands and said:—

"Baron, how can I thank you? How can we all thank you? You will have delivered this region from a plague that has scourged its inhabitants for more than a century. The horrible enemy, thank God, is at last tracked."

My father led the stranger aside, and the General followed. I knew that he had led them out of hearing, that he might relate my case, and I saw them glance often quickly at me, as the discussion proceeded.

My father came to me, kissed me again and again, and leading me from the chapel said:—

"It is time to return, but before we go home, we must add to our party the good priest, who lives but a little way from this; and persuade him to accompany us to the schloss."

In this quest we were successful: and I was glad, being unspeakably fatigued when we reached home. But my satisfaction was changed to dismay, on discovering that there were no tidings of Carmilla. Of the scene that had occurred in the ruined chapel, no explanation was offered to me, and it was clear that it was a secret which my father for the present determined to keep from me.

The sinister absence of Carmilla made the remembrance of the scene more horrible to me. The arrangements for that night were singular. Two servants and Madame were to sit up in my room that night; and the ecclesiastic with my father kept watch in the adjoining dressing-room.

The priest had performed certain solemn rites that night, the purport of which I did not understand any more than I comprehended the reason of this extraordinary precaution taken for my safety during sleep.

I saw all clearly a few days later.

The disappearance of Carmilla was followed by the discontinuance of my nightly sufferings.

You have heard, no doubt, of the appalling superstition that prevails in Upper and

Lower Styria, in Moravia, Silesia, in Turkish Servia, in Poland, even in Russia; the superstition, so we must call it, of the vampire.

If human testimony, taken with every care and solemnity, judicially, before commissions innumerable, each consisting of many members, all chosen for integrity and intelligence, and constituting reports more voluminous perhaps that exist upon anyone other class of cases, is worth anything, it is difficult to deny, or even to doubt the existence of such a phenomenon as the vampire.

For my part I have heard no theory by which to explain what I myself have witnessed and experienced, other than that supplied by the ancient and well-attested belief of the country.

The next day the formal proceedings took place in the Chapel of Karnstein. The grave of the Countess Mircalla was opened; and the General and my father recognized each his perfidious and beautiful guest, in the face now disclosed to view. The features, though a hundred and fifty years had passed since her funeral, were tinted with the warmth of life. Her eyes were open; no cadaverous smell exhaled from the coffin. The two medical men, one officially present, the other on the part of the promoter of the inquiry, attested the marvelous fact, that there was a faint, but appreciable respiration, and a corresponding action of the heart. The limbs were perfectly flexible, the flesh elastic; and the leaden coffin floated with blood, in which to a depth of seven inches, the body lay immersed. Here then, were all the admitted signs and proofs of vampirism. The body, therefore, in accordance with the ancient practice, was raised, and a sharp stake driven through the heart of the vampire, who uttered a piercing shriek at the

moment, in all respects such as might escape from a living person in the last agony. Then the head was struck off, and a torrent of blood flowed from the severed neck. The body and head were next placed on a pile of wood, and reduced to ashes, which were thrown upon the river and borne away, and that territory has never since been plagued by the visits of a vampire.

My father has a copy of the report of the Imperial Commission, with the signatures of all who were present at these proceedings, attached in verification of the statement. It is from this official paper that I have summarized my account of this last shocking scene.

CHAPTER XVI
Conclusion

I WRITE ALL this you suppose with composure. But far from it; I cannot think of it without agitation. Nothing but your earnest desire so repeatedly expressed, could have induced me to sit down to a task that has unstrung my nerves for months to come, and reinduced a shadow of the unspeakable horror which years after my deliverance continued to make my days and nights dreadful, and solitude insupportably terrific.

Let me add a word or two about that quaint Baron Vordenburg, to whose curious lore we were indebted for the discovery of the Countess Mircalla's grave.

He had taken up his abode in Gratz, where, living upon a mere pittance, which was all that remained to him of the once princely estates of his family, in Upper Styria, he devoted himself to the minute and laborious investigation of the marvelously authenticated tradition of vampirism. He had at his fingers' ends all the great and little works upon the subject. "Magia Posthuma," "Phlegon de Mirabilibus," "Augustinus de cura pro Mortuis," "Philosophicae et Christianae Cogitationes de Vampiris," by John Christofer Harenberg; and a thousand others, among which I remember only a few of those which he lent to my father."[27] He had a voluminous digest of all the judicial cases, from which he had extracted a system of principles that appear to govern—some always, and others occasionally only—the condition of the vampire. I may mention, in passing, that the deadly pallor attributed to that sort of *revenants,* is a mere melodramatic fiction. They present, in the grave, and when they show themselves in human society, the appearance of healthy life. When disclosed to light in their coffins, they exhibit all the symptoms that are enumerated as those which proved the vampire life of the long-dead Countess Karnstein.

How they escape from their graves and return to them for certain hours every day, without displacing the clay or leaving any trace of disturbance in the state of the coffin or the cerements, has always been admitted to be utterly inexplicable. The amphibious existence of the vampire is sustained by daily renewed slumber in the grave. Its horrible lust for living blood supplies the vigour of its waking existence. The vampire is prone to be fascinated with an engrossing vehemence, resembling the passion of love, by particular persons. In pursuit of these it will exercise inexhaustible patience and stratagem, for access to a particular object may be obstructed in a hundred ways. It will never desist until it has satiated its passion, and drained the very life of its coveted victim. But it will, in these cases, husband and protract its murderous enjoyment with the refinement of an epicure, and heighten it by the gradual approaches of an artful courtship. In these cases it seems to yearn for something like sympathy and consent. In ordinary ones it goes direct to its object, overpowers with violence, and strangles and exhausts often at a single feast.

The vampire is, apparently, subject, in certain situations, to special conditions. In the particular instance of which I have given you a relation, Mircalla seemed to be limited to a name which, if not her real one, should at least reproduce, without the omission or addition of a single letter, those, as we say, anagrammatically, which compose it. *Carmilla* did this; so did *Millarca.*

My father related to the Baron Vordenburg, who remained with us for two or three weeks after the expulsion of Carmilla, the story about the Moravian nobleman and the vampire at Karnstein churchyard, and then he asked the Baron how he had discovered the exact position of the long-concealed tomb of the Countess Millarca? The Baron's grotesque features puckered up into a mysterious smile; he looked down, still smiling, on his worn spectacle-case and fumbled with it. Then looking up, he said:—

---

[27] All of these titles are in fact tracts on revenants and vampires. It is surprising that Calmet's great work is not mentioned, for Le Fanu surely knew it.

"I have many journals, and other papers, written by that remarkable man; the most curious among them is one treating of the visit of which you speak, to Karnstein. The tradition, of course, discolors and distorts a little. He might have been termed a Moravian nobleman, for he had changed his abode to that territory, and was, beside, a noble. But he was, in truth, a native of Upper Styria. It is enough to say that in very early youth he had been a passionate and favored lover of the beautiful Mircalla, Countess Karnstein. Her early death plunged him into inconsolable grief. It is the nature of vampires to increase and multiply, but according to an ascertained and ghostly law.

"Assume, at starting, a territory perfectly free from that pest. How does it begin, and how does it multiply itself? I will tell you. A person, more or less wicked, puts an end to himself. A suicide, under certain circumstances, becomes a vampire. That spectre visits living people in their slumbers; *they* die, and almost invariably, in the grave, develop into vampires. This happened in the case of the beautiful Mircalla, who was haunted by one of those demons.[28] My ancestor, Vordenburg, whose title I still bear, soon discovered this, and in the course of the studies to which he devoted himself, learned a great deal more.

"Among other things, he concluded that suspicion of vampirism would probably fall, sooner or later, upon the dead Countess, who in life had been his idol. He conceived a horror, be she what she might, of her remains being profaned by the outrage of a posthumous execution. He has left a curious paper to prove that the vampire, on its expulsion from its amphibious existence, is projected into a far more horrible life; and he resolved to save his once beloved Mircalla from this.

"He adopted the stratagem of a journey here, a pretended removal of her remains, and a real obliteration of her monument. When age had stolen upon him, and from the vale of years he looked back on the scenes he was leaving, he considered, in a different spirit, what he had done; and a horror took possession of him. He made the tracings and notes which have guided me to the very spot, and drew up a confession of the deception that he had practiced. If he had intended any further action in this matter, death prevented him; and the hand of a remote descendant has, too late for many, directed the pursuit to the lair of the beast."

We talked a little more, and among other things he said was this:—

"One sign of the vampire is the power of the hand. The slender hand of Mircalla closed like a vice of steel on the General's wrist when he raised the hatchet to strike. But its power is not confined to its grasp; it leaves a numbness in the limb it seizes, which is slowly, if ever, recovered from."

The following spring my father took me a tour through Italy. We remained away for more than a year. It was long before the terror of recent events subsided; and to this hour the image of Carmilla returns to memory with ambiguous alternations—sometimes the playful, languid, beautiful girl; sometimes the

---

[28] Note that Le Fanu states that Mircalla, an innocent, was turned into a vampire in her grave when a demon entered her body. Similar origins are ascribed to the vampires in Joss Whedon's *Buffy* and *Angel* universe.

writing fiend I saw in the ruined church; and often from a reverie I have started, fancying I heard the light step of Carmilla at the drawing-room door.[29]

✄✄

[29] There is much unexplained in the story of Carmilla/Mircalla/Millarca, but the most mysterious is the identity of Madame la Comtesse, who acts the part of the vampire's "mother" in both the meeting with General Spielsdorf and the accident outside the schloss of the story. Whoever she is, she disappears without a trace, unpunished.

Anne Crawford

ANNE CRAWFORD, Baroness Erich von Rabe (1846-?), lived in
Italy as a young woman and later in Lesnian, Prussia, with her husband. Daughter of American sculptor Thomas Crawford and sister
of writer F. Marion Crawford, she and her siblings were raised as
Europeans. The "Campagna" of the title of this story is the now
densely populated region in southern Italy, the largest city of which
is Naples.

   Naples was a very sophisticated city, the capital of "the two
Sicilies" (the kingdom formed under the Congress of Vienna's
treaty of 1815), and had the first railway in Italy. This story first
appeared in 1886 in a collection called *The Witching Time: Tales for
the Year's End*, and was released later that year in *Unwin's Annual
for 1887*. It may have inspired both the tomb settings and the hypnotic elements of *Dracula*.

A MYSTERY OF THE CAMPAGNA

ANNE CRAWFORD

I.

*Martin Detaille's Account of
What Happened at the Vigna Marziali*

MARCELLO'S VOICE is pleading with me now, perhaps because after years of separation I have met an old acquaintance who had a part in his strange story. I have a longing to tell it, and have asked Monsieur Sutton to help me. He noted down the circumstances at the time, and he is willing to join his share to mine, that Marcello may be remembered.

One day, it was in spring, he appeared in my little studio amongst the laurels and green alleys of the Villa Medici. "Come, *mon enfant,*" he said, "put up your paints"; and he unceremoniously took my palette out of my hand. "I have a coach waiting outside, and we are going in search of a hermitage."[1] He was already washing my brushes as he spoke, and this softened my heart, for I hate to do it myself. Then he pulled off my velvet jacket and took down my respectable coat from a nail on the wall. I let him dress me like a child. We always did his will, and he knew it, and in a moment we were sitting in the coach, driving through the Via Sistina on our way to the Porta San Giovanni, whither he had directed the coachman to go.

I MUST TELL MY STORY as I can, for though I have been told by my comrades, who cannot know very well, that I can speak good English, writing it is another thing. Monsieur Sutton has asked me to use his tongue, because he has so far forgotten mine that he will not trust himself in it, though he has promised to correct my mistakes, that what I have to tell you may not seem ridiculous, and make people laugh when they read of Marcello.

I tell him I wish to write this for my countrymen, not his; but he reminds me that Marcello had many English friends who still

---

[1] Literally, the habitation of a hermit; here meaning a retreat, hideaway, or any secluded dwelling.

live, and that the English do not forget as we do. It is of no use to reason with him, for neither do they yield as we do, and so I have consented to his wish. I think he has a reason which he does not tell me, but let it go. I will translate it all into my own language for my own people. Your English phrases seem to me to be always walking sideways, or trying to look around the corner or stand upon their heads, and they have as many little tails as a kite. I will try not to have recourse to my own language, but he must pardon me if I forget myself. He may be sure I do not do it to offend him. Now that I have explained so much, let me go on.

When we had passed out of the Porta San Giovanni, the coachman drove as slowly as possible; but Marcello was never practical. How could he be, I ask you, with an Opera in his head? So we crawled along, and he gazed dreamily before him. At last, when we had reached the part where the little villas and vineyards begin, he began to look about him.

You all know how it is out there; iron gates with rusty names or initials over them, and beyond them straight walks bordered with roses and lavender leading up to a forlorn little casino, with trees and a wilderness behind it sloping down to the Campagna, lonely enough to be murdered in and no one to hear you cry. We stopped at several of these gates and Marcello stood looking in, but none of the places were to his taste.

He seemed not to doubt that he might have whatever pleased him, but nothing did so. He would jump out and run to the gate, and return saying, "The shape of those windows would disturb my inspiration," or, "That yellow paint would make me fail my duet in

the second Act"; and once he liked the air of the house well enough, but there were marigolds growing in the walk, and he hated them. So we drove on and on, until I thought we should find nothing more to reject. At last we came to one which suited him, though it was terribly lonely, and I should have fancied it very *agaçant*[2] to live so far away from the world with nothing but those melancholy olives and green oaks—ilexes, you call them—for company.

"I shall live here and become famous!" he said, decidedly, as he pulled the iron rod which rang a great bell inside. We waited, and then he rang again very impatiently and stamped his foot.

"No one lives here, *mon vieux!*[3] Come, it is getting late, and it is so damp out here, and you know that the damp for a tenor voice—" He stamped his foot again and interrupted me angrily.

"Why, then, have you got a tenor? You are stupid! A bass would be more sensible; nothing hurts it. But you have not got one, and you call yourself my friend! Go home without me." How could I, so far on foot? "Go and sing your lovesick songs to your lean English misses! They will thank you with a cup of abominable tea, and you will be in Paradise! This is *my* Paradise, and I shall stay until the angel comes to open it!"

He was very cross and unreasonable, and those were just the times when one loved him most, so I waited and enveloped my throat in my pocket handkerchief and sang a passage or two just to prevent my voice from becoming stiff in that damp air.

[2] Annoying, irritating.

[3] Informal greeting between friends; "old chap."

"Be still! Silence yourself!" he cried. "I cannot hear if anyone is coming."

Someone came at last, a rough-looking sort of keeper, or *guardiano* as they are called there, who looked at us as though he thought we were mad. One of us certainly was, but it was not I. Marcello spoke pretty good Italian, with a French accent, it is true, but the man understood him, especially as he held his purse in his hand. I heard him say a great many impetuously persuasive things all in one breath, then he slipped a gold piece into the *guardiano*'s horny hand, and the two turned towards the house, the man shrugging his shoulders in a resigned sort of way, and Marcello called out to me over his shoulder:—

"Go home in the cab, or you will be late for your horrible English party! I am going to stay here tonight." *Ma foi!*[4] I took his permission and left him; for a tenor voice is as tyrannical as a jealous woman. Besides, I was furious, and yet I laughed. His was the artist temperament, and appeared to us by turns absurd, sublime, and intensely irritating; but this last never for long, and we all felt that were we more like him our pictures would be worth more.

I had not got as far as the city gate when my temper had cooled, and I began to reproach myself for leaving him in that lonely place with his purse full of money, for he was not poor at all, and tempting the dark *guardiano* to murder him. Nothing could be easier than to kill him in his sleep and bury him away somewhere under the olive trees or in some old vault of a ruined catacomb, so common on the borders of the Campagna.

There were sure to be a hundred convenient places.

I stopped the coachman and told him to turn back, but he shook his head and said something about having to be in the Piazza of St. Peter at eight o'clock. His horse began to go lame, as though he had understood his master and was his accomplice. What could I do? I said to myself that it was fate, and let him take me back to the Villa Medici, where I had to pay him a pretty sum for our crazy expedition, and then he rattled off, the horse not lame at all, leaving me bewildered at this strange afternoon.

I did not sleep well that night, though my tenor song had been applauded, and the English misses had caressed me much. I tried not to think of Marcello, and he did not trouble me much until I went to bed; but then I could not sleep, as I have told you.

I fancied him already murdered, and being buried in the darkness by the *guardiano*. I saw the man dragging his body, with the beautiful head thumping against the stones, down dark passages, and at last leaving it all bloody and covered with earth under a black arch in a recess, and coming back to count the gold pieces. But then again I fell asleep, and dreamed that Marcello was standing at the gate and stamping his foot; and then I slept no more, but got up as soon as the dawn came, and dressed myself and went to my studio at the end of the laurel walk.

I took down my painting jacket, and remembered how he had pulled it off my shoulders. I took up the brushes he had washed for me; they were only half cleaned after all, and stiff with paint and soap. I felt glad to be angry with him, and *sacré'd* a little, for it made me sure that he was yet alive if I

4 "My faith!"

could scold at him. Then I pulled out my study of his head for my picture of Mucius Scaevola holding his hand in the flame,[5] and then I forgave him; for who could look upon that face and not love it?

I worked with the fire of friendship in my brush, and did my best to endow the features with the expression of scorn and obstinacy I had seen at the gate. It could not have been more suitable to my subject! Had I seen it for the last time?

You will ask me why I did not leave my work and go to see if anything had happened to him, but against this there were several reasons. Our yearly exhibition was not far off and my picture was barely painted in, and my comrades had sworn that it would not be ready. I was expecting a model for the King of the Etruscans; a man who cooked chestnuts in the Piazza Montanara, and who had consented to stoop to sit to me as a great favor; and then, to tell the truth, the morning was beginning to dispel my fancies.

I had a good northern light to work by, with nothing sentimental about it, and I was not fanciful by nature; so when I sat down to my easel I told myself that I had been a fool, and that Marcello was perfectly safe: the smell of the paints helping me to feel practical again. Indeed, I thought every moment that he would come in, tired of his caprice already, and even was preparing and practicing a little lecture for him. Some one knocked at my door, and I cried *"Entrez!"* thinking it was he at last, but no, it was Pierre Magnin.

"There is a curious man, a man of the country, who wants you," he said. "He has your address on a dirty piece of paper in Marcello's handwriting, and a letter for you, but he won't give it up. He says he must see 'il Signor Martino.' He'd make a superb model for a murderer! Come and speak to him, and keep him while I get a sketch of his head."

I followed Magnin through the garden, and outside, for the porter had not allowed him to enter, I found the *guardiano* of yesterday. He showed his white teeth, and said, 'Good day, signore,' like a Christian; and here in Rome he did not look half so murderous, only a stupid, brown, country fellow. He had a rough peasant-cart waiting, and he had tied up his shaggy horse to a ring in the wall.

I held out my hand for the letter and pretended to find it difficult to read, for I saw Magnin standing with his sketch-book in the shadow of the entrance hall. The note said this: I have it still and I will copy it. It was written in pencil on a leaf torn from his pocket-book:

Mon vieux! I have passed a good night here, and the man will keep me as long as I like. Nothing will happen to me, except that I shall be divinely quiet, and I already have a famous motif in my head. Go to my lodgings and pack up some clothes and all my manuscripts, with plenty of music paper and a few bottles of Bordeaux, and give them to my messenger. Be quick about it!

Fame is preparing to descend upon me! If you care to see me, do not come before eight days. The gate will not be opened if you come sooner. The guardiano is my slave, and he has instructions to kill any intruder who in the guise of a friend tries to get in uninvited. He

---

[5] Refers to Gaius Mucius Scaevola, a Roman youth famous for his show of bravery before the Etruscan king in 508 B.C.E. when he placed his hand over a brazier; often portrayed in classical art.

will do it, for he has confessed to me that he has murdered three men already.

(Of course this was a joke. I knew Marcello's way.)

When you come, go to the poste restante and fetch my letters. Here is my card to legitimate you. Don't forget pens and a bottle of ink! Your Marcello.

There was nothing for it but to jump into the cart, tell Magnin, who had finished his sketch, to lock up my studio, and go bumping off to obey these commands. We drove to his lodgings in the Via del Governo Vecchio, and there I made a bundle of all that I could think of; the landlady hindering me by a thousand questions about when the Signore would return. He had paid for the rooms in advance, so she had no need to be anxious about her rent.

When I told her where he was, she shook her head, and talked a great deal about the bad air out there, and said "Poor Signorino!" in a melancholy way, as though he were already buried, and looked mournfully after us from the window when we drove away. She irritated me, and made me feel superstitious.

At the corner of the Via del Tritone I jumped down and gave the man a franc out of pure sentimentality, and cried after him, "Greet the Signore!" but he did not hear me, and jogged away stupidly whilst I was longing to be with him. Marcello was a cross to us sometimes, but we loved him always.

THE EIGHT DAYS WENT by sooner than I had thought they would, and Thursday came, bright and sunny, for my expedition. At one o'clock I descended into the Piazza di Spagna, and made a bargain with a man who had a well-fed horse, remembering how dearly Marcello's want of good sense had cost me a week ago, and we drove off at a good pace to the Vigna Marziali, as I was almost forgetting to say that it was called. My heart was beating, though I did not know why I should feel so much emotion. When we reached the iron gate the *guardiano* answered my ring directly, and I had no sooner set foot in the long flower-walk than I saw Marcello hastening to meet me.

"I knew you would come," he said, drawing my arm within his, and so we walked towards the little grey house, which had a sort of portico and several balconies, and a sundial on its front. There were grated windows down to the ground floor, and the place, to my relief, looked safe and habitable. He told me that the man did not sleep there, but in a little hut down towards the Campagna, and that he, Marcello, locked himself in safely every night, which I was also relieved to know.

"What do you get to eat?" said I.

"Oh, I have goat's flesh, and dried beans and polenta, with pecorino cheese, and there is plenty of black bread and sour wine," he answered smilingly. "You see I am not starved."

"Do not overwork yourself, *mon vieux*," I said. "You are worth more than your opera will ever be."

"Do I look overworked?" he said, turning his face to me in the broad, outdoor light. He seemed a little offended at my saying that about his opera, and I was foolish to do it.

I examined his face critically, and he looked at me half defiantly. "No, not yet," I answered rather unwillingly, for I could not say that he did; but there was a restless, inward look in his eyes, and an almost imperceptible shadow lay around them. It seemed to me as though the full temples had grown slightly hollow, and a sort of faint mist layover his beauty, making it seem strange and far off. We were standing before the door, and he pushed it open, the *guardiano* following us with slow, loud-resounding steps.

"Here is my Paradise," said Marcello, and we entered the house, which was like all the others of its kind. A hall, with stucco bas-reliefs, and a stairway adorned with antique fragments, gave access to the upper rooms. Marcello ran up the steps lightly, and I heard him lock a door somewhere above and draw out the key, then he came and met me on the landing.

"This," he said, "is my workroom," and he threw open a low door. The key was in the lock, so this room could not be the one I heard him close. "Tell me I shall not write like an angel here!" he cried. I was so dazzled by the flood of bright sunshine after the dusk of the passage, that I blinked like an owl at first, and then I saw a large room, quite bare except for a rough table and chair, the chair covered with manuscript music.

"You are looking for the furniture," he said, laughing; "it is outside. Look here!" and he drew me to a rickety door of worm-eaten wood and coarse greenish glass, and flung it open on to a rusty iron balcony. He was right; the furniture was outside: that is to say, a divine view met my eyes. The Sabine Mountains, the Alban Hills, and broad Campagna, with its mediaeval towers and ruined aqueducts, and the open plain to the sea. All this glowing and yet calm in the sunlight. No wonder he could write there!

The balcony ran round the corner of the house, and to the right I looked down upon an alley of ilexes, ending in a grove of tall laurel trees—very old, apparently. There were bits of sculpture and some ancient sarcophagi standing gleaming against them, and even from so high I could hear a little stream of water pouring from an antique mask into a long, rough trough. I saw the brown *guardiano* digging at his cabbages and onions, and I laughed to think that I could fancy him a murderer!

He had a little bag of relics, which dangled to and fro over his sunburned breast, and he looked very innocent when he sat down upon an old column to eat a piece of black bread with an onion which he had just pulled out of the ground, slicing it with a knife not at all like a dagger.

But I kept my thoughts to myself, for Marcello would have laughed at them. We were standing together, looking down at the man as he drank from his hands at the running fountain, and Marcello now leaned down over the balcony, and called out a long *"Ohé!"*[6] The lazy *guardiano* looked up, nodded, and then got up slowly from the stone where he had been half-kneeling to reach the jet of water.

"We are going to dine," Marcello explained. "I have been waiting for you." Presently he heard the man's heavy tread upon the stairs, and he entered bearing a strange meal in a basket.

There came to light pecorino cheese made from ewe's milk, black bread of the consistency of a stone, a great bowl of salad apparently composed of weeds, and a sausage which filled the room with a strong smell of garlic. Then he disappeared and came back with a dish full of ragged-looking goat's flesh cooked together with a mass of smoking po-

[6] "Hey!"

lenta, and I am not sure that there was not oil in it.

"I told you I lived well, and now you see!" said Marcello. It was a terrible meal, but I had to eat it, and was glad to have some rough, sour wine to help me, which tasted of earth and roots. When we had finished I said, "And your opera! How are you getting on?"

"Not a word about that!" he cried. "You see how I have written!" and he turned over a heap of manuscript; "but do not talk to me about it. I will not lose my ideas in words." This was not like Marcello, who loved to discuss his work, and I looked at him astonished.

"Come," he said, "we will go down into the garden, and you shall tell me about the comrades. What are they doing? Has Magnin found a model for his Clytemnestra?"[7]

I humored him, as I always did, and we sat upon a stone bench behind the house, looking towards the laurel grove, talking of the pictures and the students. I wanted to walk down the ilex alley, but he stopped me.

"If you are afraid of the damp, don't go down there," he said, "the place is like a vault. Let us stay here and be thankful for this heavenly view."

"Well, let us stay here," I answered, resigned as ever. He lit a cigar and offered me one in silence. If he did not care to talk, I could be still too. From time to time he made some indifferent observation, and I answered it in the same tone. It almost seemed to me as though we, the old heart-comrades, had become strangers who had not known each other a week, or as though we had been so long apart that we had grown away from each other.

There was something about him which escaped me. Yes, the days of solitude had indeed put years and a sort of shyness, or rather ceremony, between us! It did not seem natural to me now to clap him on the back, and make the old, harmless jokes at him. He must have felt the constraint too, for we were like children who had looked forward to a game, and did not know now what to play at.

At six o'clock I left him. It was not like parting with Marcello. I felt rather as though I should find my old friend in Rome that evening, and here only left a shadowy likeness of him. He accompanied me to the gate, and pressed my hand, and for a moment the true Marcello looked out of his eyes; but we called out no last word to each other as I drove away. I had only said, "Let me know when you want me," and he said, *"Merci!"* and all the way back to Rome I felt a chill upon me, his hand had been so cold, and I thought and thought what could be the matter with him.

That evening I spoke out my anxiety to Pierre Magnin, who shook his head and declared that malaria fever must be taking hold of him, and that people often begin to show it by being a little odd.

"He must not stay there! We must get him away as soon as possible," I cried.

"We both know Marcello, and that nothing can make him stir against his will," said Pierre. "Let him alone, and he will get tired of his whim. It will not kill him to have a touch of malaria, and some evening he will turn up amongst us as merry as ever."

---

[7] In Greek legend, Clytemnestra was the wife of Agamemnon, king of the Ancient Greek kingdom of Mycenae (or Argos). In the *Oresteia* by Aeschylus, she was a seductress who murdered her husband and the Trojan princess Cassandra, whom he had taken during the sack of Troy. In Homer's *Odyssey*, her role in Agamemnon's death is unclear and her character is significantly more subdued.

But he did not. I worked hard at my picture and finished it, but for a few touches, and he had not yet appeared. Perhaps it was the extreme application, perhaps the sitting out in that damp place, for I insist upon tracing it to something more material than emotion. Well, whatever it was, I fell ill; more ill than I had even been in my life.

It was almost twilight when it overtook me, and I remember it distinctly, though I forget what happened afterwards, or, rather, I never knew, for I was found by Magnin quite unconscious, and he has told me that I remained so for some time, and then became delirious, and talked of nothing but Marcello. I have told you that it was very nearly twilight; but just at the moment when the sun is gone the colors show in their true value. Artists know this, and I was putting last touches here and there to my picture and especially to my head of Mucius Scaevola, or rather, Marcello.

The rest of the picture came out well enough; but that head, which should have been the principal one, seemed faded and sunk in. The face appeared to grow paler and paler, and to recede from me; a strange veil spread over it, and the eyes seemed to close. I am not easily frightened, and I know what tricks some peculiar methods of color will play by certain lights, for the moment I spoke of had gone, and the twilight greyness had set in; so I stepped back to look at it.

Just then the lips, which had become almost white, opened a little, and sighed! An illusion, of course. I must have been very ill and quite delirious already, for to my imagination it was a real sigh, or, rather, a sort of exhausted gasp. Then it was that I fainted, I suppose, and when I came to myself I was in my bed, with Magnin and Monsieur Sutton standing by me, and a Sœur de Charité[8] moving softly about among medicine bottles, and speaking in whispers.

I stretched out my hands, and they were thin and yellow, with long, pale nails; and I heard Magnin's voice, which sounded very far away, say, *"Dieu merci!"* And now Monsieur Sutton will tell you what I did not know until long afterwards.

II.

Robert Sutton's Account of What Happened at the Vigna Marziali

I AM ATTACHED TO Detaille, and was very glad to be of use to him, but I never fully shared his admiration for Marcello Souvestre, though I appreciated his good points. He was certainly very promising—I must say that. But he was an odd, flighty sort of fellow, not of the kind which we English care to take the trouble to understand. It is my business to write stories, but not having need of such characters I have never particularly studied them. As I say, I was glad to be of use to Detaille, who is a thorough good fellow, and I willingly gave up my work to go and sit by his bedside. Magnin knew that I was a friend of his, and very properly came to me when he found that Detaille's illness was a serious one and likely to last for a long time. I found him perfectly delirious, and raving about Marcello.

"Tell me what the *motif* is! I know it is a *Marche Funèbre!*"[9] And here he would sing a peculiar melody, which, as I have a knack at music, I noted down, it being like nothing I

---

[8] Sister of Charity.

[9] *Funeral March.*

had heard before. The Sister of Charity looked at me with severe eyes; but how could she know that all is grist for our mill, and that observation becomes with us a mechanical habit? Poor Detaille kept repeating this curious melody over and over, and then would stop and seem to be looking at his picture, crying that it was fading away.

"Marcello! Marcello! You are fading too! Let me come to you!" He was as weak as a baby, and could not have moved from his bed unless in the strength of delirium.

"I cannot come!" he went on; "they have tied me down." And here he made as though he were trying to gnaw through a rope at his wrists, and then burst into tears. "Will no one go for me and bring me a word from you? Ah! If I could know that you are alive!"

Magnin looked at me. I knew what he was thinking. He would not leave his comrade, but I must go. I don't mind acknowledging that I did not undertake this unwillingly. To sit by Detaille's bedside and listen to his ravings enervated me, and what Magnin wanted struck me as troublesome but not uninteresting to one of my craft, so I agreed to go. I had heard all about Marcello's strange seclusion from Magnin and Detaille himself, who lamented over it openly in his simple way at supper at the Academy, where I was a frequent guest.

I knew that it would be useless to ring at the gate of the Vigna Marziali. Not only should I not be admitted, but I should arouse Marcello's anger and suspicion, for I did not for a moment believe that he was not alive, though I thought it very possible that he was becoming a little crazy, as his countrymen are so easily put off their balance. Now, odd people are oddest late in the day and at evening time. Their nerves lose the power of resistance

then, and the real man gets the better of them. So I determined to try to discover something at night, reflecting also that I should be safer from detection then. I knew his liking for wandering about when he ought to be in his bed, and I did not doubt that I should get a glimpse of him, and that was really all I needed.

My first step was to take a long walk out of the Porta San Giovanni, and this I did in the early morning, tramping along steadily until I came to an iron gate on the right of the road, with VIGNA MARZIALI over it; and then I walked straight on, never stopping until I had reached a little bushy lane running down towards the Campagna to the right. It was pebbly, and quite shut in by luxuriant ivy and elder bushes, and it bore deep traces of the last heavy rains. These had evidently been effaced by no footprints, so I concluded that it was little used. Down this path I made my way cautiously, looking behind and before me, from a habit contracted in my lonely wanderings in the Abruzzi.

I had a capital revolver with me—an old friend—and I feared no man; but I began to feel a dramatic interest in my undertaking, and determined that it should not be crossed by any disagreeable surprises. The lane led me further down the plain than I had reckoned upon, for the bushy edge shut out the view; and when I had got to the bottom and faced round, the Vigna Marziali was lying quite far to my left. I saw at a glance that behind the grey casino[10] an alley of ilexes ended in a laurel grove; then there were plantations of kitchen stuff, with a sort of thatched cabin in their midst, probably that of a gardener. I looked about for a kennel, but saw none, so there was

[10] In Italy, a small country house or lodge.

no watchdog. At the end of this primitive kitchen garden was a broad patch of grass, bounded by a fence, which I could take at a spring.

Now, I knew my way, but I could not resist tracing it out a little further. It was well that I did so, for I found just within the fence a sunken stream, rather full at the time, in consequence of the rains, too deep to wade and too broad to jump. It struck me that it would be easy enough to take a board from the fence and lay it over for a bridge. I measured the breadth with my eye, and decided the board would span it; then I went back as I had come, and returned to find Detaille still raving.

As he could understand nothing it seemed to me rather a fool's errand to go off in search of comfort for him; but a conscious moment might come, and moreover, I began to be interested in my undertaking; and so I agreed with Magnin that I should go and take some food and rest and return to the Vigna that night. I told my landlady that I was going into the country and should return the next day, and I went to Nazarri's and laid in a stock of sandwiches and filled my flask with something they called sherry, for, though I was no great wine-drinker, I feared the night chill.

It was about seven o'clock when I started, and I retraced my morning's steps exactly. As I reached the lane, it occurred to me that it was still too light for me to pass unobserved over the stream, and I made a place for myself under the hedge and lay down, quite screened by the thick curtain of tangled overhanging ivy.

I must have been out of training, and tired by the morning's walk, for I fell asleep.

When I awoke it was night; the stars were shining, a dank mist made its way down my throat, and I felt stiff and cold. I took a pull at my flask, finding it nasty stuff, but it warmed me. Then I rang my repeater,[11] which struck a quarter to eleven, got up and shook myself free of the leaves and brambles, and went on down the lane. When I got to the fence I sat down and thought the thing over.

What did I expect to discover? What *was* there to discover? Nothing! Nothing but that Marcello was alive; and that was no discovery at all for I felt sure of it. I was a fool and had let myself be allured by the mere stage nonsense and mystery of the business, and a mouse would creep out of this mountain of precautions! Well, at least, I could turn it to account by describing my own absurd behavior in some story yet to be written, and, as it was not enough for a chapter, I would add to it by further experience. "Come along!" I said to myself. "You're an ass, but it may prove instructive."

I raised the top board from the fence noiselessly. There was a little stile[12] there, and the boards were easily moved. I laid down my bridge with some difficulty, and stepped carefully across, and made my way to the laurel grove as quickly and noiselessly as possible.

There all was thick darkness, and my eyes only grew slowly accustomed to it. After all there was not much to see; some stone seats in a semi-circle, and some fragments of columns set upright with antique busts upon them. Then a little to the right a sort of arch, with apparently some steps descending into the ground, probably the entrance to some discovered branch of a catacomb. In the

---

[11] A timepiece that strikes the hour.

[12] A series of steps or rungs to get over a wall or fence but remains a barrier to sheep or cattle.

midst of the enclosure, not a very large one, stood a stone table, deeply fixed in the earth. No one was there; of that I felt certain, and I sat down, having now got used to the gloom, and fell to eat my sandwiches, for I was desperately hungry.

NOW THAT I HAD come so far, was nothing to take place to repay me for my trouble? It suddenly struck me that it was absurd to expect Marcello to come out to meet me and perform any mad antics he might be meditating there before my eyes for my especial satisfaction. Why had I supposed that something would take place in the grove I do not know, except that this seemed a fit place for it. I would go and watch the house, and if I saw a light anywhere I might be sure he was within.

Any fool might have thought of that, but a novelist lays the scene of his drama and expects his characters to slide about in the grooves like puppets. It is only when mine surprise me that I feel they are alive. When I reached the end of the ilex alley I saw the house before me. There were more cabbages and onions after I had left the trees, and I saw that in this open space I could easily be perceived by anyone standing on the balcony above. As I drew back again under the ilexes, a window above, not the one on the balcony, was suddenly lighted up; but the light did not remain long, and presently a gleam shone through the glass oval over the door below.

I had just time to spring behind the thickest trunk near me when the door opened. I took advantage of its creaking to creep up the slanting tree like a cat, and lie out upon a projecting branch.

As I expected, Marcello came out. He was very pale, and moved mechanically like a sleepwalker. I was shocked to see how hollow his face had become as he held the candle still lighted in his hand, and it cast deep shadows on his sunken cheeks and fixed eyes, which burned wildly and seemed to see nothing. His lips were quite white, and so drawn that I could see his gleaming teeth.

Then the candle fell from his hand, and he came slowly and with a curiously regular step on into the darkness of the ilexes, I watching him from above. But I scarcely think he would have noticed me had I been standing in his path. When he had passed I let myself down and followed him. I had taken off my shoes, and my tread was absolutely noiseless; moreover, I felt sure he would not turn around.

On he went with the same mechanical step until he reached the grove. There I knelt behind an old sarcophagus at the entrance, and waited. What would he do? He stood perfectly still, not looking about him, but as though the clockwork within him had suddenly stopped. I felt that he was becoming psychologically interesting, after all. Suddenly he threw up his arms as men do when they are mortally wounded on the battlefield, and I expected to see him fall at full length. Instead of this he made a step forward.

I looked in the same direction, and saw a woman, who must have concealed herself there while I was waiting before the house, come from out of the gloom, and as she slowly approached and laid her head upon his shoulder, the outstretched arms clasped themselves closely around her, so that her face was hidden upon his neck.

So this was the whole matter, and I had been sent off on a wild-goose chase to spy out a common love affair! His opera and his seclusion for the sake of work, his tyrannical refusal to see Detaille unless he sent for him—all this was but a mask to a vulgar intrigue which, for reasons best known to himself, could not be indulged in, in the city. I was thoroughly angry! If Marcello passed his time mooning about in that damp hole all night, no wonder that he looked so wretchedly ill, and seemed half mad! I knew very well that Marcello was no saint. Why should he be? But I had not taken him for a fool! He had had plenty of romantic episodes, and as he was discreet without being uselessly mysterious, no one had ever unduly pried into them, nor should we have done so now. I said to myself that that mixture of French and Italian blood was at the bottom of it; French flimsiness and light-headedness and Italian love of cunning!

I looked back upon all the details of my mysterious expedition. I suppose at the root of my anger lay a certain dramatic disappointment at not finding him lying murdered, and I despised myself for all the trouble I had taken to this ridiculous end: just to see him holding a woman in his arms. I could not see her face, and her figure was enveloped from head to foot in something long and dark; but I could make out that she was tall and slender, and that a pair of white hands gleamed from her drapery.

As I was looking intently, for all my indignation, the couple moved on, and still clinging to one another descended the steps. So even the solitude of the lonely laurel grove could not satisfy Marcello's insane love of secrecy! I kept still awhile; then I stole to where they had disappeared, and listened; but all was silent, and I cautiously struck a match and peered down. I could see the steps for a short distance below me, and then the darkness seemed to rise and swallow them. It must be a catacomb as I had imagined, or an old Roman bath, perhaps, which Marcello had made comfortable enough, no doubt, and as likely as not they were having a nice little cold supper there. My empty stomach told me that I could have forgiven him even then could I have shared it; I was in truth frightfully hungry as well as angry, and sat down on one of the stone benches to finish my sandwiches.

The thought of waiting to see this lovesick pair return to upper earth never for a moment occurred to me. I had found out the whole thing, and a great humbug it was! Now I wanted to get back to Rome before my temper had cooled, and to tell Magnin on what a fool's errand he had sent me. If he liked to quarrel with me, all the better!

All the way home I composed cutting French speeches, but they suddenly cooled and petrified like a gust of lava from a volcano when I discovered that the gate was closed. I had never thought of getting a pass, and Magnin ought to have warned me. Another grievance against the fellow! I enjoyed my resentment, and it kept me warm as I patrolled up and down. There are houses, and even small eating-shops outside the gate, but no light was visible, and I did not care to attract attention by pounding at the doors in the middle of the night; so I crept behind a bit of wall. I was getting used to hiding by this time, and made myself as comfortable as I could with my ulster,[13] took another pull at my flask, and waited.

At last the gate was opened and I slipped through, trying not to look as though I had been out all night like a bandit. The guard looked at me narrowly, evidently wondering at my lack of luggage. Had I had a knapsack

[13] A man's heavy double-breasted overcoat.

I might have been taken for some innocently mad English tourist indulging in the mistaken pleasure of trudging in from Frascati or Albano; but a man in an ulster, with his hands in his pockets, sauntering in at the gate of the city at break of day as though returning from a stroll, naturally puzzled the officials, who looked at me and shrugged their shoulders.

Luckily I found an early coach in the Piazza of the Lateran, for I was dead-beat, and was soon at my lodgings in the Via della Croce, where my landlady let me in very speedily. Then at last I had the comfort of throwing off my clothes, all damp with the night dew, and turning in. My wrath had cooled to a certain point, and I did not fear to lower its temperature too greatly by yielding to an over-whelming desire for sleep. An hour or two could make no great difference to Magnin—let him fancy me still hanging about the Vigna Marziali! Sleep I must have, no matter what he thought.

I slept long, and was awakened at last by my landlady, Sora Nanna, standing over me, and saying, "There is a Signore who wants you."

"It is I, Magnin!" said a voice behind her. "I could not wait for you to come!" He looked haggard with anxiety and watching.

"Detaille is raving still," he went on, "only worse than before. Speak, for Heaven's sake! Why don't you tell me something?" And he shook me by the arm as though he thought I was still asleep.

"Have you nothing to say? You must have seen something! Did you see Marcello?"

"Oh! Yes, I saw him."

"Well?"

"Well, he was very comfortable—quite alive. He had a woman's arms around him."

I heard my door violently slammed to, a ferocious "*Sacré gamin!*"[14] and then steps springing down the stairs. I felt perfectly happy at having made such an impression, and turned and resumed my broken sleep with almost a kindly feeling towards Magnin, who was at that moment probably tearing up the Spanish Scalinata two steps at a time, and making himself horribly hot. It could not help Detaille, poor fellow! He could not understand my news. When I had slept long enough I got up, refreshed myself with a bath and something to eat, and went off to see Detaille. It was not his fault that I had been made a fool of, so I felt sorry for him.

I found him raving just as I had left him the day before, only worse, as Magnin said. He persisted in continually crying, "Marcello, take care! No one can save you!" in hoarse, weak tones, but with the regularity of a knell, keeping up a peculiar movement with his feet, as though he were weary with a long road, but must press forward to his goal. Then he would stop and break into childish sobs.

"My feet are so sore," he murmured piteously, "and I am so tired! But I will come! They are following me, but I am strong!" Then a violent struggle with his invisible pursuers, in which he would break off into that singing of his, alternating with the warning cry. The singing voice was quite another from the speaking one. He went on and on repeating the singular air which he had himself called a *Funeral March*, and which had become intensely disagreeable to me. If it was one indeed, it surely was intended for no Christian burial. As he sang, the tears kept trickling down his cheeks, and Magnin sat

[14] Literally "sacred child."

wiping them away as tenderly as a woman. Between his song he would clasp his hands, feebly enough, for he was very weak when the delirium did not make him violent, and cry in heart-rending tones, "Marcello, I shall never see you again! Why did you leave us?" At last, when he stopped for a moment, Magnin left his side, beckoning the Sister to take it, and drew me into the other room, closing the door behind him.

"Now tell me exactly how you saw Marcello," said he; so I related my whole absurd experience—forgetting, however, my personal irritation, for he looked too wretched and worn for anybody to be angry with him. He made me repeat several times my description of Marcello's face and manner as he had come out of the house. That seemed to make more impression upon him than the love-business.

"Sick people have strange intuitions," he said gravely; "and I persist in thinking that Marcello is very ill and in danger. *Tenez!*[15] And here he broke off, went to the door, and called, *"ma Sœur!"*[16] under his breath. She understood, and after having drawn the bedclothes straight, and once more dried the trickling tears, she came noiselessly to where we stood, the wet handkerchief still in her hand. She was a singularly tall and strong-looking woman, with piercing black eyes and a self-controlled manner. Strange to say, she bore the adopted name of Claudius, instead of a more feminine one.

"Ma Sœur," said Magnin, "at what o'clock was it that he sprang out of bed and we had to hold him for so long?"

"Half-past eleven and a few minutes," she answered promptly. Then he turned to me.

"At what time did Marcello come out into the garden?"

"Well, it might have been half-past eleven," I answered unwillingly. "I should say that three-quarters of an hour might possibly have passed since I rang my repeater. Mind you, I won't swear it!" I hate to have people try to prove mysterious coincidences, and this was just what they were attempting.

"Are you sure of the hour, *ma Sœur?*" I asked, a little tartly.

She looked at me calmly with her great, black eyes, and said:

"I heard the Trinità de' Monti[17] strike the half-hour just before it happened."

"Be so good as to tell Monsieur Sutton exactly what took place," said Magnin.

"One moment, Monsieur," and she went swiftly and softly to Detaille, raised him on her strong arm, and held a glass to his lips, from which he drank mechanically. Then she came and stood where she could watch him through the open door.

"He hears nothing," she said, as she hung the handkerchief to dry over a chair; and then she went on. "It was half-past eleven, and my patient had been very uneasy—that is to say, more so even than before. It might have been four or five minutes after the clock had finished striking that he became suddenly quite still, and then began to tremble all over; so that the bed shook with him." She spoke admirable English, as many of the Sisters do, so I need not translate, but will give her own words.

---

[15] "Pay attention!"

[16] Literally "my Sister"; here meaning the nurse.

[17] A late Renaissance church in Rome best known for its commanding position above the Spanish Steps, which lead down to the Piazza di Spagna.

"He went on trembling until I thought he was going to have a fit, and told Monsieur Magnin to be ready to go for the doctor, when just then the trembling stopped, he became perfectly stiff, his hair stood up upon his head, and his eyes seemed coming out of their sockets, though he could see nothing, for I passed the candle before them. All at once he sprang out of his bed and rushed to the door. I did not know he was so strong. Before he got there I had him in my arms, for he has become very light, and I carried him back to bed again, though he was struggling, like a child. Monsieur Magnin came in from the next room just as he was trying to get up again, and we held him down until it was past, but he screamed Monsieur Souvestre's name for a long time after that. Afterwards he was very cold and exhausted, of course, and I gave him some beef-tea, though it was not the hour for it."

"I think you had better tell the Sister all about it," said Magnin turning to me. "It is the best that the nurse should know everything."

"Very well," said I; "though I do not think it's much in her line." She answered me herself, "Everything which concerns our patients is our business. Nothing shocks me." Thereupon she sat down and thrust her hands into her long sleeves, prepared to listen. I repeated the whole affair as I had done to Magnin. She never took her brilliant eyes from off my face, and listened as coolly as though she had been a doctor hearing an account of a difficult case, though to me it seemed almost sacrilege to be describing the behavior of a love-stricken youth to a Sister of Charity.

"What do you say to that, *ma Sœur?*" asked Magnin, when I had done.

"I say nothing, monsieur. It is sufficient that I know it"; and she withdrew her hands from her sleeves, took up the handkerchief, which was dry by this time, and returned quietly to her place at the bedside.

"I wonder if I have shocked her, after all?" I said to Magnin.

"Oh, no," he answered. "They see many things, and a *Sœur* is as abstract as a confessor; they do not allow themselves any personal feelings. I have seen Sœur Claudius listen perfectly unmoved to the most abominable ravings, only crossing herself beneath her cape at the most hideous blasphemies. It was late summer when poor Justin Revol died. You were not here." Magnin put his hand to his forehead.

"You are looking ill yourself," I said. "Go and try to sleep, and I will stay."

"Very well," he answered; "but I cannot rest unless you promise to remember everything he says, that I may hear it when I wake"; and he threw himself down on the hard sofa like a sack, and was asleep in a moment; and I, who had felt so angry with him but a few hours ago, put a cushion under his head and made him comfortable.

I sat down in the next room and listened to Detaille's monotonous ravings, while Sœur Claudius read in her book of prayers. It was getting dusk, and several of the academicians stole in and stood over the sick man and shook their heads. They looked around for Magnin, but I pointed to the other room with my finger on my lips, and they nodded and went away on tiptoe.

It required no effort of memory to repeat Detaille's words to Magnin when he woke, for they were always the same. We had another Sister that night, and as Sœur Claudius was not to return till the next day at midday, I offered to share the watch with Magnin, who was getting very nervous and exhausted, and who seemed to think that some such attack might be expected as had occurred the night before. The new sister was a gentle, delicate-looking little woman, with tears in her soft brown eyes as she bent over the sick man, and crossed herself from time to time, grasping the crucifix which hung from the beads at her waist. Nevertheless she was calm and useful, and as punctual as Sœur Claudius herself in giving the medicines.

The doctor had come in the evening, and prescribed a change in these. He would not say what he thought of his patient, but only declared that it was necessary to wait for a crisis. Magnin sent for some supper, and we sat over it together in the silence, neither of us hungry. He kept looking at his watch.

"If the same thing happens tonight, he will die!" said he, and laid his head on his arms.

"He will die in a most foolish cause, then," I said angrily, for I thought he was going to cry, as those Frenchmen have a way of doing, and I wanted to irritate him by way of a tonic; so I went on:—

"It would be dying for a *vaurien*[18] who is making an ass of himself in a ridiculous business which will be over in a week! Souvestre may get as much fever as he likes! Only don't ask me to come and nurse him."

"It is not the fever," said he slowly, "it is a horrible nameless dread that I have; I suppose it is listening to Detaille that makes me nervous. Hark!" he added, "it strikes eleven. We must watch!"

"If you really expect another attack you had better warn the Sister," I said; so he

told her in a few words what might happen.

"Very well, monsieur," she answered, and sat down quietly near the bed, Magnin at the pillow and I near him. No sound was to be heard but Detaille's ceaseless lament.

And now, before I tell you more, I must stop to entreat you to believe me. It will be almost impossible for you to do so, I know, for I have laughed myself at such tales, and no assurances would have made me credit them. But I, Robert Sutton, swear that this thing happened. More I cannot do. It is the truth.

We had been watching Detaille intently. He was lying with closed eyes, and had been very restless. Suddenly he became quite still, and then began to tremble, exactly as Sœur Claudius had described. It was a curious, uniform trembling, apparently in every fiber, and his iron bedstead shook as though strong hands were at its head and foot. Then came the absolute rigidity she had also described, and I do not exaggerate when I say that not only did his short-cropped hair seem to stand erect, but that it literally did so. A lamp cast the shadow of his profile against the wall to the left of his bed, and as I looked at the immovable outline which seemed painted on the wall, I saw the hair slowly rise until the line where it joined the forehead was quite a different one—abrupt instead of a smooth sweep. His eyes opened wide and were frightfully fixed, then as frightfully strained, but they certainly did not see us.

We waited breathlessly for what might follow. The little Sister was standing close to him, her lips pressed together and a little pale, but very calm. "Do not be frightened, *ma Sœur*," whispered Magnin; and she answered in a business-like tone, "No, monsieur," and drew still nearer to her patient, and took his

[18] A scoundrel.

hands, which were stiff as those of a corpse, between her own to warm them. I laid mine upon his heart; it was beating so imperceptibly that I almost thought it had stopped, and as I leaned my face to his lips I could feel no breath issue from them. It seemed as though the rigor would last forever.

Suddenly, without any transition, he hurled himself with enormous force, and literally at one bound, almost into the middle of the room, scattering us aside like leaves in the wind. I was upon him in a moment, grappling with him with all my strength, to prevent him from reaching the door. Magnin had been thrown backwards against the table, and I heard the medicine bottles crash with his fall. He had flung back his hand to save himself, and rushed to help me with blood dripping from a cut in his wrist. The little Sister sprang to us. Detaille had thrown her violently back upon her knees, and now, with a nurse's instinct, she tried to throw a shawl over his bare chest. We four must have made a strange group!

Four? *We were five!* Marcello Souvestre stood before us, just within the door! We all saw him, for he was there. His bloodless face was turned towards us unmoved; his hands hung by his side as white as his face; only his eyes had life in them; they were fixed on Detaille.

"Thank God you have come at last!" I cried. "Don't stand there like a fool! Help us, can't you?" But he never moved. I was furiously angry, and, leaving my hold, sprang upon him to drag him forwards. My outstretched hands struck hard against the door, and I felt a thing like a spider's web envelop me. It seemed to draw itself over my mouth and eyes, and to blind and choke me, and then to flutter and tear and float from me.

Marcello was gone!

Detaille had slipped from Magnin's hold, and lay in a heap upon the floor, as though his limbs were broken. The Sister was trembling violently as she knelt over him and tried to raise his head. We gazed at one another, stooped and lifted him in our arms, and carried him back to his bed, while Sœur Marie quietly collected the broken phials.

"You saw it, *ma Sœur?*" I heard Magnin whisper hoarsely.

"Yes, monsieur!" she only answered, in a trembling voice, holding on to her crucifix. Then she said in a professional tone:—

"Will monsieur let me bind up his wrist?" And though her fingers trembled and his hand was shaking, the bandage was an irreproachable one.

Magnin went into the next room, and I heard him throw himself heavily into a chair. Detaille seemed to be sleeping. His breath came regularly; his eyes were closed with a look of peace about the lids, his hands lying in a natural way upon the quilt. He had not moved since we laid him there. I went softly to where Magnin was sitting in the dark. He did not move, but only said: "Marcello is dead!"

"He is either dead or dying," I answered, "and we must go to him."

"Yes," Magnin whispered, "we must go to him, but we shall not reach him."

"We will go as soon as it is light," I said, and then we were still again.

When the morning came at last he went and found a comrade to take his place, and only said to Sœur Marie, "It is not necessary to speak of this night"; and at her quiet, "You are right, monsieur," we felt we could trust her. Detaille was still sleeping. Was this the crisis the doctor had expected? Perhaps; but surely not in such fearful form. I insisted upon my companion having some breakfast before we started, and I breakfasted myself, but I cannot say I tasted what passed between my lips.

We engaged a closed carriage, for we did not know what we might bring home with us, though neither of us spoke out his thoughts. It was early morning still when we reached the Vigna Marziali, and we had not exchanged a word all the way. I rang at the bell, while the coachman looked on curiously. It was answered promptly by the *guardiano,* of whom Detaille has already told you.

"Where is the Signore?" I asked through the gate.

"*Chi lo sa?*" he answered, "He is here, of course; he has not left the Vigna. Shall I call him?"

"*Call him?*" I knew that no mortal voice could reach Marcello now, but I tried to fancy he was still alive.

"No," I said. "Let us in. We want to surprise him; he will be pleased."

The man hesitated, but he finally opened the gate, and we entered, leaving the carriage to wait outside. We went straight to the house; the door at the back was wide-open. There had been a gale in the night, and it had torn some leaves and bits of twigs from the trees and blown them into the entrance hall. They lay scattered across the threshold, and were evidence that the door had remained open ever since they had fallen. The *guardiano* left us, probably to escape Marcello's anger at having let us in, and we went up the stairs unhindered, Magnin foremost, for he knew the house better than I, from Detaille's description. He had told him about

the corner room with the balcony, and we pretended that Marcello might be there, absorbed betimes[19] in his work, but we did not call him.

He was not there. His papers were strewn over the table as though he had been writing, but the inkstand was dry and full of dust; he could not have used it for days. We went silently into the other chambers. Perhaps he was still asleep? But, no! We found his bed untouched, so he could not have lain in it that night. The rooms were all unlocked but one, and this closed door made our hearts beat. Marcello could scarcely be there, however, for there was no key in the lock; I saw the daylight shining through the key-hole. We called his name, but there came no answer. We knocked loudly; still no sign from within; so I put my shoulder to the door, which was old and cracked in several places, and succeeded in bursting it open.

Nothing was there but a sculptor's modeling-stand, with something upon it covered with a white cloth, and the modeling-tools on the floor. At the sight of the cloth, still damp, we drew a deep breath. It could have hung there for many hours, certainly not for twenty-four. We did not raise it.

"He would be vexed," said Magnin, and I nodded, for it is accounted almost a crime in the artists' world to unveil a sculptor's work behind his back. We expressed no surprise at the fact of his modeling: a ban seemed to lie upon our tongues. The cloth hung tightly to the object beneath it, and showed us the outline of a woman's head and rounded-bust, and so veiled we left her. There was a little wind-

---

[19] Here meaning "soon."

ing stair leading out of the passage, and we climbed it, to find ourselves in a sort of belvedere,[20] commanding a superb view. It was a small, open terrace, on the roof of the house, and we saw at a glance that no one was there.

We had now been all over the casino, which was small and simply built, being evidentially intended only for short summer use. As we stood leaning over the balustrade we could look down into the garden. No one was there but the *guardiano*, lying amongst his cabbages with his arms behind his head, half asleep. The laurel grove had been in my mind from the beginning, only it had seemed more natural to go to the house first. Now we descended the stairs silently and directed our steps thither.

As we approached it, the *guardiano* came towards us lazily.

"Have you seen the Signore?" he asked, and his stupidly placid face showed me that he, at least, had no hand in his disappearance.

"No, not yet," I answered, "but we shall come across him somewhere, no doubt. Perhaps he has gone to take a walk, and we will wait for him. What is this?" I went on, trying to seem careless. We were standing now by the little arch of which you know.

"This?" said he; "I have never been down there, but they say it is something old. Do the Signori want to see it? I will fetch a lantern."

I nodded, and he went off to his cabin. I had a couple of candles in my pocket, for I had intended to explore the place, should we not find Marcello. It was there that he had disappeared that night, and my thoughts

had been busy with it; but I kept my candles concealed, reflecting that they would give our search an air of premeditation which would excite curiosity.

"When did you see the Signore last?" I asked, when he had returned with the lantern.

"I brought him his supper yesterday evening."

"At what o'clock?"

"It was the *Ave Maria*, Signore," he replied. "He always sups then."

It would be useless to put any more questions. He was evidently utterly unobserving, and would lie to please us.

"Let me go first," said Magnin, taking the lantern. We set our feet upon the steps; a cold air seemed to fill our lungs and yet to choke us, and a thick darkness lay beneath. The steps, as I could see by the light of my candle, were modern, as well as the vaulting above them. A tablet was let into the wall, and in spite of my excitement I paused to read it, perhaps because I was glad to delay whatever awaited us below. It ran thus:

Questo antico sepolcro Romano scoprì il Conte Marziali nell' anno 1853, e piamente conservò. In plain English: "Count Marziali discovered this ancient Roman sepulchre in the year 1853, and piously preserved it."

I read it more quickly than it has taken time to write here, and hurried after Magnin, whose footsteps sounded faintly below me. As I hastened, a draught of cold air extinguished my candle, and I was trying to make my way down by feeling along the wall, which was horribly dark and clammy, when my heart stood still at a cry from far beneath me—a cry of horror!

---

[20] A building, or architectural feature of a building, designed and situated to look out upon a pleasing scene or vista.

"Where are you?" I shouted; but Magnin was calling my name, and could not hear me. "I am here. I am in the dark!"

I was making haste as fast as I could, but there were several turnings.

"I have found him!" came up from below.

"Alive?" I shouted. No answer.

One last short flight brought me face to face with the gleam of the lantern. It came from a low doorway, and within stood Magnin, peering into the darkness. I knew by his face, as he held the light high above him, that our fears were realized.

Yes; Marcello was there. He was lying stretched upon the floor, staring at the ceiling, dead, and already stiff, as I could see at a glance. We stood over him, saying not a word, then I knelt down and felt him, for mere form's sake, and said, as though I had not known it before, "He has been dead for some hours."

"Since yesterday evening," said Magnin, in a horror-stricken voice, yet with a certain satisfaction in it, as though to say, "You see, I was right."

Marcello was laying with his head slightly thrown back, no contortions in his handsome features; rather the look of a person who has quietly died of exhaustion—who has slipped unconsciously from life to death. His collar was thrown open and a part of his breast, of a ghastly white, was visible. Just over the heart was a small spot.

"Give me the lantern," I whispered, as I stooped over it. It was a very little spot, of a faint purplish brown, and must have changed color within the night.

I examined it intently, and should say that the blood had been sucked to the surface, and then a small prick or incision made. The slight subcutaneous effusion led me to this conclusion.

One tiny drop of coagulated blood closed the almost imperceptible wound. I probed it with the end of one of Magnin's matches. It was scarcely more than skin-deep, so it could not be the stab of a stiletto, however slender, or the track of a bullet. Still, it was strange, and with one impulse we turned to see if no one were concealed there, or if there were no second exit. It would be madness to suppose that the murderer, if there was one, would remain by his victim. Had Marcello been making love to a pretty *contadina*,[21] and was this some jealous lover's vengeance? But it was not a stab. Had one drop of poison in the little wound done this deadly work?

We peered about the place, and I saw that Magnin's eyes were blinded by tears and his face as pale as that upturned one on the floor, whose lids I had vainly tried to close. The chamber was low, and beautifully ornamented with stucco bas-reliefs, in the manner of the well-known one not far from there upon the same road. Winged genii, griffins, and arabesques,[22] modeled with marvelous lightness, covered the walls and ceiling. There was no other door than the one we had entered by. In the center stood a marble sarcophagus, with the usual subjects sculptured upon it, on the one side Hercules conducting a veiled figure, on the other a dance of nymphs and fauns. A space in the middle contained the following inscription, deeply cut in the stone, and still partially filled with red pigment:

---

[21] Literally "rustic"; here meaning a country girl.

[22] Sinuous, spiraling, undulating, or serpentine lines or linear motifs.

D. M.

VESPERTILIAE · THC · ΑΙΜΑΤΟΠΩΤΙΛΟC ·
Q · FLAVIVS · VIX · IPSE · SOSPES ·
MON · POSVIT

"What is this?" whispered Magnin. It was only a pickaxe and a long crowbar, such as the country people use in hewing out their blocks of tufa, and his foot had struck against them. Who could have brought them here? They must belong to the *guardiano* above, but he said that he had never come here, and I believed him, knowing the Italian horror of darkness and lonely places; but what had Marcello wanted with them? It did not occur to us that archaeological curiosity could have led him to attempt to open the sarcophagus, the lid of which had evidently never been raised, thus justifying the expression *piously preserved*.

As I rose from examining the tools my eyes fell upon the line of mortar where the cover joined to the stone below, and I noticed that some of it had been removed, perhaps with the pickaxe which lay at my feet. I tried it with my nails and found that it was very crumbly. Without a word I took the tool in my hand, Magnin instinctively following my movements with the lantern.

What impelled us I do not know. I had myself no thought, only an irresistible desire to see what was within. I saw that much of the mortar had been broken away, and lay in small fragments upon the ground, which I had not noticed before. It did not take long to complete the work. I snatched the lantern from Magnin's hand and set it upon the ground, where it shone full upon Marcello's dead face, and by its light I found a little break between the two masses of stone and managed to insert the end of my crowbar, driving it in with a blow of the pickaxe. The

stone chipped and then cracked a little. Magnin was shivering.

"What are you going to do?" he said, looking around at where Marcello lay.

"Help me!" I cried, and we two bore with all our might upon the crowbar. I am a strong man, and I felt a sort of blind fury as the stone refused to yield. What if the bar should snap? With another blow I drove it in still further, then using it as a lever, we weighed upon it with our outstretched arms until every muscle was at its highest tension. The stone moved a little, and almost fainting we stopped to rest.

From the ceiling hung the rusty remnant of an iron chain which must once have held a lamp. To this, by scrambling upon the sarcophagus, I contrived to make fast the lantern.

"Now!" said I, and we heaved again at the lid. It rose, and we alternately heaved and pushed until it lost its balance and fell with a thundering crash upon the other side; such a crash that the walls seemed to shake, and I was for a moment utterly deafened, while little pieces of stucco rained upon us from the ceiling. When we had paused to recover from the shock we leaned over the sarcophagus and looked in.

The light shone full upon it, and we saw—how is it possible to tell? We saw lying there, amidst folds of mouldering rags, the body of a woman, perfect as in life, with faintly rosy face, soft crimson lips, and a breast of living pearl, which seemed to heave as though stirred by some delicious dream. The rotten stuff swathed about her was in ghastly contrast to this lovely form, fresh as the morning! Her hands lay stretched at her side, the pink palms were turned a little outwards, her eyes were closed as peacefully as those of a sleeping child, and her long hair, which shone red-gold in the dim light from above, was wound around her head in numberless finely plaited tresses, beneath which little locks escaped in rings upon her brow. I could have sworn that the blue veins on that divinely perfect bosom held living blood!

We were absolutely paralyzed, and Magnin leaned gasping over the edge as pale as death, paler by far than this living, almost smiling face to which his eyes were glued. I do not doubt that I was as pale as he at this inexplicable vision. As I looked, the red lips seemed to grow redder. They *were* redder! The little pearly teeth showed between them. I had not seen them before, and now a clear ruby drop trickled down to her rounded chin and from there slipped sideways and fell upon her neck.

Horror-struck I gazed upon the living corpse, till my eyes could not bear the sight any longer. As I looked away my glance fell once more upon the inscription, but now I could *see—and read—it* all. "To Vespertilia"— that was in Latin, and even the Latin name of the woman suggested a thing of evil flitting in the dusk. But the full horror of the nature of that thing had been veiled to Roman eyes under the Greek τηςαϊματοπωτίδος, "The blood-drinker, the vampire woman." And Flavius—her *lover—vix ipse sospes,* "himself hardly saved" from that deadly embrace, had buried her here, and set a seal upon her sepulchre, trusting to the weight of stone and the strength of clinging mortar to imprison forever the beautiful monster he had loved.

"Infamous murderess!" I cried. "You have killed Marcello!" and a sudden, vengeful calm came over me.

"Give me the pickaxe," I said to Magnin; I can hear myself saying it still. He picked it up and handed it to me as in a dream; he seemed little better than an idiot, and the beads of sweat were shining on his forehead. I took my knife, and from the long wooden handle of the pickaxe I cut a fine, sharp stake. Then I clambered, scarcely feeling any repugnance, over the side of the sarcophagus, my feet amongst the folds of Vespertilia's decaying winding-sheet, which crushed like ashes beneath my boot.

I looked for one moment at that white breast, but only to choose the loveliest spot, where the network of azure veins shimmered like veiled turquoises, and then with one blow I drove the pointed stake deep down through the breathing snow and stamped it in with my heel.

An awful shriek, so ringing and horrible that I thought my ears must have burst; but even then I felt neither fear nor horror. There are times when these cannot touch us. I stopped and gazed once again at the face, now undergoing a fearful change—fearful and final!

"Foul vampire!" I said quietly in my concentrated rage. "You will do no more harm now!" And then, without looking back upon her cursed face, I clambered out of the horrible tomb.

We raised Marcello, and slowly carried him up the steep stairs—a difficult task, for the way was narrow and he was so stiff. I noticed that the steps were ancient up to the end of the second flight; above, the modern passage was somewhat broader. When we reached the top, the *guardiano* was lying upon one of the stone benches; he did not mean us to cheat him out of his fee. I gave him a couple of francs.

"You see that we have found the signore," I tried to say in a natural voice. "He is very weak, and we will carry him to the carriages." I had thrown my handkerchief over Marcello's face, but the man knew as well as I did that he was dead. Those stiff feet told their own story, but Italians are timid of being involved in such affairs. They have a childish dread of the police, and he only answered, "Poor Signori no! He is very ill; it is better to take him to Rome," and kept cautiously clear of us as we went up to the ilex alley with our icy burden, and he did not go to the gate with us, not liking to be observed by the coachman who was dozing on his box.

With difficulty we got Marcello's corpse into the carriage, the driver turning to look at us suspiciously. I explained we had found our friend very ill, and at the same time slipped a gold piece into his hand, telling him to drive to the Via del Governo Vecchio. He pocketed the money, and whipped his horses into a trot, while we sat supporting the stiff body, which swayed like a broken doll at every pebble in the road. When we reached the Via del Governo Vecchio at last, no one saw us carry him into the house. There was no step before the door, and we drew up so close to it that it was possible to screen our burden from sight. When we had brought him into his room and laid him upon his bed, we noticed that his eyes were closed; from the movement of the carriage, perhaps, though that was scarcely possible.

The landlady behaved very much as I had expected her to do, for, as I told you, I know the Italians. She pretended, too, that the signore was very ill, and made a pretense of offering to fetch a doctor, and when I thought it best to tell her that he was dead, declared that it must have happened that very moment,

for she had seen him look at us and close his eyes again. She had always told him that he ate too little and that he would be ill. Yes, it was weakness and that bad air out there which had killed him; and then he worked too hard. When she had successfully established this fiction, which we were glad enough to agree to, for neither did we wish for the publicity of an inquest, she ran out and fetched a gossip to come and keep her company.

So died Marcello Souvestre, and so died Vespertilia the blood-drinker at last.

THERE IS NOT MUCH more to tell. Marcello lay calm and beautiful upon his bed, and the students came and stood silently looking at him, then knelt down for a moment to say a prayer, crossed themselves, and left him forever.

We hastened to the Villa Medici, where Detaille was sleeping, and Sister Claudius watching him with a satisfied look on her strong face. She rose noiselessly at our entrance, and came to us at the threshold.

"He will recover," said she, softly. She was right. When he awoke and opened his eyes he knew us directly, and Magnin breathed a devout "Thank God!"

"Have I been ill, Magnin?" he asked, very feebly.

"You have had a little fever," answered Magnin, promptly; "but it is over now. Here is Monsieur Sutton come to see you."

"Has Marcello been here?" was the next question. Magnin looked at him very steadily.

"No," he only said, letting his face tell the rest.

"Is he dead, then?" Magnin only bowed his head. "Poor friend!" Detaille murmured to himself, then closed his heavy eyes and slept again.

A few days after Marcello's funeral we went to the fatal Vigna Marziali to bring back the objects which had belonged to him. As I laid the manuscript score of the opera carefully together, my eye fell upon a passage which struck me as the identical one which Detaille had so constantly sung in his delirium, and which I noted down. Strange to say, when I reminded him of it later, it was perfectly new to him, and he declared that Marcello had not let him examine his manuscript. As for the veiled bust in the other room, we left it undisturbed, and to crumble away unseen.

❧

Mary Cholmondeley

MARY CHOLMONDELEY (1859-1925) was an English novelist.
Spending her time caring for a sickly mother, she began writing,
and her first novel was published when she was twenty-six. Her
second work, *The Danvers* (1866), achieved some success, and she
wrote regularly thereafter, eventually producing more than a dozen
novels, as well as essays and short stories. The following story,
which first appeared in *Temple Bar: A London Magazine for Town
and Country Readers* in April 1890, treats an undead being that ter-
rifies a village, albeit without any blood sucking!

LET LOOSE

MARY CHOLMONDELEY

THE DEAD ABIDE WITH US!
THOUGH STARK AND COLD
EARTH SEEMS TO GRIP THEM,
THEY ARE WITH US STILL...

Some years ago I took up architecture, and made a tour through Holland, studying the buildings of that interesting country. I was not then aware that it is not enough to take up art. Art must take you up, too. I never doubted but that my passing enthusiasm for her would be returned. When I discovered that she was a stern mistress, who did not immediately respond to my attentions, I naturally transferred them to another shrine. There are other things in the world besides art. I am now a landscape gardener.

But at the time of which I write I was engaged in a violent flirtation with architecture. I had one companion on this expedition, who has since become one of the leading architects of the day. He was a thin, determined-looking man with a screwed-up face and heavy jaw, slow of speech, and absorbed in his work to a degree which I quickly found tiresome. He was possessed of a certain quiet power of overcoming obstacles which I have rarely seen equaled. He has since become my brother-in-law, so I ought to know; for my parents did not like him much and opposed the marriage, and my sister did not like him at all, and refused him over and over again; but, nevertheless, he eventually married her.

I have thought since that one of his reasons for choosing me as his travelling companion on this occasion was because he was getting up steam for what he subsequently termed "an alliance with my family," but the idea never entered my head at the time. A more careless man as to dress I have rarely met, and yet, in all the heat of July in Holland, I noticed that he never appeared without a high, starched collar, which had not even fashion to commend it at that time.

I often chaffed him about his splendid collars, and asked him why he wore them, but without eliciting any response. One evening, as we were walking back to our lodgings in

Middeburg, I attacked him for about the thirtieth time on the subject.

"Why on earth do you wear them?" I said.

"You have, I believe, asked me that question many times," he replied, in his slow, precise utterance; "but always on occasions when I was occupied. I am now at leisure, and I will tell you."

And he did.

I have put down what he said, as nearly in his own words as I can remember them.

TEN YEARS AGO, I was asked to read a paper on English Frescoes at the Institute of British Architects. I was determined to make the paper as good as I could, down to the slightest details, and I consulted many books on the subject, and studied every fresco I could find. My father, who had been an architect, had left me, at his death, all his papers and note-books on the subject of architecture. I searched them diligently, and found in one of them a slight unfinished sketch of nearly fifty years ago that specially interested me. Underneath was noted, in his clear, small hand—*Frescoed east wall of crypt. Parish Church. Wet Waste-on-the-Wolds, Yorkshire (viâ Pickering).*

The sketch had such a fascination for me that I decided to go there and see the fresco for myself. I had only a very vague idea as to where Wet Waste-on-the-Wolds was, but I was ambitious for the success of my paper; it was hot in London, and I set off on my long journey not without a certain degree of pleasure, with my dog Brian, a large nondescript brindled creature, as my only companion.

I reached Pickering, in Yorkshire,[1] in the course of the afternoon, and then began a series of experiments on local lines which ended, after several hours, in my finding myself deposited at a little out-of-the-world station within nine or ten miles of Wet Waste. As no conveyance of any kind was to be had, I shouldered my portmanteau, and set out on a long white road that stretched away into the distance over the bare, treeless wold. I must have walked for several hours, over a waste of moorland patched with heather, when a doctor passed me, and gave me a lift to within a mile of my destination.

The mile was a long one, and it was quite dark by the time I saw the feeble glimmer of lights in front of me, and found that I had reached Wet Waste. I had considerable difficulty in getting anyone to take me in; but at last I persuaded the owner of the public-house to give me a bed, and, quite tired out, I got into it as soon as possible, for fear he should change his mind, and fell asleep to the sound of a little stream below my window.

I was up early next morning, and inquired directly after breakfast the way to the clergyman's house, which I found was close at hand. At Wet Waste everything was close at hand. The whole village seemed composed of a straggling row of one-storeyed grey stone houses, the same color as the stone walls that separated the few fields enclosed from the surrounding waste, and as the little bridges over the beck[2] that ran down one side of the grey wide street. Everything was grey. The church, the low tower of which I could see at a little distance, seemed to have been built of

---

[1] Yorkshire is one of the northern counties of England, known as "God's own country" for its greenery. Pickering and Wet Waste-on-the-Wolds are fictional. A "wold" is an open range of hilly country.

[2] (North England): a brook, especially a swiftly running stream with steep banks.

the same stone; so was the parsonage when I came up to it, accompanied on my way by a mob of rough, uncouth children, who eyed me and Brian with half-defiant curiosity.

The clergyman was at home, and after a short delay I was admitted. Leaving Brian in charge of my drawing materials, I followed the servant into a low paneled room, in which, at a latticed window, a very old man was sitting. The morning light fell on his white head bent low over a litter of papers and books.

"Mr. Er—?" he said, looking up slowly, with one finger keeping his place in a book.

"Blake."

"Blake," he repeated after me, and was silent.

I told him that I was an architect; that I had come to study a fresco in the crypt of his church, and asked for the keys.

"The crypt," he said, pushing up his spectacles and peering hard at me. "The crypt has been closed for thirty years. Ever since—" and he stopped short.

"I should be much obliged for the keys," I said again.

He shook his head. "No," he said. "No one goes in there now."

"It is a pity," I remarked, "for I have come a long way with that one object"; and I told him about the paper I had been asked to read, and the trouble I was taking with it.

He became interested. "Ah!" he said, laying down his pen, and removing his finger from the page before him, "I can understand that. I also was young once, and fired with ambition. The lines have fallen to me in somewhat lonely places, and for forty years I have held the cure of souls in this place, where, truly, I have seen but little of the world, though I myself may be not unknown in the paths of literature. Possibly you may have read a pamphlet, written by myself, on the Syrian version of the *Three Authentic Epistles of Ignatius*?"[3]

"Sir," I said, "I am ashamed to confess that I have not time to read even the most celebrated books. My one object in life is my art. *Ars longa, vita brevis,*[4] you know."

"You are right, my son," said the old man, evidently disappointed, but looking at me kindly. "There are diversities of gifts, and if the Lord has entrusted you with a talent, look to it. Lay it not up in a napkin."

I said I would not do so if he would lend me the keys of the crypt. He seemed startled by my recurrence to the subject and looked undecided.

"Why not?" he murmured to himself. "The youth appears a good youth. And superstition! What is it but distrust in God!"

He got up slowly, and taking a large bunch of keys out of his pocket, opened with

---

[3] Ignatius of Antioch in Syria (*c.* 34 – *c.* 107 C.E.) was among the Apostolic Fathers, and a student of John the Apostle. En route to his martyrdom in Rome (he was sentenced to be eaten by lions in the Coliseum), Ignatius wrote a series of letters which have been preserved as an example of very early Christian theology. The authenticity of the letters has been debated throughout the history of the church, particularly in the seventeenth century. (There are fifteen letters in question; most church authorities recognize only seven, some only three, and others say all are fake, written in 250 C.E.)

[4] First two lines of the Latin translation of an aphorism by Ancient Greek physician Hippocrates; commonly understood as "art is long, life is short." Some scholars interpret "art" to mean technique or skill (referring to medicine), changing the meaning to "it takes a long time to acquire expertise, and one only has a short time to do so."

one of them an oak cupboard in the corner of the room.

"They should be here," he muttered, peering in; "but the dust of many years deceives the eye. See, my son, if among these parchments there be two keys; one of iron and very large, and the other steel, and of a long thin appearance."

I went eagerly to help him, and presently found in a back drawer two keys tied together, which he recognized at once.

"Those are they," he said. "The long one opens the first door at the bottom of the steps which go down against the outside wall of the church yard by the sword graven in the wall. The second opens (but it is hard of opening and of shutting) the iron door within the passage leading to the crypt itself. My son, is it necessary to your treatise that you should enter this crypt?"

I replied that it was absolutely necessary.

"Then take them," he said, "and in the evening you will bring them to me again."

I said I might want to go several days running, and asked if he would not allow me to keep them till I had finished my work; but on that point he was firm.

"Likewise," he added, "be careful that you lock the first door at the foot of the steps before you unlock the second, and lock the second also while you are within. Furthermore, when you come out lock the iron inner door as well as the wooden one."

I promised I would do so, and, after thanking him, hurried away, delighted at my success in obtaining the keys. Finding Brian and my sketching materials waiting for me in the porch, I eluded the vigilance of my escort of children by taking the narrow private path between the parsonage and the church which was close at hand, standing in a quadrangle of ancient yews.

The church itself was interesting, and I noticed that it must have arisen out of the ruins of a previous building, judging from the number of fragments of stone caps and arches, bearing traces of very early carving, now built into the walls. There were incised crosses, too, in some places, and one especially caught my attention, being flanked by a large sword.

It was in trying to get a nearer look at this that I stumbled, and, looking down, saw at my feet a flight of narrow stone steps green with moss and mildew. Evidently this was the entrance to the crypt. I at once descended the steps, taking care of my footing, for they were damp and slippery in the extreme. Brian accompanied me, as nothing would induce him to remain behind.

By the time I had reached the bottom of the stairs, I found myself almost in darkness, and I had to strike a light before I could find the keyhole and the proper key to fit into it. The door, which was of wood, opened inwards fairly easily, although an accumulation of mould and rubbish on the ground outside showed it had not been used for many years. Having got through it, which was not altogether an easy matter, as nothing would induce it to open more than about eighteen inches, I carefully locked it behind me, although I should have preferred to leave it open, as there is to some minds an unpleasant feeling in being locked in anywhere, in case of a sudden exit seeming advisable.

I kept my candle alight with some difficulty, and after groping my way down a low and of course exceedingly dank passage, came to another door. A toad was squatting against it, who looked as if he had been sitting there about a hundred years. As I lowered the candle to the floor, he gazed at the light with unblinking eyes, and then retreated slowly into a crevice in the wall, leaving against the door a small cavity in the dry mud which had gradually silted up round his person. I noticed that this door was of iron, and had a long bolt, which, however, was broken. Without delay, I fitted the second key into the lock, and pushing the door open after considerable difficulty, I felt the cold breath of the crypt upon my face.

I must own I experienced a momentary regret at locking the second door again as soon as I was well inside, but I felt it my duty to do so. Then, leaving the key in the lock, I seized my candle and looked round. I was standing in a low vaulted chamber with groined roof, cut out of the solid rock. It was difficult to see where the crypt ended, as further light thrown on any point only showed other rough archways or openings, cut in the rock, which had probably served at one time for family vaults.

A peculiarity of the Wet Waste crypt, which I had not noticed in other places of that description, was the tasteful arrangement of skulls and bones which were packed about four feet high on either side. The skulls were symmetrically built up to within a few inches of the top of the low archway on my left, and the shin bones were arranged in the same manner on my right. But the fresco! I looked round for it in vain. Perceiving at the further end of the crypt a very low and very massive archway, the entrance to which was not filled up with bones, I passed under it, and found myself in a second smaller chamber. Holding my candle above my head, the first object its light fell upon was—the fresco, and at a glance I saw that it was unique.

Setting down some of my things with a trembling hand on a rough stone shelf hard by, which had evidently been a Credence table,[5] I examined the work more closely. It was a reredos[6] over what had probably been the altar at the time the priests were proscribed. The fresco belonged to the earliest part of the fifteenth century, and was so perfectly preserved that I could almost trace the limits of each day's work in the plaster, as the artist had dashed it on and smoothed it out with his trowel. The subject was the Ascension, gloriously treated. I can hardly describe my elation as I stood and looked at it, and reflected that this magnificent specimen of English fresco painting would be made known to the world by myself. Recollecting myself at last, I opened my sketching bag, and, lighting all the candles I had brought with me, set to work.

Brian walked about near me, and though I was not otherwise than glad of his company in my rather lonely position, I wished several times I had left him behind. He seemed restless, and even the sight of so many bones appeared to exercise no soothing effect upon him. At last, however, after repeated commands, he lay down, watchful but motionless, on the stone floor.

I must have worked for several hours, and I was pausing to rest my eyes and hands, when I noticed for the first time the intense stillness that surrounded me. No sound from me reached the outer world. The church clock which had clanged out so loud and ponderously as I went down the steps, had not since sent the faintest whisper of its iron tongue down to me below. All was silent as the grave. This was the

[5] A small side table in the sanctuary of a Christian church used in the celebration of the Eucharist.

[6] An open hearth of a fireplace or a screen placed behind a table.

grave. Those who had come here had indeed gone down into silence. I repeated the words to myself, or rather they repeated themselves to me.

Gone down into silence.

I was awakened from my reverie by a faint sound. I sat still and listened. Bats occasionally frequent vaults and underground places.

The sound continued, a faint, stealthy, rather unpleasant sound. I do not know what kinds of sounds bats make, whether pleasant or otherwise. Suddenly there was a noise as of something falling, a momentary pause and then—an almost imperceptible but distant jangle as of a key.

I had left the key in the lock after I had turned it, and I now regretted having done so. I got up, took one of the candles, and went back into the larger crypt—for though I trust I am not so effeminate as to be rendered nervous by hearing a noise for which I cannot instantly account; still, on occasions of this kind, I must honestly say I should prefer that they did not occur. As I came towards the iron door, there was another distinct (I had almost said hurried) sound. The impression on my mind was one of great haste. When I reached the door, and held the candle near the lock to take out the key, I perceived that the other one, which hung by a short string to its fellow, was vibrating slightly. I should have preferred not to find it vibrating, as there seemed no occasion for such a course; but I put them both into my pocket, and turned to go back to my work.

As I turned, I saw on the ground what had occasioned the louder noise I had heard, namely, a skull which had evidently just slipped from its place on the top of one of the walls of bones, and had rolled almost to my feet. There, disclosing a few more inches of the top of an archway behind, was the place from which it had been dislodged. I stooped to pick it up, but fearing to displace any more skulls by meddling with the pile, and not liking to gather up its scattered teeth, I let it lie, and went back to my work, in which I was soon so completely absorbed that I was only roused at last by my candles beginning to burn low and go out one after another.

Then, with a sigh of regret, for I had not nearly finished, I turned to go. Poor Brian, who had never quite reconciled himself to the place, was beside himself with delight. As I opened the iron door he pushed past me, and a moment later I heard him whining and scratching, and I had almost added, beating, against the wooden one. I locked the iron door, and hurried down the passage as quickly as I could, and almost before I had got the other one ajar there seemed to be a rush past me into the open air, and Brian was bounding up the steps and out of sight. As I stopped to take out the key, I felt quite deserted and left behind. When I came out once more into the sunlight, there was a vague sensation all about me in the air of exultant freedom.

It was already late in the afternoon, and after I had sauntered back to the parsonage to give up the keys, I persuaded the people of the public-house to let me join in the family meal, which was spread out in the kitchen. The inhabitants of Wet Waste were primitive people, with the frank, unabashed manner that flourishes still in lonely places, especially in the wilds of Yorkshire; but I had no idea that in these days of penny posts and cheap newspapers such entire ignorance of the outer world could have existed in any corner, however remote, of Great Britain.

When I took one of the neighbor's children on my knee—a pretty little girl with the palest aureole of flaxen hair I had ever seen—and began to draw pictures for her of the birds and beasts of other countries, I was instantly surrounded by a crowd of children, and even grown-up people, while others came to their doorways and looked on from a distance, calling to each other in the strident unknown tongue which I have since discovered goes by the name of "Broad Yorkshire."

The following morning, as I came out of my room, I perceived that something was amiss in the village. A buzz of voices reached me as I passed the bar, and in the next house I could hear through the open window a high-pitched wail of lamentation.

The woman who brought me my breakfast was in tears, and in answer to my questions, told me that the neighbor's child, the little girl whom I had taken on my knee the evening before, had died in the night.

I felt sorry for the general grief that the little creature's death seemed to arouse, and the uncontrolled wailing of the poor mother took my appetite away.

I hurried off early to my work, calling on my way for the keys, and with Brian for my companion descended once more into the crypt, and drew and measured with an absorption that gave me no time that day to listen for sounds real or fancied. Brian, too, on this occasion seemed quite content, and slept peacefully beside me on the stone floor. When I had worked as long as I could, I put away my books with regret that even then I had not quite finished, as I had hoped to do. It would be necessary come again for a short time on the morrow. When I returned the keys late that afternoon, the old clergyman met me at the door, and asked me to come in and have tea with him.

"And has the work prospered?" he asked, as we sat down in the long, low room, into which I had just been ushered, and where he seemed to live entirely.

I told him it had, and showed it to him.

"You have seen the original, of course?" I said.

"Once," he replied, gazing fixedly at it. He evidently did not care to be communicative, so I turned the conversation to the age of the church.

"All here is old," he said. "When I was young, forty years ago, and came here because I had no means of mine own, and was much moved to marry at that time, I felt oppressed that all was so old; and that this place was so far removed from the world, for which I had at times longing grievous to be borne; but I had chosen my lot, and with it I was forced to be content. My son, marry not in youth, for love, which truly in that season is a mighty power, turns away the heart from study, and young children break the back of ambition. Neither marry in middle life, when woman is seen to be but a woman and her talk a weariness, so you will not be burdened with a wife in your old age."

I had my own views on the subject of marriage, for I am of opinion that a well-chosen companion of domestic tastes and docile and devoted temperament may be of material assistance to a professional man. But my opinions once formulated, it is not of moment to me to discuss them with others, so I changed the subject, and asked if the neighboring villages were as antiquated as Wet Waste.

"Yes, all about here is old," he repeated. "The paved road leading to Dyke Fens is an ancient pack road, made even in the time of the Romans. Dyke Fens, which is very near here, a matter of but four or five miles, is likewise old, and forgotten by the world. The Reformation never reached it. It stopped here. And at Dyke Fens they still have a priest and a bell, and bow down before the saints. It is a damnable heresy, and weekly I expound it as such to my people, showing them true doctrines; and I have heard that this same priest has so far yielded himself to the Evil One that he has preached against me as withholding gospel truths from my flock; but I take no heed of it, neither of his pamphlet touching the Clementine Homilies, in which he vainly contradicts that which I have plainly set forth and proven beyond doubt, concerning the word *Asaph*."[7]

The old man was fairly off on his favorite subject, and it was some time before I could get away. As it was, he followed me to the door, and I only escaped because the old clerk hobbled up at that moment, and claimed his attention.

The following morning I went for the keys for the third and last time. I had decided to leave early the next day. I was tired of Wet Waste, and a certain gloom seemed to my fancy to be gathering over the place. There was a sensation of trouble in the air, as if, although the day was bright and clear, a storm were coming.

This morning, to my astonishment, the keys were refused to me when I asked for them. I did not, however, take the refusal as final—I make it a rule never to take a refusal as final—and after a short delay I was shown into the room where, as usual, the clergyman was sitting, or rather, on this occasion, was walking up and down.

"My son," he said with vehemence, "I know wherefore you have come, but it is of no avail. I cannot lend the keys again." I replied that, on the contrary, I hoped he would give them to me at once. "It is impossible," he repeated. "I did wrong, exceeding wrong. I will never part with them again."

"Why not?"

He hesitated, and then said slowly:—

"The old clerk, Abraham Kelly, died last night." He paused, and then went on: "The doctor has just been here to tell me of that which is a mystery to him. I do not wish the people of the place to know it, and only to me he has mentioned it, but he has discovered plainly on the throat of the old man, and also, but more faintly on the child's, marks as of strangulation. None but he has observed it, and he is at a loss how to account for it. I, alas!—can account for it but in one way, but in one way!"

I did not see what all this had to do with the crypt, but to humor the old man, I asked what that way was.

"It is a long story, and, haply,[8] to a stranger it may appear but foolishness, but I will even tell it; for I perceive that unless I furnish a reason for withholding the keys, you will not cease to entreat me for them.

"I told you at first when you inquired of me concerning the crypt, that it had been closed these thirty years, and so it was. Thirty years ago a certain Sir Roger Despard departed this life, even the Lord of the manor of Wet Waste and Dyke Fens, the last of his family, which is now, thank the Lord, extinct. He was a man of a vile life, neither fearing God nor regarding man, nor having compassion or innocence, and the Lord appeared to

---

[7] Hebrew for "God has gathered"; the name of several Biblical figures.

[8] By accident or luck.

have given him over to the tormentors even in this world, for he suffered many things of his vices, more especially from drunkenness, in which seasons, and they were many, he was as one possessed by seven devils, being an abomination to his household and a root of bitterness to all, both high and low.

"And, at last, the cup of his iniquity being full to the brim, he came to die, and I went to exhort him on his death-bed; for I heard that terror had come upon him, and that evil imaginations encompassed him so thick on every side, that few of them that were with him could abide in his presence. But when I saw him I perceived that there was no place of repentance left for him, and he scoffed at me and my superstition, even as he lay dying, and swore there was no God and no angel, and all were damned even as he was.

"And the next day, towards evening, the pains of death came upon him, and he raved the more exceedingly, inasmuch as he said he was being strangled by the Evil One. Now on his table was his hunting knife, and with his last strength he crept and laid hold upon it, no man withstanding him, and swore a great oath that if he went down to burn in hell, he would leave one of his hands behind on earth, and that it would never rest until it had drawn blood from the throat of another and strangled him, even as he himself was being strangled. And he cut off his own right hand at the wrist, and no man dared go near him to stop him, and the blood went through the floor, even down to the ceiling of the room below, and thereupon he died.

"And they called me in the night, and told me of his oath, and I counseled that no man should speak of it, and I took the dead hand, which none had ventured to touch, and

I laid it beside him in his coffin; for I thought it better he should take it with him, so that he might have it, if haply some day after much tribulation he should perchance be moved to stretch forth his hands towards God. But the story got spread about, and the people were affrighted, so, when he came to be buried in the place of his fathers, he being the last of his family, and the crypt likewise full, I had it closed, and kept the keys myself, and suffered no man to enter therein any more; for truly he was a man of an evil life, and the devil is not yet wholly overcome, nor cast chained into the lake of fire.

"So in time the story died out, for in thirty years much is forgotten. And when you came and asked me for the keys, I was at the first minded to withhold them; but I thought it was a vain superstition, and I perceived that you do but ask a second time for what is first refused; so I let you have them, seeing it was not an idle curiosity, but a desire to improve the talent committed to you, that led you to require them."

The old man stopped, and I remained silent, wondering what would be the best way to get them just once more.

"Surely, sir," I said at last, "one so cultivated and deeply read as yourself cannot be biased by an idle superstition."

"I trust not," he replied, "and yet—it is a strange thing that since the crypt was opened two people have died, and the mark is plain up on the throat of the old man and visible on the young child. No blood was drawn, but the second time the grip was stronger than the first. The third time, perchance—"

"Superstition such as that," I said with authority, "is an entire want of faith in God. You once said so yourself."

I took a high moral tone which is often

efficacious with conscientious, humble-minded people.

He agreed, and accused himself of not having faith as a grain of mustard seed; but even when I had got him so far as that, I had a severe struggle for the keys. It was only when I finally explained to him that if any malign influence had been let loose the first day, at any rate, it was out now for good or evil, and no further going or coming of mine could make any difference, that I finally gained my point. I was young, and he was old; and, being much shaken by what had occurred, he gave way at last, and I wrested the keys from him.

I will not deny that I went down the steps that day with a vague, indefinable repugnance, which was only accentuated by the closing of the two doors behind me. I remembered then, for the first time, the faint jangling of the key and other sounds which I had noticed the first day, and how one of the skulls had fallen. I went to the place where it still lay. I have already said these walls of skulls were built up so high as to be within a few inches of the top of the low archways that led into more distant portions of the vault.

The displacement of the skull in question had left a small hole just large enough for me to put my hand through. I noticed for the first time, over the archway above it, a carved coat-of-arms, and the name, now almost obliterated, of Despard. This, no doubt, was the Despard vault. I could not resist moving a few more skulls and looking in, holding my candle as near the aperture as I could.

The vault was full. Piled high, one upon another, were old coffins, and remnants of coffins, and strewn bones. I attribute my present determination to be cremated to the painful impression produced on me by this spectacle. The coffin nearest the archway alone was intact, save for a large crack across the lid. I could not get a ray from my candle to fall on the brass plates, but I felt no doubt this was the coffin of the wicked Sir Roger.

I put back the skulls, including the one which had rolled down, and carefully finished my work. I was not there much more than an hour, but I was glad to get away.

If I could have left Wet Waste at once I should have done so, for I had a totally unreasonable longing to leave the place; but I found that only one train stopped during the day at the station from which I had come, and that it would not be possible to be in time for it that day.

Accordingly I submitted to the inevitable, and wandered about with Brian for the remainder of the afternoon and until late in the evening, sketching and smoking. The day was oppressively hot, and even after the sun had set across the burnt stretches of the wolds, it seemed to grow very little cooler. Not a breath stirred. In the evening, when I was tired of loitering in the lanes, I went up to my own room, and after contemplating afresh my finished study of the fresco, I suddenly set to work to write the part of my paper bearing upon it.

As a rule, I write with difficulty, but that evening words came to me with winged speed, and with them a hovering impression that I must make haste, that I was much pressed for time. I wrote and wrote, until my candles guttered out and left me trying to finish by the moonlight, which, until I endeavored to write by it, seemed as clear as day.

I had to put away my MS., and, feeling it was too early to go to bed, for the church clock was just counting out ten, I sat down by the open window and leaned out to try and catch a breath of air. It was a night of exceptional beauty; and as I looked out my nervous haste and hurry of mind were allayed. The moon, a perfect circle, was—if so poetic an expression be permissible—as it were, sailing across a calm sky. Every detail of the little village was as clearly illuminated by its beams as if it were broad day; so, also, was the adjacent church with its primeval yews, while even the wolds beyond were dimly indicated, as if through tracing paper.

I sat a long time leaning against the window-sill. The heat was still intense. I am not, as a rule, easily elated or readily cast down; but as I sat that night in the lonely village on the moors, with Brian's head against my knee, how, or why, I know not, a great depression gradually came upon me.

My mind went back to the crypt and the countless dead who had been laid there. The sight of the goal to which all human life, and strength, and beauty, travel in the end, had not affected me at the time, but now the very air about me seemed heavy with death.

What was the good, I asked myself, of working and toiling, and grinding down my heart and youth in the mill of long and strenuous effort, seeing that in the grave folly and talent, idleness and labor lie together, and are alike forgotten? Labor seemed to stretch before me till my heart ached to think of it, to stretch before me even to the end of life, and then came, as the recompense of my labor—the grave. Even if I succeeded, if, after wearing my life threadbare with toil, I succeeded, what remained to me in the end? The grave. A little sooner, while the hands and eyes were still strong to labor, or a little later, when all power and vision had been taken from them; sooner or later only—the grave.

I do not apologize for the excessively morbid tenor of these reflections, as I hold that they were caused by the lunar effects which I have endeavored to transcribe. The moon in its various quarterings has always exerted a marked influence on what I may call the sub-dominant, namely, the poetic side of my nature.

I roused myself at last, when the moon came to look in upon me where I sat, and, leaving the window open, I pulled myself together and went to bed.

I fell asleep almost immediately, but I do not fancy I could have been asleep very long when I was wakened by Brian. He was growling in a low, muffled tone, as he sometimes did in his sleep, when his nose was buried in his rug. I called out to him to shut up; and as he did not do so, turned in bed to find my match box or something to throw at him.

The moonlight was still in the room, and as I looked at him I saw him raise his head and evidently wake up. I admonished him, and was just on the point of falling asleep when he began to growl again in a low, savage manner that waked me most effectually.

Presently he shook himself and got up, and began prowling about the room. I sat up in bed and called to him, but he paid no attention. Suddenly I saw him stop short in the moonlight; he showed his teeth, and crouched down, his eyes following something in the air.

I looked at him in horror. Was he going mad? His eyes were glaring, and his head moved slightly as if he were following the rapid movements of an enemy. Then, with a furious snarl, he suddenly sprang from the ground, and rushed in great leaps across the room towards me, dashing himself against the furniture, his eyes rolling, snatching and tearing wildly in the air with his teeth.

I saw he had gone mad. I leaped out of

bed, and rushing at him, caught him by the throat. The moon had gone behind a cloud; but in the darkness I felt him turn upon me, felt him rise up, and his teeth close in my throat. I was being strangled. With all the strength of despair, I kept my grip of his neck, and, dragging him across the room, tried to crush in his head against the iron rail of my bedstead. It was my only chance. I felt the blood running down my neck. I was suffocating. After one moment of frightful struggle, I beat his head against the bar and heard his skull give way. I felt him give one strong shudder, a groan, and then I fainted away.

When I came to myself I was lying on the floor, surrounded by the people of the house, my reddened hands still clutching Brian's throat. Someone was holding a candle towards me, and the draught from the window made it flare and waver. I looked at Brian. He was stone dead. The blood from his battered head was trickling slowly over my hands. His great jaw was fixed in something that— in the uncertain light—I could not see.

They turned the light a little.

"Oh, God!" I shrieked. "There! Look! Look!"

"He's off his head," said someone, and I fainted again.

I was ill for about a fortnight without regaining consciousness, a waste of time of which even now I cannot think without poignant regret. When I did recover consciousness, I found I was being carefully nursed by the old clergyman and the people of the house. I have often heard the unkindness of the world in general inveighed against, but for my part I can honestly say that I have received many more kindnesses than I have time to repay. Country people especially are remarkably attentive to strangers in illness.

I could not rest until I had seen the doctor who attended me, and had received his assurance that I should be equal to reading my paper on the appointed day. This pressing anxiety removed, I told him of what I had seen before I fainted the second time. He listened attentively, and then assured me, in a manner that was intended to be soothing, that I was suffering from an hallucination, due, no doubt, to the shock of my dog's sudden madness.

"Did you see the dog after it was dead?" I asked. He said he did. The whole jaw was covered with blood and foam; the teeth certainly seemed convulsively fixed, but the case being evidently one of extraordinarily virulent hydrophobia,[9] owing to the intense heat, he had had the body burned immediately.

MY COMPANION STOPPED speaking as we reached our lodgings, and went upstairs. Then, lighting a candle, he slowly turned down his collar.

"You see I have the marks still," he said, "but I have no fear of dying of hydrophobia. I am told such peculiar scars could not have been made by the teeth of a dog. If you look closely you see the pressure of the five fingers. That is the reason why I wear high collars."

❧

---

[9] Rabies; especially later stages of the infection.

Mary Elizabeth Braddon

MARY ELIZABETH BRADDON (1837-1915), author of scores of sensational novels (she eventually penned seventy-five), did not begin writing until 1860, and after two obscure novels she achieved fame and fortune with the wildly popular *Lady Audley's Secret* (1862). She founded *Belgravia Magazine* in 1866 and later edited *Temple Bar Magazine*; her literary output included plays, comedies, and verse.

"Good Lady Ducayne" was first published in the February 1896 issue of *The Strand Magazine*. The story is another echo of the legendary depredations of Countess Elizabeth Bathory, who preyed on young women to prolong her vitality. Here the Lady Ducayne exhibits seemly moderation, and while she may kill her victims, she compensates them well!

GOOD LADY DUCAYNE

MARY ELIZABETH BRADDON

I.

Bella Rolleston had made up her mind that her only chance of earning her bread and helping her mother to an occasional crust was by going out into the great unknown world as companion to a lady. She was willing to go to any lady rich enough to pay her a salary and so eccentric as to wish for a hired companion.

Five shillings, told off reluctantly from one of those sovereigns which were so rare with the mother and daughter, and which melted away so quickly, five solid shillings, had been handed to a smartly-dressed lady in an office in Harbeck Street, London, W., with the hope that this very Superior Person would find a situation and a salary for Miss Rolleston.

The Superior Person glanced at the two half-crowns as they lay on the table where Bella's hand had placed them, to make sure they were neither of them florins, before she wrote a description of Bella's qualifications and requirements in a formidable-looking ledger.

"Age?" she asked, curtly.

"Eighteen, last July."

"Any accomplishments?"

"No; I am not at all accomplished. If I were I should want to be a governess—a companion seems the lowest stage."

"We have some highly accomplished ladies on our books as companions, or chaperone companions."

"Oh, I know!" babbled Bella, loquacious in her youthful candor. "But that is quite a different thing. Mother hasn't been able to afford a piano since I was twelve years old, so I'm afraid I've forgotten how to play. And I have had to help mother with her needlework, so there hasn't been much time to study."

"Please don't waste time upon explaining what you can't do, but kindly tell me anything you can do," said the Superior Person, crushingly, with her pen poised between delicate fingers waiting to write. "Can you read aloud for two or three hours at a stretch? Are you active and handy, an early riser, a good walker, sweet tempered, and obliging?"

"I can say yes to all those questions except about the sweetness. I think I have a pretty good temper, and I should be anxious to oblige anybody who paid for my services. I should want them to feel that I was really earning my salary."

"The kind of ladies who come to me would not care for a talkative companion," said the Person, severely, having finished writing in her book. "My connection lies chiefly among the aristocracy, and in that class considerable deference is expected."

"Oh, of course," said Bella; "but it's quite different when I'm talking to you. I want to tell you all about myself once and forever."

"I am glad it is to be only once!" said the Person, with the edges of her lips.

The Person was of uncertain age, tightly laced in a black silk gown. She had a powdery complexion and a handsome clump of somebody else's hair on the top of her head. It may be that Bella's girlish freshness and vivacity had an irritating effect upon nerves weakened by an eight-hour day in that overheated second floor in Harbeck Street. To Bella the official apartment, with its Brussels carpet, velvet curtains and velvet chairs, and French clock, ticking loud on the marble chimney-piece, suggested the luxury of a palace, as compared with another second floor in Walworth where Mrs. Rolleston and her daughter had managed to exist for the last six years.

"Do you think you have anything on your books that would suit me?" faltered Bella, after a pause.

"Oh, dear, no; I have nothing in view at present," answered the Person, who had swept Bella's half-crowns into a drawer, absent-mindedly, with the tips of her fingers. "You see, you are so very unformed—so much too young to be companion to a lady of posi-tion. It is a pity you have not enough education for a nursery governess; that would be more in your line."

"And do you think it will be very long before you can get me a situation?" asked Bella, doubtfully.

"I really cannot say. Have you any particular reason for being so impatient—not a love affair, I hope?"

"A love affair!" cried Bella, with flaming cheeks. "What utter nonsense. I want a situation because mother is poor, and I hate being a burden to her. I want a salary that I can share with her."

"There won't be much margin for sharing in the salary you are likely to get at your age—and with your—very—unformed manners," said the Person, who found Bella's peony[1] cheeks, bright eyes, and unbridled vivacity more and more oppressive.

"Perhaps if you'd be kind enough to give me back the fee I could take it to an agency where the connection isn't quite so aristocratic," said Bella, who—as she told her mother in her recital of the interview—was determined not to be sat upon.

"You will find no agency that can do more for you than mine," replied the Person, whose harpy fingers never relinquished coin. "You will have to wait for your opportunity. Yours is an exceptional case: but I will bear you in mind, and if anything suitable offers I will write to you. I cannot say more than that."

The half-contemptuous bend of the stately head, weighted with borrowed hair, indicated the end of the interview. Bella went back to Walworth—tramped sturdily every inch of the way in the September afternoon—and "took off" the Superior Person for the

---

[1] The state flower of Indiana.

amusement of her mother and the landlady, who lingered in the shabby little sitting-room after bringing in the tea-tray, to applaud Miss Rolleston's "taking off."

"Dear, dear, what a mimic she is!" said the landlady. "You ought to have let her go on the stage, mum. She might have made her fortune as an actress."

II.

BELLA WAITED AND HOPED, and listened for the postman's knocks which brought such store of letters for the parlors and the first floor, and so few for that humble second floor, where mother and daughter sat sewing with hand and with wheel and treadle, for the greater part of the day. Mrs. Rolleston was a lady by birth and education; but it had been her bad fortune to marry a scoundrel; for the last half-dozen years she had been that worst of widows, a wife whose husband had deserted her. Happily, she was courageous, industrious, and a clever needle-woman; and she had been able just to earn a living for herself and her only child, by making mantles and cloaks for a West-end house. It was not a luxurious living. Cheap lodgings in a shabby street off the Walworth Road, scanty dinners, homely food, well-worn raiment, had been the portion of mother and daughter; but they loved each other so dearly, and Nature had made them both so light-hearted, that they had contrived somehow to be happy.

But now this idea of going out into the world as companion to some fine lady had rooted itself into Bella's mind, and although she idolized her mother, and although the parting of mother and daughter must needs tear two loving hearts into shreds, the girl longed for enterprise and change and excitement, as the pages of old longed to be knights, and to start for the Holy Land to break a lance with the infidel.

She grew tired of racing downstairs every time the postman knocked, only to be told "nothing for you, miss," by the smudgy-faced drudge who picked up the letters from the passage floor. "Nothing for you, miss," grinned the lodging-house drudge, till at last Bella took heart of grace and walked up to Harbeck Street, and asked the Superior Person how it was that no situation had been found for her.

"You are too young," said the Person, "and you want a salary."

"Of course I do," answered Bella; "don't other people want salaries?"

"Young ladies of your age generally want a comfortable home."

"I don't," snapped Bella. "I want to help mother."

"You can call again this day week,"[2] said the Person; "or, if I hear of anything in the meantime, I will write to you."

No letter came from the Person, and in exactly a week Bella put on her neatest hat, the one that had been seldomest caught in the rain, and trudged off to Harbeck Street.

It was a dull October afternoon, and there was a greyness in the air which might turn to fog before night. The Walworth Road shops gleamed brightly through that grey atmosphere, and though to a young lady reared in Mayfair or Belgravia such shop-windows would have been unworthy of a glance, they were a snare and temptation for Bella. There were so many things that she longed for, and would never be able to buy.

Harbeck Street is apt to be empty at this dead season of the year, a long, long street, an

[2] A "day week" is a "week from today."

endless perspective of eminently respectable houses. The Person's office was at the further end, and Bella looked down that long, grey vista almost despairingly, more tired than usual with the trudge from Walworth. As she looked, a carriage passed her, an old-fashioned, yellow chariot, on C springs,[3] drawn by a pair of high grey horses, with the stateliest of coachmen driving them, and a tall footman sitting by his side.

"It looks like the fairy godmother's coach," thought Bella. "I shouldn't wonder if it began by being a pumpkin."

It was a surprise when she reached the Person's door to find the yellow chariot standing before it, and the tall footman waiting near the doorstep. She was almost afraid to go in and meet the owner of that splendid carriage. She had caught only a glimpse of its occupant as the chariot rolled by, a plumed bonnet, a patch of ermine.

The Person's smart page ushered her upstairs and knocked at the official door. "Miss Rolleston," he announced, apologetically, while Bella waited outside.

"Show her in," said the Person, quickly; and then Bella heard her murmuring something in a low voice to her client.

Bella went in fresh, blooming, a living image of youth and hope, and before she looked at the Person her gaze was riveted by the owner of the chariot.

Never had she seen anyone as old as the old lady sitting by the Person's fire: a little old figure, wrapped from chin to feet in an ermine mantle; a withered, old face under a plumed bonnet—a face so wasted by age that it seemed only a pair of eyes and a peaked chin. The nose was peaked, too, but

between the sharply pointed chin and the great, shining eyes, the small, aquiline nose was hardly visible.

"This is Miss Rolleston, Lady Ducayne."

Claw-like fingers, flashing with jewels, lifted a double eyeglass to Lady Ducayne's shining black eyes, and through the glasses Bella saw those unnaturally bright eyes magnified to a gigantic size, and glaring at her awfully.

"Miss Torpinter has told me all about you," said the old voice that belonged to the eyes. "Have you good health? Are you strong and active, able to eat well, sleep well, walk well, able to enjoy all that there is good in life?"

"I have never known what it is to be ill, or idle," answered Bella.

"Then I think you will do for me."

"Of course, in the event of references being perfectly satisfactory," put in the Person.

"I don't want references. The young woman looks frank and innocent. I'll take her on trust."

"So like you, dear Lady Ducayne," murmured Miss Torpinter.

"I want a strong young woman whose health will give me no trouble."

"You have been so unfortunate in that respect," cooed the Person, whose voice and manner were subdued to a melting sweetness by the old woman's presence.

"Yes, I've been rather unlucky," grunted Lady Ducayne.

"But I am sure Miss Rolleston will not disappoint you, though certainly after your unpleasant experience with Miss Tomson, who looked the picture of health—and Miss Blandy, who said she had never seen a doctor since she was vaccinated—"

---

[3] Not surprisingly, a spring in the shape of a letter "C." The point here is that this is an old-fashioned carriage as the newer ones had elliptical springs.

"Lies, no doubt," muttered Lady Ducayne, and then turning to Bella, she asked, curtly, "You don't mind spending the winter in Italy, I suppose?"

In Italy! The very word was magical. Bella's fair young face flushed crimson.

"It has been the dream of my life to see Italy," she gasped.

From Walworth to Italy! How far, how impossible such a journey had seemed to that romantic dreamer.

"Well, your dream will be realized. Get yourself ready to leave Charing Cross by the train deluxe[4] this day week at eleven. Be sure you are at the station a quarter before the hour. My people will look after you and your luggage."

Lady Ducayne rose from her chair, assisted by her crutch-stick, and Miss Torpinter escorted her to the door.

"And with regard to salary?" questioned the Person on the way.

"Salary, oh, the same as usual—and if the young woman wants a quarter's pay in advance you can write to me for a check," Lady Ducayne answered, carelessly.

Miss Torpinter went all the way downstairs with her client, and waited to see her seated in the yellow chariot. When she came upstairs again she was slightly out of breath, and she had resumed that superior manner which Bella had found so crushing.

"You may think yourself uncommonly lucky, Miss Rolleston," she said. "I have dozens of young ladies on my books whom I might have recommended for this situation—but I remembered having told you to call this afternoon—and I thought I would give you a chance. Old Lady Ducayne is one of the best people on my books. She gives her companion a hundred a year, and pays all traveling expenses. You will live in the lap of luxury."

"A hundred a year![5] How too lovely! Shall I have to dress very grandly? Does Lady Ducayne keep much company?"

"At her age! No, she lives in seclusion—in her own apartments—her French maid, her footman, her medical attendant, her courier."

"Why did those other companions leave her?" asked Bella.

"Their health broke down!"

"Poor things, and so they had to leave?"

"Yes, they had to leave. I suppose you would like a quarter's salary in advance?"

"Oh, yes, please. I shall have things to buy."

"Very well, I will write for Lady Ducayne's check, and I will send you the balance—after deducting my commission for the year."

"To be sure, I had forgotten the commission."

"You don't suppose I keep this office for pleasure."

"Of course not," murmured Bella, remembering the five shillings entrance fee; but nobody could expect a hundred a year and a winter in Italy for five shillings.

III.

FROM MISS ROLLESTON, at Cap Ferrino, to Mrs. Rolleston, in Beresford Street, Walworth, London.

How I wish you could see this place, dearest; the blue sky, the olive woods, the orange and lemon orchards between the cliffs and the sea—

---

[4] A train predominated by salon and dining cars (a luxurious but very expensive way to travel).

[5] This is excessive pay. In the Sherlock Holmes 1892 adventure "The Copper Beeches," the governess—note *governess*, not mere companion—is made suspicious by a salary offer of £100 per year.

sheltering in the hollow of the great hills—and with summer waves dancing up to the narrow ridge of pebbles and weeds which is the Italian idea of a beach! Oh, how I wish you could see it all, mother dear, and bask in this sunshine, that makes it so difficult to believe the date at the head of this paper. November! The air is like an English June—the sun is so hot that I can't walk a few yards without an umbrella. And to think of you at Walworth while I am here! I could cry at the thought that perhaps you will never see this lovely coast, this wonderful sea, these summer flowers that bloom in winter. There is a hedge of pink geraniums under my window, mother—a thick, rank hedge, as if the flowers grew wild— and there are Dijon roses climbing over arches and palisades all along the terrace—a rose garden full of bloom in November! Just picture it all! You could never imagine the luxury of this hotel. It is nearly new, and has been built and decorated regardless of expense. Our rooms are upholstered in pale blue satin, which shows up Lady Ducayne's parchment complexion; but as she sits all day in a corner of the balcony basking in the sun, except when she is in her carriage, and all the evening in her armchair close to the fire, and never sees anyone but her own people, her complexion matters very little.

She has the handsomest suite of rooms in the hotel. My bedroom is inside hers, the sweetest room—all blue satin and white lace—white enameled furniture, looking-glasses on every wall, till I know my pert little profile as I never knew it before. The room was really meant for Lady Ducayne's dressing-room, but she ordered one of the blue satin couches to be arranged as a bed for me—the prettiest little bed, which I can wheel near the window on sunny mornings, as it is on casters and easily moved about. I feel as if Lady Ducayne were a funny old grandmother, who had suddenly appeared in my life, very, very rich, and very, very kind.

She is not at all exacting. I read aloud to her a good deal, and she dozes and nods while I read. Sometimes I hear her moaning in her sleep—as if she had troublesome dreams. When she is tired of my reading she orders Francine, her maid, to read a French novel to her, and I hear her chuckle and groan now and then, as if she were more interested in those books than in Dickens or Scott. My French is not good enough to follow Francine, who reads very quickly. I have a great deal of liberty, for Lady Ducayne often tells me to run away and amuse myself; I roam about the hills for hours. Everything is so lovely. I lose myself in olive woods, always climbing up and up towards the pine woods above—and above the pines there are the snow mountains that just show their white peaks above the dark hills. Oh, you poor dear, how can I ever make you understand what this place is like—you, whose poor, tired eyes have only the opposite side of Beresford Street? Sometimes I go no farther than the terrace in front of the hotel, which is a favorite lounging-place with everybody. The gardens lie below, and the tennis courts where I sometimes play with a very nice girl, the only person in the hotel with whom I have made friends. She is a year older than I, and has come to Cap Ferrino with her brother, a doctor—or a medical student, who is going to be a doctor. He passed his M.B. exam. at Edinburgh[6] just before they left home, Lotta told me. He came to Italy entirely on his sister's account. She had a troublesome chest attack last summer and was ordered to winter abroad. They are orphans, quite alone in the world, and so fond of each other. It is

---

[6] Dr. Joseph Bell, a model for Sherlock Holmes, taught at Edinburgh University, and Arthur Conan Doyle received his medical degree there.

very nice for me to have such a friend as Lotta. She is so thoroughly respectable. I can't help using that word, for some of the girls in this hotel go on in a way that I know you would shudder at. Lotta was brought up by an aunt, deep down in the country, and knows hardly anything about life. Her brother won't allow her to read a novel, French or English, that he has not read and approved.[7]

"He treats me like a child," she told me, "but I don't mind, for it's nice to know somebody loves me, and cares about what I do, and even about my thoughts."

Perhaps this is what makes some girls so eager to marry—the want of someone strong and brave and honest and true to care for them and order them about. I want no one, mother darling, for I have you, and you are all the world to me. No husband could ever come between us two. If I ever were to marry he would have only the second place in my heart. But I don't suppose I ever shall marry, or even know what it is like to have an offer of marriage. No young man can afford to marry a penniless girl nowadays. Life is too expensive.

Mr. Stafford, Lotta's brother, is very clever, and very kind. He thinks it is rather hard for me to have to live with such an old woman as Lady Ducayne, but then he does not know how poor we are—you and I—and what a wonderful life this seems to me in this lovely place. I feel a selfish wretch for enjoying all my luxuries, while you, who want them so much more than I, have none of them—hardly know what they are like—do you, dearest?—for my scamp of a father began to go to the dogs soon after you were married, and since then life has been all trouble and care and struggle for you.

This letter was written when Bella had been less than a month at Cap Ferrino, before the novelty had worn off the landscape, and before the pleasure of luxurious surroundings had begun to cloy. She wrote to her mother every week, such long letters as girls who have lived in closest companionship with a mother alone can write; letters that are like a diary of heart and mind. She wrote gaily always; but when the new year began Mrs. Rolleston thought she detected a note of melancholy under all those lively details about the place and the people.

"My poor girl is getting homesick," she thought. "Her heart is in Beresford Street."

It might be that she missed her new friend and companion, Lotta Stafford, who had gone with her brother for a little tour to Genoa and Spezia, and as far as Pisa. They were to return before February; but in the meantime Bella might naturally feel very solitary among all those strangers, whose manners and doings she described so well.

The mother's instinct had been true. Bella was not so happy as she had been in that first flush of wonder and delight which followed the change from Walworth to the Riviera. Somehow, she knew not how, lassitude had crept upon her. She no longer loved to climb the hills, no longer flourished her orange stick in sheer gladness of heart as her light feet skipped over the rough ground and the coarse grass on the mountainside. The odor of rosemary and thyme, the fresh breath of the sea, no longer filled her with rapture. She thought of Beresford Street and her

---

[7] This is a sly comment on that era's popular literature, then awash in lurid "sensation" novels—a relatively new cultural phenomenon with a large and avid readership. By and large, "serious" writers applied their talents to poetry and the threatre (though there was no shortage of popular "sensation" plays as well).

mother's face with a sick longing. They were so far—so far away! And then she thought of Lady Ducayne, sitting by the heaped-up olive logs in the overheated salon—thought of that wizened-nutcracker profile, and those gleaming eyes, with an invincible horror.

Visitors at the hotel had told her that the air of Cap Ferrino was relaxing—better suited to age than to youth, to sickness than to health. No doubt it was so. She was not so well as she had been at Walworth; but she told herself that she was suffering only from the pain of separation from the dear companion of her girlhood, the mother who had been nurse, sister, friend, flatterer, all things in this world to her. She had shed many tears over that parting, had spent many a melancholy hour on the marble terrace with yearning eyes looking westward, and with her heart's desire a thousand miles away.

She was sitting in her favorite spot, an angle at the eastern end of the terrace, a quiet little nook sheltered by orange trees, when she heard a couple of Riviera habitués talking in the garden below. They were sitting on a bench against the terrace wall.

She had no idea of listening to their talk, till the sound of Lady Ducayne's name attracted her, and then she listened without any thought of wrong-doing. They were talking no secrets—just casually discussing a hotel acquaintance.

They were two elderly people whom Bella only knew by sight. An English clergyman who had wintered abroad for half his lifetime; a stout, comfortable, well-to-do spin-ster, whose chronic bronchitis obliged her to migrate annually.

"I have met her about Italy for the last ten years," said the lady; "but have never found out her real age."

"I put her down at a hundred—not a year less," replied the parson. "Her reminiscences all go back to the Regency.[8] She was evidently then in her zenith; and I have heard her say things that showed she was in Parisian society when the First Empire was at its best—before Josephine was divorced."[9]

"She doesn't talk much now."

"No; there's not much life left in her. She is wise in keeping herself secluded. I only wonder that wicked old quack, her Italian doctor, didn't finish her off years ago."

"I should think it must be the other way, and that he keeps her alive."

"My dear Miss Manders, do you think foreign quackery ever kept anybody alive?"

"Well, there she is—and she never goes anywhere without him. He certainly has an unpleasant countenance."

"Unpleasant," echoed the parson, "I don't believe the foul fiend himself can beat him in ugliness. I pity that poor young woman who has to live between old Lady Ducayne and Dr. Parravicini."

"But the old lady is very good to her companions."

"No doubt. She is very free with her cash; the servants call her good Lady Ducayne. She is a withered old female Croesus,[10] and knows she'll never be able to get through her money, and doesn't relish the

---

[8] The period in England between 1811 and 1820 when King George III was deemed unfit and his son, the Prince of Wales, ruled as his proxy as Prince Regent.

[9] Refers to "French Empire" period of 1804-1814/1815, and Joséphine de Beauharnais (1763-1814), who married Napoléon Bonaparte in 1796 (her second marriage). She was divorced by him in 1810.

[10] King of Lydia (a region in modern Turkey) from 560-547 B.C.E.; renowned for his great wealth.

idea of other people enjoying it when she's in her coffin. People who live to be as old as she is become slavishly attached to life. I daresay she's generous to those poor girls—but she can't make them happy. They die in her service."

"Don't say they, Mr. Carton; I know that one poor girl died at Mentone last spring."

"Yes, and another poor girl died in Rome three years ago. I was there at the time. Good Lady Ducayne left her there in an English family. The girl had every comfort. The old woman was very liberal to her—but she died. I tell you, Miss Manders, it is not good for any young woman to live with two such horrors as Lady Ducayne and Parravicini."

They talked of other things—but Bella hardly heard them. She sat motionless, and a cold wind seemed to come down upon her from the mountains and to creep up to her from the sea, till she shivered as she sat there in the sunshine, in the shelter of the orange trees in the midst of all that beauty and brightness.

Yes, they were uncanny, certainly, the pair of them—she so like an aristocratic witch in her withered old age; he of no particular age, with a face that was more like a waxen mask than any human countenance Bella had ever seen. What did it matter? Old age is venerable, and worthy of all reverence; and Lady Ducayne had been very kind to her. Dr. Parravicini was a harmless, inoffensive student, who seldom looked up from the book he was reading. He had his private sitting-room, where he made experiments in chemistry and natural science—perhaps in alchemy. What could it matter to Bella? He had always been polite to her, in his far-off way. She could not be more happily placed than she was—in this palatial hotel, with this rich old lady.

No doubt she missed the young English girl who had been so friendly, and it might be that she missed the girl's brother, for Mr. Stafford had talked to her a good deal—had interested himself in the books she was reading, and her manner of amusing herself when she was not on duty.

"You must come to our little salon when you are 'off,' as the hospital nurses call it, and we can have some music. No doubt you play and sing?" Upon which Bella had to own with a blush of shame that she had forgotten how to play the piano ages ago.

"Mother and I used to sing duets sometimes between the lights,[11] without accompaniment," she said, and the tears came into her eyes as she thought of the humble room, the half-hour's respite from work, the sewing machine standing where a piano ought to have been, and her mother's plaintive voice, so sweet, so true, so dear.

Sometimes she found herself wondering whether she would ever see that beloved mother again. Strange forebodings came into her mind. She was angry with herself for giving way to melancholy thoughts.

One day she questioned Lady Ducayne's French maid about those two companions who had died within three years.

"They were poor, feeble creatures," Francine told her. "They looked fresh and bright enough when they came to Milady; but they ate too much, and they were lazy. They died of luxury and idleness. Milady was too kind to them. They had nothing to do; and so they took to fancying things; fancying the air didn't suit them, that they couldn't sleep."

---

[11] That is, at twilight, between sunset and moonrise.

"I sleep well enough, but I have had a strange dream several times since I have been in Italy."

"Ah, you had better not begin to think about dreams, or you will be like those other girls. They were dreamers—and they dreamt themselves into the cemetery."

The dream troubled her a little, not because it was a ghastly or frightening dream, but on account of sensations which she had never felt before in sleep—a whirring of wheels that went round in her brain, a great noise like a whirlwind, but rhythmical like the ticking of a gigantic clock: and then in the midst of this uproar as of winds and waves she seemed to sink into a gulf of unconsciousness, out of sleep into far deeper sleep—total extinction. And then, after that black interval, there had come the sound of voices, and then again the whirr of wheels, louder and louder—and again the black—and then she awoke, feeling languid and oppressed.

She told Dr. Parravicini of her dream one day, on the only occasion when she wanted his professional advice. She had suffered rather severely from the mosquitoes before Christmas—and had been almost frightened at finding a wound upon her arm which she could only attribute to the venomous sting of one of these torturers. Parravicini put on his glasses, and scrutinized the angry mark on the round, white arm, as Bella stood before him and Lady Ducayne with her sleeve rolled up above her elbow.

"Yes, that's rather more than a joke," he said; "he has caught you on the top of a vein. What a vampire! But there's no harm done, *signorina*, nothing that a little dressing of

mine won't heal. You must always show me any bite of this nature. It might be dangerous if neglected. These creatures feed on poison and disseminate it."

"And to think that such tiny creatures can bite like this," said Bella. "My arm looks as if it had been cut by a knife."

"If I were to show you a mosquito's sting under my microscope you wouldn't be surprised at that," replied Parravicini.

Bella had to put up with the mosquito bites, even when they came on the top of a vein, and produced that ugly wound. The wound recurred now and then at longish intervals, and Bella found Dr. Parravicini's dressing a speedy cure. If he were the quack his enemies called him, he had at least a light hand and a delicate touch in performing this small operation.

"Bella Rolleston to Mrs. Rolleston—April 14th.

EVER DEAREST,

Behold the check for my second quarter's salary—five and twenty pounds. There is no one to pinch off a whole tenner for a year's commission as there was last time, so it is all for you, mother, dear. I have plenty of pocket-money in hand from the cash I brought away with me, when you insisted on my keeping more than I wanted. It isn't possible to spend money here—except on occasional tips to servants, or sous[12] to beggars and children—unless one had lots to spend, for everything one would like to buy—tortoise-shell, coral, lace—is so ridiculously dear that only a millionaire ought to look at it. Italy is a dream of beauty: but for shopping, give me Newington Causeway.

You ask me so earnestly if I am quite well that I fear my letters must have been very dull

---

[12] "Sous" here is the plural of "sou," a old French coin of small denomination (like a pence). She says, it's only possible to spend money here by giving pennies to beggars.

lately. Yes, dear, I am well—but I am not quite so strong as I was when I used to trudge to the West-end to buy half a pound of tea—just for a constitutional walk—or to Dulwich to look at the pictures. Italy is relaxing; and I feel what the people here call "slack."

But I fancy I can see your dear face looking worried as you read this. Indeed, and indeed, I am not ill. I am only a little tired of this lovely scene—as I suppose one might get tired of looking at one of Turner's pictures if it hung on a wall that was always opposite one. I think of you every hour in every day—think of you and our homely little room—our dear little shabby parlor, with the armchairs from the wreck of your old home, and Dick singing in his cage over the sewing machine. Dear, shrill, maddening Dick, who, we flattered ourselves, was so passionately fond of us. Do tell me in your next letter that he is well.

My friend Lotta and her brother never came back after all. They went from Pisa to Rome. Happy mortals! And they are to be on the Italian lakes in May; which lake was not decided when Lotta last wrote to me. She has been a charming correspondent, and has confided all her little flirtations to me. We are all to go to Bellaggio[13] next week—by Genoa and Milan. Isn't that lovely? Lady Ducayne travels by the easiest stages—except when she is bottled up in the train deluxe. We shall stop two days at Genoa and one at Milan. What a bore I shall be to you with my talk about Italy when I come home.

Love and love—and ever more love from your adoring, BELLA.

.IV.

HERBERT STAFFORD and his sister had often talked of the pretty English girl with her fresh complexion, which made such a pleasant touch of rosy color among all those sallow faces at the Grand Hotel. The young doctor thought of her with a compassionate tenderness—her utter loneliness in that great hotel where there were so many people, her bondage to that old, old woman, where everybody else was free to think of nothing but enjoying life. It was a hard fate; and the poor child was evidently devoted to her mother, and felt the pain of separation—"only two of them, and very poor, and all the world to each other," he thought.

Lotta told him one morning that they were to meet again at Bellaggio. "The old thing and her court are to be there before we are," she said. "I shall be charmed to have Bella again. She is so bright and gay—in spite of an occasional touch of homesickness. I never took to a girl on a short acquaintance as I did to her."

"I like her best when she is homesick," said Herbert; "for then I am sure she has a heart."

"What have you to do with hearts, except for dissection? Don't forget that Bella is an absolute pauper. She told me in confidence that her mother makes mantles[14] for a West-end shop. You can hardly have a lower depth than that."

"I shouldn't think any less of her if her mother made matchboxes."

"Not in the abstract—of course not. Matchboxes are honest labor. But you couldn't marry a girl whose mother makes mantles."

"We haven't come to the consideration of that question yet," answered Herbert, who liked to provoke his sister.

---

[13] Municipality in northern Italy that has been a resort area since Roman times; known as "the Pearl of Lake Como."

[14] A loose, sleeveless cloak or cape.

In two years' hospital practice he had seen too much of the grim realities of life to retain any prejudices about rank. Cancer, phthisis,[15] gangrene, leave a man with little respect for the humanity. The kernel is always the same—fearfully and wonderfully made—a subject for pity and terror.

Mr. Stafford and his sister arrived at Bellaggio in a fair May evening. The sun was going down as the steamer approached the pier; and all that glory of purple bloom which curtains every wall at this season of the year flushed and deepened in the glowing light. A group of ladies were standing on the pier watching the arrivals, and among them Herbert saw a pale face that startled him out of his wonted composure.

"There she is," murmured Lotta, at his elbow, "but how dreadfully changed. She looks a wreck."

They were shaking hands with her a few minutes later, and a flush had lighted up her poor pinched face in the pleasure of meeting.

"I thought you might come this evening," she said. "We have been here a week."

She did not add that she had been there every evening to watch the boat in, and a good many times during the day. The Grand Bretagne was close by, and it had been easy for her to creep to the pier when the boat bell rang. She felt a joy in meeting these people again; a sense of being with friends; a confidence which Lady Ducayne's goodness had never inspired in her.

"Oh, you poor darling, how awfully ill you must have been," exclaimed Lotta, as the two girls embraced.

Bella tried to answer, but her voice was choked with tears.

"What has been the matter, dear? That horrid influenza, I suppose?"

"No, no, I have not been ill—I have only felt a little weaker than I used to be. I don't think the air of Cap Ferrino quite agreed with me."

"It must have disagreed with you abominably. I never saw such a change in anyone. Do let Herbert doctor you. He is fully qualified, you know. He prescribed for ever so many influenza patients at the Londres. They were glad to get advice from an English doctor in a friendly way."

"I am sure he must be very clever!" faltered Bella, "but there is really nothing the matter. I am not ill, and if I were ill, Lady Ducayne's physician—"

"That dreadful man with the yellow face? I would as soon one of the Borgias prescribed for me.[16] I hope you haven't been taking any of his medicines."

"No, dear, I have taken nothing. I have never complained of being ill."

This was said while they were all three walking to the hotel. The Staffords' rooms had been secured in advance, pretty ground-floor rooms, opening into the garden. Lady Ducayne's statelier apartments were on the floor above.

"I believe these rooms are just under ours," said Bella.

"Then it will be all the easier for you to run down to us," replied Lotta, which was not really the case, as the grand staircase was in the center of the hotel.

---

[15] Also known as consumption or pulmonary tuberculosis. Once thought to be hereditary, this highly contagious "white plague" was a devastating scourge in the crowded urban neighborhoods of Victorian society.

[16] Meaning he'd rather take poison.

"Oh, I shall find it easy enough," said Bella. "I'm afraid you'll have too much of my society. Lady Ducayne sleeps away half the day in this warm weather, so I have a good deal of idle time; and I get awfully moped thinking of mother and home."

Her voice broke upon the last word. She could not have thought of that poor lodging which went by the name of home more tenderly had it been the most beautiful that art and wealth ever created. She moped and pined in this lovely garden, with the sunlit lake and the romantic hills spreading out their beauty before her. She was homesick and she had dreams; or, rather, an occasional recurrence of that one bad dream with all its strange sensations—it was more like a hallucination than dreaming—the whirring of wheels, the sinking into an abyss, the struggling back to consciousness. She had the dream shortly before she left Cap Ferrino, but not since she had come to Bellaggio, and she began to hope the air in this lake district suited her better, and that those strange sensations would never return.

Mr. Stafford wrote a prescription and had it made up at the chemist's near the hotel. It was a powerful tonic, and after two bottles, and a row or two on the lake, and some rambling over the hills and in the meadows where the spring flowers made earth seem paradise, Bella's spirits and looks improved as if by magic.

"It is a wonderful tonic," she said, but perhaps in her heart of hearts she knew that the doctor's kind voice, and the friendly hand that helped her in and out of the boat, and the lake, had something to do with her cure.

"I hope you don't forget that her mother makes mantles," Lotta said warningly.

"Or matchboxes; it is just the same thing, so far as I am concerned."

"You mean that in no circumstances could you think of marrying her?"

"I mean that if ever I love a woman well enough to think of marrying her, riches or rank will count for nothing with me. But I fear—I fear your poor friend may not live to be any man's wife."

"Do you think her so very ill?"

He sighed, and left the question unanswered.

One day, while they were gathering wild hyacinths in an upland meadow, Bella told Mr. Stafford about her bad dream.

"It is curious only because it is hardly like a dream," she said. "I daresay you could find some commonsense reason for it. The position of my head on my pillow, or the atmosphere, or something."

And then she described her sensations; how in the midst of sleep there came a sudden sense of suffocation; and then those whirring wheels, so loud, so terrible; and then a blank, and then a coming back to waking consciousness.

"Have you ever had chloroform given you—by a dentist, for instance?"

"Never—Dr. Parravicini asked me that question one day."

"Lately?"

"No, long ago, when we were in the train deluxe."[16]

"Has Dr. Parravicini prescribed for you since you began to feel weak and ill?"

"Oh, he has given me a tonic from time to time, but I hate medicine, and took very little of the stuff. And then I am not ill, only—weaker than I used to be. I was ridiculously strong and well when I lived at Walworth, and used to take long walks every day. Mother made me take those tramps to Dulwich or Norwood, for fear I should suffer from too much sewing machine; sometimes—but very seldom—she went with me. She was generally toiling at home while I was enjoying fresh air and exercise. And she was very careful about our food—that, however plain it was, it should be always nourishing and ample. I owe it to her care that I grew up such a great, strong creature."

"You don't look great or strong now, you poor dear," said Lotta.

"I'm afraid Italy doesn't agree with me."

"Perhaps it is not Italy, but being cooped up with Lady Ducayne that has made you ill."

"But I am never cooped up. Lady Ducayne is absurdly kind, and lets me roam about or sit in the balcony all day if I like. I have read more novels since I have been with her than in all the rest of my life."

"Then she is very different from the average old lady, who is usually a slave driver," said Stafford. "I wonder why she carries a companion about with her if she has so little need of society."

"Oh, I am only part of her state. She is inordinately rich—and the salary she gives me doesn't count. Apropos of Dr. Parravicini, I know he is a clever doctor, for he cures my horrid mosquito bites."

"A little ammonia would do that, in the early stage of the mischief. But there are no mosquitoes to trouble you now."

"Oh, yes, there are; I had a bite just before we left Cap Ferrino." She pushed up her loose lawn sleeve, and exhibited a scar, which he scrutinized intently, with a surprised and puzzled look.

"This is no mosquito bite," he said.

"Oh, yes, it is—unless there are snakes or adders at Cap Ferrino."

"It is not a bite at all. You are trifling with me. Miss Rolleston—you have allowed that wretched Italian quack to bleed you. They killed the greatest man in modern Europe that way, remember.[17] How very foolish of you."

"I was never bled in my life, Mr. Stafford."

"Nonsense! Let me look at your other arm. Are there any more mosquito bites?"

"Yes; Dr. Parravicini says I have a bad skin for healing, and that the poison acts more virulently with me than with most people."

Stafford examined both her arms in the broad sunlight, scars new and old.

"You have been very badly bitten, Miss Rolleston," he said, "and if ever I find the mosquito I shall make him smart. But, now tell me, my dear girl, on your word of honor, tell me as you would tell a friend who is sincerely anxious for your health and happiness—as you would tell your mother if she were here to question you—have you no knowledge of any cause for these scars except mosquito bites—no suspicion even?"

"No, indeed! No, upon my honor! I have never seen a mosquito biting my arm. One never does see the horrid little fiends. But I have heard them trumpeting under the curtains and I know that I have often had one of the pestilent wretches buzzing about me."

Later in the day Bella and her friends were sitting at tea in the garden, while Lady Ducayne took her afternoon drive with her doctor.

"How long do you mean to stop with Lady Ducayne, Miss Rolleston?" Herbert Stafford asked, after a thoughtful silence,

---

[17] Mr. Stafford probably alludes to the world-famous poet Lord Byron, who died in 1824 from sepsis while in Greece. It is thought that he contracted the disease via unsterilized instruments used in blood-letting treatments. The practice had lost its popularity by mid-century.

breaking suddenly upon the trivial talk of the two girls.

"As long as she will go on paying me twenty-five pounds a quarter."

"Even if you feel your health breaking down in her service?"

"It is not the service that has injured my health. You can see that I have really nothing to do—to read aloud for an hour or so once or twice a week; to write a letter once in a while to a London tradesman. I shall never have such an easy time with anybody. And nobody else would give me a hundred a year."

"Then you mean to go on till you break down; to die at your post?"

"Like the other two companions? No! If ever I feel seriously ill—really ill—I shall put myself in a train and go back to Walworth without stopping."

"What about the other two companions?"

"They both died. It was very unlucky for Lady Ducayne. That's why she engaged me; she chose me because I was ruddy and robust. She must feel rather disgusted at my having grown white and weak. By-the-bye, when I told her about the good your tonic had done me, she said she would like to see you and have a little talk with you about her own case."

"And I should like to see Lady Ducayne. When did she say this?"

"The day before yesterday."

"Will you ask her if she will see me this evening?"

"With pleasure! I wonder what you will think of her? She looks rather terrible to a stranger; but Dr. Parravicini says she was once a famous beauty."

It was nearly ten o'clock when Mr. Stafford was summoned by message from Lady Ducayne, whose courier came to conduct him to her ladyship's salon. Bella was reading aloud when the visitor was admitted; and he noticed the languor in the low, sweet tones, the evident effort.

"Shut up the book," said the querulous old voice. "You are beginning to drawl like Miss Blandy."

Stafford saw a small, bent figure crouching over the piled-up olive logs; a shrunken old figure in a gorgeous garment of black and crimson brocade, a skinny throat emerging from a mass of old Venetian lace, clasped with diamonds that flashed like fireflies as the trembling old head turned towards him.

The eyes that looked at him out of the face were almost as bright as the diamonds— the only living feature in that narrow parchment mask. He had seen terrible faces in the hospital—faces on which disease had set dreadful marks—but he had never seen a face that impressed him so painfully as this withered countenance, with its indescribable horror of death outlived, a face that should have been hidden under a coffin-lid years and years ago.

The Italian physician was standing on the other side of the fireplace, smoking a cigarette, and looking down at the little old woman brooding over the hearth as if he were proud of her.

"Good evening, Mr. Stafford; you can go to your room, Bella, and write your everlasting letter to your mother at Walworth," said Lady Ducayne. "I believe she writes a page about every wild flower she discovers in the woods and meadows. I don't know what else she can find to write about," she added, as Bella quietly withdrew to the pretty little bedroom opening out of Lady Ducayne's spacious apartment. Here, as at Cap Ferrino, she slept in a room adjoining the old lady's.

"You are a medical man, I understand, Mr. Stafford."

"I am a qualified practitioner, but I have not begun to practice."

"You have begun upon my companion, she tells me."

"I have prescribed for her, certainly, and I am happy to find my prescription has done her good; but I look upon that improvement as temporary. Her case will require more drastic treatment."

"Never mind her case. There is nothing the matter with the girl—absolutely nothing—except girlish nonsense; too much liberty and not enough work."

"I understand that two of your ladyship's previous companions died of the same disease," said Stafford, looking first at Lady Ducayne, who gave her tremulous old head an impatient jerk, and then at Parravicini, whose yellow complexion had paled a little under Stafford's scrutiny.

"Don't bother me about my companions, sir," said Lady Ducayne. "I sent for you to consult you about myself—not about a parcel of anemic girls. You are young, and medicine is a progressive science, the newspapers tell me. Where have you studied?"

"In Edinburgh—and in Paris."

"Two good schools. And know all the new-fangled theories, the modern discoveries—that remind one of the medieval witchcraft, of Albertus Magnus, and George Ripley;[18] you have studied hypnotism—electricity?"

"And the transfusion of blood," said Stafford, very slowly, looking at Parravicini.

"Have you made any discovery that teaches you to prolong human life—any elixir—any mode of treatment? I want my life prolonged, young man. That man there has been my physician for thirty years. He does all he can to keep me alive—after his lights. He studies all the new theories of all the scientists—but he is old; he gets older every day—his brainpower is going—he is bigoted—prejudiced—can't receive new ideas—can't grapple with new systems. He will let me die if I am not on my guard against him."

"You are of an unbelievable ingratitude, Ecclenza,"[19] said Parravicini.

"Oh, you needn't complain. I have paid you thousands to keep me alive. Every year of my life has swollen your hoards; you know there is nothing to come to you when I am gone. My whole fortune is left to endow a home for indigent women of quality who have reached their ninetieth year. Come, Mr. Stafford, I am a rich woman. Give me a few years more in the sunshine, a few years more above ground, and I will give you the price of a fashionable London practice—I will set you up at the West-End."

"How old are you, Lady Ducayne?"

"I was born the day Louis XVI was guillotined."[20]

"Then I think you have had your share of the sunshine and the pleasures of the earth, and that you should spend your few remaining days in repenting your sins and trying to make atonement for the young lives that have been sacrificed to your love of life."

"What do you mean by that, sir?"

---

[18] Albertus Magnus, a natural philosopher of the thirteenth century, was allegedly an alchemist, though he wrote little on the topic; Ripley was an alchemist of the fifteenth century.

[19] The word should be "Excellenza," "highness" or "excellency."

[20] That is, 1793. The story is written as a contemporary tale, so Lady Ducayne is over 100.

"Oh, Lady Ducayne, need I put your wickedness and your physician's still greater wickedness in plain words? The poor girl who is now in your employment has been reduced from robust health to a condition of absolute danger by Dr. Parravicini's experimental surgery; and I have no doubt those other two young women who broke down in your service were treated by him in the same manner. I could take upon myself to demonstrate—by most convincing evidence, to a jury of medical men—that Dr. Parravicini has been bleeding Miss Rolleston after putting her under chloroform, at intervals, ever since she has been in your service. The deterioration in the girl's health speaks for itself; the lancet marks upon the girl's arms are unmistakable; and her description of a series of sensations, which she calls a dream, points unmistakably to the administration of chloroform while she was sleeping. A practice so nefarious, so murderous, must, if exposed, result in a sentence only less severe than the punishment of murder."

"I laugh," said Parravicini, with an airy motion of his skinny fingers; "I laugh at once at your theories and at your threats. I, Parravicini Leopold, have no fear that the law can question anything I have done."

"Take the girl away, and let me hear no more of her," cried Lady Ducayne, in the thin, old voice, which so poorly matched the energy and fire of the wicked old brain that guided its utterances. "Let her go back to her mother—I want no more girls to die in my service. There are girls enough and to spare in the world, God knows."

"If you ever engage another companion—or take another English girl into your service, Lady Ducayne, I will make all England ring with the story of your wickedness."

"I want no more girls. I don't believe in his experiments. They have been full of danger for me as well as for the girl—an air bubble, and I should be gone.[21] I'll have no more of his dangerous quackery. I'll find some new man—a better man than you, sir, a discoverer like Pasteur, or Virchow,[22] a genius—to keep me alive. Take your girl away, young man. Marry her if you like. I'll write a check for a thousand pounds, and let her go and live on beef and beer, and get strong and plump again. I'll have no more such experiments. Do you hear, Parravicini?" she screamed, vindictively, the yellow, wrinkled face distorted with fury, the eyes glaring at him.

THE STAFFORDS CARRIED Bella Rolleston off to Varese next day, she very loath to leave Lady Ducayne, whose liberal salary afforded such help for the dear mother. Herbert Stafford insisted, however, treating Bella as coolly as if he had been the family physician, and she had been given over wholly to his care.

"Do you suppose your mother would let you stop here to die?" he asked. "If Mrs. Rolleston knew how ill you are, she would come post haste to fetch you."

"I shall never be well again till I get back to Walworth," answered Bella, who was low-spirited and inclined to tears this morning, a reaction after her good spirits of yesterday.

"We'll try a week or two at Varese first," said Stafford. "When you can walk halfway up Monte Generoso without palpitation of the heart, you shall go back to Walworth."

[21] An indication that Parravicini has been transfusing Lady Ducayne.
[22] Louis Pasteur (1822-1895) discovered bacteria and their role in health; Rudolf Virchow (1821-1902) is regarded as the father of modern pathology.

"Poor mother, how glad she will be to see me, and how sorry that I've lost such a good place."

This conversation took place on the boat when they were leaving Bellaggio. Lotta had gone to her friend's room at seven o'clock that morning, long before Lady Ducayne's withered eyelids had opened to the daylight, before even Francine, the French maid, was astir, and had helped to pack a Gladstone bag[23] with essentials, and hustled Bella downstairs and out of doors before she could make any strenuous resistance.

"It's all right," Lotta assured her. "Herbert had a good talk with Lady Ducayne last night, and it was settled for you to leave this morning. She doesn't like invalids, you see."

"No," sighed Bella, "she doesn't like invalids. It was very unlucky that I should break down, just like Miss Tomson and Miss Blandy."

"At any rate, you are not dead, like them," answered Lotta, "and my brother says you are not going to die."

IT SEEMED RATHER a dreadful thing to be dismissed in that off-hand way, without a word of farewell from her employer.

"I wonder what Miss Torpinter will say when I go to her for another situation," Bella speculated, ruefully, while she and her friends were breakfasting on board the steamer.

"Perhaps you may never want another situation," said Stafford.

"You mean that I may never be well enough to be useful to anybody?"

"No, I don't mean anything of the kind."

It was after dinner at Varese, when Bella had been induced to take a whole glass of Chianti, and quite sparkled after that unaccustomed stimulant, that Mr. Stafford produced a letter from his pocket.

"I forgot to give you Lady Ducayne's letter of *adieu!*" he said.

"What, did she write to me? I am so glad—I hated to leave her in such a cool way; for after all she was very kind to me, and if I didn't like her it was only because she was too dreadfully old."

She tore open the envelope. The letter was short and to the point:

Goodbye, child. Go and marry your doctor. I enclose a farewell gift for your trousseau.
—ADELINE DUCAYNE

"A hundred pounds, a whole year's salary—no—why, it's for a—a check for a thousand!" cried Bella. "What a generous old soul! She really is the dearest old thing."

"She just missed being very dear to you, Bella," said Stafford.

He had dropped into the use of her Christian name while they were on board the boat. It seemed natural now that she was to be in his charge till they all three went back to England.

"I shall take upon myself the privileges of an elder brother till we land at Dover," he said; "after that—well, it must be as you please."

The question of their future relations must have been satisfactorily settled before they crossed the Channel, for Bella's next letter to her mother communicated three startling facts.

First, that the enclosed check for £1,000 was to be invested in debenture stock in Mrs.

---

[23] A small portmanteau suitcase, typically made of stiff leather.

Rolleston's name, and was to be her very own, income and principal, for the rest of her life.

Next, that Bella was going home to Walworth immediately.

And last, that she was going to be married to Mr. Herbert Stafford in the following autumn.

"And I am sure you will adore him, mother, as much as I do," wrote Bella.

"It is all good Lady Ducayne's doing. I never could have married if I had not secured that little nest-egg for you. Herbert says we shall be able to add to it as the years go by, and that wherever we live there shall be always a room in our house for you. The word *mother-in-law* has no terrors for him."

H. B. Marriott Watson

HENRY BRERETON MARRIOTT WATSON (1863-1921), born in Australia and raised in New Zealand, came to England in 1883, where he took up journalism and writing. He became part of the circle of writers that included J. M. Barrie, Stephen Crane, Thomas Hardy, Henry James, and H. G. Wells, and he presumably knew Bram Stoker, who was well acquainted with these authors. Watson wrote more than fort novels and was best known for his romantic and swashbuckling works. He also penned many short stories and in the 1890s turned his hand to supernatural and Gothic tales, including the well-regarded "The Devil of the Marsh."

The following first appeared in 1898 in book form in *The Heart of Miranda and Other Stories, Being Mostly Winter Tales*, a collection of Marriott Watson's "creepy" tales (as characterized by the *New York Times* reviewer in 1899). While the story echoes certain elements of *Dracula* (the bat, the bite), the personality changes suffered by the vampire's victims are a unique aspect.

THE STONE CHAMBER

H. B. MARRIOTT WATSON

It was not until early summer that Warrington took possession of Marvyn Abbey.[1] He had bought the property in the preceding autumn, but the place had so fallen into decay through the disorders of time that more than six months elapsed ere it was inhabitable. The delay, however, fell out conveniently for Warrington; for the Bosanquets spent the winter abroad, and nothing must suit but he must spend it with them. There was never a man who pursued his passion with such ardor. He was ever at Miss Bosanquet's skirts, and bade fair to make her as steadfast a husband as he was attached a lover.

Thus it was not until after his return from that prolonged exile that he had the opportunity of inspecting the repairs discharged by his architect. He was nothing out of the common in character, but was full of kindly impulses and a fellow of impetuous blood. When he called upon me in my chambers he spoke with some excitement of his Abbey, as also of his approaching marriage; and finally, breaking into an exhibition of genuine affection, declared that we had been so long and so continuously intimate that I, and none other, must help him warm his house and marry his bride. It had indeed been always understood between us that I should serve him at the ceremony, but now it appeared that I must start my duties even earlier.

The prospect of a summer holiday in Utterbourne pleased me. It was a charming village, set upon the slope of a wooded hill and within call of the sea. I had a slight knowledge of the district from a riding excursion taken through that part of Devonshire; and years before, and ere Warrington had come into his money, had viewed the Abbey ruins from a distance with the polite curiosity of a passing tourist.

I examined them now with new eyes as

[1] Note that a significant episode of *Dracula* occurs at Whitby Abbey. Also, Dracula's residence in Purfleet is often mistakenly referred to as "Carfax Abbey." As the former home of monks or nuns, an abbey seems to be a favorite, if ironic, haunt of vampires.

we drove up the avenue. The face which the ancient building presented to the valley was of magnificent design, but now much worn and battered. Part of it, the right wing, I judged to be long past the uses of a dwelling, for the walls had crumbled away, huge gaps opened in the foundations, and the roof was quite dismantled. Warrington had very wisely left this portion to its own sinister decay; it was the left wing which had been restored, and which we were to inhabit.

The entrance, I will confess, was a little mean, for the large doorway had been bricked up and an ordinary modern door gave upon the spacious terrace and the winding gardens. But apart from this, the work of restoration had been undertaken with skill and piety, and the interior had retained its native dignity, while resuming an air of proper comfort. The old oak had been repaired congruous with the original designs, and the great rooms had been as little altered as was requisite to adapt them for daily use.

Warrington passed quickly from chamber to chamber in evident delight, directing my attention upon this and upon that, and eagerly requiring my congratulations and approval. My comments must have satisfied him, for the place attracted me vastly. The only criticism I ventured was to remark upon the size of the rooms and to question if they might dwarf the insignificant human figures they were to entertain.

He laughed. "Not a bit," said he. "Roaring fires in winter in those fine old fireplaces; and as for summer, the more space the better. We shall be jolly."

I followed him along the noble hall, and we stopped before a small door of very black oak.

"The bedrooms," he explained, as he turned the key, "are all upstairs, but mine is not ready yet. And besides, I am reserving it; I won't sleep in it till—you understand," he concluded, with a smiling suggestion of embarrassment.

I understood very well. He threw the door open.

"I am going to use this in the meantime," he continued. "Odd little room, isn't it? It used to be a sort of library. How do you think it looks?"

We had entered as he spoke, and stood, distributing our glances in that vague and general way in which a room is surveyed. It was a chamber of much smaller proportions than the rest, and was dimly lighted by two long narrow windows sunk in the great walls. The bed and the modern fittings looked strangely out of keeping with its ancient privacy. The walls were rudely distempered with barbaric frescos, dating, I conjectured, from the fourteenth century; and the floor was of stone, worn into grooves and hollows with the feet of many generations.

As I was taking in these facts, there came over me a sudden curiosity as to those dead Marvyns who had held the Abbey for so long. This silent chamber seemed to suggest questions of their history; it spoke eloquently of past ages and past deeds, fallen now into oblivion. Here, within these thick walls, no echo from the outer world might carry, no sound would ring within its solitary seclusion. Even the silence seemed to confer with one upon the ancient transactions of that extinct House.

Warrington stirred, and turned suddenly to me. "I hope it's not damp," said he, with a slight shiver. "It looks rather solemn. I thought furniture would brighten it up."

"I should think it would be very comfortable," said I. "You will never be disturbed by any sounds at any rate."

"No," he answered, hesitatingly; and then, quickly, on one of his impulses: "Hang it, Heywood, there's too much silence here for me." Then he laughed. "Oh, I shall do very well for a month or two." And with that appeared to return to his former placid cheerfulness.

The train of thought started in that somber chamber served to entertain me several times that day. I questioned Warrington at dinner, which we took in one of the smaller rooms, commanding a lovely prospect of dale and sea. He shook his head. Archaeological lore, as indeed anything else out of the borders of actual life, held very little interest for him.

"The Marvyns died out in 1714, I believe," he said, indifferently; "someone told me that—the man I bought it from, I think. They might just as well have kept the place up since; but I think it has been only occupied twice between then and now, and the last time was forty years ago. It would have rotted to pieces if I hadn't taken it. Perhaps Mrs. Batty could tell you. She's lived in these parts almost all her life."

To humor me, and affected, I doubt not, by a certain pride in his new possession, he put the query to his housekeeper upon her appearance subsequently; but it seemed that her knowledge was little fuller than his own, though she had gathered some vague traditions of the countryside. The Marvyns had not left a reputable name, if rumor spoke; theirs was a family to which black deeds had been credited. They were ill-starred also in their fortunes, and had become extinct suddenly; but for the rest, the events had fallen too many generations ago to be current now between the memories of the village.

Warrington, who was more eager to discuss the future than to recall the past, was vastly excited by his anticipations. St. Phara-

mond, Sir William Bosanquet's house, lay across the valley, barely five miles away; and as the family had now returned, it was easy to forgive Warrington's elation.

"What do you think?" he said, late that evening; and clapping me upon the shoulder, "You have seen Marion; here is the house. Am I not lucky? Damn it, Heywood, I'm not pious, but I am disposed to thank God! I'm not a bad fellow, but I'm no saint; it's fortunate that it's not only the virtuous that are rewarded. In fact, it's usually contrariwise. I owe this to—Lord. I don't know what I owe it to. Is it my money? Of course, Marion doesn't care a rap for that; but then, you see, I mightn't have known her without it. Of course, there's the house, too. I'm thankful I have money. At any rate, here's my new life. Just look about and take it in, old fellow. If you knew how a man may be ashamed of himself! But there, I've done. You know I'm decent at heart—you must count my life from today." And with this outbreak he lifted the glass between fingers that trembled with the warmth of his emotions, and tossed off his wine.

He did himself but justice when he claimed to be a good fellow; and, in truth, I was myself somewhat moved by his obvious feeling. I remember that we shook hands very affectionately, and my sympathy was the prelude to a long and confidential talk, which lasted until quite a late hour.

At the foot of the staircase, where we parted, he detained me.

"This is the last of my wayward days," he said, with a smile. "Late hours—liquor—all go. You shall see. Goodnight. You know your room. I shall be up long before you." And with that he vanished briskly into the darkness that hung about the lower parts of the passage.

I watched him go, and it struck me quite

vaguely what a slight impression his candle made upon that channel of opaque gloom. It seemed merely as a thread of light that illumined nothing. Warrington himself was rapt into the prevalent blackness; but long afterwards, and even when his footsteps had died away upon the heavy carpet, the tiny beam was visible, advancing and flickering in the distance.

My window, which was modern, opened upon a little balcony, where, as the night was warm and I was indisposed for sleep, I spent half an hour enjoying the air. I was in a sentimental mood, and my thoughts turned upon the suggestions which Warrington's conversation had induced. It was not until I was in bed, and had blown out the light, that they settled upon the square, dark chamber in which my host was to pass the night. As I have said, I was wakeful, owing, no doubt, to the high pitch of the emotions which we had encouraged; but presently my fancies became inarticulate and incoherent, and then I was overtaken by profound sleep.

Warrington was up before me, as he had predicted, and met me in the breakfast-room.

"What a beggar you are to sleep!" he said, with a smile. "I've hammered at your door for half an hour."

I apologized for myself, alleging the rich country air in my defense, and mentioned that I had had some difficulty in getting to sleep.

"So had I," he remarked, as we sat down to the table. "We got very excited, I suppose. Just see what you have there, Heywood. Eggs? Oh, damn it, one can have too much of eggs!" He frowned, and lifted a third cover. "Why in the name of common sense can't Mrs. Batty give us more variety," he asked, impatiently.

I deprecated his displeasure, suggesting that we should do very well indeed; his discontent seemed to me quite unnecessary. But

I supposed Warrington had been rather spoiled by many years of club life.

He settled himself without replying, and began to pick over his plate in a gingerly manner.

"There's one thing I will have here, Heywood," he observed. "I will have things well appointed. I'm not going to let life in the country mean an uncomfortable life. A man can't change the habits of a lifetime."

In contrast with his exhilarated professions of the previous evening, this struck me with a sense of amusement at the moment; and the incongruity may have occurred to him, for he went on:—

"Marion's not over strong, you know, and must have things *comme il faut*.[2] She shan't decline upon a lower level. The worst of these rustics is that they have no imagination." He held up a piece of bacon on his fork, and surveyed it with disgust "Now, look at that! Why the devil don't they take tips from civilized people like the French?"

It was so unlike him to exhibit this petulance that I put it down to a bad night, and without discovering the connection of my thoughts, asked him how he liked his bedroom.

"Oh, pretty well, pretty well," he said, indifferently. "It's not so cold as I thought. But I slept badly. I always do in a strange bed"; and pushing aside his plate, he lit a cigarette. "When you've finished that garbage, Heywood, we'll have a stroll round the Abbey," he said.

His good temper returned during our walk, and he indicated to me various improvements which he contemplated, with something of his old ardor. The left wing of the house, as I have said, was entire, but a little apart were the ruins of a chapel. Surrounded

[2] As is proper or fitting.

by a low moss-grown wall, it was full of picturesque charm; the roofless chancel was spread with ivy, but the aisles were intact. Grass grew between the stones and the floor, and many creepers had strayed through chinks in the wall into those sacred precincts.

The solemn quietude of the ruin, maintained under the spell of death, awed me a little, but upon Warrington apparently it made no impression. He was only zealous that I should properly appreciate the distinction of such a property. I stooped and drew the weeds away from one of the slabs in the aisle, and was able to trace upon it the relics of lettering, well-nigh obliterated under the corrosion of time.

"There are tombs," said I.

"Oh, yes," he answered, with a certain relish. "I understand the Marvyns used it as a mausoleum. They are all buried here. Some good brasses,[3] I am told."

The associations of the place engaged me; the aspect of the Abbey faced the past; it seemed to refuse communion with the present; and somehow the thought of those two decent humdrum lives which should be spent within its shelter savored of the incongruous. The white-capped maids and the emblazoned butlers that should tread these halls offered a ridiculous appearance beside my fancies of the ancient building. For all that, I envied Warrington his home, and so I told him, with a humorous hint that I was fitter to appreciate its glories than himself.

He laughed. "Oh, I don't know," said he. "I like the old-world look as much as you do. I have always had a notion of something venerable. It seems to serve you for ancestors." And he was undoubtedly delighted with my enthusiasm.

But at lunch again he chopped round to his previous irritation, only now quite another matter provoked his anger. He had received a letter by the second post from Miss Bosanquet, which, if I may judge from his perplexity, must have been unusually confused. He read and re-read it, his brow lowering.

"What the deuce does she mean?" he asked, testily. "She first makes an arrangement for us to ride over today, and now I can't make out whether we are to go to St. Pharamond, or they are coming to us. Just look at it, will you, Heywood?"

I glanced through the note, but could offer no final solution, whereupon he broke out again:—

"That's just like women—they never can say anything straightforwardly. Why, in the name of goodness, couldn't she leave things as they were? You see," he observed, rather in answer, as I fancied, to my silence, "we don't know what to do now; if we stay here they mayn't come, and if we go probably we shall cross them." And he snapped his fingers in annoyance.

I was cheerful enough, perhaps because the responsibility was not mine, and ventured to suggest that we might ride over, and return if we missed them. But he dismissed the subject sharply by saying:

"No, I'll stay. I'm not going on a fool's errand," and drew my attention to some point in the decoration of the room.

The Bosanquets did not arrive during the afternoon, and Warrington's ill-humor increased. His love-sick state pleaded in excuse of him, but he was certainly not a pleasant companion. He was sour and snappish, and one could introduce no statement to which he

---

[3] Engraved memorials, first popularized in the thirteenth century.

would not find a contradiction. So unamiable did he grow that at last I discovered a pretext to leave him, and rambled to the back of the Abbey into the precincts of the old chapel.

The day was falling, and the summer sun flared through the western windows upon the bare aisle. The creepers rustled upon the gaping walls, and the tall grasses waved in shadows over the bodies of the forgotten dead. As I stood contemplating the effect and meditating greatly upon the anterior fortunes of the Abbey, my attention fell upon a huge slab of marble, upon which the yellow light struck sharply. The faded lettering rose into greater definition before my eyes and I read slowly:

"Here lyeth the body of Sir Rupert Marvyn."

Beyond a date, very difficult to decipher, there was nothing more; of eulogy, of style, of record, of pious considerations such as were usual to the period, not a word. I read the numerals variously as 1723 and 1745; but however they ran it was probable that the stone covered the resting-place of the last Marvyn. The history of this futile house interested me not a little, partly for Warrington's sake, and in part from a natural bent towards ancient records; and I made a mental note of the name and date.

When I returned Warrington's surliness had entirely vanished, and had given place to an effusion of boisterous spirits. He apologized jovially for his bad temper.

"It was the disappointment of not seeing Marion," he said. "You will understand that some day, old fellow. But, anyhow, we'll go over tomorrow"; and forthwith proceeded to enliven the dinner with an ostentation of good-fellowship I had seldom witnessed in him. I began to suspect that he had heard again from St. Pharamond, though he chose to conceal the fact from me. The wine was

admirable; though Warrington himself was no great judge, he had entrusted the selection to a good palate.

We had a merry meal, drank a little more than was prudent, and smoked our cigars upon the terrace in the fresh air. Warrington was restless. He pushed his glass from him. "I'll tell you what, old chap," he broke out, "I'll give you a game of billiards. I've got a decent table."

I demurred. The air was too delicious, and I was in no humor for a sharp use of my wits. He laughed, though he seemed rather disappointed.

"It's almost sacrilege to play billiards in an Abbey," I said, whimsically. "What would the ghosts of the old Marvyns think?"

"Oh, hang the Marvyns!" he rejoined, crossly. "You're always talking of them."

He rose and entered the house, returning presently with a flagon of whiskey and some glasses.

"Try this," he said. "We've had no liqueurs"; and pouring out some spirit he swallowed it raw.

I stared, for Warrington rarely took spirits, being more of a wine drinker; moreover, he must have taken nearly the quarter of a tumbler. But he did not notice my surprise, and, seating himself, lit another cigar.

"I don't mean to have things quiet here," he observed, reflectively. "I don't believe in your stagnant rustic life. What I intend to do is to keep the place warm—plenty of house parties, things going on all the year. I shall expect you down for the shooting, Ned. The coverts[4] promise well this year."

I assented willingly enough, and he rambled on again.

"I don't know that I shall use the Abbey

---

[4] The woods in which game are found.

so much. I think I'll live in town a good deal. It's brighter there. I don't know though. I like the place. Hang it, it's a rattling good shop, there's no mistake about it. Look here," he broke off, abruptly, "bring your glass in, and I'll show you something."

I was little inclined to move, but he was so peremptory that I followed him with a sigh. We entered one of the smaller rooms which overlooked the terrace, and had been diverted into a comfortable library. He flung back the windows.

"There's air for you," he cried. "Now, sit down," and walking to a cupboard produced a second flagon of whiskey. "Irish!" he barked, clumping it on the table. "Take your choice," and turning again to the cupboard, presently sat down with his hands under the table. "Now, then, Ned," he said, with a short laugh. "Fill up, and we'll have some fun," with which he suddenly threw a pack of cards upon the board.

I opened my eyes, for I do not suppose Warrington had touched cards since his college days; but, interpreting my look in his own way, he cried:—

"Oh, I'm not married yet. Warrington's his own man still. Poker?[5] Eh?"

"Anything you like," said I, with resignation.

A peculiar expression of delight gleamed in his eyes, and he shuffled the cards feverishly.

"Cut," said he, and helped himself to more whiskey.

It was shameful to be playing there with that beautiful night without, but there seemed no help for it. Warrington had a run of luck, though he played with little skill; and his excitement grew as he won.

"Let us make it ten shillings," he suggested.

I shook my head. "You forget I'm not a millionaire," I replied. "Bah!" he cried. "I like a game worth the victory. Well, fire away." His eyes gloated upon the cards, and he fingered them with unctuous affection. The behavior of the man amazed me. I began to win.

Warrington's face slowly assumed a dull, lowering expression; he played eagerly, avariciously, he disputed my points, and was querulous.

"Oh, I've had enough!" I cried in distaste.

"By Jove, you don't!" he exclaimed, jumping to his feet. "You're the winner, Heywood, and I'll see you damned before I let you off my revenge!"

The words startled me no less than the fury which rang in his accents. I gazed at him in stupefaction. The whites of his eyes showed wildly, and a sullen, angry look determined his face. Suddenly I was arrested by the suspicion of something upon his neck.

"What's that?" I asked. "You've cut yourself."

He put his hand to his face. "Nonsense," he replied, in a surly fashion.

I looked closer, and then I saw my mistake. It was a round, faint red mark, the size of a florin,[6] upon the column of his throat, and I set it down to the accidental pressure of some button.

"Come on!" he insisted, impatiently.

"Bah! Warrington," I said, for I imagined that he had been overexcited by the whiskey he had taken. "It's only a matter of a few pounds. Why make a fuss? Tomorrow will serve."

After a moment his eyes fell, and he gave

---

[5] Americans may find a two-handed game odd, but the English played short-handed games with a reduced deck, usually twenty cards.

[6] A silver two-shilling coin, about 30 millimeters in diameter.

an awkward laugh. "Oh, well, that'll do," said he. "But I got so infernally excited."

"Whiskey," said I, sententiously.

He glanced at the bottle. "How many glasses have I had?" and he whistled. "By Jove, Ned, this won't do! I must turn over a new leaf. Come on; let's look at the night."

I was only too glad to get away from the table, and we were soon upon the terrace again. Warrington was silent, and his gaze went constantly across the valley, where the moon was rising, and in the direction in which, as he had indicated to me, St. Pharamond lay. When he said goodnight he was still preoccupied.

"I hope you will sleep better," he said

"And you, too," I added.

He smiled. "I don't suppose I shall wake the whole night through," he said; and then, as I was turning to go, he caught me quickly by the arm.

"Ned," he said, impulsively and very earnestly, "don't let me make a fool of myself again. I know it's the excitement of everything. But I want to be as good as I can for her."

I pressed his hand. "All right, old fellow," I said; and we parted.

I think I have never enjoyed sounder slumber than that night. The first thing I was aware of was the singing of thrushes outside my window. I rose and looked forth, and the sun was hanging high in the eastern sky, the grass and the young green of the trees were shining with dew. With an uncomfortable feeling that I was very late I hastily dressed and went downstairs.

Warrington was waiting for me in the breakfast-room, as upon the previous morning, and when he turned from the window at my approach, the sight of his face startled me. It was drawn and haggard, and his eyes were shot with blood; it was a face broken and savage with dissipation. He made no answer to my questioning, but seated himself with a morose air.

"Now you have come," he said, sullenly, "we may as well begin. But it's not my fault if the coffee's cold."

I examined him, critically, and passed some comment upon his appearance.

"You don't look up to much," I said. "Another bad night?"

"No; I slept well enough," he responded, ungraciously; and then, after a pause: "I'll tell you what, Heywood. You shall give me my revenge after breakfast."

"Nonsense," I said, after a momentary silence. "You're going over to St. Pharamond."

"Hang it!" was his retort, "one can't be always bothering about women. You seem mightily indisposed to meet me again."

"I certainly won't this morning," I answered, rather sharply, for the man's manner grated upon me. "This evening, if you like; and then the silly business shall end."

He said something in an undertone of grumble, and the rest of the meal passed in silence. But I entertained an uneasy suspicion of him, and after all he was my friend, with whom I was under obligation not to quarrel; and so when we rose, I approached him.

"Look here, Warrington," I said. "What's the matter with you? Have you been drinking? Remember what you asked me last night."

"Hold your damned row!" was all the answer he vouchsafed, as he whirled away from me, but with an embarrassed display of shame.

But I was not to be put off in that way, and I spoke somewhat more sharply.

"We're going to have this out, Warrington," I said. "If you are ill, let us understand that; but I'm not going to stay here with you in this cantankerous spirit."

"I'm not ill," he replied testily.

"Look at yourself," I cried, and turned him about to the mirror over the mantelpiece.

He started a little, and a frown of perplexity gathered on his forehead.

"Good Lord! I'm not like that, Ned," he said, in a different voice. "I must have been drunk last night." And with a sort of groan, he directed a piteous look at me.

"Come," I was constrained to answer, "pull yourself together. The ride will do you good. And no more whiskey."

"No, by Heaven, no!" he cried vehemently, and seemed to shiver; but then, suddenly taking my arm, he walked out of the room.

The morning lay still and golden. Warrington's eyes went forth across the valley.

"Come round to the stables, Ned," he said, impulsively. "You shall choose your own nag."

I shook my head. "I'll choose yours," said I, "but I am not going with you." He looked surprised. "No, ride by yourself. You don't want a companion on such an errand. I'll stay here, and pursue my investigations into the Marvyns."

A scowl crossed, his face, but only for an instant, and then he answered: "All right, old chap; do as you like. Anyway, I'm off at once." And presently, when his horse was brought, he was laughing merrily.

"You'll have a dull day, Ned; but it's your own fault, you duffer. You'll have to lunch by yourself, as I shan't be back till late." And, gaily flourishing his whip, he trotted down the drive.

It was some relief to me to be rid of him, for, in truth, his moods had worn my nerves, and I had not looked for a holiday of this disquieting nature. When he returned, I had no

doubt it would be with quite another face, and meanwhile I was excellent company for myself. After lunch I amused myself for half an hour with idle tricks upon the billiard-table, and, tiring of my pastime, fell upon the housekeeper as I returned along the corridor. She was a woman nearer to sixty than fifty, with a comfortable, portly figure, and an amiable expression. Her eyes invited me ever so respectfully to conversation, and stopping, I entered into talk. She inquired if I liked my room and how I slept.

" 'Tis a nice look-out you have, Sir," said she. "That was where old Lady Martin slept."

It appeared that she had served as kitchen-maid to the previous tenants of the Abbey, nearly fifty years before.

"Oh, I know the old house in and out," she asserted; "and I arranged the rooms with Mr. Warrington."

We were standing opposite the low doorway which gave entrance to Warrington's bedroom, and my eyes unconsciously shot in that direction. Mrs. Batty followed my glance.

"I didn't want him to have that," she said; "but he was set upon it. It's smallish for a bedroom, and in my opinion isn't fit for more than a lumber-room. That's what Sir William used it for."

I pushed open the door and stepped over the threshold, and the housekeeper followed me.

"No," she said, glancing round; "and it's in my mind that it's damp, Sir."

Again I had a curious feeling that the silence was speaking in my ear; the atmosphere was thick and heavy, and a musty smell, as of faded draperies, penetrated my nostrils. The whole room looked indescribably dingy, despite the new hangings. I went over to the narrow window and peered through the diamond panes. Outside, but seen dimly through that ancient and discolored glass, the ruins of the chapel confronted me, bare and stark, in the yellow sunlight. I turned.

"There are no ghosts in the Abbey, I suppose, Mrs. Batty?" I asked, whimsically.

But she took my inquiry very gravely. "I have never heard tell of one, Sir," she protested; "and if there was such a thing I should have known it."

As I was rejoining her, a strange low whining was audible, and looking up I saw in a corner of the high-arched roof a horrible face watching me out of black narrow eyes. I confess that I was very much startled at the apparition, but the next moment realized what it was. The creature hung with its ugly fleshy wings extended over a grotesque stone head that leered down upon me, its evil-looking snout projecting into the room; it lay perfectly still, returning me glance for glance, until moved by the repulsion of its presence I clapped my hands, and cried loudly; then, slowly flitting in a circle round the roof, it vanished with a flapping of wings into some darker corner of the rafters. Mrs. Batty was astounded, and expressed surprise that it had managed to conceal itself for so long.

"Oh, bats live in holes," I answered. "Probably there is some small access through the masonry." But the incident had sent an uncomfortable shiver through me all the same.

Later that day I began to recognize that, short of an abrupt return to town, my time was not likely to be spent very pleasantly. But it was the personal problem so far as it concerned Warrington himself that distressed me even more. He came back from St. Pharamond in a morose and ugly temper, quite alien to his kindly nature. It seems that he had quarreled bitterly with Miss Bosanquet, but

upon what I could not determine, nor did I press him for an explanation.

But the fumes of his anger were still rising when we met, and our dinner was a most depressing meal. He was in a degree of irritation which rendered it impossible to address him, and I soon withdrew into my thoughts. I saw, however, that he was drinking far too much, as, indeed, was plain subsequently when he invited me into the library. Once more he produced the hateful cards, and I was compelled to play, as he reminded me somewhat churlishly that I had promised him his revenge.

"Understand, Warrington," I said, firmly, "I play tonight, but never again, whatever the result. In fact, I am in half the mind to return to town tomorrow."

He gave me a look as he set down, but said nothing, and the game began. He lost heavily from the first, and as nothing would content him but we must constantly raise the stakes, in a short time I had won several hundred pounds. He bore the reverses very ill, breaking out from time to time into some angry exclamation, now petulantly questioning my playing, and muttering oaths under his breath. But I was resolved that he should have no cause of complaint against me for this one night, and disregarding his insane fits of temper, I played steadily and silently. As the tally of my gains mounted he changed color slowly, his face assuming a ghastly expression, and his eyes suspiciously denoting my actions. At length he rose, and throwing himself quickly across the table, seized my hand ferociously as I dealt a couple of cards.

"Damn you! I see your tricks," he cried, in frenzied passion. "Drop that hand, do you hear? Drop that hand, or by—"

But he got no further, for, rising myself, I wrenched my hand from his grasp, and turned upon him, in almost as great a passion as himself. But suddenly, and even as I opened my month to speak, I stopped short with a cry of horror. His face was livid to the lips, his eyes were cast with blood, and upon the dirty white of his flesh, right in the center of his throat, the round red scar, flaming and ugly as a wound, stared upon me.

"Warrington," I cried, "what is this? What have you—" And I pointed in alarm to the spot.

"Mind your own business," he said, with a sneer. "It is well to try and draw off attention from your knavery. But that trick won't answer with me."

Without another word I flung the IOU's upon the table, and turning on my heel, left the room. I was furious with him, and fully resolved to leave the Abbey in the morning. I made my way upstairs to my room, and then, seating myself upon the balcony, endeavored to recover my self-possession.

The more I considered, the more unaccountable was Warrington's behavior. He had always been a perfectly courteous man, with a great lump of kindness in his nature; whereas these last few days he had been nothing other than a savage. It seemed certain that he must be ill or going mad; and as I reflected upon this the conjecture struck me with a sense of pity. If it was that he was losing his senses, how horrible was the tragedy in face of the new and lovely prospects opening in his life.

Stimulated by this growing conviction, I resolved to go down and see him, more particularly as I now recalled his pleading voice that I should help him, on the previous evening. Was it not possible that this pathetic appeal derived from the instinct of the insane to protect themselves?

I found him still in the library: his head had fallen upon the table, and the state of the whiskey bottle by his arm showed only too clearly his condition. I shook him vigorously, and he opened his eyes.

"Warrington, you must go to bed." I said.

He smiled, and greeted me quite affectionately. Obviously he was not so drunk as I had supposed.

"What is the time, Ned?" he asked.

I told him it was one o'clock, at which he rose briskly.

"Lord, I've been asleep," he said. "Help me, Ned. I don't think I'm sober. Where have you been?"

I assisted him to his room, and he undressed slowly, and with an effort. Somehow, as I stood watching him, I yielded to an unknown impulse and said suddenly:

"Warrington, don't sleep here. Come and share my room."

"My dear fellow," he replied, with a foolish laugh, "yours is not the only room in the house. I can use half-a-dozen if I like.

"Well, use one of them." I answered.

He shook his head. "I'm going to sleep here," he returned, obstinately.

I made no further effort to influence him, for, after all, now that the words were out, I had absolutely no reason to give him or myself for my proposition. And so I left him. When I had closed the door, and was turning to go along the passage, I heard very clearly, as it seemed to me, a plaintive cry, muffled and faint, but very disturbing, which sounded from the room. Instantly I opened the door again. Warrington was in bed, and the heavy sound of his breathing told me that he was asleep. It was impossible that he could have uttered the cry. A night-light was burning by his bedside, shedding a strong illumination over the immediate vicinity, and throwing antic shadows on the walls.

As I turned to go, there was a whirring

of wings, a brief flap behind me, and the room was plunged in darkness. The obscene creature that lived in the recesses of the roof must have knocked out the tiny light with its wings. Then Warrington's breathing ceased, and there was no sound at all. And then once more the silence seemed to gather round me slowly and heavily, and whisper to me. I had a vague sense of being prevailed upon, of being enticed and lured by something in the surrounding air, a sort of horror circumscribed me, and I broke from the invisible ring and rushed from the room. The door clanged behind me, and as I hastened along the hall, once more there seemed to ring in my ears the faint and melancholy cry.

I AWOKE, IN THE SOMBER twilight that precedes the dawn, from a sleep troubled and encumbered with evil dreams. The birds had not yet begun their day, and a vast silence brooded over the Abbey gardens. Looking out of my window, I caught sight of a dark figure stealing cautiously round the corner of the ruined chapel. The furtive gait, as well as the appearance of a man at that early hour, struck me with surprise; and hastily throwing on some clothes, I ran downstairs and, opening the hall-door, went out. When I reached the porch which gave entrance to the aisle I stopped suddenly, for there before me, with his head to the ground, and peering among the tall grasses, was the object of my pursuit. Then I stepped quickly forward and laid a hand upon his shoulder. It was Warrington.

"What are you doing here?" I asked.

He turned and looked at me in bewilderment. His eyes wore a dazed expression, and he blinked in perplexity before he replied.

"It's you, is it?" he said weakly. "I thought—" and then paused. "What is it?" he asked.

"I followed you here," I explained. "I only saw your figure, and thought it might be some intruder."

He avoided my eyes. "I thought I heard a cry out here," he answered.

"Warrington," I said, with some earnestness, "come back to bed."

He made no answer, and slipping my arm in his, I led him away. On the doorstep he stopped, and lifted his face to me.

"Do you think it's possible—" he began, as if to inquire of me, and then again paused. With a slight shiver he proceeded to his room, while I followed him. He sat down upon his bed, and his eyes strayed to the barred window absently. The black shadow of the chapel was visible through the panes.

"Don't say anything about this," he said, suddenly. "Don't let Marion know."

I laughed, but it was an awkward laugh.

"Why, that you were alarmed by a cry for help, and went in search like a gentleman?" I asked, jestingly.

"You heard it, then?" he said, eagerly.

I shook my head, for I was not going to encourage his fancies. "You had better go to sleep," I replied, "and get rid of these nightmares."

He sighed and lay back upon his pillow, dressed as he was. Ere I left him he had fallen into a profound slumber.

If I had expected a surly mood in him at breakfast I was much mistaken. There was not a trace of his nocturnal dissipations; he did not seem even to remember them, and he made no allusion whatever to our adventure in the dawn. He perused a letter carefully, and threw it over to me with a grin.

"Lor', what queer sheep women are!" he exclaimed, with rather a coarse laugh.

I glanced at the letter without thinking,

but ere I had read half of it I put it aside. It was certainly not meant for my eyes, and I marveled at Warrington's indelicacy in making public, as it was, that very private matter. The note was from Miss Bosanquet, and was clearly designed for his own heart, couched as it was in the terms of warm and fond affection. No man should see such letters save he for whom they are written.

"You see, they're coming over to dine," he remarked, carelessly. "Trust a girl to make it up if you let her alone long enough."

I made no answer; but though Warrington's grossness irritated me, I reflected with satisfaction upon his return to good humor, which I attributed to the reconciliation.

When I moved out upon the terrace the maid had entered to remove the breakfast things. I was conscious of a slight exclamation behind me, and Warrington joined me presently, with a loud guffaw.

"That's a damned pretty girl!" he said, with unction. "I'm glad Mrs. Batty got her. I like to have good-looking servants."

I suddenly interpreted the incident, and shrugged my shoulders.

"You're a perfect boor this morning, Warrington," I exclaimed, irritably.

He only laughed. "You're a dull dog of a saint, Heywood," he retorted. "Come along," and dragged me out in no amiable spirit.

I had forgotten how perfect a host Warrington could be, but that evening he was displayed at his best. The Bosanquets arrived early. Sir William was an easy-going man, fond of books and of wine, and I now guessed at the taste which had decided Warrington's cellar. Miss Bosanquet was as charming as I remembered her to be; and if any objection might be taken to Warrington himself by my anxious eyes it was merely that he seemed a trifle excited, a fault which, in the circumstances, I was able to condone.

Sir William hung about the table, sipping his wine. Warrington, who had been very abstemious, grew restless, and, finally apologizing in his graceful way, left me to keep the baronet company. I was the less disinclined to do so as I was anxious not to intrude upon the lovers, and Sir William was discussing the history of the Abbey. He had an old volume somewhere in his library which related to it, and, seeing that I was interested, invited me to look it up.

We sat long, and it was not until later that the horrible affair which I must narrate occurred. The evening was close and oppressive, owing to the thunder, which already rumbled far away in the south. When we rose we found that Warrington and Miss Bosanquet were in the garden, and thither we followed. As at first we did not find them, Sir William, who had noted the approaching storm with some uneasiness, left me to make arrangements for his return; and I strolled along the paths by myself, enjoying a cigarette. I had reached the shrubbery upon the further side of the chapel, when I heard the sound of voices—a man's rough and rasping, a woman's pleading and informed with fear. A sharp cry ensued, and without hesitation I plunged through the thicket in the direction of the speakers. The sight that met me appalled me for the moment. Darkness was falling, lit with ominous flashes; and the two figures stood out distinctly in the bushes, in an attitude of struggle. I could not mistake the voices now. I heard Warrington's, brusque with anger, and almost savage in its tones, crying, "You shall!" and there followed a murmur from the girl, a little sob, and then a piercing cry. I sprang forward and seized Warrington by the arm;

when, to my horror, I perceived that he had taken her wrist in both hands and was roughly twisting it, after the cruel habit of schoolboys. The malevolent cruelty of the action so astounded me that for an instant I remained motionless; I almost heard the bones in the frail wrist cracking; and then, in a second, I had seized Warrington's hands in a grip of iron, and flung him violently to the ground. The girl fell with him, and as I picked her up he rose too, and, clenching his fists, made as though to come at me, but instead turned and went sullenly, and with a ferocious look of hate upon his face, out of the thicket.

Miss Bosanquet came to very shortly, and though the agony of the pain must have been considerable to a delicate girl, I believe it was rather the incredible horror of the act under which she swooned. For my part I had nothing to say: not one word relative to the incident dared pass my lips. I inquired if she was better, and then, putting her arm in mine, led her gently toward the house. Her heart beat hard against me, and she breathed heavily, leaning on me for support. At the chapel I stopped, feeling suddenly that I dare not let her be seen in this condition, and bewildered greatly by the whole atrocious business.

"Come and rest in here," I suggested, and we entered the chapel

I set her on a slab of marble, and stood waiting by her side. I talked fluently about anything; for lack of a subject, upon the state of the chapel and the curious tomb I had discovered. Recovering a little, she joined presently in my remarks. It was plain that she was putting a severe restraint upon herself. I moved aside the grasses, and read aloud the inscription on Sir Rupert's grave-piece, and turning to the next, which was rankly overgrown, feigned to search further.

As I was bending there, suddenly, and by what thread of thought I know not, I identified the spot with that upon which I had found Warrington stooping that morning. With a sweep of my hand I brushed back the weeds, uprooting some with my fingers, and kneeling in the twilight, pored over the monument. Suddenly a wild flare of light streamed down the sky, and a great crash of thunder followed. Miss Bosanquet started to her feet and I to mine. The heaven was lit up, as it were, with sunlight, and, as I turned, my eyes fell upon the now uncovered stone. Plainly the lettering flashed in my eyes:

"Priscilla, Lady Marvyn."

Then the clouds opened, and the rain fell in spouts, shouting and dancing upon the ancient roof overhead.

We were under a very precarious shelter, and I was uneasy that Miss Bosanquet should run the risk of that flimsy, ravaged edifice; and so in a momentary lull I managed to get her to the house. I found Sir William in a restless state of nerves. He was a timorous man, and the thunder had upset him, more particularly as he and his daughter were now storm-bound for some time. There was no possibility of venturing into those rude elements for an hour or more. Warrington was not inside, and no one had seen him. In the light Miss Bosanquet's face frightened me; her eyes were large and scared, and her color very dead white. Clearly she was very near a breakdown. I found Mrs. Batty, and told her that the young lady had been severely shaken by the storm, suggesting that she had better lie down for a little.

Returning with me, the housekeeper led off the unfortunate girl, and Sir William and I were left together. He paced the room impatiently, and constantly inquired if there were any signs of improvement in the weather. He also asked for Warrington, irritably. The burden of the whole dreadful night seemed fallen upon me. Passing through the hall I met Miss Batty again. Her usually placid features were disturbed and aghast.

"What is the matter?" I asked. "Is Miss Bosanquet—"

"No, Sir: I think she's sleeping," she replied. "She's in—she is in Mr. Warrington's room."

I started. "Are there no other rooms?" I asked, abruptly.

"There are none ready, Sir, except yours," she answered, "and I thought—"

"You should have taken her there," I said, sharply. The woman looked at me and opened her mouth. "Good heavens!" I said, irritably, "What is the matter? Everyone is mad tonight."

"Alice is gone, Sir," she blurted forth.

Alice, I remembered, was the name of one of her maids.

"What do you mean?" I asked, for her air of panic betokened something graver than her words. The thunder broke over the house and drowned her voice.

"She can't be out in this storm—she must have taken refuge somewhere," I said.

At that the strings of her tongue loosened, and she burst forth with her tale. It was an abominable narrative.

"Where is Mr. Warrington?" I asked; but she shook her head.

There was a moment's silence between us, and we eyed each other aghast. "She will be all right," I said at last, as if dismissing the subject.

The housekeeper wrung her hands. "I never would have thought it!" she repeated, dismally. "I never would have thought it!"

"There is some mistake," I said; but, somehow, I knew better. Indeed, I felt now that I had almost been prepared for it.

"She ran towards the village," whispered Mrs. Batty. "God knows where she was going! The river lies that way."

"Pooh!" I exclaimed. "Don't talk nonsense. It is all a mistake. Come, have you any brandy?"

Brought back to the material round of her duties she bustled away with a sort of briskness, and returned with a flagon and glasses. I took a strong nip, and went back to Sir William. He was feverish, and declaimed against the weather unceasingly. I had to listen to the string of misfortunes which he recounted in the season's crops. It seemed all so futile, with his daughter involved in her horrid tragedy in a neighboring room. He was better after some brandy, and grew more cheerful, but assiduously wondered about Warrington.

"Oh, he's been caught in the storm and taken refuge somewhere," I explained, vainly. I wondered if the next day would ever dawn.

By degrees that thunder rolled slowly into the northern parts of the sky, and only fitful flashes seamed the heavens. It had lasted now more than two hours. Sir William declared his intention of starting and asked for his daughter. I rang for Mrs. Batty, and sent her to rouse Miss Bosanquet. Almost immediately there was a knock upon the door, and the housekeeper was in the doorway, with an agitated expression, demanding to see me. Sir William was looking out of the window, and fortunately did not see her.

"Please come to Miss Bosanquet, Sir," she cried, very scared. "Please come at once. "

In alarm I hastily ran down the corridor and entered Warrington's room. The girl was lying upon the bed, her hair flowing upon the pillow; her eyes, wide open and filled with terror, stared at the ceiling, and her hands clutched and twined in the coverlet as if in an agony of pain. A gasping sound issued from her, as though she were struggling for breath under suffocation. Her whole appearance was as of one in the murderous grasp of an assailant.

I bent over. "Throw the light, quick," I called to Mrs. Batty; and as I put my hand on her shoulder to lift her, the creature that lived in the chamber rose suddenly from the shadow upon the further side of the bed, and sailed with a flapping noise up to the cornice. With an exclamation of horror I pulled the girl's head forward, and the candle-light glowed on her pallid face. Upon the soft flesh of the slender throat was a round red mark, the size of a florin.

At the sight I almost let her fall upon the pillow; but, commanding my nerves, I put my arms round her, and, lifting her bodily from the bed, carried her from the room. Mrs. Batty followed.

"What shall we do?" she asked, in a low voice.

"Take her away from this damned chamber!" I cried. "Anywhere—the hall, the kitchen rather."

I laid my burden upon a sofa in the dining-room, and dispatching Mrs. Batty for the brandy, gave Miss Bosanquet a draught. Slowly the horror faded from her eyes; they closed, and then she looked at me.

"What have you?—where am I?" she asked.

"You have been unwell," I said. "Pray don't disturb yourself yet."

She shuddered, and closed her eyes again.

Very little more was said. Sir William pressed for his horses, and as the sky was clearing I made no attempt to detain him, more particularly as the sooner Miss Bosanquet left the Abbey the better for herself. In half an hour she recovered sufficiently to go,

and I helped her into the carriage. She never referred to her seizure, but thanked me for my kindness. That was all. No one asked after Warrington—not even Sir William. He had forgotten everything, save his anxiety to get back. As the carriage turned from the steps I saw the mark upon the girl's throat, now grown fainter.

I waited up till late into the morning, but there was no sign of Warrington when I went to bed. Nor had he made his appearance when I descended to breakfast. A letter in his handwriting, however, and with the London postmark, awaited me. It was a pitiful scrawl, in the very penmanship of which one might trace the desperate emotions by which he was torn. He implored my forgiveness. *"Am I a devil?"* he asked. *"Am I mad? It was not I! It was not I!"* he repeated, underlining the sentence with impetuous dashes. *"You know,"* he wrote; *"and you know, therefore, that everything is at an end for me. I am going abroad today. I shall never see the Abbey again."*

It was well that he had gone, as I hardly think that I could have faced him; and yet I was loth myself to leave the matter in this horrible tangle. I felt that it was enjoined upon me to meet the problems, and I endeavored to do so as best I might.

Mrs. Batty gave me news of the girl Alice. It was bad enough, though not as bad as both of us had feared. I was able to make arrangements on the instant, which I hoped might bury that lamentable affair for the time. There remained Miss Bosanquet; but that difficulty seemed beyond me. I could see no avenue out of the tragedy. I heard nothing save that she was ill—an illness attributed upon all hands to the shock of exposure to the thunderstorm! Only I knew better, and a vague disinclination to fly from the responsibilities of the position kept me hanging on at Utterbourne.

It was in those days before my visit to St. Pharamond that I turned my attention more particularly to the thing which had forced itself relentlessly upon me. I was never a superstitious man; the gossip of old wives interested me merely as a curious and unsympathetic observer. And yet I was vaguely discomfited by the transaction in the Abbey, and it was with some reluctance that I decided to make a further test of Warrington's bedroom. Mrs. Batty received my determination to change my room easily enough, but with a protest as to the dampness of the Stone Chamber. It was plain that her suspicions had not marched with mine. On the second night after Warrington's departure I occupied the room for the first time.

I lay awake for a couple of hours, with a reading lamp by my bed, and a volume of travels in my hand, and then, feeling very tired, put out the light and went to sleep. Nothing distracted me that night; indeed, I slept more soundly and peaceably than before in that house. I rose, too, experiencing quite an exhilaration, and it was not until I was dressing before the glass that I remembered the circumstances of my mission; but then I was at once pulled up, startled swiftly out of my cheerful temper.

Faintly visible upon my throat was the same round mark which I had already seen stamped upon Warrington and Miss Bosanquet. With that, all my former doubts returned in force, augmented and militant. My mind recurred to the bat, and tales of bloodsucking by those evil creatures revived in my memory. But when I had remembered that these were of foreign beasts, and that I was in England, I dismissed them lightly enough.[7] Still the impress of that mark remained, and alarmed me. It could not come by accident; to suppose so manifold a coincidence was absurd. The puzzle dwelt with me, unresolved, and the fingers of dread slowly crept over me.

Yet I slept again in the room. Having but myself for company, and being somewhat bored and dull, I fear I took more spirit than was my custom, and the result was that I again slept profoundly.

I awoke about three in the morning, and was surprised to find the lamp still burning. I had forgotten it in my stupid state of somnolence. As I turned to put it out, the bat swept by me and circled for an instant above my head. So overpowered with torpor was I that I scarcely noticed it, and my head was no sooner at rest than I was once more unconscious. The red mark was stronger next morning, though, as on the previous day, it wore off with the fall of evening. But I merely observed the fact without any concern; indeed, now the matter of my investigation seemed to have drawn very remote. I was growing indifferent, I supposed, through familiarity. But the solitude was palling upon me, and I spent a very restless day. A sharp ride I took in the afternoon was the one agreeable experience of the day. I reflected that if this burden were to continue I must hasten up to town. I had no desire to tie myself to Warrington's apron, in his interest. So dreary was the evening, that after I had strolled round the grounds and into the chapel by moonlight, I returned to the library and endeavored to pass the time with Warrington's

---

[7] The scene echoes Quincey Morris's tale in *Dracula* of the vampire-bat of the Pampas. However, the "bloodsucking" is a myth; the vampire bat bites its victim and then laps the blood from the wound.

cards. But it was poor fun with no antagonist to pit myself against; and I was throwing down the pack in disgust when one of the manservants entered with the whiskey.

It was not until long afterwards that I fully realized the course of my action; but even at the time I was aware of a curious sub-feeling of shamefacedness. I am sure that the thing fell naturally, and that there was no awkwardness in my approaching him. Nor, after the first surprise, did he offer any objection. Later he was hardly expected to do so, seeing that he was winning very quickly. The reason of that I guessed afterwards, but during the play I was amazed to note at intervals how strangely my irritation was aroused. Finally, I swept the cards to the floor, and rose, the man, with a smile in which triumph blended with uneasiness, rose also.

"Damn you, get away!" I said, angrily.

True to his traditions to the close, he answered me with respect, and obeyed; and I sat staring at the table. With a sudden flush, the grotesque folly of the night's business came to me, and my eyes fell on the whiskey bottle. It was nearly empty. Then I went to bed.

Voices cried all night in that chamber—soft, pleading voices. There was nothing to alarm in them: they seemed in a manner to coo me to sleep. But presently a sharper cry roused me from my semi-slumber, and getting up, I flung open the window. The wind rushed round the Abbey, sweeping with noises against the corners and gables. The black chapel lay still in the moonlight, and drew my eyes. But, resisting a strange, unaccountable impulse to go further, I went back to bed.

The events of the following day are better related without comment.

At breakfast I found a letter from Sir William Bosanquet, inviting me to come over to St. Pharamond. I was at once conscious of an eager desire to do so: it seemed somehow as though I had been waiting for this. The visit assumed preposterous proportions, and I was impatient for the afternoon.

Sir William was polite, but not, as I thought, cordial. He never alluded to Warrington, from which I guessed that he had been informed of the breach, and I conjectured also that the invitation extended to me was rather an act of courtesy to a solitary stranger than due to a desire for my company. Nevertheless, when he presently suggested that I should stay to dinner, I accepted promptly. For, to say the truth, I had not yet seen Miss Bosanquet, and I experienced a strange curiosity to do so. When at last she made her appearance, I was struck, almost for the first time, by her beauty. She was certainly a handsome girl, though she had a delicate air of ill health.

After dinner Sir William remembered by accident the book on the Abbey which he had promised to show me, and after a brief hunt in the library he found it. Shortly afterwards he was called away, and with an apology left me. With a curious eagerness I turned the pages of the volume and settled down to read.

It was published early in the century, and purported to relate the history of the Abbey and its owners. But it was one chapter which specially drew my interest—that which recounted the fate of the last Marvyn. The family had become extinct through a bloody tragedy; that fact held me. The bare narrative, long since passed from the memory of tradition, was here set forth in the baldest statements. The names of Sir Rupert Marvyn and Priscilla, Lady Marvyn, shook me strangely, but particularly the latter. Some links of connection with those gravestones lying in the Abbey chapel constrained me intimately.

The history of that evil race was stained and discolored with blood, and the end was in fitting harmony—a lurid holocaust of crime. There had been two brothers, but it was hard to choose between the foulness of their lives. If either, the younger William was the worse; so at least the narrative would have it. The details of his excesses had not survived, but it was abundantly plain that they were both notorious gamblers. The story of their deaths was wrapt in doubt, the theme of conjecture only, and probability; for none was by to observe save the three veritable actors—who were at once involved together in a bloody dissolution.

Priscilla, the wife of Sir Rupert, was suspected of an intrigue with her brother-in-law. She would seem to have been tainted with the corruption of the family into which she had married. But according to a second rumor, chronicled by the author, there was some doubt if the woman were not the worst of the three. Nothing was known of her parentage; she had returned with the passionate Sir Rupert to the Abbey after one of his prolonged absences, and was accepted as his legal wife. This was the woman whose infamous beauty had brought a terrible sin between the brothers.

Upon the night which witnessed the extinction of this miserable family, the two brothers had been gambling together. It was known from the high voices that they had quarreled, and it is supposed that, heated with wine and with the lust of play, the younger had thrown some taunt at Sir Rupert in respect to his wife. Whereupon—but this is all conjecture—the elder stabbed him to death. At least, it was understood that at this point the sounds of a struggle were heard, and a bitter cry.

The report of the servants ran that upon this noise Lady Marvyn rushed into the room and locked the door behind her. Fright was busy with those servants, long used to the savage manners of the house. According to witnesses, no further sound was heard subsequently to Lady Marvyn's entrance; yet when the doors were at last broken open by the authorities, the three bodies were discovered upon the floor.

How Sir Rupert and his wife met their deaths there was no record. "This tragedy," proceeded the scribe, "took place in the Stone Chamber underneath the stairway."

I had got so far when the entrance of Miss Bosanquet disturbed me. I remember rising in a dazed condition—the room swung about me. A conviction, hitherto resisted and stealthily entertained upon compulsion, now overpowered me.

"I thought my father was here," explained Miss Bosanquet, with a quick glance round the room. I explained the circumstances, and she hesitated in my neighborhood with a slight air of embarrassment.

"I have not thanked you properly, Mr. Heywood," she said presently, in a low voice, scarcely articulate. "You have been very considerate and kind. Let me thank you now." And ended with a tiny spasmodic sob.

Somehow, an impulse overmastered my tongue. Fresh from the perusal of that chapter, queer possibilities crowded in my mind, odd considerations urged me.

"Miss Bosanquet," said I, abruptly, "let me speak of that a little. I will not touch on details."

"Please," she cried, with a shrinking notion as of one that would retreat in very alarm.

"Nay," said I, eagerly; "hear me. It is no wantonness that would press the memory upon you. You have been a witness to distressful acts; you have seen a man under the influence of temporary madness. Nay, even yourself, you have been a victim to the same unaccountable phenomena."

"What do you mean?" she cried, tensely.

"I will say no more," said I. "I should incur your laughter. No, you would not laugh, but my dim suspicions would leave you still incredulous. But if this were so, and if these were the phenomena of a brief madness, surely you would make your memory a grave to bury the past."

"I cannot do that," said she, in low tones.

"What!" I asked. "Would you turn from your lover, aye, even from a friend, because he was smitten with disease? Consider; if your dearest upon earth tossed in a fever upon his bed, and denied you in his ravings, using you despitefully, it would not be he that entreated you so. When he was quit of his madness and returned to his proper person, would you not forget—would you not rather recall his insanity with the pity of affection?"

"I do not understand you," she whispered.

"You read your Bible," said I. "You have wondered at the evil spirits that possessed poor victims. Why should you decide that these things have ceased? We are too dogmatic in our modern world. Who can say under what malign influence a soul may pass, and out of its own custody?"

She looked at me earnestly, searching my eyes.

"Yon hint at strange things," said she, very low.

But somehow, even as I met her eyes, the spirit of my mission failed me. My gaze, I felt, devoured her ruthlessly. The light shone on her pale and comely features; they burned me with an irresistible attraction. I put forth my hand and took hers gently. It was passive to my touch, as though in acknowledgment of my kindly offices.

All the while I experienced a sense of fierce elation. In my blood ran, as it had been fire, a horrible incentive, and I knew that I was holding her hand very tightly. She herself seemed to grow conscious of this, for she made an effort to withdraw her fingers, at which, the passion rushing through my body, I clutched them closer, laughing aloud. I saw a wondering look dawn in her eyes, and her bosom thinly veiled, heaved with a tiny tremor. I was aware that I was drawing her steadily to me. Suddenly her bewildered eyes, dropping from my face, lit with a flare of terror, and, wrenching her hand away, she fell back with a cry, her gaze riveted upon my throat.

"That accursed mark! What is it? What is it?—" she cried, shivering from head to foot.

In an instant, the wild blood singing in my head, I sprang towards her. What would have followed, I know not, but at that moment the door opened and Sir William returned. He regarded us with consternation; but Miss Bosanquet had fainted, and the next moment he was at her side.

I stood near, watching her come to with a certain nameless fury, as of a beast cheated of its prey. Sir William turned to me, and in his most courteous manner begged me to excuse the untoward scene. His daughter, he said, was not at all strong, and he ended by suggesting that I should leave them for a time.

Reluctantly I obeyed, but when I was out of the house, I took a sudden panic. The demoniac possession lifted, and in a craven state of trembling I saddled my horse, and rode for the Abbey as if my life depended upon my speed.

I arrived at about ten o'clock, and immediately gave orders to have my bed prepared in my old room. In my shaken condition the sinister influences of that stone chamber terrified me; and it was not until I had drunk deeply that I regained my composure.

But I was destined to get little sleep. I had steadily resolved to keep my thoughts off the matter until the morning, but the spell of the chamber was strong upon me. I awoke after midnight with an irresistible feeling drawing me to the room. I was conscious of the impulse, and combated it, but in the end succumbed; and throwing on my clothes, took a light and went downstairs.

I flung wide the door of the room and peered in, listening, as though for some voice of welcome. It was as silent as a sepulchre; but directly I crossed the threshold voices seemed to surround and coax me. I stood wavering, with a curious fascination upon me. I knew I could not return to my own room, and I now had no desire to do so.

As I stood, my candle flaring solemnly against the darkness, I noticed upon the floor an alcove bare of carpet, a large black mark, which appeared to be a stain. Bending down, I examined it, passing my fingers over the stone. It moved to my touch. Setting the candle upon the floor, I put my fingertips to the edges, and pulled hard. As I did so the sounds that were ringing in my ears died instantaneously; the next moment the slab turned with a crash, and discovered a gaping hole of impenetrable blackness.

The patch of chasm thus opened to my eyes was near a yard square. The candle held to it shed a dim light upon a stone step a foot or two below, and it was clear to me that a stairway communicated with the depths. Whether it had been used as a cellar in times gone by I could not divine, but I was soon to determine this doubt; for, stirred by a strange eagerness, I slipped my legs through the hole, and let myself cautiously down with the light in my hand.

There were a dozen steps to descend ere I reached the floor and what turned out to be a narrow passage. The vault ran forward straight as an arrow before my eyes, and slowly I moved on. Dank and chill was the air in those close confines, and the sound of my feet returned from those walls dull and sullen. But I kept on, and, with infinite care, must have penetrated quite a hundred yards along that musty corridor ere I came out upon an ampler chamber.

Here the air was freer, and I could perceive with the aid of my light that the dimensions of the place were lofty. Above, a solitary ray of moonlight, sliding through a crack, informed me that I was not far from the level of the earth. It fell upon a block of stone, which rose in the middle of the vault, and which I now inspected with interest. As the candle threw its flickering beams upon this I realized where I was. I scarcely needed the rude lettering upon the coffins to acquaint me that here was the family vault of the Marvyns. And now I began to perceive upon all sides whereon my feeble light fell the crumbling relics of the forgotten dead—coffins fallen into decay, bones and grinning skulls resting in corners, disposed by the hand of chance and time. This formidable array of the mortal remains of that poor family moved me to a shudder.

I turned from those ugly memorials once more to the central altar where the two coffins rested in this somber silence. The lid had fallen from the one, disclosing to my sight the grisly skeleton of a man, that mocked and leered at me. It seemed in a manner to my fascinated eyes to challenge my mortality, inviting me too to the rude and grotesque sleep of death. I knew, as by an instinct, that I was standing by the bones of Sir Rupert Marvyn, the protagonist in that terrible crime which had locked three souls in eternal ruin. The consideration of this miserable spectacle held me motionless for some moments, and then I moved a step closer and cast my light upon the second coffin.

As I did so I was aware of a change within myself. The grave and melancholy thoughts which I had entertained, the sober bent of my solemn reflections, gave place instantly to a strange exultation, an unholy sense of elation. My pulse swung feverishly, and, while my eyes were riveted upon the tarnished silver of the plate, I stretched forth a tremulously eager hand and touched the lid.

It rattled gently under my fingers. Disturbed by the noise, I hastily withdrew them; but whether it was the impetus offered by my touch, or through some horrible and nameless circumstance—God knows—slowly and softly a gap opened behind the lid and the body of the coffin!

Before my startled eyes the awful thing happened, and yet I was conscious of no terror, merely of surprise and—it seems terrible to admit—of a feeling of eager expectancy. The lid rose slowly on the one side, and as it lifted the dark space between it and the coffin grew gently charged with light.

At that moment my feeble candle, which had been gradually diminishing, guttered and flickered. I seemed to catch a glimpse of something, as it were, of white and shining raiment inside the coffin; and then came a rush of wings and a whirring sound within the vault. I gave a cry, and stepping back missed my foothold; the guttering candle was jerked from my grasp, and I fell prone to the floor in darkness. The next moment a sheet of flame flashed in the chamber and lit up the grotesque skeletons about me; and at the same time a piercing cry rang forth. Jumping to my feet, I gave a dazed glance at the conflagration.

The whole vault was in flames. Dazed and horror-struck, I rushed blindly to the entrance; but as I did so the horrible cry pierced my ears again, and I saw the bat swoop round and circle swiftly into the flames. Then, finding the exit, I dashed with all the speed of terror down the passage, groping my way along the walls, and striking myself a dozen times in my terrified flight.

Arrived in my room, I pushed over the stone and listened. Not a sound was audible. With a white face and a body torn and bleeding I rushed from the room, and locking the door behind me, made my way upstairs to my bedroom. Here I poured myself out a stiff glass of brandy.

IT WAS SIX MONTHS later ere Warrington returned. In the meantime he had sold the Abbey. It was inevitable that he should do so; and yet the new owner, I believe, has found no drawback in his property, and the Stone Chamber is still used for a bedroom upon occasions, being considered very old-fashioned. But there are some facts against which no appeal is possible, and so it was in his case. In my relation of the tragedy I have made no attempt at explanation, hardly even to myself; and it appears now for the first time in print, of course with suppositious names.

Dick Donovan

JAMES EDWARD PRESTON MUDDOCK (also known as Joyce Emmerson Preston Muddock; 1843-1934), wrote almost 300 stories of detection and mystery under the pseudonym of Dick Donovan between 1889 and 1922. His tough-guy detective tales, told in the first person and collected in volumes with dime-novel titles like *The Man-Hunter* (1888), *Found and Fettered* (1894), *The Adventures of Tyler Tatlock: Private Detective* (1900), and *The Triumphs of Fabian Field: Criminologist* (1912), were immensely popular, rivaling Conan Doyle. In the collection titled *Tales of Terror* (1899), Muddock ventured into the realms of the weird and horrific.

The following story, along with "The Story of Annette: Being the Sequel to The Woman with the 'Oily Eyes'" (a "prequel" in modern parlance) are soundly based in the vampire tradition, as is evident from the "Note by the Author" appended to the narrative.

THE WOMAN WITH THE "OILY EYES"

DICK DONOVAN

Although often urged to put into print the remarkable story which follows I have always strenuously refused to do so, partly on account of personal reasons and partly out of respect for the feelings of the relatives of those concerned. But after much consideration I have come to the conclusion that my original objections can no longer be urged. The principal actors are dead. I myself am well stricken in years, and before very long must pay the debt of nature which is exacted from everything that lives.

Although so long a time has elapsed since the grim tragedy I am about to record, I cannot think of it even now without a shudder. The story of the life of every man and woman is probably more or less a tragedy, but nothing I have ever heard of can compare in ghastly, weird horror with all the peculiar circumstances of the case in point. Most certainly I would never have put pen to paper to record it had it not been from a sense of duty. Long years ago certain garbled versions crept into the public journals, and though at the time I did not consider it desirable to contradict them, I do think now that the moment has come when I, the only living being fully acquainted with the facts, should make them known, otherwise lies will become history, and posterity will accept it as truth.

But there is still another reason I may venture to advance for breaking the silence of years. I think in the interest of science the case should be recorded. I have not always held this view, but when a man bends under the weight of years, and he sniffs the mould of his grave, his ideas undergo a complete change, and the opinions of his youth are not the opinions of his old age. There may be exceptions to this, but I fancy they must be very few. With these preliminary remarks I will plunge at once into my story.

It was the end of August 1857 that I acted as best man at the wedding of my friend Jack Redcar, C.E.[1] It was a memorable year, for our hold on our magnificent Indian

[1] "Civil Engineer," not "Church of England."

Empire had nearly been shaken loose by a mutiny which had threatened to spread throughout the whole of India. At the beginning of 1856 I had returned home from India after a three years' spell. I had gone out as a young medico in the service of the H.E.I.C.,[2] but my health broke down and I was compelled to resign my appointment.

A year later my friend Redcar, who had also been in the Company's service as a civil engineer, came back to England, as his father had recently died and left him a modest fortune. Jack was not only my senior in year, but I had always considered him my superior in every respect. We were at a public school together, and both went up to Oxford, though not together, for he was finishing his final year when I was a freshman.

Although erratic and a bit wild he was a brilliant fellow; and while I was considered dull and plodding, and found some difficulty in mastering my subjects, there was nothing he tackled that he failed to succeed in, and come out with flying colors. In the early stage of our acquaintance he made me his fag,[3] and patronised me, but that did not last long. A friendship sprang up. He took a great liking to me, why I know not; but it was reciprocated, and when he got his Indian appointment I resolved to follow, and by dint of hard work, and having a friend at court, I succeeded in obtaining my commission in John Company's service.[4]

Jack married Maude Vane Tremlett, as sweet a woman as ever drew God's breath of life. If I attempted to describe her in detail I am afraid it might be considered that I was exaggerating, but briefly I may say she was the perfection of physical beauty. Jack himself was an exceptionally fine fellow. A brawny giant with a singularly handsome face. At the time of his wedding he was thirty or thereabouts, while Maude was in her twenty-fifth year. There was a universal opinion that a better matched couple had never been brought together. He had a masterful nature; nevertheless was kind, gentle, and manly to a degree.

It may be thought that I speak with some bias and prejudice in Jack's favor, but I can honestly say that at the time I refer to he was as fine a fellow as ever figured as hero in song or story. He was the pink of honor,[5] and few who really knew him but would have trusted him with their honor, their fortunes, their lives. This may be strong, but I declare it's true, and I am the more anxious to emphasize it because his after life was in such marked contrast, and he presents a study in psychology that is not only deeply interesting, but extraordinary.

The wedding was a really brilliant affair, for Jack had troops of friends, who vied with each other in marking the event in a becoming manner, while his bride was idolized by a doting household. Father and mother, sisters and brothers, worshipped her. She was exceedingly well connected. Her father held an important Government appointment, and her mother came from the somewhat celebrated Yorkshire family of the Kingscotes. Students of history will remember that a Colonel King-

---

[2] Honorable East India Company.
[3] His servant (usually a junior boy).
[4] Common slang term for the H.E.I.C.
[5] A common catchphrase, based on the Welsh word "pince," meaning highest point or acme—therefore, as honorable as possible.

scote figured prominently and honorably as a royalist during the reign of the unfortunate Charles I.

No one who was present on that brilliant August morning of 1857, when Jack Redcar was united in the bonds of wedlock to beautiful Maude Tremlett, would have believed it possible that such grim and tragic events would so speedily follow. The newly-married pair left in the course of the day for the Continent, and during their honeymoon I received several charming letters from Jack, who was not only a diligent correspondent, but he possessed a power of description and a literary style that made his letter delightful reading. Another thing that marked this particular correspondence was the unstinted—I may almost say florid—praise he bestowed upon his wife. To illustrate what I mean, here is a passage from one of his letters:—

"I wish I had command of language sufficiently eloquent to speak of my darling Maude as she should be spoken of. She has a perfectly angelic nature; and though it may be true that never a human being was yet born without faults, for the life of me I can find none in my sweet wife.

"Of course you will say, old chap, that this is honeymoon gush, but, upon my soul, it isn't. I am only doing scant justice to the dear woman who has linked her fate with mine. I have sometimes wondered what I have done that the gods should have blest me in such a manner. For my own part, I don't think I was deserving of so much happiness, and I assure you I am happy—perfectly, deliciously happy. Will it last? Yes, I am sure it will.

"Maude will always be to me what she is now, a flawless woman; a woman with all the virtues that turn women into angels, and without one of the weaknesses or one of the vices which too often mar an otherwise perfect feminine character. I hope, old boy, that if ever you marry, the woman you choose will be only half as good as mine."

Had such language been used by anyone else I might have been disposed to add a good deal more than the proverbial pinch of salt before swallowing it. But, as a matter of fact, Jack was not a mere gusher. He had a thoroughly practical, as distinguished from a sentimental, mind, and he was endowed with exceptionally keen powers of observation.

And so, making all the allowances for the honeymoon romance, I was prepared to accept my friend's statement as to the merits of his wife without a quibble. Indeed, I knew her to be a most charming lady, endowed with many of the qualities which give the feminine nature its charm. But I would even go a step farther than that, and declare that Mrs. Redcar was a woman in ten thousand.

At that time I hadn't a doubt that the young couple were splendidly matched, and it seemed to me probable that the future that stretched before them was not likely to be disturbed by any of the commonplace incidents which seemed inseparable from most lives. I regarded Jack as a man of such high moral worth that his wife's happiness was safe in his keeping. I pictured them leading an ideal, poetical life—a life freed from all the vulgar details which blight the careers of so many people—a life which would prove a blessing to themselves as well as a joy to all with whom they had to deal.

When they started their tour Mr. and Mrs. Redcar anticipated being absent from England for five or six weeks only, but for several reasons they were induced to prolong their travels, and thus it chanced I was away when they returned shortly before Christmas of the year of their marriage. My own private affairs took me to America. As a matter of fact a relative had died leaving me a small property in that country, which required my personal attention; the consequence was I remained out of England for nearly three years.

For the first year or so Jack Redcar wrote to me with commendable regularity. I was duly apprised of the birth of a son and heir. This event seemed to put the crown upon their happiness, but three months later came the first note of sorrow. The baby died, and the doting parents were distracted.

Jack wrote:—

"My poor woman is absolutely pros- trated, but I tell her we were getting too happy, and this blow has been dealt to remind us that human existence must be chequered in order that we may appreciate more fully the supreme joy of that after-life which we are told we may gain for the striving. This, of course, is a pretty sentiment, but the loss of the baby mite has hit me hard. Still, Maude is left to me, and she is such a splendid woman, that I ought to feel I am more than blest."

This was the last letter I ever received from Jack, but his wife wrote at odd times. Hers were merely gossipy little chronicles of passing events, and singularly enough she never alluded to her husband, although she wrote in a light, happy vein. This set me wondering, and when I answered her I never failed to inquire about her husband. I continued to re- ceive letters from her, though at long intervals, down to the month of my departure from America, two years later.

I arrived in London in the winter, and an awful winter it was. London was indeed a city of dreadful night. Gloom and fog were every- where. Everybody one met looked miserable and despondent. Into the public houses and

gin palaces such of the poor as could scratch a few pence together crowded for the sake of the warmth and light. But in the streets sights were to be seen which made one doubt if civ- ilization is the blessing we are asked to believe it. Starving men, women and children, soaked and sodden with the soot-laden fog, prowled about in the vain hope of finding food and shelter. But the well-to-do passed them with indifference, too intent on their own affairs, and too wrapped in self-interests to bestow thought upon the great city's pariahs.

Immediately after my arrival I penned a brief note to Jack Redcar, giving him my address, and saying I would take an early op- portunity of calling, as I was longing to feel once more the hearty, honest grip of his hand- shake. A week later a note was put into my hand as I was in the very act of going out to keep an appointment in the city. Recognizing Mrs. Redcar's handwriting I tore open the envelope, and read, with what feelings may be best imagined, the following lines:

For God's sake come and see me at once. I am heart-broken and am going mad. You are the only friend in the world to whom I feel I can ap- peal. Come to me, in the name of pity.

        —MAUDE REDCAR.

I absolutely staggered as I read these brief lines, which were so pregnant with mys- tery, sorrow, and hopelessness. What did it all mean? To me, it was like a burst of thunder from a cloudless summer sky. Something was wrong, that was certain; what that something was I could only vaguely guess at. But I re- solved not to remain long in suspense. I put off my engagement, important as it was, and hailing a hansom directed the driver to go to Hampstead, where the Redcars had their residence.

The house was detached and stood in

about two acres of ground, and I could imagine it being a little Paradise in brilliant summer weather; but it seemed now in the winter murk, as if a heavy pall of sorrow and anguish enveloped it.

I was shown into an exquisitely furnished drawing room by an old and ill-favored woman, who answered my knock at the door. She gave me the impression that she was a sullen, deceptive creature, and I was at a loss to understand how such a woman could have found service with my friends—the bright and happy friends of three years ago. When I handed her my card to convey to Mrs. Redcar she impertinently turned it over, and scrutinized it, and fixed her cold bleared grey eyes on me, so that I was induced to say peremptorily, "Will you be good enough to go to your mistress at once and announce my arrival?"

"I ain't got no mistress," she growled. "I've got a master"; and with this cryptic utterance she left the room.

I waited a quarter of an hour, then the door was abruptly opened, and there stood before me Mrs. Redcar, but not the bright, sweet, radiant little woman of old. A look of premature age was in her face. Her eyes were red with weeping, and had a frightened, hunted expression. I was so astounded that I stood for a moment like one dumb-founded; but as Mrs. Redcar seized my hand and shook it, she gasped in a nervous, spasmodic way:—

"Thank God, you have come! My last hope is in you."

Then, completely overcome by emotion, she burst into hysterical sobbing, and covered her face with her handkerchief.

My astonishment was still so great, the unexpected had so completely paralyzed me for the moment, that I seemed incapable of action. But of course this spell quickly passed, and I regained my self-possession.

"How is it I find this change?" I asked. It was a natural question, and the first my brain shaped.

"It's the work of a malignant fiend," she sobbed.

This answer only deepened my mystery, and I began to think that perhaps she was literally mad. Then suddenly, as if she divined my thoughts, drew her handkerchief from her face, motioned me to be seated, and literally flung herself on to a couch.

"It's an awful story," she said, in a hoarse, hollow voice, "and I look to you, and appeal to you, and pray to you to help me."

"You can rely upon my doing anything that lies in my power," I answered. "But tell me your trouble. How is Jack? Where is he?"

"In her arms, probably," she exclaimed between her teeth; and she twisted her handkerchief up rope-wise and dragged it backward and forward through her hand with an excess of desperate, nervous energy. Her answer gave me a keynote. Jack had swerved from the path of honor, and allowed himself to be charmed by other eyes to the neglect of this woman whom he had described to me as being angelic. Although her beauty was now a little marred by tears and sorrow, she was still very beautiful and attractive, and had she been so disposed she might have taken an army of men captive.

She saw by the expression on my face that her remark was not an enigma to me, and she added quickly: "Oh, yes, it's true, and I look to you, doctor, to help me. It is an awful, dreadful story, but mind you, I don't blame Jack so much; he is not master of himself. This diabolical creature has enslaved him. She is like the creatures of old that one reads about. She is in possession of some devilish power which enables her to destroy men body and soul."

"Good God! This is awful," I involuntarily cried; for I was aghast and horror-stricken at the revelation. Could it be possible that my brilliant friend, who had won golden opinions from all sorts and conditions of men, had fallen from his pedestal to wallow in the mire of sinfulness and deception.

"It is awful," answered Mrs. Redcar. "I tell you, doctor, there is something uncanny about the whole business. The woman is an unnatural woman. She is a she-devil. And from my heart I pity and sorrow for my poor boy."

"Where is he now?" I asked.

"In Paris with her."

"How long has this been going on?"

"Since a few weeks after our marriage."

"Good heavens, you don't say so!"

"You may well look surprised, but it's true. Three weeks after our marriage, Jack and I were at Wiesbaden.[6] As we were going downstairs to dinner one evening, we met this woman coming up. A shudder of horror came over me as I looked at her, for she had the most extraordinary eyes I have ever seen. I clung to my husband in sheer fright, and I noted that he turned and looked at her, and she also turned and looked at him.

" 'What a remarkable woman,' he muttered strangely, so strangely that it was as if some other voice was using his lips. Then he broke into a laugh, and, passing his arm around my waist, said: 'Why, my dear little woman, I believe you are frightened.'

" 'I am,' I said; 'that dreadful creature has

[6] A popular spa in Germany.

startled me more than an Indian cobra would have done.'

" 'Well, upon my word,' said Jack, 'I must confess she is a strange-looking being. Did ever you see such eyes? Why, they make one think of the fairy-books and the mythical beings who flit through their pages.'

"During the whole of the dinner-time that woman's face haunted me. It was a strong, hard-featured, almost masculine face, every line of which indicated a nature that was base, cruel, and treacherous. The thin lips, the drawn nostrils, the retreating chin, could never be associated with anything that soft, gentle, or womanly. But it was the eyes that were the wonderful feature—they absolutely seemed to exercise some magic influence; they were oily eyes that gleamed and glistened, and they seemed to have in them that sinister light which is peculiar to the cobra, and other poisonous snakes. You may imagine the spell and influence they exerted over me when, on the following day, I urged my husband to leave Wiesbaden at once, notwithstanding that the place was glorious in its autumn dress, and was filled with a fashionable and light-hearted crowd. But my lightest wish then was law to Jack, so that very afternoon we were on our way to Homburg, and it was only when Wiesbaden was miles behind me that I began to breathe freely again.

"We had been in Homburg for a fortnight, and the incident of Wiesbaden had passed from my mind, when one morning, as Jack and I were on our way from the Springs, we came face to face with the woman with the oily eyes. I nearly fainted, but she smiled a hideous, cunning, cruel smile, inclined her head slightly in token of recognition, and passed on. I looked at my husband. It seemed to me he was unusually pale, and I was surprised to see him turn and gaze after her, and she had also turned and was gazing at us. Not a word was uttered by either of us, but I pressed my husband's arm and we walked rapidly away to our apartments.

" 'It's strange,' I remarked to Jack as we sat at breakfast, 'that we should meet that awful woman again.'

" 'Oh, not at all,' he laughed. 'You know at this time of the year, people move about from place to place, and it's wonderful how you keep rubbing shoulders with the same set.'

"It was quite true what Jack said, nevertheless, I could not help the feeling that the woman with the oily eyes had followed us to Homburg. If I had mentioned this then it would have been considered ridiculous, for we had only met her once, and had never spoken a word to her. What earthly interest, therefore, could she possibly take in us who were utter strangers to her. But, looked at by the light of after events, my surmise was true.

"The creature had marked Jack for her victim the moment we unhappily met on the stairs at Wiesbaden. I tell you, doctor, that that woman is a human ghoul, a vampire, who lives not only by sucking the blood of men, but by destroying their souls."

Mrs. Redcar broke down again at this stage of her narrative, and I endeavored to comfort her; but she quickly mastered her feelings sufficiently to continue her remarkable story.

"Some days later my husband and I moved along with the throng that drifted up and down the promenade listening to the band, when we met a lady whom I had known as a neighbor when I was at home with my parents. We stopped and chatted with her for some time, until Jack asked us to excuse him while he went to purchase some matches at a kiosk; he said he would be by the fountain in ten minutes, and I was to wait for him.

"My lady friend and I moved along and chatted as women will, and then she bade me good-night as she had to rejoin her friends. I at once hurried to the rendezvous at the fountain, but Jack wasn't there. I waited some time, but still he came not. I walked about impatiently and half frightened, and when nearly three quarters of an hour had passed I felt sure Jack had gone home, so with all haste I went to our apartments close by, but he was not in, and had not been in. Half distracted, I flew back to the promenade. It was nearly deserted, for the band had gone. As I hurried along, not knowing where to go to, and scarcely knowing what I was doing, I was attracted by a laugh— a laugh I knew. It was Jack's, and proceeding a few yards further I found him on a seat under a linden tree with the woman with the oily eyes.

" 'Why, my dear Maude,' he exclaimed, 'wherever have you been to? I've hunted everywhere for you.'

"A great lump came in my throat, for I felt that Jack was lying to me. I really don't know what I said or what I did, but I am conscious in a vague way that he introduced me to the woman, but the only name I caught was that of Annette. It burnt itself into my brain; it has haunted me ever since.

"Annette put out her white hand veiled by a silk net glove through which diamond rings sparkled. I believe I did touch the proffered fingers, and I shuddered, and I heard her say in a silvery voice that was quite of keeping with her appearance:

" 'If I were your husband I should take you to task. Beauty like yours, you know, ought not to go unattended in a place like this.'

"Perhaps she thought this was funny, for she laughed, and then patted me on the shoulder with her fan. But I hated her from that moment—hated her with a hatred I did not deem myself capable of.

"We continued to sit there, how long I don't know. It seemed to me a very long time, but perhaps it wasn't long. When we rose to go to the promenade was nearly deserted, only two or three couples remained. The moon was shining brilliantly; the night wind sighed pleasantly in the trees; but the beauty of the night was lost upon me. I felt ill at ease, and, for the first time in my life, unhappy. Annette walked with us nearly to our door. When the moment for parting came she again offered me the tips of her fingers, but I merely bowed frigidly, and shrank from her as I saw her oily eyes fixed upon me.

"'Ta, ta!' she said in her fatal silvery voice; 'keep a watchful guard over your husband, my dear; and you, sir, don't let your beautiful little lady stray from you again, or there will be grief between you.'

"Those wicked words, every one of which was meant to have its effect, was like the poison of asps to me; you may imagine how they stung me when I tell you I was seized with an almost irresistible desire to hurl the full weight of my body at her, and, having thrown her down, trample upon her. She had aroused in me such a feeling of horror that very little more would have begotten in me the desperation of madness, and I might have committed some act which I should have regretted all my life. But bestowing another glance of her basilisk eyes upon me she moved off, and I felt relieved; though, when I reached my room, I burst into hysterical weeping. Jack

took me in his arms, and kissed and comforted me, and all my love for him was strong again; as I lay with my head pillowed on his breast I felt once more supremely happy.

"The next day, on thinking the matter over, I came to the conclusion that my suspicions were unjust, my fears groundless, my jealousy stupid, and that my conduct had been rude in the extreme. I resolved, therefore, to be more amiable and polite to Annette when I again met her. But, strangely enough, though we remained in Homburg a fortnight longer we did not meet; but I know now my husband saw her several times.

"Of course, if it had not been for subsequent events, it would have been said that I was a victim of strong hysteria on that memorable night. Men are so ready to accuse women of hysteria because they are more sensitive, and see deeper than men do themselves. But my aversion to Annette from the instant I set eyes upon her, and the inferences I drew, were not due to hysteria, but to that eighth sense possessed by women, which had no name, and of which men know nothing. At least, I mean to say that they cannot understand it."

Again Mrs. Redcar broke off in her narrative, for emotion had got better of her. I deemed it advisable to wait. Her remarkable story had aroused all my interest, and I was anxious not to lose any connecting link of it, for from the psychological point of view it was a study.

"Of course, as I have begun the story I must finish it to its bitter end," she went on. "As I have told you, I did not see Annette again in Homburg, and when we left all my confidence in Jack was restored, and my love for him was stronger than ever if that were possible. Happiness came back to me. Oh! I was so happy, and thinking I had done a cruel, bitter wrong to Jack in even supposing for a moment that he would be unfaithful to me. I tried by every little artifice a woman is capable of to prove my devotion to him.

"Well, to make a long story short, we continued to travel about for some time, and finally returned home, and my baby was born. It seemed to me then as if God was really too good to me. I had everything in the world that a human being can reasonably want. An angel baby, a brave, handsome husband, ample means, hosts of friends. I was supremely happy. I thanked my Maker for it all every hour of my life. But suddenly amongst the roses the hiss of the serpent sounded. One day a carriage drove up to our door. It brought a lady visitor. She was shown into our drawing-room, and when asked for her name made some excuse to the servant. Of course, I hurried down to see who my caller was, and imagine my horror when on entering the room I beheld Annette.

" 'My dear Mrs. Redcar,' she gushingly exclaimed, emphasizing every word, 'I am so delighted to see you again. Being in London, I could not resist the temptation to call and renew acquaintances.'

"The voice was as silvery as ever, and her awful eyes seemed more oily. In my confusion and astonishment I did not inquire how she had got our address; but I know that I refused her proffered hand, and by my manner gave her unmistakably to understand that I did not regard her as a welcome visitor. But she seemed perfectly indifferent. She talked gaily, flippantly. She threw her fatal spell about me. She fascinated me, so that when she asked to see my baby I mechanically rang the bell, and as mechanically told the servant to send the nurse and baby in. When she came, the

damnable woman took the child from the nurse and danced him, but he suddenly broke into a scream of terror, so that I rushed forward; but the silvery voice said:—

" 'Oh, you silly little mother. The baby is all right. Look how quiet he is now.'

"She was holding him at arm's length, and gazing at him with her basilisk eyes, and he was silent. Then she hugged and fondled him, and kissed him, and all the while I felt as if my brain was on fire, but I could neither speak nor move a hand to save my precious little baby.

"At last she returned him to his nurse, who at once left the room by my orders, and then Annette kept up a cackle of conversation. Although it did not strike me then as peculiar, for I was too confused to have any clear thought about anything—it did afterwards—she never once inquired about Jack. It happened when he was out. He had gone away early that morning to the city on some important business in which he was engaged.

"At last Annette took herself off, to my intense relief. She said nothing about calling again; she gave no address, and made no request for me to call on her. Even had she done so I should not have called. I was only too thankful she had gone, and I fervently hoped I should never see her again.

"As soon as she had departed I rushed upstairs, for baby was screaming violently. I found him in the nurse's arms, and she was doing her utmost to comfort him. But he refused to be comforted, and I took him and put him to my breast, and he still fought, and struggled, and screamed, and his baby eyes seemed to me to be bulging with terror. From that moment the darling little creature began to sicken. He gradually pined and wasted, and in a few weeks was lying like a beautiful waxen doll in a bed of flowers. He was stiff, and cold, and dead.

"When Jack came home in the evening of the day of Annette's call, and I told him she had been, he did not seem in the least surprised, but merely remarked:

" 'I hope you were hospitable to her.'

"I did not answer him, for I had been anything but hospitable. I had not even invited her to partake of the conventional cup of tea.

"As our baby boy faded day by day, Jack seemed to change, and the child's death overwhelmed him. He was never absolutely unkind to me at that period, but he seemed to have entirely altered. He became sullen, silent, even morose, and he spent the whole of his days away from me. When I gently chided him, he replied that his work absorbed all his attention. And so things went on until another thunderbolt fell at my feet.

"One afternoon Jack returned home and brought Annette. He told me that he had invited her to spend a few days with us. When I urged an objection he was angry with me for the first time in our married life. I was at once silenced, for his influence over me was still great, and I thought I would try and overcome my prejudice for Annette. At any rate, as Jack's wife I resolved to be hospitable, and play the hostess with grace. But I soon found that I was regarded as of very little consequence. Annette ruled Jack, she ruled me, she ruled the household.

"*You* will perhaps ask why I did not rise up in wrath, and, asserting my position and dignity, drive the wicked creature out of my home. But I tell you, doctor, I was utterly powerless. She worked some devil's spell upon me, and I was entirely under the influence of her will.

"Her visit stretched into weeks. Our well-tried and faithful servants left. Others came, but their stay was brief; and at last the old woman who opened the door to you was installed. She is a creature of Annette's, and is a spy upon my movements.

"All this time Jack was under the spell of the charmer, as I was. Over and over again I resolved to go to my friends, appeal to them, tell them everything, and ask them to protect me; but my will failed, and I bore and suffered in silence. And my husband neglected me; he seemed to find pleasure only in Annette's company. Oh, how I fretted and gnawed my heart, and yet I could not break away from the awful life. I tell you, doctor, that that woman possessed some strange, devilish, supernatural power over me and Jack. When she looked at me I shrivelled up. When she spoke, her silvery voice seemed to sting every nerve and fibre in my body, and he was like wax in her hands. To me he became positively brutal, and he told me over and over again that I was spoiling his life. But, though she was a repulsive, mysterious, crafty, cruel woman, he seemed to find his happiness in her company.

"One morning, after a restless, horrible, feverish night, I arose, feeling strangely ill, and as if I were going mad. I worked myself up to almost a pitch of frenzy, and, spurred by desperation, I rushed into the drawing-room, and where my husband and Annette were together, and exclaimed to her:

" 'Woman, do you not see that you are killing me? Why have you come here? Why do you persecute me with your devilish wiles? You must know you are not welcome. You must feel you are an intruder.'

"Overcome by the effort this had cost me, I sank down on the floor on my knees, and wept passionately. Then I heard the silvery voice say, in tones of surprise and injured innocence:—

" 'Well, upon my word, Mrs. Redcar, this is an extraordinary way to treat your husband's guest. I really thought I was a welcome visitor instead of an intruder; but, since I am mistaken, I will go at once.'

"I looked at her through a blinding mist of tears. I met the gaze of her oily eyes, but only for a moment, and felt powerless again. I glanced at my husband. He was standing with his head bowed, and, as it seemed to me, in a pose of shame and humiliation. But suddenly he darted at me, and I heard him say: 'What do you mean by creating such a scene as this? You must understand I am master here.' Then he struck me a violent blow on the head, and there was a long blank.

"When I came to my senses I was in bed, and the hideous old hag who opened the door to you was bending over me. It was some little time before I could realize what had occurred. When I did, I asked the woman where Mr. Redcar was, and she answered sullenly:—

" 'Gone.'

" 'And the—Annette; where is she?' I asked.

" 'Gone, too,' was the answer.

"Another blank ensued. I fell very ill, and when my brain was capable of coherent thought again I learnt that I had passed through a crisis, and my life had been in jeopardy. A doctor had been attending me, and there was a professional nurse in the house; but she was a hard, dry, unsympathetic woman, and I came to the conclusion— wrongly so, probably—she, too, was one of Annette's creatures.

"I was naturally puzzled to understand why none of my relatives and friends had been to see me, but I was to learn later that many had called, but had been informed I was abroad with my husband, who had been summoned away suddenly in connection with some professional matters. And I also know now that all my letters coming for me were at once forwarded to him, and that any requiring answers he answered.

"As I grew stronger I made up my mind to keep my own counsel, and not let any of my friends know of what I had gone through and suffered; for I still loved my husband, and looked upon him as a victim to be pitied and rescued from the infernal wiles of the she-demon. When I heard of your arrival in England, I felt you were the one person in the wide world I could appeal to with safety, for you can understand how anxious I am to avoid a scandal. Will you help me? Will you save your old friend Jack? Restore him to sanity, doctor, bring him back to my arms again, which will be wide open to receive him."

I listened to poor Mrs. Redcar's story patiently, and at first was disposed to look upon it as a too common tale of human weakness. Jack Redcar had fallen into the power of an adventuress, and had been unable to resist her influence. Such things had happened before, such things will happen again, I argued with myself. There are certain women who seem capable of making men mad for a brief space; but under proper treatment they come to their senses quickly, and blush with shame as they think of their foolishness. At any rate, for the sake of my old friend, and for the sake of his poor suffering little wife, I was prepared to do anything in reason to bring back the erring husband to his right senses.

I told Mrs. Redcar this. I told her I would redress her wrongs if I could, and fight her battle to the death. She almost threw herself at my feet in her gratitude. But when I suggested that I should acquaint her family with the facts, she begged of me passionately not to do so. Her one great anxiety was to screen her husband. One thing, however, I insisted upon. That was, the old woman should be sent away, the house shut up, and that Mrs. Redcar should take apartments in a hotel, so that I might be in touch with her. She demurred to this at first, but ultimately yielded to my persuasion.

Next, I went to the old woman. She was a German Swiss—her name was Grebert. I told her to pack up her things and clear out at once. She laughed in my face, and impertinently told me to mind my own business. I took out my watch and said, "I give you half an hour. If you are not off the premises then, I will call in the police and have you turned out. Any claim you have on Mrs. Redcar, who is the mistress here—shall be settled at once."

She replied that she did not recognize my authority, that she had been placed there by Mr. Redcar, who was her master, and unless he told her to go she should remain. I made it plain to her that I was determined and would stand no nonsense. Mr. Redcar had taken himself off, I said; Mrs. Redcar was his lawful wife, and I was acting for her and on her behalf.

My arguments prevailed, and after some wrangling the hag came to the conclusion that discretion was the better part of valor, and consented to go providing we paid her twenty pounds. This we decided to do rather than have a scene, but three hours passed before we saw the last of the creature. Mrs. Redcar had already packed up such things as she required, and when I had seen the house securely fastened up I procured a cab, and conveyed the poor little lady to a quiet West-end hotel, close to my own residence, so that I could keep a watchful eye upon her.

Of course, this was only the beginning of the task I had set myself, which was to woo back the erring husband, if possible, to his wife's side, and to restore him to the position of happiness, honor, and dignity from which he had fallen. I thought this might be comparatively easy, and little dreamed of the grim events that were to follow my interference.

Three weeks later I was in Paris, and proceeded to the Hotel de l'Univers, where Mrs. Redcar had ascertained through his bankers her husband was staying. But to my chagrin, I found he had departed from his companion, and the address he had given for his letters at the post-office was Potes, in Spain. As I had taken up the running I had no alternative but to face the long, dreary journey in pursuit of the fugitives, or confess defeat at the start.

It is not necessary for me to dwell upon that awful journey in the winter time. Suffice to say I reached my destination in due course.

Potes, it is necessary to explain, is a small town magnificently situated in the Liebana Valley, in the Austrian Pyrenees, under the shadow of Pico de Europa.[7] Now, what struck me as peculiar was the fugitives coming to such a place at that time of the year. Snow lay heavily everywhere. The cold was intense. For what reason had such a spot been chosen? It was a mystery I could not hope to solve just then. There was only one small hotel in the village, and where Annette and Redcar were staying. My first impulse was not to let them know of my presence, but to keep them under observation for a time. I dismissed that

[7] A region of Spain northeast of Portugal, bounded on the north by the Bay of Biscay.

thought as soon as formed, for I was not a detective, and did not like the idea of playing the spy. But even had I been so disposed, there would have been a difficulty about finding accommodation. Moreover, it was a small place, and the presence of a foreigner at that time of year must necessarily have caused a good deal of gossip. The result was I went boldly to the hotel, engaged a room, and then inquired for Redcar. I was directed to a private room, where I found him alone. My unexpected appearance startled him, and when he realized who I was, he swore at me, and demanded to know my business.

He had altered so much that in a crowd I really might have had some difficulty in recognizing him. His face wore a drawn, anxious, nervous look, and his eyes had acquired a restless, shifty motion, while his hair was already streaked with grey. I began to reason with him. I reminded him of our old friendship, and I drew a harrowing picture of the sufferings of his dear, devoted, beautiful little wife.

At first he seemed callous; but presently he grew interested, and when I referred to his wife he burst into tears. Then suddenly he grasped my wrist with a powerful grip, and said:—

"Hush! Annette mustn't know this—mustn't hear. I tell you, Peter, she is a ghoul. She sucks my blood. She has woven a mighty spell about me, and I am powerless. Take me away; take me to dear little Maude."

I looked at him for some moments with a keen professional scrutiny, for his manner and strange words were not those of sanity. I determined to take him at his word, and, if possible, remove him from the influence of the wicked siren who had so fatally lured him.

"Yes," I said, "we will go without a mo-ment's unnecessary delay. I will see if a carriage and post-horses are to be had, so that we can drive to the nearest railway station."

He assented languidly to this, and I rose with the intention of making inquiries of the hotel people; but simultaneously with my action the door opened and Annette appeared. Up to that moment I thought that Mrs. Redcar had exaggerated in describing her, therefore I was hardly prepared to find that so far from the description being an exaggeration, it had fallen short of the fact.

Annette was slightly above the medium height, with a well developed figure, but a face that to me was absolutely repellent. There was not a single line of beauty nor a trace of womanliness in it. It was hard, coarse, cruel, with thin lips drawn tightly over even white teeth. And the eyes were the most wonderful eyes I have ever seen in a human being. Maude was right when she spoke of them as "oily eyes." They literally shone with a strange, greasy, luster, and were capable of such a marvelous expression that I felt myself falling under their peculiar fascination. I am honest and frank enough to say that, had it been her pleasure, I believe she could have lured me to destruction as she had lured my poor friend. But I was forearmed, because forewarned. Moreover, I fancy I had a much stronger will than Redcar. Anyway, I braced myself up to conquer and crush this human serpent, for such I felt her to be.

Before I could speak, her melodious voice rang out with the query, addressed to Jack:—

"Who is this gentleman? Is he a friend of yours?"

"Yes, yes," gasped Jack, like one who spoke under the influence of a nightmare.

She bowed and smiled, revealing all her

white teeth, and she held forth her hand to me, a delicately shaped hand, with clear, transparent skin, and her long lithe fingers were bejewelled with diamonds.

I drew myself up, as one does when a desperate effort is needed, and, refusing the proffered hand, I said:

"Madame, hypocrisy and deceit are useless. I am a medical man, my name is Peter Haslar, and Mr. Redcar and I have been friends from youth. I've come here to separate him from your baneful influence and carry him back to his broken-hearted wife. That is my mission. I hope I have made it clear to you?"

She showed not the slightest sign of being disturbed, but smiled on me again, and bowed gracefully and with the most perfect self-possession. And speaking in a soft gentle manner, which in such startling contrast to the woman's appearance, she said:

"Oh, yes; thank you. But, like the majority of your countrymen, you display a tendency to arrogate too much to yourself. I am a Spaniard myself, by birth, but cosmopolitan by inclination, and, believe me, I do not speak with any prejudice against your nationality, but I have yet to learn, sir, that you have any right to constitute yourself Mr. Redcar's keeper."

Her English was perfect, though she pronounced it with just a slight foreign accent. There was no anger in her tones, no defiance. She spoke softly, silvery, persuasively.

"I do not pretend to be his keeper, madam; I am his sincere friend," I answered. "and surely I need not remind you that he owes a duty to his lawful wife."

During this short conversation Jack had sat motionless on the edge of a couch, his chin resting on his hands, and apparently absorbed with some conflicting thoughts. But Annette turned to him, and, still smiling, said:—

"I think Mr. Redcar is quite capable of answering for himself. Stand up, Jack, and speak your thoughts like a man."

Although she spoke in her oily, insidious way, her request was a peremptory command. I realized at once, and I saw as Jack rose he gazed at her, and her lustrous eyes fixed him. Then he turned upon me with a furious gesture and exclaimed, with a violence of expression that startled me:

"Yes, Annette is right. I am my own master. What the devil do you mean by following me, like the sneak and cur that you are? Go back to Maude, and tell her that I loathe her. Go; relieve me of your presence, or I may forget myself and injure you."

Annette, still smiling and still perfectly self-possessed, said:

"You hear what your friend says, doctor. Need I say that if you are a gentleman you will respect his wishes?"

I could no longer contain myself. Her calm, defiant, icy manner maddened me, and her silvery voice seemed to cut down on to my most sensitive nerves, for it was so suggestive of the devilish nature of the creature. It was so incongruous when contrasted with her harsh, horribly cruel face. I placed myself between Jack and her, and meeting her weird gaze, I said, hotly:—

"Leave this room. You are an outrage on your sex; a shame and a disgrace to the very name of woman. Go, and leave me with my friend, whose reason you have stolen away."

She still smiled and was still unmoved, and suddenly I felt myself gripped in a grip of iron, and with terrific force I was hurled into a corner of the room, where, huddled up in a heap, I lay stunned for some moments. But as my senses returned I saw the awful woman smiling still, and she was waving her long white bejewelled hand before the infuriated Jack, as if she were mesmerizing him; and I saw him sink on to the sofa subdued and calmed. Then addressing me she said:—

"That is a curious way for your friend to display his friendship. I may be wrong, but perhaps as a medical man you will recognize that your presence has an irritating effect on Mr. Redcar, and if I may suggest it, I think it desirable that you should part at once and see him no more."

"Devil!" I shouted at her. "You have bewitched him, and made him forgetful of his honor and of what he owes to those that are dear to him. But I will defeat you yet."

She merely bowed and smiled, but deigned no reply; and holding her arm to Jack, he took it, and they passed out of the room. She was elegantly attired. Her raven hair was fascinatingly dressed in wavy bands. There was something regal in her carriage, and gracefulness in her every movement; and yet she filled me with a sense of indefinable horror; a dread to which I should have been ashamed to own to a little while ago.

I tried to spring up and go after them, but my body seemed a mass of pain, and my left arm hung limp and powerless. It was fractured below the elbow. There was no bell in the room, and I limped out in search of assistance. I made my way painfully along a gloomy corridor, and hearing a male voice speaking Spanish, I knocked at a door, which was opened by the landlord. I addressed him, but he shook his head and gave me to understand that he spoke no English. Unhappily, I spoke no Spanish. Then he smiled as some idea flitted through his mind, and bowing me into the room he motioned me to be seated, and hurried away. He returned in about five minutes accompanied by Annette, whom he had brought to act as interpreter. I was almost tempted to fly at her and strangle her where she stood. She was undisturbed, calm, and still smiled. She spoke to the man in Spanish, then she explained to me that she had told him I had just slipped on the polished floor, and falling over a chair had injured myself, and she had requested him to summon the village surgeon if need be.

Without waiting for me to reply she swept gracefully out of the room. Indeed, I could not reply, for I felt as if I were choking with suppressed rage. The landlord rendered me physical assistance and took me to my bedroom, where I lay down on my bed, feeling mortified, ill, and crushed. Half an hour later a queer-looking old man, with long hair twisted into ringlets, was ushered into my room, and I soon gathered that he was the village surgeon. He spoke no English, but I explained my injury by signs, and he went away, returning in a little while with the necessary bandages and splints, and he proceeded to rather clumsily bandage my broken arm.

I passed a cruel and wretched night. My physical pain was great, but my mental pain was greater. The thought forced itself upon me that I had been defeated, and that the fiendish, cunning woman was too much for me. I felt no resentment against Jack. His act of violence was the act of a madman, and I pitied him. For hours I lay revolving all sorts of schemes to try and get him away from the diabolical influence of Annette. But though I could hit upon nothing, I firmly resolved that while my life lasted I would make every effort to save my old friend, and if possible restore him to the bosom of his distracted wife.

The case altogether was a very remarkable one, and the question naturally arose, why did a man so highly gifted and so intelligent as Jack Redcar desert his charming, devoted, and beautiful wife, to follow an adventuress who entirely lacked physical beauty. Theories without number might have been suggested to account for the phenomenon, but not one would have been correct.

The true answer is, Annette was not a natural being. In the ordinary way she might be described as a woman of perverted moral character, or as a physiological freak, but that would have been rather a misleading way of putting it. She was, in short, a human monstrosity. By that I do not mean to say her body was contorted, twisted, or deformed. But into her human composition had entered a strain of the fiend; and I might go even further than this and say she was more animal than human. Though in whatever way she may be described, it is certain she was an anomaly—a human riddle.

The morning following the outrage upon me found me prostrated and ill. A night of racking pain and mental distress had told even upon my good constitution. The situation in which I found myself was a singularly unfortunate one. I was a foreigner in an out-of-the-way place, and my want of knowledge of Spanish, of course, placed me at a tremendous disadvantage.

The landlord came to me and brought his wife, and between them they attended to my wants, and did what they could for my comfort. But they were ignorant, uncultivated people, only one remove from the peasant class, and I realized that they could be of little use to me. Now the nearest important town to this Alpine village was Santander, but that was nearly a hundred miles away.

As everyone knows who has been in Spain, a hundred miles, even on a railway, is a considerable journey; but there was no railway between Santander and Potes. An old ramshackle vehicle, called a diligence, ran between two places every day in the summer and twice a week in the winter, and it took fourteen hours to do the journey. Even a well-appointed carriage and pair could not cover the distance under eight hours, as the road was infamous, and in parts was little better than a mule track.

I knew that there was a British consul in Santander, and I was hopeful that if I could communicate with him he might be able to render me some assistance. In the meantime I had to devise some scheme for holding Annette in check and saving my friend. But in my crippled and prostrate condition I could not do much. While lying in my bed, and thus revolving all these things in my mind, the door gently opened and Annette glided in— "glided" best expresses her movement, for she seemed to put forth no effort. She sat down beside the bed and laid her hand on mine.

"You are ill this morning," she said softly. "This is regrettable, but you have only yourself to blame. It is dangerous to interfere in matters in which you have no concern. My business is mine, Mr. Redcar's is his, and yours is your own, but the three won't amalgamate. Jack and I came here for the sake of the peace and quietness of these solitudes; unhappily you intrude yourself and disaster follows."

Her voice was as silvery as ever. The same calm self-possessed air characterized her; but in her oily eyes was a peculiar light, and I had to turn away, for they exerted a sort of mesmeric influence over me, and I am convinced that had I not exerted all my will power I should have thrown myself into the creature's arms. This is a fact which I have no hesitation in stating, as it serves better than any other illustration to show what a wonderful power of fascination the remarkable woman possessed. Naturally I felt disgusted and enraged, but I fully recognized that I could not fight the woman openly; I must to some extent meet her with my own weapons. She was cunning, artful, insidious, pitiless, and the basilisk-like power she possessed not only gave her a great advantage but made her a very dangerous opponent. At any rate, having regard to all the circumstances and my crippled condition, I saw that my only chance was in temporizing with her. So I tried to reason with her, and I pointed out that Redcar had been guilty of baseness in leaving his wife, who was devoted to him.

At this point of my argument, Annette interrupted me, and for the first time she displayed something like passion, and her voice became hard and raucous.

"His wife," she said with a sneer of supreme contempt. "A poor fool, a fleshly doll. At the precise instant I set my eyes upon her for the first time I felt that I should like to destroy her, because she is a type of woman who make the world commonplace and reduce all men to a common level. She hated me from the first and I hated her. She would have crushed me if she could, but she was too insignificant a worm to do that, and I crushed her."

This cold, brutal callousness enraged me; I turned fiercely upon her and exclaimed:—

"Leave me, you are a more infamous and heartless wretch than I believed you to be. You are absolutely unworthy the name of a woman, and if you irritate me much more I may even forget that you have a woman's shape."

She spoke again. All trace of passion had disappeared. She smiled the wicked insidious smile which made her so dangerous, and her voice resumed its liquid, silvery tones:

"You are very violent," she said gently, "and it will do you harm in your condition. But you see violence can be met with violence. The gentleman you are pleased to call your friend afforded you painful evidence last night that he knows how to resent unjustifiable interference, and to take care of himself. I am under his protection, and there is no doubt he will protect me."

"For God's sake, leave me!" I cried, tortured beyond endurance by her hypocrisy and wickedness.

"Oh, certainly, if you desire it," she answered, as she rose from her seat. "But I thought I might be of use. It is useless your trying to influence Mr. Redcar—absolutely useless. His destiny is linked with mine, and the human being doesn't exist who can sunder us. With this knowledge, you will do well to retrace your steps; and, if you like, I will arrange to have you comfortably conveyed to Santander, where you can get a vessel. Anyway, you will waste your time and retard your recovery by remaining here."

"I intend to remain here, nevertheless," I said, with set teeth. "And, what is more, madam, when I go my friend Redcar will accompany me."

She laughed. She patted my head as a mother might pat the head of her child. She spoke in her most insidious silvery tones.

"We shall see, *mon cher*—we shall see. You will be better tomorrow. Adieu!"

That was all she said, and she was gone. She glided out of the room as she had glided in.

I felt irritated almost into madness for some little time; but as I reflected, it was forced upon me that I had to deal with a monster of iniquity, who had so subdued the will of her victim, Redcar, that he was a mere wooden puppet in her hand. Force in such a case was worse than useless. What I had to do was to try and circumvent her, and I tried to think out some plan of action.

All that day I was compelled to keep my bed, and, owing to the clumsy way in which my arm had been bandaged, I suffered intolerable pain, and had to send for the old surgeon again to come and help me to reset the fracture. I got some ease after that, and a dose of chloral sent me to sleep, which continued for many hours.

When I awoke I managed to summon the landlord, and he brought me food, and a lantern containing a candle so that I might have light. And, in compliance with my request, he made me a large jug of lemonade, in order that I could have a drink in the night, for I was feverish, and my throat was parched. He had no sooner left the room than Annette entered to inquire if she could do anything for me. I told her that I had made the landlord understand all that I desired, and he would look after me, so she wished me good-night and left. Knowing as I did that sleep was very essential in my case, I swallowed another, though smaller, dose of chloral, and then there was a blank.

How long I slept I really don't know; but suddenly, in a dazed sort of way, I saw a strange sight. The room I occupied was a long, somewhat meagrely furnished, one. The entrance door was at the extreme end, opposite the bed. Over the doorway hung a faded curtain of green velvet. By the feeble light of the candle lantern I saw this curtain slowly pulled on one side by a white hand; then a face peered in; next Annette entered.

Her long hair was hanging down her back, and she wore a nightdress of soft, clinging substance, which outlined her figure. With never a sound she moved lightly towards the bed, and waved her hand two to three times over my face. I tried to move, to utter a sound, but couldn't; and yet what I am describing was no dream, but a reality. Slightly bending over me, she poured from a tiny phial she carried in the palm of her hand a few drops of a slightly acrid, burning liquid right into my mouth, and at that instant, I believe, it seemed to me as if a thick, heavy pall over my eyes, for all was darkness.

I awoke hours later. The winter sun was shining brightly into my room. I felt strangely languid, and had a hot, stinging sensation in my throat. I felt my pulse, and found it was only beating at the rate of fifty-eight beats in one minute. Then I recalled the extraordinary incident of the previous night, which, had it not been for my sensations, I might have regarded as a bad dream, the outcome of a disturbed state of the brain.

But as it was, I hadn't a doubt that Annette had administered some subtle slow poison to me. My medical knowledge enabled me to diagnose my own case so far, that I was convinced I was suffering from the effects of a potent poisonous drug, the action of which was to lower the action of the vital forces and weaken the heart. Being probably cumulative, a few doses more or less, according to the strength of that subject, the action of the heart would be so impeded that the organ would cease to beat.

Although this passed through my brain, I felt so weak and languid that I had neither energy nor strength to arouse myself, and when the landlord brought me in some food I took no notice of him. I knew that this symptom of languor and indifference was very characteristic of certain vegetable poisons, though what it was Annette had administered to me I could not determine.

Throughout that day I lay in a drowsy, dreamy state. At times my brain was clear enough, and I was able to think and reason; but there were blanks, marked, no doubt, by periods of sleep.

When night came I felt a little better, and I found that the heart's action had improved. It was steadier, firmer, and the pulse indicated sixty-two beats. Now I had no doubt that if it was Annette's intention to bring about my death slowly she would come again that night, and arousing myself as well as I could, and summoning all my will power, I resolved to be on the watch.

During the afternoon I had drunk milk freely, regarding it as an antidote, and when the landlord visited me for the last time that evening I made him understand that I wanted a large jug of fresh milk from the cow, if he could get it. He kept cows of his own; they were confined in a chalet on the mountain side, not far from his house, so that he was able to comply with my request.

I took a long draught of this hot milk, which revived my energies wonderfully, and then I waited for developments. I had allowed my watch to run down, consequently I had no means of knowing the time. It was a weary vigil, lying there lonely and ill, and struggling against the desire for sleep. By-and-by I saw the white hand lift the curtain again, and Annette entered, clad as she was on the previous night. When she came within reach of me I sprang up in the bed and seized her wrist.

"What do you want here?" I demanded angrily. "Do you mean to murder me?"

Her imperturbability was exasperating. She neither winced nor cried out, nor displayed the slightest sign of surprise. She merely remarked in her soft cooing voice, her white teeth showing as her thin lips parted in a smile:—

"You are evidently restless and excited tonight, and it is hardly generous of you to treat my kindly interest in such a way."

"Kindly interest!" I echoed with a sneer, as, releasing her wrist, I fell back on the bed.

"Yes; you haven't treated me well, and you are an intruder here. Nevertheless, as you are a stranger amongst strangers, and cannot speak the language of the country, I would be of service to you if I could. I have come to see if you have everything you require for the night."

"And you did the same last night," I cried in hot anger, for, knowing her infamy and wickedness, I could not keep my temper.

"Certainly," she answered, coolly; "and I found you calmly dozing, so left you."

"Yes—after you poured poison down my throat," I replied.

She broke into a laugh—a rippling laugh, with the tinkle of silver in it—and she seemed hugely amused.

"Well, well," she said; "it is obvious, sir, you are not in a fit state to be alone. Your nerves are evidently unstrung, and you are either the victim of a bad dream or some strange delusion. But there, there; I will pardon you. You are not responsible just at present for your language."

As she spoke she passed her soft white hand over my forehead. There was magic in her touch, and it seemed as if all my will had left me, and there stole over me a delightful sense of dreamy languor. I looked at her, and I saw her strange eyes change color. They became illumined, as if it were, by a violet light that fascinated me so that I could not turn from her. Indeed, I was absolutely subdued to her will now.

Everything in the room faded, and I saw nothing but those marvellous eyes glowing with violet light which seemed to fill me with a feeling of ecstasy. I have a vague idea that she kept passing her hand over my face and forehead; that she breathed upon my face; then that she pressed her face to mine, and I felt her hot breath in my neck.

Perhaps it will be said that I dreamed all this. I don't believe it was a dream. I firmly and honestly believe that every word I have written is true.

Hours afterwards my dulled brain began to awake to things mundane. The morning sun was flooding the room, and I was conscious that somebody stood over me, and soon I recognized the old surgeon, who had come to see that the splints and bandages had not shifted. I felt extraordinarily weak, and I found that my pulse was beating very slowly and feebly. Again I had the burning feeling in the throat and a strange and absolutely indescribable sensation at the side of the neck. The old doctor must have recognized that I was unusually feeble, for he went to the landlord, and returned presently with some cognac which he made me swallow, and it picked me up considerably.

After his departure I lay for some time, and tried to give definite shape to vague and dreadful thoughts that haunted me, and filled me with a shrinking horror. That Annette was a monster in human form I hadn't a doubt, and I felt equally certain that she had designs upon my life. That she had now administered poison to me on two occasions seemed to me beyond question, but I hesitated to believe that she was guilty of the unspeakable crime which my sensations suggested.

At last, unable to endure the tumult in my brain, I sprang out of bed, rushed to the looking-glass, and examined my neck. I literally staggered back, and fell prostrate on the bed, overcome by the hideous discovery I had made. It had the effect, however, of calling me back to life and energy, and I had a mental resolution that I would, at all hazards, save my friend, though I clearly recognized how powerless I was to cope with the awful creature single-handed.

I managed to dress myself, not without some difficulty; then I summoned the landlord, and made him understand that I must go immediately to Santander at any cost. My intention was to invoke the aid of the consul there. But the more I insisted, the more the old landlord shook his head. At length, in desperation, I rushed from the house, hoping to find somebody who understood French or English.

As I almost ran up the village street I came face to face with a priest. I asked him in English if he spoke my language, but he shook his head. Then I tried him with French, and to my joy he answered me that he understood a little French. I told him of my desire to start for Santander that very day, but he said that it was impossible, as, owing to the unusual hot sun in the daytime there had been a great melting of snow, with the result that a flooded river had destroyed a portion of the road; and though a gang of men had been set to repair it, it would be two or three days before it was passable.

"But is there no other way of going?" I asked.

"Only by a very hazardous route over the mountains," he answered. And he added that the risk was so great it was doubtful if anyone could be found who would act as a guide. "Besides," he went on, "you seem very ill and weak. Even a strong man might fail, but you would be certain to perish from exhaustion and exposure."

I was bound to recognize the force of his argument. It was a maddening disappointment, but there was no help for it. Then it occurred to me to take the old priest into my confidence and invoke his aid. Though, on second thoughts, I hesitated, for was it not possible—nay, highly probable—that if I told the horrible story he and others would think I was mad. Annette was a Spanish woman, and it was feasible to suppose she would secure the ear of those ignorant villagers sooner than I should. No, I would keep the ghastly business to myself for the present at any rate, and wait with such patience as I could command until I could make the journey to Santander. The priest promised me that on the morrow he would let me know if the road was passable, and, if so, he would procure me a carriage and make all the preparations for the journey.

So, thanking him, for his kindly services, I turned towards the hotel again. As I neared the house I observed two persons on the mountain path that went up among the pine trees. The sun was shining brilliantly; the sky was cloudless, the air crisp and keen. The two persons were Annette and Redcar. I watched them for some minutes until they were lost to sight amongst the trees.

Suddenly an irresistible impulse to follow them seized me. Why, I know not. Indeed, had I paused to reason with myself it would have seemed to me then a mad act, and that I was risking my life to no purpose. But I did not reason. I yielded to the impulse, though first of all I went to my room, put on a thicker pair of boots, and armed myself with a revolver which I had brought with me.

During my extensive travelling about America a revolver was a necessity, and by force of habit I put it up with my clothes when packing my things in London for my Continental journey.

Holding the weapon between my knees, I put a cartridge in each barrel, and, providing myself with a stick in addition, I went forth again and began to climb the mountain path. I was by no means a sanguinary man; even my pugnacity could only be aroused after much irritation. Nevertheless, I knew how to defend myself, and in this instance, knowing that I had to deal with a woman who was capable of any crime, and who, I felt sure, would not hesitate to take my life if she got the chance, I deemed it advisable to be on my guard against any emergency that might arise.

As regards Redcar, he had already given me forcible and painful evidence that he could be dangerous; but I did not hold him responsible for his actions. I regarded him as being temporarily insane owing to the internal influence the awful woman exercised over him. Therefore it would only have been in the very last extremity that I should have resorted to lethal weapons as a defence against him. My one sole aim, hope, desire, prayer, was to rescue him from the spell that held him in thrall and restore him to his wife, his honour, his sanity.

With respect to Annette, it was different. She was a blot on nature, a disgrace to humankind, and, rather than let her gain complete ascendency over me and my friend I would have shot her if I had reason to believe she contemplated taking my life. It might have involved me in serious trouble with the authorities at first, for in Spain the foreigner can hope for little justice. I was convinced, however, that ultimately I should be exonerated.

Such were the thoughts that filled my mind as I painfully made my way up the steep mountain side. My fractured arm was exceedingly painful. Every limb in my body ached, and I was so languid, so weak that it was with difficulty I dragged myself along.

But worse than all this was an all but irresistible desire to sleep, the result, I was certain, of the poison that had been administered to me. But it would have been fatal to have slept. I knew that, and so I fought against the inclination with all my might and main, and allowed my thoughts to dwell on poor little Maude Redcar, waiting desolate and heartbroken in London for news. This supplied me with the necessary spur and kept me going.

The trees were nearly all entirely bare of snow. It had, I was informed, been an unusually mild season, and at that time the sun's rays were very powerful. The path I was pursuing was nothing more than a rough track worn by the peasants passing between the valley and their hay chalets dotted about the mountain. Snow lay on the path where it was screened from the sun by the trees. I heard no sound, saw no sign of those I was seeking save here and there footprints in the snow. I frequently paused and listened, but the stillness was unbroken save for the subdued murmur of falling water afar off.

In my weakened condition the exertion I had endured had greatly distressed me; my heart beat tumultuously, my pulses throbbed violently, and my breathing was stertorous. I was far above the valley now, and the pine trees were straggling and sparse. The track had become very indistinct, but I still detected the footsteps of the people I was following.

Above the trees I could discern the snow-capped Pico de Europa glittering in the brilliant sun. It was a perfect Alpine scene, which, under other circumstances, I might have revelled in. But I felt strangely ill, weak, and miserable, and drowsiness began to steal upon me, so that I made a sudden effort of will and sprang up again, and resumed the ascent.

In a little time the forest ended, and before me stretched a sloping plateau which, owing to its being exposed to the full glare of the sun, as well as to all the winds that blew, was bare of snow. The plateau sloped down for probably four hundred feet, then ended abruptly at the end of a precipice. How far the precipice descended I could not tell from where I was, but far far below I could see a stream meandering through a thickly wooded gorge. I took the details of the scene in with a sudden glance of the eye, for another sight attracted and riveted my attention, and froze me with horror to the spot.

Beneath a huge boulder which had fallen from the mountain above, and lodged on the slope, were Annette and Redcar. He was lying on his back, she was stretched out beside him, and her face was buried in his neck. Even from where I stood I could see that he was ghastly pale, his features drawn and pinched, his eyes closed. Incredible as it may seem, horrible as it sounds, it is nevertheless true that that hellish woman was sucking away his life blood. She was a human vampire, and my worst fears were confirmed.

I am aware that an astounding statement of this kind should not be made lightly by a man in my position. But I take all the responsibility of it, and I declare solemnly that it is true. Moreover, the sequel which I am able to give to this story more than corroborates me, and proves Annette to have been one of those human problems which, happily for the world, are very rare, but of which there are several well authenticated cases.

As soon as I fully realized what was happening I drew my revolver from the side pocket of my jacket and fired, not at Annette, but in the air; my object being to startle her so that she would release her victim.

It had the desired effect. She sprang up, livid with rage. Blood—his blood—was oozing from the side of her mouth. Her extraordinary eyes had assumed that strange violet appearance which I had seen once before. Her whole aspect was repulsive, revolting, horrible beyond words. Rooted to the spot I stood and gazed at her, fascinated by the weird, ghastly sight. In my hand I still held the smoking revolver, levelled at her now, and resolved if she rushed towards me to shoot her, for I felt that the world would be well rid of such a hideous monster. But suddenly she stooped, seized her unfortunate victim in her arms, and tore down the slope, and when the edge of the precipice was reached they both disappeared into space.

The whole of this remarkable scene was enacted in the course of a few seconds. It was to me a maddening nightmare. I fell where I stood, and remembered no more until hours afterwards, I found myself lying in bed at the hotel, and the old surgeon and the priest sitting beside me. Gradually I learnt that the sound of the shot from the revolver, echoing and re-echoing in that mountain region, had been heard in the village, and some peasants had set off for the mountain to ascertain the cause of the firing. They found me lying on the ground still grasping the weapon, and thinking I had shot myself they carried me down to the hotel.

Naturally I was asked for explanations when I was able to talk, and I recounted the whole of the ghastly story. At first my listeners, the priest and the doctor, seemed to think I was raving in delirium, as well as they might, but I persisted in my statements, and I urged the sending out of a party to search for the bodies. If they were found my story would be corroborated.

In a short time a party of peasants started for the gorge, which was a wild, almost inaccessible, ravine through which flowed a mountain torrent amongst the debris and boulders that from time to time had fallen from the rocky heights. After some hours of searching the party discovered the crushed remains of Jack Redcar. His head had been battered to pieces against the rocks as he fell, and every bone in his body was broken.

The precipice over which he had fallen was a jagged, scarred, and irregular wall of rock at least four thousand feet in height. The search for Annette's body was continued until darkness compeled the searchers to return to the village, which they did bringing with them my poor friend's remains. Next day the search was resumed, and the day after, and for many days, but with no results. The woman's corpse was never found.

The theory was that somewhere on that frightful rock face she had been caught by a projecting pinnacle, or had got jammed into a crevice, where her unhallowed remains would moulder into dust. It was a fitting end for so frightful a life.

Of course an official inquiry was held— and officialism in Spain is appalling. It was weeks and weeks before the inevitable conclusion of the tribunal was arrived at, and I was exonerated from all blame. In the meantime Redcar's remains were committed to their eternal rest in the picturesque little Alpine village churchyard, and for all times Potes will be associated with that grim and awful tragedy.

Why Annette took her victim to that out of the way spot can only be guessed at. She knew that the death of her victim was only a question of weeks, and in that primitive and secluded hamlet it would arouse no suspicion, she being a native of Spain. It would be easy for her to say that she had taken her invalid husband there for the benefit of his health, but unhappily the splendid and bracing air had failed to save his life. In this instance, as in many others, her fiendish cunning would have enabled her to score another triumph had not destiny made me its instrument to encompass her destruction.

For long after my return to England I was very ill. The fearful ordeal I had gone through, coupled with the poison which Annette had administered to me, shattered my health; but the unremitting care and at-tention bestowed upon me by my old friend's widow pulled me through. And when at last I was restored to strength and vigor, beautiful Maude Redcar became my wife.

NOTE BY THE AUTHOR:—

The foregoing story was suggested by a tradition current in the Pyrenees, where a be-lief in ghouls and vampires is still common. The same belief is no less common throughout Styria, in some parts of Turkey, in Russia, and in India. Sir Richard Burton deals with the subject in his "Vikram and the Vampire." Years ago, when the author was in India, a poor woman was beaten to death one night in the village by a number of young men armed with cudgels. Their excuse for the crime was that the woman was a vampire, and had sucked the blood of many of their companions, whom she had first lured to her by depriving them of their will power by mesmeric influence.

☙☙

Hume Nisbet

JAMES HUME NISBET (1849-1923) was born in Scotland but emigrated to Australia at the age of 16. After seven years, he returned to his native land, paying several subsequent extended visits to Australia and New Guinea. Nisbet was a failure as a painter but wrote books on art as well as poetry, short stories, and more than forty novels. The following tale first appeared in magazine form in 1890 and was collected in book form in *Stories Weird and Wonderful* (1900). In it, the young, romantic narrator comes to the horrifying realization that all is not as rosy as it seems. Pre-dating *Dracula*, the emphasis on the hypnotic powers of the vampire maid is more reminiscent of Le Fanu's "Carmilla," and there is a strong sexual element as well.

THE VAMPIRE MAID

HUME NISBET

It was the exact kind of abode that I had been looking after for weeks, for I was in that condition of mind when absolute renunciation of society was a necessity. I had become diffident of myself, and wearied of my kind. A strange unrest was in my blood; a barren dearth in my brains. Familiar objects and faces had grown distasteful to me. I wanted to be alone. This is the mood which comes upon every sensitive and artistic mind when the possessor has been overworked or living too long in one groove. It is Nature's hint for him to seek pastures new; the sign that a retreat has become needful.

If he does not yield, he breaks down and becomes whimsical and hypochondriacal, as well as hypercritical. It is always a bad sign when a man becomes over-critical and censorious about his own or other people's work, for it means that he is losing the vital portions of work, freshness and enthusiasm.

Before I arrived at the dismal stage of criticism I hastily packed up my knapsack, and taking the train to Westmorland, I began my tramp in search of solitude, bracing air, and romantic surroundings.

Many places I came upon during that early summer wandering that appeared to have almost the required conditions, yet some petty drawback prevented me from deciding. Sometimes it was the scenery that I did not take kindly to. At other places I took sudden antipathies to the landlady or landlord, and felt I would abhor them before a week was spent under their charge. Other places which might have suited me I could not have, as they did not want a lodger. Fate was driving me to this Cottage on the Moor, and no one can resist destiny.

One day I found myself on a wide and pathless moor near the sea. I had slept the night before at a small hamlet, but that was already eight miles in my rear, and since I had turned my back upon it I had not seen any signs of humanity; I was alone with a fair sky above me, a balmy ozone-filled wind blowing over the stony and heather-clad mounds, and nothing to disturb my meditations.

How far the moor stretched I had no knowledge; I only knew that by keeping in a straight line I would come to the ocean cliffs, then perhaps after a time arrive at some fishing village. I had provisions in my knapsack, and being young did not fear a night under the stars. I was inhaling the delicious summer air and once more getting back the vigor and happiness I had lost; my city-dried brains were again becoming juicy.

Thus hour after hour slid past me, with the paces, until I had covered about fifteen miles since morning, when I saw before me in the distance a solitary stone-built cottage with roughly slated roof. "I'll camp there if possible," I said to myself as I quickened my steps towards it.

To one in search of a quiet, free life, nothing could have possibly been more suitable than this cottage. It stood on the edge of lofty cliffs, with its front door facing the moor and the backyard wall overlooking the ocean. The sound of the dancing waves struck upon my ears like a lullaby as I drew near; how they would thunder when the autumn gales came on and the seabirds fled shrieking to the shelter of the sedges.

A small garden spread in front, surrounded by a dry-stone wall just high enough for one to lean lazily upon when inclined. This garden was a flame of color, scarlet predominating, with those other soft shades that cultivated poppies take on in their blooming, for this was all that the garden grew.

As I approached, taking notice of this singular assortment of poppies, and the orderly cleanness of the windows, the front door opened and a woman appeared who impressed me at once favorably as she leisurely came along the pathway to the gate, and drew it back as if to welcome me.

She was of middle age, and when young must have been remarkably good-looking. She was tall and still shapely, with smooth clear skin, regular features and a calm expression that at once gave me a sensation of rest.

To my inquiries she said that she could give me both a sitting and bedroom, and invited me inside to see them. As I looked at her smooth black hair, and cool brown eyes, I felt that I would not be too particular about the accommodation. With such a landlady, I was sure to find what I was after here.

The rooms surpassed my expectation, dainty white curtains and bedding with the perfume of lavender about them, a sitting-room homely yet cozy without being crowded. With a sigh of infinite relief I flung down my knapsack and clinched the bargain.

She was a widow with one daughter, whom I did not see the first day, as she was unwell and confined to her own room, but on the next day she was somewhat better, and then we met.

The fare was simple, yet it suited me exactly for the time, delicious milk and butter with home-made scones, fresh eggs and bacon; after a hearty tea I went early to bed in a condition of perfect content with my quarters.

Yet happy and tired out as I was I had by no means a comfortable night. This I put down to the strange bed. I slept certainly, but my sleep was filled with dreams so that I woke late and unrefreshed; a good walk on the moor, however, restored me, and I returned with a fine appetite for breakfast.

Certain conditions of mind, with aggravating circumstances, are required before even a young man can fall in love at first sight, as Shakespeare has shown in his *Romeo and*

Juliet. In the city, where many fair faces passed me every hour, I had remained like a stoic,[1] yet no sooner did I enter the cottage after that morning walk than I succumbed instantly before the weird charms of my landlady's daughter, Ariadne Brunnell.

She was somewhat better this morning and able to meet me at breakfast, for we had our meals together while I was their lodger. Ariadne was not beautiful in the strictly classical sense, her complexion being too lividly white and her expression too set to be quite pleasant at first sight; yet, as her mother had informed me, she had been ill for some time, which accounted for that defect. Her features were not regular, her hair and eyes seemed too black with that strangely white skin, and her lips too red for any except the decadent harmonies of an Aubrey Beardsley.[2]

Yet my fantastic dreams of the preceding night, with my morning walk, had prepared me to be enthralled by this modern poster-like invalid.

The loneliness of the moor, with the singing of the ocean, had gripped my heart with a wistful longing. The incongruity of those flaunting and evanescent poppy flowers, dashing the giddy tints in the face of that sober heath, touched me with a shiver as I approached the cottage, and lastly that weird embodiment of startling contrasts completed my subjugation.

She rose from her chair as her mother introduced her, and smiled while she held out her hand. I clasped that soft snowflake, and as I did so a faint thrill tingled over me and rested on my heart, stopping for the moment its beating.

This contact seemed also to have affected her as it did me; a clear flush, like a white flame, lighted up her face, so that it glowed as if an alabaster lamp had been lit; her black eyes became softer and more humid as our glances crossed, and her scarlet lips grew moist. She was a living woman now, while before she had seemed half a corpse.

She permitted her white slender hand to remain in mine longer than most people do at an introduction, and then she slowly withdrew it, still regarding me with steadfast eyes for a second or two afterwards.

Fathomless velvety eyes these were, yet before they were shifted from mine they appeared to have absorbed all my willpower and made me her abject slave. They looked like deep dark pools of clear water, yet they filled me with fire and deprived me of strength. I sank into my chair almost as languidly as I had risen from my bed that morning.

Yet I made a good breakfast, and although she hardly tasted anything, this strange girl rose much refreshed and with a slight glow of color on her cheeks, which improved her so greatly that she appeared younger and almost beautiful.

I had come here seeking solitude, but since I had seen Ariadne it seemed as if I had come for her only. She was not very lively; indeed, thinking back, I cannot recall any spontaneous remark of hers; she answered my questions by monosyllables and left me to lead in words; yet she was insinuating and appeared

---

[1] Stoicism: an ancient Greek school of philosophy holding that virtue and happiness can be attained only by submission to destiny and the natural law; that people should be free from passion, unmoved by joy or grief, and submit without complaint to unavoidable necessity.

[2] Beardsley (1872–1898) was an English artist known for his often grotesque and erotic illustrations, especially of stories by Oscar Wilde and Edgar Allan Poe. He died of tuberculosis at age twenty-five; his work would be a major influence on the Art Nouveau movement.

to lead my thoughts in her direction and speak to me with her eyes. I cannot describe her minutely, I only know that from the first glance and touch she gave me I was bewitched and could think of nothing else.

It was a rapid, distracting, and devouring infatuation that possessed me; all day long I followed her about like a dog, every night I dreamed of that white glowing face, those steadfast black eyes, those moist scarlet lips, and each morning I rose more languid than I had been the day before. Sometimes I dreamt that she was kissing me with those red lips, while I shivered at the contact of her silky black tresses as they covered my throat; sometimes that we were floating in the air, her arms about me and her long hair enveloping us both like an inky cloud, while I lay supine and helpless.

She went with me after breakfast on that first day to the moor, and before we came back I had spoken my love and received her assent. I held her in my arms and had taken her kisses in answer to mine, nor did I think it strange that all this had happened so quickly. She was mine, or rather I was hers, without a pause. I told her it was fate that had sent me to her, for I had no doubts about my love, and she replied that I had restored her to life.

Acting upon Ariadne's advice, and also from a natural shyness, I did not inform her mother how quickly matters had progressed between us, yet although we both acted as circumspectly as possible, I had no doubt Mrs. Brunnell could see how engrossed we were in each other. Lovers are not unlike ostriches in their modes of concealment. I was not afraid of asking Mrs. Brunnell for her daughter, for she already showed her partiality towards

me, and had bestowed upon me some confidences regarding her own position in life, and I therefore knew that, so far as social position was concerned, there could be no real objection to our marriage. They lived in this lonely spot for the sake of their health, and kept no servant because they could not get any to take service so far away from other humanity. My coming had been opportune and welcome to both mother and daughter.

For the sake of decorum, however, I resolved to delay my confession for a week or two and trust to some favorable opportunity of doing it discreetly.

Meantime Ariadne and I passed our time in a thoroughly idle and lotus-eating style. Each night I retired to bed meditating starting work next day, each morning I rose languid from those disturbing dreams with no thought for anything outside my love. She grew stronger every day, while I appeared to be taking her place as the invalid, yet I was more frantically in love than ever, and only happy when with her. She was my lode-star,[3] my only joy—my life.

We did not go great distances, for I liked best to lie on the dry heath and watch her glowing face and intense eyes while I listened to the surging of the distant waves. It was love made me lazy, I thought, for unless a man has all he longs for beside him, he is apt to copy the domestic cat and bask in the sunshine.

I had been enchanted quickly. My disenchantment came as rapidly, although it was long before the poison left my blood.

One night, about a couple of weeks after my coming to the cottage, I had returned after a delicious moonlight walk with Ariadne. The night was warm and the moon at the full,

---

[3] A star used for guidance, such as Polaris (the "North Star").

therefore I left my bedroom window open to let in what little air there was.

I was more than usually weary, so that I had only strength enough to remove my boots and coat before I flung myself wearily on the coverlet and fell almost instantly asleep without tasting the nightcap draught that was constantly placed on the table, and which I had always drained thirstily.

I had a ghastly dream this night. I thought I saw a monster bat, with the face and tresses of Ariadne, fly into the open window and fasten its white teeth and scarlet lips on my arm. I tried to beat the horror away, but could not, for I seemed chained down and thralled also with drowsy delight as the beast sucked my blood with a gruesome rapture.

I looked out dreamily and saw a line of dead bodies of young men lying on the floor, each with a red mark on their arms, on the same part where the vampire was then sucking me, and I remembered having seen and wondered at such a mark on my own arm for the past fortnight. In a flash I understood the reason for my strange weakness, and at the same moment a sudden prick of pain roused me from my dreamy pleasure.

The vampire in her eagerness had bitten a little too deeply that night, unaware that I had not tasted the drugged draught. As I woke I saw her fully revealed by the midnight moon, with her black tresses flowing loosely, and with her red lips glued to my arm. With a shriek of horror I dashed her backwards, getting one last glimpse of her savage eyes, glowing white face and blood-stained red lips; then I rushed out to the night, moved on by my fear and hatred, nor did I pause in my mad flight until I had left miles between me and that accursed Cottage on the Moor.

F. G. Loring

FREDERICK GEORGE LORING (1869-1951) was a little-known British naval
officer and engineer. This story, however, published in *Pall Mall Magazine* in
December 1900, has been widely anthologized and presents a view of a confident, workman-like vampire hunter dealing with an ancient horror. Note that
the monster's shape-shifting combines werewolf-like traits with definite classical
vampiric characteristics.

THE TOMB OF SARAH

F. G. LORING

My father was the head of a celebrated firm of church restorers and decorators about sixty years ago. He took a keen interest in his work, and made an especial study of any old legends or family histories that came under his observation. He was necessarily very well read and thoroughly well posted in all questions of folk-lore and mediaeval legend. As he kept a careful record of every case he investigated the manuscripts he left at his death have a special interest. From amongst them I have selected the following, as being a particularly weird and extraordinary experience. In presenting it to the public I feel it is superfluous to apologize for its supernatural character.

MY FATHER'S DIARY

1841.—June 17th. Received a commission from my old friend Peter Grant to enlarge and restore the chancel[1] of his church at Hagarstone, in the wilds of the West Country.

July 5th. Went down to Hagarstone with my head man, Somers. A very long and tiring journey.

July 7th. Got the work well started. The old church is one of special interest to the antiquarian, and I shall endeavor while restoring it to alter the existing arrangements as little as possible. One large tomb, however, must be moved bodily ten feet at least to the southward. Curiously enough, there is a somewhat forbidding inscription upon it in Latin, and I am sorry that this particular tomb should have to be moved. It stands amongst the graves of the Kenyons, an old family which has been extinct in these parts for centuries. The inscription on it runs thus:

SARAH
1630.
FOR THE SAKE OF THE DEAD AND
THE WELFARE OF THE LIVING,
LET THIS SEPULCHRE REMAIN
UNTOUCHED AND ITS OCCUPANT

---

[1] The space around the altar in the sanctuary at the liturgical east end of a traditional Christian church building.

UNDISTURBED TILL
THE COMING OF CHRIST.
IN THE NAME OF THE FATHER,
THE SON, AND THE HOLY GHOST.

July 8th. Took counsel with Grant concerning the "Sarah Tomb." We are both very loath to disturb it, but the ground has sunk so beneath it that the safety of the church is in danger; thus we have no choice. However, the work shall be done as reverently as possible under our own direction.

Grant says there is a legend in the neighborhood that it is the tomb of the last of the Kenyons, the evil Countess Sarah, who was murdered in 1630. She lived quite alone in the old castle, whose ruins still stand three miles from here on the road to Bristol. Her reputation was an evil one even for those days. She was a witch or were-woman, the only companion of her solitude being a familiar in the shape of a huge Asiatic wolf. This creature was reputed to seize upon children, or failing these, sheep and other small animals, and convey them to the castle, where the Countess used to suck their blood.

It was popularly supposed that she could never be killed. This, however, proved a fallacy, since she was strangled one day by a mad peasant woman who had lost two children, she declaring that they had both been seized and carried off by the Countess's familiar. This is a very interesting story, since it points to a local superstition very similar to that of the Vampire, existing in Slavonic and Hungarian Europe.

The tomb is built of black marble, surmounted by an enormous slab of the same material. On the slab is a magnificent group of figures. A young and handsome woman reclines upon a couch; round her neck is a piece of rope, the end of which she holds in her hand. At her side is a gigantic dog with bared fangs and lolling tongue. The face of the reclining figure is a cruel one: the corners of the mouth are curiously lifted, showing the sharp points of long canine or dog teeth. The whole group, though magnificently executed, leaves a most unpleasant sensation.

If we move the tomb it will have to be done in two pieces, the covering slab first and then the tomb proper. We have decided to remove the covering slab tomorrow.

July 9th.—6 PM. A very strange day.

By noon everything was ready for lifting off the covering stone, and after the men's dinner we started the jacks and pulleys. The slab lifted easily enough, though it fitted closely into its seat and was further secured by some sort of mortar or putty, which must have kept the interior perfectly air-tight.

None of us were prepared for the horrible rush of foul, mouldy air that escaped as the cover lifted clear of its seating. And the contents that gradually came into view were more startling still. There lay the fully dressed body of a woman, wizened and shrunk and ghastly pale as if from starvation. Round her neck was a loose cord, and, judging by the scars still visible, the story of death by strangulation was true enough.

The most horrible part, however, was the extraordinary freshness of the body. Except for the appearance of starvation, life might have been only just extinct. The flesh was soft and white, the eyes were wide-open and seemed to stare at us with a fearful understanding in them. The body itself lay on mould, without any pretence to coffin or shell.

For several moments we gazed with horrible curiosity, and then it became too much for my work-men, who implored us to replace the covering slab. That, of course, we would not do; but I set the carpenters to work at once to make a temporary cover while we moved the tomb to its new position. This is a long job, and will take two or three days at least.

July 9th.—9 PM. Just at sunset we were startled by the howling of, seemingly, every dog in the village. It lasted for ten minutes or a quarter of an hour, and then ceased as suddenly as it began. This, and a curious mist that has risen round the church, makes me feel rather anxious about the Sarah Tomb. According to the best established traditions of the Vampire-haunted countries, the disturbance of dogs or wolves at sunset is supposed to indicate the presence of one of these fiends, and local fog is always considered to be a certain sign. The Vampire has the power of producing it for the purpose of concealing its movements near its hiding-place at any time.

I dare not mention or even hint my fears to the Rector, for he is, not unnaturally perhaps, a rank disbeliever in many things that I know, from experience, are not only possible but even probable. I must work this out alone at first, and get his aid without his knowing in what direction he is helping me. I shall now watch till midnight at least.

10:15 PM. As I feared and half expected. Just before ten there was another outburst of the hideous howling. It was commenced most distinctly by a particularly horrible and blood-curdling wail from the vicinity of the churchyard. The chorus lasted only a few minutes, however, and at the end of it I saw a large dark shape, like a huge dog, emerge from the fog and lope away at a rapid canter towards the open country. Assuming this to

be what I fear, I shall see it return soon after midnight.

12:30 AM. I was right. Almost as midnight struck I saw the beast returning. It stopped at the spot where the fog seemed to commence, and lifting up its head, gave tongue to that particularly horrible long-drawn wail that I had noticed as preceding the outburst earlier in the evening.

Tomorrow I shall tell the Rector what I have seen; and if, as I expect, we hear of some neighboring sheep-fold having been raided, I shall get him to watch with me for this nocturnal marauder. I shall also examine the Sarah Tomb for something which he may notice without any previous hint from me.

July 10th. I found the workmen this morning much disturbed in mind about the howling of the dogs. "We doan't like it, zur," one of them said to me—"we doan't like it; there was summat abroad last night that was unholy." They were still more uncomfortable when the news came round that a large dog had made a raid upon a flock of sheep, scattering them far and wide, and leaving three of them dead with torn throats in the field.

When I told the Rector of what I had seen and what was being said in the village, he immediately decided that we must try and catch or at least identify the beast I had seen. "Of course," said he, "it is some dog lately imported into the neighborhood, for I know of nothing about here nearly as large as the animal you describe, though its size may be due to the deceptive moonlight."

This afternoon I asked the Rector, as a favor, to assist me in lifting the temporary cover that was on the tomb, giving as an excuse the reason that I wished to obtain a portion of the curious mortar with which it had been sealed. After a slight demur he consented, and we raised the lid. If the sight that met our eyes gave me a shock, at least it appalled Grant.

"Great God!" he exclaimed; "the woman is alive!"

And so it seemed for a moment. The corpse had lost much of its starved appearance and looked hideously fresh and alive. It was still wrinkled and shrunken, but the lips were firm, and of the rich red hue of health. The eyes, if possible, were more appalling than ever, though fixed and staring. At one corner of the mouth I thought I noticed a slight dark-colored froth, but I said nothing about it then.

"Take your piece of mortar, Harry," gasped Grant, "and let us shut the tomb again. God help me! Parson though I am, such dead faces frighten me!"

Nor was I sorry to hide that terrible face again; but I got my bit of mortar, and I have advanced a step towards the solution of the mystery.

This afternoon the tomb was moved several feet towards its new position, but it will be two or three days yet before we shall be ready to replace the slab.

10:15 PM. Again the same howling at sunset, the same fog enveloping the church, and at ten o'clock the same great beast slipping silently out into the open country. I must get the Rector's help and watch for its return. But precautions we must take, for if things are as I believe, we take our lives in our hands when we venture out into the night to waylay the—Vampire. Why not admit it at once? For that the beast I have seen is the Vampire of that evil thing in the tomb I can have no reasonable doubt.

Not yet come to its full strength, thank Heaven!—after the starvation of nearly two centuries, for at present it can only maraud as wolf apparently. But, in a day or two, when full power returns, that dreadful woman in new strength and beauty will be able to leave her refuge. Then it would not be sheep merely that would satisfy her disgusting lust for blood, but victims that would yield their lifeblood without a murmur to her caressing touch—victims that, dying of her foul embrace, themselves must become Vampires in their turn to prey on others.

Mercifully my knowledge gives me a safeguard; for that little piece of mortar that I rescued today from the tomb contains a portion of the Sacred Host, and who holds it, humbly and firmly believing in its virtue, may pass safely through such an ordeal as I intend to submit myself and the Rector to tonight.

12:30 AM. Our adventure is over for the present, and we are back safe.

After writing the last entry recorded above, I went off to find Grant and tell him that the marauder was out on the prowl again. "But, Grant," I said, "before we start out tonight I must insist that you will let me prosecute this affair in my own way; you must promise to put yourself completely under my orders, without asking any questions as to the why and wherefore."

After a little demur, and some excusable chaff on his part at the serious view I was taking of what he called a "dog hunt," he gave me his promise. I then told him that we were to watch tonight and try and track the mysterious beast, but not to interfere with it in any way. I think, in spite of his jests, that I impressed him with the fact that there might be, after all, good reason for my precautions.

It was just after eleven when we stepped out into the still night.

Our first move was to try and penetrate

the dense fog round the church, but there was something so chilly about it, and a faint smell so disgustingly rank and loathsome, that neither our nerves nor our stomachs were proof against it. Instead, we stationed ourselves in the dark shadow of a yew tree that commanded a good view of the wicket entrance to the churchyard.

At midnight the howling of the dogs began again, and in a few minutes we saw a large grey shape, with green eyes shining like lamps, shamble swiftly down the path towards us.

The Rector started forward, but I laid a firm hand upon his arm and whispered a warning: "Remember!" Then we both stood very still and watched as the great beast cantered swiftly by. It was real enough, for we could hear the clicking of its nails on the stone flags. It passed within a few yards of us, and seemed to be nothing more nor less than a great grey wolf, thin and gaunt, with bristling hair and dripping jaws. It stopped where the mist commenced, and turned round. It was truly a horrible sight, and made one's blood run cold. The eyes burnt like fires, the upper lip was snarling and raised, showing the great canine teeth, while round the mouth hung and dripped a dark-colored froth.

It raised its head and gave tongue to its long wailing howl, which was answered from afar by the village dogs.

After standing for a few moments it turned and disappeared into the thickest part of the fog.

Very shortly afterwards the atmosphere began to clear, and within ten minutes the mist was all gone, the dogs in the village were silent, and the night seemed to reassume its normal aspect. We examined the spot where the beast had been standing and found, plainly enough

upon the stone flags, dark spots of froth and saliva.

"Well, Rector," I said, "will you admit now, in view of the things you have seen today, in consideration of the legend, the woman in the tomb, the fog, the howling dogs, and, last but not least, the mysterious beast you have seen so close, that there is something not quite normal in it all? Will you put yourself unreservedly in my hands and help me, *whatever I may do,* to first make assurance doubly sure, and finally take the necessary steps for putting an end to this horror of the night?" I saw that the uncanny influence of the night was strong upon him, and wished to impress it as much as possible.

"Needs must," he replied, "when the Devil drives: and in the face of what I have seen I must believe that some unholy forces are at work. Yet, how can they work in the sacred precincts of a church? Shall we not call rather upon Heaven to assist us in our need?"

"Grant," I said solemnly, "that we must do, each in his own way. God helps those who help themselves, and by His help and the light of my knowledge we must fight this battle for Him and the poor lost soul within."

We then returned to the rectory and to our rooms, though I have sat up to write this account while the scene is fresh in my mind.

July 11th. Found the workmen again very much disturbed in their minds, and full of a strange dog that had been seen during the night by several people, who had hunted it. Farmer Stotman, who had been watching his sheep (the same flock that had been raided the night before), had surprised it over a fresh carcass and tried to drive it off, but its size and fierceness so alarmed him that he had beaten a hasty retreat for a gun. When he returned the animal was gone, though he found that three more sheep from his flock were dead and torn.

The Sarah Tomb was moved today to its new position; but it was a long, heavy business, and there was not time to replace the covering slab. For this I was glad, as in the prosaic light of day the Rector almost disbelieves the events of the night, and is prepared to think everything to have been magnified and distorted by our imagination.

As, however, I could not possibly proceed with my war of extermination against this foul thing without assistance, and as there is nobody else I can rely upon, I appealed to him for one more night—to convince him that it was no delusion, but a ghastly, horrible truth, which must be fought and conquered for our own sakes, as well as that of all those living in the neighborhood.

"Put yourself in my hands, Rector," I said, "for tonight at least. Let us take those precautions which my study of the subject tells me are the right ones. Tonight you and I must watch in the church; and I feel assured that tomorrow you will be as convinced as I am, and be equally prepared to take those awful steps which I know to be proper, and I must warn you that we shall find a more startling change in the body lying there than you noticed yesterday."

My words came true; for on raising the wooden cover once more the rank stench of a slaughter-house arose, making us feel positively sick. There lay the Vampire, but how changed from the starved and shrunken corpse we saw two days ago for the first time!

The wrinkles had almost disappeared, the flesh was firm and full, the crimson lips grinned horribly over the long pointed teeth, and a distinct smear of blood had trickled down one corner of the mouth. We set our teeth, however, and hardened our hearts. Then we replaced the cover and put what we had collected into a safe place in the vestry. Yet even now Grant could not believe that there was any real or pressing danger concealed in that awful tomb, as he raised strenuous objections to any apparent desecration of the body without further proof. This he shall have tonight. God grant that I am not taking too much on myself! If there is any truth in old legends it would be easy enough to destroy the Vampire now; but Grant will not have it.

I hope for the best of this night's work, but the danger in waiting is very great.

6 PM. I have prepared everything: the sharp knives, the pointed stake, fresh garlic, and the wild dog-roses.[2] All these I have taken and concealed in the vestry, where we can get at them when our solemn vigil commences.

If either or both of us die with our fearful task undone, let those reading my record see that this is done. I lay it upon them as a solemn obligation. "That the Vampire be pierced through the heart with the stake, then let the Burial Service be read over the poor clay at last released from its doom. Thus shall the Vampire cease to be, and a lost soul rest."

July 12th. All is over. After the most terrible night of watching and horror one

---

2 The dog-rose (*rosa canina*) is a common plant, with thorny, clinging vines; it was the rose of medieval heraldry. Like the ash and hawthorn blossoms, it became associated with vampire prevention and was often placed in or on the coffin in Wallachia (the neighboring province to Transylvania). The smell was reputed to keep away vampires and witches, and the blossoms were said to burn the skin of the vampire.

Vampire at least will trouble the world no more. But how thankful should we be to a merciful Providence that that awful tomb was not disturbed by anyone not having the knowledge necessary to deal with its dreadful occupant! I write this with no feelings of self-complacency, but simply with a great gratitude for the years of study I have been able to devote to this special subject.

And now to my tale.

Just before sunset last night the Rector and I locked ourselves into the church, and took up our position in the pulpit. It was one of those pulpits, to be found in some churches, which is entered from the vestry, the preacher appearing at a good height through an arched opening in the wall. This gave us a sense of security (which we felt we needed), a good view of the interior, and direct access to the implements which I had concealed in the vestry.

The sun set and the twilight gradually deepened and faded. There was, so far, no sign of the usual fog, nor any howling of the dogs. At nine o'clock the moon rose, and her pale light gradually flooded the aisles, and still no sign of any kind from the "Sarah Tomb." The Rector had asked me several times what he might expect, but I was determined that no words or thought of mine should influence him, and that he should be convinced by his own senses alone.

By half-past ten we were both getting very tired, and I began to think that perhaps after all we should see nothing that night. However, soon after eleven we observed a light mist rising from the Sarah Tomb. It seemed to scintillate and sparkle as it rose, and curled in a sort of pillar or spiral.

I said nothing, but I heard the Rector give a sort of gasp as he clutched my arm feverishly. "Great Heaven!" he whispered, "it is taking shape."

And, true enough, in a very few moments we saw standing erect by the tomb the ghastly figure of the Countess Sarah!

She looked thin and haggard still, and her face was deadly white; but the crimson lips looked like a hideous gash in the pale cheeks, and her eyes glared like red coals in the gloom of the church.

It was a fearful thing to watch as she stepped unsteadily down the aisle, staggering a little as if from weakness and exhaustion. This was perhaps natural, as her body must have suffered much physically from her long incarceration, in spite of the unholy forces which kept it fresh and well.

We watched her to the door, and wondered what would happen; but it appeared to present no difficulty, for she melted through it and disappeared.

"Now, Grant," I said, "do you believe?"

"Yes," he replied, "I must. Everything is in your hands, and I will obey your commands to the letter, if you can only instruct me how to rid my poor people of this unnamable terror."

"By God's help I will," said I; "but you shall be yet more convinced first, for we have a terrible work to do, and much to answer for in the future, before we leave the church again this morning. And now to work, for in its present weak state the Vampire will not wander far, but may return at any time, and must not find us unprepared."

We stepped down from the pulpit and, taking dog-roses and garlic from the vestry, proceeded to the tomb. I arrived first and, throwing off the wooden cover, cried, "Look! It is empty!" There was nothing there! Nothing except the impress of the body in the loose damp mould!

I took the flowers and laid them in a circle round the tomb, for legend teaches us that Vampires will not pass over these particular blossoms if they can avoid it.

Then, eight or ten feet away, I made a circle on the stone pavement, large enough for the Rector and myself to stand in, and within the circle I placed the implements that I had brought into the church with me.

"Now," I said, "from this circle, which nothing unholy can step across, you shall see the Vampire face-to-face, and see her afraid to cross that other circle of garlic and dog roses to regain her unholy refuge. But on no account step beyond the holy place you stand in, for the Vampire has a fearful strength not her own, and, like a snake, can draw her victim willingly to his own destruction."

Now so far my work was done, and, calling the Rector, we stepped into the Holy Circle to await the Vampire's return.[3]

Nor was this long delayed. Presently a damp, cold odor seemed to pervade the church, which made our hair bristle and flesh to creep. And then, down the aisle with noiseless feet came that which we watched for.

I heard the Rector mutter a prayer, and I held him tightly by the arm, for he was shivering violently.

Long before we could distinguish the features we saw the glowing eyes and the crimson sensual mouth. She went straight to her tomb, but stopped short when she encountered my flowers. She walked right round the tomb seeking a place to enter, and as she walked she saw us. A spasm of diabolical hate and fury passed over her face; but it quickly vanished, and a smile of love, more devilish still, took its place. She stretched out her arms towards us. Then we saw that round her mouth gathered a bloody froth, and from under her lips long pointed teeth gleamed and champed.

She spoke: a soft soothing voice, a voice that carried a spell with it, and affected us both strangely, particularly the Rector. I wished to test as far as possible, without endangering our lives, the Vampire's power.

Her voice had a soporific effect, which I resisted easily enough, but which seemed to throw the Rector into a sort of trance. More than this: it seemed to compel him to her in spite of his efforts to resist.

"Come!" she said: "Come! I give sleep and peace—sleep and peace—sleep and peace."

She advanced a little towards us; but not far, for I noted that the Sacred Circle seemed to keep her back like an iron hand.

My companion seemed to become demoralized and spellbound. He tried to step forward and, finding me detain him, whispered, "Harry, let go! I must go! She is calling me! I must! I must! Oh, help me! Help me!" And he began to struggle.

It was time to finish.

"Grant!" I cried, in a loud, firm voice, "in the name of all that you hold sacred, have done and play the man!" He shuddered violently and gasped, "Where am I?" Then he remembered, and clung to me convulsively for a moment.

At this a look of damnable hate changed

---

[3] Van Helsing uses the same protection for Mina and himself at the conclusion of Stoker's *Dracula*.

the smiling face before us, and with a sort of shriek she staggered back.

"Back!" I cried: "back to your unholy tomb! No longer shall you molest the suffering world! Your end is near."

It was fear that now showed itself in her beautiful face (for it was beautiful in spite of its horror) as she shrank back, back and over the circlet of flowers, shivering as she did so. At last, with a low mournful cry, she appeared to melt back again into her tomb.

As she did so the first gleams of the rising sun lit up the world, and I knew all danger was over for the day.

Taking Grant by the arm, I drew him with me out of the circle and led him to the tomb. There lay the Vampire once more, still in her living death as we had a moment before seen her in her devilish life. But in the eyes remained that awful expression of hate, and cringing, appalling fear.

Grant was pulling himself together.

"Now," I said, "will you dare the last terrible act and rid the world forever of this horror?"

"By God!" he said solemnly, "I will. Tell me what to do."

"Help me to lift her out of her tomb. She can harm us no more," I replied.

With averted faces we set to our terrible task, and laid her out upon the flags.

"Now," I said, "read the Burial Service over the poor body, and then let us give it its release from this living hell that holds it."

Reverently the Rector read the beautiful words, and reverently I made the necessary responses. When it was over I took the stake and, without giving myself time to think,

plunged it with all my strength through the heart.

As though really alive, the body for a moment writhed and kicked convulsively, and an awful heart-rending shriek woke the silent church; then all was still.

Then we lifted the poor body back; and, thank God!—the consolation that legend tells is never denied to those who have to do such awful work as ours came at last. Over the face stole a great and solemn peace; the lips lost their crimson hue, the prominent sharp teeth sank back into the mouth, and for a moment we saw before us the calm, pale face of a most beautiful woman, who smiled as she slept.

A few minutes more, and she faded away to dust before our eyes as we watched. We set to work and cleaned up every trace of our work, and then departed for the rectory. Most thankful were we to step out of the church, with its horrible associations, into the rosy warmth of the summer morning.

With the above end the notes in my father's diary, though a few days later this further entry occurs:

July 15th. Since the 12th everything has been quiet and as usual. We replaced and sealed up the Sarah Tomb this morning. The workmen were surprised to find the body had disappeared, but took it to be the natural result of exposing it to the air.

One odd thing came to my ears today. It appears that the child of one of the villagers strayed from home the night of the 11th inst.,[4] and was found asleep in a coppice near the church, very pale and quite exhausted. There were two small marks on her throat, which have since disappeared.

---

4 That is, the 11th of the current month; "inst." means "instant," as in *now* or *current*.

What does this mean? I have, however, kept it to myself, as, now that the Vampire is no more, no further danger either to that child or any other is to be apprehended. It is only those who die of the Vampire's embrace that become Vampires at death in their turn.

Mary E. Wilkins-Freeman

MARY ELEANOR WILKINS-FREEMAN (1852-1930) was the product of a strict religious upbringing in Massachusetts. She began writing stories as a teenager, to help support her family, and quickly achieved success, eventually producing more than three dozen volumes of poetry and novels. She married at the age of fifty and continued to work, eventually becoming the first winner of the William Dean Howells Medal for Distinction in Fiction from the American Academy of Arts and Letters.

This story, which first appeared in *Everybody's Magazine* in December 1902, reports in completely unsensational style the tale of the no-nonsense narrator's prolonged interaction with an innocent vampire.

LUELLA MILLER

MARY E. WILKINS~FREEMAN

Close to the village street stood the one-story house in which Luella Miller, who had an evil name in the village, had dwelt. She had been dead for years, yet there were those in the village who, in spite of the clearer light which comes on a vantage-point from a long-past danger, half believed in the tale which they had heard from their childhood.

In their hearts, although they scarcely would have owned it, was a survival of the wild horror and frenzied fear of their ancestors who had dwelt in the same age with Luella Miller. Young people even would stare with a shudder at the old house as they passed, and children never played around it as was their wont around an untenanted building. Not a window in the old Miller house was broken: the panes reflected the morning sunlight in patches of emerald and blue, and the latch of the sagging front door was never lifted, although no bolt secured it.

Since Luella Miller had been carried out of it, the house had had no tenant except one friendless old soul who had no choice between that and the far-off shelter of the open sky. This old woman, who had survived her kindred and friends, lived in the house one week, then one morning no smoke came out of the chimney, and a body of neighbors, a score strong, entered and found her dead in her bed.

There were dark whispers as to the cause of her death, and there were those who testified to an expression of fear so exalted that it showed forth the state of the departing soul upon the dead face. The old woman had been hale and hearty when she entered the house, and in seven days she was dead; it seemed that she had fallen a victim to some uncanny power. The minister talked in the pulpit with covert severity against the sin of superstition; still the belief prevailed. Not a soul in the village but would have chosen the almshouse rather than that dwelling. No vagrant, if he heard the tale, would seek shelter beneath that old roof, unhallowed by nearly half a century of superstitious fear.

There was only one person in the village who had actually known Luella Miller. That person was a woman well over eighty, but a marvel of vitality and unextinct youth. Straight as an arrow, with the spring of one recently let loose from the bow of life, she moved about the streets, and she always went to church, rain or shine. She had never married, and had lived alone for years in a house across the road from Luella Miller's.

This woman had none of the garrulousness of age, but never in all her life had she ever held her tongue for any will save her own, and she never spared the truth when she essayed to present it. She it was who bore testimony to the life, evil, though possibly wittingly or designedly so, of Luella Miller, and to her personal appearance. When this old woman spoke—and she had the gift of description, although her thoughts were clothed in the rude vernacular of her native village—one could seem to see Luella Miller as she had really looked.

According to this woman, Lydia Anderson by name, Luella Miller had been a beauty of a type rather unusual in New England. She had been a slight, pliant sort of creature, as ready with a strong yielding to fate and as unbreakable as a willow. She had glimmering lengths of straight, fair hair, which she wore softly looped round a long, lovely face. She had blue eyes full of soft pleading, little slender, clinging hands, and a wonderful grace of motion and attitude.

"Luella Miller used to sit in a way nobody else could if they sat up and studied a week of Sundays," said Lydia Anderson, "and it was a sight to see her walk. If one of them willows over there on the edge of the brook could start up and get its roots free of the ground, and move off, it would go just the way Luella Miller used to. She had a green shot silk she used to wear, too, and a hat with green ribbon streamers, and a lace veil blowing across her face and out sideways, and a green ribbon flyin' from her waist. That was what she came out bride in when she married Erastus Miller. Her name before she was married was Hill. There was always a sight of *L*'s in her name, married or single.

"Erastus Miller was good-lookin', too, better lookin' than Luella. Sometimes I used to think that Luella wa'n't so handsome after all. Erastus just about worshiped her. I used to know him pretty well. He lived next door to me, and we went to school together. Folks used to say he was waitin' on me, but he wa'n't. I never thought he was except once or twice when he said things that some girls might have suspected meant somethin'. That was before Luella came here to teach the district school.

"It was funny how she came to get it, for folks said she hadn't any education, and that one of the big girls, Lottie Henderson, used to do all the teachin' for her, while she sat back and did embroidery work on a cambric[1] pocket-handkerchief. Lottie Henderson was a real smart girl, a splendid scholar, and she just set her eyes by Luella, as all the girls did. Lottie would have made a real smart woman, but she died when Luella had been here about a year—just faded away and died: nobody knew what ailed her. She dragged herself to that schoolhouse and helped Luella teach till the very last minute. The committee all knew how Luella didn't do much of the work herself, but they winked at it.

"It wa'n't long after Lottie died that Erastus married her. I always thought he hur-

---

[1] A fine white linen or cotton fabric

ried it up because she wa'n't fit to teach. One of the big boys used to help her after Lottie died, but he hadn't much government, and the school didn't do very well, and Luella might have had to give it up, for the committee couldn't have shut their eyes to things much longer. The boy that helped her was a real honest, innocent sort of fellow, and he was a good scholar, too. Folks said he over-studied, and that was the reason he was took crazy the year after Luella married, but I don't know.

"And I don't know what made Erastus Miller go into consumption of the blood the year after he was married: consumption wa'n't in his family.[2] He just grew weaker and weaker, and went almost bent double when he tried to wait on Luella, and he spoke feeble, like an old man. He worked terrible hard till the last trying to save up a little to leave Luella. I've seen him out in the worst storms on a wood-sled—he used to cut and sell wood—and he was hunched up on top lookin' more dead than alive.

"Once I couldn't stand it: I went over and helped him pitch some wood on the cart—I was always strong in my arms. I wouldn't stop for all he told me to, and I guess he was glad enough for the help. That was only a week before he died. He fell on the kitchen floor while he was gettin' breakfast. He always got the breakfast and let Luella lay abed. He did all the sweepin' and the washin' and the ironin' and most of the cookin'. He couldn't bear to have Luella lift her finger, and she let him do for her.

"She lived like a queen for all the work she did. She didn't even do her sewin'. She said it made her shoulder ache to sew, and

poor Erastus's sister Lily used to do all her sewin'. She wa'n't able to, either; she was never strong in her back, but she did it beautifully. She had to, to suit Luella, she was so dreadful particular.

"I never saw any thin' like the fagottin'[3] and hemstitchin' that Lily Miller did for Luella. She made all Luella's weddin' outfit, and that green silk dress, after Maria Babbit cut it. Maria she cut it for nothin', and she did a lot more cuttin' and fittin' for nothin' for Luella, too.

"Lily Miller went to live with Luella after Erastus died. She gave up her home, though she was real attached to it and wa'n't a mite afraid to stay alone. She rented it and she went to live with Luella right away after the funeral."

Then this old woman, Lydia Anderson, who remembered Luella Miller, would go on to relate the story of Lily Miller. It seemed that on the removal of Lily Miller to the house of her dead brother, to live with his widow, the village people first began to talk. This Lily Miller had been hardly past her first youth, and a most robust and blooming woman, rosy-cheeked, with curls of strong, black hair overshadowing round, candid temples and bright dark eyes.

It was not six months after she had taken up her residence with her sister-in-law that her rosy color faded and her pretty curves become wan hollows. White shadows began to show in the black rings of her hair, and the light died out of her eyes, her features sharpened, and there were pathetic lines at her mouth, which yet wore always an expression of utter sweetness and even happiness. She

[2] Consumption (the common name for tuberculosis at the time) was once thought to be hereditary because entire families would often be wiped out by this highly contagious lung disease.

[3] Embroidery.

was devoted to her sister; there was no doubt that she loved her with her whole heart, and was perfectly content in her service. It was her sole anxiety lest she should die and leave her alone.

"The way Lily Miller used to talk about Luella was enough to make you mad and enough to make you cry," said Lydia Anderson. "I've been in there sometimes toward the last when she was too feeble to cook and carried her some blanc-mange[4] or custard—somethin' I thought she might relish, and she'd thank me, and when I asked her how she was, say she felt better than she did yesterday, and asked me if I didn't think she looked better, dreadful pitiful, and say poor Luella had an awful time takin' care of her and doin' the work—she wa'n't strong enough to do anythin'—when all the time Luella wa'n't liftin' her finger and poor Lily didn't get any care except what the neighbors gave her, and Luella eat up everythin' that was carried in for Lily. I had it real straight that she did.

"Luella used to just sit and cry and do nothin'. She did act real fond of Lily, and she pined away considerable, too. There was those that thought she'd go into a decline herself. But after Lily died, her aunt Abby Mixter came, and then Luella picked up and grew as fat and rosy as ever. But poor Aunt Abby begun to droop just the way Lily had, and I guess somebody wrote to her married daughter, Mrs. Sam Abbot, who lived in Barre, for she wrote her mother that she must leave right away and come and make her a visit, but Aunt Abby wouldn't go.

"I can see her now. She was a real good-lookin' woman, tall and large, with a big, square face and a high forehead that looked of itself kind of benevolent and good. She just tended out on Luella as if she had been a baby, and when her married daughter sent for her she wouldn't stir one inch. She'd always thought a lot of her daughter, too, but she said Luella needed her and her married daughter didn't. Her daughter kept writin' and writin', but it didn't do any good.

Finally she came, and when she saw how bad her mother looked, she broke down and cried and all but went on her knees to have her come away. She spoke her mind out to Luella, too. She told her that she'd killed her husband and everybody that had anythin' to do with her, and she'd thank her to leave her mother alone. Luella went into hysterics, and Aunt Abby was so frightened that she called me after her daughter went. Mrs. Sam Abbot she went away fairly cryin' out loud in the buggy, the neighbors heard her, and well she might, for she never saw her mother again alive.

"I went in that night when Aunt Abby called for me, standin' in the door with her little green-checked shawl over her head. I can see her now. 'Do come over here, Miss Anderson,' she sung out, kind of gasping for breath. I didn't stop for any thin'. I put over as fast as I could, and when I got there, there was Luella laughin' and cryin' all together, and Aunt Abby trying to hush her, and all the time she herself was white as a sheet and shakin' so she could hardly stand. 'For the land sakes, Mrs. Mixter,' says I, 'you look worse than she does. You ain't fit to be up out of your bed.'

"'Oh, there ain't any thin' the matter with me,' says she. Then she went on talkin' to Luella. 'There, there, don't, don't, poor little lamb,' says she. 'Aunt Abby is here. She ain't goin' away and leave you. Don't, poor little lamb.'

---

[4] A type of pudding.

" 'Do leave her with me, Mrs. Mixter, and you get back to bed,' says I, for Aunt Abby had been layin' down considerable lately, though somehow she contrived to do the work.

" 'I'm well enough,' says she. 'Don't you think she had better have the doctor, Miss Anderson?'

" 'The doctor,' says I, 'I think *you* had better have the doctor. I think you need him much worse than some folks I could mention.' And I looked right straight at Luella Miller laughin' and cryin' and goin' on as if she was the center of all creation. All the time she was actin' so—seemed as if she was too sick to sense anythin'—she was keepin' a sharp lookout as to how we took it out of the corner of one eye. I see her. You could never cheat me about Luella Miller.

"Finally I got real mad and I run home and I got a bottle of valerian[5] I had, and I poured some boilin' hot water on a handful of catnip, and I mixed up that catnip tea with most half a wineglass of valerian, and I went with it over to Luella's. I marched right up to Luella, a-holdin' out of that cup, all smokin'. 'Now,' says I, 'Luella Miller, *you swaller this!'*

" 'What is—what is it, oh, what is it?' she sort of screeches out. Then she goes off a-laughin' enough to kill.

" 'Poor lamb, poor little lamb,' says Aunt Abby, standin' over her, all kind of tottery, and tryin' to bathe her head with camphor.

" '*You swaller this right down,*' says I. And I didn't waste any ceremony. I just took hold of Luella Miller's chin and I tipped her head back, and I caught her mouth open with laughin', and I clapped that cup to her lips and I fairly hollered at her: 'Swaller, swaller,

swaller!' and she gulped it right down. She had to, and I guess it did her good. Anyhow, she stopped cryin' and laughin' and let me put her to bed, and she went to sleep like a baby inside of half an hour.

"That was more than poor Aunt Abby did. She lay awake all that night and I stayed with her, though she tried not to have me; said she wa'n't sick enough for watchers. But I stayed, and I made some good cornmeal gruel and I fed her a teaspoon every little while all night long. It seemed to me as if she was jest dyin' from bein' all wore out. In the mornin' as soon as it was light I run over to the Bisbees and sent Johnny Bisbee for the doctor. I told him to tell the doctor to hurry, and he come pretty quick.

"Poor Aunt Abby didn't seem to know much of anythin' when he got there. You couldn't hardly tell she breathed, she was so used up. When the doctor had gone, Luella came into the room lookin' like a baby in her ruffled nightgown. I can see her now. Her eyes were as blue and her face all pink and white like a blossom, and she looked at Aunt Abby in the bed sort of innocent and surprised. 'Why,' says she, 'Aunt Abby ain't got up yet?'

" 'No, she ain't,' says I, pretty short.

" 'I thought I didn't smell the coffee,' says Luella.

" 'Coffee,' says I. 'I guess if you have coffee this mornin' you'll make it yourself.'

" 'I never made the coffee in all my life,' says she, dreadful astonished. 'Erastus always made the coffee as long as he lived, and then Lily she made it, and then Aunt Abby made it. I don't believe I *can* make the coffee, Miss Anderson.'

---

[5] Valerian root extract used as a nerve sedative and antispasmodic; herbal form of Valium.

" 'You can make it or go without, jest as you please,' says I.

" 'Ain't Aunt Abby goin' to get up?' says she.

" 'I guess she won't get up,' says I, 'sick as she is.' I was gettin' madder and madder. There was somethin' about that little pink-and-white thing standin' there and talkin' about coffee, when she had killed so many better folks than she was, and had jest killed another, that made me feel 'most as if I wished somebody would up and kill her before she had a chance to do any more harm.

" 'Is Aunt Abby sick?' says Luella, as if she was sort of aggrieved and injured.

" 'Yes,' says I, 'she's sick, and she's goin' to die, and then you'll be left alone, and you'll have to do for yourself and wait on yourself, or do without things.' I don't know but I was sort of hard, but it was the truth, and if I was any harder than Luella Miller had been I'll give up. I ain't never been sorry that I said it. Well, Luella, she up and had hysterics again at that, and I jest let her have 'em. All I did was to bundle her into the room on the other side of the entry where Aunt Abby couldn't hear her, if she wa'n't past it—I don't know but she was—and set her down hard in a chair and told her not to come back into the other room, and she minded. She had her hysterics in there till she got tired.

"When she found out that nobody was comin' to coddle her and do for her she stopped. At least I suppose she did. I had all I could do with poor Aunt Abby tryin' to keep the breath of life in her. The doctor had told me that she was dreadful low, and give me some very strong medicine to give to her in drops real often, and told me real particular about the nourishment.

"Well, I did as he told me real faithful till she wa'n't able to swaller any longer. Then I had her daughter sent for. I had begun to realize that she wouldn't last any time at all. I hadn't realized it before, though I spoke to Luella the way I did. The doctor he came, and Mrs. Sam Abbot, but when she got there it was too late; her mother was dead. Aunt Abby's daughter just give one look at her mother layin' there, then she turned sort of sharp and sudden and looked at me.

" 'Where is she?' says she, and I knew she meant Luella.

" 'She's out in the kitchen,' says I. 'She's too nervous to see folks die. She's afraid it will make her sick.'

"The Doctor he speaks up then. He was a young man. Old Doctor Park had died the year before, and this was a young fellow just out of college. 'Mrs. Miller is not strong,' says he, kind of severe, 'and she is quite right in not agitating herself.'

" 'You are another, young man; she's got her pretty claw on you,' thinks I, but I didn't say anythin' to him. I just said over to Mrs. Sam Abbot that Luella was in the kitchen, and Mrs. Sam Abbot she went out there, and I went, too, and I never heard any thin' like the way she talked to Luella Miller.

"I felt pretty hard to Luella myself, but this was more than I ever would have dared to say. Luella, she was too scared to go into hysterics. She jest flopped. She seemed to jest shrink away to nothin' in that kitchen chair, with Mrs. Sam Abbot standin' over her and talkin' and tellin' her the truth.

"I guess the truth was most too much for her and no mistake, because Luella presently actually did faint away, and there wa'n't any sham about it, the way I always suspected there was about them hysterics. She fainted dead away and we had to lay her flat on the floor, and the Doctor he came runnin' out and he said somethin' about a weak heart dreadful fierce to Mrs. Sam Abbot, but she wa'n't a mite scared. She faced him jest as white as even Luella was layin' there lookin' like death and the Doctor feelin' of her pulse.

" 'Weak heart,' says she, 'weak heart; weak fiddlesticks! There ain't nothin' weak about that woman. She's got strength enough to hang onto other folks till she kills 'em. Weak? It was my poor mother that was weak: this woman killed her as sure as if she had taken a knife to her.'

"But the Doctor he didn't pay much attention. He was bendin' over Luella layin' there with her yellow hair all streamin' and her pretty pink-and-white face all pale, and her blue eyes like stars gone out, and he was holdin' onto her hand and smoothin' her forehead, and tellin' me to get the brandy in Aunt Abby's room, and I was sure as I wanted to be that Luella had got somebody else to hang onto, now Aunt Abby was gone, and I thought of poor Erastus Miller, and I sort of pitied the poor young Doctor, led away by a pretty face, and I made up my mind I'd see what I could do.

"I waited till Aunt Abby had been dead and buried about a month, and the Doctor was goin' to see Luella steady and folks were beginnin' to talk; then one evenin', when I knew the Doctor had been called out of town and wouldn't be round, I went over to Luella's. I found her all dressed up in a blue muslin with white polka dots on it, and her hair curled jest as pretty, and there wa'n't a young girl in the place could compare with her.

"There was somethin' about Luella Miller seemed to draw the heart right out of you, but she didn't draw it out of *me*. She was settin' rocking in the chair by her sittin'-room

window, and Maria Brown had gone home. Maria Brown had been in to help her, or rather to do the work, for Luella wa'n't helped when she didn't do anythin'.

"Maria Brown was real capable and she didn't have any ties; she wa'n't married, and lived alone, so she'd offered. I couldn't see why she should do the work any more than Luella; she wa'n't any too strong; but she seemed to think she could and Luella seemed to think so, too, so she went over and did all the work—washed, and ironed, and baked, while Luella sat and rocked.

"Maria didn't live long afterward. She began to fade away just the same fashion the others had. Well, she was warned, but she acted real mad when folks said anythin': said Luella was a poor, abused woman, too delicate to help herself, and they'd ought to be ashamed, and if she died helpin' them that couldn't help themselves she would—and she did.

" 'I s'pose Maria has gone home,' says I to Luella, when I had gone in and sat down opposite her.

" 'Yes, Maria went half an hour ago; after she had got supper and washed the dishes,' says Luella, in her pretty way.

" 'I suppose she has got a lot of work to do in her own house tonight,' says I, kind of bitter, but that was all thrown away on Luella Miller. It seemed to her right that other folks that wa'n't any better able than she was herself should wait on her, and she couldn't get it through her head that anybody should think it *wa'n't* right.

" 'Yes,' says Luella, real sweet and pretty, 'yes, she said she had to do her washin' tonight. She has let it go for a fortnight along of comin' over here.'

" 'Why don't she stay home and do her

washin' instead of comin' over here and doin' *your* work, when you are just as well able, and enough sight more so, than she is to do it?' says I.

"Then Luella she looked at me like a baby who has a rattle shook at it. She sort of laughed as innocent as you please. 'Oh, I can't do the work myself, Miss Anderson,' says she. 'I never did. Maria *has* to do it.'

"Then I spoke out: 'Has to do it!' says I. 'Has to do it! She don't have to do it, either. Maria Brown has her own home and enough to live on. She ain't beholden to you to come over here and slave for you and kill herself.'

"Luella she jest set and stared at me for all the world like a doll-baby that was so abused that it was comin' to life.

" 'Yes,' says I, 'she's killin' herself. She's goin' to die just the way Erastus did, and Lily, and your Aunt Abby. You're killin' her jest as you did them. I don't know what there is about you, but you seem to bring a curse,' says I. 'You kill everybody that is fool enough to care anythin' about you and do for you.'

"She stared at me and she was pretty pale.

" 'And Maria ain't the only one you're goin' to kill,' says I. 'You're goin' to kill Doctor Malcom before you're done with him.'

"Then a red color came flamin' all over her face. 'I ain't goin' to kill him, either,' says she, and she begun to cry.

"'Yes, you *be!*' says I. Then I spoke as I had never spoke before. You see, I felt it on account of Erastus. I told her that she hadn't any business to think of another man after she'd been married to one that had died for her: that she was a dreadful woman; and she was, that's true enough, but sometimes I have wondered lately if she knew it—if she wa'n't like a baby with scissors in its hand cuttin' everybody without knowin' what it was doin'.

"Luella she kept gettin' paler and paler, and she never took her eyes off my face. There was somethin' awful about the way she looked at me and never spoke one word.

"After awhile I quit talkin' and I went home. I watched that night, but her lamp went out before nine o'clock, and when Doctor Malcom came drivin' past and sort of slowed up he see there wa'n't any light and he drove along. I saw her sort of shy out of meetin' the next Sunday, too, so he shouldn't go home with her, and I begun to think mebbe she did have some conscience after all. It was only a week after that that Maria Brown died—sort of sudden at the last, though everybody had seen it was comin'.

"Well, then there was a good deal of feelin' and pretty dark whispers. Folks said the days of witchcraft had come again, and they were pretty shy of Luella. She acted sort of offish to the Doctor and he didn't go there, and there wa'n't anybody to do anythin' for her. I don't know how she *did* get along. I wouldn't go in there and offer to help her—not because I was afraid of dyin' like the rest but I thought she was just as well able to do her own work as I was to do it for her, and I thought it was about time that she did it and stopped killin' other folks.

"But it wa'n't very long before folks began to say that Luella herself was goin' into a decline jest the way her husband, and Lily, and Aunt Abby and the others had; and I saw myself that she looked pretty bad. I used to see her goin' past from the store with a bundle as if she could hardly crawl, but I remembered how Erastus used to wait and 'tend when he couldn't hardly put one foot before the other, and I didn't go out to help her.

"But at last one afternoon I saw the Doctor come drivin' up like mad with his medicine chest, and Mrs. Babbit came in after supper and said that Luella was real sick.

" 'I'd offer to go in and nurse her,' says she, 'but I've got my children to consider, and mebbe it ain't true what they say, but it's queer how many folks that have done for her have died.'

"I didn't say anythin', but I considered how she had been Erastus's wife and how he had set his eyes by her, and I made up my mind to go in the next mornin', unless she was better, and see what I could do; but the next mornin' I see her at the window, and pretty soon she came steppin' out as spry as you please, and a little while afterward Mrs. Babbit came in and told me that the Doctor had got a girl from out of town, a Sarah Jones, to come there, and she said she was pretty sure that the Doctor was goin' to marry Luella.

"I saw him kiss her in the door that night myself, and I knew it was true. The woman came that afternoon, and the way she flew around was a caution. I don't believe Luella had swept since Maria died. She swept and dusted, and washed and ironed; wet clothes and dusters and carpets were flyin' over there all day, and every time Luella set her foot out when the Doctor wa'n't there there was that Sarah Jones helpin' of her up and down the steps, as if she hadn't learned to walk.

"Well, everybody knew that Luella and the Doctor were goin' to be married, but it wa'n't long before they began to talk about his lookin' so poorly, jest as they had about the others; and they talked about Sarah Jones, too.

"Well, the Doctor did die, and he wanted to be married first, so as to leave what little he had to Luella, but he died before the minister could get there, and Sarah Jones died a week afterward.

"Well, that wound up everything for Luella Miller. Not another soul in the whole town would lift a finger for her. There got to be a sort of panic. Then she began to droop in good earnest. She used to have to go to the store herself, for Mrs. Babbit was afraid to let Tommy go for her, and I've seen her goin' past and stoppin' every two or three steps to rest.

"Well, I stood it as long as I could, but one day I see her comin' with her arms full and stoppin' to lean against the Babbit fence, and I run out and took her bundles and carried them to her house. Then I went home and never spoke one word to her though she called after me dreadful kind of pitiful. Well, that night I was taken sick with a chill, and I was sick as I wanted to be for two weeks. Mrs. Babbit had seen me run out to help Luella and she came in and told me I was goin' to die on account of it. I didn't know whether I was or not, but I considered I had done right by Erastus's wife.

"That last two weeks Luella she had a dreadful hard time, I guess. She was pretty sick, and as near as I could make out nobody dared go near her. I don't know as she was really needin' anythin' very much, for there was enough to eat in her house and it was warm weather, and she made out to cook a little flour gruel every day, I know, but I guess she had a hard time, she that had been so petted and done for all her life.

"When I got so I could go out, I went over there one morning. Mrs. Babbit had just come in to say she hadn't seen any smoke and she didn't know but what it was somebody's duty to go in, but she couldn't help thinkin' of her children, and I got right up, though I hadn't been out of the house for two weeks, and I went in there, and Luella she was layin' on the bed, and she was dyin'.

"She lasted all that day and into the night. But I sat there after the new doctor had gone away. Nobody else dared to go there. It was about midnight that I left her for a minute to run home and get some medicine I had been takin', for I begun to feel rather bad.

"It was a full moon that night, and just as I started out of my door to cross the street back to Luella's, I stopped short, for I saw something."

Lydia Anderson at this juncture always said with a certain defiance that she did not expect to be believed, and then proceeded in a hushed voice:—

"I saw what I saw, and I know I saw it, and I will swear on my death bed that I saw it. I saw Luella Miller and Erastus Miller, and Lily, and Aunt Abby, and Maria, and the Doctor, and Sarah, all goin' out of her door, and all but Luella shone white in the moonlight, and they were all helpin' her along till she seemed to fairly fly in the midst of them. Then it all disappeared. I stood a minute with my heart, then I went over there. I thought of goin' for Mrs. Babbit, but I thought she'd be afraid. So I went alone, though I knew what

had happened. Luella was layin' real peaceful, dead on her bed."

This was the story that the old woman, Lydia Anderson, told, but the sequel was told by the people who survived her, and this is the tale which has become folklore in the village.

Lydia Anderson died when she was eighty-seven. She had continued wonderfully hale and hearty for one of her years until about two weeks before her death.

One bright moonlight evening she was sitting beside a window in her parlor when she made a sudden exclamation, and was out of the house and across the street before the neighbor who was taking care of her could stop her. She followed as fast as possible and found Lydia Anderson stretched on the ground before the door of Luella Miller's deserted house, and she was quite dead.

The next night there was a red gleam of fire athwart the moonlight and the old house of Luella Miller was burned to the ground. Nothing is now left of it except a few old cellar stones and a lilac bush, and in summer a helpless trail of morning glories among the weeds, which might be considered emblematic of Luella herself.

M. R. James

MONTAGUE RHODES JAMES (1862-1936) was a medieval scholar and provost of King's College, Cambridge (and later Eton), regarded by many as the finest writer of ghost stories in the English language. He eliminated much of the Gothic claptrap associated with the genre, preferring historical settings. Here, in a story first published in James's collection *Ghost Stories of an Antiquary* (1904), an amateur antiquarian oversteps his bounds when he seeks to meet the title figure. While there is no specific mention of Magnus's vampiric traits, he is clearly one of the undead!

COUNT MAGNUS

M. R. JAMES

By what means the papers out of which I have made a connected story came into my hands is the last point which the reader will learn from these pages. But it is necessary to prefix to my extracts from them a statement of the form in which I possess them.

They consist, then, partly of a series of collections for a book of travels, such a volume as was a common product of the forties and fifties. Horace Marryat's *Journal of a Residence in Jutland and the Danish Isles* is a fair specimen of the class to which I allude. These books usually treated of some unfamiliar district on the Continent. They were illustrated with woodcuts or steel plates. They gave details of hotel accommodation, and of means of communication, such as we now expect to find in any well-regulated guidebook, and they dealt largely in reported conversations with intelligent foreigners, racy innkeepers and garrulous peasants. In a word, they were chatty.

Begun with the idea of furnishing material for such a book, my papers as they progressed assumed the character of a record of one single personal experience, and this record was continued up to the very eve, almost, of its termination.

The writer was a Mr. Wraxall. For my knowledge of him I have to depend entirely on the evidence his writings afford, and from these I deduce that he was a man past middle age, possessed of some private means, and very much alone in the world. He had, it seems, no settled abode in England, but was a denizen of hotels and boarding-houses.

It is probable that he entertained the idea of settling down at some future time which never came; and I think it also likely that the Pantechnicon fire[1] in the early seventies must have destroyed a great deal that would have thrown light on his antecedents, for he refers once or twice to property of his that was warehoused at that establishment.

---

[1] The Pantechnicon was a large warehouse in Belgravia, London. It burnt on February 13, 1874.

It is further apparent that Mr. Wraxall had published a book, and that it treated of a holiday he had once taken in Brittany. More than this I cannot say about his work, because a diligent search in bibliographical works has convinced me that it must have appeared either anonymously or under a pseudonym.

As to his character, it is not difficult to form some superficial opinion. He must have been an intelligent and cultivated man. It seems that he was near being a Fellow of his college at Oxford—Brasenose, as I judge from the Calendar. His besetting fault was pretty clearly that of over-inquisitiveness, possibly a good fault in a traveller, certainly a fault for which this traveller paid dearly enough in the end.

On what proved to be his last expedition, he was plotting another book. Scandinavia, a region not widely known to Englishmen forty years ago, had struck him as an interesting field. He must have lighted on some old books of Swedish history or memoirs, and the idea had struck him that there was room for a book descriptive of travel in Sweden, interspersed with episodes from the history of some of the great Swedish families. He procured letters of introduction, therefore, to some persons of quality in Sweden, and set out thither in the early summer of 1863.

Of his travels in the North there is no need to speak, nor of his residence of some weeks in Stockholm. I need only mention that some *savant* resident there put him on the track of an important collection of family papers belonging to the proprietors of an ancient manor-house in Vestergothland, and

obtained for him permission to examine them.

The manor-house, or *herrgård*, in question is to be called Råbäck (pronounced something like Roebeck), though that is not its name. It is one of the best buildings of its kind in all the country, and the picture of it in Dahlenberg's *Suecia antiqua et moderna*,[2] engraved in 1694, shows it very much as the tourist may see it today. It was built soon after 1600, and is, roughly speaking, very much like an English house of that period in respect of material—red-brick with stone facings—and style. The man who built it was a scion of the great house of de la Gardie, and his descendants possess it still. De la Gardie is the name by which I will designate them when mention of them becomes necessary.

They received Mr. Wraxall with great kindness and courtesy, and pressed him to stay in the house as long as his researches lasted. But, preferring to be independent, and mistrusting his powers of conversing in Swedish, he settled himself at the village inn, which turned out quite sufficiently comfortable, at any rate during the summer months. This arrangement would entail a short walk daily to and from the manor-house of something under a mile.

The house itself stood in a park, and was protected—we should say grown up—with large old timber. Near it you found the walled garden, and then entered a close wood fringing one of the small lakes with which the whole country is pitted. Then came the wall of the demesne,[3] and you climbed a steep knoll—a knob of rock lightly covered with

---

[2] First published in 1715, Erik Dahlberg's *Suecia antiqua et hodierna* (*Sweden ancient and modern*) is the most renowned architectural and topographical documentation of Sweden during the age of imperial greatness, with some 400 copperplate engravings and etchings.

[3] The property line.

soil—and on the top of this stood the church, fenced in with tall dark trees. It was a curious building to English eyes. The nave and aisles were low, and filled with pews and galleries. In the western gallery stood the handsome old organ, gaily painted, and with silver pipes.

The ceiling was flat, and had been adorned by a seventeenth-century artist with a strange and hideous "Last Judgment," full of lurid flames, falling cities, burning ships, crying souls, and brown and smiling demons. Handsome brass coronæ hung from the roof; the pulpit was like a doll's house, covered with little painted wooden cherubs and saints; a stand with three hour-glasses was hinged to the preacher's desk. Such sights as these may be seen in many a church in Sweden now, but what distinguished this one was an addition to the original building.

At the eastern end of the north aisle the builder of the manor-house had erected a mausoleum for himself and his family. It was a largish eight-sided building, lighted by a series of oval windows, and it had a domed roof, topped by a kind of pumpkin-shaped object rising into a spire, a form in which Swedish architects greatly delighted. The roof was of copper externally, and was painted black, while the walls, in common with those of the church, were staringly white. To this mausoleum there was no access from the church. It had a portal and steps of its own on the northern side.

Past the churchyard the path to the village goes, and not more than three or four minutes bring you to the inn door.

On the first day of his stay at Råbäck, Mr. Wraxall found the church door open, and made those notes of the interior which I have epitomized. Into the mausoleum, however, he could not make his way. He could by looking through the keyhole just descry that there were fine marble effigies and sarcophagi of copper, and a wealth of armorial ornament, which made him very anxious to spend some time in investigation.

The papers he had come to examine at the manor-house proved to be of just the kind he wanted for his book. There were family correspondence, journals, and account-books of the earliest owners of the estate, very carefully kept and clearly written, full of amusing and picturesque detail.

The first de la Gardie appeared in them as a strong and capable man. Shortly after the building of the mansion there had been a period of distress in the district, and the peasants had risen and attacked several chateaux and done some damage. The owner of Råbäck took a leading part in suppressing the trouble, and there was reference to executions of ringleaders and severe punishments inflicted with no sparing hand.

The portrait of this Magnus de la Gardie was one of the best in the house, and Mr. Wraxall studied it with no little interest after his day's work. He gives no detailed description of it, but I gather that the face impressed him rather by its power than by its beauty or goodness; in fact, he writes that Count Magnus was an almost phenomenally ugly man.

On this day Mr. Wraxall took his supper with the family, and walked back in the late but still bright evening.

"I must remember," he writes, "to ask the sexton if he can let me into the mausoleum at the church. He evidently has access to it himself, for I saw him tonight standing on the steps, and, as I thought, locking or unlocking the door."

I find that early on the following day Mr. Wraxall had some conversation with his landlord. His setting it down at such length as he does surprised me at first; but I soon realized that the papers I was reading were, at least in their beginning, the materials for the book he was meditating, and that it was to have been one of those quasi-journalistic productions which admit of the introduction of an admixture of conversational matter.

His object, he says, was to find out whether any traditions of Count Magnus de la Gardie lingered on in the scenes of that gentleman's activity, and whether the popular estimate of him were favorable or not. He found that the Count was decidedly not a favorite. If his tenants came late to their work on the days which they owed to him as Lord of the Manor, they were set on the wooden horse, or flogged and branded in the manor-house yard. One or two cases there were of men who had occupied lands which encroached on the lord's domain, and whose houses had been mysteriously burnt on a winter's night, with the whole family inside. But what seemed to dwell on the innkeeper's mind most—for he returned to the subject more than once—was that the Count had been on the Black Pilgrimage, and had brought something or someone back with him.

You will naturally inquire, as Mr. Wraxall did, what the Black Pilgrimage may have been. But your curiosity on the point must remain unsatisfied for the time being, just as his did. The landlord was evidently unwilling to give a full answer, or indeed any answer, on the point, and, being called out for a moment, trotted off with obvious alacrity, only putting his head in at the door a few minutes afterwards to say that he was called away to Skara, and should not be back till evening.

So Mr. Wraxall had to go unsatisfied to his day's work at the manor-house. The papers on which he was just then engaged soon put his thoughts into another channel, for he had to occupy himself with glancing over the correspondence between Sophia Albertina in Stockholm and her married cousin Ulrica Leonora at Råbäck in the years 1705-1710. The letters were of exceptional interest from the light they threw upon the culture of that period in Sweden, as anyone can testify who has read the full edition of them in the publications of the Swedish Historical Manuscripts Commission.

In the afternoon he had done with these, and after returning the boxes in which they were kept to their places on the shelf, he proceeded, very naturally, to take down some of the volumes nearest to them, in order to determine which of them had best be his principal subject of investigation next day. The shelf he had hit upon was occupied mostly by a collection of account-books in the writing of the first Count Magnus. But one among them was not an account-book, but a book of alchemical and other tracts in another sixteenth-century hand.

Not being very familiar with alchemical literature, Mr. Wraxall spends much space which he might have spared in setting out the names and beginnings of the various treatises: The book of the Phœnix, book of the Thirty Words, book of the Toad, book of Miriam, Turba philosophorum, and so forth; and then he announces with a good deal of circumstance his delight at finding, on a leaf originally left blank near the middle of the book, some writing of Count Magnus himself headed "Liber nigræ peregrinationis."[4]

---

[4] The Book of the Black Pilgrimage. (The Pilgrimage itself is probably fictional.)

It is true that only a few lines were written, but there was quite enough to show that the landlord had that morning been referring to a belief at least as old as the time of Count Magnus, and probably shared by him. This is the English of what was written:

"If any man desires to obtain a long life, if he would obtain a faithful messenger and see the blood of his enemies, it is necessary that he should first go into the city of Chorazin, and there salute the prince…" Here there was an erasure of one word, not very thoroughly done, so that Mr. Wraxall felt pretty sure that he was right in reading it as *aëris* ("of the air").[5] But there was no more of the text copied, only a line in Latin: "Quære reliqua hujus materiei inter secretiora" (See the rest of this matter among the more private things).

It could not be denied that this threw a rather lurid light upon the tastes and beliefs of the Count; but to Mr. Wraxall, separated from him by nearly three centuries, the thought that he might have added to his general forcefulness alchemy, and to alchemy something like magic, only made him a more picturesque figure; and when, after a rather prolonged contemplation of his picture in the hall, Mr. Wraxall set out on his homeward way, his mind was full of the thought of Count Magnus. He had no eyes for his surroundings, no perception of the evening scents of the woods or the evening light on the lake; and when all of a sudden he pulled up short, he was astonished to find himself already at the gate of the churchyard, and within a few minutes of his dinner. His eyes fell on the mausoleum.

"Ah," he said, "Count Magnus, there you are. I should dearly like to see you."

"Like many solitary men," he writes, "I have a habit of talking to myself aloud; and, unlike some of the Greek and Latin particles, I do not expect an answer. Certainly, and perhaps fortunately in this case, there was neither voice nor any that regarded: only the woman who, I suppose, was cleaning up the church, dropped some metallic object on the floor, whose clang startled me. Count Magnus, I think, sleeps sound enough."

That same evening the landlord of the inn, who had heard Mr. Wraxall say that he wished to see the clerk or deacon (as he would be called in Sweden) of the parish, introduced him to that official in the inn parlor. A visit to the de la Gardie tomb-house was soon arranged for the next day, and a little general conversation ensued.

Mr. Wraxall, remembering that one function of Scandinavian deacons is to teach candidates for Confirmation, thought he would refresh his own memory on a Biblical point.

"Can you tell me," he said, "anything about Chorazin?"[6]

The deacon seemed startled, but readily reminded him how that village had once been denounced.

"To be sure," said Mr. Wraxall; "it is, I suppose, quite a ruin now?"

"So I expect," replied the deacon. "I have heard some of our old priests say that Antichrist is to be born there; and there are tales—"

"Ah! What tales are those?" Mr. Wraxall put in.

---

[5] The "prince of the power of the air" is Satan (Ephesians ii, 2).

[6] Mentioned in Matthew xi, 21-24, (and also in Luke x, 13-15), Chorazin has been identified with the village of Kerazeh, a couple of miles north of the northern end of the Sea of Galilee.

"Tales, I was going to say, which I have forgotten," said the deacon; and soon after that he said good night.

The landlord was now alone, and at Mr. Wraxall's mercy; and that inquirer was not inclined to spare him.

"Herr Nielsen," he said, "I have found out something about the Black Pilgrimage. You may as well tell me what you know. What did the Count bring back with him?"

Swedes are habitually slow, perhaps, in answering, or perhaps the landlord was an exception. I am not sure; but Mr. Wraxall notes that the landlord spent at least one minute in looking at him before he said anything at all. Then he came close up to his guest, and with a good deal of effort he spoke:—

"Mr. Wraxall, I can tell you this one little tale, and no more—not any more. You must not ask anything when I have done. In my grandfather's time—that is, ninety-two years ago—there were two men who said: 'The Count is dead; we do not care for him. We will go tonight and have a free hunt in his wood'—the long wood on the hill that you have seen behind Råbäck. Well, those that heard them say this, they said: 'No, do not go; we are sure you will meet with persons walking who should not be walking. They should be resting, not walking.' These men laughed. There were no forest-men to keep the wood, because no one wished to hunt there. The family was not here at the house. These men could do what they wished.

"Very well, they go to the wood that night. My grandfather was sitting here in this room. It was the summer, and a light night. With the window open, he could see out to the wood, and hear.

"So he sat there, and two or three men with him, and they listened. At first they hear nothing at all; then they hear someone—you know how far away it is—they hear someone scream, just as if the most inside part of his soul was twisted out of him. All of them in the room caught hold of each other, and they sat so for three-quarters of an hour. Then they hear someone else, only about three hundred ells[7] off. They hear him laugh out loud: it was not one of those two men that laughed, and, indeed, they have all of them said that it was not any man at all. After that they hear a great door shut.

"Then, when it was just light with the sun, they all went to the priest. They said to him: —

"'Father, put on your gown and your ruff, and come to bury these men, Anders Bjornsen and Hans Thorbjorn.'

"You understand that they were sure these men were dead. So they went to the wood—my grandfather never forgot this. He said they were all like so many dead men themselves. The priest, too, he was in a white fear. He said when they came to him:

"'I heard one cry in the night, and I heard one laugh afterwards. If I cannot forget that, I shall not be able to sleep again.'

"So they went to the wood, and they found these men on the edge of the wood. Hans Thorbjorn was standing with his back against a tree, and all the time he was pushing with his hands—pushing something away from him which was not there. So he was not dead. And they led him away, and took him to the house at Nykjoping, and he died before the winter; but he went on pushing with his hands. Also Anders Bjornsen was there; but

---

[7] Unit of measure (usually of cloth); the German ell is an arm's length; the English ell is twice that.

he was dead. And I tell you this about Anders Bjornsen, that he was once a beautiful man, but now his face was not there, because the flesh of it was sucked away off the bones. You understand that? My grandfather did not forget that. And they laid him on the bier which they brought, and they put a cloth over his head, and the priest walked before; and they began to sing the psalm for the dead as well as they could. So, as they were singing the end of the first verse, one fell down, who was carrying the head of the bier, and the others looked back, and they saw that the cloth had fallen off, and the eyes of Anders Bjornsen were looking up, because there was nothing to close over them. And this they could not bear. Therefore the priest laid the cloth upon him, and sent for a spade, and they buried him in that place."

The next day Mr. Wraxall records that the deacon called for him soon after his breakfast, and took him to the church and mausoleum. He noticed that the key of the latter was hung on a nail just by the pulpit, and it occurred to him that, as the church door seemed to be left unlocked as a rule, it would not be difficult for him to pay a second and more private visit to the monuments if there proved to be more of interest among them than could be digested at first. The building, when he entered it, he found not unimposing. The monuments, mostly large erections of the seventeenth and eighteenth centuries, were dignified if luxuriant, and the epitaphs and heraldry were copious.

The central space of the domed room was occupied by three copper sarcophagi, covered with finely-engraved ornament. Two of them had, as is commonly the case in Denmark and Sweden, a large metal crucifix on the lid. The third, that of Count Magnus,

as it appeared, had, instead of that, a full-length effigy engraved upon it, and round the edge were several bands of similar ornament representing various scenes. One was a battle, with cannon belching out smoke, and walled towns, and troops of pikemen. Another showed an execution. In a third, among trees, was a man running at full speed, with flying hair and outstretched hands. After him followed a strange form; it would be hard to say whether the artist had intended it for a man, and was unable to give the requisite similitude, or whether it was intentionally made as monstrous as it looked.

In view of the skill with which the rest of the drawing was done, Mr. Wraxall felt inclined to adopt the latter idea. The figure was unduly short, and was for the most part muffled in a hooded garment which swept the ground. The only part of the form which projected from that shelter was not shaped like any hand or arm. Mr. Wraxall compares it to the tentacle of a devil-fish, and continues:

"On seeing this, I said to myself, 'This, then, which is evidently an allegorical representation of some kind—a fiend pursuing a hunted soul—may be the origin of the story of Count Magnus and his mysterious companion. Let us see how the huntsman is pictured: doubtless it will be a demon blowing his horn.'" But, as it turned out, there was no such sensational figure, only the semblance of a cloaked man on a hillock, who stood leaning on a stick, and watching the hunt with an interest which the engraver had tried to express in his attitude.

Mr. Wraxall noted the finely-worked and massive steel padlocks—three in number—which secured the sarcophagus. One of them, he saw, was detached, and lay on the pavement. And then, unwilling to delay the deacon longer or to waste his own work-ing-time, he made his way onward to the manor-house.

"It is curious," he notes, "how on retrac-ing a familiar path one's thoughts engross one to the absolute exclusion of surrounding objects. Tonight, for the second time, I had entirely failed to notice where I was going (I had planned a private visit to the tomb-house to copy the epitaphs), when I suddenly, as it were, awoke to consciousness, and found my-self (as before) turning in at the churchyard gate, and, I believe, singing or chanting some such words as, 'Are you awake, Count Mag-nus? Are you asleep, Count Magnus?' and then something more which I have failed to recollect. It seemed to me that I must have been behaving in this nonsensical way for some time."

He found the key of the mausoleum where he had expected to find it, and copied the greater part of what he wanted; in fact, he stayed until the light began to fail him.

"I must have been wrong," he writes, "in saying that one of the padlocks of my Count's sarcophagus was unfastened; I see tonight that two are loose. I picked both up, and laid them carefully on the window-ledge, after trying unsuccessfully to close them. The remaining one is still firm, and, though I take it to be a spring lock, I cannot guess how it is opened. Had I succeeded in undoing it, I am almost afraid I should have taken the liberty of open-ing the sarcophagus. It is strange, the interest I feel in the personality of this, I fear, some-what ferocious and grim old noble."

The day following was, as it turned out, the last of Mr. Wraxall's stay at Råbäck. He received letters connected with certain invest-ments which made it desirable that he should return to England; his work among the papers

was practically done, and travelling was slow. He decided, therefore, to make his farewells, put some finishing touches to his notes, and be off.

These finishing touches and farewells, as it turned out, took more time than he had expected. The hospitable family insisted on his staying to dine with them—they dined at three—and it was verging on half-past six be-fore he was outside the iron gates of Råbäck. He dwelt on every step of his walk by the lake, determined to saturate himself, now that he trod it for the last time, in the sentiment of the place and hour. And when he reached the summit of the churchyard knoll, he lingered for many minutes, gazing at the limitless prospect of woods near and distant, all dark beneath a sky of liquid green.

When at last he turned to go, the thought struck him that surely he must bid farewell to Count Magnus as well as the rest of the de la Gardies. The church was but twenty yards away, and he knew where the key of the mau-soleum hung. It was not long before he was standing over the great copper coffin, and, as usual, talking to himself aloud. "You may have been a bit of a rascal in your time, Magnus," he was saying, "but for all that I should like to see you, or, rather—"

"Just at that instant," he says, "I felt a blow on my foot. Hastily enough I drew it back, and something fell on the pavement with a clash. It was the third, the last of the three padlocks which had fastened the sar-cophagus. I stooped to pick it up, and—Heaven is my witness that I am writing only the bare truth—before I had raised myself there was a sound of metal hinges creaking, and I distinctly saw the lid shifting upwards. I may have behaved like a coward, but I could not for my life stay for one moment.

"I was outside that dreadful building in less time than I can write—almost as quickly as I could have said—the words; and what frightens me yet more, I could not turn the key in the lock. As I sit here in my room noting these facts, I ask myself (it was not twenty minutes ago) whether that noise of creaking metal continued, and I cannot tell whether it did or not. I only know that there was something more than I have written that alarmed me, but whether it was sound or sight I am not able to remember. What is this that I have done?"

POOR MR. WRAXALL! He set out on his journey to England on the next day, as he had planned, and he reached England in safety; and yet, as I gather from his changed hand and inconsequent jottings, a broken man. One of several small notebooks that have come to me with his papers gives, not a key to, but a kind of inkling of, his experiences. Much of his journey was made by canal-boat, and I find not less than six painful attempts to enumerate and describe his fellow-passengers. The entries are of this kind:

> 24. Pastor of village in Skane. Usual black coat and soft black hat.
> 25. Commercial traveler from Stockholm going to Trollhattan. Black coat, brown hat.
> 26. Man in long black cloak, broad-leafed hat, very old-fashioned.

This entry is lined out, and a note added: "Perhaps identical with No. 13. Have not yet seen his face." On referring to No. 13, I find that he is a Roman priest in a cassock.

The net result of the reckoning is always the same. Twenty-eight people appear in the enumeration, one being always a man in a long black cloak and broad hat, and the other a "short figure in dark cloak and hood." On the other hand, it is always noted that only twenty-six passengers appear at meals, and that the man in the cloak is perhaps absent, and the short figure is certainly absent.

ON REACHING ENGLAND, it appears that Mr. Wraxall landed at Harwich, and that he resolved at once to put himself out of the reach of some person or persons whom he never specifies, but whom he had evidently come to regard as his pursuers. Accordingly he took a vehicle—it was a closed fly[8]—not trusting the railway, and drove across country to the village of Belchamp St. Paul. It was about nine o'clock on a moonlight August night when he neared the place.

He was sitting forward, and looking out of the window at the fields and thickets—there was little else to be seen—racing past him. Suddenly he came to a cross-road. At the corner two figures were standing motionless; both were in dark cloaks; the taller one wore a hat, the shorter a hood. He had no time to see their faces, nor did they make any motion that he could discern. Yet the horse shied violently and broke into a gallop, and Mr. Wraxall sank back into his seat in something like desperation. He had seen them before.

Arrived at Belchamp St. Paul, he was fortunate enough to find a decent furnished lodging, and for the next twenty-four hours he lived, comparatively speaking, in peace. His last notes were written on this day. They are too disjointed and exclamatory to be given here in full, but the substance of them is clear enough. He is expecting a visit from his pursuers—how or when he knows not—and his constant cry is "What has he done?" and

---

[8] A type of light hired carriage drawn by a single horse.

"Is there no hope?" Doctors, he knows, would call him mad, policemen would laugh at him. The parson is away. What can he do but lock his door and cry to God?

PEOPLE STILL REMEMBERED last year at Belchamp St. Paul how a strange gentleman came one evening in August years back; and how the next morning but one[9] he was found dead, and there was an inquest; and the jury that viewed the body fainted, seven of 'em did, and none of 'em wouldn't speak to what they see, and the verdict was visitation of God; and how the people as kep' the 'ouse moved out that same week, and went away from that part. But they do not, I think, know that any glimmer of light has ever been thrown, or could be thrown, on the mystery.

It so happened that last year the little house came into my hands as part of a legacy. It had stood empty since 1863, and there seemed no prospect of letting it; so I had it pulled down, and the papers of which I have given you an abstract were found in a forgotten cupboard under the window in the best bedroom.

❧❧

---

[9] Means "two mornings later."

F. Marion Crawford

F. MARION CRAWFORD (1854-1909), son of American sculptor Thomas Crawford and brother of writer Anne Crawford, Baroness Erich von Rabe, was born and raised in Italy and wrote many romances, including mystical tales and ghost stories. This story offers no explanation of why the vampire peasant-girl became so, and she is a pitiable creature, driven by love, saved from her fate from a peasant who fortunately knows the proper procedures for her despatch.

FOR THE BLOOD IS THE LIFE

F. MARION CRAWFORD

E HAD DINED at sunset on the broad roof of the old tower, because it was cooler there during the great heat of summer. Besides, the little kitchen was built at one corner of the great square platform, which made it more convenient than if the dishes had to be carried down the steep stone steps, broken in places and everywhere worn with age.

The tower was one of those built all down the west coast of Calabria by the Emperor Charles V early in the sixteenth century, to keep off the Barbary pirates, when the unbelievers were allied with Francis I against the Emperor and the Church. They have gone to ruin, a few still stand intact, and mine is one of the largest. How it came into my possession ten years ago, and why I spend a part of each year in it, are matters which do not concern this tale. The tower stands in one of the loneliest spots in southern Italy, at the extremity of a curving rocky promontory, which forms a small but safe natural harbor at the southern extremity of the Gulf of Policastro,

and just north of Cape Scalea, the birthplace of Judas Iscariot, according to the old local legend. The tower stands alone on this hooked spur of the rock, and there is not a house to be seen within three miles of it. When I go there I take a couple of sailors, one of whom is a fair cook, and when I am away it is in charge of a gnome-like little being who was once a miner and who attached himself to me long ago.

My friend, who sometimes visits me in my summer solitude, is an artist by profession, a Scandinavian by birth, and a cosmopolitan by force of circumstances. We had dined at sunset; the sunset glow had reddened and faded again, and the evening purple steeped the vast chain of the mountains that embrace the deep gulf to eastward and rear themselves higher and higher toward the south.

It was hot, and we sat at the landward corner of the platform, waiting for the night breeze to come down from the lower hills. The color sank out of the air, there was a little interval of deep-gray twilight, and a lamp sent a yellow streak from the open door of the kitchen, where the men were getting their supper.

Then the moon rose suddenly above the crest of the promontory, flooding the platform and lighting up every little spur of rock and knoll of grass below us, down to the edge of the motionless water. My friend lighted his pipe and sat looking at a spot on the hillside. I knew that he was looking at it, and for a long time past I had wondered whether he would ever see anything there that would fix his attention. I knew that spot well. It was clear that he was interested at last, though it was a long time before he spoke. Like most painters, he trusts to his own eyesight, as a lion trusts his strength and a stag his speed, and he is always disturbed when he cannot reconcile what he sees with what he believes that he ought to see.

"It's strange," he said. "Do you see that little mound just on this side of the boulder?"

"Yes," I said, and I guessed what was coming.

"It looks like a grave," observed Holger.

"Very true. It does look like a grave."

"Yes," continued my friend, his eyes still fixed on the spot. "But the strange thing is that I see the body lying on the top of it. Of course," continued Holger, turning his head on one side as artists do, "it must be an effect of light. In the first place, it is not a grave at all. Secondly, if it were, the body would be inside and not outside. Therefore, it's an effect of the moonlight. Don't you see it?"

"Perfectly; I always see it on moonlight nights."

"It doesn't seem to interest you much," said Holger.

"On the contrary, it does interest me, though I am used to it. You're not so far wrong, either. The mound is really a grave."

"Nonsense!" cried Holger, incredulously. "I suppose you'll tell me what I see lying on it is really a corpse!"

"No," I answered, "it's not. I know, because I have taken the trouble to go down and see."

"Then what is it?" asked Holger.

"It's nothing."

"You mean that it's an effect of light, I suppose?"

"Perhaps it is. But the inexplicable part of the matter is that it makes no difference whether the moon is rising or setting, or waxing or waning. If there's any moonlight at all, from east or west or overhead, so long as it shines on the grave you can see the outline of the body on top."

Holger stirred up his pipe with the point of his knife, and then used his finger for a stopper. When the tobacco burned well he rose from his chair.

"If you don't mind," he said, "I'll go down and take a look at it."

He left me, crossed the roof, and disappeared down the dark steps. I did not move, but sat looking down until he came out of the tower below. I heard him humming an old Danish song as he crossed the open space in the bright moonlight, going straight to the mysterious mound. When he was ten paces from it, Holger stopped short, made two steps forward, and then three or four backward, and then stopped again. I knew what that meant. He had reached the spot where the Thing ceased to be visible—where, as he would have said, the effect of light changed.

Then he went on till he reached the mound and stood upon it. I could see the Thing still, but it was no longer lying down; it was on its knees now, winding its white arms round Holger's body and looking up into his face. A cool breeze stirred my hair at that moment, as the night wind began to come down from the hills, but it felt like a breath from another world.

The Thing seemed to be trying to climb to its feet, helping itself up by Holger's body while he stood upright, quite unconscious of it and apparently looking toward the tower, which is very picturesque when the moonlight falls upon it on that side.

"Come along!" I shouted. "Don't stay there all night!"

It seemed to me that he moved reluctantly as he stepped from the mound, or else with difficulty. That was it. The Thing's arms were still round his waist, but its feet could not leave the grave. As he came slowly forward it was drawn and lengthened like a wreath of mist, thin and white, till I saw distinctly that Holger shook himself, as a man does who feels a chill. At the same instant a little wail of pain came to me on the breeze— it might have been the cry of the small owl that lives among the rocks—and the misty presence floated swiftly back from Holger's advancing figure and lay once more at its length upon the mound.

Again I felt the cool breeze in my hair, and this time an icy thrill of dread ran down my spine. I remembered very well that I had once gone down there alone in the moonlight; that presently, being near, I had seen nothing; that, like Holger, I had gone and had stood upon the mound; and I remembered how, when I came back, sure that there was nothing there, I had felt the sudden conviction that there was something after all if I would only look behind me. I remembered the strong temptation to look back, a temptation I had resisted as unworthy of a man of sense, until,

to get rid of it, I had shaken myself just as Holger did.

And now I knew that those white, misty arms had been round me too; I knew it in a flash, and I shuddered as I remembered that I had heard the night owl then too. But it had not been the night owl. It was the cry of the Thing.

I refilled my pipe and poured out a cup of strong southern wine; in less than a minute Holger was seated beside me again.

"Of course there's nothing there," he said, "but it's creepy, all the same. Do you know, when I was coming back I was so sure that there was something behind me that I wanted to turn round and look? It was an effort not to."

He laughed a little, knocked the ashes out of his pipe, and poured himself out some wine. For a while neither of us spoke, and the moon rose higher, and we both looked at the Thing that lay on the mound.

"You might make a story about that," said Holger after a long time.

"There is one," I answered. "If you're not sleepy, I'll tell it to you."

"Go ahead," said Holger, who likes stories.

OLD ALARIO WAS dying up there in the village behind the hill. You remember him, I have no doubt. They say that he made his money by selling sham jewelry in South America, and escaped with his gains when he was found out. Like all those fellows, if they bring anything back with them, he at once set to work to enlarge his house; and, as there are no masons here, he sent all the way to Paola for two workmen. They were a rough-looking pair of scoundrels—a Neapolitan who had lost one eye and a Sicilian with an old scar half an inch deep across his left cheek. I often saw them, for on Sundays they used to come down here and fish off the rocks.

When Alario caught the fever that killed him the masons were still at work. As he had agreed that part of their pay should be their board and lodging, he made them sleep in the house. His wife was dead, and he had an only son called Angelo, who was a much better sort than himself. Angelo was to marry the daughter of the richest man in the village, and, strange to say, though the marriage was arranged by their parents, the young people were said to be in love with each other.

For that matter, the whole village was in love with Angelo, and among the rest a wild, good-looking creature called Cristina, who was more like a gypsy than any girl I ever saw about here. She had very red lips and very black eyes, she was built like a greyhound, and had the tongue of the devil. But Angelo did not care a straw for her. He was rather a simple-minded fellow, quite different from his old scoundrel of a father, and under what I should call normal circumstances I really believe that he would never have looked at any girl except the nice plump little creature, with a fat dowry, whom his father meant him to marry. But things turned up which were neither normal nor natural.

On the other hand, a very handsome young shepherd from the hills above Maratea was in love with Cristina, who seems to have been quite indifferent to him. Cristina had no regular means of subsistence, but she was a good girl and willing to do any work or go on errands to any distance for the sake of a loaf of bread or a mess of beans, and permission to sleep under cover. She was especially glad when she could get something to do about the house of Angelo's father.

There is no doctor in the village, and when the neighbors saw that old Alario was dying they sent Cristina to Scalea to fetch one. That was late in the afternoon, and if they had waited so long, it was because the dying miser refused to allow any such extravagance while he was able to speak. But while Cristina was gone, matters grew rapidly worse, the priest was brought to the bedside, and when he had done what he could he gave it as his opinion to the bystanders that the old man was dead, and left the house.

You know these people. They have a physical horror of death. Until the priest spoke, the room had been full of people. The words were hardly out of his mouth before it was empty. It was night now. They hurried down the dark steps and out into the street.

Angelo was away, Cristina had not come back—the simple woman servant who had nursed the sick man fled with the rest, and the body was left alone in the flickering light of the earthen oil lamp.

Five minutes later two men looked in cautiously and crept forward toward the bed. They were the one-eyed Neapolitan mason and his Sicilian companion. They knew what they wanted. In a moment they had dragged from under the bed a small but heavy iron-bound box, and long before anyone thought of coming back to the dead man they had left the house and the village under cover of the darkness.

It was easy enough, for Alario's house is the last toward the gorge which leads down here, and the thieves merely went out by the back door, got over the stone wall, and had nothing to risk after that except the possibility of meeting some belated countryman, which was very small indeed, since few of the people use that path. They had a mattock[1] and shovel, and they made their way here without accident.

I am telling you this story as it must have happened, for, of course, there were no witnesses to this part of it. The men brought the box down by the gorge, intending to bury it until they should be able to come back and take it away in a boat. They must have been clever enough to guess that some of the money would be in paper notes, for they would otherwise have buried it on the beach in the wet sand, where it would have been much safer. But the paper would have rotted if they had been obliged to leave it there long, so they dug their hole down there, close to that boulder. Yes, just where the mound is now.

Cristina did not find the doctor in Scalea, for he had been sent for from a place up the valley, halfway to San Domenico. If she had found him, he would have come on his mule by the upper road, which is smoother but much longer. But Cristina took the short cut by the rocks, which passes about fifty feet above the mound, and goes round that corner. The men were digging when she passed, and she heard them at work. It would not have been like her to go by without finding out what the noise was, for she was never afraid of anything in her life, and, besides, the fishermen sometimes came ashore here at night to get a stone for an anchor or to gather sticks to make a little fire.

The night was dark, and Cristina probably came close to the two men before she could see what they were doing. She knew them, of course, and they knew her, and understood instantly that they were in her

power. There was only one thing to be done for their safety, and they did it. They knocked her on the head, they dug the hole deep, and they buried her quickly with the iron-bound chest.

They must have understood that their only chance of escaping suspicion lay in getting back to the village before their absence was noticed, for they returned immediately, and were found half an hour later gossiping quietly with the man who was making Alario's coffin. He was a crony of theirs, and had been working at the repairs in the old man's house. So far as I have been able to make out, the only persons who were supposed to know where Alario kept his treasure were Angelo and the one woman servant I have mentioned. Angelo was away; it was the woman who discovered the theft.

It is easy enough to understand why no one else knew where the money was. The old man kept his door locked and the key in his pocket when he was out, and did not let the woman enter to clean the place unless he was there himself. The whole village knew that he had money somewhere, however, and the masons had probably discovered the whereabouts of the chest by climbing in at the window in his absence. If the old man had not been delirious until he lost consciousness, he would have been in frightful agony of mind for his riches. The faithful woman servant forgot their existence only for a few moments when she fled with the rest, overcome by the horror of death. Twenty minutes had not passed before she returned with the two hideous old hags who are always called in to prepare the dead for burial. Even then she had not at first the courage to go near the bed with them, but she made a pretense of dropping something, went down on her

---

[1] Type of pickax with one broad end for digging.

knees as if to find it, and looked under the bedstead. The walls of the room were newly whitewashed down to the floor, and she saw at a glance that the chest was gone. It had been there in the afternoon, it had therefore been stolen in the short interval since she had left the room.

There are no carabineers[2] stationed in the village; there is not so much as a municipal watchman, for there is no municipality. There never was such a place, I believe. Scalea is supposed to look after it in some mysterious way, and it takes a couple of hours to get anybody from there. As the old woman had lived in the village all her life, it did not even occur to her to apply to any civil authority for help. She simply set up a howl and ran through the village in the dark, screaming out that her dead master's house had been robbed. Many of the people looked out, but at first no one seemed inclined to help her. Most of them, judging her by themselves, whispered to each other that she had probably stolen the money herself.

The first man to move was the father of the girl whom Angelo was to marry; having collected his household, all of whom felt a personal interest in the wealth which was to have come into the family, he declared it to be his opinion that the chest had been stolen by the two journeyman masons who lodged in the house. He headed a search for them, which naturally began in Alario's house and ended in the carpenter's workshop, where the thieves were found discussing a measure of wine with the carpenter over the half-finished coffin, by the light of one earthen lamp filled with oil and tallow.

The search party at once accused the

delinquents of the crime, and threatened to lock them up in the cellar till the carabineers could be fetched from Scalea. The two men looked at each other for one moment, and then without the slightest hesitation they put out the single light, seized the unfinished coffin between them, and using it as a sort of battering ram, dashed upon their assailants in the dark. In a few moments they were beyond pursuit.

That is the end of the first part of the story. The treasure had disappeared, and as no trace of it could be found the people naturally supposed that the thieves had succeeded in carrying it off. The old man was buried, and when Angelo came back at last he had to borrow money to pay for the miserable funeral, and had some difficulty in doing so. He hardly needed to be told that in losing his inheritance he had lost his bride. In this part of the world marriages are made on strictly business principles, and if the promised cash is not forthcoming on the appointed day the bride or the bridegroom whose parents have failed to produce it may as well take themselves off, for there will be no wedding.

Poor Angelo knew that well enough. His father had been possessed of hardly any land, and now that the hard cash which he had brought from South America was gone, there was nothing left but debts for the building materials that were to have been used for enlarging and improving the old house. Angelo was beggared, and the nice plump little creature who was to have been his turned up her nose at him in the most approved fashion.

As for Cristina, it was several days before she was missed, for no one remembered that she had been sent to Scalea for the doctor, who had never come. She often disappeared in the same way for days together, when she

---

[2] Soldiers serving as a police force.

could find a little work here and there at the distant farms among the hills. But when she did not come back at all, people began to wonder, and at last made up their minds that she had connived with the masons and had escaped with them.

I PAUSED AND emptied my glass.

"That sort of thing could not happen anywhere else," observed Holger, filling his everlasting pipe again. "It is wonderful what a natural charm there is about murder and sudden death in a romantic country like this. Deeds that would be simply brutal and disgusting anywhere else become dramatic and mysterious because this is Italy and we are living in a genuine tower of Charles V built against genuine Barbary pirates."

"There's something in that," I admitted. Holger is the most romantic man in the world inside of himself, but he always thinks it necessary to explain why he feels anything.

"I suppose they found the poor girl's body with the box," he said presently.

"As it seems to interest you," I answered, "I'll tell you the rest of the story."

The moon had risen high by this time; the outline of the Thing on the mound was clearer to our eyes than before.

THE VILLAGE VERY SOON settled down to its small, dull life. No one missed old Alario, who had been away so much on his voyages to South America that he had never been a familiar figure in his native place. Angelo lived in the half-finished house, and because he had no money to pay the old woman servant she would not stay with him, but once in a long time she would come and wash a shirt for him for old acquaintance' sake. Besides the house, he had inherited a small patch of ground at some distance from the village; he tried to cultivate it, but he had no heart in the work, for he knew he could never pay the taxes on it and on the house, which would certainly be confiscated by the Government, or seized for the debt of the building material, which the man who had supplied it refused to take back.

Angelo was very unhappy. So long as his father had been alive and rich, every girl in the village had been in love with him; but that was all changed now. It had been pleasant to be admired and courted, and invited to drink wine by fathers who had girls to marry. It was hard to be stared at coldly, and sometimes laughed at because he had been robbed of his inheritance. He cooked his miserable meals for himself, and from being sad became melancholy and morose.

At twilight, when the day's work was done, instead of hanging about in the open space before the church with young fellows of his own age, he took to wandering in lonely places on the outskirts of the village till it was quite dark. Then he slunk home and went to bed to save the expense of a light. But in those lonely twilight hours he began to have strange waking dreams.

He was not always alone, for often when he sat on the stump of a tree, where the narrow path turns down the gorge, he was sure that a woman came up noiselessly over the rough stones, as if her feet were bare; and she stood under a clump of chestnut trees only half a dozen yards down the path, and beckoned to him without speaking. Though she was in the shadow he knew that her lips were red, and that when they parted a little and smiled at him she showed two small sharp teeth. He knew this at first rather than saw it, and he knew that it was Cristina, and that she was dead. Yet he was not afraid; he only wondered whether it was a dream, for he thought that if he had been awake he should have been frightened.

Besides, the dead woman had red lips, and that could only happen in a dream. Whenever he went near the gorge after sunset she was already there waiting for him, or else she very soon appeared, and he began to be sure that she came a little nearer to him every day. At first he had only been sure of her blood-red mouth, but now each feature grew distinct, and the pale face looked at him with deep and hungry eyes.

It was the eyes that grew dim. Little by little he came to know that some day the dream would not end when he turned away to go home, but would lead him down the gorge out of which the vision rose. She was nearer now when she beckoned to him. Her cheeks were not livid like those of the dead, but pale with starvation, with the furious and unappeased physical hunger of her eyes that devoured him. They feasted on his soul and cast a spell over him, and at last they were close to his own and held them.

He could not tell whether her breath was as hot as fire or as cold as ice; he could not tell whether her red lips burned his or froze them, or whether her five fingers on his wrists seared scorching scars or bit his flesh like frost; he could not tell whether he was awake or asleep, whether she was alive or dead, but he knew that she loved him, she alone of all creatures, earthly or unearthly, and her spell had power over him.

When the moon rose high that night the shadow of that Thing was not alone down there upon the mound.

Angelo awoke in the cool dawn, drenched with dew and chilled through flesh, and blood, and bone. He opened his eyes to the faint gray light, and saw the stars still shining overhead. He was very weak, and his heart was beating so slowly that he was almost like a man fainting. Slowly he turned his head on the mound, as on a pillow, but the other face was not there. Fear seized him suddenly, a fear unspeakable and unknown; he sprang to his feet and fled up the gorge, and he never looked behind him until he reached the door of the house on the outskirts of the village. Drearily he went to his work that day, and wearily the hours dragged themselves after the sun, till at last it touched the sea and sank, and the great sharp hills above Maratea turned purple against the dove-colored eastern sky.

Angelo shouldered his heavy hoe and left the field. He felt less tired now than in the morning when he had begun to work, but he promised himself that he would go home without lingering by the gorge, and eat the best supper he could get himself, and sleep all night in his bed like a Christian man. Not again would he be tempted down the narrow way by a shadow with red lips and icy breath; not again would he dream that dream of terror and delight.

He was near the village now; it was half an hour since the sun had set, and the cracked church bell sent little discordant echoes across the rocks and ravines to tell all good people that the day was done. Angelo stood still a moment where the path forked, where it led toward the village on the left, and down to the gorge on the right, where a clump of chestnut trees overhung the narrow way. He stood still a minute, lifting his battered hat from his head and gazing at the fast-fading sea westward, and his lips moved as he silently repeated the familiar evening prayer.

His lips moved, but the words that followed them in his brain lost their meaning and turned into others, and ended in a name that he spoke aloud—Cristina! With the name, the tension of his will relaxed suddenly, reality went out and the dream took him again and bore him on swiftly and surely like a man walking in his sleep, down, down, by the steep path in the gathering darkness. And as she glided beside him, Cristina whispered strange sweet things in his ear, which somehow, if he had been awake, he knew that he could not quite have understood; but now they were the most wonderful words he had ever heard in his life.

And she kissed him also, but not upon his mouth. He felt her sharp kisses upon his white throat, and he knew that her lips were red. So the wild dream sped on through twilight and darkness and moonrise, and all the glory of the summer's night. But in the chilly dawn he lay as one half dead upon the mound down there, recalling and not recalling, drained of his blood, yet strangely longing to give those red lips more.

Then came the fear, the awful nameless panic, the mortal horror that guards the confines of the world we see not, neither know of as we know of other things, but which we feel when its icy chill freezes our bones and stirs our hair with the touch of a ghostly hand. Once more Angelo sprang from the mound and fled up the gorge in the breaking day, but his step was less sure this time, and he panted for breath as he ran; and when he came to the bright spring of water that rises halfway up the hillside, he dropped upon his knees and hands and plunged his whole face in and drank as he had never drunk before—for it was the thirst of the wounded man who has lain bleeding all night long upon the battlefield.

She had him fast now, and he could not escape her, but would come to her every evening at dusk until she had drained him of his last drop of blood. It was in vain that when the day was done he tried to take another turning and to go home by a path that did not lead near the gorge.

It was in vain that he made promises to himself each morning at dawn when he climbed the lonely way up from the shore to the village. It was all in vain, for when the sun sank burning into the sea, and the coolness of the evening stole out as from a hiding-place to delight the weary world, his feet turned toward the old way, and she was waiting for him in the shadow under the chestnut trees; and then all happened as before, and she fell to kissing his white throat even as she flitted lightly down the way, winding one arm about him.

And as his blood failed, she grew more hungry and more thirsty every day, and every day when he awoke in the early dawn it was harder to rouse himself to the effort of climbing the steep path to the village; and when he went to his work his feet dragged painfully, and there was hardly strength in his arms to wield the heavy hoe. He scarcely spoke to any one now, but the people said he was "consuming himself" for love of the girl he was to have married when he lost his inheritance; and they laughed heartily at the thought, for this is not a very romantic country.

At this time, Antonio, the man who stays here to look after the tower, returned from a visit to his people, who live near Salerno. He had been away all the time since before Alario's death and knew nothing of what had happened. He has told me that he came back late in the afternoon and shut himself up in the tower to eat and sleep, for he was very tired. It was past midnight when he awoke, and when he looked out the wailing moon was rising over the shoulder of the hill. He looked out toward the mound, and he saw something, and he did not sleep again that night. When he went out again in the morning it was broad daylight, and there was nothing to be seen on the mound but loose stones and driven sand. Yet he did not go very near it; he went straight up the path to the village and directly to the house of the old priest.

"I have seen an evil thing this night," he said; "I have seen how the dead drink the blood of the living. And the blood is the life."[3]

"Tell me what you have seen," said the priest in reply.

Antonio told him everything he had seen.

"You must bring your book and your holy water tonight," he added. "I will be here before sunset to go down with you, and if it pleases your reverence to sup with me while we wait, I will make ready."

"I will come," the priest answered, "for I have read in old books of these strange beings which are neither quick nor dead,[4] and which lie ever fresh in their graves, stealing out in the dusk to taste life and blood."

Antonio cannot read, but he was glad to see that the priest understood the business; for, of course, the books must have instructed him as to the best means of quieting the half-living Thing forever.

So Antonio went away to his work, which consists largely in sitting on the shady side of the tower, when he is not perched upon a rock with a fishing line catching nothing. But on that day he went twice to look at the mound in the bright sunlight, and he searched round and round it for some hole through which the being might get in and out; but he found none.

When the sun began to sink and the air was cooler in the shadows, he went up to fetch the old priest, carrying a little wicker basket with him; and in this they placed a bottle of holy water, and the basin, and sprinkler, and the stole which the priest would need; and they came down and waited in the door of the tower till it should be dark. But while the light still lingered very gray and faint, they saw something moving, just there, two figures, a man's that walked, and a woman's that flitted beside him, and while her head lay on his shoulder she kissed his throat.

The priest has told me that, too, and that his teeth chattered and he grasped Antonio's arm. The vision passed and disappeared into the shadow. Then Antonio got the leathern flask of strong liquor, which he kept for great occasions, and poured such a draught as made the old man feel almost young again; and he got the lantern, and his pick and shovel, and gave the priest his stole to put on and the holy water to carry, and they went out together toward the spot where the work was to be done.

Antonio says that in spite of the rum his

---

[3] This phrase appears in *Dracula* as well, spoken by Renfield. The Biblical source is a *prohibition* on the consumption of blood: "For the life of the flesh is in the blood...Therefore I said unto the children of Israel, No soul of you shall eat blood, neither shall any stranger that sojourneth among you eat blood" (Leviticus 17:11-12).

[4] "The quick and the dead" (from King James Bible, Acts 10:42, and the Apostles' Creed) refers to the *living* and the dead (not the *fast* and the dead). This meaning of "quick" comes from "the quickening," a term once used to describe the moment a baby is first felt moving in its mother's womb, when it was believed to have "come alive." The priest is describing creatures that are neither alive nor dead, namely vampires.

own knees shook together, and the priest stumbled over his Latin. For when they were yet a few yards from the mound the flickering light of the lantern fell upon Angelo's white face, unconscious as if in sleep, and on his upturned throat, over which a very thin red line of blood trickled down into his collar; and the flickering light of the lantern played upon another face that looked up from the feast— upon two deep, dead eyes that saw in spite of death—upon parted lips redder than life itself—upon two gleaming teeth on which glistened a rosy drop.

Then the priest, good old man, shut his eyes tight and showered holy water before him, and his cracked voice rose almost to a scream; and then Antonio, who is no coward after all, raised his pick in one hand and the lantern in the other, as he sprang forward, not knowing what the end should be; and then he swears that he heard a woman's cry, and the Thing was gone, and Angelo lay alone on the mound unconscious, with the red line on his throat and the beads of deathly sweat on his cold forehead.

They lifted him, half-dead as he was, and laid him on the ground close by; then Antonio went to work, and the priest helped him, though he was old and could not do much; and they dug deep, and at last Antonio, standing in the grave, stooped down with his lantern to see what he might see.

His hair used to be dark brown, with grizzled streaks about the temples; in less than a month from that day he was as gray as a badger. He was a miner when he was young, and most of these fellows have seen ugly sights now and then, when accidents have happened, but he had never seen what he saw that night—that Thing which is neither alive nor dead, that Thing that will abide neither above ground nor in the grave.

Antonio had brought something with him which the priest had not noticed. He had made it that afternoon—a sharp stake shaped from a piece of tough old driftwood. He had it with him now, and he had his heavy pick, and he had taken the lantern down into the grave. I don't think any power on earth could make him speak of what happened then, and the old priest was too frightened to look in. He says he heard Antonio breathing like a wild beast, and moving as if he were fighting with something almost as strong as himself; and he heard an evil sound also, with blows, as of something violently driven through flesh and bone; and then the most awful sound of all—a woman's shriek, the unearthly scream of a woman neither dead nor alive, but buried deep for many days.

And he, the poor old priest, could only rock himself as he knelt there in the sand, crying aloud his prayers and exorcisms to drown these dreadful sounds. Then suddenly a small iron-bound chest was thrown up and rolled over against the old man's knee, and in a moment more Antonio was beside him, his face as white as tallow in the flickering light of the lantern, shoveling the sand and pebbles into the grave with furious haste, and looking over the edge till the pit was half full; and the priest had said that there was much fresh blood on Antonio's hands and on his clothes.

I HAD COME TO the end of my story. Holger finished his wine and leaned back in his chair.

"So Angelo got his own again," he said. "Did he marry the prim and plump young person to whom he had been betrothed?"

"No; he had been badly frightened. He

went to South America, and has not been heard of since."

"And that poor thing's body is there still, I suppose," said Holger. "Is it quite dead yet, I wonder?"

I wonder, too. But whether it is dead or alive, I should hardly care to see it, even in broad daylight.

Antonio is as gray as a badger, and he has never been quite the same man since that night.

Algernon Blackwood

ALGERNON HENRY BLACKWOOD (1869-1951) was a prolific English writer of sixteen novels and over thirty volumes of ghost stories. He lived in Canada and New York for many years, returning to London at the age of thirty-six. His account of a trip up the Danube, "The Willows" (1907), was hailed by H.P. Lovecraft as the finest supernatural tale in English literature. "The Wendigo" (1910) has also achieved classic status, as did his stories about John Silence, a psychic detective.

First published in the December 1910 issue of *The Tramp* magazine, the following story perfectly combines Blackwood's twin interests in the outdoors and the occult.

THE SINGULAR DEATH OF MORTON

ALGERNON BLACKWOOD

Dusk was melting into darkness as the two men slowly made their way through the dense forest of spruce and fir that clothed the flanks of the mountain. They were weary with the long climb, for neither was in his first youth, and the July day had been a hot one. Their little inn lay further in the valley among the orchards that separated the forest from the vineyards.

Neither of them talked much. The big man led the way, carrying the knapsack, and his companion, older, shorter, evidently the more fatigued of the two, followed with small footsteps. From time to time he stumbled among the loose rocks. An exceptionally observant mind would possibly have divined that his stumbling was not entirely due to fatigue, but to an absorption of spirit that made him careless how he walked.

"All right behind?" the big man would call from time to time, half glancing back.

"Eh? What?" the other would reply, startled out of a reverie.

"Pace too fast?"

"Not a bit. I'm coming." And once he added: "You might hurry on and see to supper, if you feel like it. I shan't be long behind you."

But his big friend did not adopt the suggestion. He kept the same distance between them. He called out the same question at intervals. Once or twice he stopped and looked back too.

In this way they came at length to the skirts of the wood. A deep hush covered all the valley; the limestone ridges they had climbed gleamed down white and ghostly upon them from the fading sky. Midway in its journeys, the evening wind dropped suddenly to watch the beauty of the moonlight—to hold the branches still so that the light might slip between and weave its silver pattern on the moss below.

And, as they stood a moment to take it in, a step sounded behind them on the soft pine-needles, and the older man, still a little in the rear, turned with a start as though he had been suddenly called by name.

"There's that girl—again!" he said, and his voice expressed a curious mingling of pleasure, surprise, and—apprehension.

Into a patch of moonlight passed the figure of a young girl, looked at them as though about to stop yet thinking better of it, smiled softly, and moved on out of sight into the surrounding darkness. The moon just caught her eyes and teeth, so that they shone; the rest of her body stood in shadow; the effect was striking—almost as though head and shoulders hung alone in mid air, watching them with this shining smile, then fading away.

"Come on, for heaven's sake," the big man cried. There was impatience in his manner, not unkindness. The other lingered a moment, peering closely into the gloom where the girl had vanished. His friend repeated his injunction, and a moment later the two had emerged upon the high road with the village lights in sight beyond, and the forest left behind them like a vast mantle that held the night within its folds.

For some minutes neither of them spoke; then the big man waited for his friend to draw up alongside.

"About all this valley of the Jura," he said presently, "there seems to me something—rather weird." He shifted the knapsack vigorously on his back. It was a gesture of unconscious protest. "Something uncanny," he added, as he set a good pace.

"But extraordinarily beautiful—"

"It attracts you more than it does me, I think," was the short reply.

"The picturesque superstitions still survive here," observed the older man. "They touch the imagination in spite of oneself."

A pause followed during which the other tried to increase the pace. The subject evidently made him impatient for some reason.

"Perhaps," he said presently. "Though I think myself it's due to the curious loneliness of the place. I mean, we're in the middle of tourist-Europe here, yet so utterly remote. It's such a neglected little corner of the world. The contradiction bewilders. Then, being so near the frontier, too, with the clock changing an hour a mile from the village, makes one think of time as unreal and imaginary." He laughed. He produced several other reasons as well. His friend admitted their value, and agreed half-heartedly. He still turned occasionally to look back. The mountain ridge where they had climbed was clearly visible in the moonlight.

"Odd," he said, "but I don't see that farmhouse where we got the milk anywhere. It ought to be easily visible from here."

"Hardly—in this light. It was a queer place rather, I thought," he added. He did not deny the curiously suggestive atmosphere of the region, he merely wanted to find satisfactory explanations. "A case in point, I mean. I didn't like it quite—that farmhouse—yet I'm hanged if I know why. It made me feel uncomfortable. That girl appeared so suddenly, although the place seemed deserted. And her silence was so odd. Why in the world couldn't she answer a single question? I'm glad I didn't take the milk. I spat it out. I'd like to know where she got it from, for there was no sign of a cow or a goat to be seen anywhere!"

"I swallowed mine—in spite of the taste," said the other, half smiling at his companion's sudden volubility.

Very abruptly, then, the big man turned and faced his friend. Was it merely an effect of the moonlight, or had his skin really turned pale beneath the sunburn?

"I say, old man," he said, his face grave

and serious. "What do you think she was? What made her seem like that, and why the devil do you think she followed us?"

"I think," was the slow reply, "it was *me* she was following."

The words, and particularly the tone of conviction in which they were spoken, clearly were displeasing to the big man, who already regretted having spoken so frankly what was in his mind. With a companion so imaginative, so impressionable, so nervous, it had been foolish and unwise. He led the way home at a pace that made the other arrive five minutes in his rear, panting, limping, and perspiring as if he had been running.

"I'm rather for going on into Switzerland tomorrow, or the next day," he ventured that night in the darkness of their two-bedded room. "I think we've had enough of this place. Eh? What do you think?"

But there was no answer from the bed across the room, for its occupant was sound asleep and snoring.

"Dead tired, I suppose!" he muttered to himself, and then turned over to follow his friend's example. But for a long time sleep refused him. Strange, unwelcome thoughts and feelings kept him awake—of a kind he rarely knew, and thoroughly disliked. It was rubbish, yet it made him uncomfortable, so that his nerves tingled. He tossed about in the bed. "I'm overtired," he persuaded himself, "that's all."

The strange feelings that kept him thus awake were not easy to analyze, perhaps, but their origin was beyond all question: they grouped themselves about the picture of that deserted, tumble-down chalet on the mountain ridge where they had stopped for refreshment a few hours before. It was a farmhouse, dilapidated and dirty, and the name stood in

big black letters against a blue background on the wall above the door: "La Chenille."[1] Yet not a living soul was to be seen anywhere about it; the doors were fastened, windows shuttered; chimneys smokeless; dirt, neglect, and decay everywhere in evidence.

Then, suddenly, as they had turned to go, after much vain shouting and knocking at the door, a face appeared for an instant at a window, the shutter of which was half open. His friend saw it first, and called aloud. The face nodded in reply, and presently a young girl came round the corner of the house, apparently by a back door, and stood staring at them both from a little distance.

And from that very instant, so far as he could remember, these queer feelings had entered his heart—fear, distrust, misgiving. The thought of it now, as he lay in bed in the darkness, made his hair rise. There was something about that girl that struck cold into the soul. Yet she was a mere slip of a thing, very pretty, seductive even, with a certain serpent-like fascination about her eyes and movements; and although she only replied to their questions as to refreshment with a smile, uttering no single word, she managed to convey the impression that she was a managing little person who might make herself very disagreeable if she chose.

In spite of her undeniable charm there was about her an atmosphere of something sinister. He himself did most of the questioning, but it was his older friend who had the benefit of her smile. Her eyes hardly ever left his face, and once she had slipped quite close to him and touched his arm.

The strange part of it now seemed to him that he could not remember in the least

[1] "The Caterpillar."

how she was dressed, or what was the coloring of her eyes and hair. It was almost as though he had *felt*, rather than seen, her presence.

The milk—she produced a jug and two wooden bowls after a brief disappearance round the corner of the house—was—well, it tasted so odd that he had been unable to swallow it, and had spat it out. His friend, on the other hand, savage with thirst, had drunk his bowl to the last drop too quickly to taste it even, and, while he drank, had kept his eyes fixed on those of the girl, who stood close in front of him.

And from that moment his friend had somehow changed. On the way down he said things that were unusual, talking chiefly about the "Chenille," and the girl, and the delicious, delicate flavour of the milk, yet all phrased in such a way that it sounded singular, unfamiliar, unpleasant even. Now that he tried to recall the sentences the actual words evaded him; but the memory of the uneasiness and apprehension they caused him to feel remained. And night ever italicizes such memories!

Then, to cap it all, the girl had followed them. It was wholly foolish and absurd to feel the things he did feel, yet there the feelings were, and what was the good of arguing? That girl frightened him; the change in his friend was in some way or other a danger signal. More than this he could not tell. An explanation might come later, but for the present his chief desire was to get away from the place and to get his friend away, too.

And on this thought sleep overtook him—heavily.

The windows were wide open; outside was a garden with a rather high enclosing wall, and at the far end a gate that was kept locked because it led into private fields and so,

by a back way, to the cemetery and the little church. When it was open the guests of the inn made use of it and got lost in the network of fields and vines, for there was no proper route that way to the road or the mountains. They usually ended up prematurely in the cemetery, and got back to the village by passing through the church, which was always open; or by knocking at the kitchen doors of the other houses and explaining their position. Hence the gate was locked now to save trouble.

After several hours of hot, unrefreshing sleep the big man turned in his bed and woke. He tried to stretch, but couldn't; then sat up panting with a sense of suffocation. And by the faint starlight of the summer night, he saw next that his friend was up and moving about the room. Remembering that sometimes he walked in his sleep; he called to him gently:

"Morton, old chap," he said in a low voice, with a touch of authority in it, "go back to bed! You've walked enough for one day!"

And the figure, obeying as sleep-walkers often will, passed across the room and disappeared among the shadows over his bed. The other plunged and burrowed himself into a comfortable position again for sleep, but the heat of the room, the shortness of the bed, and this tiresome interruption of his slumbers made it difficult to lose consciousness. He forced his eyes to keep shut, and his body to cease from fidgeting, but there was something nibbling at his mind like a spirit mouse that never permitted him to cross the frontier into actual oblivion. He slept with one eye open, as the saying is. Odors of hay and flowers and baked ground stole in through the open window; with them, too, came from time to time sounds—little sounds that disturbed him without being ever loud enough to claim definite attention.

Perhaps, after all, he did lose consciousness for a moment—when, suddenly, a thought came with a sharp rush into his mind and galvanized him once more into utter wakefulness. It amazed him that he had not grasped it before. It was this: the figure he had seen was *not the figure of his friend*.

Alarm gripped him at once before he could think or argue, and a cold perspiration broke out all over his body. He fumbled for matches, couldn't find them; then, remembering there was electric light, he scraped the wall with his fingers—and turned on the little white switch. In the sudden glare that filled the room he saw instantly that his friend's bed was no longer occupied. And his mind, then acting instinctively, without process of conscious reasoning, flew like a flash to their walk of the day—to the tumble-down "Chenille," the glass of milk, the odd behavior of his friend, and—to the girl.

At the same second he noticed that the odor in the room which hitherto he had taken to be the composite odor of fields, flowers, and night was really something else: it was the odor of freshly turned earth. Immediately on the top of this discovery came another. Those slight sounds he had heard outside the window were not ordinary night-sounds, the murmur of wind and insects: they were footsteps moving softly, stealthily down the little paths of crushed granite.

He was dressed in wonderful short order, noticing as he did so that his friend's night-garments lay upon the bed, and that he, too, had therefore dressed; further—that the door had been unlocked and stood half an inch ajar. There was now no question that he *had* slept again: between the present and the moment

when he had seen the figure there had been a considerable interval.

A couple of minutes later he had made his way cautiously downstairs and was standing on the garden path in the moonlight. And as he stood there, his mind filled with the stories the proprietor had told a few days before of the superstitions that still lived in the popular imagination and haunted this little, remote pine-clad valley. The thought of that girl sickened him. The odor of newly-turned earth remained in his nostrils and made his gorge rise. Utterly and vigorously he rejected the monstrous fictions he had heard, yet for all that, could not prevent their touching his imagination as he stood there in the early hours of the morning, alone with night and silence. The spell was undeniable; only a mind without sensibility could have ignored it.

He searched the little garden from end to end. Empty! Opposite the high gate he stopped, peering through the iron bars, wet with dew to his hands. Far across the intervening fields he fancied something moved. A second later he was sure of it. Something down there to the right beyond the trees was astir. It was in the cemetery.

And this definite discovery sent a shudder of terror and disgust through him from head to foot. He framed the name of his friend with his lips, yet the sound did not come forth. Some deeper instinct warned him to hold it back. Instead, after incredible efforts, he climbed that iron gate and dropped down into the soaking grass upon the other side. Then, taking advantage of all the cover he could find, he ran, swiftly and stealthily, towards the cemetery. On the way, without quite knowing why he did so, he picked up a heavy stick; and a moment later he stood beside the low wall that separated the fields from the churchyard—stood and stared.

There, beside the tombstones, with their hideous metal wreaths and crowns of faded flowers, he made out the figure of his friend; he was stooping, crouched down upon the ground; behind him rose a couple of bushy yew trees, against the dark of which his form was easily visible. He was not alone; in front of him, bending close over him it seemed, was another figure—a slight, shadowy, slim figure.

This time the big man found his voice and called aloud:—

"Morton, Morton!" he cried. "What, in the name of heaven, are you doing? What's the matter—?"

And the instant his deep voice broke the stillness of the night with its clamor, the little figure, half hiding his friend, turned about and faced him. He saw a white face with shining eyes and teeth as the form rose; the moonlight painted it with its own strange pallor; it was weird, unreal, horrible; and across the mouth, downwards from the lips to the chin, ran a deep stain of crimson.

The next moment the figure slid with a queer, gliding motion towards the trees, and disappeared among the yews and tombstones in the direction of the church. The heavy stick, hurled whirling after it, fell harmlessly half way, knocking a metal cross from its perch upon an upright grave; and the man who had thrown it raced full speed towards the huddled up figure of his friend, hardly noticing the thin, wailing cry that rose trembling through the night air from the vanished form. Nor did he notice more particularly that several of the graves, newly made, showed signs of recent disturbance, and that the odor

of turned earth he had noticed in the room grew stronger. All his attention was concentrated upon the figure at his feet.

"Morton, man, get up! Wake for God's sake! You've been walking in—"

Then the words died upon his lips. The unnatural attitude of his friend's shoulders, and the way the head dropped back to show the neck, struck him like a blow in the face. There was no sign of movement. He lifted the body up and carried it, all limp and unresisting, by ways he never remembered afterwards, back to the inn.

It was all a dreadful nightmare—a nightmare that carried over its ghastly horror into waking life. He knew that the proprietor and his wife moved busily to and fro about the bed, and that in due course the village doctor was upon the scene, and that he was giving a muddled and feverish description of all he knew, telling how his friend was a confirmed sleepwalker and all the rest. But he did not realize the truth until he saw the face of the doctor as he straightened up from the long examination.

"Will you wake him?" he heard himself asking, "or let him sleep it out till morning?" And the doctor's expression, even before the reply came to confirm it, told him the truth. "Ah, monsieur, your friend will not ever wake again, I fear! It is the heart, you see; *hélas*,[2] it is sudden failure of the heart!"

The final scenes in the little tragedy which thus brought his holiday to so abrupt and terrible a close need no description, being in no way essential to this strange story. There were one or two curious details, however, that came to light afterwards. One was, that for some weeks before there had

[2] *French.* "Alas!"

been signs of disturbance among newly-made graves in the cemetery, which the authorities had been trying to trace to the nightly wanderings of the village madman—in vain; and another, that the morning after the death a trail of blood had been found across the church floor, as though someone had passed through from the back entrance to the front. A special service was held that very week to cleanse the holy building from the evil of that stain; for the villagers, deep in their superstitions, declared that nothing human had left that trail; nothing could have made those marks but a vampire disturbed at midnight in its awful occupation among the dead.

Apart from such idle rumors, however, the bereaved carried with him to this day certain other remarkable details which cannot be so easily dismissed. For he had a brief conversation with the doctor, it appears, that impressed him profoundly. And the doctor, an intelligent man, prosaic as granite into the bargain, had questioned him rather closely as to the recent life and habits of his dead friend. The account of their climb to the "Chenille"

he heard with an amazement he could not conceal.

"But no such chalet exists," he said. "There is no 'Chenille.' A long time ago, fifty years or more, there was such a place, but it was destroyed by the authorities on account of the evil reputation of the people who lived there. They burnt it. Nothing remains today but a few bits of broken wall and foundation."

"Evil reputation—?"

The doctor shrugged his shoulders. "Travelers, even peasants, disappeared," he said. "An old woman lived there with her daughter, and poisoned milk was supposed to be used. But the neighborhood accused them of worse than ordinary murder—"

"In what way?"

"Said the girl was a vampire," answered the doctor shortly.

And, after a moment's hesitation, he added, turning his face away as he spoke:—

"It was a curious thing, though, that tiny hole in your friend's throat, small as a pin-prick, yet so deep. And the heart—did I tell you?—was almost completely drained of blood."

⟡

E. F. Benson

EDWARD FREDERIC BENSON (1867-1940) was an English novelist, biographer, memoirist, and short story writer. Born at Wellington College to the headmaster and his wife, he was raised by his mother, a celebrated woman herself who later established an openly lesbian household. Benson was likely gay himself, and there are ample homoerotic scenes in his extensive writing. His supernatural works caught the eye of H.P. Lovecraft, who spoke highly of them in his *Supernatural Horror in Literature*.

The following story was first published in *The Room in the Tower and Other Stories* (1912) and uses the power of horrific dreams to draw the reader into a chilling encounter with the undead.

THE ROOM IN THE TOWER

E. F. BENSON

It is probable that everybody who is at all a constant dreamer has had at least one experience of an event or a sequence of circumstances which have come to his mind in sleep being subsequently realized in the material world. But, in my opinion, so far from this being a strange thing, it would be far odder if this fulfillment did not occasionally happen, since our dreams are, as a rule, concerned with people whom we know and places with which we are familiar, such as might very naturally occur in the awake and day-lit world. True, these dreams are often broken into by some absurd and fantastic incident, which puts them out of court in regard to their subsequent fulfillment, but on the mere calculation of chances, it does not appear in the least unlikely that a dream imagined by anyone who dreams constantly should occasionally come true. Not long ago, for instance, I experienced such a fulfillment of a dream which seems to me in no way remarkable and to have no kind of psychical significance. The manner of it was as follows.

A certain friend of mine, living abroad, is amiable enough to write to me about once in a fortnight. Thus, when fourteen days or thereabout have elapsed since I last heard from him, my mind, probably either consciously or subconsciously, is expectant of a letter from him. One night last week I dreamed that as I was going upstairs to dress for dinner I heard, as I often hear, the sound of the postman's knock on my nt door, and diverted my direction downstairs instead. There, among other correspondence, was a letter from him. Thereafter the fantastic entered, for on opening it I found inside the ace of diamonds, and scribbled across it in his well-known handwriting, "I am sending you this for safe custody, as you know it is running an unreasonable risk to keep aces in Italy."

The next evening I was just preparing to go upstairs to dress when I heard the postman's knock, and did precisely as I had done in my dream. There, among other letters, was one from my friend. Only it did not contain the ace of diamonds. Had it done so, I should have attached more weight to the matter, which, as it stands, seems to me a perfectly ordinary coincidence. No doubt I consciously or subconsciously expected a letter from him, and this suggested to me my dream. Similarly, the fact that my friend had not written to me for a fortnight suggested to him that he should do so. But occasionally it is not so easy to find such an explanation, and for the following story I can find no explanation at all. It came out of the dark and out of the dark it has gone again.

All my life I have been a habitual dreamer: the nights are few, that is to say, when I do not find on awaking in the morning that some mental experience has been mine, and sometimes, all night long, apparently, a series of the most dazzling adventures befall me. Almost without exception these adventures are pleasant, though often merely trivial. It is of an exception that I am going to speak.

It was when I was about sixteen that a certain dream first came to me, and this is how it befell. It opened with my being set down at the door of a big red brick house, where, I understood, I was going to stay. The servant who opened the door told me that tea was going on in the garden, and led me through a low dark-paneled hall, with a large open fireplace, on to a cheerful green lawn set round with flower beds. There were grouped about the tea table a small party of people, but they were all strangers to me except one, who was a schoolfellow called Jack Stone, clearly the son of the house, and he introduced me to his mother and father and a couple of sisters. I was, I remember, somewhat astonished to find myself there, for the boy in question was scarcely known to me, and I

rather disliked what I knew of him: moreover, he had left school nearly a year before. The afternoon was very hot, and an intolerable oppression reigned. On the far side of the lawn ran a red brick wall, with an iron gate in its center, outside which stood a walnut tree. We sat in the shadow of the house opposite a row of long windows, inside which I could see a table with cloth laid, glimmering with glass and silver. The garden front of the house was very long, and at one end of it stood a tower of three stories, which looked to me much older than the rest of the building.

Before long, Mrs. Stone, who, like the rest of the party, had sat in absolute silence, said to me, "Jack will show you your room: I have given you the room in the tower."

Quite inexplicably my heart sank at her words. I felt as if I had known that I should have the room in the tower, and that it contained something dreadful and significant. Jack instantly got up, and I understood that I had to follow him. In silence we passed through the hall, and mounted a great oak staircase with many corners, and arrived at a small landing with two doors set in it. He pushed one of these open for me to enter, and without coming himself, closed it behind me. Then I knew that my conjecture had been right: there was something awful in the room, and with the terror of nightmare growing swiftly and enveloping me, I awoke in a spasm of terror.

Now that dream, or variations on it, occurred to me intermittently for fifteen years. Most often it came in exactly this form, the arrival, the tea laid out on the lawn, the deadly silence succeeded by that one deadly sentence, the mounting with Jack Stone up to the room in the tower where horror dwelt, and it always came to a close in the nightmare of terror at that which was in the room, though I never saw what it was. At other times I experienced variations on this same theme. Occasionally, for instance, we would be sitting at dinner in the dining room, into the windows of which I had looked on the first night when the dream of this house had visited me, but wherever we were, there was the same silence, the same sense of dreadful oppression and foreboding.

And the silence I knew would always be broken by Mrs. Stone saying to me, "Jack will show you your room: I have given you the room in the tower." Upon which (this was invariable) I had to follow him up the oak staircase with many corners, and enter the place that I dreaded more and more each time that I visited it in sleep. Or, again, I would find myself playing cards still in silence in a drawing room lit with immense chandeliers that gave a blinding illumination. What the game was I have no idea; what I remember, with a sense of miserable anticipation, was that soon Mrs. Stone would get up and say to me, "Jack will show you your room: I have given you the room in the tower."

This room where we played cards was next to the dining room, and, as I have said, was always brilliantly illuminated, whereas the rest of the house was full of dusk and shadows. And yet, how often, in spite of those bouquets of lights, have I not pored over the cards that were dealt to me, scarcely able for some reason to see them. Their designs, too, were strange: there were no red suits, but all were black, and among them there were certain cards which were black all over. I hated and dreaded those.

As this dream continued to occur, I got to know the greater part of the house. There was a smoking room beyond the drawing room, at the end of a passage with a green baize door.[1] It was always very dark there, and as often as I went there I passed somebody whom I could not see in the doorway coming out. Curious developments, too, took place in the characters that peopled the dream, as might happen to living persons. Mrs. Stone, for instance, who, when I first saw her, had been black-haired, became gray, and instead of rising briskly, as she had done at first when she said, "Jack will show you your room: I have given you the room in the tower," got up feebly, as if the strength was leaving her limbs. Jack also grew up, and became a rather ill-looking young man, with a brown mustache, while one of the sisters ceased to appear, and I understood she was married.

Then it so happened that I was not visited by this dream for six months or more, and I began to hope, in such inexplicable dread did I hold it, that it had passed away for good. But one night after this interval I again found myself being shown out on the lawn for tea, and Mrs. Stone was not there, while the others were all dressed in black. At once I guessed the reason, and my heart leaped at the thought that perhaps this time I should not have to sleep in the room in the tower, and though we usually all sat in silence, on this occasion the sense of relief made me talk and laugh as I had never yet done. But even then matters were not altogether comfortable, for no one else spoke, but they all looked secretly

---

[1] Baize is a soft woolen or cotton fabric resembling felt; the door has been covered with it, like a card or billiard table, for which the cloth is primarily used.

at each other. And soon the foolish stream of my talk ran dry, and gradually an apprehension worse than anything I had previously known gained on me as the light slowly faded.

Suddenly a voice which I knew well broke the stillness, the voice of Mrs. Stone, saying, "Jack will show you your room: I have given you the room in the tower." It seemed to come from near the gate in the red brick wall that bounded the lawn, and looking up, I saw that the grass outside was sown thick with gravestones. A curious grayish light shone from them, and I could read the lettering on the grave nearest me, and it was, "In evil memory of Julia Stone." And as usual Jack got up, and again I found myself following him through the hall and up the staircase with many corners. On this occasion it was darker than usual, and when I passed into the room in the tower I could only just see the furniture, the position of which was already familiar to me. Also there was a dreadful odor of decay in the room, and I woke screaming.

The dream, with such variations and developments as I have mentioned, went on at intervals for fifteen years. Sometimes I would dream it two or three nights in succession; once, as I have said, there was an intermission of six months, but taking a reasonable average, I should say that I dreamed it quite as often as once in a month. It had, as is plain, something of nightmare about it, since it always ended in the same appalling terror, which, so far from getting less, seemed to me to gather fresh fear every time that I experienced it. There was, too, a strange and dreadful consistency about it. The characters in it, as I have mentioned, got regularly older, death and marriage visited this silent family, and I never in the dream, after Mrs. Stone died, set eyes on her again.

But it was always her voice that told me that the room in the tower was prepared for me, and whether we had tea out on the lawn, or the scene was laid in one of the rooms overlooking it, I could always see her gravestone standing just outside the iron gate. It was the same, too, with the married daughter; usually she was not present, but once or twice she returned again, in company with a man, whom I took to be her husband. He, too, like the rest of them, was always silent. But, owing to the constant repetition of the dream, I ceased to attach, in my waking hours, any significance to it. I never met Jack Stone again in all those years, nor did I ever see a house that resembled this dark house of my dream. And then something happened.

I had been in London in this year, up till the end of July, and during the first week in August went down to stay with a friend in a house he had taken for the summer months, in the Ashdown Forest district of Sussex. I left London early, for John Clinton was to meet me at Forest Row Station, and we were going to spend the day golfing, and go to his house in the evening. He had his motor with him, and we set off, about five in the afternoon, after a thoroughly delightful day, for the drive, the distance being some ten miles. As it was still so early we did not have tea at the clubhouse, but waited till we should get home.

As we drove, the weather, which up till then had been, though hot, deliciously fresh, seemed to me to alter in quality, and become very stagnant and oppressive, and I felt that indefinable sense of ominous apprehension that I am accustomed to before thunder. John, however, did not share my views, attributing my loss of lightness to the fact that I had lost both my matches. Events proved, however, that I was right, though I do not think that the thunderstorm that broke that night was the sole cause of my depression.

Our way lay through deep high-banked lanes, and before we had gone very far I fell asleep, and was only awakened by the stopping of the motor. And with a sudden thrill, partly of fear but chiefly of curiosity, I found myself standing in the doorway of my house of dream. We went, I half wondering whether or not I was dreaming still, through a low oak-paneled hall, and out on to the lawn, where tea was laid in the shadow of the house. It was set in flower beds; a red brick wall, with a gate in it, bounded one side; and out beyond that was a space of rough grass with a walnut tree. The façade of the house was very long, and at one end stood a three-storied tower, markedly older than the rest.

Here for the moment all resemblance to the repeated dream ceased. There was no silent and somehow terrible family, but a large assemblage of exceedingly cheerful persons, all of whom were known to me. And in spite of the horror with which the dream itself had always filled me, I felt nothing of it now that the scene of it was thus reproduced before me. But I felt the intensest curiosity as to what was going to happen.

Tea pursued its cheerful course, and before long, Mrs. Clinton got up. And at the moment I think I knew what she was going to say. She spoke to me, and what she said was:—

"Jack will show you your room; I have given you the room in the tower."

At that, for half a second, the horror of the dream took hold of me again. But it quickly passed, and again I felt nothing more than the most intense curiosity. It was not very long before it was amply satisfied.

John turned to me.

"Right up at the top of the house," he said, "but I think you'll be comfortable. We're absolutely full up. Would you like to go and see it now? By Jove, I believe you are right, and that we are going to have a thunderstorm. How dark it has become."

I got up and followed him. We passed through the hall, and up the perfectly familiar staircase. Then he opened the door, and I went in. And at that moment sheer unreasoning terror again possessed me. I did not know for certain what I feared: I simply feared. Then like a sudden recollection, when one remembers a name which has long escaped the memory, I knew what I feared. I feared Mrs. Stone, whose grave with the sinister inscription, "In evil memory—" I had so often seen in my dream, just beyond the lawn which lay below my window. And then once more the fear passed so completely that I wondered what there was to fear, and I found myself, sober and quiet and sane, in the room in the tower, the name of which I had so often heard in my dream, and the scene of which was so familiar.

I looked round it with a certain sense of proprietorship, and found that nothing had been changed from the dreaming nights in which I knew it so well. Just to the left of the door was the bed, lengthways along the wall, with the head of it in the angle. In a line with it was the fireplace and a small bookcase; opposite the door the outer wall was pierced by two lattice-paned windows, between which stood the dressing table, while ranged along the fourth wall was the washing stand and a big cupboard. My luggage had already been unpacked, for the furniture of dressing and undressing lay orderly on the washstand and toilet table, while my dinner clothes were spread out on the coverlet of the bed.

And then with a sudden start of unexplained dismay, I saw that there were two rather conspicuous objects which I had not seen before in my dreams: one a life-sized oil painting of Mrs. Stone, the other a black-and-white sketch of Jack Stone, representing him as he had appeared to me only a week before in the last of the series of these repeated dreams, a rather secret and evil-looking man of about thirty. His picture hung between the windows, looking straight across the room to the other portrait, which hung at the side of the bed. At that I looked next, and as I looked I felt once more the horror of nightmare seize me.

It represented Mrs. Stone as I had seen her last in my dreams: old and withered and white haired. But in spite of the evident feebleness of body, a dreadful exuberance and vitality shone through the envelope of flesh, an exuberance wholly malign, a vitality that foamed and frothed with unimaginable evil. Evil beamed from the narrow, leering eyes: it laughed in the demon-like mouth. The whole face was instinct with some secret and appalling mirth; the hands, clasped together on the knee, seemed shaking with suppressed and nameless glee. Then I saw also that it was signed in the left-hand corner, and wondering who the artist could be, I looked more closely, and read the inscription, "Julia Stone by Julia Stone."

There came a tap at the door, and John Clinton entered.

"Got everything you want?" he asked.

"Rather more than I want," I said, pointing to the picture.

He laughed.

"Hard-featured old lady," he said. "By herself, too, I remember. Anyhow she can't have flattered herself much."

"But don't you see?" said I. "It's scarcely a human face at all. It's the face of some witch, some devil."

He looked at it more closely.

"Yes; it isn't very pleasant," he agreed. "Scarcely a bedside manner, eh? Yes; I can imagine getting the nightmare, if I went to sleep with that close by my bed. I'll have it taken down if you like."

"I really wish you would," I said.

He rang the bell, and with the help of a servant we detached the picture and carried it out on to the landing, and put it with its face to the wall.

"By Jove, the old lady is a weight," said John, mopping his forehead. "I wonder if she had something on her mind."

The extraordinary weight of the picture had struck me too. I was about to reply, when I caught sight of my own hand. There was blood on it, in considerable quantities, covering the whole palm.

"I've cut myself somehow," I said.

John gave a little startled exclamation.

"Why, I have too," he said.

Simultaneously the footman took out his handkerchief and wiped his hand with it. I saw that there was blood also on his handkerchief.

John and I went back into the tower room and washed the blood off; but neither on his hand nor on mine was there the slightest trace of a scratch or cut. It seemed to me that, having ascertained this, we both, by a sort of tacit consent, did not allude to it again. Something in my case had dimly occurred to me that I did not wish to think about. It was but a conjecture, but I fancied that I knew the same thing had occurred to him.

The heat and oppression of the air, for the storm we had expected, was still undischarged, increased very much after dinner, and for some time most of the party, among whom were John Clinton and myself, sat outside on the path bounding the lawn, where we had had tea. The night was absolutely dark, and no twinkle of star or moon ray could penetrate the pall of cloud that overset the sky. By degrees our assembly thinned, the women went up to bed, the men dispersed to the smoking or billiard room, and by eleven o'clock my host and I were the only two left. All the evening I thought that he had something on his mind, and as soon as we were alone he spoke.

"The man who helped us with the picture had blood on his hand, too, did you notice?" he said. "I asked him just now if he had cut himself and he said that he supposed he must have, but that he could find no mark of it. Now where did that blood come from?"

By dint of telling myself that I was not going to think about it, I had succeeded in not doing so, and I did not want, especially just at bedtime, to be reminded of it.

"I don't know," said I, "and I don't really care so long as the picture of Mrs. Julia Stone is not by my bed."

He got up.

"But it's odd," he said. "Ha! Now you'll see another odd thing."

A dog of his, an Irish terrier by breed, had come out of the house as we talked. The door behind us into the hall was open, and a bright oblong of light shone across the lawn to the iron gate which led on to the rough grass outside, where the walnut tree stood. I saw that the dog had all his hackles up, bris-

tling with rage and fright; his lips were curled back from his teeth, as if he were ready to spring at something, and he was growling to himself. He took not the slightest notice of his master or me, but stiffly and tensely walked across the grass to the iron gate. There he stood for a moment, looking through the bars and still growling. Then of a sudden his courage seemed to desert him: he gave one long howl, and scuttled back to the house with a curious crouching sort of movement.

"He does that half a dozen times a day," said John. "He sees something which he both hates and fears."

I walked to the gate and looked over it. Something was moving on the grass outside, and soon a sound which I could not instantly identify came to my ears. Then I remembered what it was: It was the purring of a cat. I lit a match, and saw the purrer, a big blue Persian, walking round and round in a little circle just outside the gate, stepping high and ecstatically, with tail carried aloft like a banner. Its eyes were bright and shining, and every now and then it puts its head down and sniffed at the grass.

I laughed.

"The end of that mystery, I am afraid," I said. "Here's a large cat having Walpurgis Night[2] all alone."

"Yes, that's Darius," said John. "He spends half the day and all night there. But that's not the end of the dog mystery, for Toby and he are the best of friends, but the beginning of the cat mystery. What's the cat doing there? And why is Darius pleased, while Toby is terror stricken?"

---

[2] The night before May 1st, the equinox of Halloween, Walpurgis-Nacht is said to mark the final victory of spring over winter. Traditionally, before the evil spirits occupying Winter depart, they have one last gathering, on the Brocken, the highest peak in the Harz Mountains. The narrator is speaking figuratively of the coming thunderstorm; it is August, not April.

At that moment I remembered the rather horrible details of my dreams when I saw through the gate, just where the cat was now, the white tombstone with the sinister inscription. But before I could answer the rain began, as suddenly and heavily as if a tap had been turned on, and simultaneously the big cat squeezed through the bars of the gate, and came leaping across the lawn to the house for shelter. Then it sat in the doorway, looking out eagerly into the dark. It spat and struck at John with its paw, as he pushed it in, in order to close the door.

Somehow, with the portrait of Julia Stone in the passage outside, the room in the tower had absolutely no alarm for me, and as I went to bed, feeling very sleepy and heavy, I had nothing more than interest for the curious incident about our bleeding hands, and the conduct of the dog and cat. The last thing I looked at before I put out my light was the square empty space by my bed where the portrait had been. Here the paper was of its original full tint of dark red: over the rest of the walls it had faded. Then I blew out my candle and instantly fell asleep.

My awakening was equally instantaneous, and I sat bolt upright in bed under the impression that some bright light had been flashed in my face, though it was now absolutely pitch dark. I knew exactly where I was, in the room which I had dreaded in dreams, but no horror that I ever felt when asleep approached the fear that now invaded and froze my brain. Immediately after a peal of thunder crackled just above the house, but the probability that it was only a flash of lightning that awoke me gave no reassurance to my galloping heart. Something I knew was in the room with me, and instinctively I put out my right hand, which was nearest the wall, to keep it away. And my hand touched the edge of a picture-frame hanging close to me.

I sprang out of bed, upsetting the small table that stood by it, and I heard my watch, candle, and matches clatter on to the floor. But for the moment there was no need of light, for a blinding flash leaped out of the clouds, and showed me that by my bed again hung the picture of Mrs. Stone. And instantly the room went into a blackness again. But in that flash I saw another thing also, namely a figure that leaned over the end of my bed, watching me. It was dressed in some close-clinging white garment, spotted and stained with mould, and the face was that of the portrait.

Overhead the thunder cracked and roared, and when it ceased and the deathly stillness succeeded, I heard the rustle of movement coming nearer me, and, more horrible yet, perceived an odor of corruption and decay. And then a hand was laid on the side of my neck, and close beside my ear I heard quick-taken, eager breathing. Yet I knew that this thing, though it could be perceived by touch, by smell, by eye and by ear, was still not of this earth, but something that had passed out of the body and had power to make itself manifest. Then a voice, already familiar to me, spoke.

"I knew you would come to the room in the tower," it said. "I have been long waiting for you. At last you have come. Tonight I shall feast; before long we will feast together."

And the quick breathing came closer to me; I could feel it on my neck.

At that the terror, which I think had paralyzed me for the moment, gave way to the wild instinct of self-preservation. I hit wildly with both arms, kicking out at the same moment, and heard a little animal-squeal, and something soft dropped with a thud beside me. I took a couple of steps forward, nearly tripping up over whatever it was that lay there, and by the merest good luck found the handle of the door. In another second I ran out on the landing, and had banged the door behind me. Almost at the same moment I heard a door open somewhere below, and John Clinton, candle in hand, came running upstairs.

"What is it?" he asked. "I sleep just below you, and heard a noise as if—Good heavens, there's blood on your shoulder."

I stood there, so he told me afterwards, swaying from side to side, white as a sheet, with the mark on my shoulder as if a hand covered with blood had been laid there.

"It's in there," I said, pointing. "She, you know. The portrait is in there, too, hanging up on the place we took it from."

At that he laughed.

"My dear fellow, this is mere nightmare," he said.

He pushed by me, and opened the door, I standing there simply inert with terror, unable to stop him, unable to move.

"Phew! What an awful smell," he said.

Then there was silence; he had passed out of my sight behind the open door. Next moment he came out again, as white as myself, and instantly shut it.

"Yes, the portrait's there," he said, "and on the floor is a thing—a thing spotted with earth, like what they bury people in. Come away quick, come away."

How I got downstairs I hardly know. An awful shuddering and nausea of the spirit rather than of the flesh had seized me, and more than once he had to place my feet upon the steps, while every now and then he cast glances of terror and apprehension up the stairs. But in time we came to his dressing room on the floor below, and there I told him what I have described.

The sequel can be made short; indeed, some of my readers have perhaps already guessed what it was, if they remember that inexplicable affair of the churchyard at West Fawley, some eight years ago, when an attempt was made three times to bury the body of a certain woman who had committed suicide. On each occasion the coffin was found in the course of a few days again protruding from the ground. After the third attempt, in order that the thing should not be talked about, the body was buried elsewhere in unconsecrated ground. Where it was buried was just outside the iron gate of the garden belonging to the house where this woman had lived. She had committed suicide in a room at the top of the tower in that house. Her name was Julia Stone.

Subsequently the body was again secretly dug up, and the coffin was found to be full of blood.

Bram Stoker

ABRAHAM "BRAM" STOKER (1847-1912) was the Irish author of twelve novels and numerous short stories, although only *Dracula* (1897) and a handful of his short stories are read today. The following was first published in 1914 by Stoker's widow Florence (in the collection *Dracula's Guest and Other Stories*), after his death. Some scholars have mistakenly identified the tale as the "lost" first chapter of *Dracula*. It is tempting to identify the narrator of this story as Jonathan Harker, but discrepancies between this account and *Dracula* prevent a definite identification. Substantial evidence in the manuscript of *Dracula*, examined in detail in *The New Annotated Dracula* (2008), makes it plain that the story was written contemporaneously with *Dracula*, and intended to be included as the *second* chapter of that work. It is impossible to determine why the material was suppressed and later edited by Stoker into its more generic form, as it appears here. In this tale, the narrator encounters *two* vampires, one later identified in *Dracula* as a female companion of the Count's—and the other Dracula himself in wolf form!

DRACULA'S GUEST

BRAM STOKER

When we started for our drive the sun was shining brightly on Munich and the air was full of the joyousness of early summer. Just as we were about to depart, Herr Delbrück (the maître d'hôtel of the Quatre Saisons, where I was staying) came down, bareheaded, to the carriage and, after wishing me a pleasant drive, said to the coachman, still holding his hand on the handle of the carriage door: "Remember you are back by nightfall. The sky looks bright but there is a shiver in the north wind that says there may be a sudden storm. But I am sure you will not be late." Here he smiled and added, "For you know what night it is."

Johann answered with an emphatic, *"Ja, mein Herr,"* and, touching his hat, drove off quickly. When we had cleared the town, I said, after signaling to him to stop: "Tell me, Johann, what is tonight?"

He crossed himself as he answered laconically: "Walpurgisnacht."[1] Then he took

out his watch, a great, old-fashioned German silver thing as big as a turnip, and looked at it, with his eyebrows gathered together and a little impatient shrug of his shoulders. I realized that this was his way of respectfully protesting against the unnecessary delay and sank back in the carriage, merely motioning him to proceed. He started off rapidly, as if to make up for lost time.

Every now and then the horses seemed to throw up their heads and sniffed the air suspiciously. On such occasions I often looked round in alarm. The road was pretty bleak, for we were traversing a sort of high, windswept plateau. As we drove, I saw a road that looked but little used and which seemed to dip through a little, winding valley. It looked so inviting that, even at the risk of offending him, I called Johann to stop—and when he had pulled up I told him I would like to drive down that road. He made all sorts of excuses and frequently crossed himself as he spoke. This somewhat piqued my curiosity so I asked him various questions. He answered

[1] See "The Room in the Tower," note pg. 373.

fencingly and repeatedly looked at his watch in protest.

Finally I said: "Well, Johann, I want to go down this road. I shall not ask you to come unless you like; but tell me why you do not like to go, that is all I ask."

For answer he seemed to throw himself off the box, so quickly did he reach the ground. Then he stretched out his hands appealingly to me and implored me not to go. There was just enough of English mixed with the German for me to understand the drift of his talk. He seemed always just about to tell me something—the very idea of which evidently frightened him, but each time he pulled himself up, saying, as he crossed himself, "Walpurgisnacht!"

I tried to argue with him, but it was difficult to argue with a man when I did not know his language. The advantage certainly rested with him, for although he began to speak in English, of a very crude and broken kind, he always got excited and broke into his native tongue—and every time he did so he looked at his watch. Then the horses became restless and sniffed the air.

At this he grew very pale and, looking around in a frightened way, he suddenly jumped forward, took them by the bridles and led them on some twenty feet. I followed and asked why he had done this. For answer he crossed himself, pointed to the spot we had left, and drew his carriage in the direction of the other road, indicating a cross, and said, first in German, then in English:—

"Buried him—him what killed themselves."

I remembered the old custom of burying suicides at crossroads: "Ah! I see, a suicide. How interesting!"[2] But for the life of me I could not make out why the horses were frightened.

Whilst we were talking we heard a sort of sound between a yelp and a bark. It was far away, but the horses got very restless and it took Johann all his time to quiet them. He was pale and said, "It sounds like a wolf—but yet there are no wolves here now."

"No?" I said, questioning him; "isn't it long since the wolves were so near the city?"

"Long, long," he answered, "in the spring and summer, but with the snow the wolves have been here not so long."

Whilst he was petting the horses and trying to quiet them, dark clouds drifted rapidly across the sky. The sunshine passed away and a breath of cold wind seemed to drift past us. It was only a breath, however, and more in the nature of a warning than a fact, for the sun came out brightly again. Johann looked under his lifted hand at the horizon and said: "The storm of snow, he comes before long time." Then he looked at his watch again and, straightway, holding his reins firmly—for the horses were still pawing the ground restlessly and shaking their heads—he climbed to his box as though the time had come for proceeding on our journey.

I felt a little obstinate and did not at once get into the carriage.

"Tell me," I said, "about this place where the road leads," and I pointed down.

Again he crossed himself and mumbled a prayer before he answered, "It is unholy."

---

[2] According to folk tradition, criminals (including suicides, guilty of "self-murder" and accordingly denied consecrated burial) were buried at crossroads. This practice may have arisen from a belief that the roads would confuse the ghost of the deceased, preventing it returning to haunt its home. Suicides were thought to become vampires.

"What is unholy?" I enquired.

"The village."

"Then there is a village?"

"No, no. No one lives there hundreds of years." My curiosity was piqued. "But you said there was a village."

"There was."

"Where is it now?"

Whereupon he burst out into a long story in German and English, so mixed up that I could not quite understand exactly what he said, but roughly I gathered that long ago, hundreds of years, men had died there and been buried in their graves; and sounds were heard under the clay and when the graves were opened, men and women were found rosy with life, and their mouths red with blood.

And so, in haste to save their lives (aye, and their souls!—and here he crossed himself) those who were left fled away to other places, where the living lived and the dead were dead and not—not something. He was evidently afraid to speak the last words. As he proceeded with his narration he grew more and more excited. It seemed as if his imagination had got hold of him and he ended in a perfect paroxysm of fear—white-faced, perspiring, trembling and looking round him, as if expecting that some dreadful presence would manifest itself there in the bright sunshine on the open plain. Finally, in an agony of desperation, he cried: "Walpurgisnacht!" and pointed to the carriage for me to get in.

All my English blood rose at this and, standing back, I said:—

"You are afraid, Johann—you are afraid. Go home, I shall return alone; the walk will do me good." The carriage door was open. I took from the seat my oak walking-stick—which I always carry on my holiday excursions—and closed the door, pointing back to Munich, and said, "Go home, Johann—Walpurgisnacht doesn't concern Englishmen."

The horses were now more restive than ever and Johann was trying to hold them in, while excitedly imploring me not to do anything so foolish. I pitied the poor fellow, he was deeply in earnest, but all the same I could not help laughing. His English was quite gone now. In his anxiety he had forgotten that his only means of making me understand was to talk my language, so he jabbered away in his native German. It began to be a little tedious. After giving the direction, "Home!" I turned to go down the crossroad into the valley.

With a despairing gesture, Johann turned his horses towards Munich. I leaned on my stick and looked after him. He went slowly along the road for a while: then there came over the crest of the hill a man tall and thin.[3] I could see so much in the distance. When he drew near the horses, they began to jump and kick about, then to scream with terror. Johann could not hold them in; they bolted down the road, running away madly. I watched them out of sight, then looked for the stranger, but I found that he, too, was gone.

With a light heart I turned down the side road through the deepening valley to which Johann had objected. There was not the slightest reason, that I could see, for his objection, and I daresay I tramped for a couple of hours without thinking of time or distance, and certainly without seeing a person or a house. So far as the place was concerned it was desolation itself. But I did not notice this particularly till, on turning a bend in the

[3] The description fits Dracula.

road, I came upon a scattered fringe of wood; then I recognized that I had been impressed unconsciously by the desolation of the region through which I had passed.

I sat down to rest myself and began to look around. It struck me that it was considerably colder than it had been at the commencement of my walk—a sort of sighing sound seemed to be around me, with, now and then, high overhead, a sort of muffled roar. Looking upwards I noticed that great thick clouds were drifting rapidly across the sky from north to south at a great height. There were signs of coming storm in some lofty stratum of the air. I was a little chilly and, thinking that it was the sitting still after the exercise of walking, I resumed my journey.

The ground I passed over was now much more picturesque. There were no striking objects that the eye might single out, but in all there was a charm of beauty. I took little heed of time and it was only when the deepening twilight forced itself upon me that I began to think of how I should find my way home. The brightness of the day had gone. The air was cold and the drifting of clouds high overhead was more marked. They were accompanied by a sort of far-away rushing sound, through which seemed to come at intervals that mysterious cry which the driver had said came from a wolf.

For a while I hesitated. I had said I would see the deserted village, so on I went and presently came on a wide stretch of open country, shut in by hills all around. Their sides were covered with trees which spread down to the plain, dotting, in clumps, the gentler slopes and hollows which showed here and there. I followed with my eye the winding of the road and saw that it curved close to one

of the densest of these clumps and was lost behind it.

As I looked there came a cold shiver in the air and the snow began to fall. I thought of the miles and miles of bleak country I had passed and then hurried on to seek the shelter of the wood in front. Darker and darker grew the sky and faster and heavier fell the snow, till the earth before and around me was a glistening white carpet, the farther edge of which was lost in misty vagueness. The road was here but crude and when on the level its boundaries were not so marked, as when it passed through the cuttings; and in a little while I found that I must have strayed from it, for I missed underfoot the hard surface and my feet sank deeper in the grass and moss.

Then the wind grew strong and blew with ever increasing force, till I was fain to run before it. The air became icy cold and in spite of my exercise I began to suffer. The snow was now falling so thickly and whirling around me in such rapid eddies that I could hardly keep my eyes open. Every now and then the heavens were torn asunder by vivid lightning, and in the flashes I could see ahead of me a great mass of trees, chiefly yew and cypress, all heavily coated with snow.

I was soon amongst the shelter of the trees, and there, in comparative silence, I could hear the rush of the wind high overhead. Presently the blackness of the storm had become merged in the darkness of the night. By and by the storm seemed to be passing away: it now only came in fierce puffs or blasts. At such moments the weird sound of the wolf appeared to be echoed by many similar sounds around me.

Now and again, through the black mass of drifting cloud, came a straggling ray of moonlight, which lit up the expanse and showed me that I was at the edge of a dense mass of cypress and yew trees. As the snow had ceased to fall, I walked out from the shelter and began to investigate more closely. It appeared to me that, amongst so many old foundations as I had passed, there might be still standing a house in which, though in ruins, I could find some sort of shelter for a while.

As I skirted the edge of the copse I found that a low wall encircled it, and following this I presently found an opening. Here the cypresses formed an alley leading up to a square mass of some kind of building. Just as I caught sight of this, however, the drifting clouds obscured the moon and I passed up the path in darkness. The wind must have grown colder, for I felt myself shiver as I walked; but there was hope of shelter and I groped my way blindly on.

I stopped, for there was a sudden stillness. The storm had passed and, perhaps in sympathy with nature's silence, my heart seemed to cease to beat. But this was only momentarily, for suddenly the moonlight broke through the clouds, showing me that I was in a graveyard and that the square object before me was a great massive tomb of marble, as white as the snow that lay on and all around it. With the moonlight there came a fierce sigh of the storm, which appeared to resume its course with a long, low howl, as of many dogs or wolves.

I was awed and shocked and felt the cold

perceptibly grow upon me till it seemed to grip me by the heart. Then, while the flood of moonlight still fell on the marble tomb, the storm gave further evidence of renewing, as though it was returning on its track. Impelled by some sort of fascination I approached the sepulchre to see what it was and why such a thing stood alone in such a place. I walked around it and read, over the Doric door, in German:

COUNTESS DOLINGEN OF GRATZ
IN STYRIA[4]
SOUGHT AND FOUND DEATH
1801

On the top of the tomb, seemingly driven through the solid marble—for the structure was composed of a few vast blocks of stone—was a great iron spike or stake. On going to the back I saw, graven in great Russian letters:

THE DEAD TRAVEL FAST[5]

There was something so weird and uncanny about the whole thing that it gave me a turn and made me feel quite faint. I began to wish, for the first time, that I had taken Johann's advice. Here a thought struck me, which came under almost mysterious circumstances and with a terrible shock. This was Walpurgis Night!

Walpurgis Night, when, according to the belief of millions of people, the devil was abroad—when the graves were opened and the dead came forth and walked. When evil things of earth and air and water held revel. This very place the driver had specially shun-

---

[4] Styria (a province of Austria) is the setting for "Carmilla," pp. 135. The phrasing is odd here: The Countess did not die "in Styria"—the phrase "in Styria" probably modifies "Gratz," for there is another village named Gratz in Germany, not far from Munich where the events of this tale occur.

[5] This is a line from Gottfried August Bürger's 1773 poem *Lenore,* about a woman who wishes for the return of her dead lover, only to be carried off by Death. The poem was written in German; why, then, is this in Russian letters here?"

ned. This was the depopulated village of centuries ago. This was where the suicide lay; and this was the place where I was alone—unmanned, shivering with cold in a shroud of snow with a wild storm gathering again upon me! It took all my philosophy, all the religion I had been taught, all my courage, not to collapse in a paroxysm of fright.

And now a perfect tornado burst upon me. The ground shook as though thousands of horses thundered across it, and this time the storm bore on its icy wings, not snow, but great hailstones which drove with such violence that they might have come from the thongs of Balearic slingers—hailstones that beat down leaf and branch and made the shelter of the cypresses of no more avail than though their stems were standing corn.

At the first I had rushed to the nearest tree, but I was soon fain to leave it and seek the only spot that seemed to afford refuge, the deep Doric doorway of the marble tomb. There, crouching against the massive bronze door, I gained a certain amount of protection from the beating of the hailstones, for now they only drove against me as they ricocheted from the ground and the side of the marble.

As I leaned against the door it moved slightly and opened inwards. The shelter of even a tomb was welcome in that pitiless tempest and I was about to enter it when there came a flash of forked lightning that lit up the whole expanse of the heavens. In the instant, as I am a living man, I saw, as my eyes were turned into the darkness of the tomb, a beautiful woman with rounded cheeks and red lips, seemingly sleeping on a bier. As the thunder broke overhead I was grasped as by the hand of a giant and hurled out into the storm. The whole thing was so sudden that, before I could realize the shock, moral as well as physical, I found the hailstones beating me down.

At the same time I had a strange, dominating feeling that I was not alone. I looked towards the tomb. Just then there came another blinding flash, which seemed to strike the iron stake that surmounted the tomb and to pour through to the earth, blasting and crumbling the marble, as in a burst of flame. The dead woman rose for a moment of agony, while she was lapped in the flame, and her bitter scream of pain was drowned in the thunder-crash.[6]

The last thing I heard was this mingling of dreadful sound, as again I was seized in the giant-grasp and dragged away, while the hailstones beat on me, and the air around seemed reverberant with the howling of wolves. The last sight that I remembered was a vague, white, moving mass, as if all the graves around me had sent out the phantoms of their sheeted-dead, and that they were closing in on me through the white cloudiness of the driving hail.

GRADUALLY THERE CAME a sort of vague beginning of consciousness, then a sense of weariness that was dreadful. For a time I remembered nothing, but slowly my senses returned. My feet seemed positively racked with pain, yet I could not move them. They seemed to be numbed. There was an icy feeling at the back of my neck and all down my spine, and my ears, like my feet, were dead,

---

[6] Jonathan Harker meets a similar woman in Dracula's castle. Is it the Countess von Dolingen, freed from her prison?

yet in torment; but there was in my breast a sense of warmth which was, by comparison, delicious. It was as a nightmare—a physical nightmare, if one may use such an expression—for some heavy weight on my chest made it difficult for me to breathe.

This period of semi-lethargy seemed to remain a long time, and as it faded away I must have slept or swooned. Then came a sort of loathing, like the first stage of sea-sickness, and a wild desire to be free from something—I knew not what. A vast stillness enveloped me, as though all the world were asleep or dead—only broken by the low panting as of some animal close to me. I felt a warm rasping at my throat, then came a consciousness of the awful truth, which chilled me to the heart and sent the blood surging up through my brain.

Some great animal was lying on me and now licking my throat. I feared to stir, for some instinct of prudence bade me lie still, but the brute seemed to realize that there was now some change in me, for it raised its head. Through my eyelashes I saw above me the two great flaming eyes of a gigantic wolf. Its sharp white teeth gleamed in the gaping red mouth and I could feel its hot breath fierce and acrid upon me.[7]

For another spell of time I remembered no more. Then I became conscious of a low growl, followed by a yelp, renewed again and again. Then, seemingly very far away, I heard a "Holloa! Holloa!" as of many voices calling in unison. Cautiously I raised my head and looked in the direction whence the sound came, but the cemetery blocked my view. The wolf still continued to yelp in a strange way and a red glare began to move round the grove of cypresses, as though following the sound.

As the voices drew closer, the wolf yelped faster and louder. I feared to make either sound or motion. Nearer came the red glow, over the white pall which stretched into the darkness around me. Then all at once from beyond the trees there came at a trot a troop of horsemen bearing torches.

The wolf rose from my breast and made for the cemetery. I saw one of the horsemen (soldiers, by their caps and their long military cloaks) raise his carbine and take aim. A companion knocked up his arm, and I heard the ball whizz over my head. He had evidently taken my body for that of the wolf.

Another sighted the animal as it slunk away and a shot followed. Then, at a gallop, the troop rode forward—some towards me, others following the wolf as it disappeared amongst the snow-clad cypresses.

As they drew nearer I tried to move, but was powerless, although I could see and hear all that went on around me. Two or three of the soldiers jumped from their horses and knelt beside me. One of them raised my head and placed his hand over my heart.

"Good news, comrades!" he cried. "His heart still beats!"

Then some brandy was poured down my throat; it put vigor into me and I was able to open my eyes fully and look around. Lights and shadows were moving among the trees and I heard men call to one another. They drew together, uttering frightened exclama-

---

[7] Is the wolf Dracula himself? Dracula has the power to shape-shift into the form of a wolf. Or, as is more likely, is this a real wolf commanded by Dracula (as in the case of "Berserker," the wolf that invades the home of Lucy Westenra in *Dracula*)?

tions, and the lights flashed as the others came pouring out of the cemetery pell-mell, like men possessed. When the farther ones came close to us, those who were around me asked them eagerly: "Well, have you found him?"

The reply rang out hurriedly: "No! No! Come away quick—quick! This is no place to stay, and on this of all nights!"

"What was it?" was the question, asked in all manner of keys. The answer came variously and all indefinitely as though the men were moved by some common impulse to speak, yet were restrained by some common fear from giving their thoughts.

"It—it—indeed!" gibbered one, whose wits had plainly given out for the moment.

"A wolf—and yet not a wolf!" another put in shudderingly.

"No use trying for him without the sacred bullet," a third remarked in a more ordinary manner.

"Serve us right for coming out on this night! Truly we have earned our thousand marks!" were the ejaculations of a fourth.

"There was blood on the broken marble," another said after a pause—"the lightning never brought that there. And for him—is he safe? Look at his throat! See, comrades, the wolf has been lying on him and keeping his blood warm."

The officer looked at my throat and replied: "He is all right, the skin is not pierced. What does it all mean? We should never have found him but for the yelping of the wolf."

"What became of it?" asked the man who was holding up my head and who seemed the least panic stricken of the party, for his hands were steady and without tremor. On his sleeve was the chevron of a petty officer.

"It went to its home," answered the man, whose long face was pallid and who actually shook with terror as he glanced around him fearfully. "There are graves enough there in which it may lie. Come, comrades—come quickly! Let us leave this cursed spot."

The officer raised me to a sitting posture, as he uttered a word of command, then several men placed me upon a horse. He sprang to the saddle behind me, took me in his arms, gave the word to advance and, turning our faces away from the cypresses, we rode away in swift, military order.

As yet my tongue refused its office and I was perforce silent. I must have fallen asleep, for the next thing I remembered was finding myself standing up, supported by a soldier on each side of me. It was almost broad daylight and to the north a red streak of sunlight was reflected, like a path of blood, over the waste of snow. The officer was telling the men to say nothing of what they had seen, except that they found an English stranger, guarded by a large dog.

"Dog! That was no dog," cut in the man who had exhibited such fear. "I think I know a wolf when I see one."

The young officer answered calmly: "I said a dog."

"Dog!" reiterated the other ironically. It was evident that his courage was rising with the sun and, pointing to me, he said, "Look at his throat. Is that the work of a dog, master?"

Instinctively I raised my hand to my throat, and as I touched it I cried out in pain. The men crowded round to look, some stooping down from their saddles, and again there came the calm voice of the young officer: "A dog, as I said. If aught else were said we should only be laughed at."

I was then mounted behind a trooper and we rode on into the suburbs of Munich. Here we came across a stray carriage, into which I was lifted, and it was driven off to the Quatre Saisons—the young officer accompanying me, whilst a trooper followed with his horse and the others rode off to their barracks.

When we arrived, Herr Delbrück rushed so quickly down the steps to meet me that it was apparent he had been watching within. Taking me by both hands he solicitously led me in. The officer saluted me and was turning to withdraw when I recognized his purpose, and insisted that he should come to my rooms. Over a glass of wine I warmly thanked him and his brave comrades for saving me. He replied simply that he was more than glad and that Herr Delbrück had at the first taken steps to make all the searching party pleased; at which ambiguous utterance the maître d'hôtel smiled, while the officer pleaded duty and withdrew.

"But Herr Delbrück," I enquired, "how and why was it that the soldiers searched for me?"

He shrugged his shoulders, as if in depreciation of his own deed, as he replied: "I was so fortunate as to obtain leave from the commander of the regiment in which I served, to ask for volunteers."

"But how did you know I was lost?" I asked.

"The driver came hither with the remains of his carriage, which had been upset when the horses ran away."

"But surely you would not send a search party of soldiers merely on this account?"

"Oh, no!" he answered, "but even before the coachman arrived I had this telegram from the Boyar whose guest you are," and he took from his pocket a telegram which he handed to me, and I read:

BISTRITZ

Be careful of my guest—his safety is most precious to me. Should aught happen to him, or if he be missed, spare nothing to find him and ensure his safety. He is English and therefore adventurous. There are often dangers from snow and wolves and night. Lose not a moment if you suspect harm to him. I answer your zeal with my fortune.

—Dracula.

As I held the telegram in my hand the room seemed to whirl around me, and if the attentive maître d'hôtel had not caught me I think I should have fallen. There was something so strange in all this, something so weird and impossible to imagine, that there grew on me a sense of my being in some way the sport of opposite forces—the mere vague idea of which seemed in a way to paralyze me.

I was certainly under some form of mysterious protection. From a distant country had come, in the very nick of time, a message that took me out of the danger of the snow-sleep and the jaws of the wolf.[8]

[8] If the telegram was sent by Dracula from Bistritz (near his castle in Transylvania), why would he journey to Munich, as is suggested by the appearance of the tall, thin stranger?

Alice and Claude Askew

THE ENGLISH WRITERS Claude Arthur Cary Askew (1866-1917) and Alice Jane de Courcey Leake (1874-1917) married in 1900. They began almost immediately to produce almost ninety novels, many serialized, over their too-short career, which ended sadly when their ship was torpedoed in 1917. The tales of Aylmer Vance first appeared in *The Weekly Tale-Teller* in 1914 and were collected into book form as *Aylmer Vance, Ghost Seer* that year.

Vance is a combination of William Hope Hodgson's Carnacki the Ghost Finder and Sherlock Holmes, and while Vance failed to achieve the fame of those figures, here he exhibits a brisk confidence in dealing with an ancient vampire.

AYLMER VANCE AND THE VAMPIRE

ALICE AND CLAUDE ASKEW

Aylmer Vance had rooms in Dover Street, Piccadilly, and now that I had decided to follow in his footsteps and to accept him as my instructor in matters psychic, I found it convenient to lodge in the same house. Aylmer and I quickly became close friends, and he showed me how to develop that faculty of clairvoyance which I had possessed without being aware of it. And I may say at once that this particular faculty of mine proved of service on several important occasions.

At the same time I made myself useful to Vance in other ways, not the least of which was that of acting as recorder of his many strange adventures. For himself, he never cared much about publicity, and it was some time before I could persuade him, in the interests of science, to allow me to give any detailed account of his experiences to the world.

The incidents which I will now relate occurred very soon after we had taken up our residence together, and while I was still, so to speak, a novice.

It was about ten o'clock in the morning that a visitor was announced. He sent up a card which bore upon it the name of Paul Davenant.

The name was familiar to me, and I wondered if this could be the same Mr. Davenant who was so well-known for his polo playing and for his success as an amateur rider, especially over the hurdles? He was a young man of wealth and position, and I recollected that he had married, about a year ago, a girl who was reckoned the greatest beauty of the season. All the illustrated papers had given their portraits at the time, and I remember thinking what a remarkably handsome couple they made.

Mr. Davenant was ushered in, and at first I was uncertain as to whether this could be the individual whom I had in mind, so wan and pale and ill did he appear. A finely built, upstanding man at the time of his marriage, he had now acquired a languid droop of the shoulders and a shuffling gait, while his face, especially about the lips, was bloodless to an alarming degree.

And yet it was the same man, for behind all this I could recognize the shadow of the good looks that had once distinguished Paul Davenant.

He took the chair which Aylmer offered him—after the usual preliminary civilities had been exchanged—and then glanced doubtfully in my direction. "I wish to consult you privately, Mr. Vance," he said. "The matter is of considerable importance to myself, and, if I may say so, of a somewhat delicate nature."

Of course I rose immediately to withdraw from the room, but Vance laid his hand upon my arm.

"If the matter is connected with research in my particular line, Mr. Davenant," he said, "if there is any investigation you wish me to take up on your behalf, I shall be glad if you will include Mr. Dexter in your confidence. Mr. Dexter assists me in my work. But, of course—"[1]

"Oh, no," interrupted the other, "if that is the case, pray let Mr. Dexter remain. I think," he added, glancing at me with a friendly smile, "that you are an Oxford man, are you not, Mr. Dexter? It was before my time, but I have heard of your name in connection with the river. You rowed at Henley, unless I am very much mistaken."

I admitted the fact, with a pleasurable sensation of pride. I was very keen upon rowing in those days, and a man's prowess at school and college always remains dear to his heart.

After this we quickly became on friendly terms, and Paul Davenant proceeded to take Aylmer and myself into his confidence.

He began by calling attention to his personal appearance. "You would hardly recognize me for the same man I was a year ago," he said. "I've been losing flesh steadily for the last six months. I came up from Scotland about a week ago, to consult a London doctor. I've seen two—in fact they've held a sort of consultation over me—but the result, I may say, is far from satisfactory. They don't seem to know what is really the matter with me."

"Anemia—heart," suggested Vance. He was scrutinizing his visitor keenly, and yet without any particular appearance of doing so. "I believe it not infrequently happens that you athletes overdo yourselves—put too much strain upon the heart—"

"My heart is quite sound," responded Davenant. "Physically it is in perfect condition. The trouble seems to be that it hasn't enough blood to pump into my veins. The doctors wanted to know if I had met with an accident involving a great loss of blood—but I haven't. I've had no accident at all, and as for anemia, well, I don't seem to show the ordinary symptoms of it.[2] The inexplicable thing is that I've lost blood without knowing it, and apparently this has been going on for some time, for I've been getting steadily worse. It was almost imperceptible at first—not a sudden collapse, you understand, but a gradual failure of health."

"I wonder," remarked Vance slowly, "what induced you to consult me? For you know, of course, the direction in which I pursue my investigations. May I ask if you have reason to consider that your state of health

---

[1] Sherlock Holmes takes the same attitude toward his companion Dr. Watson.

[2] Significant loss of blood volume (15% to 30%), whether by wound or vampire, produces anemic symptoms—coolness, rapid heart-beat, paleness, and a narrow range between systolic and diastolic blood pressure. Even more blood loss (30% to 40%) produces changes in the mental state, loss of blood pressure, and increase in heart rate. Less than 15% blood loss produces no change in vital signs.

is due to some cause which we may describe as super-physical?"

A slight color came to Davenant's cheeks.

"There are curious circumstances," he said, in a low and earnest tone of voice. "I've been turning them over in my mind, trying to see light through them. I daresay it's all the sheerest folly—and I must tell you that I'm not in the least a superstitious sort of man. I don't mean to say that I'm absolutely incredulous, but I've never given thought to such things—I've led too active a life. But, as I have said, there are curious circumstances about my case, and that is why I decided upon consulting you."

"Will you tell me everything without reserve?" said Vance. I could see that he was interested. He was sitting up in his chair, his feet supported on a stool, his elbows on his knees, his chin in his hands—a favorite attitude of his. "Have you," he suggested slowly, "any mark upon your body, anything that you might associate, however remotely, with your present weakness and ill-health?"

"It's a curious thing that you should ask me that question," returned Davenant, "because I have got a curious mark, a sort of scar, that I can't account for. But I showed it to the doctors, and they assured me that it could have nothing whatever to do with my condition. In any case, if it had, it was something altogether outside their experience. I think they imagined it to be nothing more than a birthmark, a sort of mole, for they asked me if I'd had it all my life. But that I can swear I haven't. I only noticed it for the first time about six months ago, when my health began to fail. But you can see for yourself."

He loosened his collar and bared his throat. Vance rose and made a careful scrutiny of the suspicious mark. It was situated a very little to the left of the central line, just above the clavicle, and, as Vance pointed out, directly over the big vessels of the throat. My friend called to me so that I might examine it, too. Whatever the opinion of the doctors may have been, Aylmer was obviously deeply interested.

And yet there was very little to show. The skin was quite intact, and there was no sign of inflammation. There were two red marks, about an inch apart, each of which was inclined to be crescent in shape. They were more visible than they might otherwise have been owing to the peculiar whiteness of Davenant's skin.

"It can't be anything of importance," said Davenant, with a slightly uneasy laugh. "I'm inclined to think the marks are dying away."

"Have you ever noticed them more inflamed than they are at present?" inquired Vance. "If so, was it at any special time?"

Davenant reflected. "Yes," he replied slowly, "there have been times, usually, I think perhaps invariably, when I wake up in the morning, that I've noticed them larger and more angry looking. And I've felt a slight sensation of pain—a tingling—oh, very slight, and I've never worried about it. Only now you suggest it to my mind, I believe that those same mornings I have felt particularly tired and done up—a sensation of lassitude absolutely unusual to me. And once, Mr. Vance, I remember quite distinctly that there was a stain of blood close to the mark. I didn't think anything of it at the time, and just wiped it away."

"I see." Aylmer Vance resumed his seat and invited his visitor to do the same. "And now," he resumed, "you said, Mr. Davenant, that there are certain peculiar circumstances you wish to acquaint me with. Will you do so?"

And so Davenant readjusted his collar and proceeded to tell his story. I will tell it as far as I can, without any reference to the occasional interruptions of Vance and myself.

Paul Davenant, as I have said, was a man of wealth and position, and so, in every sense of the word, he was a suitable husband for Miss Jessica MacThane, the young lady who eventually became his wife. Before coming to the incidents attending his loss of health, he had a great deal to recount about Miss MacThane and her family history.

She was of Scottish descent, and although she had certain characteristic features of her race, she was not really Scotch in appearance. Hers was the beauty of the far South rather than that of the Highlands from which she had her origin. Names are not always suited to their owners, and Miss MacThane's was peculiarly inappropriate. She had, in fact, been christened Jessica in a sort of pathetic effort to counteract her obvious departure from normal type. There was a reason for this which we were soon to learn.

Miss MacThane was especially remarkable for her wonderful red hair, hair such as one hardly ever sees outside Italy—not the Celtic red—and it was so long that it reached to her feet, and it had an extraordinary gloss upon it, so that it seemed almost to have individual life of its own. Then she had just the complexion that one would expect with such hair, the purest ivory white, and not in the least marred by freckles, as is so often the case with red-haired girls. Her beauty was derived from an ancestress who had been brought to Scotland from some foreign shore—no one knew exactly whence.

Davenant fell in love with her almost at once, and he had every reason to believe, in spite of her many admirers, that his love was returned. At this time he knew very little about her personal history. He was aware only that she was very wealthy in her own right, an orphan, and the last representative of a race that had once been famous in the annals of history—or rather infamous, for the MacThanes had distinguished themselves more by cruelty and lust of blood than by deeds of chivalry. A clan of turbulent robbers in the past, they had helped to add many a blood-stained page to the history of their country.

Jessica had lived with her father, who owned a house in London, until his death when she was about fifteen years of age. Her mother had died in Scotland when Jessica was still a tiny child. Mr. MacThane had been so affected by his wife's death that, with his little daughter, he had abandoned his Scotch estate altogether—or so it was believed—leaving it to the management of a bailiff—though, indeed, there was but little work for the bailiff to do, since there were practically no tenants left. Blackwick Castle had borne for many years a most unenviable reputation.

After the death of her father, Miss MacThane had gone to live with a certain Mrs. Meredith, who was a connection of her mother's—on her father's side she had not a single relation left. Jessica was absolutely the last of a clan once so extensive that intermarriage had been a tradition of the family, but which for the last two hundred years had been gradually dwindling to extinction.

Mrs. Meredith took Jessica into Society—which would never have been her privilege had Mr. MacThane lived, for he was a moody, self-absorbed man, and prematurely old—one who seemed worn down by the weight of a great grief.

Well, I have said that Paul Davenant quickly fell in love with Jessica, and it was not long before he proposed for her hand. To his great surprise, for he had good reason to believe that she cared for him, he met with a refusal; nor would she give any explanation, though she burst into a flood of pitiful tears.

Bewildered and bitterly disappointed, he consulted Mrs. Meredith, with whom he happened to be on friendly terms, and from her he learnt that Jessica had already had several proposals, all from quite desirable men, but that one after another had been rejected.

Paul consoled himself with the reflection that perhaps Jessica did not love them, whereas he was quite sure that she cared for himself. Under these circumstances he determined to try again.

He did so, and with better result. Jessica admitted her love, but at the same time she repeated that she could not marry him. Love and marriage were not for her. Then, to his utter amaze, she declared that she had been born under a curse—a curse which sooner or later was bound to show itself in her, and which, moreover, must react cruelly, perhaps fatally, upon anyone with whom she linked her life. How could she allow a man she loved to take such a risk? Above all, since the evil was hereditary, there was one point upon which she had quite made up her mind: no child should ever call her mother—she must be the last of her race indeed.

Of course, Davenant was amazed, and inclined to think that Jessica had got some absurd idea into her head which a little reasoning on his part would dispel. There was only one other possible explanation. Was it lunacy she was afraid of?

But Jessica shook her head. She did not know of any lunacy in her family. The ill was deeper, more subtle than that. And then she told him all that she knew.

The curse—she made use of that word for want of a better—was attached to the ancient race from which she had her origin. Her father had suffered from it, and his father and grandfather before him. All three had taken to themselves young wives who had died mysteriously, of some wasting disease, within a few years. Had they observed the ancient family tradition of intermarriage this might possibly not have happened, but in their case, since the family was so near extinction, this had not been possible.

For the curse—or whatever it was—did not kill those who bore the name of Mac-Thane. It only rendered them a danger to others. It was as if they absorbed from the blood-soaked walls of their fatal castle a deadly taint which reacted terribly upon those with whom they were brought into contact, especially their nearest and dearest.

"Do you know what my father said we have it in us to become?" said Jessica with a shudder. "He used the word *vampires*. Paul, think of it—vampires—preying upon the lifeblood of others."

And then, when Davenant was inclined to laugh, she checked him. "No," she cried out, "it is not impossible. Think. We are a decadent race. From the earliest times our history has been marked by bloodshed and cruelty. The walls of Blackwick Castle are impregnated with evil—every stone could tell its tale of violence, pain, lust, and murder. What can one expect of those who have spent their lifetime between its walls?"

"But you have not done so," exclaimed Paul. "You have been spared that, Jessica. You were taken away after your mother died, and you have no recollection of Blackwick Castle, none at all. And you need never set foot in it again."

"I'm afraid the evil is in my blood," she replied sadly, "although I am unconscious of it now. And as for not returning to Blackwick— I'm not sure that I can help myself. At least, that is what my father warned me of. He said that there is something there, some compelling force, that will call me to it in spite of myself. But, oh, I don't know—I don't know, and that is what makes it so difficult. If I could only believe that all this is nothing but an idle superstition, I might be happy again, for I have it in me to enjoy life, and I'm young, very young; but my father told me these things when he was on his deathbed." She added the last words in a low, awe-stricken tone.

Paul pressed her to tell him all that she knew, and eventually she revealed another fragment of family history which seemed to have some bearing upon the case. It dealt with her own astonishing likeness to that ancestress of a couple of hundred years ago, whose existence seemed to have presaged the gradual downfall of the clan of the MacThanes.

A certain Robert MacThane, departing from the traditions of his family, which demanded that he should not marry outside his clan, brought home a wife from foreign shores, a woman of wonderful beauty, who was possessed of glowing masses of red hair and a complexion of ivory whiteness—such as had more or less distinguished since then every female of the race born in the direct line.

It was not long before this woman came to be regarded in the neighborhood as a witch. Queer stories were circulated abroad as to her doings, and the reputation of Blackwick Castle became worse than ever before.

And then one day she disappeared. Robert MacThane had been absent upon some business for twenty-four hours, and it was upon his return that he found her gone. The neighborhood was searched, but without avail, and then Robert, who was a violent man and who had adored his foreign wife, called together certain of his tenants whom he suspected, rightly or wrongly, of foul play, and had them murdered in cold blood. Murder was easy in those days, yet such an outcry was raised that Robert had to take flight, leaving his two children in the care of their nurse, and for a long while Blackwick Castle was without a master.

But its evil reputation persisted. It was said that Zaida, the witch, though dead, still made her presence felt. Many children of the tenantry[3] and young people of the neighborhood sickened and died—possibly of quite natural causes; but this did not prevent a mantle of terror settling upon the countryside, for it was said that Zaida had been seen—a pale woman clad in white—flitting about the cottages at night, and where she passed sickness and death were sure to supervene.

And from that time the fortune of the family gradually declined. Heir succeeded heir, but no sooner was he installed at Blackwick Castle than his nature, whatever it may previously have been, seemed to undergo a change. It was as if he absorbed into himself all the weight of evil that had stained his family name—as if he did, indeed, become a vampire, bringing blight upon any not directly connected with his own house.

And so, by degrees, Blackwick was deserted of its tenantry. The land around it was left uncultivated—the farms stood empty. This had persisted to the present day, for the superstitious peasantry still told their tales of the mysterious white woman who hovered

[3] The people who live on the land, the tenants.

about the neighborhood, and whose appearance betokened death—and possibly worse than death.

And yet it seemed that the last representatives of the MacThanes could not desert their ancestral home. Riches they had, sufficient to live happily upon elsewhere, but, drawn by some power they could not contend against, they had preferred to spend their lives in the solitude of the now half-ruined castle, shunned by their neighbours, feared and execrated by the few tenants that still clung to their soil.

So it had been with Jessica's grandfather and great-grandfather. Each of them had married a young wife, and in each case their love story had been all too brief. The vampire spirit was still abroad, expressing itself—or so it seemed—through the living representatives of bygone generations of evil, and young blood had been demanded at the sacrifice.

And to them had succeeded Jessica's father. He had not profited by their example, but had followed directly in their footsteps. And the same fate had befallen the wife whom he passionately adored. She had died of pernicious anemia—so the doctors said—but he had regarded himself as her murderer.

But, unlike his predecessors, he had torn himself away from Blackwick—and this for the sake of his child. Unknown to her, however, he had returned year after year, for there were times when the passionate longing for the gloomy, mysterious halls and corridors of the old castle, for the wild stretches of moorland, and the dark pine woods, would come upon him too strongly to be resisted. And so he knew that for his daughter, as for himself, there was no escape, and he warned her, when the relief of death was at last granted to him, of what her fate must be.

This was the tale that Jessica told the man who wished to make her his wife, and he made light of it, as such a man would, regarding it all as foolish superstition, the delusion of a mind overwrought. And at last—perhaps it was not very difficult, for she loved him with all her heart and soul—he succeeded in inducing Jessica to think as he did, to banish morbid ideas, as he called them, from her brain, and to consent to marry him at an early date.

"I'll take any risk you like," he declared. "I'll even go and live at Blackwick if you should desire it. To think of you, my lovely Jessica, a vampire! Why, I never heard such nonsense in my life."

"Father said I'm very like Zaida, the witch," she protested, but he silenced her with a kiss.

And so they were married and spent their honeymoon abroad, and in the autumn Paul accepted an invitation to a house party in Scotland for the grouse shooting, a sport to which he was absolutely devoted, and Jessica agreed with him that there was no reason why he should forgo his pleasure.

Perhaps it was an unwise thing to do, to venture to Scotland, but by this time the young couple, more deeply in love with each other than ever, had got quite over their fears. Jessica was redolent with health and spirits, and more than once she declared that if they should be anywhere in the neighborhood of Blackwick she would like to see the old castle out of curiosity, and just to show how absolutely she had got over the foolish terrors that used to assail her.

This seemed to Paul to be quite a wise plan, and so one day, since they were actually staying at no great distance, they motored over to Blackwick, and finding the bailiff, got him to show them over the castle.

It was a great castellated pile, grey with age, and in places falling into ruin. It stood on a steep hillside, with the rock of which it seemed to form part, and on one side of it there was a precipitous drop to a mountain stream a hundred feet below. The robber MacThanes of the old days could not have desired a better stronghold.

At the back, climbing up the mountain side, were dark pine woods, from which, here and there, rugged crags protruded, and these were fantastically shaped, some like gigantic and misshapen human forms, which stood up as if they mounted guard over the castle and the narrow gorge, by which alone it could be approached.

This gorge was always full of weird, uncanny sound. It might have been a storehouse for the wind, which, even on calm days, rushed up and down as if seeking an escape, and it moaned among the pines and whistled in the crags and shouted derisive laughter as it was tossed from side to side of the rocky heights. It was like the plaint of lost souls—that is the expression Davenant made use of, the plaint of lost souls.

The road, little more than a track now, passed through this gorge, and then, after skirting a small but deep lake, which hardly knew the light of the sun, so shut in was it by overhanging trees, climbed the hill to the castle.

And the castle! Davenant used but a few words to describe it, yet somehow I could see the gloomy edifice in my mind's eye, and something of the lurking horror that it contained communicated itself to my brain. Perhaps my clairvoyant sense assisted me, for when he spoke of them I seemed already acquainted with the great stone halls, the long corridors, gloomy and cold even on the bright-est and warmest of days; the dark, oak-paneled rooms, and the broad central staircase up which one of the early MacThanes had once led a dozen men on horseback in pursuit of a stag which had taken refuge within the precincts of the castle. There was the keep, too, its walls so thick that the ravages of time had made no impression upon them, and beneath the keep were dungeons which could tell terrible tales of ancient wrong and lingering pain.

Well, Mr. and Mrs. Davenant visited as much as the bailiff could show them of this ill-omened edifice, and Paul, for his part, thought pleasantly of his own Derbyshire home, the fine Georgian mansion, replete with every modern comfort, where he proposed to settle with his wife. And so he received something of a shock when, as they drove away, she slipped her hand into his and whispered:—

"Paul, you promised, didn't you, that you would refuse me nothing?"

She had been strangely silent till she spoke these words. Paul, slightly apprehensive, assured her that she only had to ask—but the speech did not come from his heart, for he guessed vaguely what she desired.

She wanted to go and live at the castle—oh, only for a little while, for she was sure she would soon tire of it. But the bailiff had told her that there were papers, documents, which she ought to examine, since the property was now hers—and, besides, she was interested in this home of her ancestors, and wanted to explore it more thoroughly. Oh, no, she wasn't in the least influenced by the old superstition—that wasn't the attraction—she had quite got over those silly ideas. Paul had cured her, and since he himself was so convinced that they were without foundation he ought not to mind granting her her whim.

This was a plausible argument, not easy to controvert. In the end Paul yielded, though it was not without a struggle. He suggested amendments. Let him at least have the place done up for her—that would take time; or let them postpone their visit till next year—in the summer—not move in just as the winter was upon them.

But Jessica did not want to delay longer than she could help, and she hated the idea of redecoration. Why, it would spoil the illusion of the old place, and, besides, it would be a waste of money since she only wished to remain there for a week or two. The Derbyshire house was not quite ready yet; they must allow time for the paper to dry on the walls.

And so, a week later, when their stay with their friends was concluded, they went to Blackwick, the bailiff having engaged a few raw servants and generally made things as comfortable for them as possible. Paul was worried and apprehensive, but he could not admit this to his wife after having so loudly proclaimed his theories on the subject of superstition.

They had been married three months at this time—nine had passed since then, and they had never left Blackwick for more than a few hours—till now Paul had come to London—alone.

"Over and over again," he declared, "my wife has begged me to go. With tears in her eyes, almost upon her knees, she has entreated me to leave her, but I have steadily refused unless she will accompany me. But that is the trouble, Mr. Vance, she cannot; there is something, some mysterious horror, that holds her there as surely as if she were bound with fetters. It holds her more strongly even than it held her father—we found out that he used to spend six months at least of every year at Blackwick—months when he pretended that he was traveling abroad. You see the spell—or whatever the accursed thing may be—never really relaxed its grip of him."

"Did you never attempt to take your wife away?" asked Vance.

"Yes, several times; but it was hopeless. She would become so ill as soon as we were beyond the limit of the estate that I invariably had to take her back. Once we got as far as Dorekirk—that is the nearest town, you know—and I thought I should be successful if only I could get through the night. But she escaped me; she climbed out of a window—she meant to go back on foot, at night, all those long miles. Then I have had doctors down; but it is I who wanted the doctors, not she. They have ordered me away, but I have refused to obey them till now."

"Is your wife changed at all—physically?" interrupted Vance.

Davenant reflected. "Changed," he said, "yes, but so subtly that hardly know how to describe it. She is more beautiful than ever—and yet it isn't the same beauty, if you can understand me. I have spoken of her white complexion, well, one is more than ever conscious of it now, because her lips have become so red—they are almost like a splash of blood upon her face. And the upper one has a peculiar curve that I don't think it had before, and when she laughs she doesn't smile—do you know what I mean? Then her hair—it has lost its wonderful gloss. Of course, I know she is fretting about me; but that is so peculiar, too, for at times, as I have told you, she will implore me to go and leave her, and then, perhaps only a few minutes later, she will wreathe her arms round my neck and say she cannot live without me. And I feel that there is a struggle going on within her, that she is only yielding slowly to the horrible influence—whatever it is—that she is herself when she begs me to go. But when she entreats me to stay—and it is then that her fascination is most intense—oh, I can't help remembering what she told me before we were married, and that word"—he lowered his voice—"the word *vampire*—"

He passed his hand over his brow that was wet with perspiration. "But that's absurd, ridiculous," he muttered; "these fantastic beliefs have been exploded years ago. We live in the twentieth century."

A pause ensued, then Vance said quietly, "Mr. Davenant, since you have taken me into your confidence, since you have found doctors of no avail, will you let me try to help you? I think I may be of some use—if it is not already too late. Should you agree, Mr. Dexter and I will accompany you, as you have suggested, to Blackwick Castle as early as possible—by tonight's mail North. Under ordinary circumstances, I should tell you, as you value your life, not to return—"

Davenant shook his head. "That is advice which I should never take," he declared. "I had already decided, under any circumstances, to travel North tonight. I am glad that you both will accompany me."

And so it was decided. We settled to meet at the station, and presently Paul Davenant took his departure. Any other details that remained to be told he would put us in possession of during the course of the journey.

"A curious and most interesting case," remarked Vance when we were alone. "What do you make of it, Dexter?"

"I suppose," I replied cautiously, "that there is such a thing as vampirism even in these days of advanced civilization? I can understand the evil influence that a very old person may have upon a young one if they happen to be in constant intercourse—the worn-out tissue sapping healthy vitality for their own support. And there are certain people—I could think of several myself—who seem to depress one and undermine one's energies, quite unconsciously of course, but one feels somehow that vitality has passed from oneself to them. And in this case, when the force is centuries old, expressing itself, in some mysterious way, through Davenant's wife, is it not feasible to believe that he may be physically affected by it, even though the whole thing is sheerly mental?"

"You think, then," demanded Vance, "that it is sheerly mental? Tell me, if that is so, how do you account for the marks on Davenant's throat?"

This was a question to which I found no reply, and though I pressed him for his views, Vance would not commit himself further just then.

Of our long journey to Scotland I need say nothing. We did not reach Blackwick Castle till late in the afternoon of the following day. The place was just as I had conceived it—as I have already described it. And a sense of gloom settled upon me as our car jolted us over the rough road that led through the Gorge of the Winds—a gloom that deepened when we penetrated into the vast cold hall of the castle.

Mrs. Davenant, who had been informed by telegram of our arrival, received us cordially. She knew nothing of our actual mission, regarding us merely as friends of her husband's. She was most solicitous on his behalf, but there was something strained about her tone, and it made me feel vaguely uneasy. The impression that I got was that the woman was impelled to everything that she said or did by some force outside herself—but, of course, this was a conclusion that the circumstances I was aware of might easily have conduced to. In every other respect she was charming, and she had an extraordinary fascination of appearance and manner that made me readily understand the force of a remark made by Davenant during our journey.

"I want to live for Jessica's sake. Get her away from Blackwick, Vance, and I feel that all will be well. I'd go through hell to have her restored to me—as she was."

And now that I have seen Mrs. Davenant I realized what he meant by those last words. Her fascination was stronger than ever, but it was not a natural fascination— not that of a normal woman, such as she had been. It was the fascination of a Circe, of a witch, of an enchantress—and as such was irresistible.

We had strong proof of the evil within her soon after our arrival. It was a test that Vance had quietly prepared. Davenant had mentioned that no flowers grew at Blackwick, and Vance declared that we must take some with us as a present for the lady of the house. He purchased a bouquet of pure white roses at the little town where we left the train, for the motor-car had been sent to meet us.

Soon after our arrival he presented these to Mrs. Davenant. She took them, it seemed to me nervously, and hardly had her hand touched them before they fell to pieces, in a shower of crumpled petals, to the floor.

"We must act at once," said Vance to me when we were descending to dinner that night. "There must be no delay."

"What are you afraid of?" I whispered.

"Davenant has been absent a week," he replied grimly. "He is stronger than when he went away, but not strong enough to sur-vive the loss of more blood. He must be protected. There is danger tonight."

"You mean from his wife?" I shuddered at the ghastliness of the suggestion.

"That is what time will show." Vance turned to me and added a few words with intense earnestness. "Mrs. Davenant, Dexter, is at present hovering between two conditions. The evil thing has not yet completely mastered her—you remember what Davenant said, how she would beg him to go away and at the next moment entreat him to stay? She has made a struggle, but she is gradually succumbing, and this last week, spent here alone, has strengthened the evil. And that is what I have got to fight, Dexter—it is to be a contest of will, a contest that will go on silently till one or the other obtains the mastery. If you watch you may see. Should a change show itself in Mrs. Davenant you will know that I have won."

Thus I knew the direction in which my friend proposed to act. It was to be a war of his will against the mysterious power that had laid its curse upon the house of MacThane. Mrs. Davenant must be released from the fatal charm that held her.

And I, knowing what was going on, was able to watch and understand. I realized that the silent contest had begun even while we sat at dinner. Mrs. Davenant ate practically nothing and seemed ill at ease; she fidgeted in her chair, talked a great deal, and laughed—it was the laugh without a smile, as Davenant had described it. And as soon as she was able she withdrew.

Later, as we sat in the drawing-room, I could still feel the clash of wills. The air in the room felt electric and heavy, charged with tremendous but invisible forces. And outside, round the castle, the wind whistled and shrieked and moaned—it was as if all the dead and gone MacThanes, a grim army, had collected to fight the battle of their race.

And all this while we four in the drawing-room were sitting and talking the ordinary commonplaces of after-dinner conversation! That was the extraordinary part of it—Paul Davenant suspected nothing, and I, who knew, had to play my part. But I hardly took my eyes from Jessica's face. When would the change come, or was it, indeed, too late?

At last Davenant rose and remarked that he was tired and would go to bed. There was no need for Jessica to hurry. He would sleep that night in his dressing-room, and did not want to be disturbed.

And it was at that moment, as his lips met hers in a good night kiss, as she wreathed her enchantress arms about him, careless of our presence, her eyes gleaming hungrily, that the change came.

It came with a fierce and threatening shriek of wind, and a rattling of the casement, as if the horde of ghosts without was about to break in upon us. A long, quivering sigh escaped from Jessica's lips, her arms fell from her husband's shoulders, and she drew back, swaying a little from side to side.

"Paul," she cried, and somehow the whole timbre of her voice was changed, "what a wretch I've been to bring you back to Blackwick, ill as you are! But we'll go away, dear; yes, I'll go, too. Oh, will you take me away—take me away tomorrow?" She spoke with an intense earnestness—unconscious all the time of what had been happening to her. Long shudders were convulsing her frame. "I don't know why I've wanted to stay here," she kept repeating. "I hate the place, really—it's evil—evil."

Having heard these words I exulted, for surely Vance's success was assured. But I was soon to learn that the danger was not yet past.

Husband and wife separated, each going to their own room. I noticed the grateful, if mystified, glance that Davenant threw at Vance, vaguely aware, as he must have been, that my friend was somehow responsible for what had happened. It was settled that plans for departure were to be discussed on the morrow.

"I have succeeded," Vance said hurriedly, when we were alone, "but the change may be transitory. I must keep watch tonight. Go you to bed, Dexter, there is nothing that you can do."

I obeyed—though I would sooner have kept watch, too—watch against a danger of which I had no understanding. I went to my room, a gloomy and sparsely furnished apartment, but I knew that it was quite impossible for me to think of sleeping. And so, dressed as I was, I went and sat by the open window, for now the wind that had raged round the castle had died down to a low moaning in the pine trees—a whimpering of time-worn agony.

And it was as I sat thus that I became aware of a white figure that stole out from the castle by a door I could not see, and, with hands clasped, ran swiftly across the terrace to the wood. I had but a momentary glance, but I felt convinced that the figure was that of Jessica Davenant.

And instinctively I knew that some great danger was imminent. It was, I think, the suggestion of despair conveyed by those clasped hands. At any rate, I did not hesitate. My window was some height from the ground, but the wall below was ivy-clad and afforded good foot-hold. The descent was quite easy. I achieved it, and was just in time to take up the pursuit in the right direction, which was into the thickness of the wood that clung to the slope of the hill.

I shall never forget that wild chase. There was just sufficient room to enable me to follow the rough path, which, luckily, since I had now lost sight of my quarry, was the only possible way that she could have taken; there were no intersecting tracks, and the wood was too thick on either side to permit of deviation.

And the wood seemed full of dreadful sound—moaning and wailing and hideous laughter. The wind, of course, and the screaming of night birds—once I felt the fluttering of wings in close proximity to my face. But I could not rid myself of the thought that I, in turn, was being pursued, that the forces of hell were combined against me.

The path came to an abrupt end on the border of the somber lake that I have already mentioned. And now I realized that I was indeed only just in time, for before me, plunging knee-deep in the water, I recognized the white-clad figure of the woman I had been pursuing. Hearing my footsteps, she turned her head, and then threw up her arms and screamed. Her red hair fell in heavy masses about her shoulders, and her face, as I saw it that moment, was hardly human for the agony of remorse that it depicted.

"Go!" she screamed. "For God's sake let me die!"

But I was by her side almost as she spoke. She struggled with me—sought vainly to tear herself from my clasp—implored me, with panting breath, to let her drown.

"It's the only way to save him!" she gasped. "Don't you understand that I am a thing accursed? For it is I—I—who have

sapped his lifeblood! I know it now, the truth has been revealed to me tonight! I am a vampire, without hope in this world or the next, so for his sake—for the sake of his unborn child—let me die—let me die!"

Was ever so terrible an appeal made? Yet I—what could I do? Gently I overcame her resistance and drew her back to shore. By the time I reached it she was lying a dead weight upon my arm. I laid her down upon a mossy bank, and, kneeling by her side, gazed into her face.

And then I knew that I had done well. For the face I looked upon was not that of Jessica the vampire, as I had seen it that afternoon, it was the face of Jessica, the woman whom Paul Davenant had loved.

And later Aylmer Vance had his tale to tell.

"I waited," he said, "until I knew that Davenant was asleep, and then I stole into his room to watch by his bedside. And presently she came, as I guessed she would, the vampire, the accursed thing that has preyed upon the souls of her kin, making them like to herself when they too have passed into Shadowland, and gathering sustenance for her horrid task from the blood of those who are alien to her race. Paul's body and Jessica's soul—it is for one and the other, Dexter, that we have fought."

"You mean," I hesitated, "Zaida, the witch!"

"Even so," he agreed. "Here is the evil spirit that has fallen like a blight upon the house of MacThane. But now I think she may be exorcised forever."

"Tell me."

"She came to Paul Davenant last night, as she must have done before, in the guise of his wife. You know that Jessica bears a strong resemblance to her ancestress. He opened his arms, but she was foiled of her prey, for I had taken my precautions; I had placed that upon Davenant's breast while he slept which robbed the vampire of her power of ill.[4]

"She sped wailing from the room—a shadow—she who a minute before had looked at him with Jessica's eyes and spoken to him with Jessica's voice. Her red lips were Jessica's lips, and they were close to his when his eyes opened and he saw her as she was—a hideous phantom of the corruption of the ages. And so the spell was removed, and she fled away to the place whence she had come—"

He paused. "And now?" I inquired.

"Blackwick Castle must be razed to the ground," he replied. "That is the only way. Every stone of it, every brick, must be ground to powder and burnt with fire, for therein is the cause of all the evil. Davenant has consented."

"And Mrs. Davenant?"

"I think," Vance answered cautiously, "that all may be well with her. The curse will be removed with the destruction of the castle. She has not—thanks to you—perished under its influence. She was less guilty than she imagined—herself preyed upon rather than preying. But can't you understand her remorse when she realized, as she was bound to realize, the part she had played? And the knowledge of the child to come—its fatal inheritance—"

"I understand," I muttered with a shudder. And then, under my breath, I whispered, "Thank God!"

❧

---

[4] Presumably a cross.

Lord Byron

GEORGE GORDON BYRON (January 22, 1788–April 19, 1824), or simply Lord Byron, is justly celebrated as a major poet in the English language. For the sake of completeness, we present as a "bonus track" the so-called "Fragment of A Novel" that Byron penned as his contribution to the ghost story challenge he proposed during the famed Haunted Summer of 1816 (see discussion of Polidori's "The Vampyre" on pg. 1). As noted earlier, Byron's influence on John Polidori's pivotal tale was profound, and thus Lord Byron may be credited with a significant role in the development of classic vampire fiction.

Sometimes reprinted as "August Darvell" or "The End of My Journey," Byron did not publish the fragment until 1819, when he included it in a publication of his long poem "Mazeppa." Keeping in mind that "The Vampire" was hugely popular when originally issued under Byron's name (apparently a ruse by the publisher), Byron may well have wished to refute that claim.

There are numerous elements common to "The Vampyre" and "A Fragment"; and Polidori admitted that his story was built upon the "foundation" of Byron's idea. Though Byron's epic narrative poems were both popular and profitable, he never produced a novel, but he had previously written about vampires; a long passage in his 1816 poem "The Giaour" describes how the titular infidel will be condemned to vampirism.

FRAGMENT OF A NOVEL

LORD BYRON

June 17, 1816.

In the year 17—, having for some time determined on a journey through countries not hitherto much frequented by travellers, I set out, accompanied by a friend, whom I shall designate by the name of Augustus Darvell. He was a few years my elder, and a man of considerable fortune and ancient family, advantages which an extensive capacity prevented him alike from undervaluing and overrating. Some peculiar circumstances in his private history had rendered him to me an object of attention, of interest, and even of regard, which neither the reserve of his manners, nor occasional indication of an inquietude at times approaching to alienation of mind, could extinguish.

I was yet young in life, which I had begun early; but my intimacy with him was of a recent date: we had been educated at the same schools and university; but his progress through these had preceded mine, and he had been deeply initiated into what is called the world, while I was yet in my novitiate. While thus engaged, I heard much both of his past and present life; and, although in these accounts there were many and irreconcilable contradictions, I could still gather from the whole that he was a being of no common order, and one who, whatever pains he might take to avoid remark, would still be remarkable. I had cultivated his acquaintance subsequently, and endeavored to obtain his friendship, but this last appeared to be unattainable: whatever affections he might have possessed seemed now, some to have been extinguished, and others to be concentered:[1] that his feelings were acute, I had sufficient opportunities of observing; for, although he could control, he could not altogether disguise them; still he had a power of giving to one passion the appearance of another, in such a manner that it was difficult to define the nature of what was working within him; and the expressions of his features would vary so rapidly, though slightly, that it was useless to trace them to their sources. It was evident that he was a prey

---

[1] Concentrated, focused.

to some cureless disquiet; but whether it arose from ambition, love, remorse, grief, from one or all of these, or merely from a morbid temperament akin to disease, I could not discover: there were circumstances alleged which might have justified the application to each of these causes; but, as I have before said, these were so contradictory and contradicted, that none could be fixed upon with accuracy. Where there is mystery, it is generally supposed that there must also be evil: I know not how this may be, but in him there certainly was the one, though I could not ascertain the extent of the other—and felt loth, as far as regarded himself, to believe in its existence. My advances were received with sufficient coldness: but I was young, and not easily discouraged, and at length succeeded in obtaining, to a certain degree, that common-place intercourse and moderate confidence of common and every-day concerns, created and cemented by similarity of pursuit and frequency of meeting, which is called intimacy, or friendship, according to the ideas of him who uses those words to express them.

Darvell had already travelled extensively; and to him I had applied for information with regard to the conduct of my intended journey. It was my secret wish that he might be prevailed on to accompany me; it was also a probable hope, founded upon the shadowy restlessness which I observed in him, and to which the animation which he appeared to feel on such subjects, and his apparent indifference to all by which he was more immediately surrounded, gave fresh strength. This wish I first hinted, and then expressed: his answer, though I had partly expected it, gave me all the pleasure of surprise—he consented; and, after the requisite arrangement, we commenced our voyages. After journeying through various countries of the south of Europe, our attention was turned towards the East, according to our original destination; and it was in my progress through these regions that the incident occurred upon which will turn what I may have to relate.

The constitution of Darvell, which must from his appearance have been in early life more than usually robust, had been for some time gradually giving away, without the intervention of any apparent disease: he had neither cough nor hectic,[2] yet he became daily more enfeebled; his habits were temperate, and he neither declined nor complained of fatigue; yet he was evidently wasting away: he became more and more silent and sleepless, and at length so seriously altered, that my alarm grew proportionate to what I conceived to be his danger.

We had determined, on our arrival at Smyrna, on an excursion to the ruins of Ephesus and Sardis,[3] from which I endeavored to dissuade him in his present state of indisposition—but in vain: there appeared to be an oppression on his mind, and a solemnity in his manner, which ill corresponded with his eagerness to proceed on what I regarded as a mere party of pleasure little suited to a valetudinarian; but I opposed him no longer—and in a few days we set off together, accompanied only by a serrugee[4] and a single janissary.

---

[2] A consumptive flush or fever; usually a symptom of tuberculosis.

[3] On the Turkish coast, Ephesus was one of the major cities of Greek and Roman times. Sardis was another important ruin in Turkey, near Ephesus in the Hermus valley. No serious archeological work had been done there before the visit Byron describes.

[4] A serrugee is a horse-tender; a janissary is a bodyguard.

We had passed halfway towards the remains of Ephesus, leaving behind us the more fertile environs of Smyrna, and were entering upon that wild and tenantless tract through the marshes and defiles which lead to the few huts yet lingering over the broken columns of Diana—the roofless walls of expelled Christianity, and the still more recent but complete desolation of abandoned mosques—when the sudden and rapid illness of my companion obliged us to halt at a Turkish cemetery, the turbaned tombstones of which were the sole indication that human life had ever been a sojourner in this wilderness. The only caravanserai we had seen was left some hours behind us, not a vestige of a town or even cottage was within sight or hope, and this "city of the dead" appeared to be the sole refuge of my unfortunate friend, who seemed on the verge of becoming the last of its inhabitants.

In this situation, I looked round for a place where he might most conveniently repose: contrary to the usual aspect of Mahometan burial-grounds, the cypresses were in this few in number, and these thinly scattered over its extent; the tombstones were mostly fallen, and worn with age: upon one of the most considerable of these, and beneath one of the most spreading trees, Darvell supported himself, in a half-reclining posture, with great difficulty. He asked for water. I had some doubts of our being able to find any, and prepared to go in search of it with hesitating despondency: but he desired me to remain; and turning to Suleiman, our janissary, who stood by us smoking with great tranquility, he said, "Suleiman, verbana su," (i.e., "bring some water") and went on describing the spot where it was to be found with great minuteness, at a small well for camels, a few hundred yards to the right: the janissary obeyed. I said to Darvell, "How did you know this?" He replied, "From our situation; you must perceive that this place was once inhabited, and could not have been so without springs: I have also been here before."

"You have been here before! How came you never to mention this to me? And what could you be doing in a place where no one would remain a moment longer than they could help it?"

To this question I received no answer. In the mean time Suleiman returned with the water, leaving the serrugee and the horses at the fountain. The quenching of his thirst had the appearance of reviving him for a moment; and I conceived hopes of his being able to proceed, or at least to return, and I urged the attempt. He was silent—and appeared to be collecting his spirits for an effort to speak. He began:—

"This is the end of my journey, and of my life; I came here to die; but I have a request to make, a command—for such my last words must be.—You will observe it?"

"Most certainly; but I have better hopes."

"I have no hopes, nor wishes, but this—conceal my death from every human being."

"I hope there will be no occasion; that you will recover, and—"

"Peace! It must be so: promise this."

"I do."

"Swear it, by all that—" He here dictated an oath of great solemnity.

"There is no occasion for this. I will observe your request; and to doubt me is—"

"It cannot be helped, you must swear."

I took the oath, it appeared to relieve him. He removed a seal ring from his finger, on which were some Arabic characters, and presented it to me. He proceeded:—

"On the ninth day of the month, at noon precisely (what month you please, but this must be the day), you must fling this ring into the salt springs which run into the Bay of Eleusis; the day after, at the same hour, you must repair to the ruins of the temple of Ceres, and wait one hour."

"Why?"

"You will see."

"The ninth day of the month, you say?"

"The ninth."

As I observed that the present was the ninth day of the month, his countenance changed, and he paused. As he sat, evidently becoming more feeble, a stork, with a snake in her beak, perched upon a tombstone near us; and, without devouring her prey, appeared to be steadfastly regarding us. I know not what impelled me to drive it away, but the attempt was useless; she made a few circles in the air, and returned exactly to the same spot. Darvell pointed to it, and smiled—he spoke— I know not whether to himself or to me—but the words were only, " 'Tis well!"

"What is well? What do you mean?"

"No matter; you must bury me here this evening, and exactly where that bird is now perched. You know the rest of my injunctions."

He then proceeded to give me several directions as to the manner in which his death might be best concealed. After these were finished, he exclaimed, "You perceive that bird?"

"Certainly."

"And the serpent writhing in her beak?"

"Doubtless: there is nothing uncommon in it; it is her natural prey. But it is odd that she does not devour it."

He smiled in a ghastly manner, and said faintly. "It is not yet time!" As he spoke, the stork[5] flew away. My eyes followed it for a moment—it could hardly be longer than ten might be counted. I felt Darvell's weight, as it were, increase upon my shoulder, and, turning to look upon his face, perceived that he was dead!

I was shocked with the sudden certainty which could not be mistaken—his countenance in a few minutes became nearly black. I should have attributed so rapid a change to poison, had I not been aware that he had no opportunity of receiving it unperceived. The day was declining, the body was rapidly altering, and nothing remained but to fulfill his request. With the aid of Suleiman's ataghan and my own sabre, we scooped a shallow grave upon the spot which Darvell had indicated: the earth easily gave way, having already received some Mahometan tenant. We dug as deeply as the time permitted us, and throwing the dry earth upon all that remained of the singular being so lately departed, we cut a few sods of greener turf from the less withered soil around us, and laid them upon his sepulchre.

Between astonishment and grief, I was tearless.

❧

---

[5] In Egyptian mythology the stork was associated with the soul.

Note on the Text

The editors of this book hope to introduce newer fans to the true origins of vampire fiction. As these works are one to two-hundred years old, the texts can seem rather daunting to those contemporary readers without a degree in Victorian literature. We feel your pain. Language is never static, and with the passage of time linguistic fashions change, and words can assume meanings or connotations that their original writers surely never intended. To retain the intended meaning, some pre-1870 texts have been edited slightly or reconfigured. Page-long paragraphs have been reformatted into more modern lengths; run-on sentences have been broken up; and a few words have been replaced when the modern usage differs markedly from the original intent.

About the Editors

LESLIE S. KLINGER is considered to be one of the world's foremost authorities on Sherlock Holmes and Dracula. He is the editor of the three-volume set *The New Annotated Sherlock Holmes*, published in 2004 and 2005. The first two volumes, *The Complete Short Stories*, won the Edgar, the highest award of the Mystery Writers of America, for "Best Critical/Biographical" work in 2005 and were short-listed for every other major mystery award. The third volume, *The Novels*, was nominated for an Edgar and a Quill award as well as every other major mystery award. In 2008, *The New Annotated Dracula* was published to critical acclaim. His current project is *The Annotated Sandman* for DC Comics, due out in 2012. He is also co-editing a collection of classic essays on Sherlock Holmes with author Laurie R. King, to be published later this year. Klinger is a member of the Baker Street Irregulars, and served as the Series Editor for the Manuscript Series of The Baker Street Irregulars; he is currently the Series Editor for the BSI's History Series. His introductions and essays have appeared in numerous books, graphic novels, academic journals, newspapers, and magazines; he also reviews books for the *Los Angeles Times*.

Les and his wife Sharon have five adult children and live in Malibu with their dog and three cats. Klinger's day job is a practice in Westwood specializing in tax, estate planning, and business law.

JEFF CONNER is a World Fantasy Award recipient for his work as editor with Scream/Press. He is currently a contributing editor for IDW Publishing, concentrating on the company's prose projects, which includes the recent *Classics Mutilated*, *GI JOE: Tales from the Cobra Wars*, and a series of stories set in the world of *Zombies vs Robots*. Jeff and his wife Melanie Dubose live in Los Angeles with their son.